Jochebed's Dream

by

J.R. Martin

Contact Information
allforhimpublishing@gmail.com

Thanks & Dedication

First of all I want to thank my Lord and Saviour Jesus Christ for His everlasting love and for His innumerable blessings upon my life. Without Him I truly could do NOTHING!

This book is dedicated to my seven beautiful, wonderful daughters (for which the book was written): Jaelyn, Janay, Jessa, Josette, Jayah, Jenya, and Jalie. I can't thank you enough for all the support and encouragement you gave me along the way as we traveled this very LONG journey together. Thank you for the exciting evenings we spent reading the latest installments and thank you for taking over the household chores so that I could, "Write, Mom. You write!" I love you all so much!

Thank you also to my unbelievable husband J. Thank you for encouraging me to publish my book and thank you so much for *everything* you did to make certain it happened. I love you - Always!

(And a special thank you to Granny for the use of your yard. ☺ - Love you! And to Janay for your time [and extra time, and EXTRA time ☺] spent editing. I can't thank you enough!!! (Also, thanks to Elise for the extra edit! And to Jaelyn, too.)

Table of Contents

DREAMING
(Chapter 1)

At first, it didn't seem real. *Could this really be happening?* I questioned.

Floods of emotion came rushing over me as I stood there staring at the ring he held up to me on bended knee.

"Will you marry me?" he asked again as I stood there frozen for what seemed like forever. "Jochebed!" he prodded, his smile slowly fading. "Are you with me? Did you hear what I asked you? …Well…*will you or won't you?*"

Will I? I thought. *Of course, I will!* But for some strange reason, the words formed in my head wouldn't come out of my mouth.

Finally, my eyes fixed on Isaac's.

What beautiful blue eyes he has, I thought, *what a perfectly handsome face, what a terribly furrowed brow! - Furrowed brow? Oh, Jochebed!* I scolded. *Get a hold of yourself before he changes his mind!*

"Yes!" I finally blurted out. "*A thousand times, yes!* I'll marry you! I will *absolutely marry you!"*

Isaac's furrowed brow turned into a soft approving one as he gently slipped the ring on my finger.

"Shoo!" he expressed with relief. "You had me worried there for a minute!" He abruptly stood up and pulled me close, holding me tightly in a warm embrace. "You've made me the happiest man in the whole world!" he whispered. He leaned back and looked at me, grinning from ear to ear. "Jochebed Lewis," he said with fervor, "that has a nice ring to it, don't you think?"

I looked up at him, smiling broadly, my heart overwhelmed with excitement, and now tears of joy streaming down my face.

"Absolutely!" I agreed. "It sounds *perfect!*"

*****

"Jochebed, JochEBED, JOCHEBED!" Samuel shouted, trying to rouse me from my sleep. "Are ya ever gonna wake up and do your chores?"

"Ohhh, go away, Samuel, and let me be!" I complained. "You've just ruined the most perfect dream! Why must you always disturb me so early?"

"Early?" Samuel quipped. "It's not early! It's seven o'clock! If Papa catches ya sleepin' in this late, he'll tan your hide!"

"*Seven o'clock!*" I exclaimed. "Samuel, why on earth did you let me sleep in so late?"

"I dunno," he replied, unconcerned, "but ya better get a move on. I've had my chores done for an hour now, and Papa'll be in from the barn any minute."

Samuel left with a big cheesy grin on his face as I quickly rolled out of bed. I hastily fixed my covers, threw on my work dress, and quickly went to the mirror to fix my hair. The day had already begun, and there I was dreaming about a man who I'm certain had never even noticed me before, much less thought about marrying me.

Get a hold of yourself now, I admonished, *it's only a dream. Besides, Isaac Lewis hasn't been around here for quite some time.*

"Still," I sighed, looking into the mirror as I pulled my hair back into a disheveled bun, "Isaac is one dream I sure wish could come true!"

"Jochebed!" Papa shouted from downstairs. "Where's my breakfast?"

"Oh, I'm coming, Papa!" I yelled back apologetically as I hurried out of my room. I scurried down the stairs, past Papa, and into the kitchen. "I'll have it prepared in a jiff!" I assured.

Papa hurried in behind me.

"What've ya been doin'?" he asked angrily. "Its past seven o'clock and I have to leave for town in less than ten minutes. How are ya gonna prepare my breakfast and me have time to eat it in that short amount of time?"

"I'm so sorry, Papa!" I apologized. "I...I overslept a bit. It won't happen again!"

Papa came close and looked me straight in the eye.

"It better not!" he reprimanded. "Ya know ya have more responsibilities around here since your mama's passin'. It's time ya grow up and start fulfillin' 'em. You're not a little girl anymore, and ya don't have the luxury of sleepin' in all day." He sighed, obviously displeased. "Now," he ranted, "I have work to do, and so do you - so get to it!" Papa grabbed some leftover cornbread and walked towards the door. "I'll see ya mid mornin'!" he stated tersely, grabbing his hat, opening the door to leave. He plopped his hat down on his head, took a bite of his cornbread, closed the door behind him, and with that he was gone.

Papa was still hurting and devastated over Mama's sudden passing (we all were...after all, it had only been a few months), and I think his pain contributed to his frustration. Still, though, it hurt me to know that I had let him down.

How could I have gotten so caught up in such a foolish dream and allowed myself to sleep in so long? I berated myself. I sighed, frustrated. *Oh well*, I reluctantly accepted, *what's done is done! No sense crying over spilt milk. You're already an hour behind on a full day's work ahead, and you'd better get started!*

Right away, I busied myself in the kitchen preparing breakfast for Samuel and myself, and while I personally could have gone without, I think Samuel thought he was going to wither away to nothing if he didn't get something to in him soon!

He came in from saddling Papa's horse, prattling on about how he was now a twelve-year-old growing boy who needed his nourishment to survive. (He had just had a birthday, turning twelve three days before.)

I, of course, just smiled at his angst, telling him that I was fairly certain he would last a few more minutes while I made his meal. I then gently reminded him that patience was a virtue and that he'd do well to learn some.

He simply rolled his eyes and scoffed (as pesky little brothers are known to do), and told me to call him when breakfast was ready. He was going back outside to do some things in the barn, and he wanted to be notified right away.

I shook my head in disbelief, and assured him that he'd be the first to know!

Samuel left, and I promptly went back to preparing breakfast.

While I was busy with the meal, my mind kept wandering back to my wonderful dream I'd had about Isaac!

Oh, how I wish I could see him again! I yearned.

He was so tall and handsome with his gorgeous blue eyes and dark wavy hair, and so kind and gentle, and so outgoing, too. He had such a wonderful sense of humor, and everyone seemed to like him, and he seemed to like everyone else as well. He'd always been very polite to me and my best friend, Naomi; however, I don't think he ever really noticed me for anything more than just an acquaintance, as I tended to be a bit shy, keeping mostly to myself. What's more, he was away at college and wouldn't be back home again until Thanksgiving break, and that was still over two months away.

~

Isaac had been at the top of his class in school, and when he finished, he felt God was calling him into the ministry. He'd been away at Bible College, out of state, now, for the past two years, and he was now back there again.

~

Why, I reasoned to myself, *would a twenty year old college student be interested in a seventeen year old schoolgirl like me?* I sighed, knowing it would likely never happen. *Ah, a girl can dream, though, I suppose!*

While I stood there stirring the oatmeal staring off into nothing, I suddenly got a whiff of something burning. Out of the corner of my eye, I caught a glimpse of black smoke starting to billow out of the oven.

"Oh no!" I shouted. "Not the biscuits!"

I quickly removed the oatmeal from the stove so as not to let that burn as well, and threw open the oven door to retrieve the now blackened biscuits that looked a bit like soot-covered rocks.

"Oh, good grief!" I lamented. "What next?"

Well, as fortune would have it, Samuel had just come back into the house to get something, and when I turned around to see who it was, he took one look at me, and nearly lost it!

"Ya look like a coal miner just come in from the mines!" he teased, immediately falling to the floor in raucous laughter. "Say, how's that diggin' goin'?"

"Oh, would you get up?!" I groused, perturbed. "Surely, it can't be worth all that!"

All of a sudden, I caught a glimpse of myself in the mirror that hung on the wall across the kitchen by the door.

"Oh my goodness!" I exclaimed at the sight as I walked over to get a closer look. "You're right! I can barely see the whites of my eyes!"

My whole face was covered in black soot from the oven, and I did look rather funny.

What's a girl to do? I thought, looking myself over.

Samuel was still chortling on the floor, and before I knew it, I too, was joining in on the laughter. We laughed and laughed and laughed some more, until we could both barely breathe!

"All right, all right!" I insisted, trying to catch my breath. "That's enough! My side is aching, and I can't take anymore! Please...stop laughing!"

Samuel tried and somewhat succeeded until he looked in my direction. Unable to withstand the sight, he burst into laughter yet again, holding his stomach, all the while rolling back and forth on the floor.

Of course, as soon as he did that I double over again, laughing so hard, I could barely see straight!

"Okay! All right! Please, stop!" I begged, trying with everything I had to sober myself. "I'm going right now to clean myself off!"

Just as I was about to turn to go to the washroom, there was an unexpected knock at the door. Completely forgetting about my current condition, I instinctively went to the door and opened it up. Much to my shock and horror, there in front of me stood none other than Isaac Lewis.

"Heelloo?" he said inquisitively with furrowed brow. "Um…is…is everything all right?"

Instantly, I felt the huge smile that was still on my face quickly disappear. All of the blood in body seemed to drain away, and my knees went wobbly and weak. My eyes got bigger and bigger as I suddenly remembered the state I was in, and as soon as that happened, all the emotions of having the man I loved standing right there in front of me, and knowing how I must look to him, I panicked, and abruptly slammed the door in his face, running wildly from the room in sheer embarrassment and humiliation!

Again, there was a knock at the door, but this time Samuel went to answer it.

"Sorry 'bout that," he said. "You can come on in."

Isaac stepped inside as Samuel closed the door.

"Sisters!" Samuel quipped, shrugging his shoulders. "What can I say?" He walked over towards the table. "Is there somethin' ya needed?" he asked.

Isaac removed his hat as his eyes searched the room, wondering where I'd gone. He shook his head, collecting his thoughts, and replied with hesitation.

"Well," he answered, "I'm actually here to speak with your father. I…" He furrowed his brow again, concerned. "Is…is she okay?" he queried.

By this time, I'd locked myself in the washroom, absolutely mortified!

Maybe he won't remember who I am! I hoped as I listened at the door.

"Who? Jochebed?" Samuel retorted.

Okay, I thought, rolling my eyes, *there goes that idea…brothers!*

"Yah," Samuel went on to say. "She'll be fine. She just burnt the biscuits is all, and now she's covered in soot. And Papa, well…he's gone right now, but he should be home in about an hour or two. You're more than welcome to stick around and wait 'til he gets here if ya want."

Gulp!

Stick around until Papa gets home? I agonized. *Is he **crazy**?*

I was horrified at the thought! To my dismay, there was the man I had dreamed of marrying standing in my now soot-covered kitchen, being told by my truly insensitive brother what a horrible cook I was, and being invited to stay in my very unkempt house, which I had not yet had time to clean due to my sleeping in dreaming about this very man! And then, just as if things couldn't get any worse, here I was barricaded in the washroom, looking like a coal miner, and in my tattered work dress to boot!

What an absolute nightmare this had become! I thought. *Awful! Just awful!*

While I'd certainly wanted to be noticed by Isaac, this was definitely NOT what I had had in mind!! It was not at all how I imagined him getting to know me, and certainly not the impression I'd hoped to make!

What must he think of me? I bemoaned. I took a deep breath and steadied myself. "Pull yourself together, Jochebed!" I bolstered as I quickly began scrubbing the soot from my face. "Things *could be* worse!" Immediately, I rolled my eyes. "Sheesh!" I whispered to myself. "What an incredibly foolish thing to say! How could things *possibly* be any worse than *this*?"

I finished wiping the soot from my face, fixed up my hair the best I could, and straightened my dress, pushing the wrinkles down and away.

"Well," I said, looking at my less-than-ideal self in the mirror, "I guess this will have to do!"

Just as I was reaching for the doorknob to leave, I paused, overcome with worry.

How can I possibly go out there and face Isaac, now? I fretted.

Fortunately, as I was contemplating what to do, I heard Isaac tell Samuel that he would be back in an hour. Samuel showed him to the door, and Isaac left.

Shoo! I breathed a huge sigh of relief. *That was close!*

Mercifully, I'd avoided the inevitable humiliation for a little while longer. At least, now I could change my clothes and tidy up a bit before Isaac came back. My hope was that by the time he arrived again, I would have a second chance to make a better impression! I slowly cracked the door and peered out.

"Is he gone?" I whispered, hoping Samuel would hear.

"Yah," he answered back. "He just left."

Thankful, I scooted on out of the washroom and back to the kitchen.

"Why on earth did ya run off like that?" Samuel queried. "It was only Isaac. What do ya care what he thinks of ya?"

As I walked over towards the sink, I replied kind of sheepishly, trying very hard not to let my true feelings show.

"Well, did you not see the way I looked?" I contended. "It was humiliating!"

Just then, I saw what seemed like a light bulb go on in Samuel's head as a big devious grin came across his face.

"Oh wow!" he charged. "Ya like him, don't ya?"

I gave him the most chagrinned look I could muster.

"Don't you have chores to do or something?" I complained.

He chuckled and glibly replied with his big cheesy grin still on his face.

"Nope!" he pointed out. "I'm still waitin' on breakfast - remember?"

I furrowed my brow, reluctantly accepting defeat.

"Oh, right!" I admitted. "Well...there's oatmeal on the stove, and you'll just have to have a piece of bread and butter to go with it, because..." I looked over at the now cold, hard, blackened biscuits that sat on the counter, "there really isn't anything I can do about these. Sorry!"

Samuel shrugged, seeming to accept it, and went to get himself a bowl.

I immediately went to cleaning like a mad woman, knowing I only had about an hour to get the house in order, change my clothes, and ready myself for Isaac's return.

Samuel sat down to eat his breakfast, all the while watching me frenzily hurry about.

"Oh yah!" he quipped with a wily grin. "Ya like him!"

I rolled my eyes and let out an *extremely* aggravated sigh!

"Oh, would you please stop!" I barked. "This is not something to be joked about!"

Samuel just grinned all the more.

"So, I'm right then," he stated with arrogance. "Not only do ya like him, but it's serious, too...isn't it?!"

I'd had it!

"Ooooo!" I groused, raising my voice in frustration. "Samuel...just eat!"

He laughed at my consternation!

"Just wait 'til Isaac hears about this!" he mischievously threatened.

My face instantly turned red with fury as I dropped what I was doing, and scurried over to him. I got right down in his face, sternly looking him in the eye, wanting to make myself *perfectly* clear!

"If a word of this leaks to **anyone**," I firmly warned, shaking my finger in his face, "I *promise you…*you will be making your own meals from here on out! *Do you understand?!?*" I knew that that would get him as he valued his meals way too much to jeopardize them!

Samuel's cheesy grin quickly turned to a look of horror.

"Sure thing!" he readily agreed, nodding his head, putting his hands up in surrender. "No…no problem! I…I got ya! These lips here," he said, pointing to his mouth, "these lips are sealed! Your secret's safe with me!"

I clenched my jaw, warily, as I squinted my eyes at him. Strangely, I was not at *all* comforted by his assurances!

Oh well! I dismissed. *No time to dwell on that now. I have too much work to do and very little time to get it done! I'll worry about him later!*

I quickly got back to work, and after about an hour or so, I heard Papa come riding up to the house.

He dismounted his horse and came inside.

"Well, now," I heard him say as I was coming down the stairs after changing my clothes, "this looks more like it! Ya've done a real fine job of cleanin', Jochebed!" He scratched his head, a bit surprised. "Although," he confessed, "I must say ya've achieved more than I thought ya would've in such a short amount of time. Ya must have really been movin'!"

Samuel glanced up from his homework that he was working on this fine Saturday morning.

"Oh, she was!" he promptly blurted out with grin.

I immediately stared at Samuel, my eyes livid and fierce! His eyes caught mine, and my gaze clearly conveyed unambiguously, *Not another word!*

Straight away, Samuel caught my drift and quickly looked back down at his paper, busying himself again with his work.

"Thank you, Papa," I said as I walked on into the kitchen, "Your praise means a lot to me!"

Papa came close and gave me a hug.

"I'm sorry about earlier, Jochebed," he apologized. "I was havin' a rough mornin', and I shouldn't have taken it out on ya. Forgive me?"

"Of course, Papa," I told him, "if you'll forgive me for sleeping in?"

He smiled down at me.

"All's forgiven," he granted. He went on. "Now," he informed, "I forgot to tell ya, Isaac Lewis is supposed to be comin' by sometime this mornin' to see if I have the right tools he needs to finish a project he's workin' on. I need to change my clothes, so I'll be upstairs for a bit. Let me know when he gets here, all right?"

"Sure thing, Papa," Samuel said, looking up from his paper, smiling. He glanced over at me, grinning from ear to ear all the while talking to Papa. "He's already been here, though," he explained. "Stopped by a little earlier. Said he'd be back by after a bit."

I couldn't believe Samuel's brazenness! I glared at him, infuriated, shaking my head.

Papa squinted his eyes, moving them back and forth between the two of us.

"What's goin' on with you two?" he questioned curiously.

"Nothing!" I answered curtly, still glaring at Samuel. *"Nothing at all!"* I immediately tried to draw Papa's attention away from Samuel's overtures. "We'll be sure to let you know when Isaac arrives," I said with a smile. "I'm sure he'll be here soon. You'd better go get changed before he gets here!"

Papa nodded and turned to go on upstairs.

"All right," he agreed.

"Papa!" I called out. "I don't mean to keep you, but…if you don't mind me asking, why is Isaac home now? I thought he wasn't due back until Thanksgiving."

Papa stopped and turned back towards me.

"Oh, he's just home for the weekend," he explained. "He's helpin' his grandparents repair a fence that was badly damaged in that big storm that came through here last week."

"Oh, I see!" I acknowledged. "Then will you be helping him repair it?"

"Sure will!" Papa replied. "In fact, it'll probably take most of the day. If ya could pack me a lunch to take with me, I'd sure appreciate it."

I smiled, delighted to help.

"No problem, Papa," I told him. "I'll have it ready to go shortly."

"Thank ya, sweetheart," he said as he turned to head on upstairs.

Just as he was about to leave the kitchen, though, there was a knock at the door.

"I'll get it!" Samuel shouted, jumping up from the table. "Bet I know who that is!" He looked at me with a big goofy grin on his face.

Papa furrowed his brow, suspicious.

"Ya sure there's nothin' goin' on with you two?" he queried again.

"Oh, you know!" I quipped, smiling nervously, hoping desperately Papa would drop the matter. "Boys will be boys!"

I nodded awkwardly, turned away, and went to prepare Papa's lunch as Samuel opened the door.

"Well, look who's here!" Samuel announced not so subtly. "Why… if it isn't Isaac Lewis!"

Papa walked over to the door.

"Come in, come in!" he encouraged as he went to shake Isaac's hand. "We were just talkin' about ya. It's good to see ya again! Been quite awhile, hasn't it?"

Isaac smiled and nodded respectfully.

"Yes, sir, it has, Mr. Lowry," he answered, stepping inside. "And it's good to see you, too."

"Well, hey," Papa suggested in a hurry, "ya make yourself at home while I go change right quick. I shouldn't be long and then we'll go out and take a look at those tools. Sure hope I have what you're needin'!"

"Oh, I'm sure you will, Mr. Lowry," Isaac bolstered. "You're the best carpenter this side of the Mississippi!"

Papa chuckled visibly embarrassed.

"Well, now," he humbly replied, "I think ya exaggerate there just a bit, Son, but…thanks nonetheless." He lifted his hands, ready to rush off. "Make yourself at home, now," he reiterated, turning to head upstairs. "I'll be back in a few minutes!"

"Yes, sir, thank you, Mr. Lowry," Isaac accepted. "I will."

Papa ran on upstairs to change while Isaac stepped on into the kitchen, walking over to Samuel (who was now back sitting at the table), and playfully tussling his hair.

"Behavin' yourself there, Sam?" he asked with a smile.

"Of course!" Samuel answered confidently. "Always!"

He went back to his homework as Isaac chuckled at his retort.

I tried hard to keep myself busy, not glancing up from my work even once, too nervous and too embarrassed to look in Isaac's direction. My heart was pounding furiously in my chest, and it seemed with every beat it was getting louder and louder and louder! I was certain everyone in the room could hear it as it seemed quite deafening to me!

Suddenly, Isaac walked over towards me, leaned in, tipped his hat, and smiled.

"And you, Jochebed," he queried. "How are you this fine day?"

I thought for sure I would swoon right there on the spot, but thankfully I managed to eke out a faint, "Fine, and you?" I never looked up as I feverishly continued to work.

"Oh, I'm good," Isaac replied politely. "It's nice to see your pretty face." He immediately realized what he'd said. "Oh, III mean...I..." he stammered, clearly flustered. "I don't mean to be forward or anything, it's just that...well...you know...it's better than it was before!" He instantly furrowed his brow, utterly mortified at what had just come out of his mouth. "Oh no!" he quickly corrected. "That sounded awful! I'm so sorry! I...I didn't mean to make it sound like you didn't look pretty before, it's just that... it's just that..."

It was more than obvious he knew he'd a dug a pretty deep whole, and that he had no idea how to get out of it!

He looked at me completely panicked!

"Okay," he said, more than a little shaken, "I think...I think I'll just stop talking now!" He hung his head and sighed. "Anyway," he offered, glancing back up at me, "it's nice to see you again!"

I chuckled at his angst as I looked up briefly, smiling.

"I understand what you mean," I told him sweetly. "And it's nice to see you, too." I shook my head. "There's no offense taken, honest!

Isaac sighed again, grateful, as he smiled back at me with those beautiful blue eyes of his.

"Still," he said as he pointed over his shoulder to the living room, "I think I'll just wait in there." He turned and walked away, not saying another word.

I couldn't help but grin to myself as I watched him disappear around the corner.

I could just melt! I thought as I went back to preparing Papa's lunch. *He called me pretty! Isaac Lewis called **me** pretty!* My heart was now fluttering in unbelievable excitement! I knew I shouldn't read too much into it, but I was so giddy about what had just happened, I simply couldn't help it! *Isaac Lewis called **me** pretty!* I exclaimed to myself yet again. I had the biggest smile on the inside, and it was all I could do to contain it on the outside.

I finished up with Papa's lunch just as he was coming down the stairs. He came over, kissed me on the forehead, grabbed his lunch sack, and called for Isaac.

Isaac sprang around the corner.

"Ready?" Papa asked.

"Ready, sir!" Isaac replied with a nod.

"All right, then," Papa said, "let's get at it!" He turned to me and Samuel before he left. "I'll see you two later on tonight," he told us as he opened the door. "Not sure when I'll be home, so don't go waitin' supper on me, okay?"

"Yes, sir," I answered. "Be safe, all right?"

"Will do!" Papa agreed as he put his hat on his head, stepping outside.

"See ya!" Samuel called out, barely looking up from his homework.

Before Isaac walked out of the house, he paused, turned to me, and tipped his hat. "Have a nice day, Jochebed," he said sweetly.

"You too, Isaac!" I echoed with a smile.

He nodded, smiled back, and left.

"Ooooo! What was that?" Samuel quipped as the door closed. "Did I detect a bit of *liiike* comin' from Isaac your way? I mean, he didn't tell *me* to have a nice day."

"Oh, Samuel!" I grumbled, so perturbed at his immaturity. "Would you please just stop it? Isaac's a gentleman…that's all!" I paused, staring longingly at the door where Isaac had just exited. "Besides," I questioned earnestly, "so what if he does like me? Would that be so terrible?"

Samuel shrugged his shoulders.

"Well," he replied with a pensive look on his face, "I guess not. I mean, I like Isaac. He seems like a decent fella. I suppose it'd be okay."

"Well, I'm so glad I have your approval!" I came back at him sarcastically.

Of course, Samuel wouldn't drop it.

"Ya plan to tell Papa?" he pressed.

I looked at him frowning, shaking my head in disbelief!

"Tell Papa what?" I exclaimed, exasperated. "We barely spoke, for goodness' sake! You make it sound as if he's asked for my hand in marriage or something!" I sighed, more than a little aggravated with him. "Again I remind you," I pointed out, "we scarcely said ten words to each other. Besides, if anything further comes of anything, I'm certain Papa will be one of the first to know!" I looked at Samuel sternly. "Now please," I said, not wanting to discuss it any further, "stop pestering me and get your homework finished!"

"Fine!" Samuel retorted, rolling his eyes. "But I bet Isaac likes ya!"

"Samuel!" I shouted, annoyed, pointing to his papers there on the table. *"To work!"*

Samuel rolled his eyes again and reluctantly started in on his homework.

I sighed, relieved, and went to cleaning the kitchen.

As I worked, trying to get everything taken care of, my mind and my heart were simply a twitter. It was all I could do to concentrate on the task at hand. I so wanted to be finished with my chores so that I could sit with my memory book and write down the events of the day - all my thoughts, my hopes, and my dreams.

Could Isaac really like me? I wondered. *Had he actually noticed me for more than just a shy little schoolgirl? Could this day be the first day of a new chapter in my life? Could my dreams really be coming true?*

MISSING MAMA
(Chapter 2)

All of these questions and so many more were racing through my mind.

Oh, how I wish Mama could be here to talk with me about such things! I lamented. *I'm positive she'd know exactly what to say. I miss her so and could really use her wisdom in these matters of the heart.* I sighed as I shook my head thinking of her. *One thing I do know she'd tell me, however,* I reminded myself, *is to always, **always** seek God!*

"In every situation," she'd say, "put Him first, and make certain you're in the center of His will!"

She taught me years ago to pray, and to pray specifically for what I would desire in a husband.

"Godliness is *key!*" she'd emphasize. "If a man loves God above all else, he'll love you the way he's supposed to love you and treat you the way you deserve to be treated."

Looking at Papa and the marriage he and Mama shared together for over twenty one years, I would say most definitely she knew exactly what she was talking about. They were such a wonderful example to Samuel and me, and I could only hope that one day, I would have a marriage that was half as loving and godly as their marriage was!

I finished cleaning up in the kitchen and headed to the sewing room to work some mending I'd been putting off for awhile. Samuel had several ripped jeans that needed patching, and I had a Sunday dress that was missing a button.

Sewing was something Mama and I always enjoyed doing together, and I missed her being here to do it with me now.

I can remember the very first time she showed me how to thread a needle, and the first time she allowed me to darn my very first sock. It seems like forever ago now, and such a simple task, but in that moment, her doing that for me made me feel so grown-up inside. Thinking back on it, it's such a precious memory that I will always cherish!

Sitting here in the sewing room, mending clothes alone is often the hardest part of the day for me. I miss the wonderful conversations Mama and I would have together, just her and me, talking about God and life and just everyday things in general. She taught me so much in those brief, busy moments, but they're things that I will never forget.

I miss the silly little screech she would let out when she'd accidentally prick her finger with a needle. I miss her loving smile and kind words of approval for a job well done, and I miss her infectious laugh when things didn't quite turn out as planned. I guess I'd have to say working here in the sewing room alone are the times I miss Mama the most!

Why God chose to take Mama home when He did and how He did, I will probably never understand, but I do know and take comfort in the fact that God will work "all things together for good to them that love God, to them who are the called according to His purpose." I know God's purpose and plan are perfect!

Mama went home to be with the Lord on June fifth. She was killed instantly when she was accidently kicked in the head by a new horse Papa had purchased. He and Mama had been trying hard that fateful day to break the horse, but it was just so strong and stubborn and willful! It was no one's fault, really, just a case of Mama being in the wrong place at the wrong time. The horse got spooked (by what we're still uncertain), but whatever it was, it caused the horse to go wild, bucking and kicking all around the pen. Mama was simply unable to get out of the way in time.

What an absolutely horrible, awful day that day was! I try hard not to dwell on it for too long, though, preferring rather to remember Mama for how she looked before all the blood and bruises. She was such a beautiful woman not only on the outside, but on the inside as well. Papa used to call her his precious flower, so lovely, so sweet!

I do take comfort in knowing, however, that she didn't suffer, and that she's now in Heaven with her loving Heavenly Father. I know that one day I'll see her again, and that makes me smile even through the tears.

Still, some days are harder than others, and I guess I would put a day like today in that category. I miss her so very much and wish, if not for just one more day, that she and I could sit and mend and talk together again.

"I miss you, Mama, so much I do, and I wish you were here!"

SURPRISES
(Chapter 3)

As I was reminiscing to myself, laughing and crying remembering Mama, I was suddenly jolted from my memories by the sound of my brother, Samuel, whooping loudly in the other room. I was so startled by his sudden outburst, I tossed the garment I was sewing straight up in the air, and it landed on the floor behind me.

"What on earth?!?" I exclaimed as I leapt from my chair, wiping the tears from my eyes and scurrying out of the room. "Samuel Michael Lowry!" I shouted as I hurried towards the kitchen. "What in the world has gotten into you? You scared the stuffing right out of me!"

As I rounded the corner going into the kitchen, my eye caught the source of my brother's excitement. There standing in the kitchen, grinning from ear to ear was Grampa and Gramma Lowry. They'd traveled all the way from North Dakota to visit us here in Pennsylvania, a visit that was totally unexpected. (Hence the whooping response from Samuel!)

Excitement thrilled my heart the moment I laid eyes on them!

~

Grampa and Gramma Lowry were always such fun to have around. Even though they were both up in years, that didn't seem to stop them for a minute! They were both spry as chickens and sharp as tacks! They were always joking and laughing, telling stories and making you feel like you were the most important person in the whole wide world! They'd been here just a few months prior for Mama's funeral and had been such a help and a blessing to us during that most difficult time, I honestly don't know what we would have done without them. One bright spot that came out of that very dark circumstance was that Gramma Lowry and I had been able to get even closer than we already had been. For that, I was grateful!

~

Needless to say, seeing them here now was quite the shock! I never ever expected them to return so soon!

"There she is!" Grampa announced cheerily, grinning from ear to ear. "There's my little Wallflower!" (He'd given me that nickname as a child because I was so shy and backwards, barely participating in anything.)

"Oh my! How are ya my dear?" Gramma called out, so excited to see me. "Come give us a hug!"

I was simply beaming!

"What an amazing surprise!" I expressed with glee, rushing to hug their necks. "Oh, Gramma, Grampa, what are you two doing here? I can hardly believe this is real! It is *so* wonderful to see you again!"

"Well, it's so good to see ya, too!" Gramma echoed as she hugged me back.

"Where's your pa?" Grampa wanted to know as I gave him a big hug.

Of course, Samuel wasted no time jumping in to taunt me some more.

"Oh, he's helpin' a *special* friend mend a fence," he told them suggestively.

Gramma looked at him circumspectly.

"A *special* friend?" she queried, curious. "And who might this *special* friend be?"

Samuel grinned his usual obnoxious, wily grin.

"Oh," he replied coyly, "I'll let Jochebed tell ya all about that!"

"Oh, good grief!" I blustered, rolling my eyes, shaking my head, trying to dismiss Samuel's mischief. "Gramma," I stated plainly, "Papa's helping Isaac Lewis mend a fence for his grandparents." I scowled at Samuel. "*That's* the *special friend* he's referring to!"

~

Grampa and Gramma Lowry had lived in Pennsylvania for many years before moving out to North Dakota. They'd been very good friends with the Lewises while they lived here, so they were very familiar with Isaac and his grandparents.

Isaac's parents had been killed in a train accident when Isaac and his younger brother, Andrew, were very little, so Isaac's grandparents, the Lewises, had taken the boys in and raised them as their own.

~

"I guess his grandparents had extensive damage after that massive storm came through here last week," I went on to explain. I paused, looking at their bags. "But enough about that," I said. "Let's get you settled in." I reached down and picked up a piece of luggage. "You can sleep in Mama and Papa's old room while you're here," I suggested - apparently much to Gramma's chagrin.

"What?" she exclaimed with concern in her voice. "Why...doesn't your Pa sleep in there?"

"Oh no, Gramma," I revealed, "not since Mama's passing. Papa's been sleeping in the guest room. He says he just can't bring himself to sleep alone in the bed that he and Mama shared for so many years."

I looked at Gramma, who was clearly worried about the situation, and tried to reassure her.

"It's okay, Gramma, really," I said. "We can talk more about it later. For now, though, Samuel and I will help you carry your bags upstairs."

Gramma reluctantly agreed, and each of us grabbed a suitcase (or two), and started trudging up the stairs with them. Honestly, that was the nice thing about Grampa and Gramma Lowry coming to visit; because they came from so far away, they generally stayed for an extended period of time.

"Oh, I know Papa will be *so* sorry he wasn't here to greet you," I said. "He'll be so surprised you're here, though. How long do you think you'll be with us this time?"

Grampa was following me up the stairs, then Gramma, then Samuel.

Grampa glanced back at Gramma smiling from ear to ear through his thick, grey mustache and said with a twinkle in his eye, "Oh now, we'll just have to see about that, won't we, dear?"

Gramma chuckled and smiled back approvingly.

"Yes, we will, dear," she replied evasively. "Yes, we will!"

"Hmmm!" I expressed with suspicion as we reached the top of the stairs. "That seems a bit fuzzy to me, doesn't it to you, Sam?" I squinted my eyes, wary. "And from the tone in your voices..." I shook my head, trying to figure it out. "Hmmm!" I said again. "What are you two up to?"

"Who? Us?" they both replied in unison as we reached the bedroom door.

"Whatever would give ya the idea that we're up to somethin'?" Grampa asked, trying to sound all innocent.

Both he and Gramma had the biggest grins I think I'd ever seen, sprawled across their faces!

My jaw nearly dropped at his audacity, as I couldn't help but smile myself.

"Well, for starters, that!" I indicted. "I mean, look at the two of you! I don't think I've ever seen you so giddy with your grins and your ever so 'innocent' sounding voices. You both look like the cat that just swallowed the canary. So give! What's going on with you two?"

Grampa just laughed in his big, bellowy way.

"My dear," he dismissed, refusing to explain, "we can talk all about that later. Why don't you and your grandma scurry on downstairs there and whip us up somethin' for lunch? This old man is near to famished! Samuel and I'll finish puttin' things away up here, won't we, Sam?"

"Sure, Grampa," Samuel agreed. "We can handle it!" Samuel glanced at me. "Hey, Jochebed," he said, half-teasingly, "can ya make sure not to burn anything this time. I really don't care much for that *extra crispy* taste!"

I shook my head with a sigh, fed-up with his impertinence.

"Samuel," I charged, "*you* are impossible!"

Gramma gave me a quizzical look, puzzled by the whole exchange.

"Come on, Gramma," I said as I let go of the bags I'd set down. "I'll tell you all about it in the kitchen."

As Gramma and I reached the bottom of the steps, Gramma impatiently inquired.

"So now," she wanted to know, "what's this about ya burnin' things? I mean, I've always known ya to be a *great* cook, and I know it," she added, "because your mama, who was a wonderful cook herself, by the way, taught ya well!"

"Well," I replied with a sigh, "I guess you could say I had somewhat of a *mishap* earlier this morning. I got a little distracted in a daydream I was having and wasn't paying enough attention to my biscuits in the oven. They got a little, well…okay…a lot burnt! We survived, though… no major damage, just a lot of smoke and perhaps a bruised ego."

Gramma chuckled as if she could relate, but she also must have noticed the slight grin on my face when I mentioned my daydream. She came close and asked with a loving smile.

"So, who is he, dear?" she asked.

I thought for a minute of simply trying to pretend that it was no one, but then I realized that Gramma would be the perfect person to talk to about such things; after all, she'd been a young lady herself once, too. I decided to share.

"Weeelll," I started sheepishly, "it's…well…it's…oh, Gramma!" I turned away, blushing. "It's just so embarrassing!"

"Now, Jochebed," Gramma reached out, trying to make me feel comfortable talking with her, "I hope ya know that you can talk to me about anything; besides, I promise, whatever it is, your secret's safe with me. Mum's the word!"

I looked at her hesitantly as she smiled so sweetly at me.

"I know, Gramma, I know," I acknowledged as I gave her a big hug. "It's just that…oh…I know it sounds so silly, but it's almost as if I feel…" I babbled awkwardly. "It's almost as if I feel…"

"As if…if ya tell someone, then perhaps the dream won't come true?" she interjected sympathetically.

I hugged her neck again.

"I'm so glad you're here!" I exclaimed. I was so relieved! I finally felt that I had someone to talk to about what I'd been feeling. "Oh, Gramma, you do understand!" I said.

"That's it! That's it exactly! It's like I'm afraid if I let the words come out of my mouth, then it's no longer just a dream. If I say them, then…then it's…it's reality!"

Gramma walked over and sat down in a chair at the table, and I went along and joined her.

"The problem is, Gramma," I continued, bemoaning what I knew to be true, "I think Samuel's starting to figure things out, and even though he says he won't tell anyone, I'm not so sure my twelve-year-old little brother is the best *secret keeper!*"

"Oh now," Gramma tried to calm, "don't ya worry any about Sam. Boys will be boys, and he may tease ya a bit, but he looks up to ya, Jochebed, that much I can tell. Despite his teasin', I know deep down inside he really loves ya a lot." She leaned over and patted my hand. "And listen," she encouraged, "ya don't have to share anything more with him unless ya feel ya want to."

I smiled, grateful.

"Thank you, Gramma," I told her. "That does help." I paused as I looked bashfully down at the floor. "My daydream," I hesitantly admitted, "it…it was…it was about Isaac Lewis."

Gramma smiled broadly as she took my face in her hands, looking lovingly into my eyes.

"He's a fine young man, Jochebed," she praised, "and a godly young man at that! I couldn't think of a finer prospect for ya." She beamed approvingly. "Do ya know if he shares these feelin's for you?"

I sighed despairingly.

"That's just it, Gramma," I lamented. "I don't! I mean, he's always very kind to me when he's around, but…oh…I don't know! I just wish I knew what to do!" I shook my head, doleful. "I've been pining away for him now for years," I revealed, "long before he ever finished school. But," I quickly clarified, "don't get me wrong…there was never anything inappropriate about it or anything, just hopes and dreams is all, it's just that…well…" I looked down, feeling ashamed, fiddling with my hands. "I…I never even told Mama about how I felt," I confessed with melancholy. "And I used to tell her *everything!*" I lifted my head, looking earnestly at Gramma. "Sometimes I feel so guilty about that," I divulged, my heart heavy, "the not telling her, but…I guess I just always thought…" Tears began to well up in my eyes as a single tear trickled down my face and onto my dress. "Oh, how I wish now that I had spoken up when I still had the chance to glean from her wisdom," I cried.

Gramma leaned in again, gently taking hold of my hand.

"I know, honey, I know!" she empathized with a look of angst. "I so wish she were here for ya, too!"

I sniffed and sniffed, wiping my tears.

"Like I said before," I continued to explain, "Isaac has always been very polite and kind to me whenever he's around, but you know me, Gramma, I'm so shy and awkward when it comes to people, and…and *even more so* when it comes to boys, I…I really don't know if he even notices me in that way, to tell you the truth." I sighed, disheartened. "I desperately want him to," I confessed, "and I hope he does, and I dream of becoming his wife someday, but…oh, I don't know! Sometimes it's all just so confusing!"

Gramma smiled tenderly.

"Love will do that to ya, my dear," she told me. "But be patient, child. Wait upon God. He *will* give ya direction if ya seek Him - of that I'm certain!" She took my hand again and gave it a squeeze. "Ya simply need to put it in His hands, Jochebed," she encouraged. "If Isaac's the right one for ya, God'll work it all out in His time."

Just then, we heard Grampa and Samuel coming down the stairs.

"So," Grampa asked as they walked into the kitchen, "what's good for lunch?"

"Oh my goodness!" Gramma shrieked, clasping her hands in dismay. "We were so busy catchin' up, we plum forgot about lunch!"

Grampa came over, leaned down, and gave Gramma a kiss on the cheek.

"You hen's a cluckin' in the kitchen," he teased lightheartedly, "enough to make a man starve to death!"

Gramma laughed and tapped Grampa on his big belly.

"Starve to death?" she jested. "Now, Ezra, I think not! Ya've got enough there to hibernate for the winter!"

Grampa let out a big, boisterous roar.

"This grizzly bear's not ready to hibernate just yet, woman!" he bantered back, grinning wildly. "Get this bear some vittles!"

We all broke out in laughter at his silliness.

"Oh, gracious!" Gramma retorted. "Now, ya boys go on now! Your *vittles* will be ready shortly!"

Samuel and Grampa headed off to the living room to play a game of checkers, while Gramma and I went to fixing lunch.

~

It was something, actually, Grampa always fancied himself the "king of checkers," so as you can imagine, any time he and Gramma came to visit, he would always challenge Samuel or Papa or, for that matter, just about anyone else to a game. I do have to confess, though, the title did seem to fit him as he was usually the one winning in the end!

~

Gramma and I worked diligently to finish the now late lunch, and when we got it all prepared, everyone sat down to enjoy turkey sandwiches, Gramma's famous apple salad, and freshly squeezed lemonade. (Gramma's was definitely the best!)

As we sat eating, we all caught up on the day-to-day news, talking about everything that had happened since Grampa and Gramma had been here last for Mama's funeral. We shared how we were all coping since her passing, shed a few tears in the process, and talked a little more about future plans. We laughed and talked and laughed some more, enjoying one another's company immensely! It was truly a fun afternoon spent with family!

*****

Before we knew it, hours had passed, and suddenly Grampa got the most bewildered look on his face. He turned to Gramma and proclaimed with furrowed brow.

"Elizabeth," he said, "this old man's hungry again!"

"Hungry?" Gramma protested. "Now how on earth can ya…" She paused as she frowned, perplexed. "Well, I'll be!" she announced, clearly surprised at what she was about to say. "I'm a little hungry myself!"

Everyone laughed at the befuddled look on Gramma's face.

Samuel looked at the clock on the wall.

"Well, there's the problem," he pointed out, drawing our attention to the time. "It's suppertime already!"

Again, laughter broke out all around! We'd been so caught up in conversation that none of us even noticed the time flying by.

"Well, for goodness' sake!" Gramma exclaimed. "Would ya look at that? I guess we'd better get these lunch dishes cleaned up and get to preparin' supper." She paused before getting up, however, looking fondly at Samuel and then to me. "I'll have to say, though," she expressed with joy in her eyes, "this has been one of the most enjoyable lunches I've had in a long while. It's been such a delight talkin' with you children." She smiled kindly. "What an absolute blessin' ya both are!" she told us. "And so grown up, too! I couldn't be prouder if I tried!"

Grampa smiled, too.

"I couldn't agree with ya more," he said. "It's been a wonderful afternoon!" His eyes suddenly lit up. "Now," he proclaimed with gusto, "LET'S EAT!"

We all broke out in laughter again.

"Grampa," Samuel snorted, "you're a hoot!"

"Challenge ya to another round of checkers, Sam?" Grampa prodded, daring Samuel to another game. "Give ya a chance to redeem yourself!"

Samuel enthusiastically took the bait.

"Grampa," he replied with confidence, "you're on! Only this time, ya better look out. I'm winnin' this round for sure!"

Grampa squinted at Samuel teasingly as if to say, *I think not!*

They both stood up, determined, and raced to the living room.

As Samuel and Grampa headed off for their rematch, Gramma and I went about cleaning the lunch dishes and making preparations for what would now be a very late supper. It felt as if I had spent nearly the entire day in the kitchen, accomplishing little, if anything else, but cooking meals and cleaning up after them. But that was fine with me, though. Having Grampa and Gramma here was a much welcomed break from the normal routine of day-to-day life. I only wished Papa could be here to enjoy the good food and laughter. I hoped he would be home soon!

*****

After almost two hours of cooking supper, it was time to eat again.

"Go wash up, boys," Gramma yelled. "Supper's on!"

Samuel and Grampa immediately jumped up from their checkers game and came rushing into the kitchen, each trying to beat the other to the sink to wash their hands. When they got there, Grampa started teasing Samuel, flicking water on him and trying to bump him out of the way. Samuel held his own, though, playfully bumping Grampa right back. Back and forth they went laughing and joking the whole time.

Gramma wrinkled her mouth.

"Now you boys quit that!" she scolded. "You're gonna get water everywhere!"

They chuckled and quickly finished up. When they'd sufficiently dried their hands, they instinctively looked at each other, somehow communicating some unspoken challenge, and bounded off towards the table, racing each other yet again.

Gramma was having none of it, though, as Grampa brushed past her, nearly knocking the platter of chicken right out of her hands.

"Now ya two slow it down there!" she demanded. "This is no place to be racin' about!"

Grampa grinned, turned on his heels, came back, and kissed her on the forehead. Carefully taking the platter of chicken from her hands, he smiled and tried to woo her.

"Sorry, my dear," he quipped. "Just can't *wait* to eat your *scrumptious* cookin'!"

Gramma pooched her lips and flashed a wary grin at Grampa.

"Flattery will get ya nowhere!" she countered teasingly. "You're worse than a little child!"

"I love ya, my dear!" Grampa replied enthusiastically, ignoring her reprimand. Gramma conceded.

"I love ya, too, ya silly old man!" she echoed back.

Grampa leaned in and gave Gramma a kiss on the lips as she lovingly kissed him back.

It was so wonderful to see the fun-loving, beautiful relationship they still had with each other even after fifty-three years of marriage. It was such an incredible example!

As we all sat eating, talking, and laughing (of course), we were all startled when suddenly the door swung open and in walked Papa.

His jaw instantly dropped, and his eyes beamed with excitement when he saw his parents sitting there at the table.

"Why, Ma, Pa, what on earth?" he questioned. "When did…what brings…what are ya doin' here?"

Grampa and Gramma jumped up from the table and ran to hug his neck.

"Michael!" they said, thrilled beyond measure. "It's so good to see ya, Son!"

"Ya look real good!" Gramma complimented with tears in her eyes.

Grampa heartily concurred.

I immediately jumped up to go grab Papa a plate and some silverware so that he could join us.

"Come on, Michael," Gramma encouraged. "We just sat down to supper. Come eat! There's gracious plenty."

Grampa and Gramma sat back down, while Papa went to lay his coat on the chair in the living room. I thought for certain I saw him wipe a tear from his face as he walked back into the kitchen.

"Let me go wash up right quick," he said, "and I'll be right in." He started towards the washroom, but stopped when he got to Gramma. He reached down from behind and put his hands on her shoulders, leaning over to kiss her cheek. "Boy," he expressed with fervor, "it's *so good* to see ya again! I can't tell ya how happy I am that you're here!"

Gramma patted his hands as tears filled her eyes yet again.

"Me too, Son!" she replied, smiling tenderly. "Me, too!"

Papa kissed her again and dashed off to wash up.

When Papa returned, Grampa asked how the day had gone at the Lewis' farm. Papa said that he and Isaac had gotten most of the fence repaired but that he'd have to go back sometime during the week to finish up.

"And Marvin and Cilia," Gramma wanted to know. "How are they gettin' along?"

"Oh," Papa answered, "they seem to be doin' all right. Marvin's still recoverin' from that nasty fall he took about a month or so ago, but other than that they seem to be doin' just fine. Don't y'all still keep in touch with 'em?"

"I try," Gramma revealed. "In fact, I'd just written to Cilia a few weeks before we decided to come out here. I hadn't yet heard back from her, though." She smiled fondly. "They're such a sweet couple," she flattered, "and dear, dear friends. I keep them in my prayers daily. It's good to hear that things are goin' better for 'em now. And Andrew and Isaac," she inquired, "how are they?"

"Well," Papa said as he stopped to contemplate, "if I remember correctly, Andrew's been workin' at the ole' Hartford Mill ever since he finished school last year, and he and his girl plan on gettin' married sometime in the spring. As for Isaac, well, he's just home from Bible College for the weekend to help his grandparents. And oh, hey! That reminds me," he went on to share excitedly, "I just about forgot! We're in for a real treat come Sunday services tomorrow."

"Oh?" Grampa queried.

"Yah," Papa explained, "Pastor Scott's asked Isaac to preach the mornin' message."

My heart suddenly lit up inside, but I instantly put my head down, trying hard not to let it show on my face so as not to give myself away.

Wow! I thought to myself. *A chance to hear Isaac preach!* I was so excited, I thought I might burst!

Gramma guardedly looked over at me and gave me a smile. I glanced over at her and quickly flashed a smile back.

"So proud of that boy Isaac!" Grampa chimed in. "He's sure come a long way! Gonna make a fine preacher boy someday, and someone a right fine husband, too!"

All at once, Samuel coughed, spewing his milk all over the table.

"What in the world, Son?" Papa shouted, scowling at Samuel's unseemly eruption. "What on earth's gotten into ya?"

By now, Samuel was, of course, grinning in my direction in a very suggestive way. I, however, was NOT returning the favor! In fact, I was vehemently staring daggers at him, willing him to keep his mouth shut! Thankfully, he got the message, immediately wiped the grin from his face, profusely apologized to everyone, and quickly went to go get a towel to clean up his mess.

"Gracious!" Papa grumbled in consternation. "Sometimes I just don't know about that boy!"

Gramma stood to her feet to help clean up the milk.

"Oh, Michael, now!" she said, trying to defend Samuel. "You used to do just as silly a things as him when you were his age."

Papa looked up with furrowed brow, clearly disagreeing.

"Well, I certainly don't remember showerin' my guests with milk!" he retorted. "And, Ma, ya just sit right on back down there. Sam can take care of his own mess."

Gramma deferentially sat back down, respecting Papa's wishes on the matter.

Just as she did, Samuel came back with the towel, and busily started cleaning up the table. As soon as he finished, he apologized again to everyone and sat back down in his seat.

"So, Pa," Papa asked, "how long do you and Ma plan on stayin' this trip?"

Grampa and Gramma coyly looked at each other, getting those same suspicious grins on their faces that they'd had earlier in the day.

"Well," Grampa said, looking at Gramma, "I suppose we might as well tell 'em, aye, Ma?"

Gramma's smile got even bigger as she nodded in approval.

"Tell us what, Pa?" Papa prodded curiously.

Grampa lightheartedly looked at Samuel.

"Ya don't have any more milk there in your mouth now, do ya, Son?" he teased. "Don't wanna trigger another mishap with my news!"

Samuel smirked a little embarrassed, but he answered nonetheless.

"No…I'm good, Grampa," he assured. "Ya can tell us."

Grampa chuckled.

"All right then, good to hear!" he quipped as he tussled Samuel's hair. Grampa looked over at Papa. "Well, Michael," he began a little more seriously, "your ma and I," he paused, taking Gramma's hand, smiling lovingly into her eyes. "Your ma and I," he reiterated, "we've…well…we've decided we're stayin' for good!"

"What?!?" Papa exclaimed in disbelief. "Are ya serious?"

"As a heart attack!" Grampa jokingly affirmed.

"Oh, Ezra!" Gramma admonished. "Don't say such things!"

"Well, it's true!" he shot back. "We bought the Bradley farm just up the road from here, and your brother Mark, and Sara, of course, will be bringin' the rest of our things from North Dakota in the next week or so. We hope to be moved in permanent within the month."

I jumped up from the table and went to hug Grampa and Gramma, so excited for the news!

"What a wonderful surprise!" I said as I hugged them tightly. "And Uncle Mark and Aunt Sara coming, too, why…this is just all too much!"

~

Uncle Mark was Papa's only sibling. Gramma always wanted to have more children but was unable to due to complications. In fact, for quite awhile after Papa was born, Grampa and Gramma began to think that he might be an only child. Eight years later, however, Uncle Mark came along and surprised them all.

Uncle Marks's wife, Aunt Sara, was a couple years younger yet than he was, and together they made such a sweet, charming, delightful couple. Aunt Sara was absolutely beautiful and vibrant and fun-loving, and she complemented Uncle Mark very well. She and I were very close, as we kept in touch often, through letters, and I looked up to her and admired her greatly! Needless to say, I was looking forward to having her and Uncle Mark around. I simply couldn't *wait* to see them again!

~

"What about the business, Pa?" Papa asked, perplexed. "Who's gonna run the store? I mean…what makes ya wanna move now?" Papa seemed almost uneasy with Grampa and Gramma's decision, sounding very hesitant and more than a little concerned. "Movin' here," he pointed out, "why…Ma, Pa, that's a pretty big deal!" He shook his head, questioning. "I don't mean to sound discouragin', but…your life's been in North Dakota now for years. Are ya sure this is what ya really wanna do?"

Gramma looked at Grampa and then answered sweetly.

"Son," she said, "ya know we're not gettin' any younger, and…well…your pa, he's just needin' to retire. Mark and Sara are plenty ready to take over the store. In fact, they're really lookin' forward to it."

Grampa jumped in, supporting Gramma's position.

"She's right, Son," he reinforced. "And truth be told, Mark and Sara have pretty much been runnin' the store by themselves for quite some time now, anyhow."

Gramma nodded, agreeing as she continued on, sounding as if she were trying to convince Papa that both she and Grampa were fine with the move.

"Now, Michael," she assured, "your pa and I have talked and talked about this a great deal - truly we have, and…well…we've finally come to the conclusion that we want to spend what years we have left closer to you and the children. Mark and Sara, why, they're just as excited as can be to run the store, and well…since…you know, they're unable to have any children of their own, and…well…since you're here all alone now with just Samuel and Jochebed we…"

Grampa interrupted, trying to clarify.

"What your ma's tryin' to say, Son, is that we love ya," he stated firmly, "and we want to be as big a help to you and the children as we possibly can be."

Papa sighed, troubled.

"But ya know that's not necessary!" he insisted, not wanting them to feel obligated just because Mama was no longer with us. "It's been tough, I'll admit, but we're gettin' along all right. I just don't want ya to feel like ya have to give up your business, and your life, to move clear across the country on the count of us."

I could tell Grampa was getting a little flustered.

"We know, Son…," he started to say forcefully.

"But we want to," Gramma finished softly, placing her hand on Grampa's arm, calming him down. Gramma paused as if she were reconsidering their decision. I could tell she didn't want to discount Papa's feelings nor intrude. "Michael," she went on to say lovingly, respecting Papa's concerns, "Son, if ya really don't want us to come, then we won't, but…" She looked at him earnestly. "I do want ya to know," she explained, "your pa and I, why…we'd talked about doin' this long before, well…long before Lydia's passin'. We really do want to be closer to you and the children - really we do!"

Samuel and I both looked at Papa with eyes pleading, both wanting desperately for Grampa and Gramma to be able to stay with us and for him to approve. He was more than a little pensive, however, as he looked at us warily and then to Grampa and Gramma. By now, they too, both had a look of longing on their faces; hoping Papa would support their decision.

We all sat there frozen, waiting for Papa to respond.

Finally, after what seemed like forever of Papa weighing the situation, a big smile made its way across his face. He looked at Samuel and me and then again to Grampa and Gramma.

"Well…" he said warmly, "welcome back to Pennsylvania! Ma, Pa, we're very blessed to have ya here!"

Everyone smiled joyously and breathed a huge sigh of relief at Papa's approval. Blissful laughter broke out as we all hugged and kissed each other, excited once more about the move!

SUNDAY MORNING
(Chapter 4)

Now that the decision for Grampa and Gramma to move back to Pennsylvania was settled, it started to sink in, and it was all a bit overwhelming, to say the least, not to mention the upcoming visit from Uncle Mark and Aunt Sara, why, that was just icing on the cake! Hence, the happy occasion made the rest of the evening fly by rather quickly!

After visiting for awhile longer, we all went about cleaning up and washing dishes and bathing for Sunday services. I helped Samuel pick out his clothes (as he was not always the best at picking things that matched), helped Papa find his missing sock, and found an extra pillow for Grampa.

By the time I finally had opportunity to lay out my own clothes for Sunday, I was exhausted and more than ready to call it a night. It had been a long, busy day, but a joyous one, and I couldn't be happier for all the events that had transpired. I got my things together, changed into my nightgown, and wearily crawled into bed. I did my nightly devotions and bowed my head to pray.

"Thank You, Lord, for my wonderful family," I expressed so very grateful, "and for bringing Grampa and Gramma back to us, too. What an incredible blessing! Thank You so much that Aunt Sara and Uncle Mark get to come for a visit, and please, Lord, please keep them safe as they travel! Thank You for keeping Papa safe today and for providing for us, and..." I paused, almost too embarrassed to utter the words. "I...I just want to say, too," I hemmed and hawed, "how...how very thankful I am that...well... that Isaac, he...he called me pretty today! It was *truly amazing!*" I was beaming as the words left my lips, absolutely giddy at the thought! "Lord," I continued with earnest, "if Isaac is who *You* would have for me, then please, Lord, help me to have wisdom and help me to trust You no matter what. I ask that You would please bless our sleep tonight and the services tomorrow, and please bless Isaac with the message that we need to hear. Thank You, I love You, Lord, In Jesus' name, Amen."

I climbed into bed and fell asleep in no time at all.

*****

Unfortunately, five-thirty came all too quickly and as much as I wanted to roll over and go back to sleep, I knew that I couldn't. I hurried and dressed, did my morning devotions, fixed my bed and my hair, and started downstairs to prepare breakfast. My hope was to have everything all ready before anyone else got up.

As soon as I opened my bedroom door to leave, however, I couldn't help but notice the most delectable smells wafting up the stairs. I quickly hustled down to the kitchen to see what was going on.

As I turned the corner into the kitchen, I was shocked to find Gramma already putting the last of the breakfast dishes on the table.

"Good mornin' dear," she said cheerfully as I walked into the kitchen. "Did ya sleep well?"

I furrowed my brow, befuddled and a little concerned.

"Yes, Gramma," I replied, "but...what on earth are you doing up so early? Did you have trouble sleeping or something?"

"Oh no, dear!" Gramma assured me. "I was up at four this mornin' -prayin' and spendin' time with the Lord. I find doin' my devotions early in the mornin' like that is the best time for me. It's usually quiet and I can spend my time really listenin' to God. When I was finished, you were still asleep, so I thought I'd come and get started with breakfast." She looked at me apprehensively. "I trust that's all right?" she hoped.

"Of course it is!" I answered hastily, not wanting to sound ungrateful. "It's just that…I was hoping to be able to extend *you* the hospitality. Regardless, though," I went on to say with a smile, walking over to her, "I really do appreciate the help!" I leaned in and gave her a kiss on the cheek. "But, Gramma," I lightly scolded, "you really didn't have to!"

"Oh, I know, sweetie," she dismissed, "but you know me, I love to cook, and I really don't mind at all!"

"Well," I complimented as I looked around at all she'd prepared, "it looks delicious! Pert near a feast, I'd say!"

"First come, first serve!" she offered with a smile. "Better dig in before the fellas start comin'."

I chuckled, delighted to oblige.

"Thanks, Gramma," I announced gladly. "I think I will! Join me?"

"Absolutely!" she accepted with a grin.

She and I sat and talked for a little while, enjoying the meal, but before we knew it, Samuel was meandering into the kitchen, rubbing his eyes, yawning and stretching, trying to wake himself up.

"Mornin'," he said, still half-asleep. "What's for breakfast?"

Gramma smiled and kindly got up to go help guide his sleepy body to the table.

"Well," she directed, "we've got bacon and eggs, biscuits with gravy, bread and butter, and some oatmeal. For drinks, we've got freshly squeezed orange juice, milk, of course, and also we've got some coffee, but I think you're a bit too young for that just yet. So," she queried happily, "what's your fancy?"

Samuel's eyes suddenly lit up with excitement when he heard the menu.

"Do I have to choose?" he asked, chomping at the bit. "Or can I sample some of everything?"

Gramma laughed at his exuberance.

"There's gracious plenty for growin' boys," she granted. "You're welcome to whatever ya can eat. Enjoy!"

Samuel immediately sat down and began piling his plate high with all kinds of food. He said a quick prayer and commenced to eating right away.

I just sat there watching him for awhile, astounded at his ferocity! Sometimes, I just couldn't believe how much food my little brother could put away!

It wasn't very long, and Papa and Grampa were coming in from the barn. Apparently, unbeknownst to me, they'd both been up since four-thirty doing chores and various and sundry of other things.

"Somethin' smells delicious!" Grampa bellowed, sniffing through the air.

"I'm with ya on that one, Pa!" Papa wholeheartedly agreed.

"Well, I sure do hope you boys are hungry," Gramma remarked, "because I made plenty!"

"Famished!" Grampa replied, wide eyed.

Papa and Grampa went to wash up, and when they returned, we all sat eating until it was time to clean up and make ourselves ready for church.

As I stood in front of my mirror, fixing my hair and primping my dress, I couldn't help but think about Isaac. I just couldn't wait to see him again and hear him preach! I said a quick prayer in my heart for him that God would calm his nerves (if he were nervous), and that God would use him in a great way. A smile stayed on my face practically the entire time as thoughts of him kept running through my mind.

It was so hard to be patient, just waiting, not knowing if Isaac thought of me in the same way as I thought of him, not knowing for certain if he was the one whom God had for me. I kept telling myself to stop worrying about it, telling myself that (*Oh, dare I even think it?*) if Isaac wasn't the one, then that would be all right, too, but it definitely wasn't easy as I cared for him a great deal! Deep down, though, I acknowledged, as hard as it would be to accept, I needed to be willing to do whatever God wanted me to do. Trying to force something that shouldn't be just wouldn't be right! I knew that it was more important for me to marry the man *God* wanted me to marry than to marry the man *I* thought I should marry. …Still, it was hard!

I bowed my head right then and there and whispered a little prayer in my heart. *Oh God,* I begged, *please give me wisdom and the patience to wait upon You!*

Suddenly, Papa called from downstairs.

"Jochebed," he shouted, "are ya ready, sweetheart? We really need to get goin', or we're gonna be late."

"Coming, Papa," I yelled back. "I'll be down in a minute." I took one more look at myself in the mirror, sprayed a little of Mama's perfume on my dress, gathered my things, and headed downstairs.

By the time I got outside, everyone was already waiting in the wagon.

"Hurry on now, child!" Papa encouraged as he jumped down to help me in.

I settled myself in the back beside Samuel, and off we went.

"Hmmm!" Samuel teased. "Someone sure smells awfully sweet this mornin'."

Gramma turned around and put her hand on my knee, smiling approvingly.

"Ya look beautiful, my dear," she complimented.

"Thank you, Gramma," I said as I shot a glance of disapproval at Samuel.

Samuel just laughed, leaned over, and mockingly quipped, "Someone's in *looove!*"

"Oh, Samuel!" I groused quietly. "Would you hush before someone hears you? Just stop it! Sit up and mind yourself!"

Of course, Samuel didn't listen, instead he kept right on teasing me and taunting me most of the way to church. Thankfully, he did, at least, have the courtesy to do it in somewhat hushed tones, keeping his foolishness just between him and me. After awhile, though, his lovesick eyes blinking at me and his obnoxious smooching sounds became quite annoying! I tried to ignore him, but he was relentless! Unmercifully, he continued on, right up until Papa happened to catch a glimpse of him smooching in my direction.

"Samuel!" he shouted in a somewhat angry tone. "Son, what in the world are ya doin'?"

Samuel immediately sat straight up stiff as a board, wiped the cheesy grin off his face, unpooched his lips, and replied in a most serious tone.

"Nothin', Papa!" he lied. He swallowed hard, nervously waiting for Papa to respond.

Papa, however, just frowned warily, turned around, and dropped the matter altogether.

I silently started to chuckle to myself, glad the ruthless teasing had finally come to an end.

Samuel, less than pleased, looked up at me, quickly stuck out his tongue, and went back to sitting there quietly.

*****

When we arrived at church, I waved to Naomi as she and her family were walking towards the church house. She politely excused herself and came running over to greet me.

~

Naomi was my best friend. We were practically like sisters. We'd known each other forever because Mama and Mrs. Anderson, Naomi's mother, had been best friends long before she and I were ever born. She and I shared many of the same interests, and we told each other *everything!* In fact, she was the only other person in the whole world that knew about Isaac. She kept my secret well, though, holding tightly to it as if it were her own. She was such a precious friend to me, and often, I truly didn't know what I would do without her!

~

Naomi cheerfully came walking up to our wagon.

"Good morning, Jochebed!" she called out. "And Mr. and Mrs. Lowry!" she exclaimed, surprised, when she noticed them sitting there. "Why, hello! How nice to see you again! I thought that was you I saw when you were driving up. I had no idea you were coming for a visit. How are you doing?"

Grampa and Gramma smiled graciously as Gramma answered.

"We're doin' just fine, dear," she replied happily. "And you Naomi, how have you and your family been?"

"Everyone is doing fine, ma'am," Naomi conveyed. "Thank you for asking."

Samuel jumped down from the wagon and ran off to find his friends, while Papa helped me down. Once I had my things, Naomi and I proceeded to walk on together towards the church building. Papa, Grampa, and Gramma followed on behind us.

As soon as we entered the church, I immediately began looking around for Isaac. At first, I didn't see him anywhere, but then, as we walked into the auditorium, there he was. He was standing upfront off to the left talking with Pastor and Mrs. Scott. I tried not to stare, but he looked so handsome with his dark wavy hair combed so neatly, standing there in his dark black suit with his white shirt and dark tie. He was simply gorgeous! Taking my eyes off of him was not easy!

It was almost time for the service to start, however, so I took my seat beside Naomi in the third pew from the front on the right-hand side of the church. Pastor Scott and Isaac took their places on the platform, and when the clock struck ten thirty, Pastor Scott got up to welcome everyone to the service. He asked everyone to stand for the opening prayer and afterwards proceeded to lead the congregation in an opening hymn. When we finished singing, Pastor Scott directed us all to sit down, gave some announcements, and then had us sing two more songs. When the last note was dampened, Pastor Scott invited Naomi to the platform where she sang a most beautiful special.

~

Without a doubt, Naomi was blessed! God had most definitely gifted her with an absolute stunning voice she had always been able to sing, and sing well, even as a child. Sometimes she and I would sing together, but I much preferred to listen to her sing alone. She sang so skillfully, and she did it with such grace and humility. To me, it was a wonderful testimony as she was willing to use her talents and abilities for the Lord!

~

When Naomi finished singing, many amens could be heard all over the auditorium. Pastor Scott walked to the lectern, thanked Naomi for her message in song, and eagerly introduced Isaac as the guest speaker.

Isaac smiled graciously, mounted the pulpit, and thanked Pastor Scott for giving him the opportunity to preach. He thanked Naomi for her beautiful song and thanked everyone for being there. After the pleasantries, he asked everyone to stand and turn in their Bibles to the book of Isaiah. He read through the passage, prayed, and seated us all so that he could begin. His sermon was strong and forceful and he delivered it quite well, and I can honestly say that I received a tremendous blessing as he preached.

Sitting there, listening intently, however, the hour seemed to fly by quickly, the minutes ticking away with ease. Before I knew it, the music was starting and the invitation was being given. Several people responded, one gentleman for salvation, (praise the Lord!), and after he'd been dealt with, Pastor Scott closed in prayer. He thanked Isaac for his powerful message, invited everyone back for the evening service, and dismissed us all for the afternoon.

What a wonderful morning in church it had been! Naomi and I talked briefly before she had to go and practice with Mrs. Grant, the piano player, as Naomi was due to sing another special in a few weeks and Mrs. Grant was going to accompany her. Before Naomi left, though, I made sure to convey to her how much I thoroughly enjoyed her song. She thanked me, we hugged, and she dashed off to practice.

I stood there a minute looking around, when suddenly, I spotted Samuel chasing about the auditorium with his friends. I was just about to go and reprimand him when Papa caught a glimpse of him as well. As soon as he did, Samuel's untoward activity quickly came to halt. As Samuel dashed by, Papa managed to get a hold of the back of his collar, promptly plopping him down in a pew there beside himself. Needless to say, neither was happy! Papa scowled angrily as he leaned down and whispered something in Samuel's ear. Whatever it was, it instantly caused a despondent look to come across Samuel's face. I can only imagine that whatever punishment was coming his way was not sitting very well with him.

~

Samuel, for the most part, was a good boy, just a bit restless and immature from time to time. He'd just turned twelve, and Papa was doing his best to keep him on the straight and narrow. Without Mama there to help him, though, Papa's job had become a whole lot harder. I tried to be an example to Samuel and help out with him where I could, but I was quickly learning that little brothers don't often like to take advice from their much older sisters. To him, I was overstepping and being bossy, and he wasn't about to listen to what I had to say. It was definitely a challenge at times!

~

I slowly started to make my way across the auditorium to Papa and Samuel, nodding politely to folks as we passed. Even though I wasn't much of a talker, I did enjoy being around others, watching them talk, and laugh, and encourage each other. Of course, I'd speak when spoken to, and while it could be a bit awkward at times, I have to admit, it was nice to have the opportunity to visit with people you rarely saw throughout the week.

As I made my way closer, I could see Grampa and Gramma talking with Mr. and Mrs. Lewis, and there beside them was Andrew, standing with his fiancée, Isabelle.

Andrew and Isabelle were such a handsome couple, and I was so excited for them and their upcoming nuptials in the spring.

I walked up and stood beside Papa, waiting patiently as he finished his conversation with Mr. Bell. (Mr. Bell was the banker in town, and he and Papa had been in school together when they were younger.) As I waited, I looked down at Samuel who was still sitting in the pew, fuming. His arms were folded, fists clenched, and he was staring angrily - kicking the floor with his foot.

I leaned over and whispered in his ear.

"It can't be all that bad, can it?" I commented, trying to cheer him.

He looked at me curtly and grumbled.

"What do you know about it?" he snapped crossly. Aggravated, he irritably looked back down at the floor and went right on moping.

I decided it'd be best to leave him be.

Soon Grampa and Gramma came walking up beside me. Just as they did, I heard Papa end his discussion with Mr. Bell.

"All right, Tom," he said, "I'll get back with ya about that later. Talk to ya soon."

Mr. Bell walked on as Papa turned around to talk with Grampa and Gramma.

As soon as Papa was turned about, Gramma put her hand on his arm.

"Son," she told him, "I hope ya don't mind, but I've invited the Lewises to join us for Sunday dinner. I know it's short notice and all, but Cilia did say she and Marvin would help with the meal. I hope it's all right?"

Papa chuckled.

"Ma," he quipped, "don't think I really have much of a choice now, do I? It'd be kind of rude of me to uninvite 'em now, don't ya think?"

Gramma looked flustered as if she'd done something wrong in inviting them without asking for Papa's permission first.

Papa noticed her angst.

"I'm just teasin' with ya, Ma," he assured her with a smile. "It's no problem. I enjoy visitin' with the Lewises."

Gramma smiled timidly, but relieved.

"All right then," she accepted, "we'd better get goin'. We have a lot of preparin' to do for dinner."

Papa sobered as he reached down and tapped Samuel on the shoulder.

"Let's go, Son!" he instructed sternly.

Samuel groused and grudgingly got up, heading for the door. Grampa and Papa followed, talking back and forth with each other, and Gramma and I walked on behind them.

As we walked, I came up right beside Gramma, taking her arm, huddling close. My heart was racing as I leaned in and whispered in her ear.

"Does this mean Isaac will be coming, too?" I asked anxiously.

Gramma smiled subtly as if she'd planned the whole thing from the start.

"Why, yes, dear," she replied innocently, "I suppose it does. I mean, it'd be impolite of me not to invite him, don't ya think?"

She walked on ahead as I paused, shaking my head at her deviousness.

Gramma, I thought, *what are you up to?*

Gramma looked back with a broad smile on her face and encouraged coyly.

"Coming, dear?" she asked.

I continued to shake my head, still questioning her intentions as I walked on.

While I knew Grampa and Gramma were good friends with the Lewises, and I knew they'd not seen each other for quite some time and wanted to catch up, somehow I felt there were ulterior motives to Gramma inviting them over today of all days. This just *happened* to be the very day Isaac was home from college. Coincidence? I think not!

Gramma, I smiled to myself, *I'm on to you!*

Pastor Scott and Isaac were both standing by the door, shaking hands with folks as they left the church. Part of me wanted to run out the side door to avoid having to say anything to Isaac, but I knew that was silly and immature. Knowing I'd have to face him, I did my best to muster up as much courage within myself as I possibly could.

As I stood there waiting my turn to leave, I rehearsed in my mind what I would say when I approached. I thought I had it down, but inching ever closer, my heart began to pound, my mouth went completely dry, and my mind suddenly went blank. As you can imagine, I was panicked! Only Papa and Samuel, and Grampa and Gramma now stood between him and me.

Suddenly, I saw Papa advance. He shook Pastor Scott's hand and complimented Isaac on his sermon, hit Samuel on the arm to get him to shake hands and be polite, (to which Samuel bristled and reluctantly complied), and then the two of them walked on out of the church together. Their encounter seemed like it only took seconds.

Once they were gone, Grampa and Gramma quickly stepped forward to offer their respects. I swallowed hard, knowing I was next! I thought I would have a few minutes to regroup, to regain my thoughts, but before I knew it, they were gone, too!

It was now my turn!

Apprehensively, I stepped forward to extend my hand to Pastor Scott. He smiled and thanked me for being there, and said something about looking forward to Naomi and me singing together again. (At least, I think that's what he said, although I can't really be certain as my mind was so preoccupied with Isaac and what I was going to say to him, my brief conversation with Pastor Scott was little more than just a blur.) I thanked him (I think), and then…there he was, Isaac, standing right in front of me! There was that gorgeous smile and those stunning blue eyes looking right into mine! I felt as if I were going to wilt as Isaac took my hand to shake it.

"Hello, Jochebed," he said politely, "it's so nice to see you this morning."

I smiled nervously, and suddenly all that courage I thought I'd built up inside of me abandoned me in one split second.

"Nice tie!" I blurted out awkwardly as I pulled my hand from his and promptly walked on.

"*Thanks!*" I heard him reply, rather bewildered and confused.

My heart sank as I realized what a blunder I had just made.

"*Nice tie?*" I berated myself as I walked towards the wagon, shaking my head in disgust. "*Nice tie? Are you kidding me? Jochebed!* **What were you thinking?** Nice tie? Not…nice delivery, not…I enjoyed your message, not…nice to see you, too, but… *nice tie? Oh, good grief!*" I hit myself in the head, *furious* with myself! "*Oh!* What Isaac must think of me?!?" I lamented.

I went on to the wagon where my family was waiting. I was *absolutely mortified* as I climbed in the back and sat down, embarrassed to the core, feeling simply awful for what had just happened!

As we started for home, I began to wonder if it was possible to ever recover from this gigantic faux paus! I couldn't help but fret, wondering how I could ever face Isaac again!

Perhaps, I thought, *this was not meant to be. After all, how could I ever marry a man that I couldn't even bring myself to properly talk to? Dear Lord,* I prayed in my heart, *please help me make it through this afternoon without making an even bigger fool of myself!*

COMMUNICATION
(Chapter 5)

When we arrived home, Papa put Samuel right to work in the barn doing extra chores, punishment for his antics at church. Papa and Grampa stood talking awhile by the woodpile, keeping an eye on him, making sure he was doing them properly.

Gramma and I went straight to work on dinner, and when I had opportunity, I straightened a few things around the house. Being busy seemed to help take my mind off the inevitable uncomfortableness I was sure to feel when Isaac arrived with his family.

As Gramma and I were finishing up with dinner, I heard the Lewis' wagon pull up outside. My heart began to pound harder and faster as I almost dreaded seeing Isaac. Grampa came inside carrying a dish for Mrs. Lewis, and she followed in behind him. Isabelle came in, too, carrying a dessert, and the men stayed outside visiting with Papa. After Grampa set down the dish he was carrying, he went back outside to join the men.

I could see Isaac through the kitchen window, and I started to think of ways that I could try to avoid him. I knew in reality that that was probably not going to be possible and would most certainly appear a bit rude, but it was, nevertheless, rather appealing.

Finally, everything was set, and Gramma sent me to call the men inside. I went to the door and yelled as loudly as I could.

"Dinner's ready!" I shouted.

They all came in, washed up, and headed for the table.

Unbeknownst to me, Gramma had decided to assign seats to everyone at the table, and it *just so happened* that Isaac was seated right next to me! If I didn't know any better, I would have thought she was trying to kill me, for I most definitely thought I was going to die on the spot when I realized what she had done!

Being the perfect gentleman that Isaac was, however, he kindly pulled out my chair for me so that I could sit down. I nervously accepted his gesture, thanked him properly, and took my seat. Once everyone was gathered round, Papa invited Isaac to say grace. He politely accepted, and offered the prayer. When he was finished, everyone began passing the food, talking, laughing, and enjoying each other's company. I, however, sat quietly, concentrating on my plate, feeling quite awkward and embarrassed from earlier.

After things had settled a bit from passing the food around the table, Isaac leaned over and tried to break the ice.

"Thank you for the compliment this morning on my tie," he said sweetly. "Of everyone that came through the line, I think you were the only one that noticed."

Instantly, I could feel the blood draining from my face in embarrassment as I wasn't quite sure if he was mocking me or just simply being polite. Nevertheless, I told him he was welcome and went right back to staring at my plate.

He politely continued on, trying to engage me in conversation.

"So, how much more schooling do you have left?" he asked.

"Two years," I said, barely looking up from my plate.

"And are you enjoying the year so far?" he queried.

"It's going well," I answered, not volunteering any more information.

He persisted, almost as if he were determined to get me to open up.

"Do you have any plans for after you've finished?" he asked considerately.

"Well," I uttered without thinking, "I would very much like to be married and raise a family someday." Then I caught myself! *Did you just say what I think you just said?* I scolded, completely horrified. *Oh, Jochebed! Why on **earth** would you say that - and to Isaac Lewis of all people!?* I suddenly wished I could disappear!

"Well," he responded kindly, "that seems like a laudable goal." He paused as he took a sip of water. "If it's not too forward of me to ask," he wondered, "do you have any prospects in mind?"

My eyes got as big as saucers as I stared even harder at my plate. I choked down the piece of meat I was chewing on, swallowed hard, and replied with a stammer.

"I'd...I'd...I'd rather not say, if that's okay?" I told him, nearly beside myself!

"Oh, that's fine!" he said apologetically. "I didn't mean to pry."

"That's all right," I assured.

And then...awkward silence!

Everyone else continued talking back and forth, enjoying one another's company. Even Samuel seemed to be engaged in conversation with others at the table. It seemed as if Isaac and I, even if for those few brief moments, were in our own little world; all the noise of the others seeming to fade away.

The uncomfortable silence between us, however, was suddenly broken when Isabelle, who was sitting on the other side of Isaac, turned to him and said, "I really enjoyed your message this morning."

"Oh, why, thank you," Isaac replied. And with that, he and she were off in conversation.

Sitting there quietly as I ate, I began to feel somewhat alone. Even though I was surrounded by plenty of other people at the table, I found it difficult to engage them in conversation. I just wished that I had enough nerve and knew what to say without feeling so embarrassed and self conscious. I was typically all right if someone spoke to me first (excluding Isaac, that is), but for me to speak to others I didn't know very well, well, that was quite another matter. Unfortunately, the Lewises were no exception. While I knew them casually through school and through church (of course), we were not at all close, and I definitely felt awkward and uncomfortable around them. I was trying to work on not being so shy, but sadly I still had a long way to go.

Feeling uneasy made the meal seem to drag on forever. So, wanting to be anywhere else but there, I quickly finished my meal and decided to busy myself, cleaning things, refilling things, and generally waiting on others; doing so, I managed to avoid having to converse with too many people directly.

Finally, after about an hour, the meal came to an end, and everyone, except the ladies, retired to the living room to visit some more. Grampa challenged our guests to a tournament of checkers, of course, and everyone but Isaac joined in the game.

As the women started cleaning off the table, I noticed Isaac walk outside by himself. I couldn't help but wonder if everything was all right. As I helped clean, going back and forth in front of the window, I could see him standing out by the big oak tree in the yard, seemingly deep in thought. I started to feel badly, hoping that I hadn't offended him in some way by my less than cordial behavior earlier at the table. He'd been so kind to try to talk to me, yet I had practically ignored him. Suddenly, and entirely out of character, I felt compelled to go outside and speak to him. At first, I fought the notion, but the more I thought on it, the more I realized it was something I needed to do.

"Gramma," I asked, "may I please be excused for a minute?"

She nodded approvingly as if she knew exactly what I was planning to do.

I smiled back, grabbed my shawl, and headed outside.

When I walked out onto the porch, there was Isaac pacing back and forth out by the tree. I made my way down off the porch and cautiously approached him. I really wasn't at all certain what I was going to say to him, but I felt I needed to say something. Not wanting to interrupt his thoughts, however, I quietly walked up and stood there, just waiting for him to notice me.

"Oh, Jochebed!" he said as he turned around. "You startled me!"

"I'm sorry," I replied, almost wanting to retreat back inside. "I didn't mean to intrude." I felt *so* shy and embarrassed.

"Is…is there something you needed?" he inquired, his brow furrowed with question.

"Nnn…no," I stammered bashfully, hemming and hawing. "I…I just saw you come out here alone, and…well…I…I was thinking back on our conversation from earlier, or…or rather our *lack* of conversation, and I guess…well…I guess I was just hoping that…well…that I hadn't…" My heart was racing a mile a minute; I was *so* unbelievably nervous! It was all I could do to force myself to finish what I was trying to say. "I…I was just hoping that I hadn't offended you in some way," I expressed with regret. "I…I just felt I needed to come out here and apologize."

Isaac looked at me completely taken aback by what I'd just told him. He shook his head, wanting to assure me.

"Oh, no…that wasn't necessary!" he quickly replied. "You didn't offend me! In fact," he said as he came a little closer, looking me in the eye, seemingly feeling guilty himself, "I was just out here thinking…" He paused, appearing a bit shy himself at this point. "I was just thinking that perhaps…well… that perhaps I'd offended you in some way?"

I immediately looked at him, astounded!

"Me?" I questioned, completely flabbergasted. "Why…why ever would you think *that?* You've always been *very kind* and *nothing* but a gentleman! I've *never* been offended by you, not even once - honestly I haven't!"

We both just stood there for a minute in awkward silence. Isaac seemed to be searching for the right words to say, and I nervously fidgeted, unsure of what to do myself.

Finally, Isaac looked at me and inquired - seemingly, genuinely confused.

"Then, Jochebed," he asked apprehensively, "I…I don't understand. Is it just me? Have I said or done something or" - he teased a bit - "am I just too boring?"

I looked at him perplexed.

"I mean, maybe you have no interest," he granted. "And…well…if that's the case, then…then I understand, but…what is it? Why won't you talk to me?"

I have to admit, he nearly bowled me over with his question. I was absolutely stunned! I instantly turned away, feeling very ashamed. I suddenly realized in that moment that Isaac *had* noticed me, but foolishly, I had been too embarrassed by my own feelings for him to even give him the proper time of day. I *wasn't* just someone he was being polite to, nor someone he just spoke to in passing, he, in fact, was actually trying to reach out to me, but I was just too blind and withdrawn to see it!

"I am so *so* sorry!" I said, feeling just awful. "I…I…" I didn't know what else to say. I was feeling too guilty and too self-conscious to even look at him.

"Jochebed," he revealed as he cautiously reached out, briefly touching my arm to get my attention. "I…I really would like to be your friend, if…if that's okay."

I was still looking away, as I couldn't bring myself to look at him.

I heard him swallow hard as he nervously began again.

"I…I really would like the chance to get to know you better," he told me. "I…" He stopped abruptly, almost as if he were embarrassed by what he'd just said. "I mean…that is…ohhh!" He punched his hand, aggravated with himself. "I'm getting this all wrong!" he blustered, looking away, clearly frustrated.

I finally looked up, trying to catch his gaze.

"Isaac," I said, trying to assure him, "I…I would very much like that, too!"

He looked back at me, pleasantly surprised.

"You would?" he asked, wanting to clarify.

I couldn't help but smile.

"Yes, Isaac," I confessed, "I would! In truth, I would love nothing more!"

A look of relief came over Isaac as a smile made its way across his face.

I nervously smiled at him, as he nervously smiled at me. We both just stood there staring at each other, not knowing what to say or do next.

After a minute or two of uneasiness between us, we both broke out into nervous laughter.

Finally, Isaac sobered and looked at me more seriously.

"Jochebed," he said, "the truth is, and I hope this isn't too soon, or even too forward, but…I would really like to ask your father's permission to…to court you. I mean…with your consent, of course."

My jaw nearly dropped in disbelief as I couldn't believe my ears!

Did he just say he wants to court **me?** I questioned to myself.

He must have sensed my complete and utter shock.

"I've overstepped, haven't I?" he apologized abruptly. "Here we were just becoming friends, and I've gone and pushed too far!"

"No, no!" I hastily answered, not wanting to give the wrong impression. "You haven't overstepped! It's just that…well…I…I never…I guess I never thought that you thought of me in that way. I mean…don't get me wrong…I wanted you to, but…" I paused, still reeling from his request. I looked at him questioning. "You would honestly consider *me* someone you would want to court?" I asked, feeling quite undeserving.

"Absolutely!" he stated emphatically, without hesitation. He looked at me intently. "I have to be honest with you, Jochebed," he confessed, "I've been thinking about this for quite some time now."

Needless to say, I was totally stunned by the disclosure! While I had dreamed of it, never in a million years did I ever think it would actually happen! I'm certain I must have looked completely dumbfounded!

Isaac continued.

"I just never had the nerve to say anything until now," he told me, "partly because I wasn't sure of …well…I wasn't sure of our age difference and all, and too, partly because…well…because you barely seemed to give me the time of day when I was around. I guess given your reluctance, I just assumed that you weren't interested in me in that way."

I stood there flabbergasted, just absolutely amazed!! I honestly couldn't believe what I was hearing! Here he and I had wasted all this time between us, and all because neither of us had the courage to say anything to the other. I was struck by the irony!

"I have to admit," Isaac revealed, "these past two days, seeing you again, being around you - it brought back all the feelings that I'd tried to bury." He shook his head, hesitant. "I hope this isn't too much for you," he said with concern, "but I felt it needed to be said. I do hope you can forgive me my cowardice for not having said it sooner."

I was just thunderstruck! Isaac truly liked me! The reality was slowly starting to sink in.

"Well," he prodded anxiously, "what do you think?"

I stood there staring at him, speechless.

"I…I just can't believe that you've felt this way about me all this time!" I expressed with dismay.

Isaac nodded, indicating that it was true.

"Well then," I said a little sheepishly, "I…I feel I have to be honest with you as well." By now, I was nearly shaking from excitement and admitted nervousness. I looked down, feeling insecure and shy. "Isaac, I…" I started to confess, my heart pounding, my hands sweating, "I like you, too. I have…I have ever since…well…ever since you were still in school." I took a deep breath, trying to calm myself, absolutely *astounded* that I was actually saying these things to Isaac Lewis. I glanced up at him, regretful and embarrassed. "I'll admit," I acknowledged, "I was just too timid and backwards and, of course, a bit reluctant to say anything to you. I didn't want to seem forward or anything."

Isaac smiled sweetly.

"Of course," he understood. "And believe me, Jochebed," he calmed, "I know exactly how you feel…about being nervous and reticent, that is…and it's okay. I'm just glad we finally talked. And, hey," he went on, "don't feel badly at all about not saying anything to me, it really wasn't your place or responsibility, it was mine, and I just wish now that I hadn't waited so long to do so."

I was so relieved that everything was finally out in the open.

Isaac seemed relieved as well.

"I've definitely learned a valuable lesson in all this," he conveyed.

"Oh," I queried, "and what's that?"

"Communication," he said, smiling. "It's absolutely key!"

We both laughed, realizing how true the statement was.

"If it's all right with you," Isaac pressed on, determined, "I'll speak to your father right away."

I smiled, delighted.

"I think that would be wonderful!" I expressed with enthusiasm and anticipation. I looked at him earnestly. "And thank you, Isaac," I said with all sincerity.

"For what?" he questioned.

"For being honest with me," I replied, "and…well…for choosing me!"

He smiled approvingly as I smiled back, giddy and overwhelmed. I just couldn't believe that this was actually happening!

Now that things were settled between us, we both headed back to the house, thrilled and eager for the prospects in front of us. There was definitely a sense of excitement in our demeanor as Isaac opened the door for me to go back inside. I hung my shawl on the peg beside the door and went back to helping the ladies in the kitchen. Isaac, smiling expectantly, went to the living room to find Papa.

When he walked in, Papa was sitting on the couch reading the newspaper, Mr. Lewis was napping in the chair across the way, and Grampa and the others were engaged in a checkers tournament in the opposite corner of the room.

"Excuse me, sir," Isaac said as he walked up to Papa. "Could I please speak to you in private for a moment?"

Papa lowered the newspaper and looked up over his glasses.

"Ya need to speak to me in private?" he asked warily.

"Yes, sir," Isaac responded nervously. "It's important."

Papa put the paper aside.

"Well," he said standing to his feet, "we can go out to the barn. No one to bother us out there."

Isaac nodded, agreeing, and he and Papa came walking into the kitchen.

When Isaac saw me and I saw him, he slyly smiled, and I returned the sentiment. I quickly sobered, however, when I heard Papa speak, afraid that he might see.

"Ma," Papa said as he grabbed his hat, "Isaac and I are goin' to the barn. We'll be back in a little while."

Gramma acknowledged, and Papa opened the door to step outside. Visibly nervous, Isaac took a deep breath and followed him out. I couldn't help but feel sorry for him. Having to confront Papa was definitely no picnic! I said a quick prayer as Isaac walked outside, closing the door behind him.

Once inside the barn, Papa turned to Isaac.

"So," he asked with little emotion, "what's on your mind, Son?"

Isaac anxiously hemmed and hawed.

"Well, you see, Mr. Lowry," he started to say, "I was just wondering…" He paused, trying to gather his courage. He swallowed hard and began again. "Well, sir," he said, "I was just wondering…"

Papa sensed his trepidation.

"What is it, Son?" he prodded. "Speak your mind!"

Isaac took a deep breath and resolved himself.

"Sir," he stated abruptly, "I want to court your daughter!"

Papa instantly furrowed his brow, none too happy with the pronouncement.

Isaac stammered to clarify.

"I…I mean…I mean," he backpedaled, "I would like your *permission* to court your daughter…that is…sir."

Papa was still reticent as he pulled at his chin.

"Jochebed?" he questioned, clearly not thrilled with the request. "Ya want to court *my* Jochebed?"

Isaac swallowed hard again as he steeled himself.

"Yes, sir," he replied, almost too nervous to speak.

Papa looked quite dour.

"You're how old, Son?" he asked sternly.

Isaac took a deep breath.

"Well, sir," he answered honestly, "I'm just twenty. I turned twenty this past June."

Papa stared at him, very uneasy with his answer.

"Twenty, huh?" he repeated apprehensively.

"Yes, sir," Isaac confirmed.

Papa stood there austerely, weighing the matter.

"And Jochebed," he wanted to know, "have ya spoken to her about all this?"

"Yes, sir," Isaac assured, a little more confident. "We've spoken."

Papa shook his head, still surly, still very apprehensive.

"She's just seventeen, ya know," Papa reminded gruffly.

"Yes, sir," Isaac replied, "I'm aware of that, sir, but…"

Papa tersely interrupted.

"You're a college man," he stated, "and she still has two years of school to go. I assume ya wantin' to court her means ya have the idea of marriage in mind one day. What about her schoolin'?"

"Oh, sir," Isaac tried to assuage, "I have no plans for marriage right away! We'd most certainly wait until after she's finished."

Papa was still clearly troubled by the whole thing.

"And you're serious about this?" he questioned. "Ya truly see my Jochebed as a potential wife for yourself?"

"Absolutely, sir!" Isaac answered doggedly. "I do! I took notice of her several years ago, and I've watched her grow into a fine young woman. She's always conducted herself with grace and strong moral character. I can see she loves God, and that's very important to me." He looked at Papa with earnest. "I promise you, sir," he said with all sincerity, "I will be honorable with your daughter and treat her with the utmost respect."

Papa just shook his head.

"Still," he countered, "you're a college man, and ya have, what, two, three more years to go?"

"Just two, sir," Isaac told him, "but that includes this one. And of course, I'll be home from time to time during the year and again next summer."

Papa shook his head more vehemently.

"But that's just it!" he stated forcefully. "You'll be away! What if in those two years ya meet a girl while at college…" He paused, concerned, looking directly at Isaac. "Ya have to understand, Son," he went on to explain, "Jochebed…well…she's been through a lot lately, what…with the sudden passin' of her ma and all. I…I don't want her gettin' hurt again."

Isaac nodded.

"I understand that, sir," he stated sympathetically, "and I assure you I have the very best intentions towards your daughter. She truly is the only one I've ever considered courting."

Papa sighed heavily as he stood there contemplating, the look on his face almost one of anger towards Isaac for even daring to ask to court his little girl. It was obvious he had his reservations.

Isaac waited anxiously yet patiently for Papa to give his consent.

After several agonizing minutes, Papa finally spoke up.

"Isaac," he flattered, "I like ya, Son, I do. I mean…ya seem like a real decent, godly young man, but…" He shook his head again. "She's my daughter," he argued, "and I need to protect her. I just don't think she's ready for this right now. …I'm sorry. You'll just have to wait!"

"But, sir!" Isaac pleaded. "I…"

"Ya have my answer, Isaac!" Papa stated firmly, abruptly cut him off. "I'm sorry. Jochebed's off limits!"

Isaac clenched his jaw, breathing heavily, shaking his head in aggravation.

"I'll respect your decision, sir," he came back at him angrily, "but with all due respect, you can't protect her forever!" Isaac was seething, more than a little frustrated and upset, but he kept his manners. "I thank your family for their hospitality," he said, trying to hold back his emotions. "Please, inform my grandparents that I'll see them at church this evening. Good day!"

Isaac left the barn, visibly disappointed and shaken. He promptly headed home.

All the while Papa and Isaac were talking, I was anxiously waiting by the window in the kitchen, my eyes fixed on the barn. The ladies had finished cleaning and had joined the men in the living room to visit, so I was all alone in the kitchen.

Gramma suddenly noticed my absence and came looking for me.

"Jochebed," she said sweetly as she walked up and put her arm around my shoulder, giving it a squeeze, "there ya are. Why don't ya come join us?"

"Oh, Gramma," I whispered back, not wanting anyone to overhear, "I'm waiting for Papa and Isaac."

"Oh?" Gramma queried expectantly.

"Yes," I answered quietly. "Today I found out that Isaac really *does* like me! And he wants to court me, Gramma - *me!*" I could scarcely contain my excitement.

Gramma got a huge, enthusiastic grin on her face, barely able to contain hers.

"Why...that's wonderful my dear!" she exclaimed. "Just wonderful!"

"He's out there right now, this very minute, asking Papa's permission!" I informed her. "I can hardly believe it, Gramma! It's all just happening so fast!"

"Why, it's what ya wanted, isn't it?" she asked a little troubled.

"Oh, of course, it is!" I assured her ardently. "It's just...well...it's just so much to take in! I've wanted this for so long that it almost doesn't seem real! I'm so afraid it's all just a wonderful dream that someone's going to wake me from."

Gramma gave me a reassuring hug, and we stood there together, watching through the window - watching, that is, right up until we both saw Isaac leave the barn abruptly, get into his buggy, and ride away.

Gramma and I immediately looked at each other with grave concern.

"What could that mean?" I asked fretfully.

"Why, I'm not sure, dear," Gramma replied, befuddled. "But," she tried to calm, "I'm sure there's a good explanation. Let's not jump to any conclusions. Come on now away from the window. We'll know soon enough."

Gramma tried to get me to go with her to the living room, but I was having none of it.

"Gramma," I resisted, so upset and full of worry, "if you don't mind, I'd like to stay here a little longer."

Gramma was hesitant, but she seemed to understand.

"All right, dear," she allowed, "but stop worrying. I'm sure everything will be fine."

She squeezed me tightly again and gave me a reassuring smile, and as much as I wanted to believe her, I just couldn't! Isaac seemed so upset, and I hadn't yet seen Papa emerge from the barn. The signs were just too ominous!

A few minutes later, the barn door opened and Papa came walking out. The look on his face was somber, and his demeanor was not at all encouraging. My countenance fell as soon as I saw him, and my heart sank deep within my chest. I could feel it begin to beat faster and faster as Papa approached the house.

I stood there at the window, breathlessly waiting, hoping against hope that maybe I had misread the situation. When Papa came through the door and looked at me, however, I knew right away that I hadn't.

"Papa," I asked anxiously, taking a step towards him, "where's Isaac?"

"He left, Jochebed," Papa answered in a harsh tone as he hung his hat on the peg by the door.

"What…why?" I questioned in dismay. "Why would he? What did you say to him, Papa? What did you do?" Tears began to well up inside of me as fear crept into my heart.

Papa turned and looked at me, sighing reluctantly.

"Jochebed," he said as he took a step towards me.

I backed away in anger, instinctively knowing what he had done.

"You're so young, sweetheart," he tried to explain, "and I…"

I immediately ran from the room, crying, scurrying as fast as I could up the stairs to my room. It was all just too much!

Gramma heard the commotion and came rushing back into the kitchen.

"Michael," she asked, worried, walking up to Papa, "what's happened? Where's Jochebed?"

"Pay it no mind, Ma!" Papa dismissed angrily. "This is between Jochebed and me! She'll get over it!" Papa shook his head in aggravation and walked on into the living room to join the guests.

Gramma didn't follow, however; instead, she came looking for me.

"Jochebed, sweetheart," she called out as she knocked softly on my bedroom door, "may I please come in?"

I was lying facedown on my bed, sobbing uncontrollably into my pillow. I couldn't understand what Papa was doing.

Why was he being so mean? I wept. *What could possibly be wrong with Isaac?*

Gramma knocked again.

"Sweetheart, please," she begged, "I really would like to talk with ya."

I just wanted to be left alone, but I knew Gramma had my best interest at heart, so I relented and told her through my tears that she could come in.

Gramma opened the door and quietly closed it behind her. She walked over to my bed, carefully sat down beside me, and gently began to stroke my hair in sympathy.

"Oh, Jochebed," she said, seeming to understand, "I'm so very sorry!"

Overwhelmed, I immediately sat up and turned to bury my head in her shoulder, bawling even harder.

"Why, Gramma?" I cried in desperation. "How could Papa do this? I've wanted this for so long!"

"There, there, child," she calmed, hugging me tightly. "There, there!" She patiently let me cry on a little while longer, but then she spoke to me in a much more serious tone. "Jochebed," she said firmly, "now I want ya to sit up here and listen to me."

I obeyed and sat up, sniffing and wiping my tears, looking up at her so heartbroken.

"Ya know that your father loves ya very much," she started.

"But it doesn't seem…" I interjected, trying to argue my case. That was as far as I got, though, because Gramma pushed right on, determined to make her point.

"Jochebed," she reiterated sternly, "your father loves ya!"

I kept quiet, and reluctantly nodded.

She went on.

"Your pa," she continued, trying to help me to see, "he's all alone now, tryin' to navigate in waters with you children that he's unfamiliar with. It's gonna take him time to figure things out. I'm certain he thought he would always have your ma here to help him with such things, *especially* with matters of the heart."

I sniffed and sniffed, trying to fight back tears, but it just hurt too much. I broke down again.

"Oh, sweetheart," Gramma comforted tenderly, wiping a tear from my cheek, "your pa…well…he's a man, and…those things just don't always come so easily to 'em. Ya need to be patient with him." She pulled me to her, cradling my head in her hands as I sobbed. "And listen," she pointed out, "ya have to remember; he knows *nothin'* of how ya feel."

I sat back up and looked at her, despondent.

She looked me square in the eye and told me honestly.

"Jochebed," she tried to explain, "for all he knows, this was all Isaac's doin' and his alone. Ya need to have the courage to talk to your pa and tell him how ya truly feel."

I sniffed again, blew my nose, and wiped away my tears. When I'd composed myself the best I could, I looked at Gramma pitifully.

"I know you're right, Gramma," I acknowledged, still fighting back tears, "it's just that…it's just that it hurts so much!" I couldn't help it; I started crying again. "What if Papa won't listen?" I cried, distraught. "What if he still says no?"

I knew how close minded and stubborn Papa could be sometimes, and in my grief, I feared the worst.

"Now, Jochebed," Gramma reprimanded, "I've always known your pa to be firm but fair! Ya need to give him a chance. Don't go borrowin' trouble where there is none! Besides, just think, *what if* he says, yes?"

Gramma sweetly took my face and held it in her hands as she smiled lovingly at me, trying to help me see that things weren't as bad as I perceived them to be. I knew she was probably right, but I was so hurt and angry with Papa that it was hard to see things from her perspective.

"Now," she said tenderly, gently prodding me to straighten up, "get yourself pulled together and clean yourself up. It's about time we were headin' off to church. You and your father will work this out," she bolstered, "I have every confidence!" She gave me a sympathetic smile. "Just talk to him, Jochebed," she encouraged, "and trust - trust that God knows what He's doin'. He's still in control, sweetheart, even in all of this!"

I sniffed and nodded, reluctantly accepting her point.

Gramma smiled kindly, patted my hand, stood to her feet, and left.

When she was gone, I sat there for a few more minutes, trying to figure everything out. As much as I just wanted to stay and cry and vent my anger, I knew that I couldn't - church was waiting.

After sitting a while longer, I decided to get myself ready to go. My heart was still heavy, but Gramma *had* given me a glimmer of hope that maybe things could still work out. I grudgingly stood up and went to look at myself in the mirror.

"Oh, goodness!" I exclaimed, lamenting my appearance.

My eyes were all puffy from crying, and my hair was a tangled mess. I straightened myself up the best I could, grabbed my things, and headed off downstairs.

As I started my decent, with every step I took, I felt myself getting angrier and angrier with Papa. I tried not to be, but the scene of Isaac driving away kept playing over and over again in my mind. The more it did, the more I felt the pain and sting of what Papa had done. Needless to say, by the time I reached the bottom of the steps, I was determined that I was not going to talk to Papa, at least, not for now. I knew that I needed to get past some of my anger before confronting him, so I decided I would do my best to avoid him if I could.

When I entered the kitchen, everyone was making their way outside to the wagons to head off to church. Fortunately, Papa had already gone outside, so I didn't have to see him. I walked over, grabbed my Bible off the shelf in the kitchen, and walked to the door to grab my shawl.

As I made my way outside, the Lewises were just pulling away, waving goodbye, and thanking us again for our hospitality. Grampa was helping Gramma into the wagon, and Samuel was running out of the barn, clumsily tucking his shirt in his pants, hopping into the wagon himself. Papa was just soberly standing there, waiting on everyone to get in.

I put my head down, hoping to avoid eye contact, and slowly started walking towards the wagon. I was simply still too angry and hurt to deal with anyone.

Of course, as I got closer, Samuel couldn't help himself. Right away, he called out to me, being meddlesome.

"What's wrong with you, Sourpuss?" he asked in a disparaging tone.

Gramma immediately turned around and chided Samuel.

Now ya sit down there, and leave your sister be, ya hear?" she instructed.

Samuel straightened up, a little surprised by Gramma's rebuke. Recognizing how serious she was, though, he quickly complied.

"Yes, ma'am, Gramma," he said, taking his seat in the back of the wagon. "I'm sorry."

"Well now, that's more like it!" she accepted, turning back around.

Papa didn't say a word as I approached the wagon, and neither did I. We simply climbed aboard, settled in, and took off.

The ride to church was unusually quiet. Grampa tried a couple of times to start a conversation, but no one, including Gramma, seemed all that interested. He finally gave up on his attempts.

When we got to church, I caught a glimpse of Isaac stepping into the building. Immediately, my heart sank, and I felt like crying all over again. I managed, however, to hold back my tears.

Because we had arrived a little late, most everyone had already gone inside. Papa, Grampa, and Samuel all got out of the wagon, and Samuel and Papa started off towards the church. Grampa waited to help Gramma from her seat.

When she was down, he turned to me, extended his hand, and cheerfully offered to help me down as well.

"Come on, Wallflower," he urged, "we're gonna be late!"

I looked up, trying not to seem too obvious about the way I was feeling. I somberly declined.

"If you don't mind, Grampa," I said, "I'll be along in a minute."

"Oh, okay dear," Grampa replied, confused by my reluctance but sensing something was wrong.

Gramma jumped in.

"You go on, Ezra," she told him. "Jochebed and I'll be along in a minute."

Grampa looked at Gramma and nodded as if he understood that something serious was afoot that needed a woman's touch. He smiled at the both of us and went on.

Once Grampa was out of earshot, Gramma turned to me as if she were going to say something. Before she could get a word out, however, I started right in.

"Gramma," I blunted, "I know what you're going to say, but I just can't!" I couldn't hold back any longer; I broke down in tears. "I just can't go in there!" I cried. "I can't face Isaac, and Papa, and…and looking like *this!* Everyone will be pointing and whispering, or worse yet, they'll be asking me what's wrong. I just can't go in there! Please don't make me go!"

Gramma looked at me with sad but understanding eyes.

"Jochebed, sweetheart," she started, trying to encourage me, "it's not the end of the world. I know you're hurtin', but…" She paused and thought for a minute. "Listen," she suggested, "most everyone's already inside. How about you and I wait a few more minutes out here and then we can just slip into the narthex undetected. We can still hear the sermon from there and get the benefit of the service without havin' to face a crowd of people. Then, later on, when the service is endin', you can slip out before anyone sees ya, and that will be that! Sound like a plan?"

I was hesitant to go in at all, but I knew Papa would be even angrier with me if I skipped out on church. I reluctantly nodded my head, unenthusiastically agreeing.

Thankfully, Gramma's plan seemed to work really well. When we sneaked into the church, everyone was already in the auditorium, standing, midway through the first hymn. Gramma and I went and sat down in some chairs just outside the auditorium, and even though the doors were already closed, we could hear and participate in the service just fine from where we were at.

I'll have to admit, it did seem a little strange not being inside with everyone else, as I had never actually spent a whole service out in the narthex before, but even though it felt a bit like playing hooky from school, it was definitely better than facing a big crowd of people in my gloomy condition. I tried to tell Gramma that she didn't have to sit with me, but she was having none of it! She stayed, supportively, right by my side.

Just as the service was winding down, Pastor Scott thanked Isaac again for the message he had given in the morning service. He said that he looked forward to Isaac coming home from college to be with us again, and then he asked Isaac to close the service in prayer. Isaac obliged.

As Isaac began to pray, I could feel tears starting to well up inside of me again. Hearing his voice and thinking about the fact that he was leaving for college today was more than I could take. I just had to get out of there!

Gramma had her head bowed for the prayer, so I subtly made my exit. I quietly closed the door behind me and ran for the wagon.

Before I got there, I was already sobbing, so overwhelmed with heartache and grief. Fortunately, our wagon was parked quite a ways out from the church and hidden somewhat under a tree. I climbed in the back and crouched down, hoping no one would notice I was there.

Soon, I could hear people exiting the church. The noise grew louder and louder as people made their way to their wagons and began to leave. I stayed hidden the best I could, hoping beyond hope that no one would spot me and hoping my family would soon come so that we could go home. I just really wanted to go home!

As I sat there for what seemed like forever, I suddenly felt a hand on my arm. I instantly froze!

"Jochebed," I heard the voice say, "I looked for you inside."

It was Isaac.

"I know you must be angry with me for leaving this afternoon," he apologized, "but I...I just didn't know what to say to you. I was too upset. I just needed to get out of there and clear my head. I'm really sorry I left, though. Forgive me?"

I really didn't want to look at him as my eyes were so puffy from crying, and my face was all red, not to mention my nose was stuffed and I sounded awful. I kept my head down, answering briefly.

"It's all right," I quickly replied, fidgeting with my handkerchief.

Isaac could tell I'd been crying.

"Oh, Jochebed!" he bemoaned, so remorseful. "I'm so sorry I hurt you!"

"No!" I blurted out, still unwilling to face him. "It's not you, really, it isn't!"

Isaac furrowed his brow, not understanding.

"Then...would you please look at me?" he implored.

"I...I can't!" I replied, too embarrassed. "I'm a mess! I've been crying and..."

"I don't care!" Isaac insisted, cutting me off. "Jochebed, I just want to see you again before I have to go."

I hesitated.

"Please!" he begged again.

I slowly and reluctantly turned my head, barely looking up to meet his eyes. When he saw mine, he smiled sweetly.

"You're simply beautiful!" he complimented without hesitation.

I shook my head timidly, humbly disagreeing.

"I know we can't talk long," he hurried, "your father will be out soon, but... please...if you can get permission...promise me you'll write to me while I'm away. I want to hear from you - really I do!" He slipped a piece of paper with his address on it into my hand. "I have to go!" he said abruptly, his eyes searching for Papa. "You do forgive me, don't you?" he asked again, his gorgeous blue eyes looking into mine.

"Of course I do!" I assured, smiling through my tears. "There was never anything to forgive!"

He smiled tenderly as he lovingly squeezed my hand, quietly slipping away into the darkness.

My heart nearly broke as I watched him disappear out of sight.

THE LONG SILENCE
(Chapter 6)

Papa and the others finally came out of the church, and when they did, I could tell Papa wasn't very happy. I watched and waited as they all started towards the wagon, Samuel running on ahead, arriving first.

"Hey, where were ya durin' church?" he asked as he climbed in beside me. "I never saw ya come in."

The sun had gone down, and it was dark outside, so mercifully Samuel couldn't see that I'd been crying.

"I was there!" I shot back tersely. "Just don't worry about it - all right!?"

"Boy!" Samuel groused. "Ya sure are moody!"

"Would you please just leave me alone?" I shouted back at him angrily.

Samuel mumbled something under his breath and promptly moved to the back of the wagon far away from me. Not long after, everyone else arrived and climbed aboard. I purposely kept my eye gaze downward, not wanting to engage with anyone, too upset and bitter to talk. My heart was shattered in what seemed like a million pieces, and nothing I could foresee could put it back together again.

Grampa and Gramma talked with Samuel a bit on the way home, but the tension between Papa and me was palpable. Neither of us uttered a single word to anyone.

As we pulled up to the house, it was a little later than usual because Grampa and Gramma had stayed after church a bit to make some final arrangements with Mr. Bell about the purchase of their new home. They apparently got everything settled, because Grampa shared with us that they were now free and clear to move in at anytime. As upset and angry as I was, I was still very happy for them.

After Papa brought the wagon to a stop, he jumped down, told Samuel to put the horses away, turned abruptly, and headed off to the barn.

Incensed, I got out of the wagon and walked straight towards the house, seething and fuming all the way! I was so infuriated with Papa, I thought I might explode!

Grampa and Gramma stood watching us, visibly troubled by the worsening situation. Gramma sighed a long, deep, disconcerted sigh, clearly worried.

Grampa put his arm around her, giving her a reassuring squeeze.

"I'll go speak with him, Elizabeth," he offered. "Don't worry!"

Gramma smiled a reluctant smile and patted Grampa on the cheek, grateful for his help. Grampa smiled back and went to the barn.

Samuel commenced to unhitching the horses, seemingly oblivious to everything that was going on, and I went on into the house, heading straight for my room. Gramma followed in behind me, but this time she let me be.

When Grampa walked into the barn to talk with Papa, Papa was leaning against a wooden desk that he'd been building for a friend. He was staring aimlessly, seemingly in agonizing thought. Grampa walked over beside him and leaned against the desk, too. They both just stood there, not saying a word.

Finally, out of frustration, Papa spoke up.

"Ya think I'm right in all this, don't ya?" he asked, wanting some assurances.

Grampa chuckled.

"Right about what, Son?" he queried. "This old man's pretty much in the dark here."

Papa sighed, aggravated.

"Right about Jochebed!" he barked, perturbed. "About Jochebed and Isaac!"

Grampa's eyes perked up.

"Jochebed and Isaac, huh?" he questioned, surprised. "Why…did somethin' happen?"

Papa shook his head, clearly upset.

"Yah, somethin' happened!" he exploded angrily. "He wants to court her!" Papa sighed heavily as he shook his head again. "A college man wantin' to court my Jochebed," he protested, "it's just not right!"

"Well," Grampa argued enthusiastically, "doesn't seem too unreasonable to me. I mean, gracious, ya can't get much better than Isaac Lewis in my opinion. He's a right good fella, and Jochebed…why…she's a *fine* young girl!"

"That's just it!" Papa shouted in consternation. "She's still a little girl! He's a grown college man, and…well…she's still in school for goodness' sake!"

"Now, Son," Grampa tried to calm, "no need to get so upset. There's really not that many years between 'em when ya think about it."

Papa nearly lost it! It was *not at all* what he wanted to hear.

"Aww, good grief, Pa!" he countered, annoyed. "Whose side are ya on now anyhow?"

Grampa started to say something, but Papa immediately cut him off.

"Oh, never mind!" he blustered, fed up with the whole thing. "I'm done talkin' about it! It's late, and I've got a lot of work in the mornin'. I'm goin' to bed!"

Papa left visibly upset just as Samuel was leading the horses into the barn. He looked over at Grampa who was still leaning against the desk, shaking his head, pulling at his chin.

"Boy," he quipped as he put the horses in their stalls, "everyone sure seems in a bad mood tonight. What's gotten into everybody?"

Grampa looked at him and gave a solemn reply.

"Life and love, Sam," he expressed with concern, "life and love."

Samuel got a confused frown on his face as Grampa left the barn, headed for the house.

"Grownups!" Samuel retorted to himself as he shook his head, befuddled. "They sure are strange!"

Grampa walked on into the house, worried and concerned.

"Where's the boy?" he asked Gramma, who was sitting at the kitchen table, reading her Bible, sipping a cup of coffee.

"He's already gone to bed, Ezra," she replied, disheartened.

Grampa pulled out a chair and sat down beside her, looking despondent and disheartened, too. He let out a long, frustrated sigh as he shook his head in aggravation.

"Would ya like some coffee?" Gramma offered.

"Sure," Grampa accepted. "That'd be fine."

Gramma got up and walked over to pour him a cup of coffee.

"I suppose ya already knew about all this?" Grampa queried.

"It all just mostly happened today," she explained as she brought his coffee to him. "And I feel just awful about it! Those two are so much alike - *stubborn!*"

"I'm with ya on that one!" Grampa heartily agreed. "Without Lydia here to bridge the gap between those two…" He paused, his eyes welling with tears. "I sure do miss that girl," he said, his heart heavy.

Gramma looked at him with anguish.

"I do, too, Ezra," she sympathized with melancholy as she put her hand on his. "I surely do miss her, too!"

Grampa wiped a tear.

"What can we do, Elizabeth?" he asked, genuinely concerned. "I think this runs deeper than just courtin'.."

"Oh, I would agree!" Gramma replied without hesitation. "Most assuredly!" She looked at Grampa intently. "I think Michael's still too hurt by the loss of Lydia to be able to think straight and far too prideful and stubborn to admit it!" She paused, taking a sip of her coffee. "And poor Jochebed," she lamented, shaking her head, "so young and yet growin' up so fast. I just don't think Michael's willin' to accept it."

Grampa nodded, conceding the point.

"But Michael's a good man and a good father," he stressed. "I've no doubt it'll take some time, but…I believe he'll figure out the right thing to do. Don't you?"

Gramma sighed, apprehensive.

"Yes," she granted, "but will Jochebed be patient enough to wait until he does?"

Grampa frowned, alarmed.

"Why…ya don't think she'd go against Michael's wishes now, do ya?" he questioned, troubled.

Gramma sighed again.

"No," she told him, less than convincing. "At least, I hope she wouldn't." She got a fretful look on her face. "But she's in love, Ezra, and ya know how that can be. She's dreamed of this for such a long, long time and…" Gramma was clearly grieved by the conflict. "Oh, I sure do hope this get's resolved soon," she worried, "before things get too far out of hand!"

"I know what ya mean," Grampa replied empathetically, "but…any advice on what we can do in the mean time?"

A smile came across Gramma's face.

"I think the only thing, and the *best thing* that we can do for 'em right now," she proposed, "is to simply pray! And of course," she quickly added, "be there for 'em when we can."

Grampa smiled back, winking in approval.

"Sure am glad I married such a wise woman," he complimented with pride. He leaned over and gave Gramma a peck on the cheek. "And a pretty one to boot!" he praised adoringly.

"Oh, Ezra!" Gramma blushed. "You're just too much!"

Just then, the door opened, and in walked Samuel, finally finished with his chores.

"Night, Grampa and Gramma," he said as he hung up his coat. "I'm plum worn out! I'm goin' to bed. See ya in the mornin'.."

"Night, Sam," Grampa echoed.

"Sweet dreams," Gramma encouraged.

*****

Unfortunately, the next morning, I woke up much earlier than usual. I think the ordeal of the previous day was still weighing heavy on my mind, and I just couldn't sleep all that well.

Lying there, contemplating the day, I definitely wasn't looking forward to having to go to school. All I really wanted to do was just curl up in bed and think and cry and write to Isaac. Since none of those things were a real option, though, I decided to go ahead and get started with my day. I did my devotions the best I could, but I'll admit, when it came time to pray, I found it very difficult - not because I didn't want to talk to God, but because I knew that I still harbored anger inside of me towards Papa, and being angry makes it very hard to pray, especially when you're trying to pray for the person you're angry with. Nevertheless, when I finished my time with God, I purposely determined that *this* day I would make an effort to talk to Papa. I knew it wouldn't be easy, but I also knew Gramma was right. Papa needed to hear my side of things.

I got up and got myself dressed and gathered my books for school.

"Today is going to be a better day," I said, trying to convince myself.

Regrettably, things didn't quite turn out the way I'd hoped, however.

As I was heading down the stairs, I could hear someone rustling around in the kitchen. I assumed it was Gramma up again at the crack of dawn making breakfast, but as I came around the corner, there stood Papa pouring a cup of coffee. He looked up, saw it was me, and went right back to what he was doing.

"Mornin'," he said with a hint of gruffness in his voice.

I took a deep breath, trying to calm myself so that I would be sure to answer in a way that wouldn't come across too disrespectful.

"Good morning," I replied in as nice a tone as I could muster. I put my books down on the edge of the counter and proceeded to walk past Papa to the sink to wash my hands to get started on breakfast.

Papa didn't say another word.

As I busied myself, and the moments ticked by, it began to feel extremely uncomfortable. There we were, both of us, standing in the same room, neither speaking, neither acknowledging the other. Needless to say, it was very unsettling and quite awkward! As unnerving as it was, however, I knew one of us needed to break the silence.

I took another deep breath and gathered as much courage as I could. I turned to face Papa and cautiously began to speak. He must have been thinking the same thing, though, because he started to say something at the exact same time that I did.

"Papa. . ."

"Jochebed. . ."

We both blurted out, talking over each other.

"Ya go first," Papa deferred.

"No, that's fine," I told him. "You can go."

"No!" Papa insisted. "What did ya wanna say?"

Breathing out a deep sigh, I reluctantly answered him.

"Well, Papa," I started in a serious tone, trying to sound mature, "I thought you should know how I feel about…"

Papa quickly interrupted.

"If this is about Isaac!" he ranted.

Immediately, I interrupted right back.

"Papa!" I shouted, beyond upset. "Please just let me finish! You haven't even heard my side of things!"

Papa snapped at me sharply.

"I don't *need* to hear your side of things!" he yelled angrily. "Isaac is a grown man, and you're still a little girl! You're not ready for marriage! End of story!"

"But, Papa!" I exclaimed, so unbelievably agitated with him. "That isn't fair! If you'll just let me explain!"

"Enough, Jochebed!" he demanded furiously. "There's nothin' more to explain! The matter's closed!"

"But, Papa!" I implored. "Please! You're being so unreasonable!"

"I said **enough**, Jochebed!" he came back at me, irate. "We're done here! Not another word!" He slammed his coffee cup down on the counter and looked at me nearly seething.

I stood there in stunned silence as he abruptly turned and headed outside. Papa had *never* spoken to me like that before, *not ever!* He was *so* cross and mean, it just wasn't like him at all! I was so shocked and stunned by what he'd done, I literally couldn't move.

Did that just happen? I asked myself, bewildered. *Papa was usually so reasonable and willing to listen, but to speak to me that way...so harshly...* I didn't know what to make of it.

Tears of hurt and anger and frustration began to well up inside of me as I stood there dealing with the fallout. I was *so livid*; I could feel my heart pounding wildly in my chest. In that moment of bitterness, I felt as if I wanted nothing more to do with Papa, not now, not ever! He wasn't being fair, not at all, and I hated him for it!

Just then, Gramma came around the corner.

"Gramma!" I exclaimed, surprised and embarrassed as I started to wipe the tears from my eyes. I immediately turned away to busy myself. "How long have you been standing there?" I wondered nervously.

"Long enough," she answered, clearly heartbroken, her countenance fallen. She took a few steps towards me. "Jochebed," she started to say.

"Don't, Gramma!" I insisted, cutting her off in an agitated, teary voice. "I don't want to talk about it! I can't!"

"But, sweetheart," she pressed, inching ever closer.

"Gramma, please!" I insisted back, even harder, too hurt and bitter to speak with her. "I know you mean well, but I...I just really want to be alone right now!"

My back still turned to her; I was trying to fight back tears as she replied with a heavy heart.

"All right, child," she accepted with sympathy. "I understand." She sighed, dispirited. "I am here if ya need me, though," she assured me tenderly.

I could hear the distress and anguish in her voice as she spoke, sounding as if she might start crying herself. I felt badly, I did, but there was just no way that I could talk to her right now, not about all this. I was far too angry and upset, and I knew I might say something I would later regret.

Disheartened, Gramma slowly turned and left the room, quietly walking back upstairs.

When I was certain she was gone, I lowered my head, overcome, grabbed hold of the sink, and began to bitterly weep. The ache in my heart was so deep and so real; I didn't know what to do with it. It felt as if my whole world was crashing down around me, and I didn't know how to stop it! *Nothing* seemed to make sense anymore, and I was beyond devastated!

Why? I questioned. *Why was Papa doing this? Why was he being so unreasonable and so **very angry** about all this? Why wouldn't he even listen to me? ...Why?* With so many agonizing and unanswered questions, my anger and aggravation grew. "That's it!" I told myself as I feverishly wiped the tears from my face and straightened myself up. "I'm done! If Papa's going to be this way, then fine! If he won't talk to me, then I won't talk to him!" I was so enraged and resentful in the moment, I determined from that point forward to speak only if spoken to!

I have to admit the Holy Spirit immediately convicted me of my rebellious, stubborn attitude, but I was so angry and so upset I foolishly pushed the conviction aside and continued on in my bitter resolve.

I finished preparing breakfast as quickly as I could, set it on the table for whoever was interested, swiftly got done with my chores, and went to my room.

After hastily getting ready for school, I decided to leave on my own so that I could just walk and think without having to deal with Papa or Samuel.

I promptly went to Samuel's room where he was still sleeping, roused him the best I could, and told him of my plans.

He grunted as if to say, *Okay, leave me alone and let me sleep!*

I shook my head, chagrinned, and did exactly that!

Grampa and Gramma were still in their bedroom, and as far as I knew, Papa was still outside somewhere, doing what I didn't know, nor did I frankly care. I gathered my things, rushed down the stairs, and swiftly left the house before being confronted by anyone else. I just wanted to get out of there and be left alone!

Fortunately, I made it out of the house without being detected and was now on my way to school by myself. Normally, Papa would take Samuel and me in the wagon as the schoolhouse was quite a distance from our place, but I knew I'd left in plenty of time to make it there on foot without being late.

*****

Back at home, everyone was now up, busily going about their morning routines, getting dressed, eating breakfast, and doing their daily chores.

Unfortunately for me, it would seem that Samuel had not been quite as awake as I thought he had been when I informed him about leaving early for school. Apparently, he had utterly failed to receive, *much less*, relay my message to Papa. Needless to say, Papa was not at all happy!

I was just about half an hour into my walk when Papa came rushing up behind me in the wagon, feverishly calling out my name.

At first, given his excitement and the frantic look on his face, I was afraid that something terrible had happened. As he approached, however, I could tell that what I mistook for frantic was actually fury!

"What on earth are ya doin', Jochebed?" he demanded to know as he pulled the wagon to an abrupt stop beside me.

"What do you mean?" I queried, thoroughly confused. "I'm on my way to school! Didn't Samuel tell you?"

Papa shook his head, infuriated.

"No, Samuel didn't tell me!" he barked crossly. "But you should've!" His face was red with anger.

"I meant no harm!" I argued, trying to defend myself.

Papa didn't seem to care, though, he was livid, and nothing I said seemed to assuage him.

"We'll deal with this when ya get home!" he announced tersely. "You'll face your punishment then!"

I could feel my anger starting to well up inside of me again as Papa's unreasonableness was making my blood boil! He was being so unfair and unduly mean, and I couldn't wait for him to leave!

Thankfully, without further ado, he immediately turned the wagon around and drove off.

As I stood there watching him go, I glared at him, beady-eyed, seething, incensed by his excessive outrage. Letting out a deep, angry sigh, and not wanting to be late, I turned on my heels, clenched my jaw, and walked on to school, fuming the whole way!

When I got to the schoolhouse, I was nearly beside myself and needed someone to vent to. Naomi was always there early, so I went directly to find her. I knew, at least, *she* would have the courtesy to listen to me!

I looked around and finally found her sitting, studying under a tree in the school yard. I immediately walked over to her and angrily plopped myself down beside her.

"Well, hello," she said, startled by my sudden interruption. She could tell by the look on my face that something was very wrong. "Are you okay?" she inquired. "You seem a bit...well...cross today. Is...is everything all right?"

I starred at her broodingly, not even sure of where to begin. So much had happened - Isaac, Papa...this *unbelievably horrible day!* I was not at all myself!

~

Normally, I wasn't an angry person...maybe a bit stubborn from time to time, that I'll admit (Mama always did say that I got my stubbornness from Papa, and *humph...seems about right given today!*).

No...usually I was sweet, and kind, and...*ohhh, I was so aggravated!!*

~

I continued to stare at Naomi, shaking my head, trying to figure out just what to say.

Growing more and more disconcerted, Naomi laid her book aside, sat straight up, and faced me square on.

"Now, Jochebed," she expressed, beyond concerned at this point, "you're starting to scare me! What on earth has gotten into you?"

I hesitated a moment longer before everything came spilling out. I explained every last bit of it in a matter of minutes!

When I finished talking, Naomi sat back against the tree with a look of utter and complete shock on her face.

I sighed, discouraged as I leaned back against the tree beside her. We both just sat there staring in silence.

After several *long* minutes of neither of us saying anything, I abruptly turned to her and questioned.

"Well!" I badgered, dearly wanting to know. "What should I do? What would *you* do?"

Naomi looked at me with a blank stare, confused and at a loss, shaking her head, indicating that she had no idea. After looking at me for a brief, but befuddled minute, she finally took a deep breath and opened her mouth as if she were about to say something.

Naturally, I instantly perked up in anticipation, hoping for some good, godly counsel from my dear, beloved friend, but much to my dismay, nothing ever came out. She aimlessly turned and went right back to staring, giving me no direction at all.

"Naomi!" I impatiently prodded, thoroughly distressed. "I'm serious! I need your advice! I *know* Papa is being *completely* unreasonable about all this!" I threw up my hands in aggravation. "It's not *my fault* he won't listen!" I asserted, trying to justify myself. I shook my head, totally frustrated! "I really don't think there would be any harm in just *writing* to Isaac, do you?" I suggested, hopeful for her approval.

Naomi quickly turned to me and looked at me as if I had lost my mind.

"Jochebed Lowry!" she exclaimed. "Are you *crazy?* I mean…I see your point about your father and all, but to write to Isaac without his permission when he expressly forbade you and Isaac to court…" She shook her head, incredulous. "Jochebed," she stressed, quite scared for my wellbeing, "if your father finds out about it…why…*I'll be short a friend!*"

"Oh, Naomi!" I dismissed, almost chuckling. "That's just silly!"

"Well, it's true!" she came back at me emphatically. "If your father is as angry with you as you say he is, then, Jochebed, he'll *kill you* if he finds out you're writing to Isaac behind his back!"

I sighed, exasperated!

"But he's being *completely* unfair!" I reminded, indignantly arguing my point, utterly infuriated at the thought. "He won't even listen to what I have to say!" I shook my head tenaciously, my mind already made up! "I won't lose Isaac because Papa's too stubborn to let me grow up!" I stated with resolve. "I won't do it, Naomi! I won't!"

Naomi was taken aback by my audacity and my uncharacteristic bent towards rebellion. In fact, she was so thrown by my defiant attitude; she almost didn't know what to say to me.

"Jochebed," she started, nearly beside herself, "I…I…this…this is *so* unlike you!" She was vehemently shaking her head, her brow furrowed as she spoke. "You…I mean…I…I don't think I have **EVER** heard you talk like this before! You…" She paused, clearly at a loss, worried and concerned for who I was becoming. She immediately tried to talk me out of it. "Your father loves you," she argued, "and I *know* you love him! You'll work this out. You will! Just *please* be patient and don't do anything rash! Isaac's not going anywhere!" she tried to convince me. "He obviously likes you *a lot* or he wouldn't want to court you. I mean, dare I say, he may even love you! You're not going to lose him, Jochebed. You won't! He'll wait for you! *I know he will!*" She was desperate to get me to see. "I'm sure your father will come around in time," she encouraged. "Please…please just be patient!"

I knew she was probably right, but I couldn't take the chance. There was just too much at stake, and I was too afraid of what might happen if I listened to her. I simply couldn't lose Isaac! I wouldn't!

I shook my head, refusing to accept her advice, stubbornly allowing my fear and anger to guide my heart rather than reason.

I was just about to argue my side of things, yet again, when the teacher rang the bell for everyone to come inside. Naomi and my conversation would have to wait. She and I had to get to class.

At lunchtime, and again after school, she and I talked passionately about the issue, and each time we talked, she never once wavered in her advice to me. She was adamant that I wait, and that I listen to Papa despite his apparent unreasonable objections. As much as I disagreed with her, I did appreciate her honesty and her concern for my well being. She was truly a faithful friend!

Truth be told, the problem wasn't with her, but with me! I just wasn't sure I wanted to heed what she was telling me to do. I was still so hurt and so angry and *so* frustrated, I couldn't see straight! Being patient and waiting on Papa to come around…well… that just seemed crazy to me! Him changing his mind about something like this was likely *never* to happen and I knew it! Once he made up his mind about something, it was nearly impossible to get him to change it.

I left the schoolhouse that day feeling frustrated and torn. I didn't like having to defy Papa, but I just couldn't see any way around it. In my mind, he'd left me with no choice. *Isaac wanted me and I wanted him and Papa would just have to accept it!*

As I made my way home, I dreaded having to face him!

*****

When I arrived at the house that evening, I was met with the punishment of having to do extra chores, even though I felt it was not at all warranted! (And privately, Gramma agreed with me.) Nevertheless, I did what I was told, albeit with a terrible attitude. As you can imagine, my anger towards Papa grew exponentially!

*****

Over the next few days, Papa and I did our best to avoid one another, barely saying two words to each other the whole time. Needless to say, it made everything and everyone very uncomfortable.

Grampa and Gramma, and even Samuel, tried from time to time to intervene and make things better between us, but it seemed with each passing day, Papa and I, both thinking the other was in the wrong, dug our heels in deeper, becoming more and more determined to stand our ground!

*****

After about the third day of our obstinacy and utter foolishness, Grampa and Gramma had finally had enough! They summarily summoned Papa and me to the living room, intent on making things right.

Papa and I both came, but we did so reluctantly, knowing full well their objective.

Childishly, he and I walked into the room and sat opposite each other, desperately trying to avoid eye contact. Gramma was sitting on the couch in between the two chairs that Papa and I were in, and Grampa was sitting there beside her, waiting.

Once Papa and I were present and settled in our seats, Grampa stood up and started into his speech.

"Now," he stated sternly, sounding rather irritated and angry, "I want the both of ya to listen and to listen well!" He looked back and forth at the two of us as he spoke. "I hope ya both realize how *ridiculous* ya've been over these past few days! And I hope ya know how much your juvenile behavior has affected *everyone* in this house! You're *both* bein' stubborn and bullheaded and it needs to stop!" He frowned in disapproval as he looked at Papa and then at me. "Just look at ya!" he indicted with bluster. "Sittin' there ignorin' each other…shame on ya!"

Papa and I hung our heads, more than a little embarrassed.

Grampa wasn't finished, though.

"Gramma and I both realize how serious and sensitive a subject matter this is," he went on to say, "but the issues at hand will never get resolved if the two of ya refuse to speak to each other!"

"We just want the two of ya to work this out!" Gramma interjected, with a hint of exasperation and irritation in her voice. "It's gone far enough, it has, and I fear what may happen if it goes much further!"

Grampa jumped back in, directly addressing Papa.

"Michael," he said with a bit more compassion, "your ma and I realize how difficult things have been for ya since Lydia's passin' and…"

"Pa!" Papa griped, stepping on his words, clearly at odds. "This has *nothing* to do with…"

"Son!" Grampa jumped right back, cutting him off, visibly upset with Papa's interruption and denial. *"Let me finish!"*

Papa shook his head, sighing in aggravation, but he kept his mouth shut. Grampa continued.

"Now!" he persisted. "I *know* it's been devastatin' for ya losin' Lydia! And dealin' with the children on your own, why, it's not somethin' ya ever thought ya'd have to do. And up 'til now…well…I'd say…"

"Aww, Pa!" Papa complained, not wanting to hear it.

"Up 'til now," Grampa plowed ahead, steadfastly determined to finish his thought, "I'd say ya've done a pretty good job! But, Son," he went on, calming himself down a bit, trying to be a little more delicate raising the subject, "your ma and I both agree that maybe, *just maybe,* you're bein' a little…well…insensitive and… unreasonable when it comes to this matter of Jochebed and Isaac courtin'."

Papa rolled his eyes and sighed as he shook his head again, obviously disagreeing with Grampa's assessment.

"Son," Grampa forcefully told him, growing ever impatient with Papa, refusing to give in to his nonverbal objections, "all Jochebed wants is a chance to present her side of things, and…**blasted**…ya *need* to be willin' to hear her out!"

I could tell Papa was not at all happy with the suggestion. He thought he was right in what he was doing, and he didn't appreciate Grampa telling him otherwise. He sat there a minute, silently fuming, trying to settle himself before speaking.

"Pa," he finally countered, in a not so agreeable tone, "I understand what you're sayin', and I know ya mean well, but…" His voice was steadily building in fury as he spoke, and it was evident Grampa was quite agitated by his tone. "Like I've said *numerous* times before," Papa ranted on, gesturing angrily, "and it hasn't changed *one iota*, Isaac's a grown man, and Jochebed's just a little girl, and there is *no way*…"

By now, Grampa's blood was boiling and he was about to come back at Papa with a heated response, but thankfully, Gramma wisely recognized the impending fallout and jumped in, trying to bring some calm to the tense situation.

"Michael," she softly pointed out, in a much more dulcet tone, "Jochebed is *not* a little girl anymore. She's a fine young lady who'll be eighteen come March. That puts less than three years between the two of 'em."

Papa vehemently shook his head, unwilling to listen.

"Ma!" he started to say, still visibly upset, "ya just don't…"

Sitting there listening to the three of them talk about me like I wasn't even there was starting to annoy me! I decided I'd had enough!

"Papa!" I shouted, trying not to sound too disrespectful, but wanting a chance to say something. "Please just let me explain my side of things! That's all I'm asking! That's all *their* asking! Just let me tell you how I feel!"

Papa looked at me crossly, but he bit his lip, keeping himself from saying anything.

I appreciated his restraint and the opportunity to finally say my piece. I took a deep breath and began to present my case.

"You have to understand, Papa," I cautiously explained, "I've had feelings for Isaac for a very long time, longer than I think he's had feelings for me. I've looked up to him and admired him for as long as I can remember. I've seen his godly character, and I've watched how he conducts himself, and he's always been very kind and respectful and a perfect gentleman." I looked away, a little embarrassed by what I was about to say, but I wanted to be completely open and honest. "I've…I've actually dreamt of one day becoming his wife," I confessed timidly. I glanced up at Papa, who seemed to be listening intently. "You see," I nervously continued, "Isaac is *exactly* what I've prayed for and desired to have in a husband. He's *exactly* the kind of man *Mama* always encouraged me to pray for!" I looked at Papa earnestly, not trying to sweet-talk him or sway him through flattery, but simply trying to be truthful. "Papa," I told him with all sincerity, "he's a lot like you!"

I could tell Papa's countenance was starting to soften a bit, and for the first time I had hope that maybe I was finally starting to get through to him. I went on.

"Over the years," I continued, "Isaac has always been very friendly and kind, sweet, in fact, but I…I just never had the courage to tell him how I really felt about him. Of course, I didn't want to be forward or anything, and…well…truthfully, I never felt it was really my place to approach him about it, but had I known he felt the same way about me as I did for him, perhaps I would have, at least, hinted about my feelings." I chuckled a bit at the irony. "The funny thing is," I revealed, "apparently he *has* had feelings for me for quite some time now, but he, too, lacked the courage to say anything."

Papa looked at me warily.

"Truly, Papa!" I conveyed adamantly, trying to convince him. "It wasn't until just this past Sunday that Isaac and I finally had the opportunity to talk openly and honestly with each other about all this. Yes," I admitted, "he was the one who ultimately broached the subject, but I was already wholeheartedly in agreement with him! We *both* share the same feelings for each other, Papa, and we *both* really want this to move forward!" I so desperately wanted him to see. "You have to believe me, Papa!" I implored. "This is not just me being influenced by an older man, or me just falling for the first person who's ever taken interest in me. I truly do have feelings for Isaac, and I have for a very long time!" I looked intently at Papa. "I would very much like the opportunity to get to know him better," I stated frankly. "And I would very much like it if you would give your consent."

Papa looked down at the floor, almost as if he were starting to realize how wrong he had been in his assumptions.

Wanting him to fully understand everything, I continued to argue my case.

"Papa," I persisted, "I know you don't want to accept it, but Gramma's right, I *am* growing up, and I'm not a little girl anymore. I know I still have a lot to learn, and *obviously* I still have areas I need to mature in, but, Papa, please…" I couldn't help it, I started to choke up. "If you could just see…I…" I tried to go on but I couldn't.

I broke down, as did Papa.

"Oh, Jochebed," he interjected, fighting back tears. "I'm so sorry! Can ya ever forgive me? I've been *so* wrong, and I've treated ya *so* badly! He wiped a tear and then another. "Your Grampa's right," he painfully admitted. He cleared his throat, trying to speak through his tears. "Losin' your ma, I..." He paused, tears streaming down his face. "It's...it's been the hardest thing I've ever had to face," he acknowledged. Papa could barely speak, he was so broken up. He sniffed and sniffed, pulling out his hanky to wipe his eyes. "I...I guess I just felt like," he confessed humbly, "I felt like if I gave ya to Isaac, then...then I'd be losin' ya, too!" He looked away in his grief, overwhelmed, pained by his selfishness and misguided intentions.

I was crying so hard at this point I could barely see straight.

Grampa and Gramma were in tears as well.

"Not only that," Papa went on to say, looking at me so sorry for what he'd done, "I felt that I needed to protect ya...to protect ya from any more pain. I know losin' your mama was so hard on ya, Jochebed, and...well...Isaac bein' a college man, I...I just didn't want him to break your heart. I just wanted to protect ya from that possibility...to protect ya from gettin' hurt again."

I looked at him, weeping, understanding now why he had acted the way he did.

"Jochebed," he admitted, "I realize now how foolish I was to think that way." He looked at me solemnly. "Oh, sweetheart," he said again, "I'm so sorry! Can ya ever forgive me?"

I immediately leapt from my chair and ran to hug Papa's neck. As I did, I cried all the more as did he.

"I love you so much, Papa!" I told him, as I hugged him tighter. "You'll never lose me! I promise! I'll always be your little girl!" I looked up at him through my tears. "I forgive you, Papa!" I assured him. "Will...will you forgive me?"

He smiled, weeping, pulling me close, and hugging me even tighter than before.

"Oh, I love ya so much, Jochebed," he stated with fervor. "So very much, I do!" He sniffed and sniffed as he tried to comfort. "All's forgiven!" he promised. "All's forgiven!" He gently lifted my chin and looked at me with such love. "Ya have my blessin', sweetheart," he said without hesitation. "Ya have my blessin' to court Isaac."

I couldn't believe my ears! Papa had actually said yes! Instantly, relief swept over me as my heart filled with joy. I got the biggest smile on my face as I hugged Papa again!

"Thank you, Papa!" I exclaimed with such gratitude. "Thank you so much for allowing this! It means the world!"

There wasn't a dry eye in the room, but now our tears were tears of joy, and not of hurt or sorrow.

Of course, as his timing was always perfect, Samuel came walking into the room just as things were winding down. What a sight we all must have been, hugging and crying and laughing together! Samuel just stood there, shaking his head with a befuddled look on his face.

Papa looked up and noticed him standing there.

"Come join us, Son," he encouraged, motioning for him to come on in the room.

Samuel frowned as he shook his head, indicating he had absolutely no interest.

"No, that's all right," he refused. "I'm good here - thanks!" He stared at all of us like we'd completely lost our minds! Not knowing what to make of it, he muttered to himself, quite disturbed. "Grownups!" he quipped. "Y'all can keep this life and love stuff!"

We all just laughed as Samuel rolled his eyes, turned, and promptly left the room.

A NEW CHAPTER
(Chapter 7)

Now that I'd received Papa's permission to court Isaac, I immediately went to amend a letter that I admittedly had already written to him but not sent. I couldn't *wait* to tell him the good news!

I was so excited, as my emotions were running away with me, I commenced to writing a letter that was nearly twelve pages long. I hoped Isaac would have enough time to read it, and I hoped he would be able to write back to me soon. I so wanted to hear from him, and to officially start our courtship. Graciously, the very next day (which was Friday) Papa mailed my letter for me. I was grateful as I wanted to get it out right away.

As Samuel and I were arriving home from school that afternoon, we were met with a wonderful surprise! Uncle Mark and Aunt Sara were at the house all the way from North Dakota with the rest of Grampa and Gramma's things. Seeing them, though, it was somewhat of a bittersweet feeling. Even though I was thrilled that they could be with us for a while, I knew that them being here meant Grampa and Gramma would soon be moving out of our house and into their own. I'd truly miss them always being around.

As we neared the house, we could see Uncle Mark, Papa, and Grampa talking and loading some of Grampa and Gramma's things into their wagon. I excitedly ran to Uncle Mark and gave him a big hug.

"Hey!" he exclaimed as he squeezed me tightly. "It's so good to see ya!" He let go and stepped back, smiling broadly. "Well, just look at ya!" he flattered. "Quite the beautiful young lady, ya are!"

I blushed at his compliment.

"Thank you, Uncle Mark," I replied demurely.

Just then, Samuel came running up.

"What'd ya bring me?" he asked eagerly, grinning in antsy anticipation.

Papa immediately looked at him, giving him a stern, disapproving frown.

"Son!" he scolded. "Ya could, *at least*, say hello first, ya know!"

~

Uncle Mark and Aunt Sara were always bringing gifts for Samuel and me when they came to visit. Nothing too elaborate, mind you, just a kind, sweet gesture on their part, an expression of their love for the two of us. I cherished each and every one!

Not surprisingly, this visit would be no exception.

~

Uncle Mark chuckled at Samuel's insolence and Papa's dismay.

"Go inside to your Aunt Sara," he directed. "She's got somethin' special for the both of ya."

Samuel immediately tore off for the house, and I followed on behind him. When we got inside, Gramma and Aunt Sara were sitting at the kitchen table, catching up on things.

"Well, here they come!" Aunt Sara announced with a huge smile on her face as she stood to her feet. She quickly came over and gave us both a big hug. "How have you been?" she asked.

"Doing well," I replied. "And you? Did you and Uncle Mark have a good trip?"

"It was all right," Aunt Sara answered. "Uneventful, and that's always a good thing. As for your Uncle Mark and me, well, we couldn't be doing any better! We're so excited to be running the store for your grandparents! We're enjoying ourselves immensely!" Aunt Sara got a great big smile on her face. "And what's this I hear?" she prodded, fishing for information. "Seems you have a bit of *good news* to tell?"

"Yah...if ya call bein' in *looove* good news," Samuel rudely butted in, rolling his eyes in disgust.

Aunt Sara laughed.

"Still the same ol' Sam I see," she remarked as she put her arm around him, squeezing him close.

Samuel squirmed a bit, looking extremely uncomfortable with her show of affection, but amazingly, he was polite and didn't pull away.

"Uhhhh...not to hurry this along or anything," he finally said, looking up at Aunt Sara, "but...Uncle Mark said somethin' about...*a gift?*"

"Samuel Michael!" Gramma reprimanded sharply, flabbergasted at his brazenness. "Ya see ya mind your manners now! Gracious!"

Aunt Sara smiled.

"It's okay, Mama Lowry," she assured. "He's right. I do have something for the both of them. But..." she paused, looking at Samuel. "I think perhaps we ought to wait for the men to come in before you open them up."

"No, problem!" Samuel said, breaking free from her arm, running straight for the door. "I'll get 'em!" He hastily opened the door and proceeded to yell at the top of his lungs for Papa, Uncle Mark, and Grampa to come inside.

Gramma was simply aghast at his appalling behavior. She shook her head in consternation as she looked over at Aunt Sara with chagrin.

Aunt Sara just smiled as she shrugged her shoulders, chuckling at Samuel's childlike impatience.

As we waited for the men to come inside, Aunt Sara walked over to a large bag she had lying on a chair beside the table. She reached inside and pulled out a small box and handed it to Samuel.

"What is it?" he asked excitedly, shaking it, chaffing at the bit to open it.

"Well," Aunt Sara answered with a chuckle, "as soon as the fellas get in here, you can open it up and find out!"

Needless to say, Samuel could barely contain himself. He stood anxiously staring at the box, turning it this way and that, and shaking it back and forth several more times. After a few more agonizing minutes, everyone finally made their way inside. As soon as the last person stepped through the door, Samuel instantly tore into his gift.

"Oh wow! Oh wow!" he shouted, clearly thrilled with the contents of the package. "I can't believe it! Is this what I think it is?"

Aunt Sara was grinning from ear to ear, pleased with his exuberance.

"Uncle Mark found it when he was cleaning out the storage room in the back of the store," she explained. "I know your father thought he'd lost it for good the last time you all were out, but when Mark moved some boxes, there it was!"

"I just can't believe it!" Samuel exclaimed. "Papa, your knife...it's your knife! The one ya said would always be mine! The one Grampa gave to you and his Pa gave to him. Look, see, here it is!"

Papa shook his head in disbelief.

"Well, would ya look at that?" he commented, absolutely stunned. He took the knife from Samuel, and started looking it over. "Huh!" he quipped, amazed. "You're right,

Sara, I *didn't* think I'd ever see it again!" He looked over at Uncle Mark. "Thanks for findin' it, little brother," he said, grateful.

"No problem," Uncle Mark replied with a shrug of the shoulder. "Can't say I was actually lookin' for it, though. Nevertheless, I am glad it all worked out. I know how much that knife means to ya, Michael."

Papa turned the knife over in his hand, examining it closer.

"After all this time," he observed, "still in great shape." He carefully opened it up and checked the blade. "Wow! Now, that's sharp!" he said, surprised. He closed it up and started to hand it back to Samuel. "Ya gotta be extra careful with that, Son," he cautioned. "That blade 'el cut ya for sure!"

Samuel nodded, taking the knife from Papa

Uncle Mark spoke up.

"Yah," he explained, "after I found it, I cleaned it up real good and sharpened the blade. Almost like new, I'd say."

"It sure is!" Papa agreed. "Thanks again for takin' care of it, Mark."

"And now," Aunt Sara interjected as she reached back into her bag, pulling out a rather large box, "this is for you, Jochebed." She handed the gift to me, smiling. "I do hope you like it," she expressed with anticipation.

I politely thanked her as I took the box from her hands, pulling out a chair at the table to sit down with it. After I was seated, I carefully began to open it up.

When the last of the paper was off, and I'd lifted the lid, there in front of me, much to my surprise and delight was the most elegant dress I think I had ever seen in my life!

"Oh, Aunt Sara!" I exclaimed, almost at a loss for words. "It's…it's stunning! Just gorgeous!" I reached inside the box and lifted the dress, unfolding it, holding it out in front of me to see it more clearly. "Did you make this?" I questioned, all the while admiring its beauty.

Aunt Sara nodded, smiling, pleased that I was pleased.

Gramma came over to take a closer look.

"Myyy!" she complimented in amazement as she ran her fingers over the dress. "Such meticulous work! Why, Sara…ya've really outdone yourself this time! It's just *beautiful!"*

I could tell Aunt Sara was a little embarrassed by all the fawning, but Uncle Mark didn't seem to mind one bit. He was beaming at his wife, proud of her amazing talents and God given abilities.

"Thank you," Aunt Sara accepted humbly. "You're all too kind." She walked over and held her hands out. "May I?" she asked.

I handed her the dress and she asked me to stand up. When I did, she took the dress and held it up against me.

"When I saw the material, Jochebed," she explained, "I immediately thought of you. I knew it would look gorgeous with your beautiful blue eyes and that marvelous dark brown hair of yours. And seeing it here against you" - she nodded in approval - "I was absolutely right! It compliments you well, and goes nicely with your complexion, too."

"Oh, Aunt Sara!" I said, giving her a big hug. "How can I ever thank you? It really is just too much! I can't wait to try it on!"

"Perhaps we could do that *after* supper," Grampa teased. "This old man's starvin'!"

"Oh, gracious, Ezra!" Gramma retorted, shaking her head. "Is there ever a time when you're *not* starvin'?"

Grampa pooched his mustache at Gramma and blew her a kiss. She shook her head at his silliness, and everyone laughed.

Putting the gifts aside, the women promptly got busy preparing supper as the men drove over to Grampa and Gramma's new place to unload some of their belongings. By the time supper was ready, the men were back and hungrier than ever.

After everyone washed up, we all sat down to the table to enjoy the wonderful meal and to talk and laugh and to catch up with Uncle Mark and Aunt Sara. Samuel, however, spent most of the meal sitting quietly, admiring his knife. I could tell he was very proud of it.

When we finished eating and everything was cleaned up, I excused myself to go upstairs to try on my new dress. I invited Aunt Sara to join me.

Once in my room, I carefully pulled the dress from the box and unfolded it yet again. It was so amazingly beautiful; I could hardly believe that it was mine!

~

The dress was a deep, dark green color, and the material was satiny and shiny. It seemed to glisten when I held it up in the light. The top part of the bodice and the sleeves were plain and smooth as was most of the bottom part of the dress, but around the neck and cuffs of the sleeves, there was an even darker green, flowery design that had been hand stitched all the way around them. That same flowery pattern cascaded down the right-hand side of the dress, starting at the waistline and ending at the floor. The ornate design (*unbelievably detailed*) was one that Aunt Sara had come up with on her own. It literally must have taken her *hours* to do the painstaking embroidery. It was absolutely breathtaking!

~

There was no doubt Aunt Sara was an extremely gifted seamstress. Mama had always envied, yet admired, her tremendous skill and ability. She would share with me sometimes as we sewed together how she wished she had half the talent that Aunt Sara had.

"She's so very good at what she does!" Mama would say. "She's a seamstress extraordinaire!"

After seeing the dress I now held out in front of me, I was inclined to agree with Mama 100 percent!

~

"Aunt Sara," I exclaimed again, as I just couldn't take my eyes off the dress, "this is almost too beautiful to put on!"

Aunt Sara blushed a bit as she smiled.

"That's very kind of you to say, Jochebed," she reluctantly accepted, "but truth be told, it's not nearly as beautiful as the girl who holds it!"

I looked away, embarrassed by the compliment.

"Well," she prodded excitedly, "let's see it on you!"

I smiled enthusiastically, eager to oblige.

Aunt Sara helped me out of my old school dress, and into the new. After she buttoned the last button, and I turned to see myself in the mirror, I could hardly believe my eyes!

"*Ohhh myyy!*" I expressed with awe as it nearly took my breath away. "How can I ever repay you?"

Aunt Sara lovingly came up behind me, smiling in the mirror at me.

"Jochebed," she said kindly, "seeing you in that dress is payment enough! It's definitely lovelier now that I see it on you!" She put her arms around my shoulders and gave me a hug.

I latched on to her arms, squeezing her back.

"Thank you so much, Aunt Sara," I said, overwhelmed. "I love you!"

"I love you too, Jochebed," she said. She smiled broadly. "Now let's go show you off!"

I smiled back, excited and thrilled to do just that!

Aunt Sara and I headed downstairs together, and when I walked into the living room where everyone had gathered to visit for awhile, there were a lot of gasps of amazement followed by many oo's and ah's. Surprisingly, even Samuel seemed impressed.

"Very exquisite!" Gramma complimented.

"Makes ya look real grown-up," Papa admired.

"A real fine young lady," Grampa remarked.

"Can I take ya on a date?" Uncle Mark teased, raising his eyebrows up and down.

I just smiled, a little bashful, and thanked everyone for their kind words.

"I'm going to cherish this for years to come, Aunt Sara," I said as I turned to hug her again. "Thank you so much for making this for me!"

"You're more than welcome, Jochebed," Aunt Sara replied as she hugged me back. "I'm just so pleased you like it!"

*****

It was getting on toward eight o'clock, and since Grampa and Gramma were not yet settled in at their new place, they decided to stay one more night with us. Uncle Mark and Aunt Sara slept in Samuel's room, and I offered for Samuel to sleep in my room on the floor. After spending one night with him, however, I realized I should have insisted he sleep downstairs on the couch, away from everyone, or better yet, out in the barn. *My*, how that boy can snore! I couldn't say for sure how much sleep I actually got, but one thing's for certain, Samuel slept like a rock!

*****

The next day was an extremely busy day. Everyone spent most of the morning at Grampa and Gramma's new place helping them move the rest of their things into the house and barn. We were in and out all morning long carrying boxes and unloading things from the wagon.

"My goodness!" Gramma kept remarking over and over again as we'd carry something else into the house. "I never realized Ezra and I had so much stuff! Perhaps we need to consider givin' some of this away!" She fretted on and off the whole time, trying to find just the right place to put everything.

~

Grampa and Gramma's house was just one story, something they were both looking forward to given their ages. They had always lived in homes with two stories, but this would be a welcomed change, much easier to get around in, and a lot less to clean. It was just big enough for company, but not too big to take care of. There were two bedrooms, a washroom, a kitchen, and a family room.

Uncle Mark and Aunt Sara planned to stay in the guest room while they were here visiting.

Papa, Grampa, and Uncle Mark were busy putting things away in the barn as Samuel was helping me, Gramma, and Aunt Sara in the house.

Aunt Sara and Samuel stepped outside to bring in the last of the boxes and hadn't been out there all that long when, all of a sudden, we heard Samuel yell at the top of his lungs.

"Help!" he shouted. "Someone, come quick! Hurry! Please! I need help!"

Everyone heard his cries and immediately came running from all directions - Gramma and I from the house, and the men from the barn. When we stepped outside, we could see Samuel kneeling down beside Aunt Sara. The terrified look on his face said it all! Something was dreadfully wrong!

Aunt Sara was lying on the ground, her body lifeless, her eyes closed shut, and her color pale and drab.

Uncle Mark sprinted to her as fast as he could go, falling down by her side.

"Sara! Sara!" he called out in a panic, lifting her body partly off the ground, holding her in his arms. "Sara, what's wrong? Sweetheart, talk to me?"

There was no response.

"Samuel!" Papa yelled as he came rushing up behind Uncle Mark. "What happened, Son?"

"I...I don't know!" Samuel stammered frantically. "I...I turned around to hand her a box, and...and when I did...she was already on the ground!"

Right away, Papa and Uncle Mark carefully lifted Aunt Sara into the back of Papa's wagon and rushed her straight to the doctor. The rest of us just stood there in stunned silence as we watched them drive away. After a minute or two, Grampa gathered all of us around; we held hands and said a prayer for Aunt Sara.

Time seemed to pass by so slowly as we all worried and waited for news about Aunt Sara. No one felt much like doing any work or anything else for that matter.

Later, when Gramma and I prepared a light lunch for everyone to eat, most of it stayed on the table. We were all just too anxious and upset to be hungry. We tried to keep a positive attitude about us, but it wasn't easy. The not knowing was agony!

"Samuel," Grampa asked again, "can ya think of anything, Son, *anything* that might've happened?"

"No, Grampa!" Samuel insisted, obviously frustrated that he couldn't. "I've been over it a thousand times in my mind, and *nothin'!* We walked outside together to get the last of the boxes, and she seemed fine. Honest she did! She and I were talkin' about some stuff when I climbed into the back of the wagon, and I was in the middle of answerin' a question she'd asked me about school or somethin', so I really didn't think much of her not talkin' right then. My back was only turned for a minute, pickin' up a box, and when I turned back around to hand it to her, she was already on the ground. I jumped down right away and called for y'all to come. She couldn't have been down for very long!"

Grampa nodded, accepting Samuel's explanation.

"Oh, I just wish we'd hear somethin', already!" Gramma fretted, as she sat ringing her hands, beyond concerned. "I can't take much more of this not knowin'!"

"There, there, Elizabeth," Grampa tried to comfort. "No need to worry. I'm sure whatever's happened, Sara's gettin' the best of care."

We waited for what seemed like an eternity, when finally, at suppertime, we could hear a wagon coming down the lane. We all jumped up and scrambled to the door to see who it was. Thankfully, it was Papa coming with news, but regrettably, he was alone. We all rushed outside on the porch to wait for him.

"What is it, Son?" Grampa asked frantically as he stepped off the porch and walked up to the wagon to meet Papa. "How's Sara?"

Papa looked somber and quite troubled. He jumped down off the wagon and walked with Grampa back towards the rest of us.

We all gathered around, anxious for what he had to say.

"Not sure, Pa," Papa explained. "Doc sent her on to the hospital, wants to run some tests on her. Mark's with her now."

I was scared, not for what Papa had just said, but for the look on his face. I'd seen that look before, and I knew it wasn't good. He looked lost and worried, similar to how he had looked the day Mama died. My heart sank in fear for Aunt Sara.

"Is she awake?" Gramma asked, almost in tears.

"Yes, Ma," Papa answered. "She did finally wake up, but she still seems very weak and extremely tired. Unfortunately, she hadn't improved all that much when I left."

"And Mark," Gramma wanted to know, "how's he holdin' up?"

Papa sighed, concerned.

"He's doin' all right," he relayed. "Worried, but he's hangin' in there. I told him we'd be by after services tomorrow. Doc wants Sara to get some rest."

"Well, we'll gather some things and sleep at your house tonight," Grampa decided. "We'll finish movin' another day."

By the time we arrived back home, it was pretty late. Everyone was subdued, and the mood was solemn and melancholy. I guess we were all just too preoccupied with thoughts of Aunt Sara and Uncle Mark. We ate a light supper, cleaned up a bit, and headed for bed. Needless to say, we were all anxious for morning to come.

As I lay there finishing my devotions, trying to pray, the events of the day kept playing over and over again in my mind. It was so difficult to focus on or think of anything else. I prayed and I prayed, begging God to keep Aunt Sara safe, and as had become my habit, I prayed for Isaac, too. I wished like everything he could be here with me during this difficult time. I missed him so much and just wanted to be with him. I continued praying the best I could until I eventually fell asleep.

*****

The next morning, I found it hard to concentrate on the service; I wanted to, but my thoughts were with Aunt Sara and Uncle Mark. I tried very hard not to worry, but it seemed nearly impossible! I didn't *want* to think the worst, but it was so hard not knowing what was going on. I caught bits and pieces of the message, but mostly I just prayed for Aunt Sara.

Immediately after the service was over, my family and I did very little talking to anyone. We wanted to be on our way as soon as possible, knowing it would be a very long trip to the hospital which was located in a big city a couple towns over. It would take us over an hour to get there.

As we were leaving, Pastor Scott told us that he would be praying for us. We thanked him, and left.

*****

When we finally arrived in the city, the streets were noisy and bustling with activity; people were simply *everywhere!* It felt so strange being in such a busy place, surrounded by all the commotion. It made me feel uneasy and terribly on edge! I much preferred the quietness and tranquility of home. Fortunately, the hospital wasn't far from the city limits, and we made it there in no time at all.

When we got to the hospital, everyone hastily got out of the wagon and waited for Papa to show us which way to go. Being in such a strange place, we all stayed close together as we made our way towards the entrance.

As we neared, I was struck by how foreboding and ominous a place the hospital seemed. It was *so* huge and imposing; I couldn't help but feel sorry for Aunt Sara that she had to be in such a place.

Once inside, it seemed no less busy in there than it had on the outside. There were nurses and doctors conversing with one another, entering and exiting rooms, and people milling about, some looking as lost as we were.

Papa looked around, and when he spotted where we needed to go, he led us to a desk off to the side in the waiting area.

When we stepped up, a nurse was sitting there, busily poring over some paperwork. Papa hoped she could help us find Aunt Sara and Uncle Mark.

"Excuse me, ma'am," he said. "Could ya tell me where I might find Sara Lowry?"

The nurse seemed oblivious to the fact that Papa was even there. She didn't even look up to acknowledge him.

Papa waited patiently for her to finish what she was doing.

"All right, sir," she eventually said, looking up, straightening the papers in front of her. "How may I help you?"

Papa politely inquired again.

"Could ya please tell me where I might find Sara Lowry?" he asked.

The nurse reached over to grab a clipboard that was lying there beside her on the desk. She set it down in front of her and began to search through the list of names that were written on it.

"Sara Lowry, Sara Lowry," she mumbled several times as she looked it over. "And how might you spell that, sir?" she asked, still searching the page.

"S - A - R - A - L - O - W - R - Y," Papa replied.

The nurse flipped the page and kept looking.

"Ah, here she is!" the nurse exclaimed, finally locating her name. She picked up a pencil and proceeded to write Aunt Sara's name and room number down on a little piece of paper. She leaned forward and handed it to Papa. "Just follow that hallway there down a ways," she instructed, pointing off to her right. "When you see the stairs, which will be on your right, follow them up to the second floor. When you reach the top, you'll want to turn right again. Her room will be down the hall on the left-hand side about halfway down."

"Thank you, ma'am," Papa said as he took the paper from her hand. We all followed Papa as he led us down the long, darkened hallway towards the stairs.

As we searched for Aunt Sara's room, I couldn't help but notice how cold and impersonal the hospital seemed. It was so drab and dreary. I hoped for Aunt Sara's sake that she wouldn't have to stay in here long.

When we finally found her room, we waited outside in the hallway as the door was closed and no one was around to let us in. Papa knocked quietly, hoping not to disturb anyone, but when he did, no one answered. He looked at the piece of paper in his hand to make certain we had the right room, and when he was sure that we did, he knocked again a little louder. This time, Uncle Mark came to the door and quietly opened it up.

"Oh, Michael!" he whispered as he slipped out into the hallway, quietly closing the door behind him. "Sorry! Sara and I have been restin'. It was such a long, tryin' night. In fact, she's still sleepin' now." He sighed as he brushed his hand through his hair. "I'm pretty sure all their testin' wore her plum out!"

Gramma walked over and gave Uncle Mark a big hug as she began to tear up.

"How are ya doin', Son?" she asked. "How's Sara?"

Uncle Mark sighed again.

"Still waitin' on test results, Ma," he answered soberly. "A couple things they thought it might be turned out not to be the case, so we're just waitin' to see about the other stuff they did this mornin'. The doc said he expects to know somethin' later this afternoon." Uncle Mark shook his head, visibly troubled. "I just don't know," he worried. "She still seems so tired and weak. I'll admit it's got me scared!"

Grampa put his hand on Uncle Mark's shoulder, trying to be a comfort.

"We've been prayin' for ya nonstop, Son," he assured. "Ya've both been in our prayers this whole time!"

Uncle Mark nodded, grateful.

"Thanks, Pa," he said. "Sara sure needs all the prayer she can get!"

UNEXPECTED NEWS
(Chapter 8)

As we stood there talking with Uncle Mark in the hallway, a nurse walked up and excused herself past us right on into Aunt Sara's room. Uncle Mark, curious, excused himself as well, and followed in behind her. We all waited in the hallway, trying to stay out of the way. After a little while, the nurse came to the door.

"She's awake now," she announced, ushering us into the room. "You can all go in to see her."

Papa nodded, and we all quietly walked in. Grampa and Gramma went first, while Samuel and I followed with Papa.

When we got inside, I was once again struck by the dreariness of this place. The room was all white, quite dim, and rather small - just a bed, side table, a couple of chairs, a few pieces of medical equipment, of course, and a small window. Unfortunately, it seemed just as sterile and cold as the rest of the hospital. Again, I felt badly for Aunt Sara having to stay in such a depressing environment.

As we all gathered in, I could see Aunt Sara laying in the bed, propped up just a bit, her head resting on a pillow. Uncle Mark was standing by her side holding her hand.

"Come in," Aunt Sara encouraged in a weak whisper of a voice. She looked so frail and not at all herself.

"Oh, Sara!" Gramma exclaimed, overcome, as she walked over to her. She tearfully leaned down and gave her a hug and a kiss on the cheek. "Ya had us all so worried! How are ya feelin', dear?"

Aunt Sara started to try to sit herself up a little more, but she just didn't seem to have the strength.

"No, no, honey!" Uncle Mark insisted. "Don't try to get up! You're fine!"

Aunt Sara took a deep breath, conceding, as she settled back down.

"The doctors haven't told us much," she went on to say, still only able to get out a whisper. "They've mostly just told us what it's not. We're hoping to know more this afternoon." She wearily took another deep breath, trying to bolster herself. "I feel so tired and run down," she conveyed, "and unfortunately, I've been a little nauseous, too. The doctors seem puzzled as to what could be wrong with me, but I do hope they can tell us something soon." Aunt Sara looked up at Uncle Mark who was clearly anxious and concerned about her condition. She managed a smile. "I'm sure I'll be up and out of here in no time," she tried to encourage.

Uncle Mark squeezed her hand and halfheartedly smiled back.

I could tell by the look on his face that he didn't share in her optimism.

We all took turns giving Aunt Sara a hug and kiss and telling her how we were all thinking about her and praying for her. She thanked us all profusely before looking up at Uncle Mark.

"I don't mean to be rude," she whispered, noticeably fatigued, "but I really am so tired and..."

"Say no more!" Papa interrupted. "We'll go! Ya get your rest. We'll get somethin' to eat and stop back by before we head for home."

Aunt Sara looked over and graciously smiled at him.

"I'll walk ya out," Uncle Mark offered.

Before he did, he leaned down and kissed Aunt Sara on the forehead, lingering for just a minute. You could tell by the look on his face that he was worried sick about her.

Aunt Sara looked so peaked and exhausted, so frail and weak. It was definitely hard seeing her that way.

Uncle Mark gave her another quick kiss before standing up again, smiling down at her with anguish in his eyes.

She smiled up at him and nodded as if to say, *it'll be all right.*

Before we could all get out of the room, she was fast asleep yet again.

"She's been like this since yesterday," Uncle Mark revealed as we stepped out into the hallway. "I just wish the doctors could tell us what's goin' on! The waitin's killin' me!"

"I know, Son," Grampa commiserated, "but ya just gotta trust the Lord. He'll take care of ya no matter what this turns out to be."

Uncle Mark didn't seem very enthused by what Grampa was saying, but he answered back, nonetheless.

"I know you're right, Pa," he admitted, "and believe me, I'm tryin'. It's just..." He paused, fighting back tears. "It's so hard when it's your wife lyin' there in a hospital bed and ya can't do anything for her. I just feel so helpless!"

Gramma walked over and gave Uncle Mark a hug.

"It'll be all right, Son," she said, trying to comfort him. "It just has to be!"

When all the hugging and tears were through, Papa asked Uncle Mark if he wanted to come with us to get something to eat. Uncle Mark thanked him for the offer, but politely declined, saying he felt he should stay with Aunt Sara just in case she needed something or in case the doctor came back with any news. Papa tried to persuade him otherwise, but Uncle Mark stood his ground, insisting he stay. Papa understood and told him we'd be back in about an hour or so. Uncle Mark gave him a hug and we left.

We all walked back down to the waiting area and found a place to sit, while Papa went to the wagon to retrieve the basket of food Gramma had prepared for our lunch. When he returned, we sat and ate and talked a bit, and by the time we all finished up and cleaned our places, it was time to go back to see Aunt Sara.

When we got to the second floor, we could see two doctors and a nurse coming out of Aunt Sara's room. They stopped for a minute in the hallway to discuss something amongst themselves, and then they turned and went their separate ways. By the looks on their faces, and the seriousness of their conversation, I hoped everything was all right.

Just as we got to Aunt Sara's room, we were met by another nurse walking out. She abruptly stopped, turned around, and told Uncle Mark and Aunt Sara that we were there. Gaining their consent, she directed us to go on inside. Once we were in the room, she promptly left.

As we gathered in, the scene was rather disconcerting. Uncle Mark was sitting on a chair beside Aunt Sara's bed holding her hand, and they were both in tears.

I took a deep breath as my heart instantly sank, fearing the worst.

Gramma, who was visibly trembling, held tightly to Grampa, who, too, seemed troubled and anxious.

Samuel stood quietly next to Papa as did I.

At first, Uncle Mark and Aunt Sara didn't look up; they seemed lost in their own little world.

Papa guardedly walked to the foot of the bed, worried.

"What is it, Mark?" he questioned in a somber tone. "What'd the doctors say?"

Uncle Mark started to shake his head as both he and Aunt Sara looked up. Through their tears, they managed a smile.

"Is everything all right? Will Sara be all right?" Gramma fretfully asked as she frantically made her way over to the bed, taking hold of Aunt Sara's other hand.

Uncle Mark seemed hesitant.

"I'll let Sara tell ya what the doctors told us," he said, sniffing and wiping his tears.

We all waited breathlessly for Aunt Sara to say something.

Still crying, looking so weak and exhausted, Aunt Sara began to explain. She looked directly at Gramma.

"You'll never believe it, Mama Lowry," she said through her tears, in her frail, whispered voice. "The doctors tell me that I…that is…that Mark and I" - she lovingly looked over at Uncle Mark and then back to Gramma - "they tell us that we're going to have a baby!"

A huge sigh of relief came flooding over all of us as whoops and hollers went up all around the room. Everyone was smiling from ear to ear, laughing, and congratulating Uncle Mark and Aunt Sara.

"But I thought ya weren't able to have children," Gramma remarked, shocked by the wonderful news.

"We thought so, too!" Uncle Mark agreed, overwhelmed with joy. "But God decided otherwise. He simply worked a miracle!"

We were all so surprised and so happy for the two of them. It was such a welcomed blessing!

"But," Uncle Mark cautioned as he paused, looking down at Aunt Sara with apprehension, "not all the news is good."

Immediately the mood dampened as we waited for what Uncle Mark had to say.

"There are some concerns for Sara and the baby," he told us.

"Concerns?" Gramma queried anxiously. "What kind of concerns?"

Uncle Mark went on to explain.

"The doctors are pretty worried, given Sara's medical history and all," he said. He tried to clarify. "They have some concerns that the stuff goin' on inside her, the stuff that was preventin' her from conceivin' in the first place, might cause problems later on. They plan to keep her here for another couple days or three to watch her, but then, if all goes well, they said she could go home." He sighed, clearly troubled. "The problem is," he continued, "they told her she has to be on strict bed rest and…" He shook his head, quite distressed. "I'm really not sure what to do," he confessed. "They don't want her goin' all the way back to North Dakota."

"Oh, Mark!" Gramma empathized. "Why ever not?"

"They said the travel'd be too much for her," he replied. "They just don't want her goin' that far. They're convinced the trip would endanger her and the baby and they don't wanna take the chance." Uncle Mark paused, looking at Grampa and Gramma, very uneasy but hopeful. "I know this is short notice and all," he started to say, "and I know it's an awful lot to ask of ya seein's how y'all are just gettin' settled in to your new place, but…"

Gramma cut him off almost as if she knew exactly what he was going to say.

"She'll stay with us!" she stated resolutely. "And that's that!"

Grampa nodded, heartily agreeing.

"Absolutely!" he confirmed. "We'd love to have ya!"

Uncle Mark furrowed his brow, still uneasy.

"You're sure?" he wanted to make certain.

"Why, as sure as I'm standin' here!" Grampa quipped with a grin.

Uncle Mark looked down at Aunt Sara as she looked up at him smiling. She squeezed his hand, nodding favorably. He squeezed back with a nod.

"Then it's settled," he approved, looking back to Grampa and Gramma. "We'll bring her home in a few days." He shook his head, touched. "Thank ya, Ma, Pa. This means a lot!"

"Yes!" Aunt Sara agreed. "It means the world! Thank you both!"

Gramma leaned down and gave Aunt Sara a kiss on the cheek as Grampa reached across the bed and shook Uncle Mark's hand.

The matter was settled. Aunt Sara would have a place to stay for the remainder of her pregnancy.

I walked over beside Aunt Sara as the others went on talking. I leaned down to give her a hug.

"I'm so happy for you and Uncle Mark," I expressed with joy, so thrilled for their good news. "I am sorry, though, that you won't be able to go home to your own place."

Aunt Sara glanced up at me with a troubled look.

"I know," she said, a bit melancholy. "Me, too!" She put her hand on her belly as she stared down at her stomach longingly. "I'm willing to do whatever it takes to keep this baby safe, though!" she stated with resolve.

"I fully understand," I told her sympathetically. I leaned down and whispered sweetly in her ear. "Selfishly, though," I confessed, "I'm glad you're staying!"

Aunt Sara managed a smile.

"I'm sure we'll have a wonderful visit while I'm here," she said, sounding so worn-out.

I could tell Aunt Sara was struggling to stay awake, so I got Papa's attention to indicate that we might want to leave.

He looked at me and nodded as if he understood.

"Come on, everybody," he announced. "We better get goin'. Let's let Sara get some rest."

There were no arguments. Everyone understood and readily agreed.

Uncle Mark and Aunt Sara thanked all of us for coming as we each took turns hugging their necks and congratulating them again. Papa reassured them that they would be in our thoughts and prayers, and we all indicated that we couldn't wait for them to be home.

Each of us slowly exited the room, and before Papa closed the door behind him, he momentarily turned back.

"I'll come in a couple of days," he said. "Hopefully by then, Sara'll be able to come home."

*****

On the ride back to our house, everyone was engaged in lively conversation.

Samuel expressed how excited he was that he was going to have a little cousin, indicating that that would finally relieve him of being the youngest in the family, Gramma just couldn't get over the amazing miracle God had performed in allowing Aunt Sara and

Uncle Mark to conceive and how He'd graciously answered our prayers concerning Aunt Sara, and Grampa and Papa were vigorously trying to figure out just how they could help Uncle Mark with the store back in North Dakota, seeing as how Aunt Sara would now have to be here with us.

I just sat, thankful, listening intently, taking it all in. I was grinning from ear to ear, my heart incredibly happy! I was so glad Aunt Sara was all right, and I was giddy at the thought of being able to spend more time with her! I smiled, too, knowing that a new little cousin was on the way. I just couldn't wait to hold it, boy or girl; I didn't care, just as long as it was healthy.

What a remarkable, wonderful day this had turned out to be! I couldn't *wait* to tell Isaac all about it!

WAITING
(Chapter 9)

During the next couple of days, while we were waiting to bring Aunt Sara home from the hospital, we finished moving Grampa and Gramma into their new house. It was hectic, but the business helped the time pass by more quickly. Before we knew it, it was time for Papa to go back to the hospital to pick up Aunt Sara and Uncle Mark.

*****

When Papa got there, the doctor agreed that Aunt Sara could be released but only under one very important condition - she *had* to be on strict bed rest! He told her he didn't want her up walking around or doing anything strenuous. He explained that the restriction was necessary given the seriousness of her condition.

"It's simply the only way!" he warned sternly. "It's what you have to do if you want to give you and your baby a chance at survival."

Aunt Sara and Uncle Mark indicated that they understood the gravity of the situation. They agreed to do their very best to comply with his wishes.

Before the doctor readied to leave, he informed Aunt Sara and Uncle Mark that he would be turning Aunt Sara's care over to Dr. Wellesley, our local doctor, saying he believed she would be in excellent hands. They agreed. He then wished her and the baby well, and asked if they had any questions.

Both Aunt Sara and Uncle Mark assured him that they had already had all their questions answered, and that they felt they were ready to go.

The doctor nodded, satisfied, shook Uncle Mark's hand, and left.

Uncle Mark and Papa grabbed Aunt Sara's things, carefully helped her out to the wagon, and when everyone was settled, they started for home.

As they traveled, Papa did his best to be extra careful, working hard to avoid big bumps and jostles so as not to upset Aunt Sara who was resting on a cot in the back of the wagon that Papa had made for her. Uncle Mark rode along side her, holding her hand, and generally trying to keep her as comfortable as possible.

*****

Back home, Samuel and I had just finished up school for the day, and Grampa had come to pick us up.

"Are they back yet, Grampa?" I asked, hopeful, climbing into the wagon.

"Not yet, Wallflower," Grampa replied, "but I'm expectin' 'em anytime now."

Sure enough, as we rode down the lane towards Grampa and Gramma's house, we could see Papa's wagon. Papa and Uncle Mark had already taken Aunt Sara inside, and Gramma and Uncle Mark were helping to settle her in the guest bedroom.

"How's Sara, Son?" Grampa asked as we walked into the house.

Papa was just coming out of the kitchen holding a glass of water.

"Seems to be doin' all right," he said as he took a sip. "She still seems awfully tired, though, and unfortunately she got sick to her stomach a couple of times on the way home." Papa shook his head. "Havin' babies sure can be rough on a woman."

"Was Mama that way with me?" Samuel queried innocently.

Papa sobered as he looked at the floor. I could tell thinking about Mama was painful for him, but he answered Samuel's question nonetheless.

"Yes, Son," he replied, looking up. "Your mama had a dreadful time with ya. She was sick for five months straight. Didn't think she'd ever get over it. But," he said, smiling, "she always said it was worth it because we ended up with you!"

Samuel had a shocked look on his face.

"Ya mean...I made Mama sick?" he questioned, surprised.

Papa nodded, affirming.

"It happens, Son," he told him, trying to explain. "Some women don't have a lick of trouble havin' babies, while others like your ma and Aunt Sara, why, they have a terrible time!"

Samuel got a look of angst on his face as he shook his head, disturbed.

"Sure am glad I'm a boy!" he quipped, relieved.

"Me, too!" I teased with a chuckle. "You'd never make it as a woman!"

"Wouldn't want to!" he retorted. "Y'all are too complicated for me!"

"Oh, now!" Grampa jested. "And what would ya know of it?"

"Weeelll," Samuel replied sheepishly, "guess I wouldn't *really* know. But they sure *seem* complicated!"

Grampa and I, along with Papa, just laughed at his consternation.

A bit embarrassed by it all, Samuel barked back.

"I'm goin' outside!" he announced. "I'm done talkin'!"

Papa grinned.

"Sounds like a good idea, Son," he said.

Samuel shook his head and started to walk away.

"And hey," Papa called out to him, "while you're out there, put your grampa's horses in the barn, all right?"

Samuel waved back, indicating he would, and ran on outside.

Just about then, Uncle Mark and Gramma came walking out of the bedroom.

"She's all settled in," Gramma stated as she went to get Aunt Sara some water.

Uncle Mark started to pace, brooding, trying to hold it all together, until Gramma was back in the room with Aunt Sara. As soon as she was, he broke down, overwhelmed by everything.

"I'm so worried for her," he said tearfully, looking so lost and afraid. "Sara's just so weak and tired and so terribly sick. What if..." He paused, shaking his head, troubled. "I just don't know what to do for her! I don't wanna lose her!"

Papa came over and put his hand on Uncle Mark's shoulder, trying to bolster him.

"She'll get through this, Mark," he told him with confidence. "Ya just wait and see!" Papa looked at him with empathy as he began to relay his own experience, trying to assure Uncle Mark that everything would work out all right. "I don't know if ya remember or not," he said, "but Lydia had an *awful* time with both Jochebed *and* Samuel, and while it was difficult for a time, she came through it just fine in the end." He nodded, assertively. "It'll be passed before ya know it, Mark," he comforted. "Just hang in there!"

Uncle Mark wiped a tear.

"I sure hope you're right, Michael," he said with trepidation. "It all just worries me somethin' awful!" He shook his head, still anxious. "It's the thought of losin' her," he confessed. "I..." He paused, fighting back tears. "I try to be happy about the baby, I do," he relayed, "but...sometimes...sometimes I'll admit it's hard. If it means I might lose Sara, I...." He broke down again.

"Now, Mark!" Grampa interjected sternly. "Son, ya gotta trust! Ya do what the Bible tells us to do and trust! Remember what it says, '*Trust* in the Lord with *all* thine heart; and *lean not* unto thine own understanding. In *all thy ways* acknowledge Him, and He shall direct thy paths.'" Grampa calmed a bit as he walked over to Uncle Mark. "I know it seems hard right now," he sympathized, "but, Son, I just *know* that God's in control of this thing! No matter what happens, ya can trust Him!"

Uncle Mark shook his head with a sigh.

"I know, Pa," he solemnly accepted. "I know. And I appreciate ya remindin' me, I do, but..." He stood there a minute, contemplating, as he wiped his tears. "I'm gonna go check on Sara," he said somberly. He turned and walked out of the room, visibly still burdened.

When I looked over at Grampa, I could see the pained look on his face. It was obvious he was concerned for his youngest son.

"He'll get through it, Pa," Papa assured. "It's all just new and unexpected. Can't say I was any less worried when Lydia was expectin' our first."

Grampa nodded, relating.

"Nor I for your Ma when she was expectin' you," he granted. "Still," he said with a sigh, "it does break my heart to see him hurtin' so."

"Just means we need to pray all the harder," Papa proffered.

"Agreed, Son!" Grampa approved enthusiastically. "Agreed!"

I sat down on the couch and thought about what Grampa had told Uncle Mark. I knew he was simply trying to help and give encouragement - that the best thing for Uncle Mark to do was to give his worries and cares to the Lord, and I *fully* understood and agreed with him, but I guess I could understand how Uncle Mark was feeling, too. The unexpected turn of events in his life was a burden weighing heavy on his heart and mind, and I knew exactly what that felt like. Having lost Mama so suddenly, I knew from my own experience that trusting God through it all was *not* an easy thing to do.

I paused and said a quick prayer in my heart for both Uncle Mark and Aunt Sara. I prayed that Aunt Sara and the baby would be safe and healthy, and that Uncle Mark would be able to lay his burdens down. I just desperately wanted everyone to be all right!

Papa and I sat and chatted a while longer with Grampa, before Papa finally decided we should get home and get some chores done. He told Grampa we'd be back later on after supper to check on things, and went to the back door to call for Samuel to come. Samuel met us around the front of the house at the wagon, and we left.

When we got home, we all went straight to work, Papa and Samuel to the barn, and me to the house. It took several hours to finish our chores, but eventually we managed to get everything accomplished.

After cleaning up the supper dishes and finishing some homework, Samuel and I went to find Papa. He was back out in the barn working on a project he'd been trying to finish for the past couple of weeks. When he finally wrapped up what he was doing, we all headed back to Grampa and Gramma's.

As we were pulling down the lane, we could see Dr. Wellesley's carriage parked in front of the house. I didn't think much of it at first, but when we got inside, I could tell something was wrong. Grampa and Uncle Mark were both in the family room looking rather troubled and anxious. Grampa was sitting in his chair, seemingly deep in thought and prayer, and Uncle Mark was up pacing back and forth, clearly worried.

"What is it, Mark?" Papa asked earnestly.

"It's Sara!" he said, panicked.

"She started bleedin' a little while ago," Grampa explained. "Was havin' some pain, too. Mark went and got the doc. He and your ma are in with her now."

Papa looked at Samuel and me and motioned for us to go sit down on the couch. We kept quiet and did as he asked.

Concerned, Papa walked over to Uncle Mark who was still pacing back and forth.

"Why don't ya come sit down, Mark," he urged. "I'm sure Doc's takin' real good care of her."

"No!" Uncle Mark insisted. "I'm good here!"

I could see the fear and trepidation in his eyes as he continued to pace back and forth, fretting, shaking his head, rubbing the back of his neck - scared to death. I felt so sorry for him, and admittedly, scared myself for Aunt Sara and the baby! I so wished there was something I could say or do to help the situation, but nothing came to mind. It was a terrible, helpless feeling! Not knowing what else to do, I decided to do the only thing I knew to do, and that was to pray.

At a loss himself, Papa came and sat down beside Samuel and me on the couch as we all waited for an update from the doctor. We waited and waited and waited some more until finally Gramma came out and walked right over to Uncle Mark.

Looking up at him with a comforting smile, gently putting her hand on his arm, she relayed the prognosis.

"She's all right, Son," she assured with a nod.

Uncle Mark breathed a huge sigh of release as he nearly staggered back, relieved.

"Doc checked her over thoroughly," Gramma went on to explain, "and he said the bleedin' was reasonably normal given everything that's goin' on with her. He said the ride home from the hospital probably caused it. It's stopped now, and she's restin' comfortably."

"Can I go see her?" Uncle Mark asked anxiously.

"Of course," Gramma answered, with an understanding smile. "She's waitin' for ya."

Uncle Mark rushed off to Aunt Sara's room as Gramma stood quietly, shaking her head, visibly grieved.

"What is it, dear?" Grampa queried. "What's botherin' ya?"

Gramma reluctantly walked over and sat down in the rocking chair next to Grampa.

"This isn't gonna be easy," she replied with a heavy-heart, "on Sara *or Mark!* I worry so for the both of 'em."

Grampa shook his head a little aggravated.

"Now, Doc said she's doin' fine, Elizabeth," he reminded with a slight reprimand. "Let's not go borrowin' trouble where it's not needed!"

Papa jumped in.

"Are ya gonna be able to handle this, Ma?" he questioned - concerned. "After all, this is a huge undertakin' for you and Pa."

"Oh, goodness!" Gramma dismissed. "Don't ya go worrin' none about us! We'll be fine!" She leaned over and patted Grampa on the leg. "We don't mind helpin' out at all," she said with enthusiasm. "Really, we don't! It's just that...well..." Another look of angst shown on her face. "I just know this is gonna be a difficult road, and I can't help but be concerned."

Grampa reached over and squeezed her hand as he gave her a sympathetic smile.

"I can understand it," Papa related. "I know it's not gonna be easy, but listen, Jochebed's available, and she'll be here to help ya whenever she can."

"That's right, Gramma!" I eagerly concurred. "Papa and I have already discussed it, and I really want to help out with Aunt Sara. I plan to be here every day after school."

"Oh, but, child!" Gramma exclaimed, very apprehensive. "Ya have your own home to run now! What about your chores and meals and your schoolwork? Why…"

"Now don't ya go worryin' about all that, Ma!" Papa insisted. "Samuel and I've agreed to help Jochebed out where we can, and she can do her homework while she's here. As for meals, why, Samuel and I can just come down here and eat with y'all. If things get to be too much, we'll make adjustments." He sat forward on the couch to emphasize his point. "It'll all work out!" he promised. "We're a family and we'll pull together to help carry the extra load!"

Gramma looked pensive.

"You're sure about this, now?" she wanted to substantiate, still not convinced. "You're sure it won't be too much or…or interfere with what ya gotta do?"

Papa stood up, walked over, and gave Gramma a kiss on the top of her head.

"It'll be fine, Ma," he calmed, smiling down at her. "Trust me!"

Gramma looked up at him, returning a hesitant smile before looking over at me.

"Well then," she said with appreciation, "thank ya, Jochebed. I welcome the help and the company."

"Then it's settled!" Papa announced. "Jochebed'll be your third set of hands."

Just then, Dr. Wellesley came out from Aunt Sara's room, bag in hand, ready to leave.

"She's asleep now," he told us, "and she'll likely sleep the night."

"Is there anything more we can do for her, Doc?" Gramma asked as she stood up, eager to know.

"No," he replied, "unfortunately for now, Mrs. Lowry, the best thing to do is to just keep her as still as possible. It's not going to be easy, and only time will tell if it'll be enough, but for now, that's my best advice. I'll be back by next week sometime to check on her, but if you need me before then, you know where to find me."

"Of course," Gramma agreed. "I thank ya for comin!"

"My pleasure, ma'am," he said. "Now, I best be going. You all have a good evening."

Papa walked Dr. Wellesley to the door to see him out, while Gramma made her way back to the bedroom to check in on Aunt Sara and Uncle Mark.

Since it was getting late and there really wasn't anything more we could do, Papa decided that he and Samuel and I should all head home. We said our goodnights to Grampa, and left.

*****

The next day after school, I hastily finished up what chores I could at home, gathered my homework to take with me, and hurried off to Grampa and Grammas' house to help with Aunt Sara. Fortunately, their new home wasn't that far down the road from our house (within walking distance), so the travel back and forth wasn't a problem.

I still hadn't had a chance to see Aunt Sara since she'd arrived home from the hospital, so I was looking forward to being able to spend some time with her. When I arrived at the house, however, she was resting, so while I waited for her to wake up, I did some reading and helped Gramma with supper.

When we were just about finished preparing the meal, Gramma sent Grampa to fetch Papa and Samuel. They were both still at home working around the house.

*****

I was standing at the counter in the kitchen, my back to the door, when suddenly Papa came up behind me, leaned around, kissed me on the cheek, and presented me with an envelope.

"Oh, Papa!" I exclaimed, putting my hand to my chest, nearly jumping out of my skin. "You startled me!"

Papa chuckled at my reaction as he stood there still holding the letter out in front of me.

It took me a minute to realize what he had, but as soon as I did, I immediately grabbed it from him, spun around, and squealed in delight!

"Is this what I think it is?" I asked in anticipation.

Papa grinned.

"I thought ya might like to have it," he said. "It was in the mail today."

"Oh, thank you, Papa!" I expressed with glee. I could hardly contain my enthusiasm!

"Go on now, child," Gramma encouraged, smiling broadly. "You go and enjoy your letter. I'll finish up in here."

I smiled, grateful.

"Thank you, Gramma," I told her, clutching the envelope to my chest. I smiled again at Papa before hurrying off to the family room to open my letter.

Once there, I promptly sat down in Gramma's rocking chair, my heart pounding wildly, eager to know the contents of Isaac's letter. I carefully, but hastily began to open the envelope, and when I had it sufficiently torn, I immediately pulled out the piece of paper that was inside, quickly unfolded it, and began to read it at once.

My dearest Jochebed,

I hope this letter finds you well.

I was so thrilled to receive your letter and to hear the good news that your father has given his permission for us to court. I look forward to getting to know you better.

I was sorry, however, to hear about your Aunt Sara. My grandparents wired me and told me that she had been taken to the hospital. I do hope everything is all right. She and your family have been in my prayers.

How are you doing? Is school going well? Are your grandparents all moved into their new home yet?

I have to admit, I can't wait to see you again! I wish Thanksgiving would hurry and arrive. I doubt I'll be able to make it home before then, but

75

I'll most definitely try. Knowing I now have you to come home to makes me long to be there all the more!

Please pray for me if you would. I have several tests coming up in the next week and a paper due at the same time. I'm busy, but grateful for the opportunity to be furthering my education here at the seminary.

I apologize that my letter is not nearly as long as yours was, but work and school have been quite demanding of my time as of late.

I'll try to write when I can, and I look forward to hearing from you again as well. Please let me know how your Aunt Sara is getting along, and please know that I'll continue to pray.

I can't wait to see you! I miss you! Be well!

Yours truly,
Isaac

My heart was simply fluttering with joy as I read the closing to his letter. My very first letter from Isaac! It was wonderful! I knew that I had to make certain I put it in my memory book to keep it always.

I held the letter close to my chest as I sat there with a smile on my face, deep in thought, a million miles away. I was enthralled, dreaming about Isaac. I reflected back over all he had written to me and contemplated what I would say in my next letter to him.

As I sat there mesmerized, mulling things over, Samuel walked in from outside.

"What's wrong with you?" he questioned with furrowed brow, looking at me suspiciously.

I didn't even hear him. My mind was too preoccupied with thoughts of Isaac.

"Jochebed!" he called out again as he walked over and snapped his fingers in my face. "Snap out of it! What's the matter with ya?"

I simply looked up at him and smiled pleasantly.

"Samuel, my little brother," I quipped as I stood up, tapping him on the nose with my letter, "you just wouldn't understand!" I happily put the letter in my apron pocket and started towards the kitchen.

Glancing back at Samuel, he was standing there staring at me with his eyebrow raised, indicating through his expression that he thought I had truly lost my mind. I didn't care, though. I was in love, and I wasn't about to let what he thought of me ruin that!

I went back to the kitchen and finished helping Gramma put everything on the table. When everyone was gathered, we prayed and commenced to eating.

We weren't long into dinner, when the conversation suddenly turned serious. Everyone was trying to figure out how Uncle Mark could go back to North Dakota and tend to the store while Aunt Sara was left behind here with us. They were trying to figure out the most efficient way for him to travel.

Would taking the train (which would cost more but be quicker) make more sense, or would driving his wagon (which would be cheaper but take much more time) be the better choice? No one seemed quite sure which would be best.

They were also trying to think of someone who might be willing and able to run the store from time to time while Uncle Mark had to be away, coming back to see Aunt Sara.

All of these things were earnestly being discussed - everyone talking back and forth and all around, trying to come to a reasonable conclusion.

Sitting there listening to all the chatter, I couldn't help but worry, *How were we going to manage this difficult situation?*

Having no solutions of my own, I finally excused myself from the table and got up to go check on Aunt Sara. I wanted to take her something to eat and to sit with her for a little while and catch up on things. I gathered her food onto a tray and went to her room.

I didn't want to disturb her if she were sleeping, so I softly knocked on her door and waited quietly for her to answer. When she did, I opened the door and walked inside.

Walking over to her, I put the serving tray of food and drink down beside her on the little table that sat next to the bed. As soon as my hands were free, I cheerfully leaned down, so happy to see her, and gave her a big hug.

"We haven't had a chance to talk since you've been home," I told her, taking a seat there beside her, anxious to speak with her. "How are you feeling?"

Aunt Sara looked up at me so weary and a little peaked.

"I'm doing all right," she replied - almost as if that were the answer she thought she should give.

I looked at her skeptical.

"The truth," I prodded.

~

Aunt Sara and I had always been able to talk with each other about anything. She was kind of like an older sister to me that I had never had. When she was around, we always enjoyed each other's company, and when she was away, we kept in touch through letters.

~

"Really, Jochebed," she came back at me, obviously trying to convince me, "I'm as good as I can be for a woman in my condition."

She seemed somewhat reticent and very emotional. She sighed deeply as she looked up at me. It appeared as if she wanted to say something more, but for some reason she refrained herself.

"What is it, Aunt Sara?" I pressed, sensing her reluctance. "You can talk to me."

She looked quite distressed, almost despondent, as she lay there quiet and still. She took a deep breath, contemplating, before finally deciding to share.

"I have to be honest," she started to say. She stopped abruptly, shaking her head, almost as though she were reconsidering. "Oh, I have to tell someone!" she blurted out, clearly upset. She again looked up at me with trepidation in her eyes. "I'm so worried, Jochebed!" she admitted. Immediately, she looked at me, frantic. "I'm trying not to be, though!" she stated quickly, trying to sound upbeat, not wanting me to think less of her somehow. "I'm trying to have faith...really I am...trying to trust the Lord in all this, but..." She turned away, attempting to hide her tears.

I couldn't help but feel badly for her as I could see the burden of guilt and fear weighing heavy on her heart. I compassionately took hold of her hand, trying to comfort her.

She turned back to me, tears streaming down her face.

"I'm just so afraid!" she cried. "I mean, I try to be strong for Mark, but when I'm alone, so tired, and *so* sick, just me and my thoughts…Oh, Jochebed," she agonized, "I've wanted this baby for so long, and now that it's finally happening, with all of the difficulties and complications, I'm just so scared! What if…what if the baby doesn't make it? What if *I* don't make it?" She shook her head, distraught. "I just don't think I can go through this!"

I looked at her, my heart rending. I knew exactly what she was feeling. I knew it, because I had lived it many times before.

Unfortunately, I knew all too well what it was like to be so worried about something and to be so consumed with fear about it that you didn't know what to do or how to cope. I knew what it was like to feel helpless in the matter, not knowing which way to turn or who to talk to or even if you were ever going to get through it. It was an awful, horrible, frightening place to be in, but it was real and I understood. I didn't judge her for it. I did, however, wish like everything that I could take her anxiety from her…but I knew that I couldn't.

"Oh, Aunt Sara," I commiserated. "I'm so sorry! I wish I could make everything all right for you!" I gently put my hand on her shoulder as she continued to cry. "I know this is difficult," I tried to console, "but…but God will see you through…I know He will!" I did what I could to encourage her. "He promises He'll never give us more than we can handle," I reminded.

Still searching for the right words to say, I drew from my own experience.

"When I lost Mama," I began. Immediately, I paused, overcome, swallowing hard, trying not to cry. I cleared my throat and did my best to continue. "When I lost Mama," I pressed on, "I clung to my favorite verse. It's found in the book of first Corinthians, chapter ten and verse thirteen. It says, 'There hath no temptation taken you but such as is common to man: but God *is faithful*, who will not suffer you to be tempted above that ye are able; but will with the temptation also make a way to escape, *that ye may be able to bear it.*' I didn't think I could handle losing Mama, Aunt Sara, but God showed Himself faithful to me during that awful time, and He continues to show Himself faithful to me now. While everyday without her is still very, very hard…" I couldn't help it, a tear escaped my eye and trickled down my cheek. "With His help," I said, sniffing, wiping the tear from my face, "I'm getting through it."

I looked at her with empathy.

"I know this trial of yours seems impossible right now," I told her, "but I *know* God is there, Aunt Sara, and I know He'll give you exactly what you need to get through it!" I squeezed her hand in support as she squeezed back. "I'm praying for you and the baby every day," I assured her. "And I'll help you in any way that I possibly can. It'll be all right" I encouraged. "I promise!"

Aunt Sara looked up at me and managed a smile through her tears.

"So grown up," she expressed with pride. "Thank you, Jochebed. You don't know how much that means to me!"

I smiled back at her, wiping my tears, as she did the same.

I sat there with Aunt Sara for quite a while longer, we talked of all sorts of things, she ate, and we enjoyed the time together immensely. I told her about my letter from Isaac and how things were going with him, and she shared with me some valuable advice regarding courtship. I so appreciated her insight about such things, especially now that I didn't have Mama to talk to anymore. Her counsel was wise, and I respected it.

Towards the end of our conversation, Papa came and knocked on the door.

"Jochebed," he said as he peeked in, "sweetheart, it's gettin' late. We need to be goin'."

"Yes, Papa," I replied. "I'll be out in a minute."

I thanked Aunt Sara for her guidance, leaned over and gave her a big hug, and told her how much I loved her. I also told her how much I couldn't *wait* to have a new little cousin!

She smiled at the thought.

"And I can't wait to be a mother," she replied.

I could tell as soon as the words left her lips that worry began to creep back into her heart. Before she could dwell on it too long, however, I quickly interjected, wanting to quell any undue concerns.

"And you'll make a *wonderful* mother, Aunt Sara!" I bolstered with a smile, "a *very*, wonderful mother!"

She brushed her angst aside and smiled back.

"Thank you, Jochebed," she said sweetly. "That means a lot!"

*****

Within the week, Uncle Mark had to say goodbye to Aunt Sara (and the rest of us, of course), and head back to North Dakota. His responsibilities awaited him, and even though they wished things could be different, and even though it was extremely hard on the two of them, deep down they knew they really had no choice.

Uncle Mark said he'd do his best to come back and visit as often as he could, but we all knew that he wouldn't be able to come very frequently nor stay for very long when he did.

Aunt Sara tried to put up a brave front, but deep down I could tell that letting him go was one of the hardest things she'd ever had to do.

It'd been decided that taking the train would be the quickest and easiest way for Uncle Mark to travel, so we all agreed to find odd jobs to help cover the expense. It wouldn't be easy, but we'd do whatever we had to do to help out.

*****

Time seemed to pass by so slowly for Aunt Sara over the next few days and weeks as she missed Uncle Mark something awful and battled her sickness and the feeling of being so tired and run-down. She did her best to stay as still as possible, lying in bed, waiting, but it wasn't at all easy for her, and while she did *extremely* well most days, there were still times when it was a struggle for her, and understandably so! Watching her tremendous dedication, though, I couldn't help but admire her strength and commitment and extraordinary resolve!

She continued to sleep quite a lot and only ate small amounts of her meals (mainly because that was all she could keep down), but despite her difficult challenges, she was slowly improving, gaining strength every day. She hadn't experienced any more bleeding since that first day she arrived home (for which we were all very thankful), and up until now, all of her doctor checkups had shown good, steady progress.

I did my best to spend as much time with Aunt Sara as I possibly could, trying to keep her spirits high, trying to encourage her while Uncle Mark was away, but sometimes it was hard as she was so lonely for him, wishing desperately that he could be there with her. I completely understood!

She had good days and bad, but overall I'd say she was dealing with her unusual circumstances quite remarkably. I could tell, however, that she was still somewhat reluctant to get too excited about her pregnancy, still fighting the fear and worry of possibly losing the baby. It was almost as if she didn't want to allow herself to get too attached to the idea of becoming a mother, afraid that if she did, her hopes and dreams would somehow be dashed. I tried to reassure her that it was all in God's hands and that He would take care of her no matter what, but I often felt my words were far too inadequate to allay her fears.

She was strong, though, and determined to get through this trial, and seeing her tenacity, I had every faith that she would. She was an amazing woman, and I respected her greatly. She was definitely a hero in my book!

COMING HOME
(Chapter 10)

It was coming on November now; the air had turned bitter cold, and Thanksgiving was just a few weeks away. Uncle Mark hadn't been back yet, choosing rather to stay in North Dakota until Thanksgiving, hoping to be able to save up enough money to stay with Aunt Sara through Christmas. It was a dreadfully long time for him to be away, but even though we all missed him terribly and couldn't wait for him to return, we understood he needed the extra time to work. Aunt Sara was doing well, so she and Grampa and Gramma all agreed to his decision.

It was hard on the two of them having to be apart from each other for so long, but Aunt Sara faithfully wrote to Uncle Mark almost every day, and he wrote back whenever he could.

Most days Aunt Sara was strong enough that she could help Gramma and me with the sewing jobs we had acquired to help with Uncle Mark's travel expenses, and given her incredible sewing abilities, she was definitely a valuable asset. She still got tired from time to time and often fought sickness, but despite her bad days, she was still a tremendous help.

As time passed, she and I could hardly contain our excitement at the thought of our fellas coming home in just a few short weeks. She was growing ever impatient and restless, as was I! It seemed Thanksgiving couldn't get here soon enough!

*****

"How's Sara today?" Papa asked Gramma as he came into the kitchen to wash up for supper.

"Oh, I don't know," Gramma bemoaned, sounding a bit worried. "I'm a little concerned about her, Michael. She seems a bit more tired today than usual, and I'm afraid she may be over doin' it with all the sewin' projects and all."

"Well, Ma," Papa tried to calm as he dried his hands and walked over to kiss Gramma on the forehead, "I'm sure she'll be fine." He threw the towel down on the counter and walked on towards the table. "Sewin' gives her somethin' to do," he explained as he took a seat. "I mean, *gracious*, I don't know how she's survived this long! I think I'd a gone plum crazy a long time ago if it was me havin' to lie still in that bed *all day*, *every day!* I admire her patience and perseverance!"

Gramma sighed as she walked over and set a dish down on the table.

"I suppose you're right," she reluctantly accepted. "But still…she worries me! Ya can never be too careful with these delicate matters."

"Aww now, Ma," Papa lightly scolded, "don't go frettin' yourself! Sara's a strong woman. If anybody can get through this, she can."

Gramma sighed again, obviously still concerned, but willing to concede the point.

Within minutes, everyone was gathered in the kitchen, ready for supper. We took our seats, Grampa prayed, and we all started in, eating and enjoying the wonderful meal that Gramma and I had prepared.

We weren't but a few minutes in, however, when suddenly Aunt Sara yelled out from the bedroom, sounding as if something were wrong.

Of course, her outburst startled all of us, and instantly we all jumped up from the table and hurried to check on her.

Hastening quickly, I made it into the bedroom first, and Papa immediately followed.

"What is it?" I exclaimed as everyone else gathered round.

"I'm not sure!" Aunt Sara moaned. "I can hardly catch my breath, and I ache so much!" She lay there on the bed, holding her stomach, turning from side to side.

"Go now and get the doctor, Michael!" Gramma insisted, wide-eyed and clearly frightened. "Ezra, bring me a cool cloth, and, Jochebed, go get some extra blankets!"

We all scurried about to do as Gramma had instructed, while Samuel stayed in the hallway out of the way.

"There, there, now!" Gramma said, trying to comfort Aunt Sara as she sat down beside her on the bed. "You'll be all right!"

When I brought the blankets over, I could tell Gramma was still fearful. I tried not to panic, but as was my tendency, I began to worry, too. I did my best not to let it show, however, not wanting to frighten Aunt Sara.

Gramma took the blankets from me, and she and I spread them over Aunt Sara. When we had her all tucked in, I took the cool cloth that Grampa had brought in from the kitchen and placed it on Aunt Sara's forehead. She was still in pain, but she did seem to be calming a bit.

"It just hurts!" she told us, grimacing.

"I know, dear," Gramma sympathized. "But just try to lie still. The doctor'll be here soon."

By now, Aunt Sara looked rather clammy and a bit pale.

"Ohhh!" she groaned. "I feel as if I might get sick!" She immediately turned and leaned to the side of the bed.

I quickly got the bucket for her, and she proceeded to throw up.

Breathing heavily, she leaned back.

"I feel so poorly," she whimpered, trying to sit up.

"No, no, dear!" Gramma insisted. "Just lie still!"

I ran to get Aunt Sara a glass of water, but before I could get back with it, she had gotten sick again.

Gramma took the cloth and wiped her brow.

"Here!" I said as I hurried back into the room. "Here's some water for her."

I handed the glass to Gramma, and she tried to get Aunt Sara to take a sip.

"I really don't think I can keep it down," Aunt Sara said, rejecting the water. "My stomach feels so awful!" She lay there sick and weak, waiting for the doctor to arrive.

In no time at all, Papa was back with Dr. Wellesley. They came to Aunt Sara's room, everyone left, and the doctor examined her.

"What do you suppose it is?" Gramma fretted as we all sat back down at the table.

"Couldn't say," Papa replied. "Let's let the doc do his job. We'll know soon enough."

We all sat and picked at our food for awhile, until Grampa decided to say a prayer for Aunt Sara. Not long after he finished, the doctor came out to speak with us.

"Well," he said, "seems she's come down with a terrible case of the flu. For now, see she gets plenty of fluids, and if she can tolerate it, see she gets something to eat."

"The baby?" Gramma asked anxiously as she stood to her feet. "Is the baby all right?"

"The baby seems fine, Mrs. Lowry," Dr. Wellesley assured with a smile. "We just need to nurse Sara through this flu. I'll check on her in a day or two and see how she's doing. Hopefully, by then, she'll be feeling better. Just keep a close eye on her for me – all right?"

"Will do, Doc," Grampa said as he stood up, walking over to him to shake his hand. "Thanks so much!" He gestured towards the front door. "I'll walk ya out," he offered kindly.

Dr. Wellesley nodded, appreciative, and he and Grampa walked out of the room.

As they left, Gramma stood there, shaking her head, almost in tears.

"Oh that poor child!" she bewailed. "How much more is she expected to endure? She's already been through so much and has so far to go!" She shook her head again, fretful. "Oh, that poor, poor dear!" she lamented, starting to tear up.

Papa looked over at Gramma.

"Ya gotta trust God in this, Ma," he told her. "He'll give her the strength she needs to get through this. And don't forget," he reminded, "we're here for her, too. She won't face it alone."

Right then, Grampa came back in from seeing the doctor out. He saw Gramma with tears in her eyes and a look of distress on her face, so he walked over to her, took her in his arms, and tried to console her.

"Now, Elizabeth," he comforted sweetly, "she's gonna be all right. No need to fret. It's just the flu, and the baby's fine."

Gramma looked up at him.

"Oh, I know you're right, Ezra," she admitted as she wiped a tear. "I just hate to see her suffer so. I just don't know how much more her poor body can take. How I wish there was somethin' more I could do for her."

"We all do, Gramma," I chimed in, sitting there feeling just as helpless.

Just then, Aunt Sara called for someone to come to her. Gramma wiped away her tears, composed herself, and she and I went to see what she wanted.

As soon as we entered the room, Aunt Sara started to apologize.

"I'm so sorry," she stressed, feeling badly. "I didn't mean to scare everyone over the flu."

"Now, don't ya worry yourself none about that," Gramma told her, walking over to the bed. "Ya just concentrate on gettin' better."

"That's right!" I concurred. "The important thing is that you get well."

Aunt Sara sighed.

"Thank you for understanding," she said, looking rather peaked. "But still, I feel so foolish!"

"No harm done," I assured her. "We're all just glad it isn't anything more serious."

*****

Over the next few days, Aunt Sara was *dreadfully* sick! She didn't feel at all like eating or drinking anything; she just couldn't keep it down. Admittedly, it was hard seeing her like that as she was *absolutely miserable!*

The doctor had been back to check on her twice, and he was troubled at what he saw. She was losing weight instead of gaining, and he was concerned not only for her, but for the baby as well. He told us he didn't want to have to move her again, but if she didn't improve within the next few days, he'd have no choice but to put her back in the hospital.

"Get her to eat something," he instructed adamantly, "even if you can only get her to sip some broth. It'd be better than nothing. She's losing ground, and I can't let it go too long!"

Gramma and I understood and we did our best to comply with his wishes.

*****

"You just have to try!" I desperately begged Aunt Sara as I attempted to get her to take some soup.

She was having none of it, though.

"Please, Jochebed," she moaned, "I feel too awful. I just can't!"

"I know you feel awful," I commiserated, "but please, do it for the baby!"

Aunt Sara could barely open her eyes at this point; she was so weak and so sick. I couldn't help but be frightened for her. I was so afraid we might lose her and the baby!

Because she was still in so much pain and so frail that she could no longer sit up on her own, I carefully put my hand under her head and lifted her forward a bit. I gently put the bowl of soup to her mouth.

"Just a sip," I prodded, trying to encourage her.

She looked up at me, desperately weary. Slowly, she opened her lips, and I was able to pour just a drop into her mouth. She swallowed slowly, and we tried again.

We went on like that for quite a while until she couldn't take any more.

"That's enough!" she resisted, turning her head, exhausted.

I carefully lowered her head to the pillow and laid the soup aside.

So worn out from it all, she immediately fell asleep.

Knowing how tired she was, I let her rest. We'd been able to get about half the broth in her, and only time would tell if she could keep it down. Thankfully, she did!

Grampa and Gramma got word to Uncle Mark about the dire situation Aunt Sara was in, and they encouraged him to come right away, even if he didn't have the money to stay until Christmas. They felt it was more important for him to be with her now, then to save up more money for later. He was on the next train out of North Dakota.

Gramma and I took turns caring for Aunt Sara, sitting with her and nursing her the best we could, but no matter what we did, she didn't seem to get any better. As you can imagine, I was worried!

When Uncle Mark finally arrived, it seemed to be exactly what Aunt Sara needed. Just having him close, her spirits were lifted, and her recovery began.

He sat with her endlessly, taking over her care - stroking her hair, talking to her, feeding her (what she would allow), and encouraging her to get well. Within a couple of days, she was slowly but steadily starting to improve.

Dr. Wellesley came at week's end to look in on her, and he was pleased with what he saw.

"You're by no means out of the woods," he informed, "but you're definitely making progress. Seems that husband of yours was all the medicine you needed!" He smiled at Aunt Sara, heartened. "You've still got a long way to go," he cautioned, "but this is certainly encouraging!" He looked at all of us, appreciative of all we'd done to care for Aunt Sara. "Keep up the good work!" he bolstered. "We'll get her through this yet!"

Needless to say, Aunt Sara's illness took a toll on all of us as she needed almost round- the-clock care for the next couple of weeks. We did what we had to do, however, to get her well again, and thankfully, our persistence paid off! By the end of that last week, Aunt Sara was all but recovered.

Oddly enough, we'd all been so keenly focused on getting Aunt Sara better; we completely failed to notice that it was the week of Thanksgiving.

*****

I was busy hanging some laundry on the line, looking rather disheveled, when all of a sudden I heard a familiar voice behind me.

"Well, there she is!" the voice said. "Your father told me I might find you here."

I spun around to see who it was that was talking to me, and much to my surprise (and delight) there stood Isaac looking so handsome in his hat and overcoat. I immediately dropped what I was doing and ran to greet him.

He smiled broadly and ran to meet me as well.

We met in the middle.

"Isaac!" I giddily queried, so thrilled and excited to see him. "What are you doing here?"

He furrowed his brow, not understanding my question.

"Umm…iitt'ss Thanksgiving," he replied, quite perplexed. "You knew I was coming home…right?"

I shook my head, confused, trying to process what he was saying. Slowly, it began to sink in.

"Thanksgiving!" I exclaimed. "It's Thanksgiving *already?*"

Isaac was more than a little confused.

"Yes," he confirmed curiously. "Jochebed is…is everything all right?"

I chuckled at the irony. Here I'd so desperately been looking forward to Thanksgiving's arrival, yet I'd been so busy that it snuck up on me without me even knowing it!

I promptly explained everything to Isaac.

"So you see," I said, "we've all been so busy caring for Aunt Sara that apparently we all lost track of time." I paused, smiling broadly. "I'm so glad you're here, though!" I expressed with glee.

"Me, too!" Isaac agreed. "And I'm glad to hear your Aunt Sara's doing much better as well."

I nodded and happily invited him into the house. We sat for a little while and visited with Grampa, Gramma, and Uncle Mark, and then I took him back to see Aunt Sara. We talked with her briefly, but didn't stay long as she was tired and needed to rest. As he and I were walking back out into the family room, I invited him to stay for supper, hoping that we would be able to spend some more time together, and although he said he would love to, he told me that he couldn't because he had already promised his grandparents that he would have supper with them. I understood and walked him out.

"I can't wait to see you again," Isaac said, smiling sweetly, staring at me with his gorgeous blue eyes. "While I've thoroughly enjoyed getting to know you better through our correspondence over these past weeks, I really do look forward to being able to just talk with you in person."

I nodded, smiling, wholeheartedly agreeing.

"I should be able to get away sometime tomorrow afternoon," he went on to say. "Can we meet then?"

My smile grew in anticipation.

"I would love that!" I replied excitedly. "I'll be back and forth between here and home, though, so you'll just have to track me down."

"It'll be my pleasure!" Isaac stated enthusiastically with a wink and a smile.

I looked away, blushing.

"See you tomorrow then," Isaac said as I shyly turned back to look at him.

He tipped his hat and stepped off the porch, proceeding to walk backwards for a while, just smiling up at me as I stood there smiling down at him.

I waved and watched as he disappeared down the lane.

Isaac's finally home! I wrote in my memory book as I caught up that night on all the events of the past few weeks. I'd been so busy with Aunt Sara, school, and chores at home and at Grampa and Gramma's that I hadn't had time to keep up with my entries.

I smiled fondly as I thought back over the day and the time I'd gotten to spend with Isaac. He was so sweet and kind and *oh so handsome!* I could hardly believe that he was finally here, and that he was actually mine!

I tried to go to sleep, but I found it nearly impossible! Even though it had been another exhausting day; I was just too giddy at the thought of being able to see Isaac again tomorrow!

GIVING THANKS
(Chapter 11)

Over the next couple of days, we all continued to marvel at the fact that it had not occurred to even one of us before now that this week was the week of Thanksgiving. Suffice it to say, we were more than a little behind on our preparations!

Each morning, Papa, Grampa, Uncle Mark, and Samuel all got up bright and early to go hunt for a turkey, hoping to find one in time for Thanksgiving Day. Normally, they'd have a little more time to do so, but given the circumstances, they'd have to make do with the days they had left.

Because we were so far behind on everything, Isaac and I only got to see each other briefly a couple of times. I was so busy helping Gramma with everything that I just couldn't get away, and he, too, was busy as he had family coming in for the holiday. I have to admit I was looking forward to the craziness settling down a bit so that he and I could spend more time together.

By midmorning on Wednesday, Gramma and I had managed to get quite a bit accomplished, but there was still a lot to do. Unfortunately, as far as we knew, the men still hadn't found a turkey and time was running out! Needless to say, I was getting a little concerned.

"We'll do what we can," Gramma encouraged with a smile, "and make the best of what we've got! I'm just so thankful Sara's doin' better and that Mark's here safe and sound and that we're all here together this year for Thanksgivin'. Turkey or not, we sure do have a lot to be thankful for!"

"You're right, Gramma," I agreed as I scurried about, trying to finish the cleaning. "We do have a lot to be thankful for!"

~

I could tell Gramma was so thrilled that she and Grampa could finally host Thanksgiving dinner for everyone this year. In the past, either they traveled the long distance to celebrate with us, or mostly we just celebrated apart due to the expense of the trip. Having us all here together was definitely one blessing I know she was very thankful for.

~

As I swept, I began to think of the wonderful time we would have - us all being together this year for Thanksgiving. I smiled at the added blessing of now having Isaac in my life, too. As my mind continued to wander, however, I couldn't help but think of Mama. An overwhelming sense of sadness overtook me as my heart began to ache at the thought of her no longer being with us.

~

Mama so enjoyed the holidays: the planning, the cooking, the sharing, the giving...she was always so happy and joyous on these special occasions. I remember her singing and humming around the house as she worked and worked, trying so hard to make everything wonderful and grand and perfect for everyone else. In truth, she loved everything about this time of year: the coolness in the air, the wonderful smells that accompanied it, but most of all, she treasured the time spent with loved ones.

"It's a time for family and friends," she'd always say. "God is just **so** good!"

Things just wouldn't be the same without her here!

~

As I stood there leaning on the handle of my broom, thinking about Mama, a tear made its way to my eye.

"Penny for your thoughts," Gramma offered as she snapped me out of my daydream.

"Oh," I said, wiping the tear from my eye, "I was just missing Mama."

Gramma walked over and gave me a sympathetic hug.

"I miss her, too, sweetheart," she commiserated. "She did so love this time of year, didn't she?"

I nodded, agreeing.

"She sure did!" I answered with fervor.

Gramma and I smiled somberly at each other as we went back to work.

*****

After about an hour or so of cleaning, I decided that I should go and check on Aunt Sara. It'd been awhile, and I wanted to make sure she was doing all right.

When I got to her room, the door was slightly ajar, so I quietly opened it, not wanting to disturb her if she were sleeping. When I saw that she wasn't, I went on inside.

As I walked on into the room, I noticed Aunt Sara sitting on her bed, just staring out the window. It looked to me as if she were crying. I abruptly stopped, not wanting to intrude, but before I could step back out of the room to give her her privacy, she turned and saw me standing there.

"Jochebed!" she said, startled, putting her hand to her chest. "I didn't even hear you come in!" She quickly began to wipe away her tears as if she were embarrassed that I had caught her crying.

"I'm sorry," I said, feeling badly. "I didn't mean to scare you. Is…is everything all right?"

She sighed with melancholy.

"You're fine," she assured. "Here…come sit down." She motioned for me to come over.

I looked at her, concerned as I made my way over to her, taking a seat on the edge of the bed there beside her. It was obvious that something was bothering her.

"Aunt Sara," I asked again, sorry to see her so down, "are…are you okay?"

"Yes, Jochebed," she replied. "I don't mean to be so sad. It's just…well…it's just hard for me right now, I guess. So much is going on - so many trials, so many emotions, and now the holidays…it's…it's just getting to me is all." She shook her head as she went on to explain. "Mark and I always took turns spending Thanksgiving with our families," she told me, "one year with his and the next with mine. Well, this year we were supposed to travel to Kansas to be with *my* family, but," she pointed to her belly, "obviously, that can't happen!" She sighed. "Mark was hoping to be able to save up enough money to buy my parents a train ticket to bring them here, but…well…since he had to leave North Dakota early on a count of me, it's…it's just not going to work out. The money's just not there! As for my parents…well…they don't have the money right now either or I know they'd come."

She looked at me, chagrinned.

"It really is just awful!" she lamented. "I mean, I know they feel terrible already not being able to be here with me during all this, but to not be able to come for Thanksgiving either, why… " She sighed again, grieved. "They've written faithfully expressing how much they love us," she went on to say, "and how we're daily in their prayers, but…it's just not the same." She looked at me with earnest. "Don't get me wrong!" she wanted to clarify. "It means the world to me that they've kept in touch, truly it does, but…it's just…" She looked down, tears filling her eyes, clearly heartbroken. "It's just been so long since I've seen them, Jochebed," she began to cry, "and I miss them *so much!* I just wish I could have them here with me, even, if only, for a short while."

I looked at her with empathy.

"I fully understand," I acknowledged. "I was just telling Gramma a little while ago how I wished Mama could be here with us this Thanksgiving, and…"

"Oh, Jochebed!" Aunt Sara abruptly interrupted. She was so apologetic. "I am so *so sorry!*" she conveyed, feeling absolutely horrible! "Here I am feeling sorry for myself, rambling on because I can't be with my family, and there you are…"

"Stop, Aunt Sara!" I insisted adamantly. "It's all right! No need to feel sorry! I miss my mama, and you miss yours. You're allowed! I mean, *gracious*, look at all you've been through and how far you still have to go! Please don't feel a bit sorry for wanting your family with you. I *know* if it were me going through all of this, I'd want my mama with me!"

I could tell Aunt Sara still felt ashamed and embarrassed that she hadn't been more sensitive to my feelings. I wanted to reassure her that I was fine.

"Aunt Sara," I went on, trying to encourage her, "really, it's okay! I understand! You've been through *so* much, and while you've been *incredibly* brave and strong through it all, you're only human. You're allowed to miss your mama!"

Aunt Sara perked up a bit.

"Thank you, Jochebed," she said as she looked at me intently - putting her hand on my arm. "I mean it! Thank you…for everything! I don't want you to think for a minute that I don't appreciate everything you and your family have done for me…because I do! You've done more for me than…"

"Aunt Sara," I interrupted with a smile, "you don't have to explain. I love you…and you're welcome! I know if it were me in your position, you'd move heaven and earth to do whatever you could for me."

She bit her lip, overcome by emotion, her eyes welling with tears.

"I love you, Jochebed," she said. "You're an amazing young lady, and I know you're mama would be *so very* proud of you. …Thank you for understanding."

Just then, Uncle Mark came bursting through the bedroom door, still dressed in his burly coat, his scarf wrapped around his face, smiling wildly with his eyes, holding the biggest dead turkey I think I'd ever seen in my life!

Aunt Sara brushed a tear from her cheek as she began to laugh -something I hadn't heard her do in a very long time.

"I see your morning hunt was a great success!" she complimented with a smile, chuckling at Uncle Mark.

He started into the room.

"Mark Adam Lowry!" Aunt Sara reprimanded sharply as she stretched out her arm, pointing to the door. "You get that dead bird out of here *right now!*"

Uncle Mark burst into laughter, tickled by her consternation.

"Thought ya might like to see what your *wonderful husband* caught for Thanksgivin' dinner," he teased, jiggling the bird out in front of him.

Immediately, she gave him a stern, disapproving look.

"That's fine!" she accepted, none too thrilled with his antics. "But I'd rather see it on my plate tomorrow than dripping blood in my bedroom today!"

Uncle Mark's smile broadened as he jiggled the bird again, knowing he'd get another rise out of her.

"Mark!" she blustered. "Stop that! You're going to make a mess!" She looked at him harshly and stated in no uncertain terms. "And I can guarantee you, mister," she warned, "if you do…your mother is going to *kill* you! And I just may help her! …Now get!"

Uncle Mark winked at her with a smile.

"Love ya, dear!" he quipped as he pulled his scarf down to blow her a kiss.

Aunt Sara shook her head with a reluctant grin, and blew him a kiss right back.

As I sat there watching, I could see in her eyes the deep, abiding love and admiration she had for him. It filled my heart with joy to see them still so in love even after everything they'd been through. It gave me a sense of comfort and hope knowing that no matter what may happen with the baby, Uncle Mark and Aunt Sara would get through it together. - There truly were *so many* things to be thankful for!

Still having so many more things to do, I excused myself from the room, and headed off to the kitchen.

As I walked down the hallway, it was evident that Uncle Mark had been caught! I could hear Gramma scolding him for having brought the turkey into the bedroom.

"Gracious, Son!" she protested, taking him to task. "Ya oughta know better than to do a thing like that! Now give me that bird and let me get to work on it!"

He tried to contain his laughter as he handed her the bird, but he just couldn't! He let out a chuckle and then another.

Gramma gave him a scowl as she took the bird from him, proceeding to bop him on the head with her hand.

"Aww, Ma!" he countered, smiling broadly. "I know ya love me!" He leaned over, grinning from ear to ear, and gave her a big kiss on the cheek.

"Oh, you get on outta here now!" she shooed, flustered.

Uncle Mark quickly kissed her again and walked on outside, still chuckling to himself.

Again, I just stood there watching, so grateful to be part of a family that truly loved each other and got along. It was a blessing I knew not everyone was able to enjoy.

"Can I help with anything, Gramma?" I asked as I walked on into the kitchen.

"Well," she answered, "why don't ya get started peelin' those apples over there so we can get goin' on some pies. I'm gonna take this gigundous turkey outback and start pluckin' it." She held it out, looking it up and down. *"Gracious!"* she grunted, trying to keep hold of it. "To look at the size of this thing, I'll be fortunate to have it *plucked* by Thanksgivin', much less dressed and cooked and ready for dinner!"

I just laughed, and went on to start peeling apples as Gramma put on her heavy shawl and took the turkey out back.

Uncle Mark and Grampa were outside by the barn chopping wood, and Papa and Samuel were home doing chores.

After acquiring a knife and placing the bushel of apples closer to the counter so I could reach them more easily, I went to the cupboard to get out Gramma's large bowl to put the apple slices in. As I stood there just ready to cut into my first apple, I was startled by a knock at the door.

I wonder who that could be, I thought to myself as I promptly put down the knife and apple, wiped my hands on my apron, and started for the front door.

Whoever was there, knocked again, so I hastened my pace to get there more quickly.

When I got to the door and opened it up, there in front of me stood a man and a woman whom, I'll admit, I didn't readily recognize.

"May I help you?" I asked.

"Is this the home of Ezra and Elizabeth Lowry?" the man inquired.

"Yes, it is," I answered, "but they're both occupied at the moment. Would you like me to go get them for you?"

"No," the woman replied. "We're actually here to see our daughter."

"Your daughter?" I questioned, a bit confused.

"Yes," the woman affirmed. "We're here to see Sara, Sara Lowry. She *is* still staying here, isn't she?"

Just then, I remembered their faces.

"You're Aunt Sara's parents!" I exclaimed, so surprised to see them. "Please, come in, come in!"

They happily walked inside as I closed the door behind them.

"I'm so sorry I didn't recognize you at first!" I said, a little embarrassed that I hadn't. I turned to greet them properly. "I'm Jochebed, Aunt Sara's niece," I reminded, grinning from ear to ear, so thrilled that they were here! "She'll be *so pleased* to see you! You wouldn't believe it, but we were just…oh, never mind!" I dismissed. I immediately pointed over to the couch "You can put your things over there for now," I directed.

Right away, they started to take off their coats.

"Here," I said, reaching my hand out. "Let me take those for you!"

They handed me their coats and I hung them up by the door as they picked up their luggage, walked over, and put it on the floor by the couch in the family room.

I couldn't keep from smiling as I turned back towards them.

"My!" I expressed with delight. "I just can't believe you're actually here!"

Once their things were all taken care of, I offered to take them to see Aunt Sara.

"Come with me," I motioned, urging them to follow. "Aunt Sara's just down the hall in her bedroom."

"How is she?" Mrs. Peters anxiously wanted to know.

"Actually, physically, she's having a pretty good day today, ma'am," I replied. I smiled, so excited! "And it's certain she'll be having an even better one when she sees the two of you!" I approached the door and knocked quietly. "She tends to sleep a lot," I explained. "I try not to disturb her when she is." I patiently waited at the door and listened.

"Come in," I heard Aunt Sara call out.

Wanting to surprise her, I only opened the door slightly, just enough to poke my head inside. I'm certain when I did, however, I must have had the biggest, most joyous grin on my face, unable to contain my enthusiasm.

Obviously, Aunt Sara noticed my unusual behavior and instantly became suspicious.

"What are you up to, Jochebed?" she questioned warily.

"Well!" I announced, rather zealous. "I have something very special to show you!"

"Oh?" Aunt Sara queried half-jokingly. "It's not another dead bird, is it? I think I've seen enough of those for one day!"

"Nope!" I promised. "It's much more wonderful than any ol' bird!"

"Ookkaayy!" Aunt Sara questioned with furrowed brow. "Then what is it?"

I gleefully swung open the door the rest of the way so that Aunt Sara could see her parents standing there.

Her face instantly lit up with joy as she screamed, elated!

"Mama! Papa! Is that really you?" she shouted as tears began to flow.

They rushed into the room and over to the bed. They hugged and wept and hugged some more.

"It's been *so* long!" Aunt Sara cried, overwhelmed. "I've missed you so much! ...Oh, I've missed you *so very much!*" She sat back, a bit curious, as she sniffed and wiped her tears. "But I," she began quite perplexed, "I...I thought... ...How...*however were you able to come?*"

Aunt Sara's parents looked at each other, questioning, as they looked back to Aunt Sara.

"Why...didn't Mark tell you, Sara?" her father asked, surprised.

Aunt Sara gave a troubled look.

"No," she answered, confused. "Tell me what?"

Mr. Peters hesitated as he looked at Mrs. Peters, unsure of what to say. It seemed he was just about to explain, but then Mrs. Peters jumped in, preventing him.

"Oh, Henry!" she dissuaded. "Don't worry the child with such things right now. Let's just enjoy our time together, all right?"

"No, Mama!" Aunt Sara insisted, wanting to understand. "What was Mark supposed to tell me?"

"Sara, honey, listen," Mrs. Peters tried to calm, "your father simply spoke too soon. There's no need to get upset. We don't want to overstep." She smiled kindly at Aunt Sara. "I really think this is something you should speak to Mark about."

I could tell Aunt Sara still wasn't happy about the situation, but she dropped the matter out of respect, not pushing the issue any further.

With the concern set aside for the moment, Aunt Sara and her parents went on talking about this and that, even asking me a few questions here and there. Not wanting to encroach on their time together, however, I felt I should leave them be to talk alone. I politely excused myself to the other room as they went on visiting.

As I was leaving Aunt Sara's room, closing the door behind me, I turned around and nearly ran right into Uncle Mark.

"Whoa!" he exclaimed. "Sorry 'bout that! Didn't mean to run ya over!"

"No, Uncle Mark," I apologized, "It's my fault. I should have been watching where I was going."

Uncle Mark suddenly furrowed his brow, stepped around me, and put his ear to the door.

"Hey!" he whispered inquisitively. "Who's she talkin' to in there?"

A smile instantly came across my face.

"You'll never believe it!" I told him excitedly. "Aunt Sara's parents...they came for a visit!"

Oddly, Uncle Mark didn't seem very enthusiastic about the news.

"Oh!" he replied, wrinkling his nose, kind of tentative like. "They…didn't happen to say anything…did they?"

I looked at him, bewildered.

"Say anything?" I questioned. "What do you mean?" I could tell by the look on Uncle Mark's face that he was anxious about something. "What is it?" I queried, trying to understand.

"Oh…never mind," he dismissed, looking fretfully at the door. "It's not important."

I wasn't buying his denial! It was *obvious* he was hiding *something!*

He paused, taking a rather deep breath, nervously blowing it out.

"Well," he said apprehensively, "guess I'd better go say hi, huh?"

I looked at him quite suspiciously.

"We'll talk later," he promised.

I slowly nodded my head.

"Sure, Uncle Mark," I replied warily. "I…hope you enjoy your visit."

Uncle Mark smiled reluctantly as he opened the door and walked inside.

Something was clearly going on with him, but I had no idea what it could possibly be, so I shrugged it off, and went to tell Grampa and Gramma that we had company. Of course, as you can imagine, they were thrilled for the good news, but they decided to keep working, wanting to give Aunt Sara and Uncle Mark some time alone with the Peterses. They would visit with them later.

Satisfied with their decision, I dutifully went back to the kitchen to start peeling apples. I washed my hands, picked up my knife and an apple, and put the knife to the peel. I was just about to cut into it when suddenly there was another knock at the door.

"Good grief!" I quipped, putting the knife and apple down, wiping my hands off on my apron yet again as I headed for the front door. "This is busier than a church social on the Fourth of July! Who on earth could this be now?"

When I opened the door, there stood Isaac, smiling kindly and looking as handsome as ever.

"Isaac!" I exclaimed, surprised, not expecting to see him so soon. I instantly started fidgeting with my hair, a little self-conscious about my appearance. "What are you doing here so early?" I asked. "I thought we weren't meeting until later."

"Weeelll," he teased as he started to turn, grinning deviously, "I can leave if you really want me to!"

"Oh, no!" I gestured desperately, reaching out to grab his arm. "I didn't mean that you had to leave!"

He glanced back at me with a wistful look.

"No, no!" he insisted, feigning rejection. "If you're too busy to see me right now, then…"

"Ohhh!" I responded in playful aggravation, pulling on his arm. "Would you stop that and get in here, please?"

He laughed as he turned and stepped inside.

"So," he questioned as he took off his hat and coat, "how are you doing this fine day?"

I closed the door behind him and answered with a bit of exhaustion.

"Very busy, actually," I replied, taking his hat and coat, "but doing well. And you?"

"I'm much better now," he intimated, smiling sweetly. "Now that I've seen you, that is!"

"Oh, Isaac!" I blushed, bashfully accepting the compliment.

"Anyway," he went on to say, "I am pretty early, so I understand if you're too busy to see me right now. I don't want to keep you from your work. I know you're behind on things."

"Well," I assured him, smiling demurely, "I do still have a lot to do, but I'd *never* turn down *your* company! You're more than welcome to stay…if you don't mind helping me in the kitchen that is."

Isaac gestured with his arm, half-bowing.

"Lead the way, my dear," he said gallantly. "I'm yours to command!"

"Oh, come on now!" I dismissed with a chuckle, smiling at his silliness.

We headed to the kitchen.

"So," I questioned as I walked over to the counter, "what brings you here so early, anyhow? I thought you said you were going to be busy with your family all day."

"Well, I was," Isaac explained as he walked up beside me, leaning on the counter, "but Grandfather and Grandmother had some errands to run and another uncle to pick up from the train station, and with all that, they weren't going to be back until evening, so I decided to come and spend the day with the one person I most wanted to be with."

"Oh," I said, trying to be as serious as I could, "then I'm afraid you've come to the wrong place."

Isaac frowned, puzzled.

"What? …What do you mean?" he queried.

"I'm afraid Samuel's at home with Papa," I told him, trying to keep a straight face. "I can go get him for you if you'd like." I couldn't help it, I started to chuckle.

Isaac looked at me, chagrinned.

"Very funny!" he retorted. "Nothing against your brother, but I'd much rather spend the day with you!"

"Well then, in that case," I said with a smile, handing him a knife and an apple, "you can help me peel these apples?"

Isaac shook his head as he smiled, taking the apple and the knife from me.

"Again I say, madam," he announced with gusto, raising the knife high in the air, "I'm yours to command!"

I laughed as I rolled my eyes, shaking my head at his playfulness. It was definitely a side of him that I'd not seen much of before, and I can honestly say, it only made me like him more! I turned, still tickled, and went to get myself a knife out of the drawer.

Once in hand, I walked back over beside Isaac, and he and I stood there talking together, peeling apples at the counter, enjoying each other's company.

As I stood there, just soaking in the moment, relishing the fact that *I* was actually standing in my Grandmother's kitchen peeling apples with none other than Isaac Lewis - the man I had dreamed of, the man I had desired for so long - I just couldn't help but reflect on how much my life had changed and in such a short amount of time. My heart was overwhelmed as I thought through all of the trials and all of the blessings of the past few months. I smiled, grateful, as I listened to Isaac talk. There truly was so much - *so very much* - to be thankful for!

THANKSGIVING DAY
(Chapter 12)

After about an hour or so of peeling apples and making lunch for everyone, Isaac and I went to let everyone know that it was time to eat. Uncle Mark and Aunt Sara were still in the bedroom visiting with Mr. and Mrs. Peters, Grampa was still outside working in the yard, and Gramma was still out there, too, wrestling with that big 'ol turkey.

Isaac went to the back door and called for them to come inside.

"Lunch is ready!" he shouted out loudly.

Both Grampa and Gramma stopped what they were doing and came inside.

While Isaac was getting Grampa and Gramma, I went to the bedroom to take Aunt Sara her lunch and to fetch Uncle Mark and the Peterses.

When I got to the bedroom door, I could hear talking back and forth, so I knocked twice, hoping someone would hear me. When no one answered, I knocked again a little louder. Still garnering no response, I opened the door slightly and stuck my head inside the room. Immediately, everyone stopped conversing and looked directly at me. I flashed an awkward smile, feeling *quite* embarrassed!

"Umm…I'm sorry," I apologized timidly as I took a step forward. "I didn't mean to interrupt. I just wanted to let you know that lunch is being served in the kitchen if…if you're interested, and…I…I also brought Aunt Sara her meal if…if that's okay."

It was an extremely uncomfortable moment, to say the least! I sensed that I had just intruded on a very serious and dire conversation. Aunt Sara was sitting there with the most furious expression on her face I think I'd ever seen, Uncle Mark was red with anger, his jaw clenched, looking as if he wanted to punch something, and Mr. and Mrs. Peters looked more than a little distressed! …And then there I was, clumsily standing there holding a meat and cheese sandwich with a glass of water on a tray. I was completely mortified!

I cleared my throat, feeling unbelievably self-conscious!

"I…I'll come back in a little while," I stammeringly suggested, motioning at the door with my head. I quickly turned to leave.

"No!" Uncle Mark shouted crossly. *"We're done here!* Sara can eat if she wants. *She could use a break!"* He scowled at Aunt Sara, who was sitting there fuming, her arms folded, staring straight ahead, clearly disregarding him - looking as if she might explode! Uncle Mark shook his head, livid, and clenched his jaw even tighter. He kept scowling at her, almost as if he was willing her to look at him. When she didn't, he sighed heavily in aggravation, mumbled something under his breath, and left the room in a huff, angrily brushing past me.

I was astounded as I turned to watch him walk away!

As I hesitantly turned back, Mr. and Mrs. Peters smiled nervously and got up to leave as well.

"We'll talk more in a little while, dear," Mrs. Peters said as she put her hand on Aunt Sara's arm.

Aunt Sara didn't move! She didn't acknowledge her mother at all!

I could tell that whatever was wrong, it was *very, **very** bad!*

"Sara Grace, *please, dear!*" her father implored a little more forcefully, obviously deeply concerned. "Let us help you and Mark resolve this!"

Aunt Sara said nothing!

"Come, Henry," Mrs. Peters urged, disheartened. "Let's let her be for awhile."

Mr. Peters shook his head, thoroughly upset, but nonetheless, he reluctantly complied. He and Mrs. Peters politely excused themselves past me, right on out the door.

They just left me standing there…all alone…in the room…with Aunt Sara!

As you can imagine, I felt incredibly uneasy not knowing what was going on. I stood there, anxious, almost trembling, unsure of what to say or do. I'd never seen Aunt Sara so angry before, and it caught me completely off guard!

I took a few nervous steps towards the bed and cautiously began to speak.

"Aunt Sara," I said tentatively, "I…I'm so sorry I interrupted. I can go if you want me to."

"Close the door!" she demanded tersely.

Startled by her forcefulness, I immediately walked back over and closed the door. Swallowing hard, I turned around, taken aback by her behavior! If I wasn't shaking before, I was visibly shaking now!

Aunt Sara was absolutely livid! She wouldn't even look at me! She just sat there, seething, shaking her head over and over again.

I'll confess…it scared me but good!

Too afraid to say anything for fear I would make things worse, I just stood there quietly, waiting to see what she would do.

Finally, after a few, *very* uncomfortable moments, Aunt Sara let it all fly!

"Oh, that man!" she exploded furiously, clenching her jaw, infuriated.

I was pretty sure she wanted to vent, so I slowly, but guardedly started towards her, lending a listening ear. As I did, she began to rant and rave.

"Do you know what he did, Jochebed?" she shouted. "Do you know what that man did? That *deceitful, conniving, selfish, EGOTISTICAL* man, do you know what he did? Do you know? Well, do you?"

I stopped abruptly in stunned silence, vehemently shaking my head, indicating that I had no idea. This was so unlike Aunt Sara; I didn't know what to do!

"And…and all while I'm lying here in this bed fighting for my life and the life of *our* baby!!" she ranted on. She was almost in tears at this point; she was so beside herself with rage! "Did he really think I was incapable of making a decision?" she questioned resentfully. "Does he really think that little of me that I'm not even *worth* consulting on such an important matter as this? I mean, *gracious!* We've talked about everything else up until now, *WHY NOT THIS?!?*" She feverishly wiped a tear from her cheek as she continued on with such hostility. "To do something like *this!*" she charged, hands flailing, scowling intently. "To go off and do something this…this *egregious!* And to do it without a word, not a *single word!* …Not one - teeny - tiny - little - itsy - bitsy - word, Jochebed! *NOT ONE!!!*"

My eyes were as big as saucers as I stood there enduring the bluster of her wrath.

"Ooooo!!!" she expressed with such ire. "I'm having a baby here! *I haven't lost my mind!!"*

She was *so* indignant; I just couldn't believe it! I stood there, flabbergasted, my mouth agape! I had never, *ever* heard Aunt Sara speak this way to anyone *or about anyone,* for that matter, *especially* about Uncle Mark! (Right about now, I was wishing like everything that I had stayed in the kitchen with Isaac!)

"And my parents!" she went on to accuse, squinting her eyes, shaking her head passionately. *"Ooooo!"* she shrieked again. "They knew all along! …*They knew all along,*

Jochebed, and they didn't say *a thing! Not one thing!* 'Didn't want to worry me,' they said. ***Worry me!?!***" She clenched her fists, shaking them wildly. "***Ohhhh!!!***" she yelled, exasperated, steam nearly pouring from her ears as her temper boiled over!

All of a sudden, out of nowhere, she turned her venom on me, looking me ardently in the eye.

"And I suppose you and your family knew about this, too?" she indicted. "I suppose you had a hand in all of this!"

"Now wait a minute, Aunt Sara!" I tried to interject, a little offended by the charge.

I wasn't able to defend myself, however, because she ran right over me, ranting on as if she hadn't even heard me speak.

"And then…and then to have the *nerve* to say that the reason I'm so upset is because I'm *having a baby!*" she shouted. "Oh my *goodness!!!* That was the ***last straw!!!***"

She was so violently irate I thought for sure she was going to come right up out of her bed.

Worried she might, I scurried to put the tray down and sat down beside her on the bed. I promptly took hold of her arms as tightly as I could and tried to calm her down.

"Aunt Sara!" I shouted sternly, not wanting to be disrespectful, but feeling the need to be forceful, nonetheless. "Stop it!" I looked her straight in the eyes, and she looked at me still seething. "Settle down and tell me what on *earth* you're talking about!" I demanded. "I'm sure whatever it is, we can work it out!"

She sat there staring at me for a moment as if she were collecting her thoughts, and then suddenly, without warning, she broke down into tears.

"Oh, Jochebed!" she cried, sobbing uncontrollably. "He sold everything…*everything* - our home, our store, our land - ***everything!***"

I looked at her utterly shocked!

*"He did **what?**"* I exclaimed in total disbelief. "Uncle Mark *did **what?**"*

Aunt Sara could hardly catch her breath, she was crying so hysterically.

"He…he…he sold all of it!" she wept bitterly. "He said he thought it was for the best!" She cried and cried and cried some more.

I was so thunderstruck; I had no words!

"He…he said he used some of the money to…to bring my parents here," she sniffed and stammered. "And then he…he said he was going to use the rest of it to…to move *us* here! But…" She broke down again. "My sister…my church…my friends…the store…*my life!*" She was so distraught. *"How could he do that? How?* He…he just sold *it all!*" She buried her face in her hands; her heart clearly broken. "He just packed it all up and took it from me, Jochebed!" she wailed. "He took it from me without a word! I just don't understand! *How could he do that?*"

I sat there holding her close, trying to console her the best I could.

She looked up at me briefly, grieved, and buried her head in my chest.

As she cried, I could feel the hurt and anguish and sadness just pouring out of her. I couldn't help but feel terrible! I wanted so badly to comfort her, to take away her pain, but I honestly didn't know what to say - truth be told, I wasn't even really sure what to think! I was so stunned and shocked by what she'd just told me, I was completely at a loss as to what to do!

Listening to Aunt Sara sob, I couldn't even begin to understand how she was feeling, although I tried. The more I did, however, the more I just couldn't wrap my mind around the fact that Uncle Mark would do such a thing! It was so life-altering, such an *enormous* decision...*to not consult Aunt Sara...*

I shook my head as I rolled it over and over again in my mind. It was so *absolutely incredible* to me, it made me want to cry, too! *And I wasn't even the one he'd done it to!*

I hugged Aunt Sara a little tighter, just letting her know that I was there for her.

After we'd sat there for a little while, her crying, letting it all out, me holding her, trying to quiet her, there was a knock at the bedroom door. Still cradling Aunt Sara, I softly told whomever it was to come in.

It was Isaac. He poked his head inside and saw me sitting there. Needless to say, he was immediately concerned. He looked at me with furrowed brow, his eyes asking, *Is everything all right? Is there anything I can do?*

I looked at him with sadness as I shook my head. Seeming to understand, he nodded and left, gently closing the door behind him.

It was just awful! Aunt Sara was inconsolable, and I was worried! She was crying so hard that no matter what I said, I just couldn't calm her down. After a while, I simply stopped talking, held her close, and let her cry.

*****

Unfortunately, as the day wore on, things didn't get any better between Aunt Sara and Uncle Mark. In fact, they seemed to be getting worse as they were no longer speaking to each other. They did seem to be hiding it well, however (mostly Uncle Mark avoided going to Aunt Sara's room, and she *definitely* refrained from requesting his presence), so for now, my family was pretty much in the dark as to what was going on. The Peterses weren't saying anything, and of course, neither was I. We just didn't feel it was our place.

Nevertheless, carrying the burden of knowing, and it starting to weigh heavily on me, I did decide to share in confidence with Isaac before he left for the evening everything I knew about the situation. I just needed someone to talk to about it, and I knew I could trust him to listen and to not say anything to anyone.

I earnestly asked him to pray for everyone involved, specifically for Aunt Sara, Uncle Mark, and for her parents. He assured me that he would, but he also made a point to tell me that he'd be praying for me as well. He knew what a precarious position I was in and that I'd need wisdom to know how to handle it.

I couldn't thank him enough for listening, for his concern, and for just being there for me. It truly did mean the world! He told me it was his pleasure and that he'd do whatever he could to help. I smiled, grateful, and we said goodnight.

*****

The next day was Thanksgiving, and given all we yet had to do, I knew it would be an extremely hectic day. Because of this, I purposely woke up extra early, had my quiet time with the Lord (making sure to say an extra prayer for Uncle Mark and Aunt Sara, of course), and hurriedly got myself dressed. When I was ready, I quickly made my way downstairs to get started on breakfast for Papa, Samuel, and the Peterses.

~

The Peterses had come to stay with us at our house because Aunt Sara and Uncle Mark were occupying Grampa and Gramma's second bedroom and there really was no extra space for them there at the house.

~

When I finished with breakfast, I placed everything on the table for whomever was interested, promptly grabbed my winter shawl, and dashed off to Grampa and Gramma's to help with the Thanksgiving meal.

I was hoping by the time I arrived at their house that things would be better between Uncle Mark and Aunt Sara, but when I opened the front door, there was Uncle Mark sleeping on the couch in the family room all by himself. I sighed, extremely disappointed, knowing precisely what that likely meant.

Discouraged, I quietly shut the door so as not to wake Uncle Mark and headed for the kitchen. When I got there, I found Grampa and Gramma sitting at the table together, enjoying a cup of coffee.

"Well, good mornin', Wallflower," Grampa welcomed with a smile.

I smiled back, walked over, and gave him a kiss on the cheek.

"Good morning, Grampa," I said, happy to see him.

"My, but you're here bright and early this mornin'!" Gramma commented. "Ya didn't have to come quite so soon."

"Oh, I know, Gramma," I replied as I went to give her a kiss, "but I wanted to get a good start on the day knowing there was so much more to do this year. You know...given we're behind and all."

"Well, thank ya, sweetheart," Gramma accepted. "You're such a dear! Ya certainly have been a huge blessin' to me over these past few months. I don't know what I'd a done without ya!"

"Well, you're welcome, Gramma," I told her as I went to hang up my shawl by the back door. "It's been my pleasure. I truly have enjoyed helping out with everything, and I have to say, I've also enjoyed getting to spend so much extra time with Aunt Sara as well. It really has been a great blessing to me!"

Grampa looked at me, kind of serious like.

"Speakin' of that, Wallflower," he asked with reserve, "ya don't happen to know what's goin' on between your Uncle Mark and Aunt Sara, do ya? Couldn't help but notice him sleepin' on the couch this mornin'." He looked worried. "I have to say it's got me a little concerned."

Gramma immediately chimed in, passionately nodding her head in agreement.

"It's got the both of us concerned!" she stated emphatically, looking just as worried.

I have to admit, their inquiry made me feel a bit awkward. On the one hand, I knew what the problem was and felt they had a right to know, but on the other hand (like the Peterses) I didn't feel it was my place to say anything. I stood there a moment, contemplating what to do.

"Weelll," I started hesitantly, "I...I..."

Grampa and Gramma could sense I was struggling.

"Jochebed, sweetheart," Gramma prodded. "What is it, dear?"

"Weelll," I started again, hemming and hawing, "I...I do know something, and...I...I...I really do think you all should know about it... and...I...well...I do want to tell you, but...it's just that...well...I really...I just really don't feel it's my place to say anything. I mean...if it's all the same to you, I...I really think it would be best if maybe...if maybe Uncle Mark or Aunt Sara told you what was going on. I hope you understand!" My eyes were pleading with them, desperately hoping they would.

At this point, Grampa and Gramma looked even more worried than they had before. Nevertheless, Grampa was gracious.

"Well, of course, we understand, Wallflower," he assured. "I'm sorry we put ya on the spot like that. I should've just waited to ask your Uncle Mark in the first place."

"That's all right, Grampa," I forgave, relieved. "I know you're just concerned."

As Grampa and Gramma finished up their coffee, I put on my apron and began making preparations for Thanksgiving dinner.

When Grampa took his last sip, he stood up with a groan, came over and put his cup in the sink, walked back over and kissed Gramma on the lips, told her he loved her, and went to put his coat on to go outside to do some work in the barn.

Shortly after, Gramma got up from the table as well, and came to help me with the meal.

She and I hadn't been working very long on things when Uncle Mark came sleepily into the kitchen, rubbing his eyes.

"Mornin," he said as he stretched and yawned, plopping himself down at the table.

Gramma immediately walked over to him, determined to get to the bottom of whatever was going.

"Care to explain yourself, Son?" she asked, disconcerted. "What's goin' on between you and Sara?"

"Ma!" Uncle Mark groused. "Can I, at least, get some coffee in me first?"

"No!" Gramma insisted. "That can wait! Ya need to explain all this!"

Uncle Mark shook his head, annoyed by her persistence.

"It's nothin', Ma, really!" he replied dismissively.

I immediately shot him a look of disapproval, appalled by his lies! I couldn't *believe* that he had just downplayed the severity of what he'd done to Aunt Sara! I clenched my jaw, *so* wanting to correct him, annoyed by his answer and tone, but I bit my tongue, turned back around, and kept right on working.

"It's between me and her," Uncle Mark contended. "I'm sure we'll work it out. Don't worry yourself none about it, all right?" He stood up and walked over to pour himself a cup of coffee. "It's Thanksgivin'," he quipped, winking at Gramma with a smile as if he hadn't a care in the world. "Let's just enjoy the day!"

I bit my lip even harder, fuming! I wanted to *throttle him!*

Gramma wasn't letting up, though; she kept right on digging.

"Well now, how are we supposed to enjoy the day," she asked in consternation, "when there's trouble between the two of ya? Obviously, *somethin's* happened if you're no longer sleepin' in the same bed as your wife!"

Uncle Mark shook his head, tired of the inquisition.

"Ma!" he snapped at her, growing perturbed.

"Ma, nothin'!" Gramma barked back, cutting him off. "*Clearly*, this is serious, and ya need to start treatin' it as such!"

Uncle Mark had had it! He looked right at Gramma and told her in no uncertain terms.

"Let it be, Ma!" he stated sternly. "It's between me and Sara!" He took his cup of coffee, grabbed his hat and coat, and huffed off outside to help Grampa.

"Well, I never!" Gramma mumbled under her breath, visibly flustered. She walked over beside me, angrily grabbed a bowl, and went to preparing her corn biscuits.

*****

A short while later, Papa, Samuel, and the Peterses arrived at the house.

"Mornin'!" Papa belted out happily as they all made their way into the kitchen.

"Not so loud, Michael!" Gramma hushed. "I think Sara's still sleepin'."

Papa put his hand to his mouth.

"Oops, sorry!" he apologized much more quietly. "Pa out back?" he asked.

"Yes," Gramma confirmed. "He said somethin' about tryin' to fix that broken wagon wheel this mornin'."

Papa smiled with a nod.

"Sounds like somethin' we can help with, right Sam?" he suggested, motioning for him to come.

Samuel sighed, less than thrilled.

"Yes, sir," he reluctantly agreed, meandering towards the back door.

"You're more than welcome to join us, Mr. Peters," Papa offered. And then he teased. "Unless ya'd rather stay in here with all these women?"

"Nope!" Mr. Peters eagerly quipped back with a hop in his step. "I'm comin' with you!" He smiled, leaned in, and gave Mrs. Peters a quick peck on the cheek before following Papa and Samuel outside.

We *women* continued working in the kitchen, preparing Thanksgiving dinner.

"Is there anything I can do to help?" Mrs. Peters politely asked.

"I could use some help peeling these potatoes," I answered with a smile.

"All right," Mrs. Peters happily agreed. She took off her hat and coat, laid them aside, and came to help.

Gramma was busy on one side of the room making her biscuits, while Mrs. Peters and I were busy on the other side with the potatoes. We all chatted a bit about this and that, but then Gramma just couldn't help herself.

"Mrs. Peters," she inquired, "I don't mean to be intrusive, but I'm quite concerned about Mark and Sara. It'd seem somethin' serious is goin' on between the two of 'em and I was just wonderin' if ya might know what that might be."

Mrs. Peters abruptly stopped what she was doing and looked at me, troubled. She sighed, disheartened, before looking back over at Gramma.

"Mrs. Lowry," she answered almost apologetically, "I have to be honest, I *do know* what's going on, but Henry and I discussed it at length last night, and…well…we concluded that due to the gravity of the situation…" She paused, sad at the thought. "We feel it's just not our place to say anything to anyone. Mark and Sara really ought to be the ones to talk to you about it. I do hope you can understand our position."

Gramma looked worried, but she seemed to understand.

"I do," she replied, disappointed. She didn't press the matter any further.

We scurried about in the kitchen, cooking and cleaning, while the men continued to work outside.

After a couple of hours or so, I was putting something away in the family room when I heard Aunt Sara call from the bedroom. I went to see what she needed.

"Oh, Jochebed!" she said, relieved, as I opened the door. "Thank goodness it's you! I really didn't feel like talking to anyone else right now!"

"Not even to Uncle Mark?" I asked, hopeful that maybe her anger had subsided towards him.

"Especially him!!" she stated emphatically.

"Oh," I replied, a bit downcast. (Clearly, nothing had changed.)

"Are my parents here yet?" she wanted to know.

"Yes," I informed her. "They've been here for awhile now. Would you like me to go and get them for you?"

She shook her head, uncertain.

"No," she expressed with reserve. "I guess I'm not really ready to talk to them right now either."

"Oh, okay," I said, feeling a bit uneasy. "Well…do you want to talk to *me?*"

Aunt Sara looked up at me, realizing my trepidation.

"I'm sorry," she apologized. "I don't mean to be this way, it's just that…it's just…well…it's just *so frustrating* right now! I feel *so betrayed…**by everyone!***" She paused, motioning for me to come over to her.

I closed the door behind me and walked to the side of her bed.

Aunt Sara took hold of my hands and looked at me earnestly.

"You never told me last night," she said, her eyes pleading, "and *please* be honest with me, Jochebed, I have to know…did…did your family know about all of this?"

"*No*, Aunt Sara!" I insisted ardently. "We didn't!"

"You're sure?" she questioned anxiously.

"Yes!" I promised. "*Honest!* We didn't know *anything* about it! And as far as I can tell, no one *still knows* anything about it!"

Aunt Sara looked at me warily.

"I'm telling you the truth, Aunt Sara!" I defended adamantly. "I haven't said *anything* to my family about *any of this*, and I can *assure you*, your parents haven't said anything as well! I mean, Grampa and Gramma have asked, but nothing's been said, and truth be told, besides the two of them, I'm not even sure Papa and Samuel realize anything's going on!"

Aunt Sara let out a huge sigh of relief.

"Good!" she replied, grateful. "I'm simply not ready for anyone to know just yet. It's all just still so painful and raw right now…I just need more time to think things through…time to figure this all out!" She looked up at me as she squeezed my hands. "Thank you, Jochebed," she told me. "I appreciate you not saying anything. Really…it means a lot!"

I sighed, admittedly discouraged.

"You're welcome…I think," I replied, disheartened. I looked at Aunt Sara with angst. "Aunt Sara," I questioned, concerned, "what are you going to do?"

She let go of my hands as she turned away, tears filling her eyes.

"I don't know," she confessed. "I stayed awake half the night last night crying and praying and thinking, trying to figure out why on *earth* Mark would do something like this! It just makes no sense to me…to change our lives so dramatically…*and to not even tell me!* I…" She shook her head as she wiped her tears. "I just can't get past it, Jochebed!" she said, a sense of foreboding in the air. "I just can't!" She sat there, angry, shaking her head over and over again in thought.

Before I could say anything to her, she started in again.

"I just don't understand what got into him!" she blurted out. "I mean, I guess I can sort of understand him telling my parents and all, I mean, I suppose he had to explain how he could suddenly afford to bring them here, and I guess I can sort of understand why my parents didn't say anything to me, *obviously* they just *assumed* that I already knew, which brings me back to my original point…*why didn't I know!!!*" She clenched her fists so tightly! *"Oh, this is so infuriating!!!"* she blustered. She was visibly shaken and upset.

I looked at her, disconcerted, at a loss as to what to say. I fully understood her anger towards Uncle Mark, because honestly, I wasn't all that happy with him right now either! It certainly made no sense to me why he'd done what he had, nor why he'd, in essence, lied to Gramma about it earlier that morning. Regardless of how I felt about him, though, I knew that this wasn't right either - Aunt Sara being so angry at Uncle Mark and him at her. I just wished like everything that they would talk things through and make things right, *especially* it being Thanksgiving Day and all! It was supposed to be a happy, thankful time, not one of hatred and anger! I sighed, hoping things would be resolved soon!

Aunt Sara asked if I would please bring her some breakfast and along with her request, she asked that I please let everyone know that she'd like to be left alone for a while.

I looked at her solemnly and reluctantly agreed.

As I walked back into the kitchen, Gramma smiled at me, and I half-smiled back at her, nervous that someone would ask me what I was doing. (I really didn't want to have to explain that Aunt Sara didn't want to see anyone.)

Mrs. Peters was busy at the sink, so I hoped she wouldn't notice me getting Aunt Sara's breakfast, but almost immediately, much to my chagrin, she all but guessed.

"Is that for Sara?" she inquired as she came walking over. "Is she awake now?"

I grudgingly turned and looked at her, very sorry for what I had to say.

"Yes, ma'am," I revealed, "she is, but…"

"Oh, then I'll go see her!" Mrs. Peters interjected enthusiastically, turning to leave.

"No, wait!" I shouted back, not meaning to sound so forceful or disrespectful, but needing to inform her of Aunt Sara's request.

All at once, Mrs. Peters stopped and looked at me inquisitively.

"I'm so sorry," I said, not wanting to have to tell her, "but…Aunt Sara…she…she asked that…well…she asked that she not be disturbed…by…by anyone."

Mrs. Peters looked so dejected and a little embarrassed.

"Oh…I see," she replied, clearly hurt.

I felt a need to bridge the gap.

"But I'm sure she'll feel like company a little later, ma'am!" I said earnestly, trying to cheer her.

"No, I understand," Mrs. Peters responded with melancholy. She shook her head, almost in tears. "I just hope this all gets resolved very soon," she expressed with grief. She didn't say anything more as she quietly went back to work.

I just couldn't help it; I stood there feeling absolutely terrible for her! Here she and Mr. Peters had come all this way to be with their daughter after being apart for so long, and then this! It truly was very sad and certainly not *at all* how I had envisioned Thanksgiving turning out!

The rest of the day was a struggle, to say the least, as everyone seemed somewhat subdued. No one really did much talking to each other as we were all too disheartened by the circumstances.

Grampa filled Papa in on what was going on, and, of course, he was concerned about the whole thing, Uncle Mark spent most of the day trying to avoid everyone (so as not to have to explain himself), and while Mr. and Mrs. Peters had tried to visit with Aunt Sara a couple of times throughout the day, neither time seemed to go all that well. They weren't in her room for very long, and when they emerged, they didn't appear to be very encouraged.

I still wasn't a hundred percent certain if they knew that I knew what was going on, but I could tell by their demeanor that they felt just as miserable about the whole situation as I did.

Before we knew it, it was dinnertime, and everyone started to gather around the table that Gramma and Mrs. Peters had so beautifully decorated. The food was plenteous and smelled delicious, and as soon as everyone was settled in their seats, Grampa stood up to give thanks.

"Thank Ya, dear Lord, for Your bountiful blessin's," he began. "Thank Ya for my wonderful family, friends that could join us, for our health, and for this wonderful new home Ya've so graciously provided for us. Thank Ya for seeing us through the many difficult trials we've faced as a family this year, and thank Ya for continuin' to see us through the ones we face today. Bless this food to our bodies, and may Ya be glorified in all that's said and done here today. In Jesus' precious name I pray, Amen."

"Amen," everyone echoed.

Right away, Grampa picked up the carving knife and began to cut the turkey as everyone else started passing food and helping their plates. There was polite but sporadic conversation, but it seemed rather awkward and uneasy as there was a definite tension that loomed in the air.

I waited for a few minutes to see if maybe Uncle Mark would take Aunt Sara something to eat, but he never budged. Instead, he just left her plate sitting empty there beside him on the table, seemingly unconcerned with whether she got something to eat or not. I'll admit it made me all the more angry at him, but I suppose it shouldn't have surprised me, after all, he hadn't been in to see her *once* all day long!

Not wanting her to have to wait a minute longer, I reached over myself and picked up Aunt Sara's plate and began to fill it with food. As I was doing so, however, I began to feel a bit on display as I could tell everyone was watching my every move. I nervously finished up what I was doing, and just as I was about to excuse myself from the table to go take Aunt Sara her meal, ***everything*** suddenly broke loose!

"Stubborn!" Gramma indicted harshly, looking straight at Uncle Mark.

"Ma, please!" he shot back, clearly not wanting to get into it. "This isn't the time or the place!"

"Then when is, Son?" Grampa asked passionately, rather perturbed himself.

"Paaa!" Uncle Mark protested, shaking his head, rolling his eyes in aggravation. Papa jumped in, frustrated himself.

"Well, why don't ya just come clean and explain to everybody what's goin' on here!" he suggested sternly. "Maybe then *we* can get to the bottom of all this and get this thing resolved!"

Uncle Mark was furious! He pushed away from the table and stood up, angrily yelling at Papa.

"Why don't ya just mind your own business, big brother?!?" he shouted crossly. "I'm more than capable of handlin' this on my own!!"

Not to be talked to that way, Papa stood up, indignant, threw his napkin down onto his plate, and yelled back at Uncle Mark!

"Well, it would appear ya *aren't* capable of handlin' this, *little brother!*" he countered sharply. "Ya haven't talked to your wife *once* today, and now it'd seem you're content to let her starve!"

Uncle Mark's face instantly turned red hot with anger as he leaned in farther, nearly face-to-face with Papa across the table.

"She's *my* wife, Michael!" he insisted, irate. "I'll deal with her how I see fit!"

Everyone sat frozen, extremely uncomfortable by the heated confrontation, afraid of what might happen next! Mr. and Mrs. Peters had their heads down, Gramma was noticeably upset, Grampa sat, angry with furrowed brow, cautiously waiting, and Samuel, who'd been in the dark up 'til now, sat there wide-eyed and shocked with his mouth agape. As for me...well...I was trembling in my seat!

Papa started back at Uncle Mark almost as if he were about to hit him.

"Deal with her how ya see fit!" he shouted, incensed. "Why ya..."

Grampa immediately stood up.

"Enough!!!" he demanded, pounding his fist on the table. *"Sit down, both of ya!"*

Papa and Uncle Mark bristled at his command, but both composed themselves and slowly sat back down, staring resentfully at each the whole time.

"Now!" Grampa started with a sigh. "As much as I don't agree with how Mark's handlin' things with Sara..."

Uncle Mark rolled his eyes, shaking his head disdainfully,

Grampa simply ignored him and went on to make his point.

"As much as I don't agree with how Mark's handlin' things," he reiterated with emphasis, "it would appear to be a matter he and Sara wish to work out on their own."

Furious, Papa interjected.

"On their own!?" he barked, incredulous at the thought. *"Pa, ya can't be serious!* I mean...*good grief!* They're not even talkin' to each other! How in the world are they gonna..."

Grampa pushed his way right back in, cutting Papa off.

"As I was sayin'..." he stated, looking directly at Papa with a scowl, "as much as I don't like this, we need to give 'em time, Michael! They know we're here if they need us!"

Uncle Mark smirked at Papa, feeling as if he'd won the round.

Grampa, however, wasn't quite finished! He quickly and soberly turned to Uncle Mark, looking him directly in the eye, clearly disappointed.

"Mark!" he reminded sternly. "Ya have a beautiful, wonderful wife in there who's carryin' your child! A wife who's been, in my opinion, *heroically* fightin' for *both* their lives now for *weeks! It'd do ya well to remember that!*" He let out a sigh. "Ya never know what tomorrow holds," he rightly pointed out, "so I *strongly* suggest that ya make things right with Sara *soon* before this thing - *whatever it is* - gets too far out of hand!"

Uncle Mark looked away, feeling embarrassed for having been upbraided by Grampa like that in front of everybody. Surprisingly, he didn't respond, though, instead, he just sat there quietly staring down at his plate.

Grampa sat back down, still unsettled as he cleared his throat.

"Now, Jochebed," he instructed as he looked at me, "take your Aunt Sara some food. And lets the rest of us," he said, looking at everyone else, "let's enjoy this wonderful meal these ladies worked so hard to prepare."

Still shaking, I nodded nervously and slowly picked up Aunt Sara's plate.

"Yes, sir," I replied, almost too frightened to move.

As I timidly got up from the table, everyone else cautiously went back to eating, not saying a word.

I made my way back to Aunt Sara's room and quietly knocked on the door even though it was slightly ajar. I wanted to be careful not to wake her if she were sleeping.

"I'm awake, Jochebed," she answered somberly. "You can come in."

I opened the door the rest of the way and walked into the room. Immediately, I noticed the look on Aunt Sara's face. She looked completely heartbroken!

"You don't have to say anything," she said despairingly. "I heard!"

I walked over and handed her the plate of food feeling absolutely miserable!

"I'm so sorry, Aunt Sara," I commiserated. "I…"

She looked away, shaking her head, fighting back tears.

My heart sank as I didn't know what to say to her.

I stood there for a minute, waiting to see if she would say anything more, but she never did. Sensing that she just wanted to be left alone, I turned, disheartened, and left the room, closing the door behind me.

As I started to step away from the door, I could hear Aunt Sara sobbing. It absolutely broke my heart! It was awful! I couldn't help but think as I made my way back to the others, what a horrible, dreadful Thanksgiving Day this had turned out to be! I couldn't wait for it to be over!

UNFORESEEN CIRCUMSTANCES
(Chapter 13)

The next morning, after breakfast was over, I was in the sewing room working on some mending when Mrs. Peters came looking for me.

"There you are," she said as she walked into the room. "I don't mean to intrude, I just wanted you to know how much I appreciate all the hospitality you and your family have shown to me and my husband over these past few days."

"Oh, you're most welcome, ma'am," I replied, more than happy to have hosted them.

"We'll be heading back to Kansas today," she informed me, quite melancholy. "We'll say goodbye to Sara, of course, but Henry really *must* get back for work. I...well...I just wanted to make sure I thanked you properly before we left."

I put my sewing aside and stood up.

"Well, again, you're welcome, ma'am," I told her with all sincerity. "I'm just sorry you have to leave so soon."

"Yes, me too," she replied somberly. "We knew coming out here that we wouldn't be able to stay long, but..." She stopped. It seemed as if she was going to say something else, but she refrained. "Anyway...like I said," she continued, disheartened, "Henry has work, and... well...given the circumstances, I'm not so sure Sara and Mark want us here much longer anyhow."

I looked at her sympathetically.

"I understand," I said, feeling badly for her. "I'm so sorry your visit wasn't more...well...pleasant."

Mrs. Peters gave a reluctant smile.

"Me, too!" she sighed, dispirited. She shook her head in contemplation. "They're both stubborn and strong willed people, you know," she remarked. She chuckled. "They say opposites attract, but that sure wasn't the case with those two!" She looked at me apprehensively. "It worries me sometimes," she confided, clearly concerned. "They're so much alike and..." She paused, sighing again. "I sure hope they get this resolved soon," she said, fretful. "Sara needs to be concentrating all her energy on staying well and protecting that baby of theirs. All this stress...it can't be good for her *or* the baby!"

Mrs. Peters then did something I wasn't at all expecting. She looked at me earnestly as she took hold of my hands.

"Learn from this, Jochebed!" she advised intently, her eyes pleading. "Don't let issues fester! 'Let not the sun go down upon your wrath.' Talk about things right away and try to resolve them quickly! The longer you let things go, the harder it becomes to work them out!"

I listened closely to what she was saying, thankful for her wisdom.

She smiled fondly at me.

"Thank you again, for everything!" she reiterated. "It really was lovely to see you and your family again. I genuinely wish you all the best!" She gave my hands a gentle squeeze. "And Jochebed," she said, "I want to thank you personally. Thank you, *truly*, for taking such good care of my Sara. It means so much to me as her mother to know she's in such loving, capable hands."

I smiled back, appreciative of her kind words.

"You're welcome, Mrs. Peters," I replied. "But honestly, it's been my pleasure! I so enjoy spending time with your daughter. She's like a big sister to me, and I love her dearly!"

Mrs. Peters gave me a hug, and I walked her out.

Mr. Peters was waiting in the wagon, ready to go to Grampa and Gramma's to say goodbye to Aunt Sara, and when they were finished there, they were heading off to the train station. It'd been nice seeing them again, but I couldn't help but feel badly that things hadn't gone better for them while they were here. I hoped their final visit with Aunt Sara would, at least, resolve the conflict between the three of them. I said a quick prayer in my heart to that end.

As I was seeing them off, I looked up, and in the distance, I could see Isaac coming down the road. I quickly stepped back inside, grabbed my winter shawl, and excitedly ran to greet him!

He smiled and waved when he saw me coming, and I waved back just as happily. He briefly paused to say goodbye to the Peterses as they passed, and then he continued on to meet me.

"Sure is a cold morning this morning," he said, rubbing his hands together, blowing on them for warmth.

"Too cold for a walk?" I asked, hopeful.

"Never!" he answered enthusiastically.

He offered me his arm, and when he did, my heart skipped a beat.

I looked up into his gorgeous blue eyes and more than willingly took hold.

"So," he began to question as we walked, "how was your Thanksgiving?"

I took a deep breath, letting it out slowly.

"Well," I replied tentatively, "I'm not really sure just where to begin."

"That bad, huh?" he teased, kind of chuckling.

I looked up at him, my expression more than confirming it.

He looked at me surprised.

"Oh!" he stated, sorry he'd misjudged. "Really...*that bad?*"

I nodded, distraught.

"Isaac," I relayed, "it was *awful!* Aunt Sara and Uncle Mark didn't say a word to each other the entire day, Papa and Uncle Mark nearly came to blows at the dinner table - I thought Grampa was going to throw both of them out on their ears - and Mr. and Mrs. Peters...well...I just feel *horrible* for them! I mean...their visit, it...it was absolutely *ruined!*"

Isaac looked at me sympathetically.

"Jochebed," he said, clearly sorry for the disaster, "I'm really sorry! I had no idea! Is there anything I can do?"

"No, sadly," I sighed. "I'm afraid there's nothing *anyone* can do...but pray, of course."

He put his arm around me and hugged me close.

"Sometimes that's the best thing we can do," he encouraged.

"I know," I replied, downcast, "but this is *huge!* It worries me, Isaac! I've never seen my Uncle Mark and Aunt Sara act like this towards each other before - *ever!* I mean, I know I'm not around them a lot, but this...this *just isn't them!*" I started to fret even more, fearful for what might happen between them. "What if this is just too much for them?" I submitted. "What if they don't resolve it? What if..."

"Now, Jochebed," Isaac interrupted, "don't go borrowing trouble! Don't even think like that! I'm sure they'll find a way to work it out in time."

I abruptly stopped walking and looked up at Isaac.

"I know we've just started courting and all," I acknowledged with apprehension, "and maybe I don't have the right to ask this of you, but… please…please promise me, Isaac, promise me that we'll always talk things out right away and be open and honest with each other! Could you…would you promise me that?"

Isaac could see the look of concern on my face, and he'd heard the worry in my voice. He looked reassuringly into my eyes and answered me sweetly.

"You have my word, Jochebed!" he told me unwaveringly. "I promise!"

In my relief, I hugged him tightly.

"Thank you, Isaac," I said, feeling much better about the situation. "That means a lot!"

As we continued on our walk, we talked back and forth a little more about Thanksgiving, about our families, and about how we were both doing in school. While on the subject, I reluctantly asked the question.

"So," I said, dreading to hear the response, "I'm not sure I really want to know the answer to this, but…when do you have to go back to school?"

Isaac sighed as he looked at me glumly.

"Well, regrettably," he informed, just as reluctant to answer as I was to ask, "I have to go back tomorrow."

"So soon?" I lamented, surprised.

"Yes," Isaac answered, going on to explain. "I told a fellow student that I would help him go over some notes from our Doctrinal class. He's been away and missed some things, so I agreed to help him out. Unfortunately, Saturday night was the only time we could meet." He paused as he looked at me longingly. "Believe me," he assured, "I'd much rather leave after services Sunday night!"

I looked up at him forlorn.

"I so wish we could have more time together," I bemoaned, downcast. "It seems as if we just get started getting to know one another better, and then we're parted again."

"I know," he agreed empathetically. "I hate that we have to be apart, too, but look at it this way, 'absence makes the heart grow fonder,' and besides, I'll be home in a few weeks for Christmas. We'll have almost a whole month to spend together then."

"Really!" I exclaimed excitedly. "A whole month?"

"Really!" he affirmed with a smile. "Of course, I will have to be away briefly during that time."

"Oh?" I queried.

"Yes," Isaac disclosed. "I've been given the opportunity to preach on two separate occasions for Pastor Landry."

I looked at him perplexed, unsure of the name.

"He pastors a small church about twenty miles from here," he clarified. "He's a good friend of my grandfather's, and he enjoys having young preacher boys in to speak to his congregation from time to time. He heard that I was going to seminary, so he asked if I'd be willing to come. Knowing it would be a tremendous experience for me, I graciously accepted the invitation. And hey, just a thought," he went on to suggest. "With your father's permission, of course, maybe you can come with me when I go."

"Oh, Isaac!" I shouted, so thrilled at the prospect, "that would be *wonderful!* I absolutely *love* hearing you preach!"

"Well, thank you," Isaac replied, a little bashful. "But I think perhaps you might be just a tad bit *biased?*"

"Maybe so," I responded demurely, "but that doesn't make you any less of a great speaker!"

"Well, I appreciate the encouragement, Jochebed," he accepted, "really I do. It means a lot coming from you."

*****

Before we knew it, time had slipped away, and it was going on noontime.

"Oh my goodness!" I exclaimed, panicked. "I was supposed to help Gramma with lunch today. I *completely* forgot! I have to get back right away!"

"No problem!" Isaac announced enthusiastically. He immediately took my hand, and we were off running. "I'll have you there in no time!" he yelled back at me. "Can you keep up?"

"I think so!" I called out, trying to get my footing.

He and I ran madly all the way back to Grampa and Gramma's, tripping and laughing and teasing each other all the way.

When we arrived, I was completely winded as was Isaac. We stood a minute at the edge of the property, trying to catch our breath.

"I think we made it in record time!" I quipped, gasping for air.

When I looked up, I was surprised to see the Peterses' wagon still parked out in front of Grampa and Gramma's. I'll admit it gave me hope, thinking that perhaps Aunt Sara and Uncle Mark and they had worked things out and were now visiting peacefully together, but as Isaac and I took a few more steps towards the house, Dr. Wellesley's wagon that was parked just beyond theirs, suddenly came into view. Instantly, my hopes were dashed as my heart sank in fear!

"Oh, no!" I cried out, frightened. "Something must be wrong with Aunt Sara!"

Isaac and I hastened our pace as we hurried on to the house.

Once there, I frantically opened the door and burst inside.

Much to my surprise, everyone was gathered in the family room, and the mood was quite dour. Papa and Uncle Mark were pacing back and forth, Grampa was sitting in the rocking chair with a grave look on his face, and Mr. and Mrs. Peters were sitting on the couch, clearly concerned. As my gaze turned towards the kitchen, there was Samuel, leaning up against the wall, looking to me as if he'd been crying.

As you can imagine, worry immediately gripped my heart as I hurried to Papa in a panic.

"Papa, what is it?" I questioned anxiously. "What's wrong? What happened?" I was fully expecting one answer but got another one altogether - one I was totally unprepared for!

"It's your Gramma," Papa replied solemnly.

"What?!?" I exclaimed in horror, shaking my head, not understanding!

Papa nodded.

"She collapsed a little while ago when she was workin' in the kitchen," he told me. "Mr. and Mrs. Peters saw her as they were leavin'. Doc's in there with her now."

Tears filled my eyes, and I broke down, crying.

"I'm so sorry, Papa," I wept, burying my face in his chest. "If I'd a been here! …Oh, Papa!"

Papa rubbed my back, trying to console me, but it did little good as I felt absolutely horrible for not having been there for Gramma!

We waited and waited for what seemed like forever, everyone worried and scared. There was a little chatter here and there between some, trying to figure out what might have happened, but mostly everyone just stared and cried and prayed, hoping for the best.

I eventually walked over and stood beside Isaac, looking up at him with tear filled eyes.

He looked down at me with compassion, putting his arm around me, trying to comfort me the best he could.

I leaned my head against his shoulder, nearly inconsolable!

Finally, Dr. Wellesley came out of the bedroom, but the look on his face was not at all encouraging!

Grampa stood up straightaway.

"Doc," he asked earnestly, "my Elizabeth…how is she?"

Dr. Wellesley shook his head sullenly.

"I'm afraid it's not good, Ezra," he answered honestly. "It seems she's suffered a stroke."

Everyone gasped as Grampa sat back down, shocked and bewildered by the news. He buried his face in his hands and began to sob.

My heart broke for him as I wept all the more, clinging desperately to Isaac.

Mrs. Peters immediately got up and went to Grampa, kneeling down beside him. She put her hand on his back and rubbed his arm, trying to console him.

"How bad is it, Doc?" Uncle Mark wanted to know.

Dr. Wellesley sighed, concerned.

"She has some paralysis on her left side," he explained. "Her speech is labored, and she's still not responding like I'd like her to. I believe it'd be best to have her transferred to the hospital to monitor her there."

Papa nodded, agreeably.

"Whatever ya think is best, Doc," he replied anxiously.

Papa, Uncle Mark, and Dr. Wellesley went at once to bring Gramma from her room, while Mr. Peters and Isaac went outside to get Grampa's wagon from the barn. Mrs. Peters and I helped Grampa out of his chair and into his coat as it was evident he was too overcome to function properly. He seemed so lost and unsure of what to do next. I worried for him!

Samuel held the door for Papa and Uncle Mark as they carried Gramma outside on a stretcher, carefully putting her into the back of Dr. Wellesley's wagon. Just as soon as she was settled, Uncle Mark climbed aboard to go with her.

"We'll meet ya there," Papa called out as they made their way down the lane.

Dr. Wellesley waved back, acknowledging, as everyone else scrambled outside and climbed into Grampa's wagon.

When we were all set, we headed for the hospital. Papa drove, Grampa sat beside him, and Samuel, Isaac, and I all rode in the back.

Graciously, Mr. and Mrs. Peters postponed their trip back to Kansas to stay at the house with Aunt Sara.

At the hospital, Dr. Wellesley immediately rushed Gramma off to an exam room while the rest of us waited in the waiting area.

Still dazed and overwhelmed, visibly beside himself with grief and distress, Grampa meandered over and sat down on a chair all by himself. Lovingly, Papa and Uncle Mark pulled up chairs and sat down beside him, just to be with him. They all sat there quietly, though, waiting and worrying.

Isaac and I sat together at a small table holding hands while Samuel restlessly milled about, unenthusiastically flipping through literature here and there, and anxiously fidgeting as he paced.

Mercifully, we didn't have a long wait. After just a few minutes, a nurse came out and asked if we were the Lowrys. When Papa indicated that we were, she led us back to see Gramma.

As we walked into the room, I could see Gramma lying there in the bed; her eyes were open, but she wasn't moving.

When Grampa walked to her side to see her, she tried to muster a smile, but the paralysis in her face didn't allow her to form a proper one.

Grampa gently took hold of her hand and smiled down at her through his tears.

"Oh Elizabeth!" he cried. "My sweet, sweet Elizabeth! Ya had us all so worried!" He tenderly stroked her hand as tears trickled down his face.

"Shhhh," I heard Gramma hush as she dotingly gazed up into his eyes. She tried to say something else, but her words were all garbled and very hard to understand.

I stood back a ways from the bed, admittedly too afraid to go near, and thankfully, Isaac stood with me. It was just so hard seeing Gramma as she now was. For the first time in my life, she suddenly looked old to me as she was so helpless, and frail, so vulnerable and weak, not at all herself anymore. Her face was distorted from the stroke, and she was struggling to move her left side. It was all just too much! I quietly wept at the sight of her lying there in her altered condition.

As I watched her, looking at her feeble, damaged body, I couldn't help but feel guilty for not having been there in the kitchen with her when she collapsed. I just kept thinking that, perhaps, somehow, I was partially to blame.

Maybe, if I hadn't lost track of time! I berated myself. *Maybe if I'd been where I was supposed to be…maybe, just maybe, I could have helped her sooner! Maybe if I could have helped her, maybe she wouldn't be as bad off as she is now!* I hung my head, fighting back tears, feeling terrible for my grievous error.

Everyone took turns talking with Gramma, giving her hugs and telling her how much they loved her, but I…I just couldn't! I felt too ashamed to face her.

Surprisingly, they allowed us to spend quite awhile with Gramma, for which we were all grateful, but then, they came and told us that they needed to get her moved to another room.

Nevertheless, before they took her, they kindly waited for Grampa and her to say their goodbyes.

He leaned down and kissed her, telling her again that he loved her and that he'd see her again real soon! He told her to mind the doctors and to get herself better, and then he kissed her again. She patted his face (with her good hand, of course), and did her best to give him a smile. I could tell it was hard on the both of them, neither wanting to be apart!

Eventually, letting go of her hand, Grampa watched intently as they wheeled her out of the room, wiping a tear from his eye as she went.

As soon as she was gone, Dr. Wellesley came in to speak to us briefly, before we left for home.

"She's going to need her rest," he informed us. "Only time will tell how much she's been affected by all that's happened. As much as I wish it weren't so, there's really nothing more we can do for her medically. How well she recuperates will depend largely on how hard she works to regain her speech and mobility. I'd like to keep her here for a day or so, just for observation, but after that she should be able to return home to begin her recovery." He looked around at everyone with query. "Will there be anyone at the house there who can help with her care?" he wanted to know. "I mean, besides you, Ezra, of course."

"There will be," Papa assured. "We'll all take turns if we have to. The important thing is to get Ma well again."

"Great!" Dr. Wellesley replied, encouraged. "Then I'll see you all in a day or two."

Papa shook the doctor's hand as did Grampa, grateful for all he'd done.

Dr. Wellesley nodded and left.

"Maybe I should stay with her," Grampa fretted. "Maybe I can help her somehow."

"Pa," Uncle Mark disagreed, "ya heard the doc. Ma needs her rest right now and that's probably what she'll be doin' - sleepin'. Besides, take it from someone who's had to stay here, unless you're the one in the hospital bed, it's a mighty uncomfortable place!"

"I agree with Mark," Papa chimed in. "Ya should come home with us for now and let Ma get her rest. I'll be sure to bring ya back to her tomorrow."

Grampa looked uncertain, but he relented.

"All right," he gave in reluctantly. "But we're comin' back at first light!"

Papa put his arm around Grampa and gave him a squeeze.

"Sure thing, Pa," he promised. "First light!"

*****

On the way home, everyone tried to stay upbeat and positive. They talked about how glad they were to still have Gramma with us and that despite everything she'd been through, she still looked good. Papa reminded us that she was a strong woman who'd overcome great challenges in her past, and he had no doubt that, in time, she would overcome this one as well.

I stayed quiet and listened, and while I understood what they were all saying, I just couldn't shake the guilty feeling that somehow Gramma was in the condition she was in because of me.

If only I had been there I lamented *if only!*

The ride home from the hospital was long, and I didn't say anything the whole way there.

About halfway, however, Isaac noticed my silence and tried to draw me out.

"Jochebed," he asked concerned, "how are you doing?"

I looked up at him, searching my mind for the right words to say, but there simply were no words to express how I was feeling. I turned away and softly began to cry.

Thankfully, Isaac didn't ask me anymore questions, seeming to understand my pain. He just put his arm around me and held me close, letting me cry.

*****

It was fairly late when we got back to Grampa and Gramma's, and no one felt much like eating, so we simply said goodnight to Grampa and Uncle Mark and headed for home.

When we got there, Isaac walked me to the door.

"I'll stop by tomorrow to say goodbye before I have to leave for school," he told me. "And please know, I'll definitely be praying for you and your family."

I nodded, thankful, as I hugged him tightly.

"Thank you for being there for me, today," I said, still hurting. "I don't know what I would have done without you!"

"Well," he replied humbly, "I don't feel I did very much, but you're more than welcome. I'm glad I could do something."

"You did more than you know," I assured him.

He nodded, smiling.

"Well," he relayed, "as much as I hate to, I really should be going. I'm sure my grandparents are wondering where I've gotten to."

"Oh, of course!" I said. "Go! I understand!"

He gave me another hug.

"I'll see you tomorrow, then," he said with a smile.

"Tomorrow," I agreed.

Isaac left and I went inside.

After hanging up my shawl, I went to get myself a glass of water.

Not long after, Samuel came inside. Uncharacteristically, he was rather quiet and distant.

"Are you all right?" I asked out of concern.

He didn't answer. He simply hung up his coat and went and plopped himself down at the table.

"Samuel," I asked again, walking over to him, sensing something more was bothering him, "are you just upset about Gramma, or...or is there something more to it?"

He immediately looked away, clearly trying to hide his tears.

Not wanting to embarrass him, I didn't push. I just sat down at the table, quietly letting him know that I was there for him.

Finally, he decided to open up a bit.

"Do...do ya think she's gonna die?" he questioned, choking back tears, his voice breaking.

"Oh, Samuel!" I replied, alarmed, reaching out, putting my hand on his arm. "What makes you think that? Gramma's hurt, yes, but...you heard the doctor, he says she can come home in a day or two! I'm sure she'll be recovered in no time!"

Samuel shook his head defiantly.

"That's what they said about Gramma Giano, too!" he blurted out angrily. "And she never came home!"

~

Gramma Giano was our mother's mother, and when Samuel was just five years old, she came down with a terrible illness. Within no time at all, whatever was ailing her, she became so sick with it that Grampa Giano and Papa had to take her to the hospital. While she was there, the doctors worked tirelessly to try to figure out what she had, but for whatever reason they could never come to any conclusions.

Thankfully, within a few days of being at the hospital, though, she miraculously started to get better, so much so, the doctors determined that she was well enough to go home. On the very day that Papa and Mama went to pick her up, however, she suddenly took a turn for the worse and died before they got there.

Grampa Giano never fully got over her death, and passed away just two months later. …I believe, from a broken heart!

~

"Oh, Samuel!" I expressed with angst, trying to explain. "Gramma Giano…her sickness…the doctors…they never really knew what she had! They didn't even know what to do for her! But Gramma Lowry…why…it's just not the same! They *know* what happened! They *know* she had a stroke!" I gave his arm a reassuring squeeze. "They know how to help her, Samuel," I told him, "and I know she's going to be all right! She just has to be!" I paused, trying to think of how to encourage him. "I get that it's frightening right now," I empathized, "and I know it's hard, and I know it doesn't make any sense, but honestly, Samuel, we really do just need to trust God in all this!"

Samuel feverishly wiped his tears, bitterly scowling at me.

"I'm *sick* of havin' to trust God in all this stuff!" he countered with such rage. "Why doesn't He just keep it from happenin' *in the first place!?* First Gramma and Grampa Giano, then Mama, then all of Aunt Sara's troubles… *now this! …It's just not fair!*" He abruptly stood up and ran off upstairs to his room.

Just as I heard him slam his bedroom door, Papa came walking in the house.

"What on earth was that?" he questioned, hearing the commotion.

I sighed, disheartened.

"It's Samuel, Papa," I answered with melancholy. "He's angry!" I shook my head as I stood up, looking off towards the stairs, commiserating with Samuel. "He doesn't understand why all these terrible things keep happening to our family," I explained. "And in truth," I confessed as I looked over at Papa, resentment welling up in my heart, "I'm not so sure I understand it either!" I angrily gathered my skirt and left the room, heading upstairs myself.

Not knowing how to respond, Papa just let me go.

*****

The next day was very stressful and busy as Mr. and Mrs. Peters had to leave to catch their train back to Kansas. They'd already delayed their trip a day to help out with everything, but now Mr. Peters really *had* to get back to his job. They got up early, packed their things, and headed off to Grampa and Gramma's to say goodbye to Aunt Sara yet again.

While they were busy with that, Papa, Uncle Mark, and Samuel left to take Grampa back to the hospital to see Gramma. With everyone leaving for the day, the task of sitting with Aunt Sara fell to me. I didn't mind really, I enjoyed her company, but with all the time I'd already spent at Grampa and Gramma's, I was feeling a little guilty that my chores at home were being neglected. Papa and Samuel helped out where they could, but there was only so much they could do.

My original plan for the day had been to catch up on some cleaning and mending and general chores around the house and then to spend some time with Isaac before he had to leave for college, but due to the unforeseen circumstances, clearly, my plans had changed!

*****

When I arrived at Grampa and Gramma's, the Peterses were still in talking with Aunt Sara so I let them be. I put the basket of mending I'd brought from home to work on down in the family room, and I headed straight for the kitchen to start on breakfast.

As I was just finishing up with everything, the Peterses came in to say their goodbyes to me.

"Thank you again, Jochebed, for all you're doing," Mrs. Peters said as she and Mr. Peters walked into the kitchen.

"Yes," Mr. Peters echoed. "We so appreciate all your hard work and effort."

"You're very welcome," I replied, grateful for the encouragement.

"We do so hope things go well with your grandmother," Mrs. Peters expressed graciously. "I pray she recuperates quickly. Sara told us that she would keep us up to date on her progress." All of a sudden, Mrs. Peters got a look of distress on her face as she looked at Mr. Peters and then back to me. "I only hope that perhaps, somehow, God will use this event to bring reconciliation between Sara and Mark," she relayed with such concern. "You'll keep praying for them, won't you?"

"Oh, yes, ma'am, *absolutely!*" I assured her. "I, too, am hoping that things will be resolved between the two of them very soon!"

Mrs. Peters came over and gave me a hug.

"You're such a dear," she said sweetly. "You take care of yourself now, all right? And our Sara, of course," she quickly added. "We'll be praying for all of you!"

"Thank you, Mrs. Peters," I accepted. "That's very kind of you. I do hope you have a safe trip back."

The Peterses gathered their things, and I saw them out.

Once they were gone, I finished up that last bit of breakfast and prepared a plate for Aunt Sara and myself.

When I got to her room, she was sitting up in her bed knitting a sweater she'd been working on for quite a while.

"Oh, hi, Jochebed," she happily greeted as I walked into the room. "Mmmm, that smells delicious!"

"Well, I hope it'll taste as good as it smells," I remarked, putting her plate down beside her.

"Oh, I'm certain it will," Aunt Sara flattered. "You're a *wonderful* cook!"

"Well, thank you," I replied with reserve.

I sat down on the chair beside Aunt Sara's bed with my plate of food, said a quick prayer, and began to eat.

"That sweater you're working on," I complimented, "it's *gorgeous!* Is it for Uncle Mark?"

Aunt Sara put the sweater aside as she took her breakfast plate.

"No!" she answered tersely. "It's not for him!"

Obviously, she was still upset with Uncle Mark, so I knew it'd be best not to push the issue any further.

I promptly let it go, and after Aunt Sara finished praying for her food, she abruptly changed the subject!

"How did Mama Lowry seem when you last saw her?" she queried, concerned.

"Umm…can I tell you in a minute?" I asked. "If it's all right with you, I'd really like to go and get the mending I brought from home. I feel I have to get caught up on it sometime!"

"Oh, no problem," Aunt Sara said, swallowing the food in her mouth. "Go right ahead!" Then she teased. "I'll be here when ya get back!" she quipped. "Sure enough, I'm not going anywhere!"

I knew Aunt Sara was just jesting, but I could tell deep down there was a part of her that was being serious, so tired of being cooped up in her room. I couldn't help but feel for her.

"I'll be back in a minute," I assured, setting my plate of food aside.

She nodded, approving, as she took another bite of her food.

As swiftly as I could, I went and gathered my things from the family room, and headed back to the bedroom.

"Now," I said as I entered, setting the basket of mending on the floor beside my chair, "where were we?"

"You were about to tell me about Mama Lowry," Aunt Sara reminded.

"Oh, yes," I recalled. I sat back down, picked up my plate of food, took a quick bite, and did my best to explain. "Well," I began, "I guess I don't really know quite how to put it. She looked...well..." I paused, sad at the thought. "She looked...she looked old to me!" I confessed. "I mean, I know she's up in years and all, but...up until now...I don't think I'd ever really thought much about her age." I shook my head, remembering. "Seeing her like that," I revealed, "lying there so helpless, so frail, struggling to speak and move, she...she just wasn't at all herself." I shrugged my shoulders. "I don't know," I said with a sigh, "I guess it all just made her seem so...so old to me somehow."

Aunt Sara nodded, seeming to understand.

"I know what you mean," she commiserated, recounting her own experience. "That happened to me with my grandfather when he had his stroke."

I looked at her totally surprised.

"Your Grampa had a stroke?" I questioned, completely unaware. "I had no idea!"

"He did," she affirmed. "It happened years ago when I was just...well...oh...I don't know, about Samuel's age, I suppose- twelve, thirteen, somewhere along in there. Anyway, it was my papa's father. He always seemed so young and spry to me, but after his stroke, suddenly, I noticed every wrinkle and frailty, something I'd never even noticed before." She sighed. "I suppose that's what illness can do to a person, though."

"It sure can!" I wholeheartedly agreed. I looked at Aunt Sara anxiously, yet hopeful. "Did...did your Grampa recover?" I asked guardedly.

"Actually," she replied encouragingly, "he did! It wasn't a full recovery, mind you, he still had some limitations, but he was definitely able to regain his ability to walk and talk. It changed him a bit, but he lived a full and happy life up until he passed away a few years ago. I think recovery kind of depends on the person and how bad of a stroke they had. My grandpa's stroke was pretty mild, and...well...hopefully, that'll be the case with Mama Lowry."

"Oh, I so hope you're right!" I expressed with apprehension. "Gramma just has to be alright!"

Aunt Sara smiled at me with confidence.

"I just know if given half a chance," she bolstered, "Mama Lowry will fight this thing tooth and nail! I can't think of a more determined woman than your grandmother!"

I was still visibly worried.

Aunt Sara tried to reassure me.

"I believe God will give her the strength she needs to get through this, Jochebed," she said, "I honestly do! And," she continued, "I have *no doubt* that Mama Lowry will work harder than *anybody* to get back to normal. Just have faith, sweetie. God's able to work miracles."

I shook my head, discouraged.

"I know, Aunt Sara," I acknowledged, "but sometimes it's just *so hard* to trust Him."

"I can understand that," she sympathized. "But don't forget, He's still in control, Jochebed, and He'll never give us more than we can handle." She smiled. "Seems I recall *someone* reminding me of that truth not too long ago!"

I halfheartedly smiled.

"You're right, Aunt Sara," I conceded. "I guess sometimes in the midst of everything it's easy to forget."

*****

Aunt Sara and I finished up breakfast and sat and talked and sewed together for quite a while. It was definitely time well spent! I shared with her about Isaac and Samuel, and thankfully, she shared with me a little about her visit with her parents. I was so glad to hear that she had forgiven them and that they had had a really good day together before her parents had to leave.

As we were talking and sharing, it seemed to me our conversation was going quite well, so much so, I decided to daringly broach the subject of her and Uncle Mark.

"Aunt Sara," I asked, hoping not to overstep, "if you don't mind me asking, how are things between you and Uncle Mark?"

Aunt Sara sighed a long, deep sigh, clearly aggravated.

"They're not!" she answered curtly. "He hasn't spoken *one word* to me in *two whole days!* **Two whole days!**" she reiterated, irate. "He sells our entire life away, and then he doesn't even speak to me!" She clenched her jaw. "He makes me *so* angry! I just don't know what to do anymore!" She shook her head, looking quite determined. "I'll be honest," she stated resolutely, "at this point...I don't *want* to talk to him! He's so proud and stubborn! He thinks he's right in his decision, and he thinks I'm wrong to even question it!" She was nearly fuming! "He sold my life, Jochebed!" she started to rant again. "My *entire life* without a single word to me until *after the fact!* I don't know what to do with that! I mean...every time I think about it, it just makes my *blood boil!* To think that he would make that kind of decision without even discussing it with me first, it just...it just *infuriates* me! I'm his wife, for goodness' sake, his partner..." She stopped abruptly, shaking her head, skeptical. "Or, at least, I *used* to be his partner!" she blurted out, doubting.

"Oh, Aunt Sara!" I interjected, taken aback by her tone. "You are still his partner! You know he loves you!"

"*Does he?*" she questioned bitterly. "If you ask me...what he's done...*that's not love!*"

I could tell she was getting pretty agitated and upset, and not wanting her to get any more stressed for the sake of the baby, I decided to try to take the discussion in a different direction,

Just as I was about to say something, however, there was a knock at the front door.

"I'm going to go see who that is," I told her, getting up out of my seat. "I'll be right back, okay?"

"And, I'll be here!" Aunt Sara retorted sarcastically, clearly tired and frustrated with her circumstances.

I gave her a look of sympathy before heading out of the room.

I must have not been quick enough to the front door, because by the time I arrived, the knocking had already stopped. Curious as to who could have been there, I decided to open the door to see if I could see anyone walking away. Much to my surprise, when I got the door open, there was no one there at all! Bewildered and perplexed by the absence, I stepped out onto the porch and looked around. Oddly, whoever had been at the door had already disappeared.

"Boy that sure is strange!" I commented to myself, still looking around, confounded. Unable to figure it out, I finally shrugged it off and went back inside.

Closing the door behind me, I happily started back towards the bedroom to finish my conversation with Aunt Sara. Just as I was about to turn the corner, however, I heard a noise at the back of the house.

"Now what on earth could that be?" I questioned inquisitively.

As I made my way into the kitchen, I instantly froze. I could tell someone was jiggling the handle to the back door, trying to get inside! I stood there, my heart pounding anxiously, uncertain as to whom it could possibly be! Fortunately, the back door was locked, and whoever it was finally gave up their attempts.

I took a deep breath and cautiously and slowly walked over to the window by the back door. Carefully pulling back the curtain, I peered out. Much to my surprise, I noticed the barn door standing wide open. I knew Papa and Uncle Mark and Grampa would never leave it that way, so I began to fear that something was amiss. Before I could think a second thought on it, though, my suspicions were instantly confirmed!

A man, someone whom I had never seen before, suddenly appeared in the doorway of the barn. He was tall and mean looking, and he wore a long coat and cowboy hat. He looked to be holding something in his hand, but from where I was standing, I couldn't tell for sure what it was.

I stood there anxiously, watching him closely, as he stood there warily looking around. All of a sudden, without warning, he looked right at me! Or, at least, that's how it seemed! Scared to death that I'd been spotted, I quickly stepped back away from the window, foolishly letting the curtain fall into place. I hoped he hadn't seen it!

My heart was beating furiously in my chest as I swallowed hard and waited. When I felt it was safe to look again, I nervously pulled back the curtain, ever so slightly, and peeked out again. Much to my surprise and horror, the man was still standing there looking in my direction. He squinted his eyes as if he suspected something, but then he abruptly turned and disappeared into the barn.

Completely frightened at this point, I quickly ran to Aunt Sara to see what we should do!

Bursting through the bedroom door in sheer panic and fear, I frantically ran to Aunt Sara's side!

"Aunt Sara, Aunt Sara!" I stuttered and stammered, whispering excitedly, almost out of breath. "There's….there's someone…someone outside! A man! In the barn! A strange man! I…I've never seen him before!"

Aunt Sara was visibly flustered, taken aback by my hysterical behavior.

"Calm down, Jochebed!" she insisted. "I can't understand you! Now, *who? Is where?*"

I took a deep breath, trying to compose myself.

"A strange man," I explained as calmly as I could, "he tried to get into the house, and now...now he's in the barn! What should I do?"

Aunt Sara immediately sat straight up, a look of shock and fright on her face.

"Can you describe him to me?" she asked anxiously.

"Um...yes!" I started to say, disconcerted, trying to recall. "He...he looked kind of tall, and...and he's got on a long, dark coat and a cowboy hat...and...um...I'm pretty sure he's got a long beard, too! And, oh, yes!" I quickly added. "He was holding something in his hand, but...I couldn't really make out what it was, though!"

Aunt Sara was beside herself!

"Well, does he know we're in here?" she asked vigorously.

"I'm not sure!" I admitted. "He was already gone from the front door when I got there, so...I don't know if he heard me open it up or not! I mean...I did step outside briefly to look around, but...I'm pretty sure he was already gone by then, at least, I think he was." I brought my hand to my forehead, distressed. "But then..." I started to say. I hesitated.

Aunt Sara was sitting there hanging on my every word, waiting with baited breath. When I didn't immediately finish my sentence, she threw up her hands in nervous anticipation!

"What, Jochebed?" she prodded fretfully. "But then *what?*"

"Well...I..." I was so scared I could barely get it out.

"Jochebed!" she pressed again impatiently, demanding to know. *"Then what?"*

I swallowed hard and did my best to answer.

"Well," I explained, absolutely terrified. "I was standing at the window by the back door, and, then...well...the man...he...he looked right at me, I mean, at least, I think he did! He was looking in my direction anyway!" I closed my eyes, trying to remember *exactly!* "Oh, I don't know!" I fretted. "I jumped back from the window as soon as he looked, so...I guess...I guess I'm not actually sure if he saw me or not!" I looked at her worried. "Oh, Aunt Sara!" I questioned, nearly beside myself. "What if he did?"

Aunt Sara shook her head, thinking.

"Quickly go to the window again," she instructed, "and..."

"What?" I interrupted incredulously. "You want me to go to the window *again?!?"*

"Yes!" Aunt Sara insisted. "We have to know what he's up to, Jochebed! But just be quiet when you do it, okay? You don't want to alert him to the fact that we're in here if he doesn't know that we are, understand?" Her expression was intense as she looked at me with earnest.

"III understand," I replied haltingly, quaking in fear. I took a deep breath and timidly turned to go back to the kitchen to check on the man.

"And, Jochebed," Aunt Sara called out, stopping me. "Do you know where Papa Lowry keeps his gun?"

"Gun?" I questioned anxiously as I promptly turned back around, looking at her with angst.

"Yes, gun!" she reiterated emphatically. "Do you know where it's at? We may need it!"

I stood there, trying to think.

"I...I'm not sure!" I stammered. "I might!" My mind was racing, trying to remember where Grampa had put it. "I'll see if I can find it!" I said hastily as I turned to leave. At this point, my whole body was trembling, I was so afraid!

"Ohhh, I wish I weren't stuck in this *awful* bed!" Aunt Sara blustered in consternation. "Please, Jochebed, be careful!!"

I nodded as I nervously left the room.

Cautiously and quietly I crept back to the kitchen and made my way to the window. Taking another deep breath to steady my nerves, I carefully opened the curtains to see if I could catch a glimpse of what was going on outside. As I looked in the direction of the barn, I could see that the door was still wide open, but what I couldn't see, was the man. I wondered if he had gone or if he was still inside the barn.

As I stood there watching and waiting, I kept trying to remember where Grampa had put his gun. I knew that in his old house in North Dakota, he had always kept it in the bedroom right next to his and Gramma's bed, but I also knew that Gramma was always a little uncomfortable having it there with them. When they moved here to Pennsylvania, I recalled Gramma telling me that Grampa had promised her he'd store it someplace else. The problem...I couldn't remember where that someplace else was!

Standing there, lost in my thoughts, I was suddenly jolted to attention when, out of nowhere, another strange man came riding up on a horse, heading straight for the barn. He slowed his horse, jumped down, and yelled out something, although I couldn't really make out what he said.

In no time at all, the other man who'd been in the barn all this time appeared in the doorway. The two of them started talking as they walked back into the barn together. It just seemed to me by the looks of them that they were up to no good. I quickly ran back to tell Aunt Sara what I'd seen.

"So, what happened?" she asked eagerly. "Is he gone? Did you get the gun?"

I was frantic and my eyes were as big as saucers!

"There...there...there's t-t-two of them now!" I stuttered.

"Two?" Aunt Sara exclaimed in disbelief.

I nodded, confirming.

"Well, where's the gun?" she queried with urgency in her voice.

I shook my head.

"I'm...I'm not sure!" I told her, completely at a loss as to where it could be. "I know where Grampa *used* to keep it, but I'm just not sure if it's still there now, now that they've moved!"

"Well, go and check where you *think* it might be!" she insisted fervently.

I nodded compliantly, and quickly left to go check Grampa and Gramma's bedroom, hoping beyond hope that Grampa still kept his gun there. As I entered their room, I hastily ran to Grampa's side of the bed, but much to my chagrin, the gun wasn't there!

"Great!" I bemoaned. "Where on earth could it be?" My eyes frantically searched the room, my mind going a million miles a minute, trying to think. "Where, *where* are you?" I found myself asking over and over again as I looked under the bed, in the closet, and behind the door.

I was just about to give up on my search, when suddenly, as if the Lord miraculously put the thought into my mind, I remembered seeing the gun in the family room beside Grampa's old chair. I promptly ran to the family room to see if it was there. Sure enough, leaning against the wall in the corner was Grampa's shotgun. I quickly grabbed it up and ran back to Aunt Sara.

"Here it is!" I announced excitedly as I entered the room.

By now, Aunt Sara was sitting on the edge of the bed, bracing herself, ready to get up.

"Aunt Sara!" I shouted in dismay. "*What are you doing?* **You can't!!**"

"Well, I can't just lie here and wait around for something bad to happen to us, now can I?!" she protested.

Before I could stop her, right before my eyes, she slowly and carefully stood up. It was obvious she was quite frail and unsteady on her feet.

"Now, give me that gun!" she insisted, almost completely out of breath.

"But Aunt Sara!" I cried out. "I can't let you do this! Think of the baby! Please, just get back in bed! I'll take care of it!"

She looked at me sternly!

"Have you ever shot a gun before?" she asked, growing rather irritated with me.

"Well, no!" I admitted. "But it can't be that hard, can it?" I stood there looking the gun over, trying to figure it out.

Aunt Sara rolled her eyes, shaking her head in aggravation as she reached out and yanked the gun from my hands.

"Now help me to the kitchen!" she demanded.

I looked at her anxiously!

"Oh, Aunt Sara!" I expressed, worried, extremely uncertain about all this. "I don't think this is such a good idea!"

"Now, Jochebed," she persisted, still trying to catch her breath, "we have no choice! – Now help me!"

Warily and reluctantly, I did as she asked.

Even though Aunt Sara had done her best to exercise her legs while in bed, they were still noticeably weak. It was clearly painful and difficult for her to stand.

"Aunt Sara, *really!*" I objected strongly as she leaned on me for support. "I just don't know about this! This just doesn't seem like the best thing to do!"

"What choice do we have?" she rightly questioned.

I looked at her, exasperated, truly having no other plan to offer.

"We have to do something!" she obstinately pushed. "Now come on! We can do this!"

I sighed grudgingly as I put my arm around her waist and she put her arm around my shoulder. Holding tightly to her, I grabbed her arm, she leaned on me, and we staggered towards the door.

After quite the effort, we finally made it down the hallway and into the kitchen.

"Oh, my goodness!" Aunt Sara groaned, completely exhausted. "I *have* to sit down!"

I directed us over to the table and managed to pull out a chair. Carefully and steadily, I helped Aunt Sara sit down as she rested the gun there beside her. She was visibly fatigued and out of breath.

"Go see!" she instructed, pointing to the window.

I quickly ran over and looked out. Much to my horror, the robbers were in the process of loading Grampa and Gramma's things into the back of Grampa's wagon.

They'd hitched his team of horses to it, ready to take off with their haul. I gasped when I realized what they were doing!

"What's happening, Jochebed?" Aunt Sara queried curiously.

"They're robbing us!" I shouted as loudly as I could in a whisper. "They've got Grampa's horses and wagon, and now they're taking things from the barn! What are we gonna do?"

As I was explaining what was going on, suddenly, I heard someone shout. Thinking it sounded an awful lot like Isaac, I immediately turned back to see. Sure enough, there he was! He was just starting around the back of the house, heading towards the barn, waving his hands, yelling at the men.

"Who are you?" he demanded to know. "What are you doing, there? Who told you you could take those things?"

The men's backs were to him, but clearly they were startled by his presence. They quickly pulled their bandannas over their faces to conceal their identity.

Surely, they'll leave now! I thought to myself.

But just as the thought crossed my mind, one of the men unexpectedly turned around, pulled out his gun, cocked back the hammer, and aimed it squarely at Isaac.

I let out a scream, but I quickly put my hand over my mouth to muffle it! I thought for sure the man was going to shoot Isaac!

"Whoa! Hold on there!" Isaac shouted, still a good ways off, abruptly stopping in his tracks, putting up his hands in a show of surrender.

The robber forcefully yelled for him to stay back.

"What is it? What's going on?" Aunt Sara asked frantically.

"It's Isaac!" I told her, panicked. "The robber...he's...he's pointing a gun at him!"

"Oh, good grief!" Aunt Sara grumbled. "You've got to be kidding me!" That was the last straw! She had had enough! She rolled her eyes, grabbed the gun, and attempted to stand to her feet.

My eyes were fixed on Isaac and the robbers the whole time, so I never saw her slowly making her way over to me. Needless to say, I nearly jumped out of my skin, when she came up beside me.

Not wasting any more time, she yanked back the curtain, assessed the situation, cocked the gun, flung the door open, and shot in the direction of the barn.

As you can imagine, the gun blast shocked and stunned the robbers who promptly forgot about Isaac, jumped into Grampa's wagon, and took off as quickly as they could!

Unfortunately, the force of the gunshot sent Aunt Sara reeling backwards. She lost her balance and went crashing to the floor.

Instantly, I ran to her side to see if she was all right.

Just as I was kneeling down, Isaac came scrambling into the house. Seeing both Aunt Sara and me on the floor, he came rushing over.

"Are you all right?" he asked, worried.

"Help me get her back to bed!" I insisted, scared to death that she had injured herself badly.

I could tell the fall was a bad one and that she was hurt much worse than she let on.

Isaac took one side, and I took the other, carefully and gently helping her to her feet.

She moaned in terrible agony as we lifted her up.

"Will you be able to make it?" I questioned, concerned.

She nodded, grimacing in pain.

Isaac and I slowly walked her back to the bedroom.

"What in the world happened here?" he asked as we made our way down the hallway.

"Let's get her settled, and I'll tell you everything!" I replied, anxious.

We managed to get Aunt Sara back to her room and into bed.

When I asked her if she needed the doctor, she insisted that she was fine and that all she needed was some rest. I didn't believe her, however, as I had witnessed her terrible fall and knew there was *no way* she was fine!

"Aunt Sara," I came back at her, almost begging. "Please, let me send Isaac to get the doctor for you!"

"No, Jochebed!" she flatly refused. "I'm fine, really. Just a little winded is all."

I could tell by the look on her face that she was desperately fighting pain. I was worried!

"Are you sure?" I pressed, extremely apprehensive.

"Yes," she insisted, trying to catch her breath, holding her side. "I'll be fine!"

I sighed, *very* reluctant!

"Well…all right," I tentatively agreed, "if you say so. But I'll be back to check on you in a little while!"

Aunt Sara took a deep breath and nodded as she winced again in obvious pain. I couldn't help but be concerned!

I looked at Isaac, troubled, and he nodded, seeming to understanding, but even so, he coaxed me to leave the room to let her rest.

I sighed again as I looked back to Aunt Sara, uneasy about the whole thing. Regardless, though, I complied, following Isaac out of the room, leaving the door slightly ajar so that I could come back and check on Aunt Sara later without disturbing her.

As soon as we were out of the room, Isaac pulled me close and gave me a reassuring hug.

"Jochebed, you're shaking," he commented. "Are you all right?"

The reality of what had just happened came crashing down on me all at once. The emotions were just too much, and I started to cry.

"I was so scared, Isaac!" I told him, overcome. "I thought we were going to die! - And then you…and then Aunt Sara…and Grampa's horses and the wagon, and…"

Isaac jumped into the middle of my meltdown, lifting my face, tenderly looking into my eyes.

"But you're safe now," he reminded, "and that's all that matters!"

I hugged him tightly as the tears flowed.

"Come on," he encouraged as he walked me to the family room.

We sat down on the couch together as I pulled a hanky from my pocket, wiping my tears, and blowing my nose.

"Jochebed," Isaac said, "I truly hate to do this, but I really should go and get the sheriff right away!"

"Oh, Isaac," I lamented, still fearful, "do you really have to go right now? What if those men decide to come back? They did leave behind one of their horses in their haste. What if they come back while you're gone? Please…please can't it wait?"

Isaac sighed, understanding my angst, but he also knew how important it was for the sheriff to be involved.

"I'm sorry, Jochebed," he explained, "but I really should go now. The sooner the sheriff knows about this, the better!"

I looked at him with dread, terribly afraid!

Isaac's compassion got the better of him.

"What if I quickly run to my place and get my brother Andrew?" he offered. "He could come and stay with you and your Aunt Sara until I get back with the sheriff. What do you say to that?"

"I don't know, Isaac," I replied, worried. "I just hate the thought of being here all alone with Aunt Sara in the condition she's in. I mean what if…"

"It only takes me about thirty minutes or so on foot," Isaac pointed out, interrupting. "And if I take the horse the robbers left behind, I can be home in no time at all. Besides, if I take their horse, and the robbers do come back looking for it, and I'm not saying they will, but, if they do, they'll see the horse is gone and figure it just ran off. It'll be fine…I promise!" He looked at me sweetly. "I'd stay myself if I could," he said, "you know that! But someone has to get the sheriff."

I knew Isaac was right, but I still hated the thought of what might happen after he left. I grudgingly agreed to his plan, though, and he gave me some quick instructions to follow while he was away.

"Make certain you lock all the doors behind me," he advised, "and keep the gun close just in case."

I looked at him warily.

"You do know how to use it, right?" he asked.

I shook my head no, indicating I had no idea.

"All right," he accepted, "come with me and let me show you how." He took my hand, and we went to the kitchen to retrieve the shotgun where he quickly gave me a lesson on how to load, aim, and take the safety off. Once he felt I was fairly certain on how to use it, he told me he would hurry and be back as soon as he could. I looked at him anxiously, as he walked to the back door. "You'll be fine!" he reassured with a smile. "I'll be back soon!"

I nodded nervously, as he opened the door.

Once he stepped outside, I quickly locked the door behind him and stood there watching as he rode away. I hesitated for a minute but then I realized that the front door was probably still unlocked. Worried that it was, I quickly ran to check! When I was certain it was secure, I headed back to the kitchen to keep an eye out for the robbers.

Trembling and terrified, I stood at the back door, frozen in place, just staring out the window, holding tightly to the gun. I was desperately watching for any strange movement, hoping beyond hope that the robbers wouldn't return!

It seemed as if I'd only been standing there for a minute or two when suddenly I was startled by a knock at the front door. (I guess time flies when you're scared out of your mind!)

After retrieving my heart from my throat, I took one more quick look out the back window and nervously forced myself to the family room. I panicked all the way, worried for whom it might be, but despite my trepidation, I knew I needed to find out who it was!

When I got to the family room, I cautiously went to the front window and peeked through the curtains. Seeing it was Andrew standing there waiting for me to let him in, I immediately felt myself relax as the tension drained from my body.

Not wanting him to have to wait any longer, I rushed to the door, unlocked it, and opened it up.

"Whoa there, don't shoot!" Andrew teased, holding up his hands in a gesture of surrender. "Don't aim to harm ya, ma'am!"

I instantly blushed with embarrassment! In my haste to let him in, I'd completely forgotten to put the shotgun down before opening the door.

"Oh, I'm so sorry!" I apologized as I put the gun aside, leaning it against the wall. "Please, come in!"

Andrew smiled as he stepped inside.

"Isaac tells me you need some company for a little while," he relayed caringly.

"Yes," I confirmed, still feeling a bit self-conscious. "That would be correct!"

"Well, I'm at your service," Andrew offered kindly. He walked on into the family room, and I locked the door behind him.

"Shall we go to the kitchen?" I suggested. "We can wait for Isaac in there."

"Sure," Andrew agreed happily, turning about. "Wherever you'd like!"

I smiled timidly and led the way.

WORRIED
(Chapter 14)

Andrew was very charming and quite nice. He was a little closer to me in age, and I knew him from school and church, of course, but we weren't particularly close. We ran in different circles, and I was busy with life as was he.

Don't get me wrong, he was always very polite and gracious whenever we'd had occasion to speak in the past, but it'd just been quite a while since I'd actually been around him. He was already finished with school and was working now and had recently become engaged to his girl, Isabelle, so I simply never saw him much anymore.

Regardless, I was very grateful that he was here with me now!

~

I'll readily admit it was a bit awkward being alone, just the two of us. I mean, Aunt Sara was in the other room and all, but still, it was just him and me alone in the kitchen, and as was my tendency, I felt extremely shy and uncomfortable. I was so nervous with Andrew there with me that I'd all but forgotten about the robbers. I sat and fidgeted, barely knowing what to say or do, when suddenly it dawned on me to do the only thing I knew to do, and that was to be hospitable. I nervously offered Andrew a drink of cold lemonade. He graciously accepted, and I went to pour him a glass.

"So," Andrew began, trying to break the ice, "I hear you've had a pretty exciting day."

"You could certainly say that," I answered shyly as I got a glass down from the cupboard. "I don't think I've ever been so frightened in all my life and hope to never be again!"

"Well, I'm sorry this happened to you and your family, Jochebed," Andrew expressed thoughtfully.

"Thank you, Andrew," I replied. "I guess being robbed was the last thing I *ever* imagined would happen today!"

Andrew nodded.

"Yes," he stated kindly, seeming to understand. He went on. "Unfortunately, I'd heard there'd been a string of robberies to the north of us, but I never thought they would make it this far south. I guess maybe the scoundrels thought that with the holidays and all, fewer people would be home. Maybe they figured they could get away with it more easily." He shook his head, disgusted. "It's sad what people will do!" he relayed.

I sighed as I walked over to him.

"Well, I certainly agree with you there," I said as I handed him his lemonade.

He thanked me for the drink and took a sip.

I sat back down and contemplated.

"Life sure has a way of changing on you when you least expect it," I found myself saying. "This whole week seems to be one of those times. Just about every day has brought a new set of problems, and with each one, everything seems to get worse! I just wish I could go back and erase the whole week and start all over again!"

"I can definitely understand that," Andrew sympathized. He took another sip of his lemonade before politely inquiring. "How is your grandmother doing?" he asked.

"I'm not really sure," I explained a bit melancholy. "We got to be with her for a while at the hospital, but...well...while she was awake and *trying* to talk, she...she was really struggling. She definitely has a lot of difficult obstacles to overcome. But," I conveyed, a little more hopeful, "the doctor did seem to think that she might be able to recover in time if she works hard at it." I smiled, heartened, thinking of Gramma. "And knowing my grandmother," I went on to say with a guarantee, "she won't quit until she's one hundred percent!"

"Well, that's encouraging!" Andrew replied with a smile. "I and my family, we've been praying for all of you since we heard the news, and please know, we'll continue to. I sincerely hope your grandmother recovers very soon!"

I thanked Andrew for his concern, and he and I talked a bit longer.

Before we knew it, Isaac was back with the sheriff.

Sheriff Bradley questioned Isaac and me as to what exactly had happened with the two men who'd come to rob Grampa and Gramma, and when he finished taking our statements, he asked if he could talk to Aunt Sara as well. Regrettably, she was sleeping at the time, so, not wanting to wake her, he told us he'd just speak to her at another time.

When he completed his inquiry, he immediately apologized, saying he wasn't very optimistic that he would be able to recover much of what was stolen. He said he'd get word out to the surrounding areas, and that he'd keep his eyes and ears to the ground, but unfortunately the men who were doing this were master thieves - extremely good at their craft, and *very* elusive!

He did thank me, however, for the description of the two men that I was able to provide, having seen their faces. He told us that most of the thefts had taken place at night or when no one was home, so no one had actually ever seen them before. The fact that I had been able to give such a detailed depiction (and Isaac a partial one, of course) was definitely the break he and surrounding law men had been looking for.

As the sheriff was explaining all of this to us, Andrew got a very troubled look on his face.

"Well, does this mean that Isaac and Jochebed are at greater risk?" he queried, concerned for our safety. "I mean, you don't think the robbers would come back and try to harm them, do you?"

Isaac must have realized what sheer terror Andrew's words would strike in my heart, because he wacked Andrew across the chest as soon as the words left his lips.

It was a gesture as if to say, *Keep your mouth shut, man! Not in front of the lady!*

Andrew looked at him, scowling.

"What on earth was that for?" he questioned, affronted.

It was too late! I was already panicked! I promptly looked at Sheriff Bradley and anxiously inquired.

"You don't think they'd come back and hurt us, do you?" I wanted to know, fearful!

Sheriff Bradley shook his head.

"Nah," he assured. "Those thieves are probably long gone from here by now. They're not likely to show their faces around here again knowin' they can potentially be identified. Don't think there's any real need for concern."

For some reason, his words were less than comforting!

By the time Sheriff Bradley left, it was later in the evening and going on suppertime.

"Oh, Isaac!" I exclaimed, realizing the lateness of the hour. "You've missed your appointment with your friend!"

"Don't worry," he said. "I was able to have Grandfather send a wire to the college to let him know that I wouldn't be able to make it." He chuckled a bit. "You know," he expounded, "I guess there really is a silver lining in every dark cloud!"

"Oh?" I questioned curiously. "And what might that be?"

Isaac smiled and came close.

"I get to spend another day with you!" he answered sweetly.

I smiled back approvingly.

"Well, I guess that is *one* redeeming factor in this truly awful day!" I said, grateful for the extra time he and I would have to spend together.

*****

Thankfully, Isaac agreed to stay with Aunt Sara and me until Papa and the others got back from the hospital. Feeling safe with him there, I went to prepare supper for everyone. Before I did, however, I made sure to invite Andrew to stay with us, but he politely declined saying he really needed to get back home. I told him I understood, and thanked him for his willingness to sit with me and Aunt Sara. He assured me it was no problem, and then Isaac saw him out.

Once Andrew was gone, Isaac came back in to help me in the kitchen.

As he and I worked to get supper around, we talked back over the harrowing events of the day. As we did, I suddenly realized what I yet had to do. Dread and fear began to creep into my heart and mind.

Sensing something was bothering me, Isaac asked what was wrong.

"What is it, Jochebed?" he queried. "What's got you so upset?"

I looked at him, worried!

"What am I going to tell Papa and Grampa and Uncle Mark?" I fretted. "How can I *possibly* tell them what happened here today? It's just so awful!"

Isaac walked over and took hold of my hand, trying to calm me.

"Just tell them the truth," he told me. "That's really all you can do."

"But I feel so terrible!" I countered. "Like maybe there was something more I could have done!"

"Don't think that way, Jochebed!" Isaac gently scolded. "No one could have stopped those men from doing what they did." He paused as a smile made its way across his face. "Although," he quipped, remembering, "I have to say…your Aunt Sara sure did do a pretty good job of it!"

We both laughed as we thought of Aunt Sara wielding that shotgun and scaring the robbers off, but then I immediately thought about the aftermath, her horrible fall, and the potential danger to the baby. I quickly sobered! …And then I thought off Uncle Mark! I looked at Isaac, fearful.

"I'm really afraid of what my Uncle Mark is going to do when he finds out what Aunt Sara did," I expressed with grave concern, knowing Uncle Mark would likely not find the situation so funny. "Oh," I just knew, "he's going to be *livid!*"

"Well, hopefully not!" Isaac argued, trying to give Uncle Mark the benefit of the doubt. "Maybe he'll see the positive side of things. She did, after all, save our lives and potentially more of your grandparent's things from being taken. I think she was brave in what she did!"

"Yes," I agreed with a sigh, "but that's you and me. Uncle Mark, well…he's a different story! As you know, he and Aunt Sara aren't exactly on the best of terms right now, and I have a feeling this isn't going to help the situation any!" I paused, pensive. "I so hope I'm wrong, though!" I conveyed, still concerned.

Isaac came closer and leaned in.

"Stop worrying!" he vigorously encouraged, in a serious yet loving tone.

I sighed again, lamenting my circumstances.

"I know," I bemoaned, "but this has to be one of the *worst weeks **ever!*** Could things possibly get any worse?"

Isaac looked at me, sorry for what I'd been through.

"Sometimes I really wish I could just go away to college with you," I said, disconcerted. "I just wish I could go away and escape all of this! It just gets to be too much sometimes!"

Isaac put his arm around me, and pulled me close.

"I can appreciate that," he replied sympathetically, "but you have to remember, Jochebed, running away only brings a new set of circumstances and challenges. God will always give you the grace you need to deal with whatever you're going through…right where you're at."

"I know," I acknowledged, "but I just wish this tidal wave of trials would come to an end sometime soon!"

Isaac squeezed me tightly.

"I'm sorry you're facing all of this," he commiserated, "but somewhere in all of this, I *know* God has a purpose!"

I looked up at him and gave a reluctant smile. Again, I knew he was right, but the turmoil of everything I was going through at the moment made it very hard to accept. I sighed, feeling frustrated, and went back to work.

When Isaac and I finished preparing the meal, Isaac sat down at the table to wait while I took Aunt Sara her supper tray.

When I entered the room, she was lying on her bed, wincing in obvious pain.

Immediately, I took the tray of food and set it on the table beside her bed.

"What is it, Aunt Sara?" I anxiously questioned. "What's going on?" Clearly, something was wrong with her.

"It's nothing," she claimed. "I'm just a little sore from earlier is all."

I was naive, but not that much so!

"I *really* think you should see the doctor, Aunt Sara!" I strongly urged. "Isaac can go get him for you right now, if you'll let him."

"I'll be fine, Jochebed!" she persisted, trying to convince me. "I think I'm just a little bruised from the shotgun blast, that's all!" She paused, grimacing in pain, trying to catch her breath. "Truthfully," she shared, "I'm more concerned about what Mark is going to do to me when he finds out about all this!" She tried to sit herself up a bit. *"Ohhhhhh!"* she cried out, instantly grabbing her side in pain.

Her shriek scared me to death and sent Isaac running to the room.

"Aunt Sara, *please!*" I begged as Isaac knocked before bursting in.

"Is everything all right in here?" he asked frantically.

"Aunt Sara needs to see the doctor!" I told him insistently. "But she's still refusing!" I quickly turned back to her. *"Please,* Aunt Sara," I implored yet again, "you just *have* to let us get the doctor for you!"

Aunt Sara could barely move, and she was having a hard time breathing. I could tell she was a lot worse off than she had let on. She gingerly laid herself back down.

"Okay, all right," she relented, fighting the pain. "You can get the doctor."

I looked at Isaac, panicked.

"I'm on my way!" he said without hesitation.

Isaac left to get the doctor, and I did what I could to ease Aunt Sara's pain. She was in such discomfort!

"Aunt Sara," I asked as I carefully put another pillow under her side, "what do you think it is?"

She clenched her jaw, cringing in pain.

"I'm not sure," she admitted, "but whatever it is, it definitely got worse when I tried to sit up." She looked up at me with such dread in her eyes. "I am in *so much trouble!*" she said with certainty.

"Don't think about that right now," I tried to calm. "I'm sure everything will be fine!" Admittedly, I was less than confident in what I was telling her, but I felt I needed to try to encourage her anyway.

Aunt Sara was buying none of it, of course!

"Jochebed," she came back at me, struggling to breathe, "I know you mean well...but...let's face it...when the doctor gets here...and finds out what I did...that'll be bad enough...but Mark...when he gets home..." She gave me a look that I'll never forget. "You might as well take that pillow, and...and put it over my face now!" she jested, yet half-serious.

"Oh, Aunt Sara!" I rebuked sharply, not finding the humor in her quip. "Don't even joke like that! – It's not funny!"

She was in a lot of pain, so I tried not to deal too harshly with her.

"Really!" I expressed in consternation. "Just, *really!*"

She looked up at me as if to say, *but you know it's true!*

I sighed heavily, shaking my head in disapproval!

*****

After I got Aunt Sara situated, I sat down beside her, and we waited for Isaac to return with the doctor.

As we sat there alone in her room, however, an eerie feeling began to come over me. I couldn't help but think what had happened the last time she and I were alone in the house together. I shuddered at the thought!

Aunt Sara must have sensed what was bothering me, because without asking a thing, she tried to reassure me.

"It's all right, Jochebed," she told me, trying to allay my fears. "They're long gone from here by now."

I gave her a reluctant smile as I nodded.

"I know," I responded unenthusiastically, trying to be brave. I took a deep breath, trying to shake it off. "Would you like to try to eat something?" I encouraged. "I could help feed you if you'd like."

"No, that's all right," she declined. "Honestly, I'm hurting so badly right now...I don't even know if I could."

"All right," I accepted. "I understand."

From then on, Aunt Sara and I pretty much sat quietly waiting for Isaac and the doctor to return. It was difficult for her to talk, and I didn't want to do anything that might make things worse for her.

*****

When Isaac and Dr. Wellesley arrived, Isaac went to the kitchen to wait while Dr. Wellesley came back to the bedroom to check on Aunt Sara. What he discovered during his examination was that she had bruised a rib pretty badly during her fall. He wrapped her up the best he could, and when he finished, he inquired as to how she could have sustained such an injury.

Assuming she had accidentally fallen out of bed, or something along those lines, as you can imagine, he was completely shocked and less than thrilled when Aunt Sara finally came clean to him as to what had *actually* happened.

He looked at her circumspectly, and administered a mild reprimand.

"I suppose I can *somewhat* understand the extenuating circumstances," he permitted. "But from now on, let's leave the shooting to someone else, shall we?"

Aunt Sara nodded, agreeing.

"You were quite fortunate!" he told her. "You could have done a lot more damage. But thankfully," he went on to say, "you'll recover, and the baby seems to be doing just fine!" He shook his head, chuckling a bit. "Seems you'll have one more remarkable story to tell this child when it's born," he conveyed, still astounded by the circumstances.

"I suppose you're right, Doctor," Aunt Sara granted with a smile. "But I promise…I'll try not to shoot any more guns until *after* the baby comes, all right?"

Dr. Wellesley chuckled again as he patted her on the arm.

"Good girl!" he quipped, approvingly. He promptly began gathering his things as he gave us some further instructions.

Aunt Sara thanked him, as did I, and I walked him out.

As Dr. Wellesley and I were making our way out of the bedroom towards the family room, I thought I heard someone coming into the house. Sure enough, when we rounded the corner, there was Uncle Mark rushing towards us.

"Everything okay, Doc?" he questioned frantically, concerned.

"Yes," Dr. Wellesley assured, "Sara will be fine." He smiled with a shake of his head, still in disbelief. "But I'll let *her* tell you what happened!" he said, not offering any details. He turned to me. "I left instructions with Jochebed here, and I know Sara will be in very capable hands." He walked on towards the door. "I'll check back in in a day or two to see how Sara's getting along, but until then, see that she gets her rest." Dr. Wellesley opened the door to leave. "Take care now!" he said, "I'll talk to you soon!" With that, he left, closing the door behind him.

A soon as he was gone, Uncle Mark abruptly turned to me.

"So, what's goin' on?" he demanded to know.

A bit taken aback by his tone, and admittedly, not wanting to be the one to have to tell him, I immediately directed him to Aunt Sara.

"I really think you should ask her," I suggested.

It was clear Uncle Mark wasn't too happy with the idea.

"But I'm askin' *you*, Jochebed!" he came back at me a little perturbed. "Now tell me what happened?"

Now *I* wasn't too happy!

"Uncle Mark," I replied somewhat forcefully, "I mean no disrespect, but I don't feel it's my place. Please, just go talk to her!"

He looked at me, clearly agitated, shaking his head in aggravation. I could tell the *last thing* he wanted to do was go talk to Aunt Sara.

"So you're really not gonna tell me, huh?" he snapped angrily.

"No, sir!" I persisted, standing my ground.

Unfortunately for Uncle Mark, Papa had already come in the back door and was in the kitchen with Isaac and had overheard our conversation. Needless to say, he'd heard quite enough!

"Go talk to your wife, Mark!" he demanded gruffly as he walked into the family room, Isaac following.

The look on Papa's face was stern and quite serious. I could tell by his tone and demeanor that he was fed up with Uncle Mark and how he'd been treating Aunt Sara (and everyone else for that matter).

Uncle Mark scowled at Papa, clenching his jaw, fuming! It was obvious he didn't appreciate Papa's interference.

Despite Uncle Mark's petulance, however, Papa didn't back down one bit! He stood there glaring at him unsympathetically and resolute!

After a few tension filled moments, Uncle Mark huffed, conceding, and angrily walked off to talk with Aunt Sara.

Papa sighed and shook his head in frustration as he watched Uncle Mark leave the room. Once he was gone, however, Papa, letting his aggravation go, turned to me and Isaac and informed us that he'd already dropped Samuel off at home and that Grampa had decided to stay at the hospital with Gramma (despite he and Uncle Mark's arguing to the contrary). He said that Grampa was insistent that he stay this time, and that there was just no changing his mind.

I nodded, understanding Grampa's desire to want to be with Gramma.

"I do have some good news, though," he said with a smile. "The docs say Gramma's doin' well and that she should be able to come home on Monday!"

I smiled, excited for the news!

"They believe her stroke was a mild one," he went on to say, "and they fully expect her to make a good recovery in time."

I was so thrilled for what Papa had just told us, I almost hated to have to divulge what had happened while he was away.

Knowing I couldn't avoid the inevitable, though, I reluctantly disclosed the whole terrible ordeal to him.

"Well, I was wonderin' where Grampa's team of horses and wagon got to," Papa remarked as he came over to give me a hug. "Are ya all right, sweetheart?" he asked, concerned.

"I'm fine, Papa," I assured, sickened by the situation. "I'm just so sorry Grampa and Gramma lost their things."

"It's just stuff, Jochebed," Papa encouraged as he hugged me tighter. "You and Sara are safe, that's the important thing!"

I was so relieved that Papa understood and that he wasn't angry. Unfortunately, I couldn't say the same for Uncle Mark!

As Papa and I stood hugging, all of a sudden, we could hear Uncle Mark and Aunt Sara going at it. Their voices got angrier and louder as they yelled back and forth at each other.

"Why would ya do that, Sara?" Uncle Mark shouted. "Have ya gone and lost your mind?"

Aunt Sara shouted back.

"I was trying to save our lives, Mark!" she defended. "I'd think you could try to understand that!"

"One task!" Uncle Mark indicted, irate. "Ya had *one task! ONE! Stay in bed! That's it!* Stay in bed...and ya couldn't even do *that!"*

Aunt Sara immediately came back at him, seething, her voice fighting pain.

"Did you even hear what I said, Mark?" she argued. "I was trying..."

"Tryin' to do what, Sara?" Uncle Mark berated, stepping on her words. "Ya could have lost the baby, or...or do ya even care about that anymore?"

Aunt Sara nearly came unglued!

"Ohhhh, how ***dare*** *you!!!"* she screamed, infuriated. *"Of course,* I care about this baby!! I can't believe you just stood there and said that to me! I mean, seriously...*now who's lost their mind?!?* I've been sacrificing literally *for weeks* to protect this baby, Mark - over *two months now* to be exact!" She was rightfully incensed! *"Ohhhh,* how ***dare*** *you!!!"* she blew up at him again.

"How dare *I?"* Uncle Mark countered furiously. "How dare *you!* What if somethin' bad had happened, Sara? Then what? *Huh? Then what?"*

"But it didn't, Mark!" Aunt Sara pointed out, shouting ever more feverishly, bolstering her argument. "The baby's *fine!* The doctor said so! And thanks, by the way, for asking about me! It's so nice to see how much you care! ...Oh, that's right, I forgot, apparently, I don't *mean* that much to you anymore!"

"Oh, come on!" Uncle Mark griped. "Here we go again! This is about the property, isn't it?"

"It's *not* just about the property, Mark!" Aunt Sara argued. "You sold our lives and..."

"I *didn't* sell our lives, Sara!" Uncle Mark protested, clearly tired of the accusation. "I made a decision; a decision to move us here! What's so bad about that? *Huh?* I thought ya liked it here!"

"I do, Mark!" Aunt Sara granted. "But that's *not the point!* I...*we* had a life in North Dakota! We had the store, our church, our friends, my sister..."

"And we have family *here!"* Uncle Mark fought back.

"But, Mark..." Aunt Sara went on.

My heart sank as we all stood anguished, listening to them quarrel back and forth. Neither one seemed to be listening to the other, and nothing seemed to be getting resolved. In fact, it sounded like things were getting worse!

Isaac looked at me sympathetically as I looked at him, forlorn.

Papa, on the other hand, was fed up! He'd had all he could take!

"That's it!" he stated angrily. "It's time to put an end to this nonsense!"

He started towards the bedroom, but before he could get very far, Uncle Mark came storming out of the room, slamming the door behind him, jarring the entire house. He furiously walked down the hallway into the kitchen and out the back door.

Right away, Papa and Isaac went after him as I hastened to the bedroom to check on Aunt Sara.

When I walked into the room, she was lying in her bed, absolutely livid! Her face was beat red, and instantly, she put up her hand to stop me from saying anything.

"Jochebed," she said more furiously than I think I had ever heard her before, ***"don't!*** I won't discuss this now! *I can't!* I'm afraid if I do I might just say something I'll later regret! Please...just let me be!"

Trying to be considerate of her feelings, I decided to respect her wishes. Disappointed and discouraged, I turned to leave. As I started for the door, however, I suddenly felt compelled to say something. I turned back around to face Aunt Sara.

"Aunt Sara," I said, hoping to get through. "I know you may not want to hear this, but somewhere deep in your heart, I know you still love him, and I know he still loves you! 'Charity shall cover the multitude of sins'," I reminded her. "I know what Uncle Mark did was inconsiderate, and I know how he's handling it is wrong, but please...please, try to be the better person! Please be willing to forgive! I love you both, and it breaks my heart to see you like this. Please, Aunt Sara, please?"

With all my might, I begged her, wanting so desperately for things to be resolved between her and Uncle Mark, but as I stood there, she never looked at me once, nor answered me back.

Heartbroken, and feeling I'd done all I could do, I decided to leave her be.

Outside, Papa and Isaac were confronting Uncle Mark.

Papa yelled, incensed.

"What do ya think you're doin', Mark?" he questioned, finally understanding the rift between Uncle Mark and Aunt Sara. "Ya mean to tell me ya sold everything in North Dakota to move out here without even consultin' your *wife first!?* What in the world? What were ya thinkin'?"

"I'm thinkin' it's *none* of your business!" Uncle Mark shouted, rushing up to Papa, irate!

"Right!" Papa came back at him sarcastically, trying to keep his cool. "Ya keep tellin' me that, but the problem is ya keep makin' it my business when ya carry on like ya do in front of everybody!"

"Oh, just leave me alone!" Uncle Mark complained, dismissing the charge. "I'll deal with *my* wife when and where and *how* I see fit!!" He turned to walk away.

"No, ya won't!" Papa argued back, reaching out to grab his arm. "I don't appreciate the way you're treatin' *your* wife! It's not how things are supposed to be, Mark, *and ya know it!* Not to mention, you're settin' a *lousy* example for my children!"

Uncle Mark heatedly pulled his arm away from Papa, stepping back as Papa continued talking.

"They look up to ya, Mark," he upbraided. "It's about time ya grow up and start actin' like a man and bein' the example ya oughta be!"

Uncle Mark was *absolutely furious!* His face instantly turned red with anger as he clenched his jaw and fist. Without warning, he drew back, swung violently, and hit Papa square in the mouth.

Totally unprepared for that kind of retaliation, Papa went spinning backwards, falling to the ground - hard! Stunned, he sat there for a second, dazed by the blow. Once he'd come to his senses, he quickly shook it off, wiped blood from his lip, and scrambled to his feet. He stared at Uncle Mark, seething!

Uncle Mark put up his fists, readying himself for a fight.

Shocked by the sudden turn of events, Isaac, who'd witnessed the whole thing, started to jump in the middle of the two of them to prevent a brawl.

Papa immediately put up his hand, however, indicating he had no intentions of fighting.

Isaac stopped, stepped back, and waited and watched.

Papa shook his head, spitting blood to the ground as he glared at Uncle Mark. More than a little upset, he walked right up to him and got in his face, practically nose to nose.

"You're a fool!" he stated bluntly with tears in his eyes. "I'd give *anything* to be able to talk to my wife just one more time! And here ya stand - *arrogant*, with a wife who's *very much alive*, who loves ya, and who just wants ya to listen to her and love her!" He sniffed, his lip quivering, angry and emotional. "Ya've lost your mind!" he charged as he poked Uncle Mark in the chest. "Ya've lost your mind if ya let your pride and stubbornness get in the way of makin' this right! Don't wait, Mark!" he implored, fighting back tears. "I'm tellin' ya…do it now! Do it now before…before somethin' bad happens and…and ya don't get another chance!" Papa turned away, broken, and walked to the house.

Completely caught off guard, Uncle Mark and Isaac just stood there, unsure of what to do.

After Papa was inside, feeling a bit uncomfortable, yet feeling he should try to say something to help, Isaac turned to Uncle Mark.

"I know I don't know you very well," he began hesitantly, "but I do love your family, and…with all due respect…I believe your brother's right. You really should resolve this conflict with your wife sooner rather than later." He shook his head, conceding. "I know I'm not an authority or anything," he admitted, "after all, I've never even been married, but I do believe I know enough about the Bible to know what it says about marriage and husbands and wives, and how things should be."

He looked at Uncle Mark with all seriousness.

"You're the head of your wife, Mr. Lowry," he boldly stated. "And I don't mean to overstep, but being the head means you have to lead, and right now, from what I can see, maybe you need to be willing to lead in humility and understanding and forgiveness. I know your wife loves you, and she needs you now more than ever, *especially now* given her condition." Isaac shook his head again. "Just be willing to lead, Mr. Lowry," he encouraged. "Show your wife that you still love her and that she still matters to you!"

"But I was leadin'!" Uncle Mark argued angrily. "And she needs to respect my decisions!"

"I get that," Isaac expressed kindly, trying to be respectful, yet honest. "But the way I figure, if you lose your wife because of your unwillingness to bend, because of your arrogant need to be right, your insensitivity, your pride…then you won't *have* anyone *to* respect you! How can she respect someone who won't respect her?" He paused, contemplating, considering his words carefully. "I guess what I'm asking you to do, Mr. Lowry, is to try to see it from your wife's point of view," he said, reasoning it out, hoping Uncle Mark would understand. "I mean wow! You took her life away, everything that was familiar to her. You stole it right out from under her without a single word!"

Uncle Mark shook his head, still upset and unrelenting. It was obvious he didn't want to accept what Isaac was saying, but regardless of how he felt, he did keep quiet and continued listening.

"I realize you had all the best intensions," Isaac granted, "but, I think maybe you need to consider for a minute how your wife must feel about all of it. My understanding is you came here to help your parents move…that was all…right? Staying here permanently was *never* part of the plan."

Uncle Mark reluctantly nodded, conceding the point.

"All right, then," Isaac went on. "If you think about it, all of a sudden your wife finds herself sick and weak and stuck in a strange bed, having a baby she never thought she could have, in a place she never thought she would be." Isaac looked at him intently, sighing, feeling a bit inadequate to be offering the advice he was giving. "Again," he admitted humbly, "I realize I don't have the experience of being married yet, so again, maybe it's not my place to say anything, but…"

He paused, pulling at his chin, wondering if he should say anything more. Finally, after weighing it out, he decided, experience or no, he was going to say his piece in hopes that it might somehow help the situation.

"Mr. Lowry," he pointed out, "the way I see it, your wife is sacrificing *everything* to keep your baby safe, and she's doing it here, in unfamiliar surroundings, in a place that's not her own. I'm sure part of what sustained her in the beginning, in those really difficult days, was the knowledge that one day, after the baby arrived, she'd be able to go home - to her home! But now, suddenly, out of nowhere, she finds out that the place she called home no longer exists; that you, without consulting her, without showing her an ounce of respect by talking it over with her first, decided to take it all away!" Isaac shrugged. "I imagine in her mind she already had a room all decorated for the baby, in *her* house, in North Dakota. How do you think she feels, knowing she now has *nothing?*"

Uncle Mark's defenses seemed to be coming down a bit, his demeanor slowly changing. It seemed almost, as if, he were finally beginning to understand.

"I know you think you were right in what you did," Isaac went on to say, "but, Mr. Lowry, stop and think about what you *really* did - what you did to your wife. You took away her comfort, her security, her place of belonging, and those things are very important to a woman. Again, I know I've never been married, but I think I've observed enough and heard enough messages on the subject to have gained, at least, in my opinion, a fairly good understanding about these things." He pressed on. "I know I can't speak for your wife directly, but I imagine she would've supported, and maybe even loved and respected your decision, *if* you had respected her enough to include her in it."

Isaac paused again and thought for a minute.

"Mr. Lowry," he acknowledged, "you're right. You are the head of your family, and as the head you have the final say, but when you make decisions, especially those that don't include your wife, you need to realize that they have consequences. Again, with all due respect, if you're going to be man enough to make the decisions, then in my estimation, you need to be man enough to deal with the fallout *from* those decisions."

At first, Uncle Mark didn't say anything. He just stood there starring at Isaac, mulling everything over.

Isaac stood there, too, worried that perhaps he'd overstepped.

It was an awkward moment between the two of them, to say the least!

Thankfully, Uncle Mark finally responded.

"I appreciate what ya said," he told Isaac, his attitude seemingly humbled. "You're gonna make a great pastor someday. And a great husband, too! …Jochebed's blessed to have ya." He put his hand on Isaac's shoulder as he passed, looking him in the eye, nodding, grateful.

Isaac nodded back, relieved as Uncle Mark walked on to the house.

RECONCILIATION
(Chapter 15)

Uncle Mark opened the back door and walked inside, looking tentatively at Papa and me. We were at the table tending to Papa's split lip and both of us looked at him warily, wondering what he would do. It appeared by the look on his face that something had changed, but he quietly closed the door behind him and walked on to Aunt Sara's room without saying a word to either of us.

Papa just shook his head and sighed as I went back to trying to treat his lip.

When Uncle Mark got to Aunt Sara's bedroom, he lightly knocked on the door and went inside.

"Sara," he asked as he entered the room, "are ya awake?"

Aunt Sara was lying half-turned on her side, facing away from the door.

"What do you want?" she asked tersely, trying to sound as if she hadn't been crying.

Uncle Mark sighed, remorseful.

"I wanna talk," he replied solemnly.

"Haven't we talked enough?" she came back at him, distraught. "I don't think my heart can take any more of our talking!" Aunt Sara couldn't hold back, she broke down again, crying.

Uncle Mark lowered his head, ashamed, as he went to the side of her bed, kneeling down.

"Sara," he said regretfully. "I'm so sorry! I've handled this all so badly and...and I realize now that I...I was wrong to take everything away from ya like I did. I...." Tears began to well up in his eyes as he tried to explain. "I didn't think it would..." He stopped abruptly, realizing his mistake. "I didn't think!" he admitted honestly. He sniffed and wiped a tear, feeling horribly! "Oh, Sara!" he conveyed intensely as he put his hand on her arm, her back still to him. "I love ya *so much!* Please, just hear me out!"

Aunt Sara didn't respond.

Hurt, but determined to share his reasoning, Uncle Mark pressed on.

"I just thought," he truthfully conveyed, "I thought I was doin' what was best for us. I knew ya'd have to be here for a long time, waitin' on the baby and all, and that we'd have to be away from each other a lot durin' that time, so...so I thought if I just sold everything and moved us here then...well...then we wouldn't have to be apart." He looked up, desperate for her to believe him. "I honestly thought it would be the best thing for us, Sara!" he cried. "Honest I did!" He shook his head, worried, afraid he wasn't getting through to her. "I was so excited about bein' able to be here with ya," he told her, "that...I'll admit...it didn't even *once* cross my mind to talk to ya about it first." He was nearly pleading. "I...I just wanted to be with ya, Sara!" he stated earnestly. "Honest I did! Please, ya've gotta believe me! I did all this *for us!* ...Out of love!" He sniffed again, feeling guilty. "I guess I...I guess I never figured on...on how it'd affect you!" he admitted

He buried his face in his hands, crying, leaning on the bed there beside Aunt Sara.

"I'm so sorry, Sara!" he wept. "Can ya ever forgive me?"

Feeling guilty herself, tears streaming down her face, Aunt Sara tried to turn, putting her hand on Uncle Mark's back in a consoling way.

He looked up at her, broken.

"I never should've yelled at ya," he went on to say, "and I'm sorry. I let my pride get in the way, and…" He shook his head in tears. "I'm so sorry, Sara!" he apologized. "Ya didn't deserve that!"

At this point, Aunt Sara could barely speak; she was so overcome by emotion.

"Mark, I…" she sniffed and stammered, "I…I'm sorry, too! I love you *so much*, and I…I *do* forgive you!" She wiped a tear. "Will you," she asked, just as desperate as he, "will you forgive me?"

Uncle Mark furrowed his brow, shaking his head vigorously.

"Sara," he stated emphatically, "there's nothin' to forgive! This was my fault from the beginnin' and mine alone! Ya had *every right* to be angry with me for what I did and how I treated ya! I see that now. …Ya did nothin' wrong!" He wiped her tears as he lovingly looked into her eyes. "I know that what I did, it…it hurt ya so much," he confessed, "but…I promise ya, Sara…if you'll let me…somehow…someway, I'm gonna make this up to ya! I will!" He fought back tears as he mustered a reluctant smile. "I know I can't get our life back in North Dakota," he acknowledged, "but…but I promise ya…I'll do *everything* I can to make the best life for us here…you…me…*and the baby!*"

Aunt Sara smiled approvingly as she wiped her tears…tears that were now tears of joy. She put her hand to Uncle Mark's face.

"I love you so much!" she expressed affectionately. "As long as I'm with you…that's all that matters!"

Uncle Mark gathered Aunt Sara in his arms and hugged her tightly as they kissed, so grateful they had finally talked and worked things out.

After holding each other for several minutes, Uncle Mark leaned back and looked at her intently.

"There's somethin' I really need to do," he said with urgency in his voice as he slowly stood to his feet. "I'll be right back, okay?"

Aunt Sara nodded, accepting, seeming to understand.

Feeling the need to apologize, Uncle Mark promptly left the room and headed to the kitchen.

By now, Papa's bleeding had stopped, and he and I were sitting at the kitchen table together having a cup of coffee.

Papa briefly glanced up when Uncle Mark walked into the room, but immediately looked back down, staring into his cup.

"So?" he questioned gruffly as Uncle Mark made his way over to him.

Uncle Mark looked at me, woeful; it was obvious he'd been crying, but honestly, I didn't know what to make of it. I quickly looked away, feeling badly, and admittedly a bit angry for everything that had transpired.

Turning his attention back to Papa, he took a deep breath and revealed what had happened between him and Aunt Sara.

"Sara and I," he told us, "we…we worked things out."

"Good!" Papa replied abruptly, not looking up from his coffee.

Uncle Mark took another deep breath, feeling terrible for what he'd done, and embarrassed and ashamed for how he'd been acting. After a long, uncomfortable silence, he cleared his throat, nervously mustering the courage to speak.

"I owe ya an apology, Michael," he finally admitted. "I shouldn't have hit ya, and…I'm sorry. I let my anger get the best of me, and I know it was wrong and…and I'm sorry! And Jochebed…Michael," he went on to say, "I owe ya both an apology for the way I've been actin' lately. I was stubborn and pigheaded, and…I was wrong. …Forgive me?"

Papa sighed as he looked up at Uncle Mark, slowly shaking his head.

"You're forgiven," he assured. "Just don't let it happen again!"

He graciously extended his hand to Uncle Mark in a gesture of forgiveness, but when he did, Uncle Mark took hold and pulled Papa right up out of his seat and into an embrace.

"I love ya, big brother!" he expressed sincerely, patting him on the back.

"I love ya, too, ya big brute!" Papa teased, smiling.

We all laughed at the retort.

"I could've taken ya if I'd a wanted to!" Papa claimed with confidence, half-smiling, looking Uncle Mark in the eye.

"Yah, I don't think so, ya old man!" Uncle Mark teased back.

We all laughed again, but then Papa got quite serious.

"I'm really glad you and Sara got things right," he said. "Ya had us all a little worried."

"Me, too," Uncle Mark agreed. "But it's all good!!" He looked over at me again. "Jochebed," he conveyed, feeling badly, "I also need to apologize to ya for…well…for lettin' ya get stuck in the middle of all this. I should've seen what it was doin' to ya, and…I'm really sorry!" He sighed, clearly upset with himself. "I guess you're pretty disappointed in your ol' Uncle Mark, aren't ya?" he questioned, concerned.

I shook my head, smiling.

"No, Uncle Mark!" I assured him. "I'm just thankful you and Aunt Sara are all right!"

He smiled, agreeing.

"I am, too," he replied, relieved. He looked around, bewildered. "Hey," he queried, "where's that fella of yours, Isaac? I need to apologize to him, too."

I furrowed my brow.

"I'm actually not sure," I answered, a little perplexed. "He must have gone on home. He never came back inside after you two talked."

"Well," Uncle Mark advocated, "I have to say ya have a good man there, Jochebed. Ya need to hang on to that one, ya hear?"

I blushed at his comment.

"Yes, sir, Uncle Mark," I replied demurely. "I plan to!" I glanced over at Papa, and thankfully, he smiled back.

"Well, come on, sweetheart," Papa urged, "this old man needs to get to bed, and so do you. Sunday sunrise is gonna come mighty early! Sure hope, Sam's asleep by now."

I looked at him, doubtful.

"It's Samuel, Papa!" I quipped as I stood up, gathering the coffee cups.

Papa smirked, nodding, conceding the point.

I went and put the coffee cups in the sink, and before I went to gather my things, I walked over and gave Uncle Mark a big hug.

"Please, tell Aunt Sara I said goodnight," I requested. "And please let her know I'll be by to see her tomorrow after church, all right?"

"I sure will," Uncle Mark promised. "We'll see ya then!"

Papa hugged Uncle Mark again and we said goodnight.

*****

As Papa and I were heading home, I decided to talk to him about something that had been weighing heavy on my mind.

"Papa," I asked nervously, "is…is everything all right between us?"

Papa frowned as he looked over at me, more than a little confused.

"As far as I know it is, sweetheart," he answered. "Why do ya ask?"

"Well," I hesitated, "I guess after everything that's happened over the last few days, I just wanted to make sure you and I were okay. We haven't had a chance to talk much, and I know I was late that day getting back when Gramma had her stroke, and I…"

Papa stopped me midsentence.

"Jochebed!" he stated emphatically. "I don't blame ya for that if that's what you're thinkin'! No one's to blame! It just happened!"

I pressed my point.

"But if I had been there!" I argued. "Then maybe…maybe I could have seen something! …Maybe I would've found her sooner!"

Papa slowed the wagon, bringing it to a stop. Looking at me directly, he told me in no uncertain terms.

"Don't do that to yourself, Jochebed!" he insisted ardently. "Ya bein' there wouldn't have changed a thing! The doctor was quite clear that oftentimes there's subtle signs before a stroke that no one ever notices. This was gonna happen to your gramma *regardless* of who was or wasn't there! And as to findin' her sooner," Papa pointed out, "Jochebed, Mr. Peters said he and Mrs. Peters were walkin' into the kitchen right as she fell. I don't think even you bein' there could've been any sooner than that. God had the Peterses leavin' at just the right time, sweetheart, and He's in control, even of all the little details. And look," he continued. "There's plenty of positives: Gramma's alive, she's strong, and she gets to come home day after tomorrow!" He smiled, rejoicing. "I mean, we've gotta give glory where glories due," he said, amazed and thankful. "Praise God her stroke was a mild one! And I have *every confidence*," he added, "knowin' my ma, she's not gonna rest 'til she's up managin' everybody and everything!"

He gently lifted my chin.

"I love ya, Jochebed!" he told me without hesitation. "And me and you… we're just fine…all right?"

I smiled, appreciative and very relieved.

"I love you, too, Papa!" I echoed. "And thank you!"

SAYING GOODBYE
(Chapter 16)

The next day was Sunday, and I was looking forward to seeing Isaac again, but I was dreading him having to go back to college. I couldn't wait for Christmas break to arrive so that we could have several weeks to spend together.

When we got to church, I immediately looked around for him, and spotting his grandparents' carriage, I knew he was likely already inside.

Sure enough, when I walked in, he was waiting for me in the narthex.

"Good morning," I said as I walked up to him. "What happened to you last night? You just disappeared."

Isaac looked a little somber as he explained.

"After everything that happened," he told me, "I guess I just felt like your family needed time to be alone...time to talk and work things out. I didn't want to intrude any more than I already had, and...well..." He looked at me, sorry. "I'm afraid I may have overstepped in talking with your Uncle Mark. I said some pretty harsh things to him. Anyway, I knew I'd see you today, so I decided to go on home." He paused, looking somewhat anxious. "I'm almost afraid to ask," he admitted, "but...how did things go after I left?"

"Really well!" I informed him enthusiastically. "And you didn't overstep at all. Whatever you said to Uncle Mark, Isaac, it worked! He and Aunt Sara reconciled, and then Uncle Mark came and made things right with Papa and me. He even said he wanted to apologize to you, but...you'd already gone."

Isaac looked surprised.

"Me?" he questioned. "I'm not quite sure why he'd feel the need to apologize to me; I mean...if anybody needs to apologize, I feel like I do! Regardless, though," he went on to say, "I am glad to hear that things are better for you and your family."

I nodded, smiling, wholeheartedly agreeing.

He smiled back, amazed.

"God sure is good!" he stated with conviction. "He really does work miracles!"

"I know!" I expressed, grateful. "But," I lamented, "I sure wish He'd work a miracle right now!"

Isaac furrowed his brow not understanding.

I looked up at him, smiling all dreamy like.

"I wish He'd work a miracle so that you wouldn't have to leave," I said bashfully.

Isaac grinned.

"Now that's a miracle I'd *love* to see happen!" he heartily approved.

We left off talking, and walked into church together, deciding to sit with Naomi and her family close to the front of the church. Before the service started, we were able to have a brief but nice visit with them, and when the service ended, we talked a bit more before Isaac and I decided to leave.

As we were heading out, Papa came over to us and informed us that he was going to find Samuel, and once he did, they were leaving directly to go to the hospital to visit with Gramma and to pick up Grampa. He asked me if I wanted to go with them, but I told him that I had planned to spend some time with Isaac before he had to leave for college, and then I was going to go sit with Aunt Sara for awhile. I did, however, offer to go along if he needed me to.

He just smiled and kissed me on the forehead.

"Enjoy your time together, sweetheart," he said. "We'll see ya when we get back."

I thanked him, told him to be careful, and we parted ways.

Isaac promptly invited me to go with him to his house for lunch, and I, of course, happily accepted the invitation!

Giddy and exuberant, I couldn't wait! It would be the first time going to the Lewis' home alone without Papa and Mama and Samuel. We'd been there together as a family before (the Lewises had hosted a church picnic that we had attended), but it had been almost a year since the event, and I'd not been back since.

As you can imagine, it was thrilling riding with Isaac and his grandparents back to their house. Sometimes being with him, I still had to pinch myself to make sure I wasn't dreaming! I had fantasized of being with him for so long; sometimes it just didn't seem real!

It was a beautiful, sunny, unusually warm day for late November, and Isaac took full advantage of the nice weather. When we got to the Lewis' house, he took my hand immediately and whisked me away on a walk before I could even offer my help in the kitchen.

"Isaac!" I worried, a little embarrassed as I stopped in my tracts, pulling my hand away. "Don't you think I should help with the meal? After all, I don't want your family to think badly of me!"

"Oh, stop fretting!" Isaac insisted, scolding me a bit. "Grandmother was young once, too! Besides, I happen to know that Isabelle and Andrew are coming today, and they said they'd take care of all the preparations."

"You're sure?" I questioned, hesitant.

"I'm positive!" he assured, smiling. "Now stop worrying! I already told them I planned to have you all to myself today!"

"Oh, Isaac!" I blushed, still wavering. "I'll go…but…only if you're *certain!*"

"I am!" he persisted, grinning wildly, taking hold of my hand once again. "Now come on!"

With that, we were off on our walk!

*****

We had such a lovely time together, he and I. We talked about all sorts of things: likes and dislikes, pet peeves, favorite things, and future plans. I couldn't have asked for a lovelier day together! Time, however, seemed to fly by all too quickly, but then again, I'd noticed being alone with Isaac seemed to have that effect!

Needing to get back for the noon meal, he and I hurried to his house and when we arrived, we enjoyed a lovely dinner with his grandparents, and Andrew and Isabelle, engaging in wonderful conversation. It was a delight to see Isaac interacting with his family, and it was nice to get to know them a little better, too.

Andrew and Isabelle talked about their plans for their upcoming nuptials, and I could tell they were very much in love and very much looking forward to being married.

Mr. and Mrs. Lewis kindly asked about Grampa and Gramma, and told me they planned to visit as soon as Gramma was home.

Before I knew it, it was going on three o'clock, and I needed to get back to help Uncle Mark with Aunt Sara. Unfortunately, it was also time for Isaac to go back to college as well.

I thanked the Lewises for their hospitality, and they said they were pleased to have me, and that they were looking forward to me coming back.

When we'd said our goodbyes, Isaac borrowed their horse and buggy and took me back to Grampa and Gramma's.

As we drove, I couldn't help but be thankful! It had been such an amazing, enjoyable day, absolutely perfect! I so wished it didn't have to come to an end!

At Grampa and Gramma's, Isaac came inside with me to say hello and goodbye to Uncle Mark and Aunt Sara, and when he did, Uncle Mark took the occasion to apologize to him for his poor testimony and behavior the night before. Isaac explained that it really wasn't necessary, but he graciously accepted the apology, nonetheless.

Still feeling a little guilty himself, though, Isaac too, apologized to Uncle Mark, saying again he hoped he hadn't overstepped in how he'd addressed him.

Wanting to put his mind at ease, Uncle Mark assured him that he hadn't.

"In truth," he told him, "I'm glad ya said what ya did. I needed to be reminded!"

With the issue settled between them, we all talked for a few minutes longer, before Isaac said he really needed to get going. He had some last-minute things to attend to at home before leaving for school, and he felt he should get to them before it got to be too late.

I reluctantly walked him out.

"This is the part I absolutely hate!" Isaac bemoaned as he took my hands and looked longingly into my eyes. "Leaving you behind is getting harder and harder! I already can't wait to see you again!"

I looked back into his beautiful blue eyes.

"I know," I agreed, feeling miserable at the thought of his departure. "I can feel my heart aching already! These next couple weeks can't pass soon enough!"

Isaac smiled, expectantly.

"I can't wait for your first letter!" he said sincerely.

"I'll be sure to write the first chance I get!" I assured. "I promise! And please, promise me you'll be safe going back and that you'll write to me, too, just as soon as you can!"

Isaac pulled me close.

"I promise," he replied sweetly.

He hugged me tightly and told me that he'd miss me terribly, and I echoed the same.

"I'll be praying for you and your family," he said with earnest. "Please keep me informed as to how everyone's doing."

Again, I assured him that I would, we said a quick prayer together, and hugged one last time.

Smiling warmly, Isaac walked to his buggy, climbed aboard, and waved goodbye as he took off for home.

I stood there, heartbroken, waving back, trying to hold in my tears. It was so hard watching him go! Nevertheless, knowing I had to move forward with him gone, as soon as he disappeared out of sight, I wiped my tears, composed myself the best I could, and walked back inside the house.

Just as I was closing the door behind me, Uncle Mark walked into the family room.

"He really is the cream of the crop, Jochebed," he complimented. "Ya have a great fella there!" He paused as he got a mischievous smirk on his face. "So when's the weddin'?" he asked.

"Uncle Mark!" I exclaimed, completely embarrassed. "We've just started courting for goodness' sake!"

He chuckled, tickled at my reaction.

"I know," he said, grinning from ear to ear. "I'm just teasin' with ya! But honestly," he went on to say much more seriously, "I can tell ya two have somethin' real special."

I looked down bashfully, embarrassed by the comment.

"Well, thank you, Uncle Mark," I replied demurely. "I like to think so, too." I walked over and gave him a hug and a kiss on the cheek.

Uncle Mark looked down at me as he hugged me back.

"And, Jochebed," he said kindly, "Isaac's a blessed fella as well!"

I just smiled, appreciative, and walked on into the kitchen.

*****

The rest of the afternoon seemed to fly by as I helped Uncle Mark with Aunt Sara. She was still in so much pain from her bruised rib; simply trying to sit up or lie down in bed seemed an immense chore. I helped feed her an early dinner and cleaned up her room a bit for her, but by the time I finished with all that, it was time for me to get ready for the evening service.

Just about the time I was ready to leave to go back home, however, Papa, Grampa, and Samuel came driving up to the house.

Uncle Mark and I ran out to greet them.

"How's Ma doin'?" Uncle Mark asked anxiously as we walked out onto the porch.

"Better!" Grampa relayed wearily as he got down off the wagon.

I could tell from his demeanor that the last few days had taken quite a toll on him.

He came up onto the porch and gave me a big hug and as soon as he did, he looked over at Uncle Mark. The look on his face was one of concern and noticeable displeasure.

"I hope things have come to a resolution here, Son," he stated sternly, looking him right in the eye.

Uncle Mark replied, embarrassed and feeling guilty.

"They have, Pa," he assured. "And I'm sorry it took me so long to come around."

Grampa firmly took hold of Uncle Mark's hand and pulled him in close.

"Me and your ma raised ya better than that, Mark," he told him. "I trust it won't happen again!"

"It won't, Pa!" Uncle Mark answered back, almost as if he were a little boy again. "I've learned a valuable lesson, and I intend to do better!"

"Good!" Grampa replied, relieved. "All's forgiven!"

They hugged, and we all went back inside.

Papa helped get Grampa settled a bit, and then he and I and Samuel all left to go back home. Papa wanted to check on some things before we headed to church, and I still wanted to freshen up a bit.

When we got home, Papa went straight to the barn, and Samuel and I went to the house.

"Hey, little brother," I commented as we walked inside, trying to engage him in conversation. "You haven't said much since you and Papa got back from the hospital. Is everything all right?"

Samuel didn't really answer. He just grunted and shrugged his shoulders.

"Samuel!" I called out again, trying to get his attention as he kept on walking.

He rudely ignored me and went on upstairs.

I have to admit his behavior troubled me. He still seemed quite angry and not at all himself. I followed right behind him up the stairs, but he never once acknowledged that I was there.

When he reached the top of the steps, he walked straight to his room, went inside, and abruptly slammed the door behind him.

Needless to say, I paused, disheartened and concerned.

Unsure of what to do, I proceeded on to my bedroom, hesitating at the door.

Should I go talk to him? I wondered. I stood there, troubled, contemplating what to do. Finally, after debating with myself, I decided that I should, at least, try. I went to his door and quietly knocked.

"Samuel," I requested softly, "may I come in?"

"Go away and leave me alone!" he barked. "I don't wanna talk to ya!"

I was a bit taken aback by his response, but I persisted.

"Samuel, please," I implored, "I just want to talk!"

I could hear Samuel coming towards the door, so I waited. Suddenly, he threw the door open and shouted directly in my face.

"What about 'go away' don't ya understand!?!" he yelled, irate.

I stood there, completely stunned by his actions, but he didn't seem to care one bit! He proceeded to slam the door right in my face.

Now, I was furious! He was *not* going to talk to me like that, nor treat me that way! Immediately, I vigorously started pounding on the door, screaming loudly.

"Samuel, you let me in right now!" I insisted heatedly.

I could feel his strong resistance as he leaned against the door, trying to prevent me from getting inside.

I kept on pushing as hard as I could, trying to open the door.

"Samuel!" I demanded. "Stop this right now and let me in!"

"No!" he shouted back angrily, still resisting with all his might.

"Yes!" I yelled back adamantly, still leaning hard against the door.

I was just about to say something else to him when, all of a sudden, the door gave way, and I went hurling through the bedroom like a freight train! Propelled by the force of my pushing, I couldn't stop my momentum! I summarily went crashing into the dresser on the other side of the room, bounced off, stumbled backwards, and finally fell to the floor with a thud, landing hard on my backside.

Samuel, not caring a wit, just stood there with his arms crossed, staring at me, perturbed!

"Serves ya right!" he quipped tersely. "Next time maybe you'll leave me alone!"

He left the room and slammed the door behind him as I sat there flustered, trying to collect my thoughts. I felt about to see if I was hurt and noticed a small gash on my arm from where I had hit the dresser. It was bleeding a little, but my concerns were more for Samuel than for myself. I took a deep breath, shook off what had just happened, and stood to my feet. When I got up and tried to walk, I immediately noticed my leg was sore, but I hobbled to the door and opened it up, nonetheless. When I peered out into the hallway, Samuel had already gone, and Papa was just coming up the stairs.

"What are ya doin' in there?" Papa asked a bit puzzled.

I proceeded to limp on out of the room.

"What on earth happened to ya?" Papa questioned, concerned, as he came over to me. "Gracious, child, are ya all right?"

"I'm fine, Papa," I assured him, covering the cut on my arm, trying to stop the bleeding.

"Well, it doesn't look like you're fine!" he disagreed, taking hold of my arm. "What's goin' on here?" He helped lead me down to the wash room to help bandage me up.

"It's Samuel, Papa," I said with a sigh.

"What?" Papa exploded, quite upset. "Samuel did this to ya?"

"No, no!" I answered quickly. "I mean…not really!"

Papa furrowed his brow, looking at me suspiciously.

I sighed again and tried to explain.

"Truth is," I confessed, "it was just as much my fault as it was his. I was trying to get into his room to talk to him." I grimaced as Papa applied the rag he'd wet to my arm. "Something's not right with him, Papa," I expressed with angst. "I really think you should talk to him."

"Talk to him about what, Jochebed?" Papa wanted to know.

I winced in pain as he began to wipe the blood away.

"I…I think he's still angry about everything," I told him, watching anxiously as he kept rubbing. I cringed in pain as he wiped across the cut, obviously not realizing the amount of pressure he was applying. Not able to take it anymore, I abruptly grabbed the rag from his hand. "Thank you!" I said kindly. "But if it's all the same to you, I can take over from here."

"Oh, all right!" Papa agreed.

I went on to share my concerns as I cleaned my wound.

"I can't say for sure that that's what's bothering him, Papa," I admitted, "but if I had to guess, I'd say that that's what it is. He just needs some attention, I think."

"All right," Papa reluctantly granted. "I'll talk to him. You're sure ya don't need any more help here?"

"No, Papa," I quickly replied. "I've got it! I'll clean up and get ready to go."

Papa nodded and went to find Samuel.

*****

Papa looked around all over the place: in the house, outside - *everywhere*, calling and searching for Samuel. When he got no response, he came scrambling back into the house.

"Jochebed!" he yelled up the stairs, less than thrilled that he hadn't found Samuel yet. "Is Samuel up there with you?"

I promptly walked to the top of the stairs and called back down to him.

"No, Papa," I replied. "I'm sorry, I haven't seen him."

I could tell Papa was angry, yet a little worried.

"Isn't he outside?" I asked as I hurried down the stairs a little concerned myself at this point.

"Not that I could find him," Papa told me with a troubled look on his face. He shook his head as he pulled at his chin. "Where on earth could that boy be?" he questioned. "He *knows better* than to just run off like this!"

"Well, maybe he headed back over to Grampa and Gramma's," I suggested, trying to be of help.

Papa nodded.

"Yah, you're probably right," he conceded with a sigh, clearly upset with the situation. "I'll head over there right now. Ya stay here, though, in case he comes back, all right?"

"Yes, Papa," I agreed. "I'll wait here."

Papa shook his head in disgust as he started to leave.

"If that boy makes us late for church," I heard him grumble as he headed out the door, "I'm gonna tan his hide!"

THE BLIZZARD
(Chapter 17)

I stood there, my mind racing, trying not to worry.

Where could Samuel be? I thought to myself. *It's not like him to just run off!* I tried not to let my worry run away with me, but admittedly it was hard.

Hoping to keep my mind off of things, I proceeded back upstairs to finish getting ready for church. I thought perhaps if I kept myself busy, I wouldn't fret as much. Regrettably, it didn't really work, though, as I couldn't shake the feeling that something was dreadfully wrong. It was getting darker, and with each passing minute, I could hear the wind picking up outside as it swirled around, causing the trees to scrape up against the side of the house. Needless to say, it only added to my concern!

"Oh, Jochebed!" I told myself, trying to calm my nerves. "Stop worrying so! I'm sure Samuel's safe and sound at Grampa and Gramma's!"

I finished getting ready and headed downstairs to wait in the kitchen for Papa and Samuel to arrive. By the time I got there, however, the wind was howling terribly, and I could see out the kitchen window that snow was just starting to fall.

"My!" I quipped. "How *quickly* the weather does change this time of year!"

I fidgeted a bit and straightened up a bit and sat a bit and paced a bit, and then I sat some more. I kept glancing at the clock on the wall and going to the window to look out, but every time I did, there was *nothing,* just blackness, and wind, and more snow!

Surely, I fretted, *Papa should be back by **now!***

I tried to reassure myself that he was probably just talking with Samuel at Grampa and Gramma's, reprimanding him for running off, and that they'd be back any minute, but as I sat there anxiously waiting, the minutes only seemed to tick away faster and faster, and still, there was no Papa or Samuel! As you can imagine, with each passing minute, my worry began to grow exponentially!

Suddenly, there was a big gust of wind, and my heart sank! Rushing to the window yet again and peering out, there was no doubt a snowstorm was blowing in.

After about an hour of waiting, *way past* the time to make it to church, I decided I couldn't wait any longer! The not knowing was killing me and I had to go see what was going on! Against Papa's wishes, I gathered my winter shawl and started over to Grampa and Gramma's.

As soon as I left the house, though, I was immediately struck by the drastic change in the temperature. What had been an unusually warm day for November had rapidly turned into a very cold, blustery, snowy night. Instantly chilled, I decided to go back inside to grab my winter coat and gloves. My shawl simply wouldn't do on this chilly, stormy night!

Being in a hurry, I quickly grabbed my things and put them on as I went. I bundled up as tightly as I could, but the farther away I got from the house, the more the cold began to affect me. The wind and the snow kept pelting me in my face, and I was already chilled to the bone! While I was very thankful I had changed into my winter coat and gloves (as they were helping a little), I was definitely beginning to regret that I'd not taken the time to change from my bonnet to my winter hat. My head and ears were freezing!

As I hastened along in the bitter cold, the thought of Papa and Samuel possibly being out in this gathering storm made me hurry and worry all the more!

"Oh, please let them be there! Please let them be there!" I kept praying over and over again.

As I got closer to Grampa and Gramma's, not seeing Papa's wagon, I began to lose hope! I knew I hadn't passed him on the way, so likely that meant he was off somewhere else.

I quickly ran towards the porch, but as I got closer, I noticed the house seemed unusually dark. I scurried up the steps to the front door to go inside to see if maybe Grampa was just napping or something, but curiously, the door was locked. Remembering where Grampa and Gramma kept their hidden key, I went to get it and unlocked the door.

When I entered the house, much to my surprise, no one was in the family room. Thinking perhaps they might be in the kitchen, I ran to look in there. It was dark, and I didn't hold out much hope, but I thought I'd better check, nonetheless. When I got to the kitchen, however, sure enough, my suspicions were confirmed. No one was in there either! Hoping that maybe someone might be outside by the barn or something, I rushed to the back window to look out. Again, no one was there!

Starting to feel miserably alone, I quickly turned and ran down the hallway towards Aunt Sara's room.

She, at least, had better be here, I kept thinking to myself the whole way there, *or I'm in trouble!* I knocked and opened the door all at the same time, frantic to talk to someone!

Startled, Aunt Sara immediately turned to look at me, her hand instinctively reaching for the shotgun that was leaning up against her bed.

"Oh, good grief, Jochebed!" she said, putting her hand to her chest. "You nearly scared me to death!"

I could tell that the sudden turning had caused her great discomfort. She put her hand to her side, grimacing in pain, holding it gingerly, trying to catch her breath.

"I'm so sorry, Aunt Sara!" I apologized still in a panic. "I didn't mean to scare you, but Papa never came back for me! What's going on? Did he find Samuel? Where is everyone?"

Aunt Sara shook her head, confused.

"Wait a minute, slow down. What are you talking about?" she questioned.

"Papa," I clarified, "didn't he come here looking for Samuel? Awhile ago, didn't he come?"

Aunt Sara shook her head again.

"Jochebed, I'm sorry," she told me, "I've been asleep. Your Grampa and Uncle Mark left for church well over an hour ago, and I've not seen your father or Samuel."

"What!?" I exclaimed fretfully. "You mean Papa never came?"

"Jochebed, sweetheart, you're not hearing me!" Aunt Sara insisted, trying to get me to calm down and listen. "I've been asleep! I persuaded your Uncle Mark to take Papa Lowry to church this evening, and after much cajoling, he eventually acquiesced. I knew I was tired and would likely sleep the night, so I convinced him that I'd be all right here alone for the short time they'd be away. If your Papa and Samuel were here, sweetie, I'm sorry, I never heard nor saw them!"

I stood there shaking my head, bewildered and disheartened.

Aunt Sara sensed I was troubled.

"Jochebed," she queried, "I don't quite understand. Why would Samuel and your father have come here tonight anyhow? I thought you all were going to church."

I looked at her beleaguered.

"Oh, Aunt Sara!" I explained, almost in tears at this point, completely beside myself with worry. "I'm afraid something awful's happened! Samuel's run away, and Papa went looking for him! We thought maybe he came here, but...now... Oh, Aunt Sara!" I went and collapsed by her bed, sobbing into her lap.

She put her hand on my head, trying to console me.

"There, there!" she comforted. "I'm sure everything will be all right." As she tried to get me to calm down, she inquired again. "Now, let me get this straight," she questioned. "Samuel ran away and your father went looking for him, that much I understand, but...why would Samuel run away in the first place?"

I managed to get my crying under control and explained *everything* that had happened with Samuel since Gramma's stroke.

"I'm so sorry, Jochebed," Aunt Sara expressed with concern. "I wasn't aware that things had gotten so bad." Seeing everything more clearly now, and growing concerned herself, she prodded me to think. "Is there anywhere he likes to go when he just wants to be alone?" she asked. "It's possible he could have gone there!"

I wiped my tears as I sat back to answer her.

"That's just it!" I bemoaned, quite frustrated with myself. "I've tried and tried to think of somewhere he could have gone, but nowhere...*nowhere* comes to mind!"

"Now there has to be *someplace!*" Aunt Sara insisted. *"Think!"*

I sat there trying to rack my brain.

"Well...there is *one place* he might go," I divulged, "but..." I hesitated.

"Well, where Jochebed?" Aunt Sara pressed. "Where would he go?"

I looked at her uncertain.

"Maybe...maybe to Mama's grave?" I suggested.

All of a sudden, a big gust of wind kicked up outside, whistling through the cracks in the house.

"*All the way out there*, on this cold and windy night?" Aunt Sara exclaimed, distressed. "Why...he'd freeze to death!"

"Well, I don't know that that's where he went for sure!" I defended. "It's just a guess! But, honestly, it's the only place I can think of where he might go to think and be by himself!"

"Well, would your father know to look there?" Aunt Sara questioned.

I shook my head tentatively.

"That's just it," I told her, "I really don't know! He might, but it's doubtful."

Aunt Sara looked at me anxiously.

"Then I think it's worth a look!" she urged. "I'd say to wait for your Uncle Mark and Grampa to get home, but from the sound of that wind..." She paused as she looked towards the window, clearly concerned. "If he *is* out there all by himself," she worried, "then he needs to get home and get warm right away!"

I knew she was right, but I wasn't sure what I should do.

"Oh, I wish I knew where Papa was!" I fretted. "Do you think it'd be okay for me to go all the way out there by myself?"

Aunt Sara seemed ambivalent as she sat there weighing the situation, her face filled with angst. Sighing heavily, she looked up at me.

"I hate to say for sure not knowing the conditions out there," she admitted. "I mean…it does sound like it's getting worse, but…" She shook her head, frustrated. "Oh, I don't know!" she said warily. "How did things seem when you were walking over here?"

"Well," I revealed, trying to be honest yet trying not to make things sound too terribly bad, "the wind *was* blowing pretty hard, but it was *just* starting to snow so…if I had to say…I'm fairly certain I could make it out to Mama's grave to check for Samuel and be back before things get *too* bad." At this point, I was simply trying to reassure Aunt Sara and admittedly convince myself that things would be fine.

Aunt Sara looked uneasy and more than a little hesitant.

"Oh, Jochebed," she lamented, still unsure, "I just don't know!"

It seemed to me she was rethinking her suggestion to have me go look for Samuel.

"Your brother does need to be found before it gets too bad out there," she concluded. "But…I just don't want anything bad to happen to you in the process of trying to find him!" She looked at me, troubled. "Maybe he'll make it back on his own!" she offered, hopeful.

I looked at her dubiously.

Aunt Sara sighed, becoming more and more agitated.

"How I wish I weren't confined to this blasted bed!" she protested angrily. "If I weren't, I'd go out there myself!"

Clearly, Aunt Sara going was out of the question, and even though the thought of venturing out into the dark, cold, snowy night on my own was worrisome and not at all appealing, deep down I knew the responsibility fell to me. It would be some time yet before Uncle Mark and Grampa would arrive home from church, and I had absolutely *no idea* where Papa was or when he'd be back. If Samuel *was* out there on his own, contemplating who knows what, I needed to go find him and bring him home, after all, the alternative just wasn't acceptable! The thought of him being out in the gathering storm all by himself, possibly freezing to death, was more than I could bear!

As much as it made me nervous to go, and even though I wasn't at all certain he'd be out there, I knew for Samuel's sake, I needed to, at least, try. I nodded, bolstering myself, determined to put my fears aside and go help find him!

"I'll go!" I said resolutely as I stood to my feet, a sudden burst of confidence welling up inside of me.

"Jochebed, are you sure?" Aunt Sara questioned, looking at me apprehensively.

"Yes!" I replied with resolve. "I'll do it! I'll go!"

Just then, the storm blew a branch up against the side of the house, causing a big thud.

"Oh, I don't know about this, Jochebed!" Aunt Sara worried. "Maybe you shouldn't go! I mean, now that I hear the fierceness of that wind, maybe you *should* wait for your Uncle Mark!"

I clenched my fists, settled.

"No!" I insisted. "There's just no time to wait! It's getting later and darker and worse out there by the minute, and if I'm going to go, I should go now!" I looked at her intently, trying to assure her. "Everything will be all right, Aunt Sara," I said. "Mama's graves not *that far*. Hopefully, Samuel will be there, and this will all be over soon!"

Aunt Sara was more than a little reluctant, but she eventually agreed.

"All right," she relented. "But please, please be careful, Jochebed! I'd never forgive myself if something bad happened to you!"

I leaned over and gave her a hug.

"Samuel needs to be found," I reminded, trying to persuade her that my mission was justified, "and if I can help do that, then I will!" I stood back up. "I'll be fine!" I reassured, trying to allay any fears (admittedly, hers *and* mine). "I'll be back as soon as I can!"

Aunt Sara looked at me anxiously as I started to leave the room.

I smiled back, blew her a kiss, and closed the door behind me.

"I'll be praying!" Aunt Sara yelled out as I hastened down the hallway towards the kitchen. "Please hurry back! And please...please be careful!"

I quickly found a lantern next to the back door, lit it, and headed outside.

Immediately upon opening the door, the wind and snow and cold nearly took my breath away!

"I can do this!" I told myself, trying to muster my courage. "I have to find Samuel!" I grabbed my bonnet strings, holding them tightly under my chin, closed the door behind me, and headed out into the blustery night.

The wind was howling and the snow was flying and it was turning into a real blizzard, and even though the severity of the weather gave me pause, as soon as I thought of Samuel being out in this storm all by himself, potentially scared and all alone, I knew I had to press on!

As I struggled against the wind and the snow, at times I could barely see two steps in front of me. It was awful! I knew Mama's grave was almost half a mile away in a little grave yard that was accessed by a long winding path, and I knew I knew the way like the back of my hand, but in the black of night, with the whirling snow, I was starting to doubt whether or not I could actually find it. For Samuel's sake, though, I knew I had to try!

~

The grave yard was just a little family plot that had been in our family for years, and it sat in a little carved out area next to a big wood. It wasn't much, but it was ours, and I hoped to get there safely!

~

I was fairly certain I was walking in the right direction, but with the noise of the wind and with the blinding snow, it made it nearly impossible for me to get my bearings. I just kept hoping and praying as I continued on that I would make it to Mama's grave all right!

Back at Grampa and Gramma's Aunt Sara was fretting and praying as the storm outside kept building and building.

Fortunately, not long after I left, Uncle Mark and Grampa made it home.

Still covered in snow, but wanting to check on Aunt Sara before he put things away, Uncle Mark walked back to her bedroom. Seeing she was awake, he walked on in.

"Whew!" he commented, amazed. "I wasn't sure we'd make it back here! That storm came up quick, and it sure is a doozy! I helped Pa in the house, but I still have to put the horses away in the barn. Just wanted to check in on ya first and see how ya were doin'."

Aunt Sara looked up at him pale with fright.

Uncle Mark furrowed his brow, perplexed.

"What is it, Sara?" he asked. "What's wrong? You're white as a ghost!"

"Is it really that bad out there?" she questioned, fearful.

"Yah, it is," Uncle Mark confirmed. "But sweetheart," he tried to calm, "Pa and I, we're here now…we're safe! Everything's fine!"

Aunt Sara started to tear up.

"But it's not fine, Mark!" she wailed. "You don't understand!"

Uncle Mark walked over to her, confused.

"What do ya mean, Sara?" he queried. "What's goin' on?"

Aunt Sara broke down.

"It's Jochebed!" she wept, looking up at Uncle Mark, feeling absolutely guilty and afraid. "She's…she's out there!"

"In this!?!" Uncle Mark blustered in disbelief.

Aunt Sara hung her head, nodding in affirmation.

"But why?" he demanded to know. "Why on earth would she be out there in *this?"* He scowled at Aunt Sara, furious! "What's goin' on, Sara?" he questioned again, angrily. "Why is she out there?"

Aunt Sara regretfully explained to Uncle Mark all that had happened, and as she talked, Uncle Mark just shook his head in incredulity! He simply couldn't believe what he was hearing! Needless to say, by the time she finished telling him everything, he was absolutely beside himself and hopping mad!

"Michael and Samuel were at church, Sara!" he shouted furiously. "Jochebed was *supposed* to be at home waitin' for 'em! I mean…*good gracious*…they left right after we did! They're most likely home by now, and probably wonderin' *where on earth she's at!"* He huffed in aggravation. *"Unbelievable!"* he ranted. "I just can't believe this! How could ya have sent her out in this kinda weather? Ya should've known better, Sara! Ya just should've known better!

Aunt Sara sat sobbing, devastated by his thoughtless words!

"But Mark," she cried, "that's not fair! I had no way of knowing it was that bad out there! I *NEVER* would have let her go if I had! We didn't know about Samuel and Michael…we didn't know where they were at!" She did her best to get him to see. "Mark," she told him, trying to defend her decision, "you have to understand…we were scared! We were scared that Samuel was lost…lost out in this gathering storm! Jochebed *assured me* she could make it out to Lydia's grave and back before things got too bad, and I trusted her judgment!" She looked at him, pleading. "Please, Mark!" she implored. "You have to believe me! I am so sorr…"

"We'll deal with this later!" he barked, infuriated, cutting her off mid-sentence! "Time's a wastin! We've got a missin' girl on our hands, and Michael needs to know!" He clenched his jaw as he shook his head again, hastily starting for the door. "And ya better hope we find her, too!" he stated crossly, glancing back at Aunt Sara.

When Uncle Mark left the room, he slammed the door behind him, leaving Aunt Sara to herself. Immediately, she buried her face in her hands, and began to cry uncontrollably.

Uncle Mark hurried on to the kitchen and promptly informed Grampa as to what was happening. Worried and concerned, Grampa quickly gathered his things so that he could go with Uncle Mark to tell Papa. Just as they were getting ready to leave, however, Papa and Samuel came bursting through the front door.

"Is Jochebed here?" Papa asked in a panic. "She's not at home and we can't find her anywhere!"

"Michael," Uncle Mark rushed to answer, "I'm sorry to have to tell ya this, but…she's out in this storm!"

"What? Why?" Papa exclaimed. He shook his head, not understanding! "Why would she be out in this?" he questioned anxiously.

"She went to look for Samuel at Lydia's grave," Uncle Mark explained.

"But…*why?*" Papa wanted to know. "I *explicitly* told her to wait at home! She *knows* better than to go out in this kind of weather alone!" Papa was frantic. "We have to find her, Mark!" he said with urgency in his voice, his eyes filled with fear and dread. "She won't survive out there for long!"

"I'm goin' with ya!" Samuel insisted. "She wouldn't be out there if it wasn't for me!"

Papa hesitated for a minute, visibly shaken and worried.

"All right, Son," he allowed, "you can come. But ya have to *promise* you'll stay close!"

"I promise!" Samuel agreed.

Everyone quickly gathered lanterns, extra blankets, and bundled themselves up tightly. Before heading out into the storm that had now turned into a raging blizzard, however, they decided the best course of action would be to tie ropes to each other for safety. It was just too dangerous to venture out alone!

When they got outside and started searching, the visibility was almost zero. Uncle Mark and Grampa were linked together with one rope, and Papa and Samuel were linked together with another. While they'd agreed to try to stay close to each other, it was nearly impossible! The snow was just too thick and the wind too strong. They could barely see each other, much less me!

As they made their way past the barn, all yelling out my name, they finally came to the conclusion that they were going to need a lot more help if they were to have any hope of finding me in all this mess.

Uncle Mark shouted to Papa over the noise of the wind.

"I'll head back with Pa to the church and ring the bell for help!" he called out. "You and Samuel keep lookin'! *But be careful!* Don't go doin' anything foolish!"

Papa waved, indicating he'd heard.

"Y'all be careful, too!" he yelled back. "*But hurry!* We have to find her soon! She can't possibly last much longer out here!"

"Be safe!" Uncle Mark hollered out at the top of his lungs.

Papa and Samuel went on as Uncle Mark and Grampa made their way back to the wagon.

Not surprisingly, it took them quite awhile just to find their way back to the house. Once they did, though, they followed it around to the front where they'd left the horses and the wagon sitting. Eventually, coming upon the wagon, they climbed aboard and immediately took off for the church, hastening as fast as they could go!

On the way, they had a terrible time keeping the horses on the road due to the blinding snow and strong, swirling winds. It was slow going and arduous, but finally they managed to make it into town.

When they arrived at the church, Pastor Scott and his wife, Addie, were just locking up for the night, getting ready to leave to go home.

Uncle Mark and Grampa came rushing up to the steps yelling all the way.

"Ring the bell! Ring the bell!" they shouted frantically.

Mrs. Scott turned around as soon as she heard them calling.

"What's wrong?" she inquired, concerned. "What's happened?"

"It's Jochebed!" Uncle Mark blurted out anxiously. "She's missin' out in this storm, and we need help findin' her!"

"Oh, no!" Mrs. Scott gasped in horror, bringing her hands to her face. "That poor girl! Out all alone in *this!*" She looked to the heavens. "Oh please, dear Lord," she prayed, "please be with her and let her be all right!"

Pastor Scott swiftly unlocked the door and ran back inside to ring the bell. He rang it and rang it, and rang it some more, hoping to summon help.

Within minutes, people from all around the area started showing up to the church.

"What's going on, Mark?" Mr. Bell asked, who'd shown up first with his wife, Madeline.

"It's Jochebed!" Uncle Mark explained. "She's lost out in this storm!"

As he began to give details, eight more people showed up, then six more, and then three. Since everyone was curious as to why they'd been beckoned, he decided to wait until everyone was gathered around before he continued. When everyone was in and settled, he explained the dire situation.

"It's Jochebed Lowry," he told everyone with grave concern in his voice. "She's lost out in this blizzard! Michael and Sam are out in it now lookin' for her, but we need your help if we're gonna find her in time. The last we knew, she was headed for her mama's grave, but that was a while ago, and with a storm like this, y'all know how easily it is to be thrown off course." He shook his head, worried. "Truthfully, given the severity of this storm," he offered candidly, "I'd be surprised if she made it all the way out there, so with that bein' said, just know, she could be *anywhere* by now!" He went on. "We'll use my pa's house as a meetin' place," he suggested, "and let's everyone team up so no one else gets lost. Check in periodically, if ya would, so we can know you're safe and where ya've already searched. My wife, Sara, will be there, and ya can update her on your progress."

"I'll go and stay with her!" Mrs. Bell volunteered.

"I will, too!" Isabelle offered. (She and Andrew had shown up together to help.)

"I'll go with them as well," Mrs. Scott chimed in.

"All right then," Uncle Mark agreed. "Let's get goin'! And hey… everyone, *please* be careful!"

Everybody initially set out together in a caravan, but then split into groups once they reached Grampa and Gramma's.

The night was getting darker and colder, and the storm was still raging on!

While all this was happening in town, Papa and Samuel had continued walking on towards the grave site looking for me. Their search was slow and grueling due to the inclement weather, but they were determined to find me so they kept right on going, fighting the harsh winds and blinding snow, calling my name over and over again. Their efforts, however, garnered no response.

After about an hour or so of Papa and Samuel searching on their own, the area became flooded with men and their dogs, lanterns, and horses. Everyone was in a full-out search, trying to find me.

"Anything?" Mr. Bell called out to Papa as he and Mr. Sithe came riding up beside him.

"No!" Papa yelled back over the noise of the wind. "I can't find her anywhere, and she won't answer!"

The snow was pouring out of the sky, whirling about, landing everywhere like a thick blanket covering everything! In fact, it had drifted so high in spots, Papa and Samuel were almost up to their knees, trying to wade through it.

"Can ya take Sam with ya on your horse?" Papa asked. "I don't think he can go much further on foot."

"No, Papa!" Samuel insisted. "I'm fine! I have to help find her! I have to!"

"Samuel," Mr. Bell interjected, "Son, you can still help find your sister, but I think it'd be best if you came with me on horseback."

"No, Papa, please!" Samuel begged. "I wanna stay with you! I can do this, I promise. Please?"

Papa looked at Samuel, reluctantly, and then to Mr. Bell.

"It'll be all right, Tom," Papa decided. "Sam can stay with me."

"All right, then," Mr. Bell agreed. "Where to next?"

"I think we'll finish lookin' around here and then head south towards the Motter's place," Papa replied. "I'm hopin' maybe she found her way to their house to get warm."

"Okay," Mr. Bell approved. "Charles and I'll go north to the Wellesley's and then head east towards the river. - Don't worry, Michael, with everyone searching, I'm sure we'll find her soon!"

Mr. Bell turned to go, but before he could take off, his horse reared back on his hind legs, almost throwing Mr. Bell off his saddle.

"Whoa, there, Jack!" Mr. Bell bellowed. "What's wrong with you, boy?"

Jack reared back again, this time snorting and shaking his head defiantly.

"Enough of this!" Mr. Bell demanded, growing angry at his horse's resistance. "Now get on with ya!"

Jack stubbornly refused to move, firmly holding his ground.

Curious, Papa lifted his lantern to see what the horse was balking at. There on the other side of him was a mound of snow, and laying beside it a lantern that had clearly gone out.

"Tom!" Papa yelled fretfully. "Is that her?" Papa hurriedly ran over to the pile of snow and promptly knelt down. Fearing it was me under there, he feverishly began digging.

Seeing Papa's franticness, Mr. Bell immediately jumped off his horse and rushed to help, as did Samuel and Mr. Sithe.

The snow was piled up rather deep, but suddenly Papa shouted, "It's a glove!"

Everyone continued to dig as fast and furiously as they could!

"Jochebed! Jochebed!" Papa kept shouting as he threw handfuls of snow aside. "Jochebed, answer me!"

"Please be all right!" Samuel cried out as he dug. "Please be alive!"

After digging for several heart-pounding minutes, they were finally able to reach me.

Grabbing hold of my shoulders, Papa turned me over, face up, and scooped me up into his arms.

Mr. Bell shined his lantern on my face.

"She's blue!" Papa cried out, panicked at the sight. "I can't hear her breathin'!"

Mr. Bell scooted over quickly and leaned down over my face.

"She may just be too cold, Michael!" he submitted, trying to sound hopeful. "We need to get her warmed up as soon as possible!"

Samuel scrambled to get the blankets that he and Papa had brought from Grampa and Gramma's and handed them to Mr. Bell. Together, they worked quickly to get me all wrapped up as tightly as they could.

While they were doing that, Papa was vigorously rubbing my face and body, trying to get me warm.

When I was sufficiently wrapped, Mr. Bell untied the rope connecting Papa and Samuel and tied Samuel to himself.

"You take my horse, Michael!" Mr. Bell insisted. "Get her home as fast as you can! Charles and I'll bring Samuel along behind you."

Papa nodded, instantly jumped to his feet, and climbed up on Mr. Bell's horse. When he was situated, Mr. Bell, Mr. Sithe, and Samuel all helped to lift my motionless body up to Papa. As soon as Papa had me in his arms, we were off!

Worried sick, Papa hastened the horse along, compelling him to go faster and faster. Following his commands, the horse obeyed!

As we went, Papa held me tightly, talking in my ear the whole way.

"Ya hang on Jochebed, ya hear me?" he desperately begged. "Don't ya die! Ya hang on! Just hang on! ...I love ya, sweetheart, so much...so does Sam, and we need ya! ...Please...please don't die! Just hang on!" Over and over again, he kept reiterating this to me until we reached Grampa and Gramma's.

When we arrived, Mrs. Bell, Mrs. Scott, and Isabelle were all at the house with Aunt Sara just as they said they would be. They were anxiously waiting for any news and providing food and coffee to all those who were out searching. All of the men were in teams, and each came back to the house to check in after a half hour or so. They would come to get updates and to refresh themselves before heading out again.

When Papa came into view of the house, he noticed a few men milling about by the back door, preparing their horses to go out and search again. In need of help, he yelled out as loudly as he could, hoping someone would hear. Unfortunately, the noise of the storm was too great, and it drowned out his pleas. As he got a little closer, he shouted out again.

"Help her!" he demanded as he came barreling up to the back door. He pulled up on the reins to slow the horse. "Help her!" he insisted passionately. "Please, somebody help her!"

Finally able to see him and hear his cries, the men promptly ran to his aid. Right away, they reached up and carefully took hold of my lifeless body, gently lowering me down. Once in hand, they rushed me inside as quickly as they could.

Papa immediately dismounted and followed in behind them.

When the men came bursting through the back door, the women in the kitchen were startled by their sudden entry. As soon as they realized what was happening, though, they instantly scurried to help.

"How long has she been unconscious?" Mrs. Bell wanted to know. (She was a nurse and had some training as to know what to do.)

"I don't know!" Papa told her anxiously. It was clear from the look on his face that he was panicked and deeply worried.

The men carried my body to the couch in the family room and gently laid me down.

Mrs. Bell quickly took over my care.

"Someone go get Dr. Wellesley right now!" she demanded, assessing my condition. "And someone get me a tub of warm water!" She looked directly at Isabelle. "You heat up some rags for warming!" she instructed. "And, Addie, you help me get her out of these wet clothes!" She quickly looked around at the men who'd brought me in. "And you," she stated bluntly, "get!"

Papa went with Mr. Trussle (a dear old friend of the family) to get the tub, and Mrs. Scott helped to unwrap me from my blankets.

"We have to get her out of these wet things!" Mrs. Bell insisted, helping to undress me. "We need to warm her up right away! Her breathing is much labored, and her color isn't good at all! I fear we may be losing her!"

When they had me almost undressed, Isabelle ran in with some warm rags that she had heated on the wood stove.

"Here!" she said, handing them to Mrs. Bell. "Will these help?"

"Yes!" Mrs. Bell replied, taking them from her. "These will do just fine!" She took the rags and had Mrs. Scott help to lay them out over my body. "Get some more if you can, Isabelle!" Mrs. Bell requested. "It'll take a while to heat that water for the tub, and I want to keep her as warm as possible!" Mrs. Bell quickly turned to Mrs. Scott. "Addie," she said, "go ask Sara where they keep the extra blankets...*gracious*, pull one off a bed if you have to! This child needs all the warmth she can get!"

Mrs. Scott nodded compliantly.

"I'm on it!" she agreed jumping up, scurrying off to find the blankets.

Mrs. Bell knelt down beside me and stroked my face. Leaning in close, she whispered in my ear.

"You fight for me, Jochebed, you hear?" she pleaded. "No one's dying on my watch! No one!" She kept rubbing my arms and legs, trying to warm me up.

After a few minutes, Mrs. Scott came rushing back in with several blankets, and Isabelle soon returned with more warm cloths.

"The water's almost ready," Isabelle informed. "And they have the tub ready to bring in as well."

"Then have them bring it on," Mrs. Bell approved. "That way it's here when the water's ready." She sighed, frustrated, feeling somewhat helpless. "I'm afraid that's all we can do for now," she bemoaned. She shook her head as she looked worriedly into my face. "This poor child's frozen, through!" she remarked with angst. "I just pray she'll come to once she thaws a bit!"

All the ladies sat there in the room with me, waiting nervously and praying desperately as they tried to warm me up.

Finally, Papa and Mr. Trussle came in with the tub, and not long after, Isabelle brought the water from the kitchen to fill it up.

"All right now," Mrs. Bell announced, "we need to get her into this water! You men get on outta here, and make certain no one else comes in!"

Papa and Mr. Trussle did what Mrs. Bell asked, and as soon as they were gone, all the ladies gently lifted me from the couch and placed me into the tub.

After just a few minutes in the warm water, I began to shiver and shake.

"That's a good sign!" Mrs. Bell said, cautiously optimistic. "That's the most response we've gotten from her yet!"

"Look!" Isabelle exclaimed excitedly. "I can see some color returning to her face!"

"I can, too!" Mrs. Scott enthusiastically agreed.

Mrs. Bell was kneeling down beside me, watching me like a hawk.

"That's a girl, Jochebed!" she praised, encouraging me on. "You keep fighting! Just keep fighting!" She looked up at the other ladies. "It sounds like her breathing may be improving a bit as well," she relayed. "It's still slow and labored, but it does seem steadier."

My color was improving, but my breathing was still strenuous, and I hadn't come to as of yet.

After about twenty minutes of sitting in the warm water, Mrs. Bell asked Mrs. Scott to get me some dry clothes, and she asked Isabelle to see if there was a bed that they could lay me in.

Both ladies went off to fulfill their tasks.

After a few minutes, Mrs. Scott came back with a gown and robe borrowed from Aunt Sara, and Isabelle came back and said that Papa would help to move me into Grampa and Gramma's room for now.

They got me out of the tub, dried off and dressed, and called Papa to come and get me. When he came, he gently lifted me from the couch and carried be back to the bedroom. Mrs. Bell quickly followed.

*****

"Do ya think she'll be all right?" Papa asked as Mrs. Bell settled me in.

"Honestly, Michael, I really don't know," she answered, uncertain. "Her color looks better, but I'm still concerned that she hasn't come to as of yet. I'm hoping Dr. Wellesley can tell us more when he arrives."

Papa nodded somberly as he took a seat there beside me on the bed. Gently taking hold of my hand, he sat watching me, overwhelmed with worry and emotion. He sniffed as he fought back tears.

"Thank ya for all ya've done, Madeline," he said to Mrs. Bell who was still sitting there on the other side of the bed.

She gave a reluctant smile as she stood to her feet, wanting to give Papa some time alone with me.

"You're welcome, Michael," she replied, melancholy. "I only wish it could have been more. I'll let you know when the doctor arrives."

Papa nodded as she started for the door.

Just as she was leaving, Samuel came to the door, peering in.

"Is she gonna be okay?" he asked her, his face clearly showing the worry in his heart.

Mrs. Bell smiled tenderly and patted his cheek.

"Go be with your sister," she encouraged. "She needs all the love and prayers she can get."

Samuel looked up at her, hesitant, as he cautiously walked into the room.

"Papa," he questioned as he stood a ways back from the bed, "is…is she okay?"

"Come and see, Son," Papa said, motioning for Samuel to come closer.

"I…I don't want to!" Samuel refused. "I'm afraid to see her like that."

"It's all right, Son," Papa assured. "She's still with us. She just looks like she's sleepin'. Come on…come see your sister."

Samuel slowly and tentatively made his way to the side of the bed. As he approached, he looked down at me, very uneasy, and unsure of what to think.

"She…she looks so peaceful," he commented.

Papa looked down at me with tears in his eyes, nodding in agreement. Fighting back tears, he wondered aloud.

"I…I just don't understand," he said distraught. "Why…*why would she do such a thing?*"

Samuel shook his head, feeling guilty.

"I'm so sorry, Papa!" he cried, taking the blame. "It's all my fault! If I hadn't a run away…if I…"

Papa stood up and walked to him, taking hold of his shoulders, looking him in the eyes.

"This isn't your fault, Son!" he insisted. "Don't ya go doin' that to yourself! If anyone's to blame, it's me! I should've gotten word to her that I'd found ya…that you were all right!" Papa teared up as he pulled Samuel close. "It's not your fault, Son," he said, overcome. "It's not your fault!"

Samuel hugged Papa tightly and cried.

Papa did his best to console him.

Just then, Uncle Mark and Grampa came bursting anxiously into the room.

"How is she, Michael?" Uncle Mark asked frantically. "We just heard when we came in from the search!"

"Not sure," Papa answered glumly, looking down at my motionless body. "She has a little more color than before, but she still hasn't come to. We won't know anything for sure 'til Doc gets here. Mr. Sithe and Mr. Bell went to fetch him." He wiped his tears. "Are all the teams back yet?" he wanted to know, concerned.

"Most!" Grampa answered, walking to the side of the bed. "I think there's just one or two still out searchin'. They should be rotatin' in here pretty soon, though."

"Good!" Papa replied. "The sooner we get everybody in out of this storm, the better I'll feel."

"I agree, Michael," Uncle Mark commented. "I'll go tell everyone still waitin' out in the other room that they can go whenever they'd like."

"Thanks, Mark," Papa appreciated. "And please…make sure to thank 'em for me, won't ya?"

"Of course!" Uncle Mark assured. "I'll let 'em know."

Just as Uncle Mark was leaving the room, Dr. Wellesley came to the bedroom door, snow-covered and still bundled up tightly.

"Doc!" Uncle Mark exclaimed, almost running into him. "Thank goodness you're here! They're waitin' on ya!"

Dr. Wellesley nodded and walked on into the room, shedding his hat and coat as he came. Setting them aside, he quickly made his way to the bed to examine me.

Papa stepped out of the way while Grampa motioned to Samuel for him to come with him into the other room.

Readily complying, Samuel and Grampa left, but Papa stayed.

"How's she look, Doc?" he questioned earnestly as Dr. Wellesley began his examination.

"Well," he said with a sigh, "the best I can tell, she seems to be frozen through. Nurse Bell did the right thing in warming her, and I do think she has a chance to recover, but it'll take some time before we can know for sure. Not knowing how long she was out there and in this condition, it's just too hard to say definitively." Dr. Wellesley leaned in to listen to my chest.

Papa looked on anxiously.

"Her heart, Doc," he asked, "is it all right?"

Dr. Wellesley sighed again as he looked up at Papa.

"I'll be honest with you, Michael," he replied, putting his stethoscope around his neck, "it sounds weaker than I'd like it to."

Papa furrowed his brow, worried!

Dr. Wellesley shook his head, concerned.

"My hope is it'll get stronger with time," he went on to say, "but..." He paused, pensive. "We'll just have to keep an eye on it for now." He looked over at Papa. "It's really all we can do," he relayed. "I'm afraid we just have to wait this thing out."

Papa was quite upset and troubled.

"Well...will she wake up?" he wanted to know, fearful.

Dr. Wellesley shook his head again, clearly bothered by his limitations.

"I'm very sorry, Michael," he humbly admitted, "I just don't know. I wish I could tell you that she'll be fine, but right now, it's just too early to tell." He looked back to me, trying to point out the positives. "Her vitals are weak but they are stable," he stressed, "and she is breathing steadily, which is a good sign, so...well...hopefully, as she continues to warm, her body will allow her to wake up."

Papa sighed, less than encouraged.

Dr. Wellesley stood to his feet turning towards Papa.

"Time will give us a better picture, Michael," he said. "We just have to wait and see."

Papa nodded, reluctantly accepting what he'd been told.

"Keep her warm and comfortable," Dr. Wellesley instructed, as he turned back to put his equipment into his bag. "And come get me right away if she comes to!"

Papa was frustrated that the doctor couldn't do more, but he understood.

"Will do, Doc," he assured solemnly. "And...and thanks."

Dr. Wellesley finished gathering his things.

"I'll walk ya out," Papa offered.

"No need," Dr. Wellesley told him. "You stay. I'll find my way."

Papa nodded, appreciative, as Dr. Wellesley walked towards the door.

As soon as Dr. Wellesley started to leave, Papa promptly sat back down next to me on the bed, again taking my hand in his, as tears filled his eyes. His heart was wrenching in grief as he brought my hand to his lips, kissing it gently. Holding it tightly, he poured his heart out to God.

"Oh please, dear God," he begged, "please let her be all right!"

After Dr. Wellesley left the room, he decided that while he was there, he would check in on Aunt Sara, who, understandably, was beside herself with guilt and grief for having let me go out into the cold. He tried to console her, sharing with her that he felt I would recover in time, but nothing he said seemed to make her feel any better.

Having said all he could say on the matter, he left off and examined her rib to see how it was healing, and also checked the progress of the baby.

Uncle Mark walked into the room just as he was finishing his exam.

"How's she look, Doc?" he asked.

"Surprisingly well!" Dr. Wellesley commented, sounding quite encouraged. "Your wife's a very strong lady. Her rib seems to be healing nicely, and the baby's progress looks great! So much so," he continued with a smile, "I'm going to allow her a little more leeway."

Aunt Sara perked up a bit.

"What are ya sayin', Doc?" Uncle Mark queried.

"Well, I think if she's extremely careful," the doctor explained, "she could spend some time in a wheelchair, maybe have an opportunity to get out of this room for a little while."

Aunt Sara couldn't believe it!

"Do you really mean it?" she questioned in disbelief.

"Absolutely!" Dr. Wellesley replied with a chuckle. *"But listen!"* he emphasized, looking at her more seriously. "This is *not* a license to go places and do things! You still need to take it easy, especially now with that bruised rib of yours. But, if you're careful, I see no reason why you couldn't get out of here for short periods of time."

Aunt Sara could hardly contain herself; she was so elated! She looked at Dr. Wellesley.

"I can't thank you enough!" she said. "You don't know how much this means to me! I feel as if I've just had my prison sentence commuted."

Dr. Wellesley chuckled again.

"Well," he replied, smiling, "I'm just glad I could bring *some* good news today. But again," he reminded, looking Aunt Sara firmly in the eye, "I can't stress this enough - this is *not* permission to do whatever you want, Sara! You still need to take it extremely easy, and you need to mind that you listen to your body and not overdue. If things start to go south with you or the baby, I'll have no choice but to confine you back to bed. Do you understand?"

"Yes, of course, Doctor!" Aunt Sara confirmed, excitedly. "I'll be careful!"

"I'll make sure she doesn't overdue, Doc," Uncle Mark chimed in, assuring him.

"Well, good!" Dr. Wellesley approved as he gathered his bag. "I'll have a wheelchair sent over just as soon as this blizzard passes."

Aunt Sara grabbed his hand, grateful.

"Thank you again, Doctor," she said, overjoyed. "This means the world!"

"Yes, thank ya, Doc," Uncle Mark echoed.

Dr. Wellesley nodded as he left.

"You take care now," he encouraged, looking back at Aunt Sara.

Uncle Mark walked him out.

"Be careful goin' home, Doc," Uncle Mark advised as he shook Dr. Wellesley's hand.

"I will, Mark," he assured. "And hey!" he added as he slipped on his hat and coat, bundling up. "You take good care of that wife of yours, and be *sure* to let me know right away if anything changes with Jochebed, all right?"

"Will do," Uncle Mark agreed. "You'll be the first to know!"

Dr. Wellesley left (as had most everyone else who had come to help search for me), and, in fact, once he was gone, the only ones that remained (besides family, of course) were Pastor Scott and his wife, Addie. They were in the family room talking with Grampa and Samuel, and after seeing Dr. Wellesley out, Uncle Mark decided to join them.

"Before you sit down, Mark," Pastor Scott requested, "could you please ask Michael to come join us for a moment?"

Uncle Mark nodded.

"Sure," he said. "I'll go get him." Uncle Mark walked to the bedroom and knocked softly on the door as he came in the room.

"Michael," he called out.

Papa looked up.

"I think Pastor Scott wants to talk to us in the other room for a minute," he said. "He'd like it if ya could come join us."

Papa looked back to me, heartbroken and torn.

"Sure," he finally agreed, reluctant to leave me alone. He leaned over and kissed me on the forehead as he let go of my hand. Wiping tears from his eyes, he got up and somberly walked to the family room with Uncle Mark.

"Pastor Scott," Papa commented as he walked into the family room, surprised to still see him there. "You and Addie...ya didn't have to stay!"

"Oh, I know, Michael," Pastor Scott acknowledged. "But if it's all right with you, I just wanted to take a minute or two to talk with you and your family."

Papa nodded, agreeing.

"That'd be fine," he granted as he went to take a seat in one of the chairs Grampa had brought in from the kitchen.

When Papa and Uncle Mark were seated, Pastor Scott began.

"Well," he said with a heavy heart, "I can't begin to tell you how very sorry we are, and by we, I mean Addie and me, we're...we're so very sorry for all the *many* trials you and your family have been facing of late. I know it seems incomprehensible that one family should have to endure so many difficult things, and I don't begin to understand why they're happening, but I do know that God has a special purpose and plan for your lives. And even though right now the valley seems deep and the road dark and long, I'm confident that God *will* bring you through *all of this* in time!"

He pulled out his Bible that he'd brought along with him.

"I'm reminded of the words in the book of James chapter one," he said as he flipped through the pages, finding the passage. Settling on the verse, he started to read. "It says here in verse two and following, 'My brethren, count it all joy when ye fall into divers temptations; Knowing this, that the trying of your faith worketh patience.' And Romans chapter eight and verse twenty eight tells us, and I quote, 'And we know that all things work together for good to them that love God, to them who are the called according to His purpose.'" Pastor Scott paused attentively. "I don't want to sound like I'm preaching at you," he said, "because I know you know this, but...don't ever forget that even in the midst of what makes no sense to us, we can take heart in knowing that it all makes perfect sense to God. Again, I know you've heard this all before, but I guess my hope is that maybe by being reminded of these truths, it'll be a help and comfort and an encouragement to you."

He looked around at everyone, grieved.

"Please know we love you and your family very much," he conveyed with sincerity, "and that we're praying for *all of you!* And please, please know that we're here for you *whatever* you need! Don't hesitate for a moment to call on us for help!"

When Pastor Scott finished, Papa was tearing up, and Grampa and Uncle Mark were fighting back tears as well.

"Just one more thing," Pastor Scott added, "if it's all right, I'd like to say a prayer on your behalf. And then," he said, looking over at his wife, "Addie and I, we'll...we'll be on our way."

Grampa nodded favorably, as did Papa and Uncle Mark, and everyone bowed their heads.

"Oh, dear Heavenly Father," Pastor Scott began, "I want to thank You for this dear family. They're beloved brothers and sisters in Christ, and when one in the body is hurting, we all hurt. We come to You now not knowing why all these terrible things keep happening to them, but, Father, we take comfort in knowing that You do and that You have a perfect purpose and plan for it all and that You are in control and that *in Your time* You will help us to see. Please be with the Lowry family right now and in the days ahead, comfort them, strengthen them, and increase their faith to trust You through this difficult valley, and help them to be drawn closer to You through it all. Right now, I pray that You would *please* touch Jochebed's body and allow her a full and swift recovery. Please continue to be with Mrs. Lowry and allow her to come back to us soon, and Lord, we also pray for Sara and the baby. Please keep them safe, and bring that little one into the world healthy and strong! Oh, Lord, we thank You for what You've already done, and we thank You in advance for what we know You're going to do. We put all things into Your hands. Have Your perfect will and way. Increase our faith. Help us, Lord, to trust You! We love You! In Jesus' precious name we pray. Amen."

Everyone echoed amen as they stood to their feet, wiping their tears.

Papa, Uncle Mark, and Grampa all took turns shaking Pastor Scott's hand.

"We can't thank ya enough for all ya've done for us," Papa told him.

"Well, it's the least we can do," Pastor Scott replied.

"And again, please don't hesitate to call on us if you need *anything!*" Mrs. Scott interjected, reminding them.

"We won't, Miss Addie," Grampa assured. "And thank ya!"

Papa and Grampa saw the Scotts to the door and said goodnight as the Scotts courteously bid them farewell and made their way out into the blustery night.

Since I was still unconscious in Grampa and Gramma's bedroom, Papa and Uncle Mark set up a cot in the family room for Grampa to sleep on. Samuel curled up on the couch, and Papa slept on the floor right next to me. He wanted to be there just in case I came to in the middle of the night.

Completely exhausted from the events of the day, everyone slept a good sleep as the storm outside raged on.

COMING TO
(Chapter 18)

Sometime during the night, I felt myself start to shiver uncontrollably. I couldn't seem to get myself warm. I felt as if I was in a dream, and I couldn't wake myself up. It felt like I had a weight on my chest, and no matter how hard I tried, I couldn't take a breath. I tried to gasp for air over and over again, but it just seemed like I was flailing under water.

Then, almost without warning, after struggling for what seemed like forever, my body suddenly jerked and I took in a huge, deep breath of air. My eyes opened wide, and I lay there, anxious, my heart pounding wildly, feeling as if I'd just run a very long race.

Disoriented, I felt lost and very confused. It was terribly dark and cold...so very cold, but I couldn't figure out why. I darted my eyes back and forth, looking here and there, trying to determine where I was at, but in the darkness, nothing *at all* looked familiar!

Laying there, trembling, I began to feel overwhelming fear and panic welling up inside of me, and all I *desperately* wanted to do was run away! Every time I tried to move, though, all I could feel was pain, *unbelievable* pain! I just didn't understand! I hurt *so badly*, and the cold...I just couldn't shake the cold!

In my quest to understand what was going on, I must have been making some noise because suddenly Papa's face came into view. I instantly screamed, and continued to scream, frightened, not realizing who he was.

"It's all right, Jochebed!" Papa assured, leaning over me, trying to calm me down. "It's all right! It's just me, Papa! You're all right!"

All the commotion woke Uncle Mark, and he came running into the room.

"What is it, Michael?" he asked, panicked. "What's wrong?" Seeing the struggle between me and Papa, Uncle Mark rushed over to try to help calm me.

Out of fear and pain and confusion, I kept screaming and fighting, eventually waking everyone in the house.

Within seconds, Samuel and Grampa were bursting into the room as well to see what was going on.

"Someone get a light in here!" Papa demanded, still wrestling with me, trying to get me quieted.

Grampa hurried to get a lantern so I could see my surroundings.

"Jochebed!" Papa kept shouting. "Stop fighting, child! You're all right! It's Papa and your Uncle Mark! You're at Grampa and Gramma's! Please...it's all right!"

I was so afraid I didn't know what to do, and I was screaming so loudly and fighting so furiously, I couldn't hear what Papa was saying. I just didn't understand what was going on! Uncle Mark was trying to hold my legs, and Papa was holding my wrists, and I was struggling to get myself free from the both of them!

Finally, Grampa came back into the room with the lantern and brought it up close to the bed. As soon as the light fell across Papa's face I immediately stopped screaming and struggling. I stared at him, bewildered. It was strange. I knew I knew him...he seemed so familiar to me, but for the life of me I couldn't place him.

Overcome with anxiety, I started to breathe heavily, frightened and confused! My head was pounding and my heart was racing, and I just wanted them to go away! I jerked my wrists from Papa's hands and held them close to my chest, afraid for what he might do to me next!

When I'd settled and stopped fighting, Uncle Mark let go of my ankles, for which I was thankful, but still, I didn't know what to do! I was in so much pain and so cold and so afraid, I just laid there, trembling, staring at everyone!

Papa started to come close, but I shook my head vigorously, indicating I wanted him to stay back! He must have seen the look of shear panic on my face because he immediately stopped.

"Jochebed," he said softy, "sweetheart, it's Papa. Don't ya know who I am?"

Still breathing heavily, I looked up at him, anxious, trying hard to remember, but no matter how long I stared at him, I just couldn't! Again, I feverishly shook my head, signifying I had no idea who he was.

Hoping that perhaps I might recognize him, Grampa decided to put the light up close to his face.

"Jochebed," he asked, holding the lantern up beside himself, "do ya know *me?*"

I nervously looked over at him and tried to focus. His voice sounded familiar, but I couldn't place him either. Again, I shook my head no. I was *completely terrified!* It just made no sense! I didn't understand where I was, how I had gotten here, who these people were, or what was going on!

Papa looked worriedly at Uncle Mark who was standing there shaking his head just as distressed.

"Go get the doc!" Papa urged, frightened. "Get him here *now!*"

Uncle Mark immediately left!

Not knowing what else to do, and hoping perhaps I'd recognize Samuel, Papa told him to come over to the side of the bed.

Given everything that had just transpired, as you can imagine, Samuel was rather reluctant. Still, he did what he was told and walked over. Nervous and uneasy, he paused before stepping into the light.

"Samuel!" I exclaimed in a whispered, raspy voice. "You're here! Where have you been?"

Immediately, his eyes lit up, taken a back.

"Ya...ya know me?" he questioned, completely surprised by my response.

"Of course I do!" I answered, trying to reach my hand out to his. "Where were you? I...I was so afraid!"

Samuel looked nervously at Papa, unsure of what to do.

Papa nodded back at him as if to say, *Talk to her, Son.*

Samuel swallowed hard as he looked back to me with an anxious, hesitant look on his face.

His reluctance confused me, but I didn't dwell on it.

"I...I was at church," he blurted out, offering nothing more.

I managed a painful smile.

"Well, I'm just glad you're safe," I whispered, fighting pain and the urge to go to sleep. I was shivering terribly from the cold, and my body ached so badly it hurt to talk. My eyelids felt like lead, and I found it hard to keep them open. Before I knew it, I had slipped back into a coma.

Assuming that I had just fallen asleep, not realizing that I was actually unconscious again, Papa, Grampa, and Samuel decided to let me be. They left the room and went to wait for the doctor to arrive.

Before joining Grampa and Samuel in the family room, Papa looked in on Aunt Sara to see if she knew what was happening, and she explained that Uncle Mark had informed her before he left to go get the doctor. Beside himself with concern, Papa asked her if she would be praying. She promptly assured him that she already had been and that she would continue. He nodded, grateful, and solemnly left the room.

Sitting around waiting for Uncle Mark to get back with Dr. Wellesley, Grampa, Samuel and Papa sat quietly, dazed and admittedly scared. No one was quite sure what to say or think.

"What's wrong with her, Papa?" Samuel finally questioned, confused. "Why'd she know me but not any of you?"

Papa looked over at Samuel, dejected and troubled.

"I...I don't know, Son," he admitted somberly. "The brain's a funny thing and..." He sighed. "I just don't know. Hopefully, Doc can tell us more when he gets here."

"Well, if ya ask me, it was just eerie!" Samuel expressed with a shiver. "I've never seen anybody like that before! I mean...it was like she was there but...but she really wasn't!" He shook his head. "Scared me but good!" he confessed.

Papa nodded, conceding the point.

"I know what ya mean, Son," he agreed. "I was scared, too. I think we all were!"

Samuel looked down and sighed as he and Papa left off talking.

Silence once again settled over the room as they waited.

Finally, after what seemed like an eternity, Uncle Mark arrived back with Dr. Wellesley.

"So what's this I hear about Jochebed waking up?" Dr. Wellesley asked as he came inside, shaking the snow from his coat.

Papa immediately jumped up and walked over to him

"She's back asleep now, Doc," he informed. "She was only awake for just a few minutes. I think all the flailin' about and fightin' wore her plum out."

Dr. Wellesley looked quite troubled.

"Let me see her!" he insisted earnestly.

Papa quickly walked him to the room and over to the bed.

Dr. Wellesley leaned down to check me to see how I was doing.

"Get me some more blankets!" he sternly demanded. "She's cold as ice!"

Dr. Wellesley called my name several times, trying to rouse me, but I gave no response. He listened to my heart and lungs, took my temperature, and felt my pulse. When he finished, he turned to Papa who was now standing with the blankets he'd gathered, promptly took the blankets from him, and began to cover me up.

"It would appear she's unconscious again," Dr. Wellesley explained, tucking the blankets in around me. "Tell me again exactly what happened."

Papa recounted the whole dreadful ordeal to him.

Dr. Wellesley listened intently.

"Well," he said with a sigh, "I know it's hard to accept, but I believe she's still suffering the effects of being out in the cold for so long. Again, not knowing how long she was down out there makes it much more difficult to predict how soon or how full of a recovery she'll make. All I can tell you for now is to keep an eye on her and keep her warm. She'll probably be in pain as the cold wears off as her body's still in shock from what happened, but if she wakes up again," he instructed, "don't try to push her. She may or may not remember everything, but...just give her time and space to process things, all right?"

Papa was clearly troubled.

Dr. Wellesley sighed again as he shook his head, obviously feeling helpless in the face of my injuries.

"I'm sorry, Michael," he said as he looked down at me. "I wish I could tell you more, but not knowing how things have affected her brain, I...I just don't know how this will all play out."

Papa looked at him anxiously, his heart overwhelmed with grief and fear!

"Are...are ya sayin' she'll never remember us, Doc?!?" he questioned, panicked.

"No," Dr. Wellesley replied, "that's not what I'm saying, but I do have to caution you, Michael," he relayed, very disheartened, trying to be completely honest with him, "I am afraid that...it *is* a possibility."

Papa nearly went weak at the disclosure!

Dr. Wellesley shook his head, feeling badly.

"I'm sorry I can't be more certain one way or the other," he told him, "but unfortunately, there's still so much we just don't know about the brain."

Needless to say, upon hearing the doctor's assessment, Papa was beside himself with worry!

Sensing Papa's grave concern, Dr. Wellesley tried to put things in a little better light.

"On the bright side," he bolstered, "her waking up at all and knowing Samuel like she did, why, that's a good sign! Hopefully, it's an indication her memory will return with time." He again sighed in frustration. "Like I told you earlier," he expressed with aggravation, "I wish I could tell you that everything will be all right, Michael, really I do, and..." He paused, looking at me. "I wish like everything there was something more I could do for her, but..." he looked back to Papa. "Regrettably, we just have to wait and see."

Papa shook his head, angry and upset, as tears welled up in his eyes.

"I just want my little girl back!" he raged as a tear escaped his eye and trickled down his face.

Dr. Wellesley stood up and walked over to Papa, putting his hand on his shoulder in sympathy.

"I know you do, Michael," he tried to comfort. "And I want that for you, too! And I promise...I'll do *everything* I can to help your daughter. You have my word!"

Papa calmed a bit as he looked at Dr. Wellesley.

"I know ya will, Doc," he acknowledged. "I don't mean it to sound like I'm blamin' ya. I'm not. It's just so hard, the not knowin'."

"I understand," Dr. Wellesley accepted with a sigh.

Before leaving, Dr. Wellesley leaned down and caringly made sure I was covered up good and tight. He checked my heart and lungs one more time, shook his head (discouraged that there wasn't more he could do), packed up his things, and went on his way.

By the time Dr. Wellesley left, the sun was just peeking over the horizon, and the snow and wind had all but stopped.

Papa, knowing he was supposed to go pick up Gramma today, decided to try to go into town to see if he could wire the hospital to let them know that he wouldn't be able to make it due to the aftereffects of the storm. The snow was just too deep and the trip too long for him to try to attempt it. He hoped that perhaps by tomorrow things would be cleared a bit and he could go then. He'd just have to wait and see.

Unfortunately, I was still unconscious when Papa was preparing to go into town. With a very heavy heart, he kissed me on the forehead and went on.

Samuel, who was off from school today due to the storm (not that Papa would have made him go anyhow given the circumstances), decided to go along with him.

Uncle Mark was up and about, too, getting ready to go help Grampa in the barn, but just as he was tying his last shoe lace, there was a knock at the front door.

"I'll go see who it is," he told Aunt Sara.

Quickly tying the knot, Uncle Mark left the bedroom and went to the door. When he opened it up, Mr. Trussle was standing there on the porch with a wheelchair beside him.

"Someone order a wheelchair?" he asked, smiling.

"You better believe it!" Uncle Mark replied. "Come on in. Sara'll be thrilled!"

Mr. Trussle pushed the wheelchair into the family room as Uncle Mark closed the door behind him.

"Doc asked me to deliver it at my earliest convenience," he said, "but when I heard it was for Sara, I made a special effort."

"That was kind of ya," Uncle Mark told him.

Mr. Trussle shook his head.

"Well," he sympathized, "I sure can't imagine bein' cooped up like that for as long as she has, why...I bet she's goin' absolutely crazy! I know I'd be!"

"Oh, yah! Ya better believe it!" Uncle Mark quipped. "She can't *wait* to be free of that room!"

Mr. Trussle chuckled.

"Well, I'm glad I can be of help to her," he said with a smile. "Say," he queried, "how's Jochebed doin' this mornin'? Any improvement?"

Uncle Mark's smile immediately turned to concern as he looked at Mr. Trussle solemnly.

"She had a *terrible* night," he revealed. "She woke up briefly, but..." He shook his head, worried and troubled by what he'd witnessed. "It was hard to see her like that," he explained with melancholy. "She was scared to death and *incredibly* confused. It caught us all off guard. Doc came and took a look at her, but...well...she'd fallen back unconscious, and...unfortunately, so far today, she hasn't come to yet."

Mr. Trussle looked grieved.

"I'm very sorry to hear that, Mark," he conveyed with sympathy. "I'll be sure to let the folks in town know. Everybody's been prayin' and askin' about her, of that I can assure ya!"

"Well, I can't tell ya how much I appreciate it," Uncle Mark said, grateful. "We all do!"

"Well, you're welcome," Mr. Trussle replied humbly. "And, hey," he offered, "if ya folks need anything, ya just let me and the Mrs. know right away, all right?"

"Sure will, Mr. Trussle. Thanks!" Uncle Mark responded. "And, too, thanks again for bringin' Sara's wheelchair by so quickly. I know she'll surely appreciate it."

Mrs. Trussle smiled.

"Not a problem," he assured as he headed for the door. "It was my pleasure! Hope she enjoys her new found freedom."

"Oh, I know she will!" Uncle Mark replied.

Mr. Trussle left, and Uncle Mark pushed the wheelchair to Aunt Sara's bedroom door.

"Got a little surprise for ya," he said as he pushed the door open.

Aunt Sara squealed in delight as soon as she saw the chair.

"Oh, Mark!" she exclaimed excitedly. "May I sit in it, please?"

Uncle Mark smiled and rolled the chair over to the side of the bed where he gently and carefully helped Aunt Sara into it.

She grimaced in pain from her bruised rib and let out a groan as she gingerly settled in.

"Are ya sure ya wanna do this, Sara?" Uncle Mark questioned, a little hesitant.

"Are you kidding me? Of course, I do!" Aunt Sara replied emphatically. "Bruised rib or not, I'm getting out of this room!"

Uncle Mark shook his head with a grin as he pulled a blanket from their bed to cover her legs with it.

After he got her all situated, he asked, "So, how do ya feel?"

Aunt Sara was sitting there with her hand to her head.

"A bit lightheaded," she admitted. "But I'll be fine!"

Uncle Mark warily looked at her.

"Don't worry," she assured, determined, "I'm fine! *No way* are you getting me back into that bed now!"

Uncle Mark chuckled with a shake of his head.

"All right," he relented, smiling. "Where do ya wanna go first?"

Aunt Sara got quiet as she looked down at the floor glumly.

"I…I want to see Jochebed," she said, her heart aching from guilt and remorse.

Uncle Mark sighed heavily as he understood Aunt Sara's desire to see me. He was also sighing because he felt guilty himself for having been so hard on her when all this first happened. He hadn't brought it up, realizing just how dreadful she felt about the whole situation, but deep down he knew he owed her an apology for how he'd treated her. He decided to take the occasion to offer one.

"Sara," he said tenderly as he pushed her towards my room, "I…I wanna apologize for…for yellin' at ya like I did yesterday, about…about Jochebed."

Aunt Sara stopped him.

"No!" she insisted, feeling to blame. "You were right! I should've known better!" She dropped her head, grieved, as she shook it vehemently. "And that's just it!" she scolded herself. "I think there was a part of me that *did know*, Mark! But I let my fear for Samuel override my better judgment and now…now I can *never* forgive myself for what's happened!"

Uncle Mark abruptly stopped the wheelchair and knelt down beside Aunt Sara.

"Sara," he said firmly as he lifted her face, "this is *not* your fault! And I never should have made it seem so! Jochebed's a big girl, and she knew…"

"Don't, Mark!" Aunt Sara interrupted angrily. "Don't you *dare* blame this on Jochebed! I was the adult! I should have known better!"

"That's enough, Sara!" Uncle Mark shouted angrily. "I wasn't tryin' to blame Jochebed! I'm not tryin' to blame *anyone! It's no one's fault!*" He looked at Aunt Sara with consternation. "Besides," he pointed out, "even if there is fault, there's *plenty* to go around!" He took a deep breath, calming a bit. "Sara," he tried to comfort, "it just happened! Bad things happen!"

Aunt Sara was too upset to accept it.

"Can we not talk about this right now?" she requested tersely. "I just really want to see Jochebed!"

Uncle Mark hung his head, sighing, realizing he wasn't going to convince her.

"Yah," he allowed, standing to his feet. "I'll take ya to her."

Uncle Mark wheeled Aunt Sara into the room and right up next to the bed where she could hold my hand and talk to me. Instantly, upon seeing me, she started to cry.

I was still unconscious, lying motionless and quiet.

"Oh, Mark!" Aunt Sara wept hysterically, burying her face in her hands. "What have I done?"

Uncle Mark tried to console her, but she was too despondent.

"I can't live with myself if she doesn't recover!" she sobbed.

Feeling helpless, and still like he was partially to blame for Aunt Sara's feelings of overwhelming guilt, Uncle Mark stood there quietly and let her cry. After a few minutes, he worryingly suggested.

"Let me take ya back to bed," he urged, concerned this all might be too much for her.

"No!" Aunt Sara defiantly refused. "I want to sit with her for a while! ...Please?"

Uncle Mark was reluctant, but he relented.

"All right then," he agreed. "I'll give ya some time with her. I'll be back after a bit."

Aunt Sara nodded, acknowledging, and Uncle Mark left the room to go help Grampa outside.

Overcome, Aunt Sara sat for a minute just watching me as I lay there, so peaceful and still. She was beside herself with heartache and regret. Lovingly, she reached out and took hold of my hand.

"Please, Jochebed!" she begged, tears streaming down her face. "Please forgive me! I'm *so* sorry...so *very, very* sorry!" She squeezed my hand tightly, absolutely distraught. "Please be all right!" she implored. "You just *have to be all right!*" She sniffed and stammered, confessing her faults. "I...I never should have let you go!" she cried. "I...I should have known better! I am *so, so sorry!*" She leaned forward, laying her head on my chest, sobbing uncontrollably.

As she lay there crying, strangely I began to feel cold again...so very, very cold! It seemed the same thing that had happened to me earlier was now happening to me again. Once more, I felt like I was underwater and I couldn't breathe, and I found myself fighting and struggling to get a breath! Within seconds, I started to feel unbelievable pain, and then suddenly, I jerked awake, but only briefly, gasping for air.

Of course, when I moved, it startled Aunt Sara. She immediately sat up and looked at me, anxious and hopeful!

"Jochebed!" she queried frantically. "Are you awake? Are you okay?"

By the time she sat up, my eyes were already closed again.

As I lay there, however, I thought for sure I could hear voices, but they seemed so distant and garbled. Confused, and trying to make them out, again, I began to feel like I was underwater and fighting for air.

"Jochebed! Jochebed!" Aunt Sara kept pleading. "Please, come back to us! Please wake up!"

I struggled and struggled, but it seemed no matter what I did, I just couldn't break through the heavy fog I was in. I just couldn't take a breath!

Just as I felt I had no more fight in me, suddenly, without warning, my body jolted awake again and I gasped for air.

"Jochebed!" Aunt Sara cried out, holding my hand, looking into my eyes. "Stay with me! You're all right, sweetheart! Please, look at me! You can do it!"

I lay there a second, completely disoriented, not knowing again where I was at or what was happening to me. Scared and confused, my eyes immediately began to frantically search the room for something familiar. As I could settle on nothing, my heart began to race, and before I knew it, horrible pain was coursing through my body. I moaned as it hurt so badly!

Recognizing my panic, Aunt Sara tried to calm me.

"It's all right, Jochebed," she said in a soothing, quiet tone. "You're safe! There's no need to be afraid."

I looked at her with utter bewilderment as I felt for sure that I knew her. Her voice I recognized, and I had no doubt in my mind that I had seen her somewhere before, but still, no matter how hard I tried, I just couldn't remember who she was! For some reason, though, whether it was her gentle smile, or her calming, familiar voice, I didn't feel the least bit threatened by her. In fact, there was something comforting and reassuring about her.

"Where's Samuel?" I asked in a whispered, weary voice, assuming somehow that she'd know.

"He's safe, Jochebed," she assured. "He's with your father."

I lay there shivering, unable to shake the cold that was enveloping my body. I hurt and I was confused and I just wanted answers!

"Where's Mama?" I inquired, trembling and aching terribly.

Aunt Sara's face went ashen as she looked at me, fearful.

"Mama?" she questioned with trepidation.

"Yes," I whispered back. "Where's Mama? Why isn't she here?"

Aunt Sara's eyes filled with tears as she looked at me with incredible sadness and grief.

Needless to say, I didn't understand her response. I furrowed my brow, waiting.

Heartbroken and unsure of how to answer me (and truthfully, not even sure if she should), Aunt Sara sat quietly, contemplating, as a tear trickled down her cheek.

I looked at her, perplexed. Her reluctance was confusing and made no sense to me at all. She had known about Samuel, *surely* she would know about Mama! The longer she sat there saying nothing, though, the more upset I became! Wanting an answer and growing ever more impatient, I asked her again more forcefully.

"Where's Mama?!?" I demanded to know. "Where is she?!?"

Aunt Sara bit her lip as she shook her head, reticent.

"Oh, Jochebed, sweetheart," she disclosed somberly, "your mama, she...she passed away months ago."

I frowned, shaking my head adamantly, not wanting to accept her answer.

"No!" I said breathing heavily. "It's not true! You're lying! Where's Mama?"

Aunt Sara sighed as she looked at me with such sympathy.

"Sweetie," she tried to explain, her voice patient and kind, "I'm afraid it is true. Your mama, she's…she's gone. She was killed in a terrible accident this past summer."

I swallowed hard as I looked at her, trying to process what she was saying. It just didn't seem real! *It just couldn't be!*

As I lay there rolling the information over and over again in my mind, suddenly, out of nowhere, I began to feel such an overwhelming sense of loss. Floods of emotion came welling up inside of me as I slowly began to remember Mama's horrible death. Not knowing what to do with the memory or how to handle what I was feeling, I broke down in tears, sobbing.

"Oh, sweetheart!" Aunt Sara wept, trying to console me. "I'm so sorry! I'm so, very, very sorry!"

We both cried and cried, and cried some more, and then, as if I'd never asked before, I queried in a whispered, raspy voice, "Where's Samuel?"

Startled, Aunt Sara looked at me with such pity and concern, tears streaming down her face. She knew in that moment that something was dreadfully wrong! She shook her head, worried sick, as she gently moved a wisp of hair from my forehead.

"Jochebed, sweetheart," she answered patiently. "Samuel…he's safe. He's with your papa."

FAMILIAR STRANGERS
(Chapter 19)

I was able to stay awake a little longer this time, but eventually I slipped back into unconsciousness. It didn't seem to me that I was out for very long, but when I suddenly jerked awake again, I could tell time had passed; Aunt Sara was gone, and it was dark like nighttime.

As I became more aware, I began to look around again, searching my surroundings. Things seemed familiar to me, like I'd been here before, but unfortunately, I was still very confused, and for some reason, this time, my head was throbbing in an *enormous* amount of pain! Thankfully, I didn't feel as cold as I had in the past, but even though that part seemed somewhat better, I was still hurting all over, and my heart was racing with a sense of fear and panic.

I looked across the way, and much to my surprise, Grampa was napping in a chair on the other side of the room. He had a little light sitting beside him as if he had been reading and simply fell asleep.

I tried to call out to him, but my voice would only manage a whisper.

"Grampa," I found myself saying, over and over again. "Grampa!"

He was sound asleep, but my incessant calling was eventually enough to rouse him awake.

"What…what's goin' on here?" he blustered, startling from his sleep. He seemed a little dazed and befuddled.

"Grampa," I whispered again.

Not sure if he'd heard right, or if he was just dreaming, he rubbed his eyes, grabbed the light, and stood to his feet. Cautiously making his way over to the side of the bed, he leaned in with the lantern and held it out over me.

"Did ya say somethin', Wallflower?" he asked, hopeful.

I flinched at the light as I looked up at him.

"Grampa," I said again. "Is that you?"

Instantly, the biggest grin made its way across his face as he shouted out *quite loudly!*

"Michael, get in here! Quick!" he yelled.

All his excitement alarmed me, and I panicked, not understanding.

Within seconds, Papa, Uncle Mark, and even Samuel came rushing into the room. Needless to say, all the commotion scared me half to death!

"Say it again, dear!" Grampa urged, leaning down over my face. He looked up at Papa, thrilled! "She said my name, Son," he revealed excitedly. "She knew who I was!"

"Jochebed!" Papa questioned, hopeful. "Is that true? Do ya know him? Do ya know me?"

By now, with all the uproar, I was absolutely petrified, and I wasn't sure what to say. Everyone was crowding in around me, staring at me in anticipation. (All but Samuel that is, he was standing off back by the door out of view.) I began to feel trapped! I looked back and forth at everyone, trying to figure things out, but I felt so lost and confused! *Nothing* made sense to me, and I was *completely terrified* of Papa and Uncle Mark! I just wanted them to go away! I looked squarely at Grampa, frightened.

"Please!" I insisted. "What's going on? Why are they here?"

Papa could tell I was nervous and scared, so he told Uncle Mark to back off.

Grampa looked up, almost in despair.

"She just doesn't know us yet, Pa," Papa explained. "But she does you. Talk to her."

Papa stepped back out of sight and stood with Samuel and Uncle Mark.

Disheartened, Grampa came close again and forced a smile.

"Everything's all right, Wallflower," he assured in such a comforting way as he looked down at me. "You're safe and sound. No one's gonna hurt ya."

"Where's Samuel?" I asked, fretful, unable to shake the feeling that something terrible had happened to him.

"Why, he's right here, sweetheart," Grampa said as he motioned for Samuel to come close.

At first, Samuel shook his head out of fear, reluctant to go, but Papa encouraged him on.

Not really wanting to, but seeing he had no choice, he timidly stepped out of the darkness and into the light of the lantern where I could see him.

"Oh, Samuel!" I exclaimed, so relieved that he was all right. "You're here! You're safe! Where have you been?"

Samuel frowned angrily and shook his head, not understanding what was wrong with me. Frightened and upset, he ran from the room.

Papa went after him.

"Samuel!" Papa called out as he reached to grab his arm. He took hold and pulled Samuel to himself.

By now, Samuel was crying. He buried his head in Papa and hugged him tightly.

"What's wrong with her, Papa?" he questioned. "I thought she knew me! Why didn't she remember?"

Papa tried to calm him and explain.

"Son, it's like she's sick," he told him. "Her mind…it's…it's just not right right now. It can't remember certain things, but Sam," he said, taking hold of his arms, looking him in the eye, "she *does* remember you! She just doesn't remember what happened."

"But I told her last night what happened!" Samuel came back at him crossly, "and now she's askin' all over again! It's like…it's like I never said a thing!"

"I know, Son!" Papa commiserated. "And I know it doesn't make any sense right now, but it's like…well…it's like her mind is stuck. She only remembers to a certain point and then…then *nothing!* But," he tried to bolster, "the important thing is that she does know ya! Ya just have to be patient with her and give her time to recover."

Samuel looked away, still bothered by it all.

"Son," Papa tried to encourage, "last night she didn't know Grampa, but today she does. Maybe tomorrow she'll remember someone or somethin' else. Just give her time. Can ya do that?"

Samuel nodded and wiped his tears.

"I guess so," he replied. "It's just so…so frightin' and…and strange! I want her to be like she was!" he insisted. "I want my sister back!"

Papa hugged Samuel again.

"I know, ya do, Son, and so do I!" he empathized. "It's just gonna take some time."

Samuel looked up at him and nodded.

"Hey," Papa asked, trying to take Samuel's mind off of things, "tomorrow, ya wanna go with me to pick up your Gramma from the hospital?"

"Sure, Papa," Samuel agreed. "But what about school?"

Papa smiled as he tussled Sam's hair.

"I think they'll understand if ya miss one more day," he told him.

Samuel hugged Papa again and went back to the couch to lie down.

Once he was settled, Papa walked back to the bedroom to check on me, passing Uncle Mark who was just heading out to go back to bed. As they passed in the doorway, they just looked at each other, troubled.

When Papa stepped back into the room, Grampa was still sitting on the bed beside me, talking to me about this and that. Some things I understood, but most things I had no idea what he was talking about. I didn't say much, though. I basically just listened.

"How's she doin', Pa?" Papa asked in a hushed tone as he quietly made his way towards the bed, careful to stay out of the light so as not to scare me.

Grampa looked up, a little discouraged.

"Well," he replied, standing to his feet, walking over towards Papa, "she hasn't said but two words to me, but she does seem to be listenin'. "And," he added optimistically, "she's still awake, so...that's a good sign!"

"That is good, Pa," Papa agreed, sounding heartened, yet sad. He looked dejected and a bit heartbroken. "I'm gonna turn in for the night," he said. "Sam's stayin' here on the couch, but I think I'm gonna head on home. If ya need me, y'all know where to find me."

Grampa felt badly for Papa, but he understood.

"All right, Son," he accepted. "I'll walk ya out in a minute."

Papa nodded solemnly and left the room.

Grampa turned and walked back to me, sitting down again, and taking hold of my hand.

"I love ya, Wallflower," he expressed with a smile as he leaned over to kiss my forehead. "I'll be right back, okay?"

I looked up at him and nodded.

He smiled again and stood to his feet, heading off to go find Papa.

"Do ya plan to go get your ma tomorrow?" Grampa inquired as he walked into the kitchen where Papa was waiting.

"That's my plan," Papa confirmed. "The problem is where to put her. She really should be in familiar surroundin's to try to regain her strength, but there's just no room for her here."

"I know," Grampa sighed. "I've been thinkin' on that myself. Maybe we could set up a small bed in the family room for now, and I could stay with you at your house."

"Oh, Pa, that's nonsense!" Papa groused. "Ya need to be here with Ma!"

"Well," Grampa shot back, affronted, "I'm open to suggestions!"

Papa sighed in consternation as he scowled and shook his head, unsure of what to do.

"Maybe we should try to move Jochebed home," he purposed.

"What!?" Grampa exclaimed. "Now who's talkin' foolish? That child's confused enough! If we try movin' her now, why..."

"All right, all right, Pa!" Papa snapped, cutting him off, tired and aggravated by the whole thing. "I get it!" Papa shook his head again and sighed, frustrated! "Oh, I don't know!" he grumbled angrily. *"Blasted everything!"*

Grampa and he just stood there in silence, neither knowing what to say.

"I'll think on it tonight," Papa finally said, worn out and disheartened from the day. "We'll figure somethin' out! I'll talk to ya tomorrow before I leave."

"All right, Son," Grampa agreed, sympathetic to his anger and discouragement. "Get some sleep. I'll see ya in the mornin'."

After Papa left, Grampa came back into the bedroom to say goodnight to me. After he tucked me in, he went to bed himself.

When he was gone, I lay there in the dark, feeling so lost and alone. It seemed the world was moving around me, but I was just standing still. It was the most frustrating feeling I'd ever had, and I didn't know what to do about it. I tried to think, but my thoughts were all jumbled. I remembered bits and pieces, moments in time, some making sense to me and others not. I remembered Mama, her smile, her laugh, I remembered her reading to me as a child and sewing with her when I got older, but then I'd remember something random, something I'd heard in a message years ago and none of it seemed connected. I remembered burning biscuits and laughing with Samuel and…

"Oh, Samuel!" I worried. Immediately, my heart began to race with fear as I remembered that he was lost. "Where's Samuel?" I wanted to know. I knew I needed to find him! I was frantic! Just as I was about to go find him, though, my mind wondered to something else. "Oh, Mama!" I agonized, my heart heavy, suddenly remembering that she had died. It made me so sad and I wanted to cry, but then I remembered earnestly looking for Samuel. *Did I find him?* I fretted. *Was he safe? Was he gone, too?* My heart began to pound faster and faster as I panicked, wondering.

All of these thoughts kept racing through my mind, taking me here and there, and then back again. Too overwhelmed by it all, I started to cry.

My body ached and my head hurt so badly and I could *barely* keep my eyes open from the pain and I *just wanted* to run away from it all, but I couldn't! I felt too weak and too tired to even move. Finally, out of sheer exhaustion, I fell asleep, only this time, it was actually sleep and not unconsciousness.

*****

The next morning, Papa came by early to pick up Samuel to go get Gramma from the hospital. Grampa had planned to go with him, but everyone thought it best he stay back with Aunt Sara and me, seeing as how I recognized him and not the others.

Before Papa left, however, he came in to check on me.

When he entered the room, I was still fast asleep, so he walked over to the bed and stood quietly, just watching me. He gently stroked my hair and cautiously leaned down to give me a kiss.

Even though he was trying to be careful, it was enough to rouse me awake, and when I came to, I nearly jumped out of my skin! Right away, I started breathing heavily, panicked, and I almost screamed out again in fear. For some reason, though, this time, I didn't. I just warily looked up at him as he stood there looking down at me.

"I'm sorry, Jochebed," he apologized. "I didn't mean to wake ya."

I swallowed hard, shaking my head, terrified, still breathing heavily, just wanting him to go away!

"Jochebed, sweetheart!" he implored, desperately wanting me to remember him. "It's Papa! I'm not gonna hurt ya!"

I could hear the distress and plea in his voice and he looked so sad to me and I wanted so badly to remember him, but try as I might, I just couldn't. He sounded kind, he did, but something about him still frightened me, and I didn't like him being there! I shook my head again, vehemently, indicating that I wanted him to leave!

He looked completely dejected, but he wisely recognized my fear, and without saying another word, he left.

"How is she this mornin'?" Uncle Mark queried as Papa was coming out of the room.

"'Bout the same," he relayed, cut deep by my rejection.

Uncle Mark put his hand on Papa's shoulder.

"Give her time, Michael," he tried to encourage, "she'll come around."

Papa shook his head, not so sure.

"I hope you're right," he said, nearly in tears. "Ya just can't imagine how hard it is to look into your child's eyes and have her look back at ya completely lost and absolutely *terrified* that you're standin' there!" He wiped a tear, fighting his emotions. "I want so badly to help her, Mark," he cried, his lip quivering. "She's my little girl, and...I love her so much, but...I can't even get *close to her!* I'm tired of feelin' so *helpless!*" He stopped and cleared his throat as he sniffed and wiped his tears. "I've gotta go pick up Ma," he announced abruptly. "Ya comin'?"

Uncle Mark patted him on his shoulder in sympathy.

"Yah," he replied solemnly, feeling badly for Papa. "Just let me get a cup of coffee in me first."

Papa nodded and followed Uncle Mark to the kitchen.

When Papa and Uncle Mark walked into the kitchen, Samuel and Grampa were already there eating breakfast.

Papa and Uncle Mark walked over, poured themselves a cup of coffee, and joined Grampa and Sam at the table.

"Well," Papa started as he sat down, "here's what I'm thinkin'. I figure Mark and I can move the chairs in the family room out to the barn. We'll set up Lydia's and my old bed in there for Ma and Pa temporarily until Jochebed's well enough to move back home; that way everyone can stay where they're at, and Ma and Pa can be together. I know it'll be tight quarters for a while, but hopefully it won't be for long."

"Sounds like a plan!" Grampa agreed enthusiastically. "But why don't ya leave Sam here with me today and while you two go get your Ma he and I can take care of settin' things up."

Papa looked over at Samuel.

"Well, what do ya say, Son?" he asked. "Ya wanna stay here and help your Grampa?"

Samuel shrugged his shoulder and contemplated.

"If you'd rather go with us, ya can," Papa assured, sensing his reluctance. "It shouldn't take long for your Uncle Mark and me to set things up when we get back."

Samuel shook his head.

"No, Papa," he finally accepted, "it's fine. I'll stay. Things should be ready for Gramma when she comes home."

"You're sure?" Papa questioned.

Samuel nodded, confirming.

"All right then, Mark," Papa said, taking one last sip of his coffee, standing to his feet, "we better get goin'!"

*****

Before he left, Uncle Mark wheeled Aunt Sara to the family room where she could watch and visit with Grampa and Samuel as they worked. She and Uncle Mark kissed goodbye, Uncle Mark grabbed his coat, and he and Papa left.

While I lay alone in the bedroom, falling in and out of sleep, Grampa and Samuel went straight to work getting things situated for Gramma's arrival.

*****

Unfortunately, as I lay in bed, time seemed to pass by so slowly. When I'd wake, all I could do is just lie there and think, and when I wasn't thinking, it seemed I was sleeping.

When I did have thoughts, though, the memories would still come and go, and they were still just as scattered and jumbled as ever. The only constant seemed to be Samuel. I just wanted to find him and make sure he was all right!

Lying there, though, I began to hear noises in the other room, and it piqued my curiosity. The more I heard them, the more I wanted to know what was going on.

Too confused to know that I should just stay put (after all my head was pounding horribly, and I felt incredibly weak and sore), I determined to try to sit myself up. I pushed down on the bed with my hands and tried to lift my head off the pillow. As I lifted it up more and more, though, I thought for sure my head was going to explode! I was in sheer agony!

I paused, taking a deep breath, and eventually managed to get myself partway up. By the time I got myself all the way up, however, I was in tears from the unbearable pain I was in!

Still determined to go see what was happening, I refused to lie back down. Instead, I just sat there for a moment, trying not to throw up! I was so sick to my stomach by this point; I thought for sure I was going to lose it!

Thankfully, I managed to keep everything down, and when I recovered enough, I flung the covers off of myself and carefully swung my legs over the side of the bed. Slowly and carefully, I scooted myself to the edge and just sat there. I *had* to rest! I was so exhausted and completely out of breath I wasn't sure I could go on. I waited, trying to breathe, but as I sat there, I noticed how unbelievably weak I felt and how terribly my head was pounding! It was as if someone was hitting me with a hammer or something! My vision was blurred and doubled all at the same time, and, of course, that made it very hard to see.

Still confused, and not thinking straight, however, I pressed on.

I squinted and strained, trying to focus, and even though it was difficult and I was *completely* miserable, I wasn't going to let that deter me on bit! My mind was set; I was going to go find Samuel one way or the other!

I put my hands on the nightstand beside the bed and tried to lift myself up, but as soon as I stood to my feet, I immediately blacked out and fell to the floor, hitting my head on the chair that was sitting there next to the bed.

*****

"What on earth?" Aunt Sara said to herself, startled by the commotion.

Grampa and Samuel had just left to go to our house to load up Mama and Papa's bed, and Aunt Sara was there alone in the family room, working on some mending.

She promptly lay the mending aside, gathered the blanket that was resting over her lap, threw it onto the couch, and wheeled herself towards the bedroom. When she got there, my door was slightly ajar, so she pushed it open and came right in. Seeing me there in a heap on the floor, she instantly gasped in fright!

"Jochebed!" she shouted, frantically trying to get to me. She wheeled her chair as close to me as she possibly could, and reached down to turn my head. "Oh, no!" she exclaimed. "You're bleeding!" She looked around to see if there was anything she could use to stop it, but there was nothing within reach. "Oh, this chair!" she blustered in frustration.

She knew better, but she lifted herself out of her wheelchair, grimacing in pain as she did. She carefully and slowly knelt down beside me and pulled a blanket from my bed, tucking it under my face, wanting to get my head off the cold, hard floor. She attempted to roll me over, but the pain from her bruised rib prevented her from doing so, so unable to do much more, she decided to use a portion of the blanket to try to stop the bleeding. The gash on my head was fairly deep, though, and no matter how hard she pressed, the bleeding just wouldn't stop! She sat, panicked, trying to figure out what to do.

"Please, dear Lord," she begged, "You've *got* to help me! Please stop this bleeding and help me to know what to do!"

Thinking she would try to go find something else to wrap my head with, she grabbed hold of her wheelchair and painfully lifted herself back up to her feet. Standing there, hurting, she held her side, trying to catch her breath. She was just about to sit herself back down in her wheelchair when suddenly; there was an unexpected knock at the front door.

"Oh, thank You, Lord!" she praised, quickly sitting back down, and wheeling herself out of the room. The whole way to the front door, she prayed and prayed that whoever was there wouldn't go away before she could get to them.

Unfortunately, the person knocked a couple more times, and stopped, assuming no one was coming to answer the door.

"Oh, please, don't let them leave!" she begged, turning her wheels as fast as she could.

When she finally got to the family room and over to the door, she hastily opened it up and looked outside. Much to her surprise and relief, Dr. Wellesley was just stepping off the porch, heading towards his rig.

"Doctor!" she shouted hysterically. "I'm here! Come quick!"

Dr. Wellesley immediately turned and ran back up onto the porch, hurrying inside.

"Are you all right?" he questioned anxiously, looking at her earnestly. "What's wrong?"

"It's Jochebed!" Aunt Sara explained excitedly. "She's fallen and she's bleeding badly!"

Dr. Wellesley rushed to the bedroom, with Aunt Sara following behind him.

Upon entering the room and seeing me lying there, Dr. Wellesley raced over as quickly as he could and turned me over. Grabbing gauze from his bag, he began to apply pressure to my wound, hoping to stop the bleeding. Once he had it somewhat under control, he lifted me back into bed and tended to my cut. He cleaned it well, and began to stitch it up.

"There!" he said as he clipped the thread from the last stitch. "That ought to hold it." He promptly turned to Aunt Sara. "How in the *world* did she end up on the floor?" he wanted to know.

"Honestly, I can't say," Aunt Sara admitted. "She must have tried to get out of bed on her own. I was in the other room, tending to some mending when I heard a thud. Right away, I dropped what I was doing and came to see what was happening. When I got here, she was already on the floor, bleeding."

"Well, I'm glad it wasn't any worse than it is," Dr. Wellesley commented as he cleaned up his things. As he checked my vitals and looked me over to make sure I hadn't injured myself further, he questioned Aunt Sara as to how I'd been doing.

"Better, I guess," Aunt Sara offered, a little unsure. "She seems to be staying awake for longer periods of time, but we're finding that her memory is sketchy at best. For instance, she recognizes Samuel when she can see him but then keeps asking about him, worried he's still lost, when she can't. And yesterday she didn't recognize Papa Lowry, but today she suddenly does. And oh, yes!" Aunt Sara continued, remembering. "Worst of all, regrettably, she thought her mama was still alive. I had to explain to her that she had passed and when it all came rushing back to her, she broke down sobbing as if it had just happened all over again. It was heart wrenching to watch, to say the least! She's yet to recognize her own father or Mark, and there's still no indication that she even knows who *I am!*" Aunt Sara shook her head, grieved. "It's just all so confusing, Doctor!" she confessed.

"Well, unfortunately, Sara," Dr. Wellesley explained, "it's all too common with injuries to the brain. We'll just have to wait and see and hope she continues to improve. I've seen some patients who never remember a thing, and others who, suddenly, out of nowhere, remember everything! And then there are yet others, who are somewhere in between. We'll just hope for the best for Jochebed."

Aunt Sara nodded, agreeing.

"She may be out for a while," Dr. Wellesley warned, putting the rest of his things away, "so don't let that alarm you. She did take a pretty nasty fall." He looked at Aunt Sara. "Has she been eating at all?" he questioned curiously.

"No, nothing so far," Aunt Sara replied. "She's been so in and out, we really haven't been able to give her anything."

"Well, see if you can't get her to eat something when she comes to," Dr. Wellesley instructed. "She needs to rebuild her strength so that she can get better. And by all means, *keep a close eye on her!* In her state of mind, it's hard to tell what she might do! Until she's more stable, she shouldn't be trying to get out of bed, *especially* on her own!"

"I understand, Doctor," Aunt Sara assured. "I'll be certain to let everyone know we need to watch her more closely."

"Sounds good!" Dr. Wellesley agreed. "I'll stop in tomorrow to check her again." He stood up to leave. "By the way," he asked as he and Aunt Sara made their way to the front door, "how are you feeling?"

"Still pretty sore," Aunt Sara confessed, "but loving my newfound freedom!"

"Well, you be sure to take it easy," Dr. Wellesley cautioned. "You've got precious cargo there that needs protecting."

"Oh, I know!" Aunt Sara replied as she put her hand on her belly, smiling up at Dr. Wellesley. "I'm minding to take care!"

"That's good to hear!" he approved, smiling back. "I'll see you tomorrow." He opened the door to leave.

"Thank you so much, Doctor," Aunt Sara said as he stepped outside.

You're welcome," Dr. Wellesley answered back as he turned to leave, clasping the collar of his coat to protect himself from the cold.

Aunt Sara closed the door behind him and wheeled herself back to my room to sit with me until I woke up.

COPING
(Chapter 20)

I was out for about a half hour, and when I came to, Aunt Sara was sitting there dutifully, patiently waiting for me to wake up.

"There you are," she said with a smile as I painfully opened my eyes. "How are you feeling, sweetie?"

I was a little groggy and my head was in a tremendous amount of pain and I was still very confused, so I didn't really answer her.

"What happened?" I asked, bringing my hand to my forehead, feeling the bandage that covered my wound.

"You fell and hit your head," Aunt Sara informed me. "You passed out for a while, but the doctor came and fixed you up."

"I fell?" I queried, not remembering. "But how?"

"I think you were trying to get out of bed," Aunt Sara explained. "You must've tripped or blacked out or something, because you fell and hit your head on the chair. Dr. Wellesley said you really ought to stay in bed and rest for a while, at least, until you get your strength back."

I looked at Aunt Sara feeling terribly lost as my mind began to race. I just stared at her and watched her for the longest time. Something she said, it was like I had heard it before, only I couldn't place it.

You really ought to stay in bed. You really ought to stay in bed. That phrase kept whirling around in my mind.

"Jochebed," Aunt Sara questioned, "sweetheart, are you all right?"

"It's you!" I exclaimed out of the blue as my mind cleared a bit.

"It's me?" Aunt Sara wondered aloud, not understanding. "What do you mean, it's me?"

"It's you!" I replied earnestly. "It...it was you! *You were the one* who was supposed to stay in bed! *You were the one* the doctor talked to! I...*I remember!*"

Aunt Sara got a look of excitement on her face.

"You're exactly right, Jochebed!" she told me enthusiastically. "Do you remember who I am?"

Regretfully, I didn't. I shook my head no, embarrassed that I couldn't remember. It was obvious to me by the look on her face and by the tone in her voice that I was *supposed* to know who she was, my mind, however, was completely blank. I felt (as her look of excitement turned to one of disappointment) that I had let her down.

"I'm really sorry," I said, feeling awful. "I'm sorry I don't know who you are!"

"Oh no, sweetie," Aunt Sara assured. "It's all right. You're continuing to remember things, and that's all that matters. Don't let it get to you. In time, I have every confidence you'll remember everything!"

I looked up at her, feeling discouraged and hopeless.

"Maybe you're right," I whispered, my head still throbbing. "But I really just want to rest right now, if that's okay?"

"Well, actually," Aunt Sara suggested, "you really should try to eat something. The doctor said you need to build up your strength. I can make something for you if you'd like?"

I didn't feel the least bit hungry; in fact, I felt a little sick to my stomach from the amount of pain I was in. I looked at Aunt Sara, wearily.

"I'm really not hungry at all," I told her, just wanting to go to sleep.

"Please, Jochebed," she begged. "It's been so long since you've had anything. Try something…won't you?"

I felt horrible, but I relented.

Aunt Sara left right away to get me something to eat.

*****

Grampa and Samuel had finally returned with the bed from our house, and were now busily setting it up in the family room.

They were putting the last part of it together when Aunt Sara came out of the bedroom.

"How's she doin'?" Grampa asked, hopeful.

"She seems to be doing all right given the circumstances," Aunt Sara replied.

She then commenced to telling Grampa and Samuel everything that had happened.

"Oh, my gracious!" Grampa expressed with concern. "You're sure she's all right?"

"Yes, Papa Lowry," Aunt Sara reassured. "She's as *all right* as she can be."

Worried, Grampa put down the tool he was holding in his hand.

"I'm gonna go look in on her," he said.

"All right," Aunt Sara agreed. "I'm off to make her something to eat."

"She's hungry?" Grampa asked enthusiastically. "Well, that's good to hear!"

"Well, not actually," Aunt Sara confessed. "I think she's doing it more out of obligation than actual hunger."

"Oh, I see," Grampa came back a bit dejected. "Well, maybe by the time ya get things fixed, she'll feel more like eatin'."

"I do hope you're right," Aunt Sara replied. "She seems so weak and frail. She really does need the nourishment."

Grampa walked over and put his hand on Aunt Sara's shoulder, sympathetic to her concerns.

"This may be a long, slow process," he reminded, smiling down at her, trying to lift her spirits, "but I just know that one of these day's we're gonna have our old Jochebed back!"

"Sure hope that's true, Grampa," Samuel chimed in. "I miss her!"

Grampa looked across the room to Samuel and nodded, agreeing.

"I miss her, too, Sam," he said, "but God'll see her through this…I know He will! We just have to trust Him!"

Grampa walked off towards the bedroom and Aunt Sara wheeled herself to the kitchen to make me something to eat.

"Can I help with anything?" Samuel asked as he followed her into the kitchen.

"Oh, I think I can manage," Aunt Sara answered. "But thank you for asking."

"You're sure?" Samuel pushed. "'Cause I can help ya if ya want?"

Although Aunt Sara could manage quite well on her own, except for reaching things up high, of course, she could sense that Samuel wanted to be of use.

"Well, I do need some things from the cupboards," she said, smiling at Samuel. "If you could fetch me a plate and the serving tray that would be great!"

A smile came across Samuel's face as he went to get the things Aunt Sara had requested.

While they were busy in the kitchen, Grampa visited with me for a short while in the bedroom. He didn't stay very long, however, because he really needed to get Gramma's bed all set up for her before she arrived home from the hospital.

After making sure I was all right, he told me he loved me, gave me a kiss on the cheek, and headed back to the family room.

As soon as Samuel noticed Grampa was back, he excused himself from the kitchen and went to help him.

Aunt Sara finished up my lunch, gathered everything onto a tray, and brought it to me along with a glass of milk. Unfortunately, by the time she got to my room, I was already fast asleep.

Still feeling I should eat something, she wheeled herself over to the side of my bed and set the tray on the table there beside me. Leaning over, she gently tried to wake me.

I startled at her prompting and nearly screamed.

"I'm sorry, Jochebed," she calmed. "I didn't mean to scare you, but I have your food here for you. Do you think you can sit up and try to eat something?"

I looked at her feeling so miserable, still not the least bit hungry, but she'd gone to all the trouble, so I felt obliged. I tried to sit myself up, but my head was throbbing mercilessly and made it nearly impossible. Every time I went to move, it seemed to get worse.

"I really don't think I can," I told her fighting the pain.

"Here, then," Aunt Sara offered. "Let me see if I can help you." She leaned over and slipped her hand gently under my head, lifting it carefully from my pillow.

I immediately cried out!

"I can't!" I insisted, my eyes closed, breathing heavily.

Aunt Sara gently lowered my head back down and sat back.

"Well now," she said, concerned, "we have to try to get something in you. Maybe if I just pinch off a little of your sandwich at a time, I could feed it to you bit by bit that way."

I swallowed hard and glanced at her.

"All right," I whispered reluctantly. "We can try."

She reached over and took a small portion of the sandwich and brought it to my mouth. Surprisingly, I managed to get it down. She pinched off a little more and fed it to me, and, again, a little more. While it was a long, arduous, slow process, I eventually got about half the sandwich eaten.

"Can we please stop now?" I begged after going on like that for quite awhile. "I'm so exhausted. I just want to sleep!"

"You're sure you don't want to try to eat just a little more?" Aunt Sara encouraged.

"No!" I replied, certain. "I really do just want to rest." (It seemed falling asleep was the only thing that helped to ease the pain in my head.)

"All right," Aunt Sara conceded, "but I'll be back to check on you in a little while." She looked at me sternly. "And no trying to get out of bed this time, all right?" she instructed.

"I promise," I agreed.

Aunt Sara started gathering everything to take with her, when suddenly I asked in a random thought.

"Is Gramma home yet?" I queried.

Clearly, my question caught her completely off guard.

"What did you say?" she questioned, not sure she'd heard me correctly.

"Is...is Gramma home yet?" I asked again.

Aunt Sara looked at me, shocked yet excited!

"You remember!?" she exclaimed.

I looked at her, perplexed, confused by her reaction.

"Yes," I replied, now wondering if I'd said something wrong. "She was sick, a stroke, right? Wasn't she supposed to come home from the hospital soon?"

Aunt Sara got the biggest smile on her face as she looked at me so proudly.

"Yes, Jochebed," she answered sweetly, "you're absolutely right! Gramma did have a stroke, and she's coming home today. Your papa and Uncle Mark went to get her."

"I...I have to get out of her bed!" I insisted frantically, trying to sit myself up.

"No, no, no!" Aunt Sara resisted, gently coaxing me back down. "You rest. Grampa and Samuel are setting up a bed for her in the family room. She'll be fine in there until you get better."

The mention of Samuel's name instantly brought fear to my heart!

"Samuel!" I asked in a panic. "Is...is he all right? Is he safe? We have to find him!"

Aunt Sara got an anguished look on her face as she sighed, disheartened. I could tell by her reaction that what I'd said had discouraged her. Managing a smile, though, she looked at me sweetly, and assured me yet again.

"He's fine, Jochebed," she told me. "Samuel's here and he's safe."

"Well...can I see him?" I queried, anxious to make sure he was all right. "Please! I really want to see him!"

Sensing my angst, and not wanting to upset me further, she reluctantly agreed.

"I'll ask him to come in right away," she promised somberly, setting the lunch tray on her lap to take with her. Once she was set, she rolled herself over to the door and left.

I lay there, waiting restlessly, desperately wanting to see Samuel!

By now, Grampa and Samuel had finished putting the bed together for Gramma, and Grampa was napping on the couch.

Not wanting to disturb him, Samuel was quietly sitting on the floor, looking at a book.

When Aunt Sara came into the room, Samuel looked up, and Aunt Sara motioned for him to come over to her.

He willingly complied.

"Samuel," she whispered, so as not to wake Grampa. "Jochebed's awake, and she'd really like to see you."

Samuel frowned and looked at her warily.

"Does she remember?" he wanted to know.

Aunt Sara shook her head.

"I'm sorry, Samuel, but no," she relayed with sadness. "She still thinks you're missing. She wants to see for herself that you're all right."

Samuel sighed, aggravated as he looked down at the floor.

"Fine!" he conceded, visibly upset. "I'll go see her to ease her mind."

Aunt Sara looked at him sympathetically.

"You're a good brother to do this," she encouraged.

Samuel shrugged his shoulders, sloughing off the compliment.

"I'm sorry she doesn't remember," Aunt Sara commiserated. "Would you like me to go with you?"

Samuel sighed again.

"No," he replied glumly. "I think I can do this."

Aunt Sara gave him an understanding smile as she lovingly squeezed his arm.

Samuel took a deep breath, and slowly walked to the bedroom, poking his head inside the door. Needless to say, he was very disinclined and hesitant to come inside.

"Samuel," I called out in horrible pain, forcing myself to sit up a bit so I could see him better. "Is that you?"

Samuel straightened himself and walked on into the room, but he only came partway before stopping.

I furrowed my brow, not understand.

"Come here, silly!" I urged, so excited to see him, my speech arduous and at a whisper. "Come here and let me see you!" My head was pounding, but I didn't care! Samuel was actually here and safe and that was all that mattered to me!

Strangely, Samuel looked anxious and wary of coming any closer.

"What's wrong?" I questioned, puzzled by his reluctance.

Samuel didn't budge nor say anything. He just stared at me, unsure of what to do.

"Please, Samuel!" I begged. "Come over here so I can see you!"

Slowly, Samuel began to saunter over a little closer to the bed.

"Come on!" I prodded, reaching out to him. "I want to give you a hug. I just can't believe you're really here! Where were you?"

Something I said must have bothered him, because he suddenly stopped, and began to back away bit by bit.

"Samuel!" I called out again, grimacing in pain, squinting my eyes, trying to focus. "What's wrong?"

He looked at me, so furious, and yelled at me with a vengeance.

"Why don't you remember!?" he shrieked angrily. *"**Just remember!!**"*

I startled, taken aback by his outburst. Confused, I shook my head, not understanding what he meant.

He was fuming!

"You know all this already!" he insisted, shouting vehemently, tears welling up in his eyes. ***"Why can't you just remember?!?"***

I started to say something, but before I could get a word out, he immediately turned and ran from the room.

Aunt Sara must have heard the uproar because she was already on her way in just as Samuel was running out.

He raced past her before she could catch him.

"Samuel!" she called out, concerned.

"Leave me alone!" he yelled back in tears.

Distressed, but understanding, Aunt Sara let him go. She wheeled herself into the room and over to my bed where I was now lying there crying.

"What happened?" she asked, worried.

"I...I don't know!" I cried, rubbing my forehead, my eyes closed in pain. My head was killing me and crying only made it worse, but I couldn't help it! I was so hurt and confused by what had just happened I didn't know what else to do! "Why is Samuel so angry with me?" I sobbed, not understanding. "Why did he yell at me like that? What did I do wrong? *What did I do?*"

Aunt Sara came up close and put her hand on my arm.

"Oh, sweetie!" she tried to console. "You didn't do anything wrong." Her voice was sympathetic and kind. "Samuel, he...well...he just doesn't know how to deal with you right now," she explained. "That's all!"

"But...but why?" I sniffed and stammered, wanting to understand. "What's wrong with me?"

Aunt Sara did her best to explain that I was not the Jochebed that Samuel knew, that I had had a terrible accident and was, for lack of a better term, sick for now. She tried to encourage me that, with time, Samuel would come to accept me, but that I just needed to be patient until he did. She told me not to worry and just to concentrate on getting better, but the more she talked, the more confused I became. None of it made any sense to me at all!

Discouraged and lost, I closed my eyes and tried to rest.

Aunt Sara graciously sat with me until I eventually fell asleep.

*****

It was early afternoon when Papa and Uncle Mark returned home with Gramma, and when she arrived, as you can imagine, Grampa was elated to see her! They carefully helped her inside and got her into her bed in the family room, and when she was settled, she remarked how good it was to be home again! Interestingly enough, she had a wheelchair of her own, and when Aunt Sara saw it, she joked with Gramma that when she was feeling better, maybe they could race each other. Gramma smiled and winked at her.

"You wait, see," she promised. "I beat you!"

~

It was amazing how much improved Gramma seemed. The doctors and nurses had been working with her at the hospital, and she was well on her way to recovery.

~

"I determined to get better!" she announced as she smiled up at Grampa who was dotingly standing beside her, holding her hand.

"I know ya are, dear," he replied as he leaned down and gave her a kiss. "I'm just so glad to have ya home!"

~

Gramma's left side was still a little weak, and paralyzed, but she said that the feeling was slowly starting to come back a little.

~

"In no time at all," she teased with Grampa, "I be up chasing you 'round the house!"

Grampa just laughed.

"That's my Elizabeth!" he quipped.

Suddenly, Gramma realized that Samuel and I were missing from her homecoming.

"Where Jochebed, Samuel?" she queried. "I not see them yet."

"Yah," Papa wondered, "where is Sam? I haven't seen him either."

Aunt Sara answered, trying not to give too much away as they hadn't yet told Gramma about my condition.

"I think he got a little upset earlier," she said motioning her head in the direction of my bedroom, hoping Papa would catch the drift. "I think he may have gone back to your place."

Papa nodded, indicating that he understood.

Gramma asked again.

"Jochebed, where she?" she wanted to know.

Grampa turned and looked at Papa, his eyes asking, *What should I say?*

Papa shook his head, realizing that there was no keeping it from her.

"She needs to know, Pa," he said bluntly. "She'll find out eventually."

Gramma furrowed her brow, questioning.

"Find out what?" she asked, anxious to understand. "What you keeping from me? What going on? Where Jochebed?"

Grampa reluctantly turned back to Gramma, loathe to have to tell her. He took hold of her hand yet again, letting out a long, mournful sigh.

"Elizabeth," he explained somberly, "Jochebed, she…well…she had a horrible accident, sweetheart."

Gramma gasped, terribly upset!

"Accident?" she exclaimed, frightened. "Why…she okay?"

"Well now," Grampa answered, trying to calm her, "she seems to be slowly improvin' physically, but…well…it's her memory we're the most concerned about. She seems to be havin' a hard time rememberin' things."

Gramma squeezed Grampa's hand, dismayed, as she looked at him with deep concern.

"Oh, poor dear!" she expressed with angst. "Where she at? Can I see her?"

"In time, Mama Lowry," Aunt Sara replied. "She's resting right now. Besides, you need to get some rest yourself after your long trip."

"You not tell me what to do!" Gramma snapped at her, angrily.

"Elizabeth!" Grampa admonished, shocked and taken aback by her tone. "That's not like ya to talk to Sara that way!"

"It's all right, Papa Lowry," Aunt Sara assured, not taking any offense. "The same thing happened with my grandfather when he had his stroke. It changed his personality somewhat. She doesn't mean anything by it."

"It's true, Pa," Uncle Mark jumped in, backing her up. "The doc's told us we might see some changes in her personality and that they're probably permanent, but they also said not to worry about it. Apparently, it's somethin' that often happens in people who've had strokes."

Grampa looked back at Gramma, worried, nonetheless, and quite uneasy about the whole thing.

"Stop talking me like I not here!" Gramma barked tersely.

"Now, now, dear," Grampa tried to calm, "we know you're here. Ya can go see Jochebed later on. Sara's right, she needs her rest and so do you."

Gramma sighed, chagrinned.

"Well…all right," she grudgingly agreed as she settled down in her bed. "I sleep then."

Everyone left the room to give her some peace and quiet.

"Now, what's this about Samuel?" Papa asked Aunt Sara as they started into the kitchen.

"Well," Aunt Sara explained with solemnity, "Jochebed was asking about Samuel again, and she insisted on seeing him. I *warned Samuel* before he went in there that she couldn't remember, but he said he thought he could handle it." She shook her head clearly troubled. "Something must have upset him, though," she divulged, "because he ended up yelling at Jochebed something awful right before he ran off. I assume he headed back to your house because I haven't seen him around here since."

Papa sighed, frustrated.

"I suppose I better go check on him," he said. "I just wish he'd understand." Papa left right away to go find Samuel, and sure enough, when he got back to our place, he found him sulking in his room.

"Son," Papa called out as he knocked on Samuel's bedroom door, starting to open it up. "Ya in there?"

"Yah, Papa," Samuel answered as he sat up on his bed. "I'm here."

Papa walked in and sat down beside him on the bed.

"We got Gramma home safe," he informed, hoping to break the ice with some good news.

Samuel nodded as he stared down at his hands.

Papa went on.

"She'd really like to see ya, Son," he told him. "She's been askin' for ya."

"Hmmm," Samuel retorted, "I guess, at least, *she* remembers who I am!"

Papa shook his head, sighing, a little aggravated with Samuel.

"Son!" he came back at him, rebuking him a bit. "I thought I explained all of this to ya before! Your sister, she…"

"Ya don't have to explain!" Samuel interrupted angrily, shouting tersely. "*I know!* It's just that…well…she…I mean…she just *scares me!* It's like…it's like I see her, and she looks like my sister, but then…then she says somethin', and…well…it's like…it's like she's not even really there!" He shook his head, clearly annoyed and disconcerted by the whole situation. "I don't know how to be around her, Papa!" he admitted. "I feel like I'm talkin' to a *ghost* or somethin'!"

Papa sighed again as he put his arm around Samuel.

"I understand," he said, "and I won't force ya to see her if ya don't want to. But, Sam, your sister's still there. She's just a bit lost right now, that's all! But one thing's for sure, she loves ya a lot. The fact that she's still concerned about ya and askin for ya is proof of that to me!" He paused and thought for a minute. "Really, all we can do for now is just keep prayin' for her," he advised. "Hopefully, one day real soon she'll remember for keeps."

"I *am* prayin'!" Samuel insisted, perturbed. "Have been ever since all this happened, but…" He looked down at the floor, feeling guilty. "I just keep thinkin'…if only she could've known I was safe at church with you." He looked up at Papa with tears in his eyes. "I just wish she'd a stayed at home, Papa!" he bemoaned, upset with me that I hadn't listened. "Why couldn't she just have stayed at home!?"

Papa pulled Samuel close.

"I don't know, Son," he replied, hugging him tightly, fighting back tears. "I wish she would've stayed home, too, but…she didn't." He shook his head. "We can't dwell on that now, though," he pointed out. "What's done is done, and we're at where we're at! The only thing we can do is try to move forward from here."

Samuel wiped a tear from his eye.

"I am sorry I yelled at her, Papa," he said feeling badly for not having been more sensitive to my condition.

"I know ya are, Son," he acknowledged. "And I'm sure she'll understand when she's better. It's just gonna take some time!"

THE SURGERY
(Chapter 21)

After Papa and Samuel talked, they decided they should get some things done around the house, so Papa went to finish some projects that were due to be delivered to his customers within the next few days, and Samuel went to do his chores and some of mine. They both worked hard right up until it was time to go join the others at Grampa and Gramma's for the evening meal.

"There he is!" Gramma exclaimed excitedly as Samuel came through the door. "You come see me!"

Samuel ran over and gave Gramma a big hug and a kiss.

"It's good to have ya home, Gramma," he said, smiling. "Ya look real good!"

"Well, thank ya!" Gramma replied. "It good be here!" Abruptly changing course, she looked around and impertinently demanded, "Now, someone take me see Jochebed!"

"Are ya sure ya wouldn't rather wait 'til after supper?" Grampa asked as he came into the family room from the kitchen.

"I wait long enough!" Gramma insisted tersely. "Now take me to her!"

"All right then," Grampa conceded with a sigh.

Papa, who was standing there in the family room as well, watching, quickly got the wheelchair and brought it to the side of the bed.

"No need hold so tight!" Gramma sniped as Papa and Grampa tried to help her into the wheelchair. "I can do myself!"

"Now, woman!" Grampa snapped back. "You'll let us help ya, or you're goin' *right back in that bed!*"

Gramma frowned at Grampa.

"You cantankerous!" she charged.

"Me!?" Grampa strongly objected. "Why...I think you're talkin' to the *wrong person* there, missy!"

"Oh, you be quiet!" Gramma hushed. "Just get me in chair and take me Jochebed!"

Papa couldn't help but chuckled at their banter back and forth.

"This is gonna be *some* recovery!" he quipped as he winked at Grampa.

Grampa rolled his eyes.

"Humph!" he groused. "Some recovery indeed!"

Gramma got situated in her chair and was ready to go.

"Well," she prodded impatiently, "chair not move itself!"

"Uh-huh!" Grampa nodded, exasperated, as he took the handles of the wheelchair. "Some recovery *indeed!*"

Papa grinned as he shook his head, nearly chuckling.

Grampa summarily wheeled Gramma to the bedroom, and Papa followed behind them.

When they came in, I was lying in the bed, resting.

Grampa pushed Gramma right up next to me.

"Jochebed," Gramma sweetly called out. "I hear you not well."

I opened my eyes as soon as I heard her voice, turning my head the best I could to look at her.

"Gramma!" I exclaimed in a painful whisper, so thrilled to see her. "When did you get here?"

"While ago," she answered, sneering as she glanced at Grampa and Papa. "No one let me come see you 'til now, though!" She turned back to me. "How you feel?" she asked kindly.

"I'm well," I responded without pause, obviously not fully comprehending my current condition. "I plan to be out of here by tomorrow."

"Oh, do ya now?" Grampa quipped sarcastically. "And just how do ya plan to manage that?"

"Oh, bother!" Gramma dismissed. "Don't listen him. He killjoy!"

"Woman!" Grampa grumbled, a little perturbed yet half-teasing, "I've just about had it with ya, now! I'm gonna have Michael here take ya back to the hospital if ya keep goin' like this!"

Gramma smiled broadly.

"See," she insisted, "killjoy!"

I managed a smile, but only briefly. Any little movement seemed to make my head hurt so much worse, and with my thinking not right, it never occurred to me once to say anything to anyone about the tremendous pain I was in. I guess I just assumed that everyone already knew. Evidently, they had no idea, though, because no one ever offered or gave me anything to help ease my discomfort.

*****

Papa and Grampa left Gramma to visit with me for awhile while they went on to supper. Grampa was going to take Gramma with them, but she rather *strongly insisted* that he leave her there with me. Not wanting an argument, Grampa agreed!

*****

Gramma and I talked back and forth the best we could, but her speech was not quite back to normal, and my speech was still labored due to the level of pain I was in. As difficult as it was for both of us to converse, though, we did manage a conversation, albeit an unusual one. Some things she talked about I understood (others were still a mystery), and due to my continued confusion, I don't think she always understand what I was trying to say. Nevertheless, despite our varied obstacles, I did so enjoy her company!

After about a half hour or so, Grampa came back into the bedroom to check on Gramma.

"All right now," he announced as he walked in, "time to break this hen fest up! Ya both need somethin' to eat!"

"Already?" Gramma questioned, having lost track of time. "Why, I not even hungry!"

Grampa walked up behind her wheelchair and took hold of the handles.

"Well, you're not the only one in the room, my dear," he reminded playfully as he smiled and winked at me.

Without warning, totally out of the blue, Gramma suddenly broke down into tears.

"I sorry," she said, lowering her head, fretful.

Grampa was thrown by the sudden change in her emotions. He knelt down beside her to talk with her.

"Elizabeth," he assured, feeling awful he'd upset her so. "Sweetheart, I didn't mean anything by it. I was just teasin' with ya!"

"Well, you not funny!" Gramma told him, pouting. "Take me to bed!"

Grampa looked astonished as he stood to his feet.

"All right, dear," he replied, compliant. He looked at me. "I'll have your Aunt Sara bring some food for ya right away, all right, Wallflower?" he said as they started to leave.

"Who?" I questioned, not remembering who Aunt Sara was.

"Your Aunt Sara," Grampa explained. "Ya know, the nice lady who's been helpin' to take care of ya."

"Oh, her," I recalled. "Sure, that would be fine."

Grampa and Gramma left the room, and I lay there waiting in pain.

A few minutes later, Aunt Sara came into the room carrying a tray of food on her lap for me.

"Brought you something to eat," she said, smiling as she wheeled herself over to the bed. "Are you hungry?"

"A little," I answered.

"Well, that's good to hear!" Aunt Sara expressed, thankful. "I brought you soup this time. Do you think you can sit up and eat it?"

"No," I replied honestly.

"Still feeling weak and tired?" she assumed.

"Some," I replied. "But…truthfully… it's my head! I can barely stand the pain it hurts *so badly!* Every time I try to move the least little bit, it feels as if it might explode, and I can scarcely see straight because of it! If it's all the same to you I…I think I'll just lie here."

Aunt Sara looked at me shocked and obviously very concerned.

"Oh, sweetie!" she lamented. "How long have you been feeling this way? Since you fell and hit your head?"

"No," I revealed. "It's never stopped hurting since…since I first woke up. I think the fall just made it worse."

"Oh, my goodness, Jochebed!" Aunt Sara exclaimed with angst. "Why didn't you say something!? We could've told the doctor a long time ago! Surely he could've given you some medicines for the pain!"

"I'm sorry," I said. "I guess I thought you knew."

Aunt Sara shook her head, grieved, feeling badly.

"No sweetie, we didn't," she told me. "But, I'm going right now to have your Uncle Mark get the doctor. You sit tight, all right? I'll be right back!"

Aunt Sara left the room, and after she did, I must have fallen asleep because the next sound I heard was the voice of Dr. Wellesley calling my name, trying to rouse me awake.

"Jochebed!" he kept saying over and over again. "Can you hear me? Can you open your eyes for me?"

Once I was aware that he was there and that he was calling my name, I tried the best I could to open my eyes, but I could barely get them open; the pain was just too intense! When I did finally manage to open them a crack, I tried to focus, but my eyes wouldn't let me. Everything looked hazy and dark and very blurred!

Lying there, I didn't think it was possible, but the pain in my head seemed to be getting worse!

"I'm going to shine a light in your eyes," Dr. Wellesley informed me as he pulled my eyelid up a bit, and held the light there.

Instantly, I thought I was going to be sick!

"Stop!" I begged in agony, trying to push his hand away.

Dr. Wellesley put the light down and gently began to feel all around my head. When he got to the right side, immediately, I cried out in excruciating pain! Needless to say, he was quite surprised and very concerned. He took my vitals one more time and turned to Aunt Sara who was there in the room with us.

"I need to talk to Michael right away!" he requested earnestly.

Aunt Sara could tell by the look on Dr. Wellesley's face that whatever was wrong with me, it was very serious! Without delay, she rushed from the room to go find Papa.

"Where's Michael?" she asked frantically as she wheeled herself into the family room.

Uncle Mark was there, sitting on the couch, perusing the newspaper.

"He took Sam back to the house. Why?" he questioned, standing to his feet, concerned, hearing the urgency in Aunt Sara's voice. "What's goin' on?"

"Go get him, Mark!" Aunt Sara insisted, nearly in tears. "I think something's really wrong with Jochebed! Dr. Wellesley needs to talk to him *now!*"

Uncle Mark nodded, understanding, as he took off at once to go get Papa.

*****

When Papa arrived back at Grampa and Gramma's with Uncle Mark, he ran straight to the bedroom in a panic.

"What is it, Doc?" he asked frightened, bursting in the room. "Is she okay?"

Dr. Wellesley stood up somberly as Papa raced over to him.

"Let's talk over there," he suggested, directing Papa away from the bed.

"What is it?" Papa wanted to know, nearly beside himself with worry at this point. "What's wrong?"

"Michael," Dr. Wellesley queried. "When you found Jochebed, had she hit her head on anything?"

Papa furrowed his brow, taken aback by the question, trying to think. He looked down at the floor as he ran his hand through his hair, trying to remember.

"I…I don't know!" he blurted out anxiously. "The snow it…it was so deep, and…and the wind was blowin' so hard. I…I really couldn't say. Why?"

Dr. Wellesley shook his head, clearly troubled by what he'd discovered.

"I honestly don't know how I missed it, Michael," he confessed, "and I'm so very sorry that I did, but Jochebed has a soft spot on the right side of her head. I fear it's a fracture that's causing pressure to build on her brain. More than likely it's what's causing her headaches and her memory loss."

"What?!?" Papa exclaimed, astounded by the disclosure, unable to take it all in. "What…what are ya sayin', Doc?"

"She needs to be operated on, Michael," Dr. Wellesley answered succinctly.

Papa stood there stunned and confused.

"Operated on!" he came back at him, trying to wrap his mind around it. "Ya mean…wait a minute…are ya sayin'…are ya sayin' she needs…*brain surgery?*"

"Yes, Michael," Dr. Wellesley replied. "It's crucial that we relieve the pressure right away!"

Papa stood there shaking his head in disbelief. He was speechless!

"Michael!" Dr. Wellesley stated emphatically, shaking Papa from his fog. "I'm not asking your permission! She needs this surgery right away, or she'll die!"

Aunt Sara was sitting in her wheelchair by the bedroom door with Uncle Mark there by her side. They'd overheard the conversation, and Aunt Sara was already in tears.

Papa, dazed and heartbroken, slowly walked over to the bed.

My eyes were closed in pain, so I didn't see him standing there.

Gently, he reached down and put his hand on my arm, tears rolling down his face.

"I love ya, sweetheart," he whispered completely overwhelmed. "We're gonna get ya well!"

*****

Needless to say, everyone quickly began making preparations to transport me to the hospital. Papa made up a comfortable bed in the back of the wagon, and Aunt Sara packed some food for the trip. Uncle Mark hitched up the horses, and Papa had the doctor and Grampa carefully lift me onto a stretcher to take me out to the wagon, as I was still very leery of him and Uncle Mark.

When I was sufficiently settled in, Dr. Wellesley climbed aboard and rode along with me in the back of the wagon. Before we left on our trip to the hospital, however, he insisted we stop by the Bell's home (as it was on the way), and pick up Mrs. Bell. She was a nurse and he knew she could be of assistance.

"You boys be careful, ya hear?" Grampa called out as Uncle Mark climbed up onto the wagon seat there beside Papa. "Ya have precious cargo you're carryin'! Bring us back news as soon as ya can. We'll be prayin'!"

"Will do, Pa!" Papa called back, waving his hand. "We'll get word when we can!"

As soon as we were off, Grampa left to go get Samuel from home so that he could spend the night with them.

When we stopped at Mrs. Bell's house, she didn't hesitate for a minute to come with us. She quickly gathered her things and climbed into the back of the wagon to sit next to me and Dr. Wellesley.

As we travelled along to the hospital, she and Dr. Wellesley tended to me the best they could, trying to keep me warm and as still as possible. The longer we drove on, however, the more my pain intensified, and the more disoriented I became. Once again, I began to drift in and out of consciousness. There was no doubt, I was steadily getting worse!

Because I was unconscious most of the way, I don't really remember much about the trip. I vaguely remember a bump here and there and Mrs. Bell smiling down at me when I'd briefly come to, but beyond that, everything else was just a blur.

When we arrived at the hospital, I was quickly rushed into surgery. They operated late into the night and Papa and Uncle Mark anxiously waited, pacing and praying in the waiting room until the surgery was over.

After waiting for hours, Dr. Wellesley and Mrs. Bell finally came to find them.

"How is she?" Papa asked nervously, racing up to them as they walked into the room.

"She's resting comfortably," Dr. Wellesley informed. "Best I can tell the surgery went well. We won't know for sure, though, until she starts to wake up."

Thrilled for the news, Uncle Mark hugged Papa, and they both breathed a huge sigh of relief.

Mrs. Bell smiled.

"Come with me," she encouraged. "I'll take you to her."

Papa shook Dr. Wellesley's hand, and he and Uncle Mark followed Mrs. Bell down a long corridor, around a corner, and into a small, dimly lit room.

It was very white, sterile, and cold, and I was lying in a bed, covered with blankets, still unconscious with my head all wrapped in bandages.

Mrs. Bell walked over beside the bed and motioned for Papa and Uncle Mark to come, too.

"It's all right," she assured, sensing their reluctance. "You can talk to her."

Papa and Uncle Mark cautiously walked over towards me.

"You're sure it's all right?" Papa questioned, worried.

"Absolutely!" Mrs. Bell replied. She compassionately looked down at me before excusing herself from the room, wanting to give Papa and Uncle Mark some time alone with me.

Papa and Uncle Mark both came over and stood by the bed.

Putting his hand tenderly on my arm, gently stroking it, Papa fought hard to hold back his tears.

"I can't lose her, Mark!" he said, looking down at my frail body, his heart aching with grief.

"And ya won't big brother!" Uncle Mark tried to bolster. "Doc says things went well, and I trust his judgment."

Papa couldn't hold it in any longer. He broke down; the stress of everything crashing in on him.

"Why, Mark?" he questioned bitterly through his tears. "I just can't understand it! Why is all this happenin'? I know I'm supposed to trust God through all this, but…I'll confess it…it's gettin' real hard to do! I try to set the right example for Sam and Jochebed, but …"

"You're a fine example, Michael!" Uncle Mark interjected. "Ya've been through a lot. We all have! It's understandable ya'd question. I know I have!" He shook his head, sympathetic. "Believe me," he relayed, "I get that none of this makes sense right now, I mean…it just doesn't! But I gotta believe that Pastor Scott was right when he told us the other night that God has a reason and a purpose for all this."

Papa stood crying, overwhelmed by it all.

"I…I just want my little girl back!" he wept.

"I know ya do, Michael," Uncle Mark comforted. "I want her back, too!"

I was unconscious for the rest of the night and into the next, and as days continued to pass that I didn't wake up, the doctors grew more and more concerned.

Understandably, Papa was worried, too!

"It's not totally unprecedented for some patients to take longer than others to come to," they told Papa. "We'll just have to wait and see and keep an eye on her in the meantime."

The knowledge was of little comfort to Papa as he sat anxiously, diligently by my bed, day after day, waiting for any signs of consciousness.

Obviously, Uncle Mark, Dr. Wellesley, and Mrs. Bell had all gone home by now, but Papa dutifully stayed, not wanting to leave my side.

Of course, everyone at home was praying for me and wishing me well, and every time Uncle Mark came back to visit, he came bearing gifts and flowers and various sundry of other things.

The best gift of all, though, was when, that next week, Isaac came to see me.

~

Isaac's grandparents had gotten word to him of my terrible accident and subsequent trip to the hospital, so, as quickly as he could, he made arrangements to leave school. He would have come sooner, but he simply wasn't able to get away.

When he finally did arrive at the hospital, he shared with Papa, (who'd met him in the hallway) how badly he felt for having had to wait so long to get there. Papa, however, encouraged him that he was just glad he could come at all.

~

On the way to my room, Papa explained to Isaac that there was a very good chance that when I woke up I may not remember him. Papa said he couldn't be certain, of course, but that Isaac should prepare himself for the possibility just in case.

As you can imagine, Isaac was devastated by the thought, but he understood.

When they got to my room, they walked inside, and Isaac immediately rushed to my side and sat down next to me in the chair there beside my bed. I was still unconscious; my status unchanged, doing no better, no worse. Everyone was just waiting, hoping I would wake up soon.

Isaac sweetly took hold of my hand, and, overcome at the sight, began to cry.

Understanding how difficult it was for Isaac to see me this way for the very first time, and wanting to give him some time alone with me, Papa kindly stepped out of the room to leave us be for awhile.

"Oh, Jochebed!" Isaac wept. "I'm here! I'm here now! You just have to be all right! Please…I can't imagine my life without you! You just have to be all right!" Right then and there, he bowed his head, squeezing my hand even tighter, tears streaming down his face. "Oh, dear, God," he prayed, pleading, "please bring her back to us! Even if she can't remember me, please…please just let her live!" He sat crying, begging God over and over again to spare my life. "I love her, Lord!" he admitted through his tears. "Truly I do! And I believe with all of my heart that she's the one You have for me. Oh, God, I promise, I promise God, if she doesn't remember me, I'll do *everything*… ***everything*** I can to win her back! Just please, please let her be all right! Please just let her live!"

Papa was standing just outside the door and overheard Isaac's declaration of love for me, and in that moment, any concerns or reservations that he may have had about Isaac and me being together quickly disappeared from his thoughts. He was convinced of the sincerity in Isaac's heart, and he knew that I would be in good hands.

*****

For the next two days, Isaac never left my side, even when Papa had had to return home a couple of times, Isaac stayed.

Knowing Isaac was an honorable man, Papa had no qualms about letting him do so.

*****

When Friday morning arrived, the doctor who had operated on me came in to do his daily exam. When he finished, he informed Isaac that he didn't think there was anything more he could do for me.

"I'm sorry," he conveyed. "It is perplexing. I just can't explain why she hasn't come to yet. The swelling appears to be going down, and her wound is healing nicely, but for some reason…" He shook his head, clearly discouraged. "We'll just have to continue to wait and watch and hope for the best," he said.

His words were less than encouraging, but Isaac tried to remain positive.

As the day wore on, Isaac sat with me and read me Scripture, prayed with me, and talked to me, hoping beyond hope that something would get through to me.

"I have a wonderful surprise to show you in the spring," he revealed with excitement. "I can't wait for you to see it! It's something my grandparents and I have been working on for quite some time now. I think you'll *absolutely* love it! I know I do! Too," he went on, "I've been thinking a lot about us lately. I know I haven't talked this over with you, or with your father yet either, for that matter, but I was thinking that maybe we could…"

Just then, I stirred, and immediately Isaac leapt from his chair, leaned down, and got right in my face.

"Jochebed!" he shouted eagerly. "Can you hear me?"

I stirred a bit more, feeling extremely groggy and tired, trying to open my eyes, but unfortunately, it felt again as if there were weights on my eyelids.

"Jochebed! Jochebed!" Isaac kept calling, trying to rouse me. "That's it! You can do it! Come on! Just open those beautiful blue eyes of yours!"

After struggling for several minutes, my eyes slowly began to open, but only slightly. I was completely disoriented, and still not quite fully awake. I tried to move my head, but it hurt too badly, and when I tried to speak, I could only manage a moan.

When my eyes finally *did* open, and I *could* see more clearly, there stood Isaac staring down at me with his piercing blue eyes, his dark wavy hair partially in his face, and his gorgeous smile, smiling at me!

"That's my girl!" he grinned excitedly. "I knew you could do it!" He wiped a tear from his eye.

Naturally, I didn't understand what was happening nor did I have any clue as to where I was at or why I was even here. I tried to think, tried to focus, but I was completely lost. Wanting some answers, I attempted to speak again.

"Where…where am I?" I whispered.

"You're in the hospital," Isaac explained. "They had to operate on you."

"Operate?" I questioned, at a loss. "Am…am I okay?"

"Well, that depends," Isaac quipped, smiling. "Do you know who I am?"

I frowned as I looked at him, bewildered. He wasn't making a lick of sense.

"Of…of course I do," I replied absolutely perplexed by his question. "Why would you ask me such a thing?"

"All right then," he pressed, "who am I?"

Needless to say, at this point, I was beyond confused! Isaac asking me who he was made absolutely no sense to me at all!

Why would he think I wouldn't know who he was? I thought to myself. I stared at him, totally baffled, beginning to wonder if perhaps there was something wrong with *him!*

"Well!" Isaac prodded insistently. "Tell me, who am I?"

I cocked my eyebrow, looking at him curiously, thinking *surely* he'd lost his mind!

He just stood there smiling down at me, impatiently anticipating my answer.

I frowned, befuddled, and stated very matter-of-factly, "You're Isaac!"

"Whooooooweee!!!" he shouted, nearly giving me a heart attack! "I love you, Jochebed Lowry!" he exclaimed in excitement as he leaned down to give me a hug.

I groaned and winced in pain when he did.

"Oh, I'm sorry!" he said, carefully letting me go. "I didn't mean to hurt you! It's just that you...*you know me!* You know who I am!"

He seemed so ecstatic by the fact, but I couldn't figure out for the life of me why!

Taking hold of my hand, he sat back down in his chair, grinning from ear to ear. Tears were in his eyes, but I could tell they were tears of joy. He lovingly brought my hand to his lips and sweetly kissed it.

"You're here!" he expressed with such gratitude. "You're really, really here! And you know who I am!" He squeezed my hand as he looked up. "Thank You Lord!!" he exclaimed, elated.

I looked at him like he'd gone completely mad! To be honest, I was beginning to worry a little.

Why was me knowing him such a big deal? I wondered. It just made no sense! *Of course, I knew him!*

Obviously, I had no idea the significance of what had just happened.

Isaac sat there beaming at me, absolutely thrilled by my reply.

Suddenly, a nurse who'd overheard the commotion came running into the room.

"Is everything all right?" she asked as she hastened towards the bed.

"Everything's great!" Isaac exclaimed. "She woke up! Jochebed...she's awake, and she knows who I am!"

The nurse smiled as she looked down at me.

"Why, hello there, young lady," she said kindly. "We've been wondering when you'd join us." She proceeded to check my vitals and to look me over. "Looks good," she commented, "but I know the doctor will want to take a look at you, too. I'll go get him and be right back." She smiled at me again and patted me on the hand. "So glad to finally see those beautiful eyes of yours," she complimented.

I managed a reluctant smile as she left to go get the doctor.

I have to admit I was still confused as to why everyone was so excited to see me awake. I had no recollection of what I'd been through in the past two weeks, no recollection of the surgery, no recollection of what had happened to get me here. Truthfully, it was an eerie, helpless, empty feeling, and I just wanted to understand. I looked over at Isaac after the nurse left, and he was still smiling, looking at me so thankful and so overjoyed!

*What **had** happened?* I questioned. *Why **was** I here?* If only I could make sense of it all.

Isaac leaned forward on the bed and started to talk to me.

"You had us all so worried, Jochebed," he revealed, squeezing my hand tightly. "We just didn't know if you were ever going to wake up, but now..." He smiled. "I'm so thankful God answers prayers!"

I just lay there listening, staring at him with a blank stare, wishing I understood what he was talking about. I was happy that he was so happy, but not really understanding why was very frustrating.

I was just about to ask him to explain everything when all of a sudden the door opened and in walked the doctor and nurse to check on me.

The doctor did a thorough examination and asked if I was in any pain. I confessed that I was, and he ordered the nurse to bring me some medicine.

After she left, to comply with his instructions, the doctor asked me a critical question.

"Jochebed," he queried, "do you remember what happened to you?"

I looked at him, unsure of what he meant.

"Isaac told me I had surgery?" I replied, wondering if that was what he wanted to know. "I'll admit, though, I don't remember it, and I don't know why I had to have it either."

The doctor nodded.

"Well," he told me, "that's understandable. You've been through a very traumatic experience." He paused a minute before questioning me further. "Tell me," he asked curiously, "what *is* the last thing you remember?"

I stared at him a minute, thinking, before looking over at Isaac. When I did, I noticed Isaac's demeanor had changed from one of excitement to one of concern as he waited.

Laying there a minute longer, I searched my mind for my last memory. I looked back to the doctor.

"Can you tell me?" the doctor prodded.

My head was throbbing, and I just wanted to sleep, but I did my best to answer his question.

"Samuel," I whispered, slowly starting to recall, "he...he was lost. I...I had to find him." I paused, trying to fight through the pain. "It...it was cold...I think," I recounted. I looked back to Isaac as panic began to set in.

He looked me in the eyes and squeezed my hand again as if to say, *You're safe now! It's all right!*

I nodded slowly and continued on.

"I...I was looking for him," I eked out, my voice still weak and raspy. "I...I think I went to Mama's grave to try to find him." The memories were sketchy and seemed to come in fragments and tiny, unconnected pieces. I did my best to patch them together. "I...I *had to find him!*" I insisted again, getting more anxious as I remembered. My heart began to race, and before I knew it, floods of fear and emotion came sweeping over me, and I broke down into tears. "I...I'm *so sorry*, Isaac!" I said, frantically looking into his eyes as I slowly began to realize what I'd done. "Papa told me to stay home, but I... ...Oh, Isaac, I...I should have listened! I...I *never* should have left the house! Can...can you ever forgive me? I'm *so, so sorry!*"

"Shhh!" Isaac sweetly consoled, trying to calm me. "It's all right. You're all right! I understand."

Memories continued to swirl around in my head as I tried to explain what had happened.

"I...I...I lost my way," I sniffed and stammered, feeling so guilty and ashamed. "But I...I *needed to find Samuel!* He was lost and..." I looked back to the doctor as my memories began to fade. "I...I don't really remember anything else," I confessed. "It just seems as if my mind is blank." I put my hands to my face and sobbed for what I'd done, and for fear that Samuel had never been found.

"It's all right, Jochebed," Isaac told me as he leaned in, rubbing my arm to try to calm me. "It's all right! It'll be all right!"

"But Samuel!" I cried in desperation. "Did they find him? Is he all right? Is he safe?"

Isaac nodded, a reassuring smile making its way across his face.

"He's fine, Jochebed," he promised in such a comforting way. "They found him and he's safe and he's at home right now with your father."

I took a deep breath as I wiped my tears.

"You're…you're sure?" I questioned, still worried. "You're absolutely certain?"

"Positive!" Isaac guaranteed as he looked me in the eye. "You don't have to worry, Jochebed. Everything's fine!"

I nodded (the best I could) relieved that Samuel was okay.

The doctor asked me a few more questions, checked my vitals again, and indicated that he was pleased with what he saw. Nonetheless, he made it clear that I was not out of the woods yet, and that I still had a very long road of recovery ahead of me.

He instructed me to stay in bed for the time being and said that the nurse should be back any minute to administer my medicine.

"I promise to get word to your father that you've come to," the doctor said as he headed towards the door to leave. "I'll check back in on you later."

I thanked him, and he walked out.

Not long after he'd left the room, a nurse came in and gave me some medicine. After she'd administered the dose, she made sure I had enough blankets and that I was comfortable, asked if I needed anything else (to which I replied that I didn't), and said she'd be checking back in periodically throughout the day.

I nodded and she left.

After she was gone, Isaac sat with me and held my hand as I drifted in and out of sleep. He talked with me when I was awake and helped feed me when they brought me my meals. I can't begin to tell you how thankful I was to have him there with me through this most difficult ordeal, as I couldn't *imagine* having to face it all alone!

SLOW RECOVERY
(Chapter 22)

It was going on suppertime when suddenly there was a knock at my door. Isaac quietly got up to go see who it was, and when he opened the door, there stood Papa, Samuel, and Uncle Mark anxious to see me. Isaac slipped out quietly and partially closed the door behind him.

"She's asleep right now," he whispered. "She's had a pretty rough day of it so far. She's doing better though, and the doctor seems hopeful."

Papa was thankful that I was now conscience, but he was understandably concerned as to whether or not I could remember anything. He looked at Isaac, apprehensive.

"How's her mind?" he asked, worried. "What, if anything, does she remember?"

"Bits and pieces, sir," Isaac explained. "She seemed to remember searching for Samuel and that you told her not to go, but beyond that, she didn't remember much."

"Did she ask about Sam?" Papa questioned.

"Yes, sir," Isaac replied. "She was beside herself with worry as to whether or not he'd been found and whether or not he was safe."

Papa and Samuel looked at each other quite disheartened.

Isaac noticed and tried to assure them.

"Oh, but I let her know that he was all right, sir," Isaac quickly blurted out.

Papa sighed.

"No," he explained. "Ya don't understand. We've told her time and time again that Sam's all right, but just as soon as he leaves her sight, she forgets. She just keeps askin' over and over again where he's at and if he's safe. I guess I was just hopin' that maybe...maybe she'd remember."

Isaac felt badly that he hadn't known.

"Oh, I see, sir," he sympathized. "But, Mr. Lowry," he continued, "I've been talking with Jochebed on and off all day now, and to me...well...she seems to be aware of most things. I mean, I could be wrong, but to me she seems as normal as can be expected."

"Did she know ya?" Uncle Mark queried.

Isaac nodded happily.

"Yes!" he replied enthusiastically. "She knew right away!"

"Well, that's a hopeful sign," Papa commented. "I guess we'll have to wait..."

"Isaac!" I called out. "Where are you?"

Everyone was still in the hallway, and I couldn't hear them because they were talking so quietly, trying not to disturb me.

Samuel, who was standing right beside Isaac at the door, heard me calling.

"Sounds like she might be awake," he said as he put his ear to the door.

Isaac turned around, cracked the door open, and poked his head inside.

"You're right," he acknowledged, turning back to Papa and the others, "she's awake." He opened the door for everyone to go inside, but Papa was hesitant. "Mr. Lowry?" Isaac questioned with furrowed brow, not understanding his reluctance.

Papa sighed as he tried to explain.

"She didn't know me before," he said somberly. "And she was *terrified* of me whenever I was around. I...I'm just afraid that..."

"Go to her, Michael," Uncle Mark urged. "Ya need to see your daughter whether she's afraid of ya or not. Samuel and I'll stay out here for a while so we don't overwhelm her. It'll give ya a chance to talk with her."

Papa was still unsure as he looked at Uncle Mark and Samuel.

"I agree with him, sir," Isaac interjected. "She needs to see you."

"Isaac!" I called out again wondering where he could be and feeling a bit frightened. "Where are you?" It was still very painful for me to turn my head too far in any direction, so I couldn't see him standing at the door. I thought I'd heard his voice, but I wasn't sure.

"I'm here!" he answered as he walked into the room towards the bed. "I'm here, Jochebed! No need to fret!" He came over and took hold of my hand.

"I thought you'd left me!" I told him, so relieved to see his face.

"Never!" he smiled reassuringly. "Hey, I have someone here who wants to see you."

"You do?" I questioned. "Who?"

Isaac motioned for Papa, who was standing at the door, to come over to my bed. Slowly and tentatively he walked towards me.

As he eventually came into view, I immediately began to cry.

"Papa!" I exclaimed so happy to see him, and so sorry for what I'd done. "Where have you been?"

Isaac stepped back, smiling, as Papa, overwhelmed with joy, rushed to my side. He took my hand and held it tightly as he leaned down and smiled, his eyes filling with tears.

"Ya remember!" he said, overcome. He looked up. "Thank Ya Lord," he cried out, grateful. "Thank Ya for bringin' my little girl back to me!" He bent down and kissed my cheek and as he did I could feel the wetness of his tears against my face. "Oh, Jochebed!" he wept. "I have ya back!"

I was still a little confused as to what he meant by all that, but I knew that I was glad to see him and that I owed him an apology for what I'd done.

"I'm so sorry," I said as tears rolled down my face. "I'm so sorry, Papa! I'm sorry I disobeyed you! Can you ever forgive me for all of this?"

Papa shook his head dismissing the notion that I needed to apologize.

"Oh, sweetheart," he comforted as he wiped my tears, "all's forgiven. You're here and you're safe and you're my little girl again…that's all that matters to me!" He leaned down and carefully lifted me to himself and held me close, squeezing me tightly. It was as if he never wanted to let me go. After several minutes, he gently laid me back down and smiled at me as he wiped his tears. "Ya can tell 'em to come on in," Papa instructed Isaac. "They need to see that we have our Jochebed back."

Isaac nodded, smiling, as he walked over to the door to open it up for Uncle Mark and Samuel.

Uncle Mark walked in the room first and over to my bed while Samuel lingered back a ways, out of sight.

"There's my favorite niece!" Uncle Mark announced cheerily, grinning from ear to ear.

"Uncle Mark!" I replied, trying to smile through the pain. "It's so good to see you!"

"Hey, would ya look at that!" he quipped, elated, looking over at Papa. "She knows who I am!"

Papa nodded, smiling broadly, so happy and proud that I could remember.

"Samuel," Papa encouraged, motioning for him to come. "Come over here, Son. Come see your sister!"

I perked up a bit.

"Samuel's here?" I questioned anxiously, not realizing that he was in the room. I so desperately wanted to see him, to see for myself that he was all right! "Is he really here?" I pressed.

Samuel scowled at Papa warily, none too eager to see me. It was understandable, though, given everything I'd put him through before. Still, knowing he needed to obey Papa, he slowly began to meander over towards the bed.

"Samuel!" I cried out, tearing up again as he came into view. "You're here! It's really you! I'm so glad you're all right!"

Samuel didn't say anything; instead, he just gave me a halfhearted smirk, indicating he really didn't want to be there.

Of course, I had no way of knowing why he felt the way he did, but I chose to overlook it, simply thankful that he was safe.

"Where were you?" I asked, not realizing he'd already told me before.

Samuel closed his eyes and sighed, agitated that I was asking him again. He looked at Papa and shook his head, thinking that nothing had changed.

Papa, however, encouraged him to answer.

"Go on, Son," he urged. "Tell your sister what happened."

Samuel sighed again, visibly frustrated, clearly none too happy, but he reluctantly complied, hemming and hawing the whole time.

"I…I was angry that night," he begrudgingly explained. "So I…I took off for church early and…well…I know I shouldn't have, but I…I was hopin' to…to talk to Pastor Scott about…ya know…about all the bad stuff that's been happenin' to us lately. And… well…" He paused, looking down at the floor, guiltily. "Anyway," he haltingly went on, "I'm…I'm sorry ya got hurt and all. I…I never meant for that to happen."

It was obvious Samuel felt responsible for what had happened to me, and I wanted to assure him that I didn't blame him in any way.

"Samuel," I conveyed, "I know you didn't mean for any of this to happen. And truth be told, if I had listened to Papa and stayed at home like I was supposed to, none of this *would* have happened! I'm just glad you're all right!"

Samuel glanced up briefly, but I could tell by the look on his face that he was skeptical. He didn't say anything, though; he just went back to staring at the floor.

There was an awkward moment of silence until Uncle Mark finally spoke up and asked, "So, how ya feelin'?"

My head was pounding and I felt rather tired, but I looked at Uncle Mark and attempted an answer.

"Well," I quipped, still struggling to speak, "I've definitely been better!"

Uncle Mark chuckled a bit.

"Well, I can certainly understand that!" he replied still smiling.

*****

As we talked, it became clear that even though I remembered some things, other things were a complete blank. For instance, Papa and Uncle Mark had to explain to me what had happened when I was at Grampa and Gramma's house after my accident, because those days were completely gone from my memory. I had no recollection at all of *anything* that had taken place during that time! It was simply gone, erased from my mind as if it had never happened. I'll admit it felt very strange being told of things that I had said and done, yet I had no memory of ever saying or doing them. I slowly began to accept it, though, simply being grateful for the things that I *could* remember! I hoped that maybe time would eventually fill in the gaps.

Finally, after talking for about an hour or so, I just couldn't hold my eyes open any longer. My head was still in a lot of pain from the surgery and even though the medicine they gave me seemed to ease the throbbing, it also made me very drowsy. I simply drifted off to sleep during the conversation.

Once everyone realized I was no longer awake, they quietly left the room to let me rest.

"Can ya let Jochebed know we'll be back tomorrow?" Papa asked Isaac.

"Of course, Mr. Lowry," he agreed. "I'll tell her."

They all said goodnight, and Papa, Samuel and Uncle Mark left for home.

*****

Sometime late in the night, I suddenly jolted awake. There was a pounding in my head that just wouldn't go away, and I was certain that that was what woke me. I lay there trying to deal with the pain the best I could, trying to go back to sleep, but the throbbing was so intense, I just couldn't! Not wanting to wake Isaac to go get a nurse (it had been such a long day, and I knew he was terribly exhausted), I decided to wait it out. I closed my eyes and lay there, thinking and praying, hoping beyond hope that maybe I would eventually fall back to sleep.

As I waited, I thought about all that had happened to me and about everything that I'd been told. I recalled what Papa and Uncle Mark had relayed about my accident; how so many people had searched for me and how so many more had prayed for me and how they were *still* praying for me now, and I smiled at the thought of Samuel being safe! As I listened to Isaac breathing from across the room, sleeping in a chair next to the window, I couldn't help but be touched by how much he cared for me. It amazed me that he would be willing to sacrifice so much to stay with me here in the hospital.

Naturally, thinking about all these things, I became overwhelmed, realizing how truly blessed I was to have so many wonderful, caring people in my life. I decided to take some time to simply thank the Lord for all His incredible blessings!

Before I knew it, I had drifted off back to sleep.

*****

The next day, very early in the morning, the doctor came in to check on my progress. When he opened the door, it was enough to stir both Isaac and me awake.

"Good morning," he said as he came over to me. "How are you feeling today?"

I tried to open my eyes, but my head hurt and it was hard to focus when it was so bright in the room.

"Can you open those eyes for me?" the doctor asked as he listened to my heart.

By now Isaac was wide awake and by my side.

"Honestly, I don't think I can," I told the doctor. "I have such a terrible headache and opening my eyes only seems to make it worse."

Isaac jumped in to support what I was saying.

"I did notice she was moaning a lot during the night, Doctor," he said, concerned, taking hold of my hand to let me know he was there. "I didn't want to wake her, but it did seem to me that she was in *a lot* of pain."

"Well," the doctor replied, "let's take a peek under those bandages and see how things are looking." Very carefully and gently he began to unwrap the bandages from my head. Laying them aside, he leaned in and looked intently at the place where he'd made the incision. "Hmmm," he observed. "Looks like a bit of infection may be setting in. I'll clean the wound and redress it, and we'll see if that won't take care of the problem. In the meantime, I'll have the nurse bring you some more medicine for the pain."

He walked to the door and yelled for one of the nurses to come, and when she did, he instructed her as to what kind and how much medicine to bring for me. When she was sure of his wishes, she left immediately, and the doctor came back over to the bed to tend to my wound.

Needless to say, I grimaced in terrible discomfort every time he touched me.

"Is it bad?" Isaac asked the doctor, worried, allowing me to squeeze his hand to cope with the pain.

"No, I don't think so," the doctor assured as he continued to work. "I think we caught it in time. It doesn't appear that it's gone too deep; just on the surface as far as I can tell. A thorough cleaning ought to take care of it."

"What about her headaches?" Isaac wanted to know. "I mean, they seem so severe. Will they go away?"

"Well, I'm optimistic," the doctor answered. "But I'll be honest, sometimes with head injuries it's hard to say. There's still a small amount of swelling from the surgery, so until that goes down, we won't know for sure. Once it does go away, however, hopefully the headaches will too!" He paused what he was doing and looked over at Isaac. "I will caution you, though," he said, "with everything that's happened, there is a slight chance she may have to deal with them from now on."

"Will they be constant?" I whispered, deeply concerned by the prognosis. (I was hurting so badly at the moment, I *dearly* wanted to know!)

"No, I doubt it," the doctor answered, trying to allay any fears. "More than likely they'll come and go. … *If you have them at all!* Let's try to stay positive, all right? Hopefully, as things improve, the headaches will go away on their own."

"When can she go home?" Isaac inquired.

"Well, now…that's another story," the doctor replied. "With this type of surgery, I like to monitor my patients until I'm certain they're able to get around comfortably on their own." He paused and thought for a minute. "I figure we're looking at…oh…at least, a week, if not two," he calculated. "Of course, a lot will depend on how well Jochebed progresses."

That was not at all what I wanted to hear!

"A week or two?" I bemoaned, wanting desperately to be back home. "Will it really be that long?"

"Oh, I'm afraid so," the doctor confirmed. "Don't forget, you just had major surgery, and that takes a while to recover from. I want to make certain that you're fully recuperated before I send you home. I surely wouldn't want you reinjuring yourself or hurting yourself worse."

I looked at Isaac chagrinned as the doctor continued rewrapping my head. When he was finished, he left, and a nurse brought me my medicine. I took it, and within a short time I began to feel very tired and groggy. I was able to stay awake for a little while longer, talking with Isaac, but eventually I just couldn't keep my eyes open anymore and promptly fell asleep.

About forty-five minutes or so into my nap, Papa and Uncle Mark showed up at the hospital to see me. When they came into the room, Isaac was asleep in a chair across the way. As soon as he heard the door, though, he woke up.

"Mr. Lowry," he whispered as he stood to his feet yawning. "Sorry to be sleeping but the doctor was by pretty early this morning to check on Jochebed, and I was plum worn out."

"Oh, I understand," Papa whispered back. "How's she doin' today?"

"Maybe we should talk in the hallway," Isaac suggested.

Papa and Uncle Mark agreed, so they left the room, Isaac following. He quietly closed the door behind him.

"The doctor said she has a small infection in her incision," Isaac disclosed.

Immediately, Papa furrowed his brow, concerned.

"But, he doesn't seem overly concerned about it," Isaac quickly added, trying to dispel any fears. "He treated it and he seems to think it should clear up soon."

Papa sighed, relieved.

"Well, that's good," he replied. "How's she feelin' otherwise?"

Isaac looked apprehensive.

"Well, sir," he replied, "she's still having terrible headaches, in fact, she seems to be in a lot of pain most of the time. I know she tries to put on a brave face, but...I can tell she's suffering."

Papa again looked worried and a bit disheartened.

Isaac explained further.

"The doctor seems to think that the headaches may be due to some swelling from the surgery that hasn't gone down yet," he clarified. "So..."

"So they should clear up when she recovers?" Papa interjected, hopeful.

"Well, possibly," Isaac relayed. "But to be honest, Mr. Lowry, the doctor's not really sure. He hopes they will, but..."

"What do ya mean he *hopes* they will?" Papa asked unhappily.

"Well," Isaac answered hesitantly, not wanting to be the bearer of bad news, "he did mention that there's a possibility the headaches could be permanent...because of everything she's been through."

Papa closed his eyes, sighing, clearly upset.

"Well...did he happen to say when she could come home?" he wanted to know.

Again, Isaac reluctantly answered, not wanting to give Papa the bad news.

"Unfortunately, sir," he told him, "the doctor said she'll probably have to stay another week or two."

"A week or two?" Papa questioned, astounded by the length of time. "I figured she'd have to stay for awhile, but...why so long?"

"Well," Isaac explained, "the doctor wants to make sure she's fully recovered before he sends her home. He's afraid if he lets her go too soon she could hurt herself again."

Papa shook his head, pulling at his chin, frustrated at the thought of me having to be in the hospital for so long.

"If it's what she needs, Michael, then it's what's best," Uncle Mark advocated.

Papa sighed, reluctantly accepting it.

Since I was still asleep, Papa, Uncle Mark, and Isaac decided to go and get a late breakfast together. By the time they got back to the room, I was awake and a nurse was in tending to me, trying to get me to eat something. (Although, I was not cooperating very well as I was not the least bit hungry!)

"Oh, good your back!" she commented as Papa, Isaac, and Uncle Mark walked into the room. "Could I get one of you to help me sit her up? I want to see if we can get her upright today."

Still feeling weak, and in a bit of pain, I cringed at the thought!

Papa walked to the side of the bed, leaned over, and gave me a kiss on the cheek.

"Hi, sweetheart," he said, smiling down at me.

I managed a brief smile back.

With medicine in me now (it starting to take effect), my pain was getting a little better and it made it much easier for me to open my eyes.

"All right, then," the nurse instructed, "if you'll grab under her arm there, I'll grab under this one. On the count of three we'll gently lift her up. Ready?"

Papa nodded, indicating that he was.

"All right," the nurse said, "here we go. One, two, three, *lift!*"

On her count, she and Papa slowly began to pull me up, and with the amount of pain and pressure it caused, I nearly passed out! I didn't think it was possible to feel any worse than I already did, but clearly I was wrong! My head felt like it weighed a hundred pounds and I felt very sick to my stomach.

"Careful! Careful! Slowly!" the nurse cautioned as she could tell I was really struggling.

Finally, *thankfully*, it was over! I was sitting up at a slight angle in the bed, trying to cope.

"There!" the nurse declared, pleased, as she slipped an extra pillow in behind me to help prop me up. "How's that?"

I sat clenching my jaws, hurting something awful, my eyes tightly closed in pain. I thought for sure my head was going to fall off!

"Is this pressure normal!?" I asked, my hand to my head, trying not to get sick.

"Unfortunately, yes," the nurse explained. "You've been lying flat for days now; it may take a minute or two, but it should lessen."

Desperately hoping she was right, I sat there waiting for the throbbing to stop. I swallowed hard and took a few deep breaths, doing what I could to keep everything down. With the pain and the dizziness, however, it definitely wasn't easy! I squeezed Papa's hand with all my might, trying to get through it!

Finally, after what seemed like forever, the pressure did slowly start to subside a bit. I still felt terrible, but I managed a whisper.

"I do think it's getting a little better now," I told the nurse.

"Good!" she replied cheerfully. "Now how about trying to eat something?"

I was amazed at her persistence! I hadn't felt like eating anything before, and I *certainly* didn't feel like eating anything now!

I took a deep breath and almost begged her.

"May I *please* just sit here for a minute?" I implored.

"Of course," she agreed kindly. "I understand. I'll leave your meal. You can try to eat something when you feel up to it."

"Thank you," I replied, relieved.

The nurse left and I just sat there frozen, trying not to move. The pressure was subsiding, but I still felt lightheaded and sick to my stomach.

"Sweetheart," Papa asked softly, "is there anything we can get for ya?"

"Water," I answered, dying of thirst. "I could use some water."

Isaac went over to the pitcher of water that was there in my room and poured me a glass. Bringing it over, he carefully brought it to my lips.

"Here you go," he said sweetly as he helped me take a sip and then another.

I felt simply dreadful and just wanted to lie back down, but I knew the nurse wanted me sitting so I tried to put the thought from my mind. Trying to endure, I just sat there with my eyes closed, almost trembling, I felt so miserable. It was the worst I think I'd ever felt!

Feeling badly for me, but really unable to help me, everyone just stood there quietly, watching and waiting.

"I'm sorry to hear ya might have to be in here for a while," Uncle Mark finally said, as he patted me on the leg.

I squinted up at him, managing a reply.

"I know," I agreed, breathing deeply. "I was pretty disappointed when the doctor told us. I'm determined, though, to work as hard as ever to..." I paused, struggling. "I plan to...to get out of here as soon as I can," I eventually finished. "I need to get well again so...so that I can help out with...with Aunt Sara and with...with Gramma."

"Jochebed," Uncle Mark urged, "don't ya worry any about your Aunt Sara, she's doin' good, so much so, Dr. Wellesley gave her permission to be up in a wheelchair, and I assure ya, she's takin' every advantage of it. She and the baby are doin' just fine!"

"And as for your Gramma," Papa interjected, continuing Uncle Mark's line of thinking, "she's doin' a lot better, too! Every day we're seein' great improvements from her, and your Grampa's able to tend to her just fine along with the rest of us. There's no need for ya to be worryin' about anything other than gettin' yourself better! You just concentrate on that, ya hear? I don't want ya pushin' yourself too hard too fast and hurtin' yourself worse!"

I glanced up at Papa.

"You're sure you can manage without me?" I questioned, feeling a little guilty.

"Sweetheart," Papa assured, "I'm *absolutely* positive! As much as I'd love to take ya home with me right now, I want ya healed first! That's the most important thing!"

I sighed deeply as I looked down at the bed, my eyes partially closed.

Papa could tell something was wrong beyond just my pain.

"What is it, Jochebed?" he queried.

"Well," I told him, a little embarrassed, "it's just...it's just..." I hesitated.

"What, Jochebed?" Papa pressed. "What is it? What's botherin' ya?"

"Well..." I started again, "I guess...I guess I'm just not looking forward to being here all by myself for so long. I so wish you could stay with me!"

Papa looked at me, dispirited.

"Ya know I'd stay if I could, sweetheart," he told me, feeling badly that he couldn't. "But with Samuel and work and..." He paused, giving me a kiss on the forehead. "I'll visit ya as often as I can," he promised. "And ya know you'll be in my constant prayers!"

"And hey, I'll visit ya, too!" Uncle Mark chimed in with a smile, trying to encourage me. "Besides, with all that hard work you'll be doin', why…I bet the days'll just fly by!"

I understood, but still I felt like crying. I dreaded the thought of being left all alone in such a strange, unfamiliar place. I tried to push my feelings aside, though, trying to put on a brave face, but deep down I couldn't help but worry!

"Mr. Lowry," Isaac spoke up, as he took hold of my hand. "I know this may be an unusual request, but…with your permission, and Jochebed's of course, I…I'd really like the opportunity to stay with her and to help her with her recovery."

"*What? No!*" I insisted. "How can you? Your schooling it…it would be too much!"

"Jochebed's right, Son," Papa agreed. "Ya shouldn't jeopardize your schoolin'."

"I'm sure I can work something out with my professors," Isaac proffered. "I only have about a week or so left before Christmas break anyhow. I'm certain they'll understand given the circumstances." He looked at me longingly and back to Papa. "Sir," he stated confidently. "I *know* I can make up the work! It won't be a problem! I'd very much like to stay and help if I may. I don't want her to have to be alone!"

Papa pulled at his chin, mulling it over.

"You're *sure* it wouldn't be too much of an imposition?" he wanted to make certain.

"Not at all, sir!" Isaac guaranteed.

"And you'll be above reproach with my daughter!?" Papa questioned, staring at Isaac stringently. (Well…it was more like he was threatening, really, rather than questioning!)

"*Absolutely, sir!*" Isaac promised. "You can be assured that I'll be an *absolute* gentleman *at all times!*"

Papa looked at me, reluctant, seriously contemplating the matter, as I looked at him intently, willing him to say yes. He could tell by the look on my face that I desperately wanted *someone* to be with me through this difficult ordeal.

Finally, he sighed, commiserating, feeling for my dilemma. He knew Isaac was an honorable man and that he could trust him, but still, I was his little girl. He thought for a minute longer before looking back to Isaac.

"All right, Son," he agreed, giving his consent. "If ya promise me you'll be decent and respectful and if ya can work things out with your professors, then…well…ya have my permission."

"Thank you, sir!" Isaac replied sincerely. "I will!" Isaac looked at me, smiling. "I promise to take good care of her!" he pledged earnestly.

THE HOSPITAL STAY
(Chapter 23)

I was so thankful and pleased with Papa that he was allowing Isaac to stay with me in the hospital. It was such a relief knowing that I wouldn't have to face my daunting recovery alone.

Knowing, though, that he was now going to be with me for awhile, Isaac needed to go home to get some of his things and to get other things taken care of regarding his school. Kindly, Uncle Mark offered to go with him, and they left right away.

When the hospital staff learned of what Isaac was planning on doing, they generously offered to provide him a room near mine. I was grateful as it meant he'd no longer have to sleep in an uncomfortable chair, and Papa was grateful, too, as it made him feel a bit more at ease with the decision he'd made to allow Isaac to stay with me.

*****

While Isaac and Uncle Mark were away for the day, Papa graciously waited with me. I was still in a lot of pain, but despite the obstacle, I managed to sit up for over half the day. In that time, Papa was able to convince me to eat something, albeit not very much as I was still a little sick to my stomach due to being dizzy on and off. Papa was very kind and patient with me, though, not pushing me too hard.

Ever vigilant and keeping a watchful eye on me during this time, every few minutes Papa would ask me how I was doing.

After quite awhile of his persistent asking, it got to the point where I finally had to politely tell him, "Papa, nothing much has changed since the last time you asked me two minutes ago."

He'd smile and apologize, saying he just wanted to make sure that I was comfortable and that I didn't need anything. While I appreciated his due diligence, I explained to him that, at least for now, being comfortable just wasn't possible!

Nevertheless, despite his over protectiveness, I did so enjoy our time together. It had been such a long time since he and I had had an uninterrupted opportunity to talk.

"How's Samuel doing with all of this?" I asked, still troubled by his behavior when he'd visited last.

"He's gettin' along," Papa replied, "but truthfully, with everything that's happened, he's just tryin' to make sense of it all."

"I suppose I can understand that," I accepted. "Was...was that why he was so distant with me yesterday?"

Papa looked at me somberly.

"Jochebed," he reminded, "it's like your Uncle Mark and I told ya. ...After you're accident, when ya were at Grampa and Gramma's, ya...well...ya just weren't at all yourself. You were there, yes, but ya really weren't, and by that I mean, it was like ya were lost or somethin' - terribly confused. It was very disconcertin' for Samuel to see ya like that; as it was for all of us!" He sighed as he shook his head. "I just think Sam's havin' a real hard time dealin' with everything is all," he conveyed with concern. "And I guess it didn't help much that when he was here yesterday, ya said some of the same things to him that ya'd said to him several times before. To him it just didn't seem like anything had changed."

I looked at Papa, feeling badly.

"I'm sorry, Papa," I told him. "I had no idea! Would you please tell Samuel that I didn't mean anything by it?"

"Believe me, sweetheart," he assured, "I already have. I just think until he can be around ya more and see for himself that ya really have changed, he's gonna have a hard time acceptin' it. Don't worry, though," Papa encouraged, "I have no doubt he'll come around in time."

"But…I guess I don't understand, Papa," I pointed out, confused. "Samuel was around me for quite awhile yesterday here at the hospital, I mean…couldn't he see the change in me then?"

"No, sweetheart," Papa answered matter-of-factly. "He never left your sight."

I furrowed my brow, not understanding.

"But, what do you mean?" I queried, at a loss. "Why would that matter?"

Papa came close and took my hand, smiling at me in a reassuring way.

"Jochebed," he explained, "ya have to understand…at home ya'd talk and act more…well…normal, kinda like ya did here yesterday, and at home, as long as Samuel was in the room with ya, ya'd recognize him, ya'd talk to him, but then, just as soon as he'd leave your sight…well…ya'd forget everything that had just happened and go on worryin' bout him. Within just a short amount of time, ya'd be askin' about him all over again – where he was at, if he was safe, all of it! That cycle went on for two days, so when Sam came to see ya here…well…"

I sighed, connecting the dots.

"I did it again!" I interrupted, feeling even worse. "I get it."

Papa nodded, confirming.

"But, hey," he reminded, noticing my angst, "like I told ya before, Sam'll come around…ya wait and see! Don't worry yourself any about it, all right? It'll all work out, I know it will!"

I looked down, shaking my head none too sure.

"Yes, Papa," I reluctantly agreed. "If you say so."

"Well, I do!" Papa stated enthusiastically, trying to cheer me. "Now," he continued, changing the subject, "how are you and Isaac doin' since all this?"

His question threw me a bit as I bashfully smiled.

"I know it may sound crazy, Papa," I replied, "but just watching his concern for me through all of this, and now his willingness to sacrifice so much more…" I paused, almost finding it hard to express what I was feeling. "If I can say it," I conveyed with reserve, "I didn't think it was possible, but…I think I love him even more!"

Papa's eyes got wide, reeling from my response.

"*Love?*" he questioned warily.

"Yes, sir," I blushed. "I truly, honestly believe that he's the one God has for me. I just *know* we'll marry one day!"

"Now, hold on there!" Papa came back at me, taken aback by my certainty. "Ya've only just started courtin'! Are ya sure ya should be thinkin' that far down the road at this point?"

"Well…" I started to explain.

Papa didn't give me much of a chance, though. He immediately jumped right back in, expressing his concern.

"And Isaac," he wanted to know, "he feels the same way?"

"Weelll, I suppose I can't say that for sure," I admitted. "I mean, it's not like we've actually said anything to one another officially, but… well…I believe he cares a great deal for me, and …"

Papa looked at me circumspectly and interrupted yet again.

"He's a fine man, Jochebed," he said with reserve, "but I think ya'd best make certain of these feelin's before ya go makin' any definite plans. Give yourselves time to grow together. If you're truly meant to be, then God'll solidify it in both your hearts."

"Oh, I know, Papa!" I assured. "I know He will! And I'm not pushing anything, honest!"

Papa nodded, apprehensive, but accepting.

My head was hurting, so we left off talking, and in no time, I was fast asleep.

Tired himself, Papa ended up dozing off, too, resting in the chair there beside my bed.

*****

Come later that evening, I was awake and in a lot of pain, so much so, I was in need of some more medicine. Papa promptly left to go find a nurse, and while he was gone, Isaac came walking into the room.

"I bring greetings from Andrew and Isabelle," he announced as he came to the side of the bed. "And my grandparents send their love and prayers as well."

I hurt so badly that I could barely turn my head to look at him.

"Having a headache again?" he queried, concerned, noticing the distress on my face.

"Yes," I whispered, "a bad one! Papa's getting the nurse, though."

Isaac gently brushed a hair from my forehead as he leaned in a bit.

"I'm sorry, Jochebed," he sympathized. "Is there anything I can do?"

"No," I grimaced in pain. "I just need my medicine."

"Well, maybe this will help lift your spirits," he said as he sat down beside me. "I have a gift here from Isabelle. You can open it later, though, when you're feeling up to it."

He started to place the box at the foot of my bed.

"Will you open it for me?" I asked.

"You're sure you don't want to wait and do it yourself?" he questioned.

"No!" I insisted. "I'd like to see what it is."

"All right," Isaac agreed.

He took the box and opened it up, and when he did, inside was the loveliest afghan. He reached in and pulled it out, unfolded it, and stood up to show me the beautiful colors and design.

"It's *so* beautiful!" I whispered. "Please be sure to thank Isabelle for me. I definitely appreciate it!"

I winced again as pain coursed through my head. It was all I could do to bear it! I took a deep breath and swallowed.

"Would you spread it over me, please?" I asked wearily. "These hospital blankets are so thin I can barely keep warm."

"Sure," Isaac said sweetly. He gently spread the blanket over the top +of me, sat back down, and took hold of my hand.

"Thank you," I told him, grateful, as I lay there, trying to cope.

"You're welcome," he replied as he leaned in a little closer. He looked at me with such concern and compassion. "I so wish I could take your pain from you!" he expressed earnestly. "I'd take it from you in a minute if I could!"

"I know you would," I replied appreciatively. "But, honestly, I wouldn't wish this agony on my worst enemy!"

Isaac gave a reluctant smile.

"I just hate seeing you like this," he conveyed with worry in his eyes.

Just then, Papa came back with the nurse, and Uncle Mark came in behind them.

The nurse hurried over and administered some medicine to me, taking care to be as gentle with me as she could as she lifted my head to help me take it. She checked my heart and lungs, the dressing on my head, gathered her things, and left.

Not long after, Papa informed me that he and Uncle Mark really had to get going as it was getting quite late and they still had a long trip ahead of them. As much as I hated to see them go, I understood. They both came over and gave me a kiss goodbye, told me to get well soon, and Papa shook Isaac's hand, telling him to take good care of me. Isaac, of course, assured Papa once again that he would.

Before finally saying goodbye, Papa gave me one last kiss on the forehead, told me he loved me, I returned the sentiment, and then he and Uncle Mark left for home.

*****

It always seemed to take awhile for the medicine to take effect, but thankfully, when it did, it really did seem to help.

When I began to feel a little better, Isaac and I were able to talk for quite awhile.

As we were in the middle of a conversation, however, the nurse who'd been caring for me unexpectedly came back into my room and informed me that she wanted to try to get me up and out of bed. At first, I thought she must be joking, but much to my surprise, she wasn't!

She came right over to the bed and abruptly asked, "Ready for your first walk?"

I looked up at her thinking, *surely*, she must be crazy, but much to my chagrin, she was dead serious!

She dutifully leaned over and proceeded to throw my covers off, and when they were clear, she, with Isaac's help, carefully sat me up.

When I was upright, she came around and grabbed my legs, slowly swinging them over the side of the bed.

Graciously, Isaac helped to steady me as she did.

"All right," she announced, "here we go!"

I looked at Isaac with sheer panic and dread in my eyes, but he smiled lovingly at me, and whispered in my ear.

"It'll be all right," he assured. "I've got you!"

Isaac got under one arm as the nurse got under the other, and they helped scoot me forward a bit on the bed until I could feel my foot on the cold, hard floor.

"Carefully, now!" the nurse urged. "Just take it slowly!"

All at once, Isaac and the nurse began to lift me up, but as my feet rested on the floor, I could tell my legs were very weak and unstable. It'd been so long since I'd been out of bed; I wasn't at all sure I could even stand.

Gently, Isaac and the nurse pulled me up until I was standing upright.

Wobbly and frail, I put my full weight on the two of them, afraid I was going to fall! Uneasy about the whole thing, and extremely hesitant, I tried to take my first step. As soon as I put my foot forward, however, putting any weight on it, my leg gave way and I nearly fell. Thankfully, Isaac and the nurse caught me, holding me tightly, propping me up.

"That's all right," the nurse told me. "Just try again."

I took a deep breath, glancing at Isaac, my look indicating a desire to quit.

He smiled back as he nodded.

"You can do it!" he encouraged.

I took another deep breath, putting my foot out again to try. It was so hard and somewhat painful, but I managed.

"I did it!" I exclaimed, so proud of myself.

"All right…again!" the nurse demanded. "Let's try to make it over to the wall there and back."

Fortunately, the wall wasn't very far from the bed, and even though it took me quite a while, I did finally make it over to it.

When I got there, I wanted to rest and catch my breath, but the nurse wasn't waiting. She wasted no time turning me around.

"Now back to the bed," she insisted.

"You can do it!" Isaac encouraged again. "Just think of our walks back home."

I breathed a sigh as I determined one foot in front of the other, and even though I was completely exhausted, I could feel my legs getting a little stronger with every step.

When I finally made it back to the bed, I thought for sure I was through. Unfortunately, I was wrong!

"Now, one more time!" the nurse instructed.

"Really?" I questioned, wanting desperately to lie back down.

"Really," the nurse kindly replied. "I want to get you moving while your headache is subsided. The exercise will do you good!"

I shook my head and looked at Isaac completely discouraged and distressed.

He smiled at me with his beautiful blue eyes and gorgeous face and cheered me on.

"I know you can do this, Jochebed!" he bolstered. "We'll do it together!"

Not wanting to disappoint, I gathered as much energy as I possibly could and began again. I leaned on Isaac and the nurse more heavily this time for support as I felt very weak and tired, but after what seemed like a monumental struggle, I did finally make it all the way to the wall and back.

"Good girl!" the nurse praised, thrilled for the accomplishment.

She and Isaac carefully helped me back into bed.

"Tomorrow we try to go farther!" she informed with enthusiasm.

I gave Isaac the most pitiful look as I was not at all looking forward to it, but he just shook his head and smiled, knowing it would be all right!

*****

The next day was Sunday, and I have to admit, it felt so strange not being able to go to church. Early in the morning, though, Isaac came knocking on my door to ask if I would pray and do devotions with him. Of course, I eagerly agreed!

It was such a blessing as we shared the most precious time together reading God's Word and praying. I felt like every time Isaac prayed I got to see a little deeper into his heart, and he said he felt the same way about me. Needless to say, I so cherished our time together!

Just as Isaac and I were finishing up our devotions, however, the nurse who had been tending to me walked in and inadvertently interrupted us.

"Oh, I'm sorry," she apologized as she saw we were praying. "I didn't mean to intrude. I can come back in a few minutes."

"No, that's fine," Isaac assured. "We were just finishing up."

The nurse seemed pessimistic and almost bitter as she walked over to the bed, commenting rather glibly as she laid down the gauze and scissors she was carrying.

"You believe in God, huh!" she quipped cynically.

"Absolutely, ma'am," Isaac affirmed without hesitation. "With all of our hearts we do! Don't you?"

"Oh, no!" she confessed quite passionately. "I don't go for that religion stuff! I see way too much pain and suffering and death around here to believe in that nonsense!"

Not surprisingly, Isaac saw this as a perfect opportunity to share the gospel with my nurse. He proceeded to ask her, since she saw so much death, if she knew for sure where she would go if *she* were to die.

She honestly admitted that she didn't, but then again she said, "I really try hard not to think about it. It just seems so morbid and frightening to me."

Isaac nodded, understanding, but then he began to share with her that death didn't have to be so terrifying if she knew for sure where she was going when she died.

"And the Bible tells us that we *can know for sure*," he explained. "Would you be willing to let me show you?"

She seemed a bit reluctant at first, but eventually indulged him out of kindness.

They walked over and sat down in the chairs across the room.

Isaac opened his Bible and took her to Romans chapter three and verse twenty three.

"For all have sinned, and come short of the glory of God;" he read to her. He explained how that she was a sinner, and how that because of that sin she was separated from God and deserved to go to hell. He took her next to Romans six and verse twenty three to solidify the point. "For the wages of sin is death," he showed her, pointing to the verse, allowing her to see it for herself.

She looked pensive and a bit uneasy.

He continued.

"There is *absolutely nothing* you can do to earn your way into heaven!" he stated emphatically. "*None* of your good works will ever get you there! The fact that you're a nurse: helping people, being kind to them, all of it...it can never be enough to get you into heaven."

She looked at him, perplexed.

"You see," he went on, "God tells us right here in the book of Titus chapter three and verse five that it is, 'Not by works of righteousness which we have done, but according to His mercy He saved us, by the washing of regeneration, and renewing of the Holy Ghost;' and again in Ephesians chapter two verses eight and nine, 'For by grace are ye saved through faith; and that not of yourselves: it is the gift of God: Not of works, lest any man should boast.'"

She seemed to be listening intently, hanging on his every word as if she had never heard the truth of the gospel before. It was truly something to behold!

"You may be wondering by now," he pressed on, "that if you can't work your way into heaven, then how does one get there?"

She cocked her head back and forth indicating that the thought had crossed her mind.

Isaac smiled.

"Well," he emphasized enthusiastically, "that's the good news of the gospel!" He quickly turned in his Bible to the book of John chapter three. "You see right here," he said, pointing to the verse, "John chapter three and verse sixteen tells us, 'For God so loved the world, that He gave His only begotten Son, that whosoever believeth in Him should not perish, but have everlasting life.'" He looked up at her with compassion in his eyes. "God loved you so much," he expressed with earnest, "that He sent His only Son to die on the cross of Calvary for your sins. He took our place - yours and mine! He paid the penalty! He paid the price! Why? Because you and I couldn't! Jesus Christ was the spotless, sinless Lamb that shed His innocent blood for the sins of the *whole world!*"

Isaac began to flip through his Bible yet again, this time to the Old Testament.

"Here," he said, "look with me in Isaiah. It says here in chapter fifty three and verse six that, 'All we like sheep have gone astray; we have turned every one to his own way; and the LORD hath laid on Him the iniquity of us all.'" Isaac graciously expounded on the verse. "The *Him* the verse is referring to there is Christ, God's only Son," he explained. "God laid on Christ all of our sins - past, present, and future. He died, was buried, and then He rose again the third day, and now He lives in Heaven, preparing a *wonderful* place for all those who believe! That means, for all those who are willing to put their faith and trust in Christ *alone* for salvation - salvation being a free gift He offers to all! And I'm sorry," Isaac queried. "May I ask your name?"

"It's Evelyn," the nurse answered. "Miss Evelyn Wilford."

"Well, Miss Wilford," Isaac went on, "God offers the free gift of salvation to *you!*" He paused, looking at her kindly. "Can you tell me," he questioned, "what do you do with a gift that someone is offering to you?"

"Well," she thought for a minute, "I suppose you take it from them."

"Yes, ma'am, you're exactly right!" Isaac affirmed. "You receive it! And do you know how you receive this free gift?"

The nurse shook her head, indicating that she didn't know.

"Well," Isaac told her, "you receive it by faith…faith in Christ alone! Again, Ephesians chapter two, verses eight and nine tell us, 'For by grace are ye saved through faith; and that not of yourselves: it is the gift of God: Not of works, lest any man should boast.' And back in Romans chapter ten and verse nine and ten, and also in verse thirteen, it says, 'That if thou shalt confess with thy mouth the Lord Jesus, and shalt believe in thine heart that God hath raised Him from the dead, thou shalt be saved. For with the heart man believeth unto righteousness; and with the mouth confession is made unto salvation.' And verse thirteen, 'For whosoever shall call upon the name of the Lord shall be saved.'" Isaac looked over at the nurse. "Miss Wilford," he asked sincerely, "would you like to receive this free gift of salvation and have assurance in your heart that if you were to die today you'd be in heaven?"

I sat there watching and praying intently the whole time as Isaac shared the gospel, asking the Lord to help my nurse see her need of salvation, and begging the Holy Spirit's conviction upon her heart. I so desperately wanted her to get saved!

As I watched, I could see tears begin to well up in her eyes as she began to realize her sinful state and her need of a Saviour.

She wiped a tear and inquired.

"What do I need to do?" she wanted to know.

Isaac smiled, more than happy to tell her.

"It's simple," he replied. "All you need to do is repent and believe in your heart that Jesus Christ died and that He rose again and that He lives today and that He is the *only* way to get to heaven. Simply put your faith and trust in Christ *alone* for salvation and ask Him to come into your heart and life to be your personal Lord and Saviour."

She looked at Isaac and then at me.

"I want to do that!" she stated through her tears. "I finally understand, and...I want to do that!"

Isaac gladly led her in a simple prayer as she bowed her head right there in my hospital room and accepted Christ as her personal Lord and Saviour.

My heart was filled with such joy as I sat there listening to this dear lady - *my* nurse - pray and receive Christ!

When she said amen, she leaned over and gave Isaac a big hug, thanking him profusely. She said she had always been afraid to die, but now she knew she didn't have to fear death.

"Thank you! Thank you! Thank you!" she kept saying over and over again. "I feel as if a huge weight has been lifted from my shoulders. I have such peace...a peace like I've never known before!" She stood up and came over to the bed, wiping away tears of joy.

I smiled at her, so thrilled for her decision.

"Congratulations!" I expressed with delight. "I'm so happy for you!"

"Thank you!" she replied as she gave me a hug. "You've helped change my life!"

I smiled at her excitedly as she continued to wipe her tears. It was evident that something truly genuine had changed in her.

Needing to continue on with her duties, however, she composed herself and proceeded to change my bandage and to check my vitals. When she finished, she gave me my medicine with a sip of water, all the while beaming with joy. It was the first time I'd ever really seen her happy since my stay in the hospital, and I was ecstatic!

As she left the room, she made sure to thank both Isaac and me again.

After she left, Isaac came over to the bed and took hold of my hand.

"God sure is amazing, isn't He?" he declared with wonder and awe.

"He sure is!" I agreed wholeheartedly.

I sat there a minute reflecting on the miracle that had just taken place.

"That's it!" I suddenly blurted out.

"What's it?" Isaac questioned, a little confused.

"Me!" I exclaimed.

"You?" Isaac queried, completely lost.

"Yes!" I insisted excitedly, looking into his eyes. "Me getting hurt, me being here in the hospital, it was all for *that* - all so that *my* nurse could hear the gospel and be saved! God took my tragedy and turned it into a miracle! He really did work it all out for good!"

Isaac nodded, smiling.

"You're right," he said, agreeing with my assessment. "He truly is amazing!"

From then on, whenever my nurse, Nurse Wilford, would come into my room, it seemed she always had a smile on her face, and she was full of spiritual questions. I would answer some of them when Isaac wasn't around, and he would answer others when I was asleep.

We really did seem to work well together, he and I, and I was so happy that we had the opportunity to help Nurse Wilford grow in the Lord.

*****

Over the next week, my recovery was very slow and painful and oftentimes quite difficult, and, of course, having headaches on top of everything else most *definitely* didn't help! While the swelling from my surgery had all but gone down, unfortunately, my headaches hadn't gone away! While some days were better than others, many days the pain was so intense that I could barely get out of bed! Thankfully, though, when I would have one of those terribly, awful days, Isaac would graciously sit with me, rub my forehead, and quietly pray for me. He was such a blessing!

Papa and Uncle Mark came to visit me several times during the week, and on one occasion, Papa even brought Grampa with him. Needless to say, I was so happy see him as it had been such a long time!

While Grampa was there visiting, he gave me a great report on Gramma, telling me how she was improving more and more every day. It definitely encouraged my spirits to know that she was slowly getting better.

As you can imagine, I very much cherished the visits with my family as they were such an incredible support to me during this difficult, trying time. I have to admit, though, I was a little saddened that Samuel never again came to visit me while I was in the hospital. While it bothered me greatly, I did try my best not to let my disappointment show, especially when Papa was around. I didn't want him worrying or feeling badly about the situation. I simply prayed that things would be resolved between Samuel and me when I got home.

*****

When the doctor checked on me at the end of the first week, he informed me that my infection had completely cleared and that the incision was healing nicely. All the swelling had gone down, and he was pleased with my progress. He was happy that I was able to sit up and get out of bed on my own (although, I still needed assistance walking), and he was glad to see that the strength in my legs was coming back, but, unfortunately, it was coming back slower than he'd expected. When I asked him why, he explained that there may have been some slight damage to my nerves due to the extended exposure to the cold. He was hopeful, though, that it would resolve itself in time.

"Can I go home soon?" I asked, desperately wanting to be back with my family.

"Well," he told me, "I'd like to see you walking better, preferably without assistance. I don't want to take the chance of you falling and reinjuring yourself."

"I understand, Doctor," I replied, disheartened.

*****

I have to admit I was pretty discouraged at the end of that first week, wanting *so badly* to be able to go home! I was just so tired of being in the hospital and wanted to put it all behind me! I suppose the only redeeming factor of staying was getting to disciple my nurse and getting to spend more quality time with Isaac. Still, I just wanted to go home!

Sensing my depression, Isaac tried to cheer me.

"Besides going home, of course," he queried, "what do you want for Christmas this year?"

"Oh, wow, Christmas!" I exclaimed, nearly forgetting its soon arrival. "With everything that's happened, I guess I haven't even thought about it!"

"Well, think!" he prodded cheerfully. "What do you think you'd like?"

"Umm, I don't know," I answered, genuinely unable to think of a thing. "How about you? …What do you want?"

"No, no!" Isaac insisted as he got up out of his chair across the way and walked over to the side of my bed. "What do you *really* want?"

I looked up at his handsome face and got lost in his smile and beautiful blue eyes. I smiled back and blushed a bit.

"Truthfully," I revealed, looking deep into his eyes, "I already received my Christmas gift!"

He cocked his eyebrow, quite perplexed.

"Oh, you did?" he questioned. "And when was this?"

I smiled broadly.

"The day you told me you loved me!" I answered giddily.

Isaac looked completely dumbfounded and more than a little embarrassed. He clearly didn't think that I would remember him making his declaration of love to me as I was still coming out of my coma.

"You…you heard that?" he asked, as he looked at me with angst.

"I did!" I confirmed, somewhat teasing. "But don't worry," I assured, trying to ease his mind, "I won't hold you to it! I know you were just caught up in the moment - excited about me waking up and knowing you. I know you didn't really intend to…"

Isaac's face sobered instantly.

"Jochebed," he abruptly interrupted, "I hope you won't think this too forward…I mean…I know we haven't been courting for very long, but…well…the more I get to know you, and all this time we've been able to spend together, I…I've watched you, and I …" He paused in a long dramatic pause.

Immediately, I thought my heart was going to burst in anticipation of what he was going to say next! Speechless, I breathlessly waited for him to finish his statement. Thankfully, he finally did!

"I…I do love you, Jochebed," he stated earnestly. "Very much I do!"

My eyes got as big as saucers as I sat there stunned - my mouth agape. I certainly wasn't expecting to hear that!

Isaac shook his head, apologetic.

"I've said too much, haven't I?" he lamented. "I'm sorry, Jochebed, just forget…"

"I love you, too!" I blurted back, almost as if the words had a will of their own and couldn't be contained.

Isaac looked at me, shocked, completely taken aback by my response, but as it slowly began to sink in, a grin slowly made its way across his face. His eyes lit up with elation.

"You do!?" he exclaimed, overjoyed.

I nodded my head, smiling in affirmation.

"I do!" I confirmed. "I love you! I think deep down I always have!"

He leaned in and came close to my face, smiling broadly, looking at me with his piercing blue eyes.

"This truly *is* the best Christmas present ever!" he announced with excitement.

"It is!" I enthusiastically agreed.

HARD WORK
(Chapter 24)

I was more determined now than ever to get myself well enough to go home! Every day was a challenge, and I got discouraged easily, but with Isaac by my side, it made it easier to press on. He worked with me every day, several times a day, helping me walk, his arms around my waist, supporting me as I tried to move forward. We'd walk across the room and back together, and then he'd have me do it again. It got to the point where I could go back and forth quite a few times (with help, of course).

*****

"I can't do this!" I insisted, scared to death to move. I stood there beside the bed, grasping Isaac's hands, trying to hold myself steady. "I mean it, Isaac!" I told him, in no uncertain terms. "I can't do this on my own!"

"Yes, you can!" he encouraged.

I shook my head, terrified!

"Jochebed," he stated firmly, "look at me!"

Reluctantly, I looked up at him with absolute trepidation in my heart! This was the first time he wasn't standing beside me supporting my weight. Instead, he was standing in front of me, simply holding my hands. I felt very uneasy and vulnerable. I was convinced I was going to fall!

"Isaac!" I protested, too afraid to move. "I can't! I'll fall!"

"No you won't!" he insisted, not letting me off the hook. "I've got you! You can do this! Now, trust me! Just one small step!"

I squeezed his hands so tightly that my knuckles started to turn white.

"Isaac," I worried, "I just don't know!"

"Well, I do!" he conveyed with confidence. "Your father's coming today, and you're going to show him how much progress you've made. Now come on!"

I took a deep breath and let it out slowly, still very reticent!

"You're sure you've got me?" I questioned, extremely wary.

Isaac looked at me in incredulity.

"Of course I do!" he stated assuredly. "Trust me!"

I took another deep breath and cautiously put my foot out to take a step. I wobbled a bit, but Isaac steadied me with his strong hands.

"That's it!" he encouraged. "Keep going!"

I took another shaky step and then another.

"Good, Jochebed!" he praised excitedly. "You're doing it!"

I focused hard, concentrating on every step, and even though I never left the room, it felt like the longest walk I'd ever taken! It was exhausting!

"Please don't make me go back!" I begged as soon as we made it to the other side of the room. "My head's throbbing something awful, and my legs are hurting, too!"

"All right," Isaac relented. "I understand. We'll try again tomorrow." He carefully scooped me up into his arms and carried me back to bed.

After I was settled, he went and got the nurse.

She brought me some medicine for my headache, and not long after I took it, I fell fast asleep.

Not surprisingly, I slept right up until Papa came to visit later that evening.

When he arrived, Isaac met him in the hallway.

"She's had a pretty rough day today, sir," Isaac told him. "But she's been working harder than anyone I know and she's made great strides! I couldn't be prouder!"

"Well, I can't thank ya enough for everything ya've done for my daughter," Papa relayed with gratitude. "Don't know how I can ever repay ya."

"It's not necessary, sir," Isaac assured. "I'd do it again in a heartbeat! It really has been my pleasure! I've enjoyed my time with Jochebed immensely, getting to know her better, seeing her strengths and her weaknesses…it's definitely caused me to admire her even more than I had before. You truly do have an amazing daughter, sir," Isaac complimented. "You should be proud!"

Papa put his hand on Isaac's shoulder.

"I am!" he stated emphatically. "And you're a good man, Isaac! …Thank you!"

Isaac opened the door to my room, and he and Papa walked inside.

Isaac was a little surprised that I was still asleep.

"Wow!" he whispered to Papa. "She's been asleep now for three hours. I thought for sure she'd be awake by now." He quietly walked over to the side of my bed. "Jochebed," he called out, trying to rouse me. "Your father's here."

I slowly and groggily opened my eyes.

"What?" I asked, trying to wake.

"Your father," Isaac repeated, "he's here to see you."

Papa came over.

"Hi, sweetheart," he said as he looked down at me, smiling.

I tried to open my eyes, but my headache was back with a vengeance.

"Isaac tells me ya've been workin' real hard today," Papa complimented.

"Yes, sir," I whispered, struggling with the pain. "I just wish with all my progress, the doctor would let me go home!"

"Me, too!" Papa commiserated. "Me, too!" He lovingly put his hand on my arm. "Everyone misses ya a lot," he told me, "especially your Aunt Sara and Gramma. They're both just beside themselves that they can't come see ya."

"Oh, I miss them, too!" I expressed with distress, longing to be home.

Papa smiled, trying to lift my spirits.

"I have something for ya, though," he said. "It's from your Aunt Sara." He reached into his coat and pulled out a beautiful gown. "She made this for ya," he explained as he handed it to me. "She thought maybe ya'd feel more comfortable in it than in those ol' hospital gowns."

I reached out the best I could and took the gown from Papa. It felt so soft and warm as it was flannel, and, of course, it was quite stunning!

"I wish I could tell her thank you myself," I lamented. "But you'll be sure to let her know for me, won't you?"

"Sure, I'll tell her," Papa promised.

Still reeling from the pain in my head, I turned to Isaac.

"Isaac," I whispered, trying to open my eyes a little more, "could you *please* go and get the nurse! I *desperately* need something for this headache! I feel as if I might get sick!"

"I'll go find her now!" Isaac told me. "I'll be right back!"

"Oh, sweetheart," Papa sympathized as Isaac left to go get the nurse. "I hate to see ya in so much pain. I sure wish there was somethin' I could do to take it from ya."

"Just pray, Papa," I suggested, feeling absolutely miserable. "I believe God's the only One that can help me get over these terrible headaches."

Papa gently took hold of my hand.

"I am prayin', sweetheart," he assured, "and I'm not gonna stop 'til you're better!"

Just then, Isaac came back with the nurse.

"How are you doing?" she asked as she came over to the bed.

"Not very well," I explained. "My head hurts so badly that I feel sick to my stomach."

"Well, I'm sorry sweetie," she told me, looking at my chart and then to the clock on the wall. "Unfortunately, I can't give you any more medicine for another hour or so. Is there anything else I can get for your stomach, some juice, perhaps, or water? Maybe something to eat?"

"No," I rejected. "I don't think I could keep anything down."

The nurse sighed, concerned.

"If you're sure?" she questioned, hesitant.

"I am," I replied.

"All right then," she instructed, "just try to rest. I'll bring the medicine as soon as time permits."

I painfully nodded, understanding her limitations.

She kindly patted me on the arm, and left.

Isaac came over beside the bed and started to rub my forehead. For some reason, it seemed to help, and I appreciated his willingness to do it.

"Well," Papa remarked, "it looks like ya could use some peace and quiet, sweetheart, so I'll go and let ya rest."

"No, Papa!" I insisted, desperately wanting him to stay. "You came all this way to see me. Please don't go! I'm sure I'll feel better in a little while!"

Papa leaned down and kissed my cheek.

"It's all right, Jochebed," he comforted. "No need to feel badly. We'll have all the time in the world to spend together just as soon as you're well enough to come home."

"I know, Papa," I bemoaned, quite upset and thoroughly disappointed. "But I so wanted to visit with you!"

"I know, Jochebed," Papa agreed, "I did, too! But it's all right, really! Ya just get to feelin' better, okay? We'll talk soon enough."

I sighed, frustrated.

"Okay, Papa," I unenthusiastically relented. "I love you!"

Papa gave me another kiss on the cheek.

"I love ya, too," he echoed. "I'll see ya real soon!" He reached across, shook Isaac's hand, kissed me one more time on the cheek, and left.

After he was gone, I tried really hard not to cry as it only made my head hurt worse, but I felt so miserable, and was so upset that Papa had to leave, the tears just started to flow.

It had truly been a exasperating and trying day, and I just wanted to be better so that I could go home!

Lying there in pain, so hurt and angry that I couldn't leave, I resolved within myself that, no matter what, I was going home at the end of the week if it was the last thing I did!

*****

That Friday morning, bright and early, my doctor came in to check on my progress.

"How are we doing today?" he asked enthusiastically as he came into the room.

Isaac was standing beside my bed as I was just about to try to get up for my first walk of the day.

"My nurse tells me you're becoming quite mobile," he shared.

"I am!" I confirmed. "I've been working really hard at it all this past week."

"Well," he said in anticipation, "how about you show me what you can do."

Eager to show him, I pulled the covers back and put my legs over the side of the bed. I carefully eased myself up and stood there a minute, making sure I had my footing. Isaac was there in front of me, but this time he was only there in case I needed him.

I lifted my foot and took a step all on my own. No wobble, no shaking! I was ready for my next step. I lifted my other foot and stepped forward. So far so good! Isaac had his hands out just in case I needed to grab hold, but I never did! Amazingly, I made it all the way to the wall all by myself!

"That's my girl!" Isaac exclaimed, so proud of me.

I stood there holding onto the wall, trying to catch my breath. When I felt strong enough, I slowly turned myself around and stood there.

"Can you make it back?" the doctor queried.

"Yes!" I answered resolutely.

I wanted to show him that I could do it! Admittedly, I'd only done it one other time on my own without help, but my hope was that if I could prove to him that I could make it, then maybe, just maybe, he'd let me go home!

Supportively, Isaac cheered me on.

"Come on, Jochebed, you can do it!" he cheered. He backed up a little, his hands out in front of me just in case.

I slowly took a step and then another (well, it was more of a shuffle, really, than a step this time), but nevertheless, I did it! I made it all the way back to the bed on my own with absolutely no help! I was so proud of myself, as was Isaac.

He sweetly helped me back into bed as the doctor walked over to talk with me.

"Good job, young lady," the doctor praised as he started to unwrap my head to check my incision. "You've definitely come a long way!"

"Enough to go home?" I asked impatiently, hoping beyond hope that he'd say yes.

He didn't answer, though; instead, he proceeded to examine me.

I waited anxiously for him to respond.

"Hmmm," he said as he checked my head, then again he let out another, "hmmm," as he listened to my heart and lungs.

I could tell that Isaac was just as anxious as I was as we waited for him to finish.

Finally, the doctor stood up from having been leaned over me, and stepped back a little.

"Well," he said as he took the stethoscope from his ears, "it all sounds good...*very* good, in fact. And your incision's healed nicely as well. No more wraps!"

"Thank goodness!" I exclaimed, thrilled for the good news. "But about going home?" I prodded, very much wanting an answer. "Will you let me go?"

The doctor looked at me, contemplating.

"I'll be honest with you, Jochebed," he confessed, "I wish you were a little farther along in your recovery, but…" He paused, looking at me circumspectly. "I think if you promise to continue to work hard," he went on to say, "and if you'll promise me you'll be careful, and by that I mean, taking it easy, not pushing too hard, then…well…" He smiled. "I suppose I can let you go home tomorrow."

"Woohoo!" Isaac shouted as I leaned forward and hugged the doctor.

"Thank you! Thank you! Thank you!" I said, so elated. "I just can't wait!"

"Now, you still have a long ways to go," the doctor cautioned. "And like I said, you'll need to take it easy. I don't want you reinjuring yourself and landing back here in the hospital."

"Oh, I know, Doctor," I assured. "I promise I'll be careful! No one wants to keep me out of here more than I do!"

"All right then," the doctor smiled. "I'll get word to your father, and he can make arrangements to pick you up sometime tomorrow morning. Sound like a plan?"

"Absolutely!" I agreed enthusiastically. "It can't get here fast enough!"

ARRIVING HOME
(Chapter 25)

As you can imagine, I could barely sleep that Friday night, I was so excited! I tossed and turned the whole night through, thrilled to finally be going home!

Early the next morning, Isaac helped me gather my things, packing them up for me, getting them all ready to go. When he finished with my things, he went to his room to get his stuff together. Once everything was all set, he brought his bag into my room, and he and I sat, waiting, anticipating the doctor's arrival. He was to do his final exam, and then officially release me.

We waited and waited for what seemed like forever, but finally, there was a knock at the door. Both Isaac and I looked, expecting to see the doctor walk in, but instead, it was nurse Wilford.

"Is it all right to come in for a minute?" she asked as she stood in the doorway.

"Of course," I said, smiling, motioning for her to come in. "You're always welcome!"

She walked on into the room, closing the door behind her, making her way over to the bed.

"I just wanted to say thank you again," she expressed, so appreciative, as she looked at Isaac and me. "I can't begin to tell you how grateful I am that the two of you cared enough about me to tell me about the Lord Jesus Christ. It *truly* has changed my life in so many ways, but there's simply not time enough for me to share with you just how many!" She beamed as she went on. "I was able to talk with my sister in Ohio the other day," she told us, "and much to my delight, she decided to accept Christ as her Saviour, too!"

Isaac and I both smiled broadly, overjoyed at the news.

"I also got the chance to talk to my neighbor about what happened to me," Nurse Wilford shared, "and she and her husband have agreed to come to church with me this Sunday. I just can't wait! I'm so excited!" She fought back tears of joy as she went on to express her gratitude. "I feel I've learned so much from the two of you in the short time we've had together," she relayed, "and it means the world! You two will always have a very special place in my heart!" She wiped a tear, smiling. "Again, I just can't thank you enough!" she said. "You're both just so wonderful! I'm going to miss you terribly! I wish you both the very best!"

"That's very kind of you," Isaac replied graciously. "And thank you for sharing with us. It's great to hear how the Lord's been working in your life and how He's using you to reach others for Him! Praise the Lord for His transforming power!"

"I agree one hundred percent!" I chimed in enthusiastically, so amazed at what God had already begun to do in my nurse's life. "Nurse Wilford, that's simply remarkable! I'm so happy for you!" I smiled, pleased. "You'll be in my prayers for certain," I told her, "and if you ever have any questions, or if you just want to talk, I hope you'll not hesitate to write to me."

Nurse Wilford smiled back, appreciative.

"Thank you, Miss Jochebed," she said. "I won't! In fact, I'd like that very much!" She looked at Isaac, and then back to me. "Well, again," she expressed with kindness, "I wish you two all the best. You make a very nice couple, and I'm sure that God will continue to use the both of you to help change others lives. God bless you both!" With that, she leaned over and gave me a big hug, wishing me well, before walking around to the other side of the bed to hug Isaac.

We all had tears in our eyes as we had to say goodbye. It was definitely bittersweet.

Before Nurse Wilford left, however, I jotted down my address for her, and she did the same for me. We exchanged them, hugged one last time, and she turned to leave. Just as she was heading out the door, the doctor was walking in.

"So," he quipped with a smile as he walked over to the bed, "are you ready to get out of this place?"

"You can't imagine!" I replied, chafing at the bit to leave.

"Well, let's have one more look and listen here before you go, shall we?" he said, leaning in. "I'll sign the papers to let you go home when I finish my exam."

I nodded, agreeing, and he proceeded to look me over.

When he was through, he smiled approvingly.

"Still looks good," he conveyed, pleased. "I'll have the release nurse bring you your medicine, which you'll need to take with you, and I'm also sending you home with a wheelchair. You'll need to use it until you're stronger and much steadier on your feet." He looked at me very seriously and quite sternly. "Jochebed," he instructed, "I want you to listen to me very carefully. You need to work hard to get well, but I *don't* want you pushing things too far, too fast! You have to take it easy and allow yourself time to heal. Listen to your body. It'll usually tell you when it's time to quit." He went on. "I wish I could tell you that your headaches will get better," he said a bit downcast, "and I suppose there's always a chance that they could, but…honestly, short of a miracle, I'm afraid that's not likely to happen. Your medicine should help, though, but remember, you need to make sure you're keeping track of when you take it. It's a pretty powerful substance, and I don't want you harmed by it."

I nodded as I listened to his directives.

"Also," he continued, "I don't want you alone when you're trying to walk. You're not quite where you should be, and building up your strength is going to take some time. Just take it slow and let yourself recover, and I'm sure if you do, eventually you'll be fine."

"I understand, Doctor," I assured. "I'll be as careful as I can be. And thank you…thank you for saving my life!"

"You're most welcome," he replied with a smile. "I'm just glad that I was able to." He reached out and shook my hand, and then Isaac's. "You take care, now," he told me as he walked towards the door. "And, oh, Jochebed, one more thing."

I perked up, listening intently.

"I've left instructions that you're to follow up with your doctor, Dr. Wellesley," he said. "He has all your information, and should know how to treat you from here."

"Of course," I agreed.

The doctor smiled again before leaving.

"I don't want to see you back here again, all right?" he stated kindly.

"Believe me!" I replied emphatically. "I'm not planning *any* return trips!"

The doctor chuckled lightheartedly and left.

Once he was gone, Isaac and I sat again, waiting, but this time for Papa to arrive. Needless to say, I was so excited and antsy, I could hardly sit still!

"I thought he would be here by now!" I complained, raring to go.

"Patience," Isaac gently encouraged. "I'm sure he'll be here any minute."

I took a deep breath, keeping my eyes fixed on the door, unbelievably fidgety and restless, more than anxious to leave!

"So," Isaac queried, trying to take my mind off of things, "what are you looking forward to the most when you get home, besides seeing your family, of course?"

"Besides seeing my family," I replied without hesitation, "*definitely* being in my own bed! I can't *wait* to finally be comfortable again!"

Isaac nodded, agreeing.

"I can see where that would be appealing," he said. "After sleeping here myself, my bed's sounding *pretty* good about now!" He thought for a minute. "Sooo," he went on to question coyly. "What will you miss the most?"

"Well, that's a silly thing to ask," I lightly admonished. "I'll miss being with you every day, of course!"

He smiled, delighted.

"I was kind of hoping you'd say that," he admitted. "I'll definitely miss seeing you every day, too."

Just then, there was a knock at the door and Papa poked his head inside the room.

"Anybody in here in need of a ride?" he asked cheerfully as he pushed my wheelchair on in.

"Oh, Papa!" I exclaimed, so excited to see him. "You're finally here! How soon can we leave?"

"Right now," he informed me. "That is…if you're ready."

"If I'm ready?" I immediately came back at him, wanting to jump off the bed and into the wheelchair on my own. "Are you joking? I've been ready since last week. Please…let's get out of here!"

Papa laughed at my eagerness.

"I kinda thought ya'd feel that way," he commented happily as he wheeled the chair closer. "Good thing I've already signed the papers to bust ya outta here."

I grinned at his humor.

He felt his coat pocket.

"Yep," he quipped, "got your medicine right here and the escape route all planned out!"

I laughed as he and Isaac helped me out of bed and into the wheelchair.

When I was situated, they gathered my things, and wanting to help, I offered to carry something. Papa accepted, and placed a few things in my lap while Isaac grabbed the rest, including his bag.

Papa took hold of my wheelchair and wheeled me out with Isaac following.

When we got outside, I was struck by how bitter cold it was out there. The snow was just starting to fall, and the wind kept pelting snowflakes at my face. Out of nowhere, I suddenly began to feel anxious and afraid, like I just wanted to run away to safety. I'll admit, I was taken aback by the strange feeling as I didn't understand it!

I'd always liked the wintertime before, I thought. *Why was I so frightened now?*

My heart began racing, and I felt extremely panicked as I found myself holding more tightly to my things, wishing Papa would just hurry on faster. I knew in my mind that I was safe - Papa and Isaac were with me - but I still felt this overwhelming sense of dread. I can't begin to tell you how relieved I was when we finally reached the wagon.

Papa and Isaac carefully helped me inside, and I lay down on a cot that Papa had prepared for me in the back. Isaac sat with me, and Papa climbed aboard in the front. Once we were all settled, Papa took off for home.

Thankfully, I began to feel a little better once we got moving, but I could tell the anxiety was still there. I could hear the wind howling as it whipped the sides of the covering, and I could see the snow falling behind us as we drove away from the hospital. I tried not to focus on my fear, choosing rather to focus on being home, but the panic I was feeling was very real and it kept surging through my body every time the wind would jostle the wagon about. I was scared, and I didn't know why. Worst of all, I didn't know how to make it stop!

I think Isaac could sense something was wrong because after watching me for a little while, he asked if I was all right. I tried to assure him (and admittedly, myself) that I was, but deep down I was still fighting, trying to quell the uneasiness inside of me.

Isaac gently took hold of my hand and whispered.

"I love you, Jochebed," he said so sweetly.

I smiled up at him as if to say, *I love you, too.*

Having him there did seem to help, so I tried to concentrate on him and on being home instead of on my fears.

As we went, I could hardly believe that I was finally on my way home. I had begun to feel as if I'd never make it back. The trip was long and bumpy, and all of the jarring caused a slight headache to come on, but I didn't care. I just wanted this ordeal to be over and to be back in the safety of my own home!

*****

When we finally arrived, Papa and Isaac helped me out of the back of the wagon and into my wheelchair. By now, the snow was coming down something fierce, and the wind was still blowing viciously! My heart began to race again as the snow blew hard in my face, the wind nearly taking my breath away. The feelings of anxiety I'd felt before came flooding back, and I just wanted to run away. It just made no sense to me!

Why was this bothering me so much? I questioned apprehensively.

"Please get me inside!" I begged, not wanting to be out in the storm for one more minute.

Isaac quickly wheeled me up towards the house as fast as he could, and Papa followed behind with some of my things.

"Oh, Papa!" I yelled out upon seeing it, completely amazed. "When did you build this?"

Isaac started me up a ramp that Papa had built for me.

"I've been workin' on it for awhile now," Papa called out over the roar of the wind. "We can talk about it inside."

Isaac pushed me up the ramp, and Papa came hurrying up around us to open the door.

As soon as Isaac wheeled me inside, much to my surprise, everyone shouted, "Welcome home!"

I thought for sure I was going to have a heart attack right there on the spot!

"Oh, my goodness!" I exclaimed, overwhelmed by the reception. "You all scared me to death!"

Aunt Sara was sitting in her wheelchair by the kitchen table, smiling from ear to ear, holding a beautifully decorated cake that she had prepared.

"It's so good to see you again, Jochebed," she said. "I'm so glad you're home!"

Grampa came walking up to me with Gramma on his arm. She was very unsteady on her feet, but she was walking!

"Oh, Gramma!" I shouted, elated to see her. "Look at you up and about!"

She reached down smiling as she took my hand and gave it a squeeze.

"I miss you so much, my Jochebed," she said with love. "I so glad you back!"

I smiled up at her, grinning from ear to ear. I was so proud of the progress she'd made.

"No wheelchair?" I queried.

"Not if I help it!" Gramma declared adamantly.

Grampa patted her on the hand and winked at me.

"Only when she gets tired," he told me, smiling. He got a broader grin on his face. "It's so good to have ya back safe and sound, Wallflower," he said, so happy to have me home.

Uncle Mark came up after Grampa and Gramma and gave me a big hug.

"It's good to see ya, Jochebed!" he expressed with a smile. "Glad ya finally made it back!"

"Me, too!" I heartily agreed, grinning happily.

I was so overwhelmed by my family's welcome and so thrilled to be back in my own house again that my anxiety over the storm that was raging outside seemed to dissipate.

"Well, come on now," Papa prodded everyone, "let the poor child get inside the house."

Isaac pushed me on into the kitchen where everything was decorated so nicely with ribbons and flowers.

"Who'd like some cake?" Aunt Sara asked as she set it down on the table.

"Count me in!" Grampa accepted excitedly as he and Gramma slowly made their way over to the table.

"Ya don't have to ask me twice!" Uncle Mark quipped as he headed for the knife to cut a piece.

Aunt Sara laughed at their eagerness.

Everyone gathered round the table for a piece of cake as Papa put my things in the living room.

Isaac and I waited back a ways as Aunt Sara made her way over beside me to give me a proper greeting.

"Give me a hug!" she insisted as she put her arms out.

I enthusiastically leaned over and we hugged and hugged.

"It is *so good* to see you!" she whispered in my ear as she started to tear up. "Jochebed," she said, struggling to express how she was feeling, "I...I am *so sorry* this happened to you! Can you ever forgive me?"

I sat back and looked at her a bit puzzled.

"Please don't cry, Aunt Sara," I encouraged with dismay. "I don't blame you for this. I don't blame *anyone* except myself. I should've listened to Papa and stayed home that night. If I had, none of this would've happened."

"No, Jochebed!" Aunt Sara disagreed ardently, yet quietly enough so that no one else could hear our conversation. "I'll not let you blame yourself for this! I should've stopped you from going! I should've known better!"

Just then, Papa came back into the room and offered to get me some cake. I don't think he realized he'd interrupted Aunt Sara's and my conversation, but nevertheless he did, so she and I left off talking about the incident.

"I'll be there in a minute, Papa," I replied.

He smiled and went on to the table.

"Another time," Aunt Sara said discreetly, wiping her tears, not wanting anyone else to see. "We'll talk later."

I nodded, agreeing.

"Get on over here you two and get ya some of this *scrumptious* cake!" Grampa insisted, motioning to Isaac and me. "Better hurry too before your Gramma eats it all!" He looked at her and winked, as he put a great big bite of cake in his mouth.

"Me!?" Gramma protested, agitated by Grampa's assertions. "Oh now, you stop, Ezra! You eat half mine!"

Everyone laughed as Isaac wheeled me over to the table.

Aunt Sara smiled as she composed herself and came over, too.

It was so wonderful as we all sat talking, enjoying a piece of Aunt Sara's delicious cake.

*****

The welcome home party lasted well into the evening, all of us laughing and talking and catching up. Everyone filled me in on everything that I'd missed while I was away, and Isaac and I shared how we were able to lead my nurse, Nurse Wilford, to the Lord. As you can imagine, everyone was thrilled for the news!

I shared some details about my recovery and how I'd survived my stay in the hospital, and I also profusely thanked Isaac in front of everyone for all he'd sacrificed for me. Of course, he was humbled, and a bit embarrassed by the praise, but I didn't care! I wanted everyone to know what a wonderful and amazing man he truly was!

I can't begin to tell you how delightful an evening it was spending time with my family again, and, obviously, with Isaac. I was *so thankful* and *overjoyed* to finally be home!

Unfortunately, the only person missing from the evening's festivities was Samuel, and when I had a chance to ask Papa about it, he told me that he was upstairs in his room.

"Just leave him be for now," Papa encouraged. "You two can talk about things later."

I wasn't happy about it, but I accepted it.

"All right, Papa," I reluctantly agreed. "He and I can talk later."

Papa nodded and went on.

Me, however, I sat there a bit chagrinned. I really wanted to see Samuel as I felt terrible that my ordeal had affected our relationship the way it had. I just wanted an opportunity to make things right between us again. I hoped I could talk to him soon!

MY FIRST NIGHT ALONE
(Chapter 26)

After everyone left for the evening, Papa went outside to tend to some things in the barn, and Isaac and I sat alone in the kitchen.

"I hate this," he said, taking hold of my hands. "I don't want to leave you!"

"I don't want you to leave either," I told him, sad at the thought.

"As much as I hated you being in that hospital," he continued, "I loved spending all that time with you."

I smiled lovingly at him as I put my hand to his face.

"I can't ever thank you enough for all you've done for me, Isaac," I expressed, again, with sincere gratitude. "I don't think I would have made it if not for you. I love you with all of my heart!"

Isaac smiled back at me so tenderly.

"I love you, too," he echoed. "And it was my pleasure to be by your side every step of the way. I wouldn't have wanted to be anywhere else."

I smiled back as he and I sat there gazing into each other's eyes.

As we were sitting there, unexpectedly, Samuel came down the stairs and around the corner. When he saw Isaac and me sitting there, he abruptly turned and ran back upstairs.

"Samuel!" I called out. "Samuel, please...come back!"

It was too late. He was already gone.

"Do you want me to go talk to him?" Isaac offered.

"No," I said shaking my head, frustrated. "This is something he and I will have to work out. But thank you for asking."

"Well, all right then," Isaac agreed. He sighed as he stood to his feet. "As much as I hate to," he lamented, "I really ought to be going."

"I understand," I unenthusiastically accepted. "Will I see you tomorrow?"

"Of course!" he answered, without reservation. "You really didn't think you were going to get rid of me that easily, now did you?"

I smiled up at him, giddy over his devotion.

"I love you, Isaac Lewis!" I announced with fervor.

He smiled back at me as he walked to the door.

"I love you, too, Jochebed Lowry," he announced just as passionately. "I'll let your father know I'm leaving so he can come help you to bed."

"Please be careful going home, Isaac," I said. "And thank you again for everything! I'll see you tomorrow!"

Isaac nodded and left, and as soon as he closed the door, a sense of anxiety washed over me as I felt strangely alone. Papa was still outside in the barn, and even though I knew Samuel was right upstairs, sitting there in my wheelchair by myself in the stillness and quietness of the house, unable to just get up and move about, made me feel extremely vulnerable and helpless. In the hospital, there were always doctors and nurses in and out and Isaac, of course, and I guess I just got used to the noise and the security of others being around if I needed something, but here...now...well...I was on my own! I tried not to get too carried away with my fears, but still...I couldn't wait for Papa to come back inside!

I sat waiting for several minutes, thinking he would be right in, but much to my dismay, he never came. I tried to move my wheelchair, but…*oh gracious*…what an experience that was! My arms were still a little weak, and maneuvering was not *nearly* as easy as Aunt Sara had made it seem. I pushed this way and that, trying to work my way over to the stairs so that I could call up to Samuel, hoping we could talk, but by the time I got there, I was so exhausted and out of breath, I wasn't even sure I could yell loud enough for him to hear me. Needless to say, I sat there a minute, trying to recuperate.

Once I felt like I could get his attention, I called out as loudly as I could for Samuel to come. I waited, but I got no response.

"Samuel!" I yelled a little louder… still…no response. "Samuel Michael Lowry!" I ended up shouting at the top of my lungs. "I know you're up there! Would you *please* come down here so I can talk to you?"

At last, I could hear some movement. I was hopeful that maybe he would come. Thankfully, after about a minute or two of waiting, he finally appeared at the top of the stairs.

"There you are!" I called out a little aggravated at his reluctance. "Would you please come down here so that I can talk to you?"

Petulant, Samuel didn't budge. He just stood there at the top of the stairs looking down at me, saying nothing.

It was irritating to say the last!

"Samuel, I know you can hear me!" I shouted to him angrily. "Now please, come down here so I don't have to yell! I really want to talk to you and work things out!"

Samuel was clearly hesitant, but eventually he started to slowly meander down the steps. He only made it down just a couple when he abruptly stopped.

"Where's Papa?" he wanted to know, sounding somewhat afraid to be alone with me.

"He's outside in the barn," I answered, "but he should be in any minute now."

Samuel ambled down a few more steps, staring at me extremely warily the entire time.

"Samuel," I tried to convince him. "There's nothing to be afraid of! It's just me! I'm not going to hurt you! I just want to talk!"

It didn't seem to matter a wit what I said to him, he was determined to be obstinate, flatly refusing to take another step.

"Fine then!" I came back at him a little perturbed. "If that's all the farther you'll come, then I guess I'll just talk to you from there!" I cleared my throat and proceeded to say my piece. "Samuel, I know that I wasn't myself before when I was at Grampa and Gramma's," I started to explain, "maybe even a little frightening in how I acted, but…I assure you…I'm better now…I promise! Papa explained to me at the hospital how I was back then, and truthfully, I probably would've been scared of me, too! But honest…that's not me anymore, *I really am better!* I've changed, Samuel, I have, and I would really appreciate it if you would, at least, give me a half a chance to show you. I couldn't remember things before, but now I can, so please…*just talk to me!*"

Samuel was quite somber as he stood there listening.

"Then prove it!" he blurted out angrily. "Prove that ya really remember!"

"All right!" I agreed, determined to get the matter settled. "I remember you coming to visit me in the hospital! I even remember what you said to me. You explained to me where you were at on that terrible night and what you were doing - talking to Pastor

Scott. I remember that you would barely look at me, much less speak to me while you were there at the hospital, and I *definitely* remember you never coming back to visit!"

Samuel seemed to be intently listening, weighing the validity of what I was telling him as he hesitantly took another step down the stairs.

"You see, Samuel," I insisted sharply, "I do remember! I remember that you weren't at my welcome home party tonight, and I remember…"

As I continued through a litany of things that I could recall, Samuel began to slowly make his way down the stairs towards me, almost as if the cloud of uncertainty and suspicion was starting to lift. It seemed the more I proved myself to him, the more he warmed up to me.

"I don't know what else you want me to say to convince you that I'm all right!" I finally told him, quite aggravated. "No, I'm not one hundred percent, but I'm better…much better!" I was almost in tears; I wanted so badly for him to accept me again.

By the time I finished talking, he was standing on the floor at the bottom of the stairs right in front of me.

"Ya promise you're okay?" he questioned, still a little unsure.

I nodded, indicating that I was.

"Ya promise ya won't go away like that again?" he wanted to know.

I reached out, taking hold of his hand.

"Samuel," I replied as tears welled up in my eyes, "I can't promise you that nothing bad will ever happen to me again, but I do promise you that, no matter what, I'll always love you."

Surprisingly, Samuel got a tear in his eye, too.

"Jochebed," he said, leaning down, hugging me tightly. "I don't ever wanna lose ya again, all right?"

I hugged him back as tightly as I could.

"And I don't ever want to be lost again!" I assured him.

We hugged for a minute, and then he stood up abruptly.

"I hope you're not mad at me for all of this," he stated concerned, clearly afraid that I might be.

"Samuel," I gently scolded, "of course not! Don't think for a minute that I blame you for any of this, because I don't! In fact, I don't blame anyone other than myself."

Samuel got a little quiet.

"I…I know Papa said that it wasn't my fault," he confessed, "but I just feel guilty knowin' that if I hadn't run away that night, then…then you'd a never have come lookin' for me and…"

"But Samuel," I interjected, "everyone has bad days from time to time, and you running away…well…okay, maybe you shouldn't have done that or, at the very least, maybe you should have let someone know where you were going, but listen, I was supposed to stay home that night and wait for you and Papa to come back. Papa left clear instructions, and I didn't listen. I let my worry and my fear get the best of me, and I did a really foolish thing! Yes, I did it out of love, but nevertheless, I disobeyed, and unfortunately, I paid a very big price for it!" I looked at Samuel, trying to convince him. "I don't blame you at all," I reiterated. "Honest, I don't! Besides, I don't know if you heard or not, but God was able to take this horrific tragedy and bring some good from it."

Samuel cocked his head, listening.

"My nurse at the hospital, Nurse Wilford," I explained, "Samuel…she got saved as a result of me being there! That may not have happened if I hadn't needed brain surgery! So you see, it wasn't all for nothing! Don't get me wrong, it's been difficult, definitely, and it'll continue to be difficult I'm sure, but that right there, my nurse getting saved, and, oh yah, I almost forgot to tell you, Nurse Wilford, she was able to lead her sister to the Lord as well, and on top of that, she now has neighbors willing to go to church with her!" I sighed, trying to drive the point home. "Samuel, believe me," I admitted, "it stinks that this happened to me, *to us*, but people coming to know the Lord as a result of it…well…that makes it all worthwhile somehow."

Samuel shrugged his shoulders as he nodded, beginning to see the bigger picture.

"I suppose you're right," he conceded. "I guess I never really thought of it like that before."

I smiled up at him.

"I love you, Samuel," I told him sincerely. "Please, don't ever forget that!" I paused. "So," I asked curiously, "are we okay now?"

Samuel reluctantly nodded.

"Yah, we're good," he assured me as he shot me a smile. "And, oh, by the way," he apologized, a bit bashful. "I'm sorry about that whole door thing in my room the other day. I shouldn't have …"

I furrowed my brow, looking at him as if I were at a loss.

"Door thing?" I interrupted, sounding rather perplexed. "What door thing?"

Samuel's face instantly went pale as he scowled at me, worried.

"You…you remember, don't ya?" he questioned anxiously. "Ya know…a while back…when you were pushin' on my door…tryin' to get in my room…I was pushin' back hard tryin' to stop ya, and…well…I let go, and…and ya went flyin' across the room!"

I looked at him with the most bewildered, confused look I could muster.

"Jochebed," he recounted, visibly growing more and more concerned that maybe I'd forgotten, worried that maybe I wasn't really as 'okay' as I'd claimed to be. "Ya…ya hurt your arm!" he stammered nervously. "It was right before I ran away! How could ya not remember it?"

I sat there with a blank stare on my face, making it seem as if I had absolutely no recollection of the event whatsoever.

More than a little apprehensive at this point, Samuel gradually began to back away from me, panicked.

Sensing his trepidation, and not wanting to push the ruse too far, I slowly started to smile.

"I'm just teasing with you, little brother," I confessed with a chuckle. "I remember!"

Samuel clenched his jaw, fuming!

"Jochebed!" he shouted, aggravated. "That's not funny! Ya had me goin' good there for a minute! I thought for sure ya were still messed up or somethin!"

"I know," I replied, laughing. "Serves you right, though," I said, rubbing my arm. "That really hurt!"

Samuel shook his head as he pointed his finger at me.

"I'll get ya for that!" he threatened playfully.

I simply smiled and teased right back.

"Oh, yah!" I quipped. "I dare ya!"

We both laughed.

Samuel then sobered, becoming quite serious.

"I am glad you're back, though, Jochebed," he told me. "I really have missed ya!"

I looked at him, nodding.

"I can't tell you how glad I am to be back!" I expressed with relief. "And, Samuel," I admitted just as sincerely, "I really missed you, too!"

I couldn't believe it, but Samuel and I were so caught up in our conversation with each other, neither of us had even noticed that Papa had come back into the house. I have no idea how long he'd been standing there, but he came around the corner just as Samuel and I finished talking.

"I'm glad to see the two of ya have mended things," he told us, looking at Samuel and me. "But it's late, and we should be gettin' to bed."

"Yes, Papa," Samuel complied, giving Papa a hug, and then me. "I love ya both," he said in a very uncharacteristic, heartfelt moment.

"We love ya, too, Son," Papa replied, somewhat surprised by Samuel's unexpected sentiment.

With that, Samuel ran on upstairs to his room while Papa turned to me, nodding, giving me a look of approval, happy that Samuel seemed to be doing better.

Once Samuel was gone, Papa suggested that I, too, turn in for the night.

"Ya've had a long day, sweetheart," he said. "Let's get ya off to bed."

"But, Papa," I wondered, "how? I certainly don't want you carrying me up and down the stairs every night. It'll be too much!"

Papa grinned.

"Wouldn't think of it!" he quipped, motioning with his head. "Come with me."

I looked at him circumspectly as he stepped around to the back of my wheelchair and started pushing me down the hall towards the sewing room.

"Where are we going, Papa?" I questioned curiously. "Why are we headed down here?"

"You'll see!" Papa answered coyly.

When we got to the door, Papa stopped, walked around, opened it up, and stepped inside. He promptly lit a lamp before coming back to get me. As we entered the room, I couldn't believe my eyes!

"Oh, Papa!" I exclaimed in amazement. "This is incredible! How did you…"

"It was your Aunt Sara's idea," Papa explained. "She thought ya'd want some privacy when ya got back home, so instead of settin' up your bed in the livin' room, she suggested we rearrange some things in here to make it your own. What do ya think?"

I looked around, simply astonished!

"I love it!" I replied, so surprised by all the changes. "The handle rail, the table, the chair…oh, Papa, it's just perfect!"

"Well, I knew ya'd need some help at first, walkin' and all," Papa told me, explaining his thinking, "so I installed this rail along the wall here so ya'd have somethin' to hang on to…just 'til ya get your balance back, of course, and then…see there," he commented, pointing across the way, "I installed another one over there by the bed so that ya can get in and out more easily. I hope it'll help."

"Oh, I know it will, Papa!" I assured, delighted, admiring the room. "I just can't believe you did all this for me! Thank you!"

Papa smiled, pleased that I was pleased.

"I'm glad ya like it!" he expressed with satisfaction. "And see here," he pointed out, walking over to the nightstand on the other side of the bed, "I put this bell here so just in case ya need anything, ya can ring it, and we'll come runnin' to help ya."

I shook my head, astounded!

"You really have thought of everything, haven't you?" I complimented.

"Well," Papa admitted, "the bell was actually Sam's idea."

"Then I'll be sure to thank him in the morning," I promised. "Speaking of the morning," I wondered, redirecting my thoughts, "what are we going to do about church?"

"I thought what I'd do is take ya over to Grampa and Gramma's so ya can spend the mornin' with them," Papa started to explain as he walked back over towards me. "Grampa's plannin' on stayin' back with Gramma and Aunt Sara anyway, so, if you're up to it, then. ..."

"I'm up for it!" I interrupted, excited for the opportunity. "I definitely want to go!"

"All right, then," Papa agreed, grinning at my enthusiasm. "That's what we'll do!"

Papa proceeded to help me get into bed before tucking me in, and I have to admit, I felt like a little girl again. It had been so long since Papa had done that for me.

Once I was settled, we said goodnight, and Papa left for bed, leaving the door slightly ajar just in case.

After Papa was gone, feeling tired, I tried my best to go to sleep, but no matter what I did I just couldn't. My mind was simply too preoccupied with the events of the day: too excited that I was finally back home, thankful that Samuel and I had been able to resolve our issues, and *thrilled* to be back in my own comfortable bed!

Of course, the happy memories *would have been* a perfect ending to a most wonderful day, but as I continued to lie there, hoping sleep would come, a very sharp pain suddenly went piercing through my head. Instantly, my heart sank, knowing full well what that meant. Another headache was coming on!

Right away, I began to pray, hoping beyond hope that the headache would simply go away on its own (as sometimes they did), but the longer I lay there, regrettably, the pain got worse!

Thinking I would just take some medicine to relieve the pain, it suddenly dawned on me that neither Papa nor I had remembered to put my medicine in the room with me, which meant, more than likely, it was still in my hospital bag all the way out in the living room. I thought about getting up and trying to go get it myself, but recognizing my own limitations, I promptly put the idea out of my mind. I considered ringing the bell (after all, that's what it was there for), but I was too afraid that ringing it this late would wake everyone, and I didn't want to do that either!

Very frustrated, I sighed in quite the quandary.

What was I going to do? I agonized.

Lying there, contemplating, the decision was quickly made for me as the pain in my head suddenly became so unbearable I thought for sure I was going to be sick! I needed help, and I knew it, and as much as I hated to do it, I would have to ring the bell to get someone's attention.

As I slowly and carefully turned myself to reach for the bell, however, almost instantaneously the room started spinning - *terribly!* Immediately, I closed my eyes and swallowed hard, breathing heavily, waiting, hoping that somehow it would stop!

It was awful! I struggled and struggled to keep everything down as I was getting dizzier and dizzier by the minute!

*Oh, this is **not** going to be easy!* I lamented, growing ever more sick to my stomach.

Finally, after a couple of minutes, things settled a bit and I was able to reach for the bell. Grabbing hold, I picked it up and started to ring it, but when I did, I instantly regretted it! As soon as the first clang filtered out into the air, the noise of it was so piercing, intensifying the pounding in my head even more, I felt like throwing the bell across the room! Gritting my teeth in pain, I refrained, however, realizing my dire need for someone to come and help me. Bracing myself, I reluctantly rang the bell again. I rang and I rang and I rang it some more, eventually yelling out, thinking *surely* someone would come. Unfortunately, no one ever did, though, and now in *excruciating pain*, I just had to stop! The pressure in my head was building up so much; I was convinced my head was going to explode!

After exhausting every possible option I could think of, I decided I had no choice but to try to get my medicine on my own. I needed it badly, and I didn't know what else to do!

Papa had left my wheelchair close by, so I knew that if I used the handrail that he had installed, I could probably make my way over to it.

Knowing it was the only way, I tried to sit myself up, but when I did, I nearly threw up from the severe pain and dizziness. I kept taking deep breaths, trying to keep everything down, but it was nearly impossible as I felt absolutely horrible!

Thankfully, after a few minutes of fighting it, my stomach did seem to settle a bit, and the room slowly stopped spinning.

Determined to keep moving, I removed the covers from off my legs and carefully swung them to the side of the bed. Unfortunately, when I did, the movement only started things spinning again. Instantly, I closed my eyes and sat there very still, clenching the bed sheets, trying to steady myself.

Again, after a few agonizing minutes, the dizziness finally subsided and I regrouped. I took a deep breath, and when I felt that I could, I opened my eyes the best I could to assess the situation.

Still struggling, I could just make out the handrail and the wheelchair as judging distances was often very hard for me when I had a headache. Sometimes they would cause my vision to blur, making it quite difficult for me to focus. I did the best I could, however, blinking and straining, the moonlight streaming in the window helping a little, but to no avail. No matter how hard I tried, everything still seemed distorted and hazy. I'll admit I was tempted to give up, but the pain was just too intense and I wanted it to go away! I knew the only thing that was going to accomplish that was getting to my medicine, so despite the obstacles, I resolved to keep trying.

Taking another deep breath, I leaned a bit and reached for the rail by my bed. Entirely misjudging it, however, I missed it completely and collapsed onto my pillow. Needless to say, that didn't help with my pain any!

In utter and complete agony, I lay there just trying to breathe.

"How will I ever make it all the way out to the living room?" I moaned.

Mustering what strength I had, when I felt I could move again, I scooted myself a little closer to the wall and tried to reach for the handrail yet again. Mercifully, this time, I was able to take hold, grasping it as tightly as I could. Gripping it firmly with one hand, I turned myself slightly so that I could grab hold with the other. Once I had a strong grasp, I slowly and painfully lifted myself up out of the bed. I was bent over in pain, but I was standing.

All of a sudden, though, without any warning, *everything* came up! I got sick everywhere - all over the floor, a little on the wall…it was absolutely terrible! My head was now throbbing even more than it had been before, and I was close to passing out.

Could things possibly get any worse!! I bemoaned.

Standing there, trying to cope, I tried calling out for help again, but I was so weak, and my call so faint, no one could hear me.

Finally, I found a little more energy and decided to press on. The only problem…now there was a big mess in front of me, and I didn't know what to do. I knew it needed to be cleaned up, but I knew I needed my medicine more. The mess would just have to wait, and I'd simply have to do my best to work around it.

Starting to feel sick again, I cried out in desperation.

"Please, dear Lord!" I begged. "Please, You've got to help me!"

I so felt like breaking down into tears, but I knew if I did it would only make things worse, so I bit my lip and closed my eyes, breathing hard, doing my best to suppress my emotions. It took some doing, but thankfully, I was able to keep myself from crying.

Swallowing hard, I composed myself, and tried to move forward (around the mess, of course) towards my wheelchair. I kept tight hold of the rail along the wall so as not to fall, shuffling my feet along the floor, coming right up next to the chair.

Now, I thought to myself, standing there half dizzy and sick to my stomach, *how in the world do I get in the chair without falling?*

Hesitant, I let go of the rail with my right hand, still holding tightly with my left, and reached out towards the side of the chair. Feeling the edge of it with my fingertips, I leaned myself out a little more and took hold. The chair was a bit unsteady, but I quickly took a step towards it, releasing my left hand from the rail as I did, and, all in one motion, I turned and swung myself into the chair. I'd made it! Unfortunately, I got sick all over again.

It was truly beginning to feel a bit like torture to me. I was in absolute misery, almost wishing I could die; it seemed more than I could take! Not only was I in severe and unbearable pain at this point, weak and exhausted, but now I was covered in disgusting vomit, too! All I could do was just sit there and cry. I didn't want to, but I just couldn't help it anymore! It was all simply too much!

"Please, Lord!" I cried out again. "*Please…**please** help me through this!"

I was so depleted sitting there, nearly at the end of my rope, I didn't know what to do. I tried to think of some other way, *any other way* to solve my problem, but there just wasn't one! Getting to my medicine was the only solution.

I took a deep breath and forced myself to push with all my might on the wheels of my chair. It was a struggle, but eventually I managed to back myself up to the door. Maneuvering over, I grabbed hold of the edge of the door, flinging it open just wide enough so that I could get out of the room. I turned the wheelchair the best I could, and pushed myself through the doorway, out into the little hallway that led to the kitchen. By the time I'd gotten this far, I was so worn out and in so much pain, I *had* to stop and rest!

When I felt I could go on, I grabbed the wheels of my chair again and inched myself a little further down the hallway. Not surprisingly, I didn't get very far before I had to stop and rest again. It went on like this for me, over and over again, until I finally made it into the kitchen.

By the time I wheeled myself partway across the kitchen floor, I was in so much pain and so exhausted, mercifully, I either passed out or simply fell asleep, I'm not certain which.

I must have been out for quite awhile, though, because the next thing I remember is suddenly being awakened by Papa rubbing my arm, trying to wake me, frantically calling my name!

"Jochebed! Jochebed!" he kept saying over and over again. "Are ya all right? Sweetheart, can ya hear me? Are ya all right?"

I opened my eyes the best I could and tried to focus on him, but it took me a minute to realize where I was at and what had happened.

"Papa," I whispered as I began to remember, the pain still pulsing through my head, "I really need my medicine!"

Papa ran as quickly as he could to the living room and found my hospital bag, frantically searching through it for my medicine. Once in hand, he hurried back into the kitchen, mixed it in a glass of water, and brought it to me.

"Here, sweetheart," he urged as he put the glass to my mouth. "Drink it down."

He tipped the glass so that I could drink, and when I was finished, he put the glass on the table and promptly turned my chair around.

"Let's get ya back to bed!" he said anxiously.

Gently pushing me back to my room, and carefully helping me into bed, Papa cleaned me up the best he could and tucked me in.

In no time at all, I was fast asleep out of sheer exhaustion.

After making sure I was all right, Papa finished cleaning up the mess I'd made, and quietly left so that I could sleep.

AN UNUSUAL SUNDAY
(Chapter 27)

After the horrendous night I'd had, I was out for nearly half the day (although I wasn't aware of it). In fact, the sun was up and already shining brightly through my window by the time I finally woke up.

When I opened my eyes, though, I have to admit, I was a little disoriented at first. I was so used to waking up in the hospital; I literally had to think for a minute where I was at and what day it was. When I finally remembered, I realized that my headache was gone and that I was *incredibly* hungry! Not wanting to attempt another trip to the kitchen just yet, I looked around for the bell that Papa had provided for me. When I found it, I grabbed it and rang it, hoping *this time* someone would hear.

Within minutes, Papa came to the door with a warm smile.

"Hey, sleepyhead, how ya feelin'?" he asked as he came into the room.

"Morning, Papa," I replied back with a grateful smile.

"Mornin'?" Papa teased. "I'd say more like good afternoon!"

"Afternoon? Really?" I exclaimed, completely mortified that I'd slept in so late. "You mean I've slept half the day away!? Oh, Papa, I'm sorry! You and Samuel, did you have to miss church?"

"Now don't ya go worryin' none about that," Papa quieted. "Sam ran down to Grampa and Gramma's and rode along with Uncle Mark, and I stayed behind and had my own special time with God."

"But still," I lamented, "me sleeping so long!"

"It's only a little after lunchtime," Papa calmed. "No need to fret! You're still recoverin', and in the state I found ya this mornin', ya needed your rest." Papa walked over to the bed and sat down beside me. "Speakin' of that," he queried, "what happened? Why didn't ya ring the bell for help? Ya know the doctor told ya not to be out of bed on your own."

"But Papa," I defended, "I did ring the bell! Over and over again I rang it, but no one ever came! I even tried yelling, but no one heard me. I lay here for as long as I could, really I did, but the pain was just too much. I didn't know what else to do, and I desperately needed my medicine. I had to try!"

Papa looked at me sympathetically.

"I'm sorry, sweetheart," he apologized. "I should've thought that through more carefully. I'm so sorry ya had to go through all that. I'll make certain it never happens again! If I have to sleep down here myself, I will!"

It was obvious he felt to blame.

"Papa," I assured, "it's not your fault. I forgot, too. I should have remembered to ask you to put my medicine in here with me where I could get to it. You couldn't have known that you wouldn't be able to hear me."

"But that's just it," Papa corrected. "When Samuel had the idea for the bell, we actually tested it out to see if we could hear it from upstairs, and we could just fine. I guess we just never factored in us bein' asleep."

I snickered at the thought.

"Yes," I chimed in, teasing. "And as loud as Samuel snores, it's *no wonder* you never heard it!"

Papa laughed.

"That boy can saw some logs now, can't he?" he quipped.

Neither Papa nor I had heard Samuel come to the door.

"Hey!" Samuel protested, feigning offense, as he stepped into the room. "Are you two talkin' about me?"

We all just laughed as Samuel walked over towards us.

"How ya feelin'?" he asked as I scooted myself up in the bed.

"Better now, thank you," I told him. "And thanks, by the way, for thinking of the bell. It's a wonderful idea!"

"Oh, you're welcome," he replied. "I actually got the idea from Billy Thorn, ya know, my friend from school."

I nodded, indicating I remembered who he was.

"Well," Samuel went on to explain, "he was tellin' me one day all about how that when his father had to have surgery and was recoverin' at home and all, his ma put a bell in his pa's room so he could ring it whenever he needed somethin'. I thought it was a neat idea, so I told Papa about it."

I smiled, appreciative.

"Well, regardless of whose idea it was," I stated, grateful, "I like it!"

"Good!" Samuel nodded, pleased. "And..." He started to say something else, but Papa must not have heard him because he abruptly interrupted.

"Ya've already had a visitor today," Papa informed me.

"Oh, who?" I queried.

"Isaac," he answered with a grin. He teased. "If I didn't know any better, I'd think that boy likes ya or somethin'."

"Oh, Papa!" I blushed, embarrassed.

"He came by earlier this mornin' right after church askin' 'bout ya," Papa went on to say. "Said he'd be back sometime this afternoon. I imagine he'll be along any minute now."

"Excuse me, Papa," Samuel tried to jump back in.

I ran right over him, though, not even acknowledging his attempts to speak.

"Any minute!" I fretted, anxious about my deplorable appearance. I started frantically looking around at the room and at my nightgown, and patting my hair, trying to get it to lay down a bit. "Can you *please* help me get cleaned up and...and get me a change of clothes and...and a brush for my hair...and...and... ...*Ohhh!* I really don't want Isaac to see me like this!" I still had on my soiled nightclothes, and my hair was an atrocious mess, not to mention the aroma in the room was...well...less than pleasant! (Truthfully, I'm not sure why I was so worried about what Isaac would think of me; I mean, he had just spent two weeks in the hospital with me, seeing me at my worst. But still, I felt self-conscious and wanted to look my best for him.)

Papa leaned in, taking hold of my hands, trying to calm me down.

"Now don't go gettin' yourself all worked up," he gently admonished. "I'd already thought about all that! I had Sam ask Mrs. Bell this mornin' at church if she'd come by today and help ya with a bath. She agreed and said she'd be by after lunch." He looked at me, hoping he'd done the right thing. "I assume that's all right with ya?" he queried.

"Excuse me, Papa," Samuel said, again trying to get his attention.

"In a minute, Son," Papa hushed, holding up his finger for Samuel to wait. "So is that all right with ya, Jochebed?" Papa wanted to know.

My face lit up, thrilled!

"Yes, Papa, thank you," I replied, very relieved. "That'll be wonderful! I really wasn't sure how I was going to manage everything on my own."

"Excuse me, Papa!" Samuel interjected a lot more forcefully this time, determined to have his say.

Finally Papa turned to listen.

"Yes, Son," he questioned. "What is it?"

"That's what I've been tryin' to tell ya!" he revealed, frustrated.

"What is?" Papa asked.

"Mrs. Bell," he blurted out. "She's already here! She's been waitin' for ya in the kitchen all this time!"

"What? Well, Son!" Papa chided, a little perturbed, scrambling to his feet. "Don't ya think that should've been the *first thing* out of your mouth when ya came in the room!? I mean, *gracious!* Next time speak up! It's *rude* to keep our guests waitin'!" He quickly left the room to go greet Mrs. Bell.

Samuel immediately looked at me rather annoyed by Papa's inequitable accusation.

"He's gotta be jokin' - right?" he protested."I mean…ya saw he wouldn't let me talk?"

I couldn't help but chuckle.

"Way to go little brother!" I teased.

He shook his head, rolling his eyes, disgusted, as he summarily waved me off, and left.

*****

"Madeline!" Papa said a little embarrassed as he came around the corner into the kitchen. "I'm so sorry ya had to wait!"

"Oh, that's fine!" Mrs. Bell assured. "No problem. I haven't been here all that long. How's Jochebed doing?"

Papa nodded, grateful for her understanding and concern.

"She seems a lot better now," he explained. "But she had a real rough night. She's been gettin' these terrible headaches, and they really debilitate her somethin' awful!"

Mrs. Bell instantly got a look of distress on her face.

"Oh, I'm so sorry to hear that, Michael!" she sympathized. "I had no idea!" She sighed, optimistic. "Well, hopefully," she added, "as Jochebed continues to heal, they'll go away with time. I'll definitely be praying to that end!"

"Well, thank ya," Papa replied. "I appreciate the prayers. And I sure hope you're right…it's just so hard seein' her in such pain." He shook his head, fretful, as he sighed. "Well, anyway," he went on, "if ya wanna come with me, she's right down the hall here waitin' on us."

Mrs. Bell smiled graciously, and Papa led her to the sewing room.

"Well, good day, Miss Jochebed!" Mrs. Bell greeted cheerfully as she and Papa came into the room. "It's so good to see you awake and out of that hospital bed! I'm so very glad you're home and doing better."

"Thank you, ma'am," I replied, grateful. I looked at her a bit timid. "I…I hear I owe you a great debt of gratitude for helping to save my life," I told her. "I…I honestly don't think I can ever repay you for what you did for me!"

"Oh, no need for that," Mrs. Bell downplayed humbly. "I was just doing my part. Many others played a much bigger role than I."

"Now, Madeline," Papa interjected, "you're much too modest! If it hadn't been for your quick thinkin' that night…" He paused, fighting back tears. "If…if it hadn't of been for you," he pointed out, his voice full of emotion, "I…I'd hate to think where we might be."

"Well," Mrs. Bell responded demurely, a little embarrassed by the compliment, "I'm just glad Jochebed's here and recovering. Now," she went on, clearly wanting to change the subject, "how about we get you all freshened up for that beau of yours?"

Papa smiled as he wiped a tear.

"That's my cue to leave," he quipped as he headed for the door. "I'll go fetch the tub and get the water goin' for ya."

"Thank you, Papa," I called out as he left.

Mrs. Bell wasted no time as she proceeded to ask me what I needed and where she might find them. I told her that I needed my hair brush, some hair bows, my stockings, and a dress. (Ah, a dress! I couldn't *wait* to be back in a dress again! I'd been in gowns for so long that I was looking forward to feeling normal again, or, at least, as close to normal as I could get for now.) I explained to her exactly where she could find them in my room upstairs, and she immediately set her things down and went to retrieve what I had requested.

After Mrs. Bell had gotten my things, she stopped in the kitchen to help Papa warm up the water for my bath.

I waited and waited, looking forward to finally getting clean!

When Mrs. Bell came back into the room, she happily announced, "Your fella's here!"

"What?" I fretted. "Isaac's here *already?* Why…he can't see me like *this!*"

"Now, don't you go worrying yourself!" she calmed. "I told him to go wait in the barn along with your father and brother. We have the house to ourselves." She smiled. "So…ready for that bath?"

I breathed a huge sigh of relief.

"Yes, ma'am!" I smiled back, thankful. "I am!"

Mrs. Bell helped me out of bed and into my wheelchair, and once I was settled, she pushed me to the living room where Papa had set up the bathing tub for me. When she was certain the curtains were closed tightly and the door was locked securely, she helped me undress and, holding tightly to her, I carefully climbed into the tub.

Sitting there in the warm water, I can't begin to tell you how good it felt to finally be able to bathe. While the bed baths at the hospital had been refreshing and served their purpose, they just weren't the same, and I had grown quite tired of them. This was simply another reason for me to be thankful that I was home!

I tried to hurry, not wanting to keep Isaac waiting any longer than I had to, so I scrubbed and washed as quickly as I could, and when I was ready, Mrs. Bell helped me rinse.

Getting the last of the suds out of my hair, Mrs. Bell set the water pot aside, extended her hand to me, and carefully helped me out of the tub. I dried, she helped me dress, and then she graciously brushed my hair and brought a mirror for me so that I could fix my bows.

When I was all set, she went outside to fetch Papa, Samuel, and Isaac from the barn.

*****

"Wow, you look beautiful!" Isaac complimented as he came inside.

"Thank you," I replied bashfully. "I'm sorry you had to wait so long."

"I'd wait all day for you if I had to!" Isaac told me, smiling, as he came over and knelt down beside me.

Just then, Mrs. Bell and Papa came walking back into the house.

"Ya look real nice, sweetheart," Papa remarked as he walked inside.

"Thank you, Papa," I accepted. "And thank you, Mrs. Bell, for *all* of your help! You've been *more* than kind!"

"Well, it was my pleasure," she assured with a smile. "And listen," she added thoughtfully, "don't hesitate to call on me again if you need me - for *anything*…all right?"

"Yes, ma'am, I won't," I promised.

"Now," Mrs. Bell went on to say, "I really do need to be going. Tom will be wanting his dinner before service tonight."

She promptly went and gathered her things, we all thanked her again for her help, and she left.

"Where's Samuel?" I asked Papa, noticing his absence.

"Oh, he went on over to Grampa and Gramma's," Papa explained. "He's just gonna eat supper over there and go on to church with Uncle Mark."

"Oh, I see," I acknowledged.

Papa looked around.

"Well," he announced, "I'd better get this tub taken care of. You two gonna be all right in here on your own?" He smiled teasingly.

"Papa!" I declared, somewhat embarrassed and mildly scolding him.

He just winked at me and went on to take care of things.

"Naomi's been asking about you a lot," Isaac told me. "She wanted me to tell you that she's sorry she never got a chance to come visit you while you were in the hospital. She feels pretty badly about it."

"Oh, no…I understand!" I assured.

"Well," Isaac went on, "she was wondering if you, at least, received her letter she sent? The one she gave your father to give to you."

I nodded, indicating that I had.

"Yes, I received it," I affirmed. "I just never had the opportunity to write her back. Please tell her I'm sorry and that I miss her a lot and that I hope to see her real soon!"

"Well," Isaac shared, "when I talked with her this morning at church, she said she wasn't sure if she should come by and visit just yet. I told her I'd be seeing you today, and that I'd ask if it'd be all right."

"Oh, please, yes!" I replied assuredly. "Tell her to come by any time!"

"All right," Isaac chuckled. "I'll let her know tonight at church." He then changed the subject rather abruptly. "Now, what's this I hear about an adventurous night last night?" he questioned with concern.

"Oh, that," I recalled, sighing loudly. "It was *truly* an awful, *awful* ordeal! Definitely one I hope to *never* go through again! I think Papa and I have worked out a solution, though."

"Well, that's good to hear!" Isaac commented, thankful. "I just hate to think of all you had to go through, and all alone at that!"

"Well, I appreciate your concern," I relayed. "But I do feel much better today."

"I'm glad," Isaac expressed with a smile.

*****

Isaac and I sat and talked for a while, Papa came in and made me something to eat, I ate what I could, and when I finished, Isaac and I enjoyed the rest of the afternoon together.

Unfortunately, as is usually the case when you're enjoying someone's company so, time absolutely flew by! Before we knew it, the hours had ticked away and it was time for Isaac to leave for the evening service. He told me he had some things he needed to do with his family after church so he couldn't come back by to visit me yet this evening, but he assured me that he would be back to see me in the morning.

He wished me a better night, I thanked him, and we said our goodbyes.

After he was gone, Papa and I spent the evening talking and having devotions together, and I have to admit, it was really nice being able to spend some time alone with him, just he and I.

It felt so good to be home!

CHRISTMAS DECORATIONS
(Chapter 28)

Over the next week, I continued to work very hard at trying to walk and to regain my strength, and by the end of that week it seemed all of my hard work and efforts were finally starting to pay off. I *was* getting stronger (I could feel it), and my ability to walk *was* improving, at least, somewhat. I was still a bit wobbly and unsteady on my feet (and still needed assistance, of course), but I was definitely able to go greater distances without tiring and without feeling like I was going to fall at every turn.

On days that my headaches were severe, I mostly just stayed in bed and tried to endure the best I could, but thankfully, my medicine did seem to help, for the most part, although, sometimes it didn't seem to help at all, especially if I waited too long to take it.

During that same week, I'd become quite proficient at using my wheelchair and was fairly independent with it now around the house, and to help me out, Papa had moved downstairs to the couch in the living room so that he could hear me if I needed anything during the night. Isaac continued to visit me every day, and Naomi, too, was now stopping by each day after school to bring me my homework and to keep me apprised as to what was going on in the classroom. Her help was such a tremendous blessing to me as I hated that I had to miss so much school, but there was just no way that I could attend, at least, not yet.

Over at Grampa and Gramma's, Gramma was continuing to amaze everyone with the huge strides she was making in her recovery. She was already up walking short distances with a cane, and Papa said she was determined to be completely wheelchair free by Christmas. I was so proud of her for all she'd accomplished, but admittedly, I envied her progress, wishing that I were as far along as she was!

Amazingly, Aunt Sara and the baby were doing great, too! She was even starting to show a little, and I was so excited for her and Uncle Mark. I just couldn't *wait* to see my new little cousin!

~

I had other cousins, ones on Mama's side, but we rarely got to see them because they lived so far away in California. Mama's two older brothers, Uncle Samuel and Uncle John, had moved out there many years ago, long before Samuel and I were ever born. They were quite a bit older than Mama, and they never made it back very often.

Uncle Samuel and his wife, Mary, had three children - Otis, Esther, and Violet, and they were all older than I was. Uncle John and his wife, Caroline, had five children - Markus; Luke; Paul (who was my age); Ellie, (who was a year younger than me); and James (who was just a year younger than that).

I had only ever seen pictures of my older cousins, and the last time I saw my Uncle John's children was when they came for a visit right after Samuel was born.

I got to see my two uncles at Mama's funeral, but when they came, they came alone as they just couldn't afford to bring everyone with them.

Mama had an older sister, Esther, who lived in Florida and who had also come for the funeral, but she was a spinster and had no children.

Needless to say, I was excited for what it would be like to have a cousin I could actually be around and get to know!

~

Christmas was now just a week away and I was looking forward to spending time with family and with Isaac, of course, but I couldn't help but feel sad that Mama wasn't here to share in the festivities. Just like Thanksgiving, this would be our first Christmas without her and I was heartbroken at the thought.

We had always adorned the house so beautifully each year, but this year with everything going on, no one had taken the time to do so. I missed the festive décor, especially the tree Papa and Samuel would always cut down and bring home for us to trim. We always decorated it together as a family, and then when we would finished, we would sit around and sing Christmas carols, enjoying hot cocoa well into the night.

Things just wouldn't be the same this year without Mama!

My, how quickly life can change, I wrote in my memory book. *A year ago, we were all whole and together as a family, and yet this year it feels as if we're all in pieces, trying to put things back together again. Oh, how I wish Mama was here! How I wish she could be the one to help me bathe and recuperate! How I wish she could know that I was in love with Isaac and how well things were going between us! How I wish she could know about Aunt Sara and Uncle Mark and their new little bundle of joy on the way! I know she would be overjoyed and so elated for the both of them!*

I found myself missing Mama something terrible as I looked up from my memory book and stared out the window on this cold, snowy day. I couldn't help but cry as I thought about her being gone!

Just then, there was a knock at the front door, startling me from my thoughts. Samuel was away at school (this was his last day before Christmas break), and Papa was working in the barn. (He was always good about checking in on me every half hour or so when no one else was with me, but he'd just been in a few minutes earlier, so I was alone in the house.) I wiped my tears and made my way to the door to see who it was.

Before I could get to it, however, Isaac opened the door and peeked in.

"Oh, hi," I said upon seeing him, motioning to him. "Come on in."

Isaac came inside and closed the door behind him.

"How are you feeling today?" he asked as he hung up his hat and coat.

"Oh, I'm all right, I guess," I answered, still a bit melancholy.

"Having another headache?" Isaac queried, noticing that I wasn't myself.

"No," I replied, "so far, today's been a pretty good day, as far as that's concerned. It's just that…well…I guess I'm…I'm just upset about the holidays…you know…missing Mama and all."

Isaac sighed sympathetically.

"I'm sorry, Jochebed," he commiserated as he came over and knelt down in front of me. He took my hands and looked me in the eyes. "I know this can be a really difficult time of the year," he conveyed with compassion. "Is there anything I can do?"

I looked at him glumly.

"No, but thanks," I replied. "I'm sure I'll be all right in time. It's just that…everything just seems so broken this year - me, Gramma, Mama being gone…I don't know…everything's just so different! Papa hasn't even mentioned Christmas gifts, much less a Christmas tree, and me…well…I haven't been able to get out to get any material to make anything for *anyone!*" I shook my head, nearly in tears. "I don't know, Isaac," I lamented. "It all just seems so sad to me!"

Isaac tenderly squeezed my hands, letting me know he cared.

"I genuinely wish I could make things better for you," he told me feeling badly. He paused and thought for a minute. "Hey!" he suddenly queried eagerly. "Where do you keep your Christmas decorations?"

I looked at him a little bewildered.

"What? Why?" I asked. "I don't think Papa really wants to put them up this year."

"Well," Isaac explained excitedly, "that doesn't mean you and I can't put them up! Come on!" he urged, standing to his feet. "Where do you keep them? Let's try to get them up before Samuel gets home! What do you say?"

I sat there, wary, contemplating his suggestion. I just wasn't sure how Papa would feel about us doing such a thing. I didn't know if it would be too much of a reminder to him of Mama; after all, it was always she who decorated everything so magnificently.

"Oh, I don't know," I questioned reluctantly.

"Come on!" Isaac pushed enthusiastically. "It'll be fun! Now where do you keep them?"

"Oh, all right!" I finally relented, giving into his zeal. "You win! They're in the closet in the sewing room."

Isaac was off to the sewing room in a flash, and I followed in my wheelchair right on his heels.

When he opened the door to what was now *my room*, he couldn't help but take the occasion to tease about the disarray the room was in.

"Why, Jochebed Lowry!" he quipped, joking as he walked into the room, "I'm *shocked* at you, keeping such a messy room! Why...I thought you'd take better care than this!"

I squinted my eyes at him, perturbed by the implication.

"*Ooooo*, Isaac Lewis!" I came back at him. "That's mean! You *know* I can't keep things as tidy as I'd like them to be! Besides, half of this stuff isn't even mine! This *is* still a sewing room after all!"

He chuckled at my consternation.

"Still," he teased on as he picked up an old sock of Samuel's that needed darning, "leaving dirty, ol', holey socks lying about - *really!?* Why...that's just *so unlike you!*"

I had had quite enough of his deliberate poking fun at me. Aggravated, I summarily leaned over, picked up my pillow from off my bed, and flung it at him, trying to hit him. Unfortunately, it missed him by a mile!

Instantly, he broke out into raucous laughter.

"Isaac Lewis!" I blustered, getting more frustrated by the minute. "Now you stop that!"

By now he was doubled over laughing uncontrollably.

"You throw like a little girl!" he indicted as he picked the pillow up off the floor and threw it back at me.

The pillow hit me right in the head!

"Ohhh, that's it!" I exclaimed, instantly grabbing the pillow. "Throw like a little girl? I'll show you who's a little girl!"

I took the pillow, lined it up, and threw it back at him as hard as I possibly could. This time, it hit him dead on in the face!

Unprepared for the impact, he went stumbling back, tripped over some laundry that was lying on the floor, and fell right into a basket there behind him. Completely stunned, he sat there, dazed, his arms and legs hanging out of the basket. Before he could even respond, though, - crack, snap - the basket broke, shattering into pieces, and he...he went crashing to the floor.

Needless to say, I was practically in tears at this point as I was in stitches, laughing at the scene before me. I did my best to roll over to him, but when I got there, I could barely speak I was laughing so hard!

"Are you...are you okay?" I questioned, trying to compose myself.

He looked up at me with the most befuddled look on his face.

I couldn't help it; I lost it again!

"Uncle!" he cried out, surrendering. "I cry uncle! I take back everything I said!" He picked himself up off the floor and looked at the basket. "Whoops!" he quipped. "I guess I owe you a new basket!"

I wiped my tears.

"Oh, my!" I exclaimed, surveying the damage. "I guess you do!"

We both started laughing again.

"Shall we...shall we get what we came in here for?" I asked, trying to calm myself.

"And what was that again?" he queried, barely able to speak he was laughing so hard. "I think you knocked it clean out of me!"

We both doubled over, laughing even harder.

"All right, all right!" he finally gave in, holding his side, trying to settle himself down. "Now let's get serious here! We have work to do!" He stood up sniffing and wiping his tears. "Now," he calmed, "where did you say those decorations were at?"

I wiped a tear and then another, finally composing myself enough to answer.

"They're in the closet there," I reminded, pointing to the door behind him. "They should be in a box on the top shelf marked 'Christmas'. That's where Mama always kept them."

Isaac pulled out his hanky and blew his nose as he turned to open the door. Stepping over the pieces of the broken laundry basket, he made his way into the closet.

As I waited, I could hear him moving this and that, searching here and there, and after a while, it seemed to me he was taking way longer than necessary. I was beginning to wonder about him!

"Did you get lost in there or something?" I called out curiously. "Can you see okay? Is the box in there?"

Eventually, Isaac answered.

"Yah, I found it," he assured. "I'm coming. Here it is!"

After a couple more seconds, he finally emerged carrying the Christmas box.

"Yep, that's it!" I confirmed. "But we'd better get a move on if we're going to clean up this mess and get these Christmas decorations up before Samuel gets home!"

Isaac nodded, agreeing as he carried the box to the kitchen for me so that I could get started on things while he went back to the sewing room to clean up the broken basket. When he finished, he came to join me and we spent the next few hours decorating the entire house.

I have to admit it was rather nice spending the time with Isaac, making the house look festive, but with each item I took from the box, I had mixed emotions; it was definitely bittersweet as it brought back *so* many memories! In the end, however, even though seeing some of the items and heirlooms was rather difficult, it was wonderful to see the house so full of Christmas cheer again. I couldn't *wait* for Papa and Samuel to see it!

"Now," I pointed out as I put the last ribbon in place, "the only thing missing is a Christmas tree!"

"Well," Isaac replied, hopeful, "maybe when your father sees the decorations, he'll feel like getting one."

"Oh, I so hope you're right!" I expressed with longing. "It just wouldn't feel like Christmas without one."

Thankfully, Papa had stayed out in the barn the whole time while Isaac and I worked to get the house ready. He hadn't come back inside to check on me because he knew Isaac was with me. I was glad for it, though, because now that meant the decorations would be a complete surprise to both him *and* Samuel.

Now that everything was in place, however, I'll confess it was very hard to wait. I was just so excited for Samuel and Papa to see what Isaac and I had accomplished. I hoped they'd come soon!

THE MOST WONDERFUL NIGHT
(Chapter 29)

After waiting for what seemed like forever, Papa and Samuel finally came. Both were amazed and completely surprised at what Isaac and I had done.

"I just about forgot how beautiful this house could be," Papa remarked with tears in his eyes. "Your mama would be right proud, Jochebed."

"Thank you, Papa," I acknowledged.

I waited, not wanting to push things about the Christmas tree, hoping that maybe Papa would notice its absence and say something about it himself, but, regrettably, he never did. Disappointed, but understanding, I just let it go.

*****

The next morning, I had another miserable start to the day as I woke up once again in pain. Unfortunately, my medicine was running low, and Papa couldn't afford to get me anymore as of yet. He told me that he'd just delivered a project to a customer, and that he was awaiting payment, but he said it would probably be another several days before he could get the money. He said he'd do what he could, but that for now I'd just have to make do with what I had.

I'll admit I was worried because I knew what it meant for me if I ran out of medicine. I prayed *desperately* that I would have enough to get me through!

Some headaches were worse than others, some simply passed on their own, and I knew that, so with this one I was having this morning, I decided to wait and see. Generally, within a short amount of time, I could tell which way things were going to go. Sorry to say, the longer I lay there, though, the worse things got. I began to hurt so badly that I could barely move. There was no doubt; I needed my medicine for this one!

Before I could set myself up to get it, however, I suddenly began to feel dizzy and sick to my stomach, and I felt so sick, I wasn't even sure I could muster the energy to put my medicine together. I wearily reached for the bell and rang it.

Thankfully, Samuel came running.

"Did ya need somethin', Jochebed?" he asked as he came into the room.

"Please, go get Papa," I whispered back, my speech labored, fighting the pain.

Samuel could tell I was in bad shape, so right away, he took off for the barn, yelling for Papa the whole way.

Papa heard him and came rushing out.

"What is it, Son?" he asked in a panic. "What's wrong?"

"It's Jochebed, Papa!" Samuel relayed, nearly out of breath.

He hadn't but got my name out of his mouth, and Papa was off. He tore off for the house, running straight to my room.

When he got there, I had already gotten sick all over, and it was evident I was in desperate shape. I needed my medicine right away, and as soon as Papa saw me, he knew it. I'd been down this road several times before, and he'd helped me through it every time.

Immediately, he came to my bedside, grabbed the glass of water and medicine off my nightstand, mixed them together, and brought the glass to my mouth to help me drink.

Thankfully, within a short while, the medicine began to take effect, and I began to feel a tad bit better.

Papa sat with me until I did.

I couldn't help but feel badly when I got so sick like I did. Most days my headaches were manageable, but when they got to the point where I couldn't care for myself, it was miserable on everyone.

"I'm so sorry, Papa," I whispered as I lay there struggling with the pain.

"Don't ya apologize, Jochebed," Papa insisted. "I know ya can't help it. Ya bear the brunt of these horrible episodes and it breaks my heart somethin' awful that there's not more I can do for ya. I just keep prayin' God'll have mercy and take 'em away from ya soon!"

I thanked Papa for understanding and for his prayers, but still I felt terrible that he had to clean up after me and tend to me like he did.

He didn't seem to mind, though. He lovingly smiled, kissed me on my forehead, and went about cleaning up. When he finished, he patiently waited with me until I drifted off to sleep.

*****

Later on in the day, Isaac came to visit and, thankfully, I was feeling much better. Since I was, he decided it would be a good time for me to walk for awhile to build up my strength even more. I didn't mind, really, as I could now walk beside him, only needing his arm for support every once in a while.

As he helped me up out of my wheelchair to begin our walk, he told me how proud he was of me for how hard I was working and for how far I had come since the hospital. Grateful, I thanked him profusely for standing by me through it all!

Walking there beside him, back and forth through the house, I couldn't help but think about what a truly wonderful man Isaac was. I knew that he really loved me, not only because he had told me so, but because he had demonstrated it to me over and over again and continued to demonstrate it to me every day. I knew that it would have been easy for him to have moved on to someone else, someone who wasn't as sick or as damaged as I was, but he hadn't! He was standing steadfast by my side and continuing to love me despite all my challenges…despite all the issues that I now faced. I just smiled as we walked, thinking about how truly blessed I was to have him in my life.

"What are you thinking about?" he asked when he noticed me smiling.

I got an even bigger smile on my face as I answered.

"You!" I said proudly.

"Me?" Isaac questioned, surprised. "What about me?"

"Oh, I was just thinking about how wonderful you are!" I expressed with admiration.

"Oh, you were, now?" he quipped modestly. "And what makes *me* so wonderful?"

"Everything!" I answered with all sincerity, beaming up at him.

"Everything?" Isaac chuckled. "Wow! I sure have pulled the wool over your eyes now, haven't I?"

I wasn't buying any of his self-deprecation.

"Nope!" I countered succinctly. "I can see quite clearly, and I *definitely* like what I see!"

Isaac smiled over at me.

"Well, I definitely like what I see, too!" he gushed sweetly.

I blushed a bit as he walked me back to my wheelchair.

Once I was seated and settled, Isaac knelt down beside me.

"I want you to do something for me," he said, somewhat excitedly, taking hold of my hand.

"Oh, what's that?" I queried.

"I want you to get yourself all fixed up," he instructed. "I want you to put on your best dress and meet me here in this kitchen at seven o'clock this evening. Can you do that for me?"

I furrowed my brow, starring at him warily.

"Why? What for?" I wanted to know.

"You ask too many questions!" he indicted, remaining rather evasive. "Can you make it or not?"

I sat there still wary, trying to figure out what he was up to.

"Well!" he pressed. "Will you do it?"

I was so suspicious of him; I wasn't quite sure how to respond, but even though I was hesitant and a bit apprehensive, I answered, nonetheless.

"I…I think I can manage it," I replied. "But…I sure wish you would tell me what's going on!"

As soon as Isaac had my answer, he abruptly stood to his feet with a cagey grin on his face, walked over, and put on his hat and coat.

"See you tonight at seven, my dear!" he called out happily.

I shook my head, thoroughly confused, my eyes questioning his motives.

He tipped his head with a wink and a smile, opened up the door, and left.

After he'd gone, I sat there a minute, unsure of what to think.

What was he up to? I wondered. As I sat there contemplating, trying to figure it out, I happened to glance at the clock on the wall. "Oh, my!" I exclaimed. "It's already a quarter after five. I'd better get moving!" I quickly wheeled myself to the bottom of the stairs. "Samuel!" I shouted. "Would you please come down here?"

Samuel came to the top of the stairs.

"What do ya need?" he asked impatiently.

"Could you please go to the barn and ask Papa to come inside for a minute?" I requested.

"Sure," he reluctantly agreed. "I'll be right down. Just let me grab my coat." Samuel ran to his room, grabbed his coat, and came dashing down the stairs. As he passed me, he slipped on his coat, and headed for the door. "Everything all right?" he called back before he left.

"Yes," I told him. "I just need Papa's help with something is all."

Samuel shrugged and went on outside.

*****

When Papa came in the house, I asked him if he would help me get some things from my room, and if he would be willing to go and get Aunt Sara for me. When he asked me why, I told him that I needed her help getting ready for Isaac's surprise.

"Surprise, huh?" Papa questioned.

I explained, and he willingly agreed.

Thankfully, Aunt Sara was more than happy to come and help me get ready, although, as you can imagine, it was quite the sight, she in her wheelchair and I in mine! Somehow, though, we did manage!

Aunt Sara helped me into my dress the best she could, and after we got it all fastened and situated, she helped me fix my hair up all fancy like.

"Why, Jochebed Lowry!" she complimented as she put the last ribbon in my hair. "You are *simply breathtaking! Just **breathtaking!** Isaac is a very* blessed man!"

I leaned over and gave her a big hug.

"Thank you so much, Aunt Sara," I said sincerely. "None of this would've been possible without you...none of it!"

"Oh now," she deflected modestly, "my role was a minor one. It's the girl inside that makes all the difference." She took my hand, smiling broadly, and gave it a squeeze.

I squeezed back, smiling tepidly, nervous as all get out!

Taking a deep breath, I blew it out slowly, unsure of what Isaac would think of me, and anxious for what he had planned.

"Seven o'clock!" I announced apprehensively. "Isaac should be here by now."

Aunt Sara smiled, sensing my trepidation.

"You'll be fine!" she assured with another squeeze of the hand.

I reluctantly nodded and wheeled myself out of the room as Aunt Sara followed behind me.

As I made my way down the little hallway towards the kitchen, I could hear voices talking back and forth. As I neared, I could tell it was Papa and Isaac.

When I came around the corner and Isaac saw me, he immediately fell speechless. His eyes got really wide, and his jaw dropped open in astonishment.

I smiled up at him demurely as I rolled towards him.

He walked over to meet me.

"Jochebed!" he commented, overwhelmed. "You look ...you look...*incredible! Absolutely stunning! Just...just beautiful! Wow!*"

~

My hair was done up in a loose bun with ringlets on the sides and white ribbons hanging to the back and to the sides, and I was wearing the dark green satiny dress that Aunt Sara had made for me. My first opportunity to wear it, and the very first time Isaac had ever seen me in it.

~

"You said to wear my best," I countered. "I hope it's not too much."

"No, not at all!" Isaac assured. "You look...*perfect!* Just...*amazing!* Are...are you ready to go?"

"Go?" I questioned, looking up at Papa, wondering what was going on.

I hadn't been out of the house since I'd arrived home, and I wasn't sure I wanted to leave just yet. I guess it never crossed my mind that what Isaac was planning might include me having to go outside. The thought of wondering out into the wind and snow sent chills through my body as I feared that the anxiety I had felt before would return and I didn't want anyone to know!

I looked at Papa thinking that *surely* he'd be against it, but he just smiled at me as if to say, *It's fine with me.*

I deduced that he must have already okayed Isaac's plans.

I nervously looked back at Isaac and tried not to show my apprehension, but I guess I didn't do such a great job of it.

"You still want to go, don't you?" he asked, a little concerned.

I just sat there, unsure of what to do. I didn't want to ruin Isaac's surprise, but I wasn't sure I was ready to face my fears either. I swallowed hard, anxiously starring at him, not knowing how to answer.

Noticing my reluctance, Papa walked over and knelt down beside me.

"Jochebed," he said sweetly, "I think this would be good for ya. Ya've come a long way in your recovery, and I want ya to go and have a wonderful time." He took hold of my hand and smiled. "Ya have my permission, sweetheart," he assured. "It's all right for ya to go."

I tentatively smiled back as I nodded, very uneasy.

"Thank you, Papa," I replied hesitantly. "III appreciate it."

I looked up at Isaac, still apprehensive, as I took another deep breath. When I gazed into his gorgeous blue eyes that were smiling down at me, however, I instantly melted! He looked so handsome and debonair in his top hat and overcoat.

How could I say no? I thought to myself. In that moment, I determined that, anxiety or no, I was going! "All right then," I announced unwaveringly, "I'm ready!"

Isaac's smile broadened as he took my hand.

"Come with me then," he invited gallantly. "Your chariot awaits!"

I furrowed my brow absolutely bewildered as to what he had planned. I couldn't figure out for the life of me what he was up to!

Needless to say, when he reached down and took hold of my other hand, gently lifting me from my wheelchair, I was *completely* taken aback!

"I'm...I'm going without my chair?" I questioned, slowly standing to my feet, looking over at Papa, astonished.

Again, Papa just smiled, nodding approvingly as he walked over to get my winter shawl. Bringing it back over to me, he helped me put it on. "Ya look real beautiful, sweetheart," he complimented with pride, leaning in, gently kissing me on the cheek. "Enjoy your evenin'!"

"Thank you, Papa," I accepted with reserve as I kissed him back.

Isaac stepped up.

"Ready?" he asked.

I took another deep breath and tried to put on a brave face even though I could feel panic starting to well up inside of me.

"Yes," I answered, letting out a sigh. "I'm ready."

Isaac nodded sweetly as he put his arm around me, taking hold of my hand to help me.

Papa graciously opened the door for us as Isaac led me out onto the porch.

When we stepped outside, the air was bitter cold, snow was just starting to fall, and the wind was blowing ever so gently. Nervous, I held tightly to Isaac, trying not to let my anxiety overtake me.

Why was this bothering me so much? I wondered, not at all understanding the reason for my angst. I tried to stay focused on Isaac.

As we made our way carefully down the steps, Isaac made sure to hold extra tightly to me so I wouldn't fall. It was slow-going as I hadn't walked down stairs yet, but eventually, I made it.

When I looked up, there in front of me was the most gorgeous sleigh I had ever seen! It was decorated brilliantly with greenery and poinsettias and it had a large, white, fluffy blanket spread over the seat, and a big, bright, red blanket for Isaac and me to sit under. There was even a driver to drive us.

"Oh, Isaac!" I gasped, so overwhelmed. "How did you...?"

"Never you mind that!" he told me. "Let's get you tucked in and warm."

Isaac carefully helped me into the sleigh before running around to get in on the other side himself. When he was in and settled, he motioned to the driver, and we were off.

Isaac and I snuggled close together under the blanket to keep warm.

The moon was peeking through the clouds, and despite the cold, it *was* a very beautiful night! The snow was falling ever so gently and the air was crisp and smelled of evergreen.

Amazed by it all, I just sat there next to Isaac taking it all in. Thankfully, my anxiety seemed to dissipate as I was distracted by the wonderful experience.

I still wasn't sure where we were going, but to be honest, I didn't really care! If we only drove around for a few more minutes, and then headed back to my house that would be fine with me! The night had already been more than I could have ever imagined!

Isaac kept his arm around me the whole way, helping to keep me warm, and, of course, I was very grateful, as it was becoming rather blustery out.

As we rode, we talked, both commenting on how cold but how beautiful everything looked all snow-covered and icy.

Suddenly, Isaac looked over at me.

"Nothing, though," he complimented so sweetly, "looks as beautiful as you do tonight!"

I blushed a bit and thanked him timidly.

"You look very handsome, too," I complimented back.

~

Isaac was wearing a dark black suit with long tails and a top hat, and he had on a white shirt and a black bow tie which complemented it perfectly! I'd never seen him so dressed up before.

~

"I feel as if we're going to a grand ball!" I told him excitedly as we drove on.

"You'll see!" Isaac replied cheerfully. "I just hope you'll like it."

I smiled longingly at him.

"I'm with you!" I expressed with contentment. "We could be going to an old, dirty barn for dinner, and I wouldn't care."

"Well," Isaac replied affably, "you're sweet! But hopefully this will be better than any 'ol barn!"

*****

Sure enough, before I knew it, we were pulling up to Isaac's grandparents' house. There were candles in the windows, and the whole place looked unbelievably amazing!

Isaac carefully helped me down off the sleigh and held tightly to me as he led me to the house.

When we got to the door, surprisingly, Andrew was there to greet us.

"Good evening, ma'am," he welcomed, all dressed up like a butler. "Won't you please come in?"

I smiled curiously at him as I was still in the dark as to what was going on.

Andrew didn't say another word, however, as he ushered Isaac and me inside, taking my shawl for me and Isaac's top hat and overcoat.

I thanked him politely, as did Isaac, and then Isaac offered me his arm, ceremoniously leading me into the dining room.

As we walked, I couldn't get over how lovely and exquisite the entire house appeared! It was decorated so opulently with all kinds of Christmas ornaments and ribbons, and the smells...oh, how it smelled of all the best smells! There was a huge

Christmas tree adorned *stunningly*, standing in the front window, and a fire crackling in the fireplace with garland draped across the hearth, red bows and bells hanging in between, and candles lit everywhere! It was as if I'd stepped into a fairytale!

~

The lavishness of the home, while grand and beyond what I had ever seen before, didn't really surprise me, though. Isaac's grandparents were *very well off* and could easily afford such nice things.

Now don't get me wrong, Isaac never acted like he was well-to-do or anything, and neither did his family, in fact, they were very modest people who were always very generous with their money, but they were quite wealthy and their home reflected their innumerable blessings.

~

Needless to say, I couldn't believe how absolutely breathtaking everything was as Isaac walked me over to the table and helped me sit down. After he pushed my chair up to the table, he walked into the other room without saying a word. I sat there waiting, wondering what he was up to.

~

The table was lit by candlelight and decorated with more garland and beautiful poinsettias. It was so elegant! The tablecloth was silk, as were the napkins, and the table was set with fine china. The silverware was polished crystal clear, and the glasses glistened in the candlelight. I felt as if I were dining as royalty!

~

As I sat there admiring everything, Isaac suddenly appeared around the corner carrying the biggest laundry basket I think I had ever seen! I immediately put my hand to my mouth, smiling, as I couldn't help but let out a giggle. The basket had a huge red bow tied around the top, and it was filled with the most stunning, long stem, white roses!

Isaac walked right up to me and presented it to me in the most gallant, courteous way.

"I do believe this belongs to you, my lady," he said as he bowed, extending the basket out to me.

I couldn't help but chuckle at the sight.

Isaac looked up at me, grinning, delighted that I was pleased.

I politely took the basket from him and placed it on the floor beside me.

"Why, thank you, kind sir," I replied, playing along. "It's just what I've always wanted!"

"Well, you're most welcome, my lady," he countered as he went and sat down across the table from me. "I do hope this to be a might sturdier than the last. Of course, I...sat in it first just to make certain."

Obviously, he was just jesting, and we both laughed heartily at the quip.

"Oh, Isaac!" I exclaimed so overwhelmed by everything. "This is just too much! It's the most amazing, wonderful night *ever!*"

He smiled, satisfied and so happy that I was enjoying myself.

Just then, Isabelle emerged from the kitchen carrying a tray with two covered plates on it. She carefully put one plate down in front of me, and set the other down in front of Isaac.

When she removed the covers, it revealed the most delectable food I had ever seen!

"Enjoy!" she encouraged with a smile as she nodded at Isaac and me. She dutifully turned and walked back into the kitchen where Andrew joined her.

Isaac smiled and reached across the table, taking hold of my hands. I smiled back, we bowed our heads, and he prayed. When he said amen, he smiled again, lovingly squeezed my hands, and he and I commenced to eating - enjoying the delicious meal that Isabelle and Isaac's grandmother had prepared for us.

As I sat there, overwhelmed by it all, I just couldn't get over how much trouble Isaac had gone to to make this evening so special for me. It was so much more than I could ever imagine!

"I don't know how to thank you for all of this, Isaac!" I conveyed with sincerity. "And to think...I almost didn't come."

Isaac looked at me inquisitively.

"What do you mean?" he queried.

I was hesitant to say anything, but I knew Isaac would understand.

"Well," I awkwardly began, trying to explain, "ever since I left the hospital...well...when I'm out in the cold and the snow, I seem to get this overwhelming sense of panic, and I don't know why! I used to love the winter, but now...I...I just don't understand what's gotten into me."

Isaac looked concerned, but he was very understanding.

"Jochebed," he asked curiously, "how much do you remember about the night of your accident?"

I looked at him, a bit confused, unsure of what that had to do with anything, but I answered him, nonetheless.

"Well," I began, "I can remember looking for Samuel...and that I wasn't supposed to, and...I...I think it was cold that night, too, but..." I paused as I closed my eyes, trying to force the memories to come. I looked over at Isaac with a furrowed brow. "I...I'm almost certain I was on my way to Mama's grave that night," I relayed. "But...somehow I...I think I got lost." I stopped, shaking my head, confounded at what I'd just said. It honestly made no sense to me. "For the life of me, though," I went on to confess, thoroughly confused, "I really have no idea why I got lost! I've been to Mama's grave *lots of times!* I know I know the way!" I shook my head again. "But...anyway," I continued, "I got lost, and then...well...I woke up in the hospital." I looked at Isaac questioning. "Why do you ask?" I wanted to know. "What does it matter?"

Isaac looked at me earnestly.

"Is that all you remember?" he asked, concerned.

I sat and thought again.

"I think so," I replied. "But honestly, it's all really very sketchy. I can only actually recall bits and pieces of things."

Isaac sighed, accepting it.

"Well, if I can try to explain," he revealed, "the night of your accident, there was a terrible blizzard. It was snowing and blowing so hard that you couldn't see two feet in front of your face. On your way to your mama's grave, you got lost in all that snow. Didn't your father tell you?"

"Maybe," I admitted, trying to remember. "I'm sure he probably did. I know he and Uncle Mark told me several things about that night, but, truthfully, even that seems a bit hazy to me now. I guess I just don't know if I was told or not."

"Well," Isaac proffered, "if I had to guess, I'd imagine that's why you have such anxiety when you're out in the snow and cold. Probably deep down it brings back terrible feelings of that horrible night."

I sat there listening, almost in tears.

"I...I guess it never crossed my mind," I replied with angst.

"But you're safe now, Jochebed!" Isaac reminded. "You don't have to be afraid anymore!"

I nodded, acknowledging what he was saying. I knew he was right, but still....

"Do you think it'll ever go away?" I questioned, worried that I might always feel this way.

Isaac smiled reassuringly.

"I know it will!" he announced with confidence. "God can take any burden if you're willing to give it to Him!"

I reluctantly smiled back, hesitating, bashfully looking down at the table. I'll admit I foolishly felt embarrassed to ask.

"Well...would you...would you please pray for me?" I asked, almost pleading. "Would you pray that I'll be *able* to let it go?"

"Jochebed," Isaac assured, coaxing me to look at him, "of course, I will. I love you, and I'll help you in any way I can!"

Looking into his patient, caring, loving eyes, I was reminded once again of what a truly amazing, remarkable man Isaac was. I shook my head, unable to wrap my mind around it all.

"What did I ever do to deserve you?" I questioned, feeling so unworthy. I smiled at Isaac, my heart filled with gratitude. "I can't thank you enough for being so understanding about all of this," I said as I reached across the table, taking hold of his hand. "I truly am so very blessed to have you in my life, Isaac...truly I am!"

"As am I you," he echoed, tenderly squeezing my hand in confirmation. "We'll get through this together," he promised. "We will!"

I nodded and smiled, appreciative, as he and I went back to talking, immensely enjoying our meal and our time together.

As you can imagine, I so didn't want this enchanted evening to come to an end, but unfortunately, about halfway through our perfect night together, I began to feel pangs of a headache coming on.

"Isaac," I said reluctantly, so disheartened by what I knew was likely coming.

"What is it, Jochebed?" he questioned, sensing something was wrong.

"I'm so sorry to have to say this," I told him, feeling awful about ruining everything, "but I feel a headache coming on, and I don't know how long I have before it gets really bad. If it's all the same to you, I ..."

"Say no more!" Isaac interrupted, abruptly standing to his feet. "I'll get you home!" Isaac hurried to get our things as he called for Andrew to help.

Andrew and Isabelle both came, and after Isaac returned, Isabelle graciously helped me with my shawl.

"Thank you all so much for everything," I told them as Isaac helped me to the door. "This was such an amazing night and I can't begin to thank you enough for all that you've done! And thank you, too," I quickly added, "for all of your prayers for me over this past month. They mean more than you know!"

Isabelle walked up and gave me a hug as she put her hand to my cheek sympathetically.

"You just feel better, all right?" she encouraged.

I managed a smile.

"I'll try," I replied, the pain slowly starting to build in my head.

Isaac and Andrew helped me outside and into the sleigh, but by the time I got in and settled, I was exponentially worse, feeling quite sick to my stomach. I was desperately praying that I would be able to make it all the way home without losing it!

Once Isaac and I were nestled under the blanket together, the driver promptly came and we started out for my house.

As we went, I was growing ever tired, fighting to stay awake, battling the pain in my head, and trying to keep everything down all at the same time. I was absolutely miserable! I just wanted my medicine and my bed! I rested my head on Isaac's shoulder the whole way home, trying my best not to get sick, and feeling so badly that our most romantic, beautiful evening had to be ruined by one of my terrible, debilitating headaches.

"I'm so sorry," I whispered to Isaac. "I wish things had turned out differently!"

Isaac gently stroked my cheek.

"Don't feel badly," he replied sweetly. "I just want you to be all right!"

I wanted to talk with him, but I just couldn't. I was too sick to even move!

*****

When we finally arrived home, the driver pulled up to the house, but I was far too weak and in too much pain to walk inside.

"Do you think you can step down?" Isaac asked me as he'd come around to help me down off the sleigh.

"I'll try," I answered back, grimacing in pain.

Isaac took hold of my hands and carefully helped me down, but standing there, I began to feel so dizzy I couldn't even open my eyes. Isaac tried to steady me with his hands.

"Can you walk?" he questioned, concerned.

I just stood there, squeezing his hands with all my might, clenching my jaw, trying not to move, trying not to get sick!

Isaac understood without me even saying a word and carefully swept me off my feet and into his arms.

"Come with me," he instructed the driver.

Isaac carried me to the house as quickly as he could, and the driver followed behind.

"The door!" Isaac prodded.

The driver quickly went around and opened it up.

As soon as the door swung open, Papa, who'd been sitting in the living room, waiting, quickly jumped up and came to see what was going on.

"Is she all right?" he asked anxiously.

"It's one of her headaches, sir," Isaac informed. Isaac proceeded to carry me straight to my room where he laid me down on my bed as gently as he could.

Papa followed, and immediately went to my nightstand to get me some medicine, but when he started to measure out the dose, he discovered that there wasn't enough. Knowing I needed something, however, he decided to give me what he had.

I took what he gave me, but honestly, it really didn't do anything to lessen the pain. In fact, after Isaac and Papa left to give me some privacy and to let me rest, I lay there, shaking, writhing in terrible pain. Thankfully, eventually, I ended up falling asleep.

"Is that the last of her medicine, sir?" Isaac asked Papa as they walked out into the kitchen.

"Yes," Papa admitted with a sigh, "and I just don't know when I'll be able to get her anymore." He looked down, embarrassed to have to say. "Money's tight right now," he confessed. "I'm waitin' on payment from a few customers, but they've not come through as of yet. I just hope she can hold on 'til I can get the money."

Isaac looked at Papa deeply concerned.

"I'm prayin' for a miracle!" Papa went on to say with earnest.

Isaac nodded, acknowledging, but still he was worried.

"Sir," he jumped in, graciously offering, "I don't mean to overstep my bounds, but…if you'd allow me to I…I'd very much like to pay for Jochebed's medicine."

Immediately, Papa allowed his pride to overtake him, and he rejected the proposal outright!

"No!" he insisted stubbornly. "I'm her father and I'll provide for her needs!"

"I understand that, sir," Isaac countered respectfully. "But…"

"No buts'!" Papa stated adamantly. "I appreciate the offer, Son, I do, but we can manage on our own just fine!"

Isaac could clearly see that Papa was not about to relent nor budge on the issue. He wisely chose not to push.

"Yes, sir," he conceded, sorry he couldn't help. "I understand."

Papa and Isaac stood there for a minute longer in awkward silence, until Isaac, sensing that he ought to go, spoke up.

"Well, sir," he said hesitantly, "thank you for allowing me to take Jochebed out this evening. I…I believe she had a really nice time, despite…well…despite everything."

Papa nodded austerely.

"You're welcome, Son," he replied curtly. "I'm just sorry it had to come to this end."

"Me too, sir," Isaac agreed with a bit of melancholy. He paused nervously, and again there was another moment of awkward silence between the two of them. "Well, sir," Isaac finally said, feeling more than a little uncomfortable, "if there's nothing more I can do, then…well…I'll…I'll be going. I'll come by tomorrow to see Jochebed if…if that's all right with you?"

"That'd be fine!" Papa approved, not offering anything more.

Isaac took a deep breath, letting it out slowly.

"Well, all right then," he commented uneasily as he started for the door. "You, umm…you have a goodnight, sir."

Papa nodded, seemingly still upset, choosing not to verbally respond.

Isaac flashed a nervous grin, and left.

CHRISTMAS EVE
(Chapter 30)

I was so exhausted from the evening out with Isaac and from dealing with my headache that, thankfully, I slept soundly the rest of the night, nothing stirring me from my sleep.

By morning, I was feeling somewhat better, but I was still in my dress, and the ribbons in my hair were barely clinging to my head.

When I was awake enough, I rang the bell for Papa to come and help me.

"How ya doin' this mornin'?" he asked as he came into the room.

"Better," I sighed, frustrated. "I just wish I hadn't ruined the evening with Isaac."

"Aww, I suspect nothin' was ruined, sweetheart," Papa tried to encourage. He smiled kindly. "Did ya, at least, enjoy yourself?" he queried

"Oh yes, Papa, immensely!" I expressed with delight. "It was the most *wonderful* night ever! It really did feel like a dream…just like a fairytale! Thank you so much for letting me go!"

"Well, you're welcome," Papa replied as he walked over, leaning down to give me a hug. "I'm glad ya had a good time." He stood back up. "I'll go and get your Aunt Sara so she can help ya out of your things."

"Oh no, Papa!" I stated confidently. "No need! I think I can manage. Getting out of the dress is a little easier than getting into it."

"You're sure?" Papa questioned.

"I'm sure," I said as I started to take the ribbons from my hair. "But if you could take these for me and put them away upstairs on my dresser," I requested, handing the ribbons to him. "They were Mama's, and I don't want them getting lost."

"Of course!" Papa agreed taking them from me. Once he had all the ribbons in hand, he wanted to make sure that that was all I needed. "And that's it?" he questioned, readying to leave.

I was reluctant to say, but I needed to know.

"Well…I guess there is one more thing," I timidly replied.

"Ok, what's that?" Papa asked curiously.

"Well…umm," I hemmed and hawed, more than a little scared to ask. "I…I couldn't help but notice that my…my medicine bottle it…it looks empty. Is…is it completely gone?"

Papa sighed, disheartened, as he hung his head.

"I'm afraid it is, sweetheart," he reluctantly admitted. "But I'm tryin' hard to get the money. I should have it real soon."

I could tell Papa felt horrible about the situation, so I tried not to let it show how worried I was about it.

"I know you're trying, Papa," I assured him, trying to sound supportive. "I'm sure I'll be fine."

Papa looked up at me, and even though I was doing my best to mask my concern, he could tell by the look on my face that I was troubled. He leaned down and put his hand to my face.

"Don't worry, Jochebed," he said, determined. "I'll get that medicine for ya somehow!"

I nodded and forced a smile as he gave me a kiss on the forehead.

After standing back up, he smiled sympathetically, and left.

Honestly, I wanted to believe that everything would be all right, but deep down I was afraid that it wouldn't be!

~

Papa was a wonderful father, but he was a proud and stubborn man who always prided himself on being able to provide for the needs of his family. He was always very reluctant to ask *anyone* (including family) for *anything*, so knowing him like I did, I knew there was just *no way* he would ever ask for money, no matter *how desperately* we were in need of it!

Needless to say, I worried that my headaches would return before he was able to get any medicine for me, although, I hoped and prayed that I was wrong!

*****

It was Sunday, and Samuel was off to church with Uncle Mark, while Grampa and Gramma remained home with Aunt Sara. Papa and I had our own devotional time together as we had done before, and, as you can imagine, given my present predicament, I was praying *extra hard* that I would *not* get another horrible headache, at least, until I had medicine to help me if I did!

It was hard to believe, but Christmas was now just two days away, and unfortunately, instead of looking forward to it, I was feeling rather down about it. I had no gifts of my own to give to anyone, and for whatever reason, Papa still hadn't seen fit to get a Christmas tree for the house.

Sitting at breakfast together, Papa happened to notice my dour demeanor and asked me what was bothering me.

"Is it another headache, sweetheart?" he queried.

"No, Papa, not really," I replied.

"Well then, what's botherin' ya?" he prodded, recognizing that *something* had me down.

I sighed.

"It's nothing, Papa," I answered, being less than honest, not wanting him to feel badly.

Papa wasn't buying it!

"Now, Jochebed," he stated sternly, leaning towards me, "I may not know much, but I can tell when somethin's botherin' my little girl. Now tell me, what is it?"

"Really, Papa!" I insisted adamantly, giving a half-hearted smile, "it's nothing. I'll be fine!"

Papa raised his eyebrow, looking at me warily, unsure if he believed my answer. He didn't say anything more, though, choosing to let it go.

We continued eating our breakfast in silence, and when Papa was finished, he told me that he had some things he needed to do in the barn. I nodded, acknowledging, and he excused himself from the table. Before he went outside, however, he asked if I'd be all right for awhile on my own. I assured him that I would, and he left.

After I finished eating, I did what I could to clean up around the kitchen, and before I knew it, Samuel was running through the door.

"Hey!" he said when he saw me. "How was your evenin' out with Isaac last night?"

"It was really wonderful!" I relayed with a smile. "That is," my countenance changing to one of melancholy, "right up until I got sick and had to come home."

"Sorry, Jochebed," Samuel replied, unusually sincere. "Everybody at church has been askin' about ya, and they say to tell ya they're prayin' for ya, too." He thought for a minute. "Ya know," he suggested, "the way I see it, with all those prayers bein' said for ya, ya oughta be recovered in no time at all."

I chuckled, seeing his point.

"Thanks, Sam," I acknowledged with a grin. "It's nice to know so many people care about me. I just hope I'll get the chance to thank them soon." I started to turn my chair, but then I wondered. "Hey, did Isaac happen to say anything about coming over today?" I asked as I looked back towards Samuel.

"Nope!" he answered succinctly as he walked over to make himself a sandwich. "He wasn't there today."

"What do you mean he wasn't there?" I questioned, surprised. "It's not like Isaac not to go to church. Do you know why?"

"Nope!" he answered again just as succinctly. "His grandparents weren't there either."

"Oh no!" I exclaimed, concerned. "I do hope everything's all right! Isaac never said anything last night about not going to church!"

"Well, maybe he did, and ya were just too sick to remember," Samuel proposed as he finished making his sandwich.

"I *suppose* that could be the case," I halfheartedly accepted. "But I'm pretty sure I would have remembered if he had said something."

Samuel shrugged his shoulders, seemingly uninterested as he walked off, eating his sandwich.

"Hey!" I yelled out as he disappeared around the corner and started up the stairs. "Aren't ya gonna clean up your mess?"

He gave no response, instead, continuing right on up the stairs to his room.

I huffed, exasperated by his rudeness.

"Brothers!" I groused in consternation. Shaking my head, I rolled myself over, and started putting things away for him.

*****

About an hour later, I was reading a book in the living room when Isaac came over to see me.

"How's my girl today?" he asked as he came in and sat down beside me on the couch.

"I'm doing better, thank you," I replied. "And you?"

"Great, actually!" he answered excitedly. "The service went really well, if I do say so myself!"

"Service?" I questioned with a furrowed brow. "What service? Samuel said you and your family weren't *in* church today."

"Oh no!" Isaac corrected. "Don't you remember? I had one of those speaking engagements at Pastor Landry's church today."

I had no idea what he was talking about.

"Pastor who?" I asked as I shook my head not understanding. "You did what?"

"You remember," he encouraged. "I told you about the speaking engagements at Thanksgiving."

I scratched my head, completely baffled.

"No, Isaac, really," I told him, feeling a bit foolish. "I...I honestly don't know what you're talking about!" I searched my mind for any hint of a memory. "You...you say we talked about it at Thanksgiving?" I queried, still bothered that I couldn't recall.

Isaac could tell that I truly had no recollection of our conversation.

"It's all right," he assured. "No need to fret. I had a couple speaking engagements scheduled for when I was home on Christmas break is all, and today was one of them."

"Oh!" I replied, sorry and frustrated and discouraged that I couldn't remember.

For some reason, I had most of my memory, but from time to time, I realized that there were gaps. *This* was evidently one of those times, and it was rather upsetting to me!

"Don't worry about it!" Isaac told me, sensing my angst. "It's fine, really!"

"Only it's not fine!" I snapped back at him, so aggravated with my limitations. "Sometimes it gets *so maddening* when I can't remember things! Like the other day for instance," I revealed, "I went to get something out of the kitchen, the kitchen I've grown up in my *whole life*, the kitchen I've cooked in, cleaned in - *forever*, and when I got there, I couldn't remember *for the life of me* where I could find the thing I was looking for! I embarrassingly had to ask Samuel to come and help me. I felt like such a fool!"

"Now stop it!" Isaac reprimanded. "You're not a fool! You suffered a brain injury, Jochebed, it's to be expected! You need to stop being so hard on yourself! I'm just glad you're here and that you can remember the important things - *like me!*" He winked and grinned, leaning into me, trying to cheer me up.

"All right," I conceded as I teasingly pushed him away. "You win!"

Isaac and I spent the rest of the afternoon together as Samuel and Papa spent the day outside.

*****

Just as Isaac was getting ready to leave for church, Papa and Samuel came walking in the house, carrying an unexpected surprise.

"Oh, Papa!" I exclaimed with excitement. "It's beautiful!"

There in front of me was a huge Christmas tree that he and Samuel had cut down.

"Thought this house was missin' somethin'," Papa quipped with a smile. "Thought we could decorate it tonight after church."

I sighed, disheartened.

"Oh, I sure wish I could go!" I replied, desiring to be back in the services.

"I know ya do, sweetheart," Papa sympathized. "But soon! I just don't think you're ready right now, especially bein' out of medicine and all."

I was disappointed, but I knew Papa was right.

"I understand, Papa," I reluctantly acknowledged. "Hopefully, soon!"

Papa turned to Isaac.

"Will ya join us to decorate the tree tonight?" he invited.

"Absolutely! I'd love to, sir," Isaac accepted. "Thank you for asking."

*****

As soon as Samuel and Isaac returned home from church, we all commenced to decorating the Christmas tree. It took us quite a while, but when we finished, the tree looked *absolutely beautiful!*

I so cherished the wonderful time spent with Papa and Samuel and Isaac; it had truly been a lovely evening, but my heart couldn't help but ache missing Mama. Things just weren't the same without her here!

*****

The next day was Christmas Eve, and it was growing colder outside as it seemed another bad snowstorm was moving in. I tried not to worry, but I'll confess it wasn't easy. The winds were howling something fierce, and the shutters kept clanging against the house, and every time there was a rush of wind or the banging of a branch, another wave of anxiety would roll over me. I tried to push it aside, but it seemed nearly impossible.

I sat there at the kitchen window, fretful, watching the snow fall fast and furious. Papa was working in the barn, trying to finish up projects before Christmas, and Samuel was sitting in the living room reading a book. All of a sudden the wind slammed a limb into the side of the house making an awful racket.

"Whoa!" Samuel shouted as he came scurrying into the kitchen. "Did ya hear that?" He rushed over next to me and peered out the window.

"Yes, I heard it!" I answered curtly, my heart racing with fear.

"It *sure* sounds bad out there, doesn't it?" Samuel commented, not helping my current condition any. "Sure hope everyone'll still be able to come for the Christmas Eve gatherin' tonight."

"Yes me, too," I replied, concerned.

Samuel stared out the window, watching the snow swirl about as the wind howled on.

"Gramma's sure gonna be disappointed if she can't come see ya again after all this time," he remarked as he shook his head. "She's been lookin' forward to it for quite awhile. I know she misses ya somethin' awful!"

"And I miss her!" I agreed with longing. "But," I hesitated, looking out at the gathering storm, concerned for everyone's safety, "maybe it'd be best if they didn't come."

"Are ya kiddin'? No way!" Samuel bulked. "We gotta have Christmas Eve! It wouldn't seem like Christmas without it! Besides, I'm sure Papa and Uncle Mark'll figure out a way to get everybody here."

"I suppose you're right," I acknowledged, still worried about the storm. "But still…it does seem awfully bad out there."

Samuel stared at me with a frown.

"I'm surprised at ya, Jochebed," he indicted. "You're usually the *first* one excited about our Christmas Eve gatherin'. What's gotten into ya?"

"Nothing!" I answered evasively, trying to avoid the subject. "Don't worry about it! I…I'm just concerned for everyone's safety, that's all!"

I abruptly turned from the window and rolled myself over to the counter, hoping to avoid any further confrontation. Thankfully, it worked! I don't know whether or not Samuel actually believed what I'd told him, but, at least for now, he dropped the matter. I know I wasn't being completely honest with him, but I certainly wasn't about to reveal to my twelve-year-old brother how I was now terrified of snowstorms. I really didn't think he'd understand.

I decided to get busy with preparations, hoping to distract myself from my worries and to be ready just in case things worked out that everyone could come for the Christmas Eve festivities. Being limited on what I could do, I decided to enlist Samuel's help. *My*, that was a challenge and a decision I would later come to regret!

We cleaned up the house together, which took several hours, and that wasn't too terribly bad, but then we moved into the kitchen to begin work on the meal. …I thought *for sure* I was going to lose my mind!

"No, Samuel!" I barked completely frustrated. "That doesn't go in there!"

"But ya said to add salt!" he complained.

"Not in that pot!" I corrected, pointing feverishly. "It goes in *that pot!*"

"This one?" he questioned.

"Yes, that one!" I answered, more than a little perturbed at his lack of aptitude. "Now please, dump it in there, stir it up, and then go get the milk. We need to put some in the potatoes."

"No, no, no Samuel!" I shouted. "You can't just go pouring it in! You need to stir it in *slowly* so they get nice and fluffy."

"Fluffy!?" Samuel protested with a look of disbelief. "Who cares about *fluff?*"

"Oh, good grief, Samuel!" I insisted. "Give me that milk! You go take the biscuits out of the oven!"

"Sheesh, you're bossy!" Samuel groused.

"Look, I'm the cook here! You're the help!" I reminded him in no uncertain terms. I was completely infuriated with his sheer incompetence! "If the meal turns out badly," I pointed out, "it reflects poorly on me, so please, just do as I ask!"

Samuel rolled his eyes and went to get the biscuits.

"There!" he said, slamming them down on the counter. "Now what?"

"Okay," I instructed, "now you can get the bread basket out and put them in there. …No, no, no, Samuel, not that basket, *that one!* You should know by now what basket we use for bread. You eat enough of it!"

"Like I pay any attention to what the basket looks like!" Samuel argued, growing ever annoyed with my constant correction. "I'm concentratin' on the bread, for goodness' sake, not some dumb ol' basket!"

I rolled my eyes in complete aggravation as I went back to stirring the potatoes.

As I slowly poured the rest of the milk in, I thought to myself, *Now I know why I never saw Samuel in the kitchen helping Mama! She had better sense then to let him anywhere **near it**!!!*

"There!" he announced so proud of himself. "How's that?"

I turned around to find the biscuits piled one on top of the other like a huge hay stack ready to topple over.

"Seriously, Samuel!" I exclaimed in consternation, utterly flabbergasted. "You're kidding me, right?"

Samuel looked at the biscuits.

"What's wrong with it?" he quipped. "I think it looks neat. I added my own *flare!*" He ended his presentation with a flurry of his hands.

I couldn't believe it! I was absolutely incredulous! I put my face in my hands, shaking my head, nearly beside myself with rage at this point. I tried not to scream as I felt my blood starting to boil, but it wasn't easy!

I took a deep breath and tried to calm myself.

"Samuel, dear brother," I started in dulcet tones, "we're making dinner, not building a barn. Would you *please* place the biscuits in the basket properly so they won't fall all over the floor?"

"You're no fun!" Samuel complained as he grumpily started to rearrange the biscuits.

I glared at him a minute and turned to tend to things on the stove.

"All right, there!" Samuel stated in a huff. "Your boring ol' biscuits are done. Now what?"

I took another deep breath, trying not to get angry.

I'll admit, I hesitated to give him another task given the fiasco he'd already been, but I thought I'd give it one more try…something simple perhaps, something he wouldn't be able to mess up.

"All right," I answered, "would you please start cutting up some apples for the pies?"

"Sure thing!" he agreed. "No problem!"

I turned back to the stove and began working again when suddenly I realized Samuel was making strange grunting noises. It sounded almost as if he were struggling with the apples or something, but I couldn't imagine for the life of me what he could possibly be having so much trouble with. I took another deep breath and sighed as I shook my head, exasperated. I have to admit part of me didn't want to find out what the problem was, but the other part of me knew that I needed to.

I braced myself for what I might see as I reluctantly turned around.

"Aaaaaa!" I screamed at my wits end. It was all I could take!

Samuel startled at my sudden outburst and threw his apple straight up in the air.

"What is *wrong* with you?" he shouted with a scowl, hastily turning to look at me.

I shook my head in total disbelief!

"*What* is in your hand?" I questioned, thoroughly bewildered and astounded by what I was seeing.

Samuel held up the utensil he'd been using to cut the apples.

"Is that what I think it is?" I asked, rolling myself over to where he was standing.

Samuel started to back away slowly, noticing the absolute fury in my eyes.

It took everything within me not to strangle him.

"Samuel!" I asked with clenched jaw, my anger welling inside of me. "What on earth…are you doing…with a fork?"

Samuel looked at me, and then at the fork. Standing there a minute, he frowned before answering me as if I were the one who was crazy for asking.

"I was scrappin' the peel off the apples so I could cut 'em up," he told me so matter-of-factly.

I was completely dumbfounded, almost at a loss for words!

"*Surely*," I shouted, losing my composure, "**surely**, you know that you *don't* use a…You know what, never mind! I don't even want to know! - Out!" I demanded, pointing to the door. *"Out!* Get out of my kitchen *now!"*

Samuel could tell I was serious so he quickly handed me the fork and immediately left the room.

I just sat there shaking my head.

"Unbelievable!" I quipped. "Just *absolutely unbelievable!!!* How could **anyone** be so inept in the kitchen? I mean, *really!* How is it even possible!?!"

I huffed in utter dismay as I collected myself the best I could before going back to work. I determined that after the harrowing experience I had just had, I would *never again* work in the kitchen with Samuel - *ever!* Beyond making a sandwich, he was pretty much useless! I felt sorry for his future wife!

As the day wore on, the snow outside continued to fall, and I was getting more and more worried with each passing minute.

Eventually, Papa came stomping into the house from outside, shaking snow from his coat.

"Gracious!" he commented, shuddering. "It's becomin' a real mess out there!"

Samuel came running in from the living room.

"We're gonna be able to have our party, aren't we?" he asked anxiously. "I mean, I worked real hard on the meal and…and *everything!*"

I scowled at him as if to say, *You've **got** to be kidding me!* I bit my tongue, however, and refrained myself from saying something I might later regret.

Papa looked at Samuel and smiled.

"Don't ya worry about the party, Son," he calmed. "We're spendin' Christmas Eve together for sure! In fact, I was just comin' to tell ya that I'm goin' right now to help your Uncle Mark bring everybody over. I'll be back in a little while, all right?"

"All right, Papa," I acknowledged. "But please be careful!"

"I will, sweetheart," he promised. "Don't worry!" He bundled up tightly again, and left.

Samuel looked over at me with a big grin on his face, but it quickly dissipated when he saw the look on mine. He could tell that I was still less than happy with him! …He quickly disappeared into the other room.

*****

Everything was ready. It took most of the day, but Samuel and I had finally managed to get everything accomplished that we'd set out to do.

After waiting for quite awhile, Papa eventually made it back with Uncle Mark and Aunt Sara and with Grampa and Gramma as well.

Needless to say, I was so thrilled to see everyone, but especially Gramma. I'd seen the others on and off since I'd been home, but Gramma hadn't been able to make it back since my homecoming party due to her own recovery. Watching her, listening to her, I was amazed at how much progress she had made in that short amount of time. Her speech was about the same, but she was free of her wheelchair like she'd determined to be by Christmas, and she was now up walking with her cane, and walking quite well at that!

"Oh, Gramma!" I exclaimed as she walked over to me. "You look incredible!"

"I do look incredible, don't I!" she teased, puffing out her chest.

I laughed, and we hugged.

"You look good, too," she complimented. "When you get out of that thing?"

"I don't know Gramma," I replied. "But hopefully soon!"

"You be up in no time," she bolstered. "I sure of it!"

"Thank you, Gramma," I said. "I do hope you're right." I smiled broadly. "It sure is good to see you again!" I remarked, so happy in the moment.

"And *me?*" Grampa asked as he came over to give me a kiss and to take Gramma's coat.

"Of course, Grampa," I assured, grinning at his quip. "It's *always* good to see you!"

As we were catching up, there was an unexpected knock at the door. Papa went to answer it, and when he opened it up, there stood Isaac snow-covered and cold, but he was here.

"Glad ya could make it, Son," Papa told him as he took his hat and coat.

"Me, too!" Isaac agreed as he winked at me. "Thank you again for inviting me."

*****

We all sat and ate and laughed and visited and had the most wonderful time together! We shared stories of Christmases past, and Papa read the Christmas story to us, as was our tradition. It was such a lovely but far too brief evening as no one could stay very late due to the storm. Despite having to cut our Christmas Eve celebration short, though, it was still a joyous time spent with loved ones.

As I lay in bed that Christmas Eve night, I reflected back over the entirety of the day. For me, it had been a great day in spite of all the worry and in spite of all the frustrating moments with Samuel. All in all, everything had been good and I was thankful! I got to spend time with the people I loved, and it was the first whole day I had gone without a headache. I was hopeful that it was a sign I was getting better.

Unfortunately, Christmas Day would prove me very wrong!

THE CHRISTMAS PRESENT
(Chapter 31)

The next morning, the snowstorm had ended, and there was a beautiful, thick blanket of white, covering everywhere the eye could see. It was absolutely breathtaking!

Samuel had been up since the crack of dawn, impatiently waiting, but now, he could wait no longer. He ran in and woke Papa up, and he wanted to come and wake me up, too, but Papa refused to let him. He reminded him that I was still recovering and that just because it was Christmas, that didn't mean I didn't still need my rest. Samuel was chagrinned, but he complied.

Papa decided since he was already awake that he would start on breakfast for me. Fortunately, Papa was much more adept in the kitchen than Samuel, which was a good thing; otherwise, they probably would have starved to death while I was away.

He wasn't long into his preparation when I was awakened by the smell of bacon wafting through the air. It reminded me of waking up on Christmas Day when Mama was alive. She always woke before dawn and prepared a grand breakfast for everyone to enjoy. I missed her already!

Wanting to be of help, I made my way into my wheelchair and joined Papa and Samuel in the kitchen.

"Oh good, she's awake!" Samuel announced with enthusiasm as soon as he saw me coming. "Let's go open presents!"

"Son, sit down!" Papa instructed. "I really don't think those gifts are goin' anywhere. We're gonna sit right here and enjoy our breakfast together before we go openin' presents."

Samuel sighed, disheartened, as he reluctantly came back and plopped himself down in his chair.

"Merry Christmas, sweetheart!" Papa said as he came over and gave me a kiss good morning.

"Merry Christmas, Papa," I echoed back. "You didn't have to do all this!"

"It was my pleasure," Papa smiled. "Hope ya enjoy it! Now go join your brother," he encouraged.

I smiled, appreciative, and made my way over to the table.

"Merry Christmas, Samuel," I said as I took my place.

"Can we please just hurry and eat?" he urged impatiently.

"Son, why don't ya come help put things on the table," Papa strongly suggested. "That might just help move things along a little faster."

Liking the sound of that, Samuel quickly jumped up and hastily started putting things on the table. When everything was set and ready, Papa asked him to say the blessing. He agreed, but he prayed so fast, I barely caught a word of what he said.

"Well, now," Papa quipped, looking warily at Samuel, "I certainly hope it's blessed!"

Samuel grinned, shrugged his shoulders, picked up his fork, and dug right in.

As I sat there scooping eggs onto my plate, my heart suddenly sank as a twinge of pain went piercing through my head. Instantly, I was gripped by fear for what it might bring, especially knowing I had no more medicine. Yesterday had been such a good day, and I had been so hopeful, but now...I silently prayed to myself that it wouldn't be a bad one, but deep down I knew that it had been a few days since I had had one, and I feared I was due. I tried not to let on that anything was wrong, though, as I didn't want to spoil the day for everyone else.

Sitting there, trying to deal with the pain, trying to act as normal as possible, I watched in amazement as Samuel sat scarfing down his food. It astounded me how much he could put away and in such a short amount of time! I thought for sure he was going to inhale his entire breakfast whole!

Papa couldn't help but notice it, too, as Samuel was making such an incredible racket!

"Slow down there, Son!" he lightheartedly scolded. "Ya might actually enjoy it more if ya tasted it first!"

Samuel didn't seem to care; he was on a mission to finish, and he wasn't about to stop for anything!

I on the other hand, was finding it hard to eat at all. My headache was getting worse, and I was afraid if I ate too much, I would end up getting sick.

"Everything taste all right?" Papa questioned when he noticed I was barely touching my food.

"Yes, Papa," I assured. "It's fine, really. I'm just not that hungry right now, I guess."

"All right," Papa smiled. "Then if you're finished…"

"She is!" Samuel jumped in eagerly, answering for me, hopping up out of his seat, downing his last sip of milk.

Papa just shook his head and chuckled.

"All right, Son," he gave in. "We can go and open presents."

"Yes!" Samuel shouted excitedly. He immediately tore off for the living room, urging Papa and me to follow.

Papa wiped his mouth and got up from the table.

"I'll clear these dishes later," he told me as he grabbed his cup of coffee and started for the other room. "Ya comin', sweetheart?"

My head was now throbbing mercilessly and I was starting to feel sick to my stomach, but I didn't want to ruin Christmas for Papa and Samuel. Even though it hurt terribly and it was growing increasingly more difficult to focus, I did my best to mask my pain. I took a deep breath and managed a smile.

"Yes, Papa," I replied, putting on a brave face. "I'm coming." I clenched my jaw, swallowing hard, as I slowly wheeled myself into the living room to join Papa and Samuel.

"Come on, slowpoke!" Samuel yelled at me impatiently. "You're takin' forever!"

I painfully smiled, still trying to hide my condition as I hurried on the best I could.

Once I was present and settled, Papa gave his permission.

"All right, Sam," he allowed, "ya can hand out the gifts."

Samuel scurried towards the tree and quickly grabbed a couple of boxes. He looked at the tags, gave one to me, and kept the other for himself.

"Thank you, Papa," I said as I took the present from Samuel.

It was wrapped so beautifully, I almost hated to open it up.

Papa smiled.

"I hope ya like it, sweetheart," he replied.

I carefully pulled the paper back and opened the box. Inside was the most brilliantly, hand carved, jewelry box I had ever seen! Papa had made it for me and had even etched my name into the top of it. I just couldn't get over how beautiful it was!

"Oh, Papa, it's just gorgeous!" I exclaimed as I ran my fingers over the top of it, admiring it greatly. "Thank you so much! It's wonderful! I love it!"

Papa was grinning from ear to ear.

"I'm glad!" he expressed with joy, pleased that I was pleased.

Of course, Samuel wasted no time tearing into his gift. He frantically tore the paper, flinging it aside as he attempted to rip off the lid of the box.

"What is it? What is it?" he wanted to know as he anxiously tried to open it up. Finally, he got the lid off, and inside was a new rifle that he had been wanting for quite some time. "Oh, wow, Papa! I can't believe it! I can't believe it!" he shouted, elated. "I've wanted this for so long!"

Papa smiled broadly.

"I've had it bought since before Thanksgivin'," he revealed. "Mr. Trussle gave me a great deal on it. I hope ya like it, Son."

"Like it?" Samuel exclaimed. "I love it! Thank ya, Papa, thank ya!" Samuel ran over and gave Papa a huge hug.

"Love ya, Son," Papa told him. "I expect next year ya can shoot the Christmas turkey."

"Really!? Really, Papa?" Samuel questioned in disbelief. "Oh wow! I can't believe it! I can't wait 'til next Christmas!"

I don't think I had ever seen Samuel so excited about anything!

I could tell Papa was contented, but still, I felt badly for him.

"I'm sorry I couldn't make anything for you this year, Papa," I expressed with regret, wishing Papa had a gift of his own to open.

"Jochebed," Papa tried to assure, "just havin' you children here with me and seein' your faces light up at your gifts is all the Christmas present I need. I love ya two more than ya know!"

"We love you, too, Papa," I replied with a smile.

Papa nodded approvingly.

"Well," he said, standing to his feet, "I expect I better get those dishes cleaned up. Wanna get it done before I go help get the rest of the family over here."

"I can do it, Papa," I offered (although, I confess with the amount of pain I was now in I wasn't quite sure how I was going to manage).

"Nope!" Papa refused. "Ya go on and relax and enjoy your day, sweetheart! It's part of my Christmas gift to ya. I'll take care of it!"

I sighed, more than a little relieved.

"That's sweet of you, Papa," I said, grateful. "Thank you!" I was in so much pain at this point; I didn't know what to do. I swallowed hard, trying not to be obvious about it. "Then if you don't mind, Papa," I went on to say, "I think I'm going to go and get out of this nightgown before everyone arrives."

"Sure thing," Papa agreed.

I gave a reluctant smile as I nodded and slowly started to wheel myself out of the room.

"Jochebed," Papa stopped me, sensing something was wrong. "Is everything all right?"

"I'm fine, Papa," I lied. "I just want to get changed is all."

Papa looked at me warily, almost as if he suspected that I wasn't being completely honest.

"Okay," he answered guardedly. "But you'll let me know if ya need anything…right?"

I flashed a halfhearted grin as I nodded and proceeded on to my room. As I wheeled myself back, I felt awful for having lied to Papa, but I was determined that I was *not* going to ruin Christmas for everyone!

Being out of medicine, I didn't want Papa to feel badly that he couldn't afford to get me any more right now. I thought that if I could just go and lie down for a little while, perhaps my headache would pass. At least, that was my hope!

As I gradually wheeled myself down the little hallway towards the sewing room door, however, my head felt like it was going to explode and my stomach was in terrible knots. It was all I could do not to get sick right then and there!

When I finally got inside the room, I was so weak and dizzy and in so much pain, I could barely sit up straight, much less, stand. Somehow, though, I did manage to get myself up and out of my wheelchair by grabbing hold and hanging on tightly to the handrails in my room.

As soon as I stood up, however, everything went dark and I passed out, collapsing in a heap on the floor, hitting my head as I fell.

I don't know for sure how long I'd been out, but it must have been a while because when I came to, I could hear voices talking in the other room. I knew then that everyone had arrived for Christmas.

I wasn't sure what had happened to me, but I did know that I was still in a tremendous amount of pain, and that I still felt sick and very weak. I tried to lift myself up, but I just had no strength. I lay there on the floor, trying desperately not to get sick.

Regrettably, that plan didn't work for very long, though, as I ended up throwing up all over the floor. I was so dizzy and lightheaded that I just couldn't stop. I got sick over and over again until nothing else would come up. I was absolutely miserable! I couldn't even muster enough energy to yell for help, and the bell was simply too far out of reach for me to get to. I came to the conclusion that I would just have to lie there on the floor until someone came looking for me.

*****

"Merry Christmas!" Uncle Mark yelled out as he pushed Aunt Sara into the house.

"Merry Christmas!" everyone echoed back.

There was hustle and bustle, and everyone was excited to be there and to be, soon, opening more gifts.

Uncle Mark and Aunt Sara put the food they'd brought down in the kitchen and went to join everyone in the living room.

Samuel was showing Grampa and Gramma his rifle, and when he saw Uncle Mark come into the room, he ran over to show him as well.

"What ya got there?" Uncle Mark queried as Samuel came running up to him.

"It's the rifle I've been wantin' for two years now!" he answered with enthusiasm. "Can ya believe it?"

"That's great, Sam!" Uncle Mark expressed, happy for him. "Looks like a real dandy!"

"Yah!" Samuel agreed. "And Papa said I can kill the Christmas turkey next year, too!"

"Oh, he did now?" Uncle Mark commented as he smiled at Papa.

Samuel nodded excitedly.

"Well, maybe after lunch," Uncle Mark offered, "you and I can go out and get to practicin' for next year."

"Really!" Samuel shouted eagerly. "Ya mean it?"

Uncle Mark nodded.

"Sure do!" he said. "Ya clear it with your Pa first and I'll take ya out."

"Oh, boy!" Samuel exclaimed, running over to Papa. "Can I, Papa? Can I? Please?"

"We'll see, Son," Papa answered with a chuckle. "We'll see!"

"Where Jochebed?" Gramma queried. "I not see her yet."

"Oh, she went to change, Ma," Papa explained. "She should be out any time now, though."

Gramma nodded, satisfied with the answer.

Everyone sat and talked and talked until finally Papa realized that I hadn't come out yet.

Aunt Sara had gone into the kitchen to help Uncle Mark prepare things for lunch, so Papa went in to find her.

"Sara," he requested, a little concerned, "Jochebed went to her room to change, and well…she's been in there for quite awhile now. Could ya go check on her and see if maybe she needs some help?"

"Sure, Michael, no problem," Aunt Sara agreed, more than happy to do it. "You know us women, always wanting to look our best!"

Papa nodded, smiling.

"Thank ya, Sara," he said. "I appreciate it."

I was still lying on the floor, barely able to move, when Aunt Sara came, lightly knocking on the door.

"Jochebed," she called out, "it's Aunt Sara. May I come in?"

I was relieved that someone had finally come, but I could only manage a whisper and Aunt Sara couldn't hear me.

Growing a little concerned, she carefully and quietly opened the door. As soon as she saw me lying there on the floor, she immediately shouted for Papa and rushed to my side.

"Michael!" she yelled again as loudly as she could. "Michael, get in here quick! Jochebed needs help!"

Right away, Papa and Uncle Mark came rushing to the room.

I was lying on the floor, a mess, crying; I was in so much pain!

"Michael!" Aunt Sara questioned frantically. "Where's her medicine? I'll go get it!"

"She's out!" Papa revealed as he and Uncle Mark lifted me up and onto the bed. "Get me a cloth to clean her," Papa instructed.

Uncle Mark ran to the wash room to get Papa a rag, and by now, everyone else had gathered to see what all the commotion was about. They stood at the door peering in, while Uncle Mark hurried back. As everyone stood watching, I felt a bit on display, completely mortified and embarrassed for the horrendous condition I was in.

"Michael!" Aunt Sara reprimanded tersely. "Why does this poor child have no medicine?"

"Never you mind that right now!" Papa came back at her. "Just please, help me get her changed!"

Uncle Mark motioned for everyone to step back as he stepped out of the room himself, closing the door behind him to give me some privacy.

Papa turned momentarily as Aunt Sara went to helping me out of my nightgown, but it was obvious she was beside herself, visibly furious and livid with Papa for having let my medication run out. She laid my soiled garment aside, and when I was properly covered again, she told Papa that he could turn back around. Immediately, he knelt down and started to wipe my face and hair, trying to help clean me off.

"Jochebed," Papa asked, "sweetheart, is there anything I can do?"

I was so weak and so sick, and my head was spinning so badly that I had my eyes closed, just trying not to get sick again.

"Papa!" I begged in a whisper. "Please, *please* just make it stop!" I had never felt so sick - not ever!

"Michael Lowry!" Aunt Sara demanded crossly as she watched me lie there writhing in pain. "You go this very minute and find Dr. Wellesley and get this poor child some medicine!!"

"Sara!" Papa came back at her a little perturbed. "Ya don't understand! I just don't have the money right now to get her any!"

Aunt Sara shot Papa a look that could kill! Stiffening her jaw, she let him have it!

"I don't care what it takes, Michael!" she shouted, infuriated. "If you have to beg, then beg! If you have to borrow, then borrow! If you have to take that shiny new rifle of Samuel's and hold Dr. Wellesley at gunpoint, then *do it!* I don't care what method you choose...*just get this child some medicine!!!*"

Papa was taken aback by Aunt Sara's tone, but he knew she was right. I needed something, and I needed it now!

"I'll see what I can do," Papa agreed. "I'll be back as quickly as I can."

Papa went off to get the doctor, and Aunt Sara sat with me, trying her best to comfort me until Papa returned.

Everyone else went to the living room to wait.

*****

When Papa and the doctor arrived, I was still terribly, horribly sick. Dr. Wellesley brought some medicine with him and gave it to me right away, but because I'd had had to wait so long to take it, and because things seemed to be so much more worse this time, it took the medicine a lot longer to take effect. When it finally did, however, I was able to fall asleep.

"Doctor," Aunt Sara started, as she and Papa and Dr. Wellesley made their way into the kitchen, "this just isn't right! This poor girl gets violently ill every time she has one of these awful headaches, and it seems like they're getting worse! I understand her having headaches and all, but *not like this!* Surely there's *something more* that can be done for her!"

Dr. Wellesley nodded with a sigh.

"I agree with you, Sara," he commented. "She shouldn't still be suffering to this degree." He contemplated. "I do have a good friend who's a professor at a large medical school," he disclosed. "I believe he knows a specialist who deals with just this sort of thing. I'll contact him as soon as possible, and we'll get Jochebed some help. In the meantime, Michael," he said, turning to Papa, "I'm going to leave the rest of this medicine with you. You can pay me for it whenever you can. I know you're good for it."

Papa was grateful.

"Thanks, Doc," he replied as he took the bottle from him. "I should have the money for ya real soon."

Dr. Wellesley nodded, accepting.

"And," Papa continued apologetically, "thanks for comin' all the way out here on Christmas Day. I'm sorry we had to take ya away from your family."

"No trouble," Dr. Wellesley assured. "I'm just glad we could get her some relief." He put his hat and coat on, grabbed his bag, and headed for the door. "You all have a Merry Christmas now," he said with a smile. "I'll be in touch just as soon as I know something."

"Thanks, Doc," Papa called out. "And Merry Christmas to ya as well!"

Once the doctor was gone, Aunt Sara turned to Papa, feeling guilty for how she had acted.

"I'm sorry, Michael," she conveyed with regret. "I shouldn't have yelled at you like I did. Sometimes I let my passion run away with me, and I just…"

"No apologies needed," Papa interrupted. "You were right, Sara. I shouldn't have let my pride get in the way. I should've gotten that medicine for Jochebed days ago when I knew she was runnin' low." He sighed, feeling responsible for what I'd had to endure. "I just hope she'll forgive me," he said with melancholy.

"I'm sure she will," Aunt Sara encouraged.

Papa walked over to Aunt Sara and put his hand on her shoulder.

"I can't thank ya enough for carin' so deeply about my daughter," he told her as he started to tear up. "I miss Lydia *so much* and I think it's times like these that I miss her the most. I so wish she were here right now to help tend to our little girl. I just feel so inadequate to care for her myself sometimes." Papa tried hard to fight back his tears. "I'm grateful she has ya, Sara," he said with a nod. "Really I am!"

Aunt Sara teared up herself.

"I love her as if she were my own, Michael," she stated earnestly. "I'll be here for her however I can."

Papa took a deep breath, letting it out slowly as he nodded again.

"I know ya will," he acknowledged. "And thank ya!"

Papa and Aunt Sara took a moment to compose themselves before rejoining the others in the living room.

"How she doing?" Gramma asked immediately upon seeing them.

"Better, Ma," Papa replied as he walked in and took a seat across the way. "Thankfully, she's asleep now, gettin' some rest. And too," he went on. "Doc says he knows a specialist that may be able to help her."

"Oh, that a relief!" Gramma expressed, thankful. "That poor child been through enough. My goodness! I feel for her!"

"What are we gonna do about Christmas, Papa?" Samuel queried, worried.

"Well, Son," Papa suggested, "I say we go ahead and eat lunch and wait for Jochebed to wake up. We can open gifts later. Besides, there's somethin' extra special for her this year, and I don't want her to miss out."

"Sounds all right to me, Papa," Samuel agreed. "It just wouldn't feel right to open stuff without her."

Everyone got up and went to the kitchen to gather round the table to enjoy a delicious meal and good conversation. When they finished, Aunt Sara and Uncle Mark cleared and cleaned the lunch dishes, while Papa and Samuel went outside to try his new gun.

While they were busy with all that, I slept on; in fact, I slept for nearly three hours. By the time I finally awoke, Isaac had already arrived, coming to join us for Christmas.

Wanting to see how I was doing, Aunt Sara excused herself from the others and came to check on me. Carefully, opening the door so as not to wake me if I were still sleeping, she quietly made her way into the room.

Fortunately, I had just woken up, and was rubbing the sleep from my eyes.

"How are you feeling, sweetie," she asked as she wheeled herself over to my bed.

"So much better, thank you," I replied as I sat myself up. "I'm *so sorry* I ruined everyone's Christmas! I really thought I could handle my headache without any medicine."

"Now, you haven't ruined anyone's Christmas," Aunt Sara assured. "You just delayed it a bit, that's all. No harm done! I'm just glad you're feeling better. You had me pretty worried there for a minute!"

"You and me both!" I revealed, being completely honest. I looked at her intently. "I really thought I might die, Aunt Sara," I confessed. "I was *so scared!* I've *never* felt like that before - *ever!* I mean, I've had some really bad headaches, but that...that was the *absolute worst!*"

"Well, there may be a specialist who can help you," Aunt Sara informed me, "but we'll talk about that later. For now, why don't you get yourself changed? That fella of yours is here, and I don't think your brother can wait much longer to open gifts." She smiled. "Sam's put up a good front up 'til now, but I think I'm starting to notice a few cracks."

I chuckled.

"All right, Aunt Sara," I agreed. "I'll be out in a minute."

"Do you need any help?" she asked thoughtfully.

"No, I think I can manage," I told her. "But thank you!"

"All right," Aunt Sara replied. "Then I'll see you in a bit."

Aunt Sara left, and I proceeded to do my best to get myself dressed. I was so thankful to be feeling better, and thankful that that *awful* ordeal was finally passed. I praised the Lord for seeing me through it, but I also begged His mercy to help me overcome my headaches. I *never* wanted to go through anything like that ever again!

It took me a while to finish dressing, but when I felt I was presentable, I wheeled myself out to greet everyone.

"There she is!" Grampa bellowed with a smile as I came around the corner into the kitchen.

Everyone perked up, and Isaac came over to see me.

"I hear you've had a pretty rough Christmas so far," he sympathized, taking hold of my chair. "Are you feeling any better?"

"Much better, thank you," I replied. "But this is *not at all* how I saw my day going!"

Isaac pushed me over towards the table.

"Well, hopefully things will get better from here," he encouraged.

Before I could offer a reply, Samuel jumped in.

"Present time!" he loudly proclaimed, motioning for everybody to come. "Everyone to the livin' room!"

We all just laughed at his exuberance and anxious anticipation.

"Well," Papa quipped with a smile, "ya heard the boy. Everyone to the livin' room!"

We all gathered in, and once we were settled and quiet, Grampa offered a prayer. As soon he finished, we all went around, taking turns, giving testimony as to what we were thankful for. After the last person spoke, Papa began handing out presents to everyone.

Grampa went first opening his gift and he was thrilled for what he received. Inside a carefully wrapped box was a brand new Bible, something he had needed for years. His old one was extremely tattered and torn and in desperate need of replacing. He couldn't thank everyone enough for the generous gift.

When Grampa was finished, Gramma went next, opening two boxes. In the first, there was a beautiful sweater handmade by Aunt Sara, and in the second, there was an ornate cane carved by Papa, per Grampa's request. Gramma, too, was delighted!

"Thank ya so much, Sara," she said. "And thank ya, too, Michael, it beautiful!" Papa nodded, smiling.

"You're welcome, Ma," he said, "but it was Pa's idea."

Gramma smiled up at Grampa, who was sitting there beside her on the couch.

"Thank ya, Ezra," she relayed, grateful. "It right thoughtful of you!" She leaned over and gave him a kiss on the cheek, and I couldn't help but smile at his playful reaction. As soon as she kissed him, he grinned and shuttered all over, acting as if he were a giddy school boy again. It was really sweet and endearing to see!

Gramma held out the cane, admiring it.

"I not need this for long, though," she insisted. "I be better in no time!"

Grampa put his arm around her, giving her an approving squeeze.

Everyone else went on to take their turns opening their gifts. Samuel got a case for his gun and a new shirt, Papa received a new shirt as well along with a Sunday tie, Uncle Mark got a new knife and a new harness for his horse, and Aunt Sara received a beautifully carved baby crib that Papa had made for her.

When it was my turn, I opened a box to discover a new apron that Aunt Sara had made for me, and in yet another box, there was a bracelet with a charm on it from Isaac which was absolutely stunning! I thanked them both profusely for their thoughtful gifts!

When everyone was finished opening presents, unexpectedly, Papa and Isaac got up and walked over by the Christmas tree together.

"If I could have everyone's attention," Isaac requested, trying to quiet everyone. "I have something here that I found the other day, and as soon as I saw it, I knew it shouldn't stay hidden. I spoke to Mr. Lowry about it, and he agreed that Jochebed should have it."

Needless to say, I was rather surprised by his announcement, and couldn't imagine what in the world it could possibly be.

Reaching down behind the Christmas tree, Isaac pulled out the most beautifully wrapped present I think I had ever seen. It was wrapped in white silky paper with a red ribbon tied around it, culminating in a rather large bow.

I looked at Isaac, questioning, as he brought the present over to me.

What on earth could it be? I thought as he laid the gift in my lap.

Everyone was watching so intently, curious themselves as to what the box could hold.

I looked around at everyone, and then down at the gift. Sticking out from underneath the bow was a small tag with something written on it.

Examining it closer, I noticed what it said. *To: Jochebed, From: Mama*, it read.

Immediately, my eyes filled with tears as my heart began to ache - bitter pain mixed with joy. I looked up quickly to Papa first and then to Isaac. I thought for certain it *must* be a mistake! Anxiously, I looked again at the package, and there it was. I had read it correctly. It was staring up at me plain as day.

To: Jochebed, From: Mama, the tag read. I looked up again, bewildered.

Papa and Isaac seemed breathless as they waited for me to open the gift. It was almost as if they were willing me with their eyes to do so.

I didn't understand how it could be possible, but right there, right in front of me was a gift from my mother. I took a deep breath, feeling nervous and excited all at the same time!

Slowly and deliberately I began to tear away the paper as my heart pounded furiously in anticipation. As I shed the paper away, there beneath the wrapping lay a book. As I pulled off the last of the paper, I could see inscribed on the front cover, in Mama's own handwriting, the words, *My Memories of Jochebed*.

Tears immediately began to stream down my face as I ran my fingers over the lettering. I shook my head in disbelief as it just didn't seem real! It was as if somehow Mama were actually here with us again.

I looked up, overwhelmed; there wasn't a dry eye in the place. Everyone was speechless!

I looked back down at the book and slowly opened it up, carefully flipping through its pages. I couldn't believe it; each one was *filled* with Mama's handwriting. I glanced at a few entries before looking up at Papa. I was crying so hard, I could barely speak.

"How?" I desperately wanted to know. "Where?"

Papa deferred to Isaac, who went on to explain.

"The other day when we were looking for the Christmas decorations," he revealed, "I found the book on a shelf in the closet behind some boxes. Your mama must have hid it there. I knew right away when I saw it that it was something she intended for you to have someday, so I asked your father about it. He said he had no idea the book even existed, but he agreed with me that you should have it, and he felt today would be the perfect day to give it to you, so…"

I shook my head simply amazed as I looked back down at the book, admiring it through my tears. I couldn't speak! I was just so moved by this *incredible* gift! I couldn't *wait* to read through its pages, to have the chance…just one more time…to be alone with my Mama!

AN UNWELOMED GUEST
(Chapter 32)

Despite my horrific start to the day, this had turned out to be one of the greatest Christmases I had ever had. I couldn't believe this extraordinary gift that had been given to me!

That night after everyone had left, and I was alone in the sewing room, the room in which Mama and I had spent so many hours together in, I took out Mama's memory book and opened it up to the very first page.

There at the top was an inscription that read, *"To my dearest Jochebed Faith, my joy, my delight, a precious gift from God."*

I was already in tears!

I flipped to the next page, wiping my eyes, and began to read.

"Today I brought my Jochebed Faith into the world." Mama wrote. *"It was a difficult delivery, but she is here, and she is safe, and she is strong! When I look at her, I see her father's eyes and my mama's mouth. She is so beautiful, and so tiny! She has the sweetest face and the most beautiful hair, the tiniest little nose, and long skinny fingers like me. She is absolutely perfect! I just can't believe that she's finally here and that she's actually mine! Thank You, God, for this most precious gift that is my daughter, Jochebed."*

I was crying so hard at this point, I could scarcely read. My heart was aching so much with happiness and longing as I missed Mama so much...so very much! I just didn't know if I could go on reading, I was so overcome with emotion.

I closed the book and laid it to my heart, holding it tightly, weeping, as I thought of Mama. I cried and I cried until I finally fell asleep.

*****

The next morning when I woke up, I had another terrible headache, but fortunately, I now had medicine I could take, so I was able to head it off before it got much worse.

As I lay there waiting for the pain to pass, I decided I would try to read some more from Mama's memory book. Unfortunately, though, during the night it had slipped from my hands and landed on the floor beside my bed. I thought that I could just lean over and pick it up, but trying to do so was a mistake! As I went to lean down, my head began to throb something fierce, and I felt myself starting to pass out. Sitting back up quickly, I averted the problem, but the memory book would have to wait.

My stomach started to feel a bit queasy, but I took a few deep breaths and swallowed hard, managing to keep everything down.

Knowing I had to wait a while longer, I went ahead and said my prayers, did my devotions, and planned the rest of my day. When I finally felt like I was strong enough, I got myself out of bed, got myself dressed, and knelt down to pick up the memory book. Carefully laying it on my pillow, I smiled, looking forward to returning to its pages later on. For now, though, I needed to get going. I had a busy day ahead and I knew the sooner I got started the better.

As I was just about to grab my wheelchair to set myself down in it, I suddenly realized that I was standing there on my own, not holding on to a thing. I looked at my wheelchair and then back to my bed and then back to the wheelchair yet again. Growing ever more confident, I decided that I felt strong enough to try to go it alone. I wasn't so foolish as to try to walk without the support of *something*, however (just in case), but I *was* determined that I was going to *walk* to the kitchen all by myself!

I carefully made my way over to the wall where Papa had installed the handrail for me, and grabbing hold, I followed it along the wall over to the door. When the rail came to an end, I put my hand on the wall, and steadying myself, I walked along until I was past the door so I could open it.

Flinging the door wide open, I started to make my way down the little hallway towards the kitchen, relying, of course, on the wall for support as I went.

As I walked, I could hear Papa busy in the kitchen with breakfast, but I wasn't at all sure where Samuel was at. My curiosity didn't last long, though, as he suddenly came scurrying down the stairs, rounding the corner. As soon as he spotted me moving along the wall by myself, his eyes got big as saucers, and he came rushing over to me, frantic!

"Are ya crazy or somethin'?" he whispered, his expression strongly encouraging me to immediately stop what I was doing and head back to my room. "If Papa catches ya," he warned, "you're as good as dead!"

"Oh, Samuel!" I hushed. "Stop being so dramatic! I can do this! I feel fine!"

"Yah right!" he quipped sarcastically. "Ya look real fine, *huggin' the wall there!*"

"Oh, would you stop!" I insisted. "Just go on and let me be!"

He shook his head as he rolled his eyes, exasperated with my obstinacy.

"Fine!" he relented. "But don't say I didn't warn ya!" He shook his head again, leering at me the whole time as he walked on to the kitchen.

"Mornin', Son," I heard Papa say to him. "Ready to eat?"

"Yah, sure," Samuel answered as he went and sat down at the table.

While Samuel was busy eating, I was still methodically making my way down the hallway towards the kitchen. It was slow going, but I was doing it!

My progress must not have been fast enough for Samuel's liking, however, because after a few minutes, he excused himself from the table and came peeking around the corner.

I looked at him sternly as if to say, *What?*

He just rolled his eyes again and went back to the table. Nevertheless, after taking a few more bites of his food and drinking some of his juice, he excused himself a second time, and came peeking around the corner again.

I was a little farther down the hallway this time, but still not quite to the end. When I saw him staring at me, I got rather upset.

"What are you doing?" I whispered angrily. "Would you just *go?*"

He shook his head, clearly disagreeing with my foolish decision to keep on doing what I was doing.

"You're gonna be in *so much trouble!*" he whispered back.

Just then, Papa called to him.

"Samuel!" he wanted to know. "What are ya doin', Son? What's goin' on?"

Samuel instantly turned around, feigning innocence.

"Nothin', Papa!" he answered unconvincingly. "I just...I just thought I saw somethin' but...it was nothin'! Everything's fine!"

I rolled my eyes, utterly unimpressed with his persuasive powers. ...I could have thumped him!

Of course, Samuel's weak response was enough to peak Papa's suspicion and he summarily walked over and rounded the corner.

Needless to say, when he saw me standing there on my own, up against the wall, no wheelchair in sight, I was certain he was going to explode right there on the spot! I watched his face go from ashen to beet red within seconds!

"Now, Papa!" I started, trying to minimize the blast I knew was coming. "I wanted to…" That was all the farther I was able to get in my defense.

Papa immediately came rushing over to me, angrily grabbing me by the arm.

"Jochebed Faith Lowry!" he shouted, irate. "What in the *world* do ya think you're doin'? *Where's your chair?* Is it broke? *Because it better be!!* …Why on *earth* are ya out here on your own?!?" He abruptly turned and looked at Samuel, who was trying to slowly tip toe back into the kitchen. "Hold it right there, Son!" he sternly demanded.

Samuel stood straight up and nervously turned back to face Papa.

"Ya knew all along that your sister was walkin' down here on her own and ya just let her go!" he blustered. "What on earth were *you* thinkin'? Have ya *both lost your minds?!?"*

Yep! He was not at all happy!

"Papa," I started again, "please calm down. I'm fine!"

He looked at me, still infuriated, clearly not caring a whit!

"Ya *know* you're not to be out walkin' on your own!" he harshly reprimanded. "The doctor was *very clear* on that instruction, Jochebed - *very clear!*" He turned back to Samuel. "Ya both know that!" he scolded furiously. He turned back to me. "Ya could've fallen and hurt yourself *worse!* And after yesterday's episode, I would've *thought* ya would've had better sense!"

"But, Papa!" I countered, trying to explain. "I feel so much stronger now! I can get around my room almost flawlessly. I …"

"*I don't care,* Jochebed!" Papa dismissed. "It's not about ya bein' strong enough to stand or even walk! It's about your headaches and the potential of ya passin' out! Even with your medicine in ya, ya *know* it always makes ya groggy!" He sighed as he shook his head, trying to calm himself down a bit. "I know you're strong, sweetheart," he said, "but your head isn't where it should be, and until ya see the specialist, I *forbid ya* to walk on your own without assistance. *Do ya understand?"*

I hung my head, feeling somewhat guilty for what I'd done.

"Yes, Papa," I conceded, disappointed, but accepting that he was right. "I understand, and…I'm sorry."

Papa promptly helped me back to my room and into my wheelchair.

Pushing me into the kitchen, we all sat and ate our breakfast in silence. Papa was still visibly upset, as was Samuel (for having been yelled at), and recognizing I was the cause of it all, I thought it best not to say anything so as not to make things worse.

*****

Later on in the day, I was sitting by myself in the living room, trying to catch up on some schoolwork, when suddenly there was a knock at the door. Papa was in the barn, and Samuel was off somewhere shooting his new rifle, so I wheeled myself over to see who was there.

When I opened up the door, much to my surprise, there was a man standing there in front of me, someone whom I didn't readily recognize, but who did look vaguely familiar to me.

"May I help you, sir?" I asked as he stood there staring at me with a very ill-tempered, stern look on his face.

"Ya here alone?" he inquired gruffly.

His odd behavior and question threw me and I began to feel a little uncomfortable talking with him having no one else around. Still, I tried to be polite, answering his question the best I could.

"No, sir," I relayed, wondering what he could possibly want. "I'm not alone. My Papa's in the barn, and my brother's around here somewhere. Is...is there something you needed?"

"Not right now there isn't!" he replied evasively, nervously glancing over his shoulder, almost as if he were afraid someone would see him standing there. When he was sure no one had seen him, he abruptly turned back to me with a scowl on his face and a strange resolve in his eyes. "I'll be back!" he stated bluntly, giving no further explanation or reason for his being there in the first place. He gave me another strange look before turning and walking down off the porch. He immediately mounted his horse and took off down the road.

I thought the whole encounter was rather odd and a little unsettling, but I quickly dismissed it, closed the door, and went back to my homework.

I worked and worked and worked some more, diligently trying to catch up on all the school work Naomi had brought to me before Christmas break. I had had to put it off for various sundry of reasons, but now I *needed* to get it completed. School was starting back up tomorrow, and I knew more homework would be coming my way.

While I was so very thankful my teacher was willing to let me do my work at home to keep up with everything, I was a little frustrated that I couldn't be in the classroom to hear the actual instruction firsthand. Trying to get the information through Naomi, while helpful, was just not the same. I managed the best I could, but I couldn't help but worry that my grades may suffer because of it.

Just as I was finishing up, putting my books away, Isaac came over to visit.

"It's so good to see you!" I said, exhausted from all my schoolwork.

"It's good to see you, too!" he replied with his usual handsome smile. "How's your day been?"

"Well, not so great!" I admitted. "I've been catching up on homework most of the day, but...to be honest...that's really not been the worst of it."

"Oh?" Isaac queried inquisitively. "Care to explain."

"Weeelll," I revealed sheepishly. "I...I kind of managed to make Papa pretty angry with me this morning."

"Oh really?" Isaac quipped as he hung up his hat and coat. "And how'd you manage to do that?"

I looked at him anxiously.

"If I tell you," I hemmed and hawed, "will...will *you* promise not to get upset with me?"

Isaac furrowed his brow as he looked at me suspiciously.

"What did you do, Jochebed?" he questioned, growing ever more concerned.

"Weeelll," I answered again, trying to put the best light on things. "I...I walked a little!"

Isaac shrugged his shoulders, not seeing the conflict.

"Well, that doesn't sound so bad," he accepted. "You've walked before. What's the big deal? I don't see your father getting upset about *that*."

I smiled reticently before divulging the whole truth.

"I walked down the hallway by myself!" I blurted out as quickly as I could, hoping perhaps I could sneak the indiscretion right past him.

Of course, I couldn't, and immediately his approving look turned to one of...well...not so approving!

"You did *what?*" he exclaimed.

"Now, please don't be angry!" I implored, trying to calm the situation. "I thought I could do it, and I *was* doing it...that is...well...until Papa caught me."

Isaac came over and knelt down in front of me.

"Jochebed," he said, taking hold of my hands, shaking his head, looking into my eyes, "I'm not angry with you, I'm just...I'm just worried for you! You're strong, no doubt, and getting stronger every day, but...well...I worry about your headaches. They're *so* severe! If one comes on you and you fall, why...you could hurt yourself worse than you did before!"

"I know, I know!" I relented, so frustrated with the whole matter. "Papa pretty much said the same thing. ...It's just that...well...I...I just *so* want to be past all of this! I just want to be *normal again!*"

"I know you do," Isaac sympathized, putting his hand to my cheek. "And I have every confidence that you will be back to 'normal' soon enough. But you've *got to* be *patient*, Jochebed! What happened to you was no small thing! It's just going to take some time for you to fully recover. Maybe after you see that specialist you told me about, maybe then you'll be able to get out of this wheelchair."

Admittedly, I was feeling sorry for myself, but Isaac was right, and I knew it. I sighed as I looked up at him, forlorn.

"It's just so hard to be patient sometimes," I confessed. "I feel as if my life is on hold."

Isaac nodded, smiling compassionately as if he understood.

"How about I work with you for awhile?" he suggested. "Helping you walk, getting you stronger for when you *can* be on your own? What do you say to that?"

I sighed again reluctantly, squeezing his hand.

"I suppose I can pretend we're on one of our walks," I said, trying to make the best of it.

Isaac grinned.

"That's my girl!" he told me happily. "Now you're talking!" He stood to his feet and carefully helped me up out of my chair. "And where would you like to go walking today, my dear?" he asked gallantly.

I smiled playfully and shook my head.

"Take me to the meadows, dear fellow!" I proposed with a chuckle. "I so love the smell of the flowers and the tall grass blowing in the breeze."

"Ah!" Isaac nodded, quite agreeably. "Very good choice! Your wish is my command!" He sweetly offered me his arm. "Right this way madam!" he encouraged. "The meadow awaits!"

We both laughed at our silliness.

Isaac and I spent quite a while walking back and forth in the kitchen and down the little hallway and back again. We laughed and talked the whole time, and even though we were only in the meadow in our minds, it was a lovely walk, and we enjoyed our time together immensely.

Isaac ended up staying and eating supper with us and left to go home after he helped me clean up the supper dishes. Papa made Samuel bathe and go to bed extra early because he had to get up for school the next day, and while Samuel was less than thrilled about it, he obeyed, albeit, reluctantly. I was rather tired myself, so I decided that I would turn in early as well. I had my devotions, read a little more from Mama's memory book, and soon fell fast asleep.

It was the middle of the night, and as I slept, I began to toss and turn something awful. I tossed and turned, moaning and groaning, having a *terrible* nightmare. Suddenly, I jolted awake, aroused by the sound of my screams. I sat straight up and continued screaming at the top of my lungs absolutely panicked!

Papa, of course, heard the commotion and frantically came rushing into my room.

"Jochebed! Jochebed! What is it?" he questioned as he ran over, taking hold of my shoulders.

I was shaking terribly in a cold sweat as I looked up at him wide eyed and frightened!

"Jochebed!" Papa reiterated. "What is it? What happened?"

I was so shaken and scared, I was having a hard time catching my breath.

"Papa," I sputtered and stammered, beside myself with fear, "it was…it was…it was *him!*" I started to cry as leaned forward, clinging to Papa.

Papa sat down on the edge of my bed, holding me tightly, trying to calm me.

"It was who?" he asked as he sat me back up. He looked me straight in the eyes. "Jochebed," he questioned again, not understanding, "it was who?"

I swallowed hard, trying to compose myself.

"He…he was here, Papa!" I tried to explain. "Today…the man…the man at the door."

Papa shook his head clearly lost.

"What man, Jochebed?" he queried, confused. "You're not makin' any sense!"

I calmed myself the best I could, still physically shaking I was so afraid.

"Papa," I slowly started to reveal, "it was him…the man…the one who robbed Grampa and Gramma. It was him! He was here today…at our door! He was here!"

"What!? When!?" Papa questioned with angst. "Are ya sure?"

"Yes, Papa!" I stated adamantly. I started to shake my head, angry and frustrated with myself. "I…I didn't recognize him at the time," I confessed, "my memory…*I forgot!* But now…now *I'm sure of it!* I know it was him, Papa. *I know it was!*" I clung to Papa again, fretful and in tears. "Oh, Papa!" I cried, terrified. "What are we going to do?"

Papa hugged me tightly again, trying to console me.

"It'll be all right, sweetheart," he assured. "It's all right! Tomorrow, I'll go straight to the sheriff and let him know."

"Papa," I sobbed, "please, don't make me sleep in here alone. I'm so afraid he'll come back for me."

Papa sighed, understanding.

"All right," he accepted. "Let me go check the door and check on Samuel. I'll come back and sleep on the floor here beside ya." He gave me a reassuring smile. "It'll be okay, sweetheart," he said calmly. "I promise! I'll be right back."

I nodded, wiping my tears as Papa leaned over and gave me a kiss on the cheek. He flashed another reassuring smile as he got up and left to go check on things.

When he left, I tried not to let my fears run away with me, but I couldn't help it! I sat there shaking, petrified! I couldn't get that awful man's face out of my mind, and my heart was pounding furiously, worried sick that he would come back for me! Regrettably, all the stress caused another headache to come on, so I quickly put my medicine together and drank it down, hoping to keep the pain at bay. Crawling under my blankets, I lay back down, anxiously waiting for Papa to return.

Lying there, waiting and waiting, it seemed as if Papa was taking forever! Thankfully, *finally*, he came back in and lay down on the floor beside me. I felt so much better having him there, but still I had a hard time falling back to sleep. I couldn't stop thinking about what the man in the hat had said to me.

"I'll be back," he'd told me, with such resolve in his voice.

Those words continued to echo over and over again in my mind, and no matter how hard I tried, I just couldn't seem to shake them! I tossed and turned all night, wishing morning would soon arrive!

*****

The next day, Papa had the sheriff come out to the house and he took my statement of what had happened and agreed that it sounded like the man they were looking for. When we were finished, Papa walked the sheriff out, and I rolled myself over to the window by the door to watch the sheriff leave. When I did, I could hear Papa and the sheriff talking back and forth about the incident.

"I thought for sure he'd be long gone by now," the sheriff said in a disconcerted tone. "He must be pretty brazen to come showin' his face back around here knowin' he can be identified." He looked at Papa intently. "Ya keep a close eye on that girl of yours, Michael," he warned. "He knows where she lives now. She just might be in danger!"

"Ya don't have to worry about that, Sheriff," Papa assured. "I'll make certain someone's around at all times."

"Good!" the sheriff replied. "And I'll ride back by from time to time to help keep an eye out myself. Ya just never know what a man like that might do!"

Papa shook the sheriff's hand, grateful.

"Thanks, Sheriff," he said. "I appreciate ya comin' out."

Sheriff Bradley tipped his hat, mounted his horse, and took off.

As he did, I swallowed hard, fretful. I knew the conversation the sheriff had had with Papa wasn't meant for me to hear, but I *had* heard it, and now I was more terrified than ever! The man in the hat had as much as told me that he would be back, and I knew it was just a matter of time before he would return. My heart sank in absolute fear!

After a few minutes, Papa came back into the house and as soon as he saw me, he could tell by the look on my face that I had overheard his conversation with Sheriff Bradley. Recognizing that I was frightened, he walked over and tried to reassure me.

"It'll be all right, Jochebed," he explained. "Samuel and I'll keep a close eye on ya. Ya don't have to worry. Sam has his gun now, and I'll keep mine on me at all times. You'll be safe, I promise! I'll add another lock to the front door, and we'll make sure we lock up every time we leave the house, all right?"

I nodded, acknowledging.

"And one last thing," Papa added, looking at me sternly. "I forbid ya to answer the door alone, ya hear?"

While I heard what Papa was saying, it was of little comfort. I felt as if I had a price on my head, and somehow, someway the man in the hat was going to come to collect.

"Jochebed!" Papa called to me, snapping me from my thoughts. "Did ya hear me? Ya don't answer this door alone, all right?"

I slowly nodded, accepting his directive.

"Yes, sir," I told him. "I heard you. I won't."

Papa looked over at Samuel who'd been sitting at the kitchen table, listening to the whole thing.

"Ya keep your gun handy, ya hear, Son?" he instructed. "I'm countin' on ya to help protect your sister until this is over."

"Sure, Papa," Samuel agreed. "I'll watch out for her."

In that moment, Samuel sounded so grown-up, but even though I knew I would be under the watchful eye of my brother and my father, I was still overwhelmed with fear.

Samuel looked over at me as I looked up at him. Our eyes met.

"I'll protect ya, Jochebed!" he said with fervor. "No need to worry."

I just looked at him and smiled. For the first time, I felt as if I was his younger sister and he was my older brother. He really was growing up and maturing.

Me on the other hand, I felt so weak and vulnerable, like a helpless little girl that needed defending. I hoped that Samuel and Papa would be able to do just that.

TAKING CARE OF BUSINESS
(Chapter 33)

Over the next few days, it was all I could do not to sit at the window and stare out, waiting for the man in the hat to return. Papa had informed Uncle Mark and Grampa of the situation, and they were on guard, along with the rest of the family, and I, of course, had told Isaac about what had happened. He sweetly tried to spend as much time with me as he possibly could, wanting to help keep me safe, but also wanting to help take my mind off of things. I was grateful!

Papa still had to work in the barn, but he insisted on keeping the barn door open, even though it was bitter cold outside. He was going to keep an eye out no matter what! Samuel stayed home from school to help keep watch, too, but after a couple of days, Papa decided he shouldn't miss any more school and had him return to class.

While Samuel was away at school, and when Isaac couldn't be with me, Uncle Mark often brought Aunt Sara over so that she could sit with me. Everyone knew that she was pretty handy with a gun, so Papa felt safe having the two of us alone in the house.

*****

It was a crazy time. I was still battling headaches, and the stress of everything was not helping *at all!* Everyone was on edge and more than a little concerned. I couldn't help but feel angry and miserable all at the same time as we continued to deal with the situation on a daily basis. I was miserable due to my headaches and angry because I felt as if the man in the hat had stolen away my family's sense of security and safety. Part of me just wished he would show up so that it could all be over! I was so tired of feeling like a prisoner in my own home! It just wasn't fair! I had done nothing wrong, he had, and he should be the one in jail, not me!

*****

The routine of this round-the-clock protection for me went on until New Years Day. The only change was that Isaac had to return to school the day after.

*****

It was early in the morning on that day, and Papa and Samuel were upstairs getting dressed and I was sitting at the kitchen table by myself, trying to finish my breakfast. I was barely able to eat, however, because I felt sick - not from a headache, mind you, but sick from the thought of having to say goodbye to Isaac. He was supposed to come by after breakfast, and I think there was a part of me that thought that maybe if I didn't eat my food, breakfast wouldn't end and Isaac wouldn't have to leave. It was a silly thought, I know, but I wished it could be so.

Why is it, I thought to myself, *that when you're excited and looking forward to something happening, time seems to tick by so slowly, but when you're dreading something happening, time seems to fly by at unbelievable speed?*

Sure enough, as I was sitting there just moving the food around on my plate, there was a knock at the door. Papa and Samuel were right upstairs, so I didn't think anything of going to answer the door by myself. My mind was so distracted with thoughts of Isaac, that I completely forgot about Papa's instructions not to answer the door on my own. I foolishly went to the door and began to unlock it, not even looking out the window to see who it might be. I guess I just assumed that it was Isaac, and I went to let him in.

I proceeded to unlock the door and reached to grab the doorknob to open it up, but before I could even turn it, the door suddenly swung open. There right in front of me stood the man in the hat. He had a gun in his hand and a bandana over his face.

Needless to say, my heart instantly began to beat furiously, terrified, as I let out a frenzied scream.

The man in the hat immediately rushed me, putting the gun to my head and his hand over my mouth. He quickly kicked the door closed behind him and pushed me all the way across the kitchen until I slammed into the kitchen cabinets.

"Keep your mouth shut!" he barked furiously. He pushed up against me even harder. "Now," he said crossly, getting right in my face, "I believe you and me has some unfinished business to take care of!"

My eyes widened as I starred anxiously into his. I thought for sure I was going to die! My mind raced as I thought of my family and of Isaac. I couldn't imagine being taken from them. Scared out of my mind, I couldn't help but cry.

"Hush!" he demanded angrily, his eyes shifting back and forth as he looked around nervously. "You're alone, right?" he questioned, almost as if he'd been watching the house.

I knew it was a lie, but I didn't want Samuel or Papa to be hurt, so I nodded my head yes.

"Good!" he came back at me. "Then this should be easy."

Unbeknownst to me, Papa and Samuel had both heard my scream. They immediately suspected something was wrong because they knew I wasn't one to just scream out about anything. Hearing the subsequent commotion, they were *sure* something was amiss. Assuming the worst, Papa lowered Samuel out of the upstairs window down onto the roof that jutted out over the sewing room in the back. Once there, Samuel jumped down and ran as fast as he could to go get Uncle Mark and Grampa. In the mean time, Papa was slowly and quietly making his way down the stairs, pistol in hand.

The man in the hat was still hovering over me with his hand over my mouth and his gun at my head. I was sitting there frozen stiff, looking up at him, beside myself with fear!

"So ya think ya know who I am, do ya?" he charged angrily.

I furrowed my brow, trying to feign ignorance. Again, I felt it prudent to lie. I shook my head no, but he wasn't buying it!

"Don't lie to me!" he demanded, irate, jamming the gun into my temple. "I knew when ya came to the door the other day that you was that girl from the other house we robbed a few months back. Ya gonna tell me ya didn't recognize me, too?"

Again, I shook my head no, but he didn't seem to care. He had it settled in his mind who I was, and he was determined to exact his revenge.

"Don't think I didn't see ya talkin' to that there sheriff either," he revealed, his beady eyes staring right into mine. "I saw ya, clear as day I did!" He was so angry! "Ya think ya can just turn me in? Well...ya got another thing comin'!" Slowly, he began to cock back the hammer on his gun. "Pity for you," he said, "I was just comin' to rob ya the other day, but...now look at what ya've gone and made me do." He got right in my face and looked at me sternly. "I don't take kindly to snitches, little lady!" he stated with contempt. A devious grin slowly made its way across his face. "Was just waitin' for the right moment," he divulged, seemingly with pleasure, "and it looks like I've finally found it! Gonna be able to kill me two birds with one stone...get rid of *you* and make off with as much lute as I can in the process!" He chuckled. "Can't get much better than that now can it, girly?" He grinned sadistically. "Why," he said leaning in again, "one could say this is my *lucky day!*"

By now, my heart was nearly pounding out of my chest I was so desperately afraid! I could tell from the looks of the man that he was a vicious, hateful person. His eyes were shifty, and he smelled of booze, and he was wearing leather gloves, a long, tattered, leather coat, and an old cowboy hat that was frayed and worn. His beard hung down below his bandana, and his pants looked weathered like he'd spent a lot of time traveling. He was mean and angry, and I didn't know what to do. I thought for sure he was going to kill me right then and there!

Just as he was saying his last hateful words to me, I caught a glimpse of Papa out of the corner of my eye. He had his gun drawn, and he was slowly, steadily making his way into the kitchen. Because the man had pushed me all the way back up against the kitchen cabinets, his back was to the rest of the room. He was too busy starring me in the face, spewing his spiteful, malicious, rancor to even notice Papa coming up behind him.

"Get that gun away from my daughter, now!" Papa demanded crossly as he put his gun to the robbers head and cocked back the hammer.

The robber didn't flinch. He just got a demonic grin on his face and started to laugh.

"Well now," he said to Papa as he kept his gun trained on my head. "I guess we got us a little bit of a preee-dicament here, now don't we?" He laughed again. "Someone's not walkin' outta here today," he quipped, "and I don't plan on it bein' me! So...why don't ya just drop that gun of yours there before I blow a hole clean through your little girl's head?"

Papa shoved his pistol even harder into the back of the man's skull.

"I'm not tellin' ya again!" he stated with determination. "Let my daughter go!"

"Do it!" I suddenly heard Uncle Mark yell out as he came through the door with his shotgun aimed right at the robber. He walked over and stood to the left of Papa.

"Ya heard 'em, mister!" Grampa shouted tersely as he quickly walked to the right of Papa, his rifle pointed at the man as well.

Everyone stood there, guns drawn, ready to fire. I was *so* unbelievably scared and nervous I could barely breathe! The man was still leaning over me with his hand over my mouth and his gun pointed at my head. I could feel his breath on my face and the cold steel of the gun against my temple. I was staring directly into his evil eyes as he was staring angrily into mine.

After several *very* tense moments, he snarled underneath his bandana as he leaned in and whispered in my ear.

"We're not finished, me and you!" he stated confidently with a devilish look on his face. He slowly and gradually lifted his hand off my mouth.

I was so terrified; I couldn't take my eyes off of him! He was still so close; I could see my reflection in the blackness of his eyes. I didn't dare move!

Finally, after a few more seconds, figuring he was outnumbered, the man reluctantly un-cocked his gun and slowly withdrew it from my head.

Grampa quickly moved in and grabbed the gun out of his hand while Papa swiftly holstered his.

Seething, Papa instantly threw his arms around the robber and pulled him off of me. Beyond livid, he violently threw him to the floor and jumped on top of him, grabbing hold of his collar. The man didn't have a chance! Papa immediately, mercilessly, began pounding him in the face with his fist.

I was shocked! I had never *ever* seen Papa act like that before!

He just kept hitting the man over and over again until the man was bleeding and almost unconscious.

Uncle Mark was yelling at Papa to stop, but it was as if Papa couldn't even hear him. He just kept pummeling the man, beating him senseless!

Finally, Uncle Mark had to move in and pull Papa off.

"Stop it, Michael!" he shouted. "Enough! Let the sheriff deal with him!"

Papa suddenly stopped, almost as if he'd been jolted from a trance. He looked down at the man who was lying there bleeding, barely conscious. He let go of his coat collar and threw him to the floor. He shook his head; almost as if he couldn't believe what he had just done. He rolled off to the side and sat there a minute somewhat dazed.

After shaking it off, he looked up at me and scrambled to my side.

"Oh, Jochebed!" he said, frantically looking me over. "Are ya all right?"

"Yes, Papa," I assured, tearfully, still shaking from the ordeal.

"Did he hurt ya? Are ya hurt?" Papa questioned anxiously.

"No!" I answered. "I'm all right."

Just then, Samuel showed up to the house with the sheriff. He came inside with his gun drawn and walked over to the man. Seeing he was subdued, he holstered his weapon and jerked the man up off the floor. He immediately tied his hands behind his back, making sure he was secured.

"Is everyone all right?" the sheriff asked.

We all assured him that we were, so he took the man straight away.

Papa was still on his knees beside me as the sheriff walked the man out.

Papa hugged me tightly as I wept.

"It's over, sweetheart!" he kept saying as he stroked my hair, trying to calm me down. "It's over now! You're safe! It's all over!"

I looked up through my tears, still hugging Papa, as Isaac was just coming into the house.

"What on earth?" he questioned as he rushed over to me. "Was that who I think it was?"

"Yes!" Grampa confirmed. "But he won't be comin' 'round here anymore!"

Papa left off hugging me as Isaac stepped in. He hugged me so tightly as the reality of what had just happened began to set in.

"Are you all right?" he asked anxiously.

I slowly nodded, still in shock. I just didn't know what to think. This awful nightmare had just happened, yet somehow it didn't seem real. I was shaking uncontrollably, terrified by the whole ordeal!

I sat there for a minute just hugging Isaac, crying. He held me close, trying to console me. Papa and Uncle Mark and Grampa stood discussing everything, while Samuel watched on the front porch as the sheriff road away with the horrible man in custody.

Isaac leaned back and looked at me, lovingly wiping the tears from my face.

"It's all over now, Jochebed," he assured. "You're safe!"

I nodded, knowing he was right, but I just couldn't help it; there was still terror deep in my heart. Even though I'd seen the man taken away, and I knew he was going to jail, I was still afraid. What he'd whispered to me before he let me go kept ringing in my ears. I wanted to feel safe, but I just didn't!

MOVING FORWARD
(Chapter 34)

I was pretty quiet for the next two days. I'd said goodbye to Isaac, who hated like everything to have to leave, but he had to get back to school, and I understood. I knew he had told me that he loved me and that he'd be praying for me, and I knew I had returned the sentiment, but somehow it all seemed like such a blur. I was so traumatized by what had happened to me, I just couldn't seem to shake the dark cloud I was under no matter how hard I tried.

Papa and Samuel tried to get me to talk about it, but I just felt like being alone. I spent most of my time by myself in my room.

Papa was content to let it go for a while, but after several days of it, his concern grew, and he went to talk to Aunt Sara about it.

"I'm really startin' to worry about Jochebed," he relayed as he walked into the kitchen at Grampa and Gramma's. "What happened to her, it..." He sighed as he shook his head, disheartened. "It's...it's changed her," he conveyed. He looked at Aunt Sara, worried. "Would ya be willin' to talk with her?" he asked, hopeful.

"Say no more!" Aunt Sara agreed. "I'll get my things."

Grampa and Gramma, who were in the kitchen as well listening to it all, spoke up.

"She just need time, Michael," Gramma encouraged. "She been through lot. She be okay. She strong girl."

"I know, Ma," Papa granted, "but she seems so distant and not at all herself. I just wish she'd *talk* to somebody! She's been havin' more headaches, and I'm afraid the stress of it all is makin' 'em worse!"

"Well, if anybody can get her to open up," Grampa bolstered, "it's Sara. I'm sure Jochebed just needs a woman's touch is all."

Papa sighed.

"I sure hope your right, Pa," he said. "I just don't know what else to do. Samuel and I have tried talkin' with her, but...she'll barely speak to us. She claims everything's fine, and then goes to her room where she spends most of the day." He hung his head. "I'm not gonna lie," he confessed, "she has me worried somethin' awful!"

Just then, Aunt Sara came back into the room.

"I'm ready when you are, Michael," she said, tightening her bonnet.

Papa brought Aunt Sara to the house, and she wheeled herself back to my room, knocking softly on the door before opening it.

When she came inside, I was lying on the bed, just staring out the window, battling yet another headache, and waiting for my medicine to take effect.

She rolled herself over beside my bed.

"Jochebed, sweetie," she queried as she came close, "how are you doing?"

"Fine!" I answered curtly, less than truthful, not even turning to look at her.

"How have your headaches been?" she asked, already knowing the answer from Papa, but trying to break the ice.

"Fine!" I answered again, still not turning to look at her.

Aunt Sara sighed a little frustrated.

"Jochebed," she rightly stated, "I know you're *not fine!* Your Papa's worried sick about you, and frankly so am I. Please...tell me what's going on!"

"I'm fine!" I insisted yet again rather tersely, just wanting to be left alone.

Aunt Sara wasn't backing down.

"Jochebed," she said sweetly but sternly, "there's clearly something bothering you. You're not yourself and…" She sighed again. "Would you *please* just turn over here and look at me? I really think you need to talk to somebody about what happened to you."

I didn't budge, nor say anything. I felt like crying, but I didn't. I didn't want to be rude to Aunt Sara, but I really didn't feel like talking either.

"Aunt Sara," I finally told her, as I turned my head slightly to look at her out of the corner of my eye, "I'm fine, really! I…I just can't talk about it…all right?" I turned back to staring out the window. As I did, a single tear escaped my eye and trickled down my cheek.

"Oh, Jochebed," Aunt Sara replied sympathetically. "Sweetie, I know you went through a horrific experience. It was frightening and cruel and a *terrible* thing! You faced death at the hands of a very awful man and…"

"You don't have to remind me of what happened!" I blurted out angrily, fighting back tears. "I know! I was there! Remember!?!"

Aunt Sara came closer so that she could put her hand on my arm.

"I know you were there," she said. "I didn't mean to…" She took a deep breath and let it out slowly. "Jochebed," she tried to convey, "we're just concerned about you is all. It's obvious that you're upset, and it's understandable, but…you can't keep pushing everyone away. You need to open up about this – *please!* We love you, sweetie, and we just want you to be all right."

I lay there weeping silently, my head pounding, feeling tired.

There was no doubt that something inside of me had changed that horrifying day, I knew it…I could feel it. I was clearly withdrawn and growing ever more angry. I was still scared and worried for what the man in the hat might do to me, but with all of these feelings churning inside of me, I just didn't know how to express them to anyone else.

At this point, Aunt Sara was almost in tears herself. She rubbed my back, trying to console me.

"Oh, Jochebed," she pleaded, "please…please just talk to me! I just can't bear to see you like this! …Please say *something!*"

I hesitated a while longer while Aunt Sara sat patiently waiting.

After a few more minutes of deafening silence, though, her patience began to wear thin. She folded her arms, growing ever more upset at my unwillingness to talk things out, and finally, she had had it!

"I'm not going away until you talk to me!" she stated emphatically, desperately wanting to help me.

I knew Aunt Sara's tenacity, so I knew she wasn't kidding! She'd sit there until we were both old and grey if she had to.

I reluctantly wiped a tear and carefully turned myself to face her.

"You're right!" I finally admitted. "I am angry, but…maybe not at what you think."

"Okay," she conceded. "I'm listening."

"I *am* angry at the man in the hat!" I confessed. "I'm angry that he hurt me and that he took away my sense of security! I'm angry that I was foolish, *again*, and let him inside the house without thinking! I'm angry that I couldn't get away because I'm *sick* and *stuck* in that *awful wheelchair!* I'm angry that I can't forget his face or the smell on his clothes! I'm angry that I wake up at night in a cold sweat from the dreadful nightmares I still have of that terrible day! I'm angry that I can't forget the words he said to me! I'm angry that I can't get up and walk around when I want to because of these *horrendous headaches*, and I'm so *sick* of being in *pain!*" It was as if I couldn't help it; all of my anger and frustration just came pouring out. "And I'm angry that Gramma got sick!" I wept. "And I'm angry that Isaac's gone and that Mama died!" And then the whole truth of it finally came spilling out. "*I'm just so angry with God!*" I shouted, confused and bitter and broken.

By now, tears were streaming down my face as I tried to make sense of it all. I stuttered and stammered, venting on angrily.

"I'm tired, Aunt Sara!" I said, sniffing, trying to wipe my tears. "I'm just so tired of it *all!* It's...it's...it's *ridiculous!* Why? Why all these things, these *awful, unfair* things? *Why us? What did we do?* We're not bad people!" I reasoned. "We go to church, we pray...*why? What did we do to deserve all this?*" I put my hands over my face, crying uncontrollably.

Aunt Sara sat there, quietly listening. She wisely understood that I needed to get it all out.

When I'd finished talking, she reached out and stroked my arm in sympathy.

"There, there!" she consoled. "It's all right."

I sobbed and sobbed until I couldn't shed any more tears. It was the first time since the incident that I had let myself really cry. I have to admit it felt good to finally let go of it all!

"I'm sorry," I apologized as I calmed myself down.

She handed me a handkerchief to blow my nose.

"I'm sorry I'm so angry," I told her. "I know it's wrong. I know it is, but..."

"But understandable," Aunt Sara interjected with empathy. "Jochebed, sweetheart..." She shook her head and gave a sympathetic smile. "Oh, sweetie, listen," she began, "I know I don't have all the answers, but you know, sometimes when we go through these things, it's easy to get upset and angry and question why. We're human, and I believe God understands that, but no matter what, we have to remember that God is a good God, and that He's in control of all things, and that He's right in *everything* He does. Regardless of how we feel about it, and regardless of how much we understand it, we need to trust Him!"

I wiped a tear and blew my nose, calming down a bit, and I *was* listening, but I was still hurt and upset.

Sensing that, Aunt Sara continued to try to encourage me.

"I'll be the first to admit," she said, "it does seem like our family has had our share of 'bad' things happening to us lately, but, to be honest," she added, "I guess I don't really see them as being bad."

I looked at her perplexed, confused by her perception.

How could she not see them as bad? I wondered. *What else could they possibly be?*

"What I do see is life," she went on to explain. "Life happening to us just as it does to everyone else. Our problems are just different than theirs is all. But you know," she continued with a smile, "to me, the blessing we have through it all is that...*we know God*, unfortunately so many others facing their problems, don't." She sighed. "We live in a fallen, sin-cursed world, Jochebed," she told me, "bad things are going to happen to *everyone!*" She shrugged. "Okay, again, I'll admit our problems seem to have all piled up here all at once, but in spite of when they happen or how often they happen, everyone faces trials in their lives. The wonderful thing is that we can take comfort in a God Who loves us and Who promises He'll never give us more than we can handle and Who promises to be with us through it all."

I lay there contemplating her wisdom, and while I understood it, it was still hard to accept. I shook my head, still questioning - still discouraged.

Aunt Sara smiled lovingly as she put her hand on my shoulder.

"Jochebed," she pointed out so sweetly, "you could have died. *Several times* you could have died, I mean, with *everything you've been through...*" She nodded. "Praise God, He protected you *each* and *every* time! To me, that's a blessing, not something bad!"

She went on.

"You know," she encouraged, "God must see something very special in you to have allowed you to go through so many trials." She leaned in close. "I believe He's allowed so many things in your life so that you can use them one day to be a help and a blessing to someone else. I know it doesn't make sense right now, but it will. Trust Him! Be patient and allow God to work in and through you. Who knows," she said, beaming, "maybe, just maybe, God's preparing you to be a preacher's wife."

I looked away, blushing.

"Listen," Aunt Sara continued, "I don't understand it all, but I do understand your anger. We all get angry from time to time, but don't blame God. He has it all worked out even before it happens, and He has it all worked out for our good."

As I lay there listening to Aunt Sara, I could feel some of my anger starting to dissipate. What she was saying I already knew; I'd heard it before in one way or another, but I guess with all the trials piling up, I had just lost sight of it all.

I began to think long and hard about where I was at, and while I did try to let go of some of what I was feeling, I'll confess, despite being reminded of the spiritual aspects of everything, it was still very difficult to do.

"Aunt Sara," I interjected, "I know what you're saying is true...I do, but...it's just so hard. I guess when you're in the midst of something so terrible, it's easy to look at all the bad stuff and forget about the good. ...I know God has and is seeing us through everything, it's just that...well...I'm *so afraid*, and I don't deal very well with fear!" I shook my head. "I guess...well..." I revealed, feeling guilty, "unfortunately, I...I think my fear and anger have started to turn into bitterness and depression. I know I need to give it all to the Lord, I do...but again, *it's just so hard sometimes!*" I paused as I thought about everything I was going through. "I...I can't say I'm over everything, because I'm not," I admitted, "but I do want you to know, what you said...it...it has helped me, and I promise...I'll try to deal with things – honest I will! Please, just don't be angry with me!"

Aunt Sara shook her head.

"Oh, sweetie, I could never be angry with you," she assured. "I know it's going to take time. You're a wonderful girl who's had to face a lot in her short lifetime, but listen, don't let it get you down. Let it make you stronger!"

I looked at her, wanting desperately to do what she said, but I struggled with how to let it all go.

"All I can say is I'll try," I promised, wanting to reassure her.

"And that's all anyone can ask," Aunt Sara accepted.

I wiped my nose again as I sighed in pain. With all my crying, the medicine I'd taken earlier wasn't helping my headache at all, in fact, the pain seemed to be getting worse. I looked at Aunt Sara, struggling.

"Aunt Sara," I said, "I do appreciate you talking with me, but…" I brought my hand to my forehead as I closed my eyes. "I hurt so badly right now. I really do need to rest."

"I understand," she replied. "I hope you feel better, soon." She turned herself to leave, but before she did, she briefly turned back. "Jochebed," she conveyed, "I love you, and I know things *will* get better!"

I managed a reluctant smile, and she left the room.

Aunt Sara quietly closed the door behind her and wheeled herself out to the kitchen where Papa was waiting.

"How is she?" he asked, concerned.

Aunt Sara looked solemnly at Papa as she shared what she could.

"She's angry, Michael," she explained, "but I think she'll get through it. She's just been through *so* much, and I think she's simply weary of it all." Aunt Sara sighed, sympathetic to my feelings. "It's understandable, though," she submitted. "It definitely hasn't been easy for her over these past few months. She's just trying to figure out how to deal with everything is all." She nodded with an encouraging smile. "We did have a good talk, though," she assured Papa. "And I'd say she's doing a little better now. It's just going to take her some time, that's all…and a lot of prayer, of course." Aunt Sara paused as she sobered. "Michael," she added, quite seriously, "I feel you need to know, too, that…she's still *really* scared. You need to help her feel safe again."

Papa furrowed his brow, at a loss.

"I guess I just don't understand, Sara," he remarked, shaking his head. "The man's gone! He's in jail now! She saw him bein' taken away. She *is* safe! What's she got to be so afraid of?"

"Oh, Michael!" Aunt Sara expressed with concern as she tried to help him see. "*Everything* - her home, her privacy, her security - all of it was violated the day that evil man attacked her! She's having a hard time getting all of that out of her head. You weren't there, and neither was I. We don't know what he did to her or…or what he said to her for that matter, *but she does*, and that's not something you can easily forget!"

Papa nodded as if he were starting to understand.

"I believe she'll get past it," Aunt Sara reiterated, "it's simply going to take time. The best thing you can do for her in the meantime, though, is just be there for her, comfort her when she'll let you, and let her talk if she needs to talk. And …" Aunt Sara sighed. "Don't push her to get past this too soon, Michael. She needs time to heal, and that may take longer than you think."

"All right," Papa acknowledged. "I'll do what I can. I just want what's best for her. I just want her to be okay again."

"I know you do," Aunt Sara agreed, "and so do I." She paused as she looked earnestly at Papa. "Love her, Michael!" she encouraged. "Be there for her! That's really all you can do for now."

Papa nodded again, accepting, as he took a deep breath, looking over at Aunt Sara.

"Again, I can't thank ya enough," he said, grateful. "I really don't know what I'd do without ya. She needs more than I can give her sometimes, and…I really do appreciate the help."

"Well, you're more than welcome," Aunt Sara replied. "She means the world to me, and I'm more than happy to do it!"

FEAR
(Chapter 35)

I have to admit the next few days and weeks were simply awful! I tried my best to put up a good front, but deep down I was gripped by fear. It got to the point where I could only sleep for short periods of time at night because I was having terrible nightmares that the man in the hat would return. The lack of sleep made my headaches so much worse, which in turn caused me to have to stay in bed most of the time, which in turn caused Papa to worry all the more. I prayed and prayed to God that He would help my fears go away, but they only seemed to increase. I was withdrawn and quiet most of the time, but whenever I *had* to be around people, I did my best to pretend that things were fine.

It'd been almost three weeks since the incident with the man in the hat, and since Isaac had returned to college, and, regrettably, I hadn't left the house for anything, not even once. I just couldn't stop thinking about what that awful man had whispered to me on that horrible day.

"We're not finished, me and you!" he'd told me.

Every time those words raced through my mind, it sent chills down my spine and struck fear deep in my heart. I was utterly paralyzed by his ominous threat. Even though I knew he was in jail, I'd convinced myself that somehow, someway, he would get out and find me and eventually kill me. I was terrified!

Despite my crushing worry and debilitating fear, though, I hadn't told a single soul what he had said to me, not even Isaac. I was foolishly trying to deal with it on my own.

I'd written to Isaac in those three weeks, but only once (which was highly unusual for me as I would usually write to him, at least, once or twice a week), and the letter I'd sent was very brief. I'd included nothing too deep or informative as I just couldn't bring myself to write to him about what was happening to me.

He wrote back (*several* times, in fact) expressing his concern, obviously noticing the change in me, but I didn't know how to respond. My intent wasn't to be hurtful or rude; I just didn't know how to (and couldn't) talk to anyone about what I was going through, and that included Isaac. I'd retreated within my fear, and I didn't know how to emerge.

Nevertheless, with all of this swirling around me, this coming Friday posed a huge dilemma for me. I had a scheduled appointment with the specialist Dr. Wellesley had recommended I go see, and, unfortunately, that meant I would have to leave the house, something I did *not* want to do! The thought of having to leave the comfort and security of my own home was more than I could take! Needless to say, I battled anxiety, *terribly*, in anticipation of having to go!

Sadly, though, I knew I had no choice, there was just no way to avoid it. Isaac was coming home to go with me, and Papa had already rearranged his day so that he could take me. It was awful, and I just didn't know what to do!

How can I possibly make it all the way to my appointment feeling this way? I questioned anxiously. *And how…how am I ever going to face Isaac?* I worried and fretted and worried some more as I was in a horrible predicament! How on earth was I going to get out of *this?*

*****

"Now, Sara!" Papa stated a little upset as he sat down at the kitchen table at Grampa and Gramma's. "I did what ya said! I've tried to give Jochebed time, tried to talk to her, tried to be there for her, but nothin'...*nothin's* worked, and *blasted*, it's got me worried! It's *obvious* she's not herself, even though she tries to pretend she's fine, but...*I know she's not!* Her headaches are gettin' worse and..." He sighed, frustrated. "I just don't know what to do for her anymore!"

Aunt Sara nodded, seeming to understand.

"I know, Michael," she lamented. "I wholeheartedly agree. I've noticed it, too. She seems quieter than usual and even more withdrawn than she did before. I mean, normally, she'd jump at a chance to get out of the house, but when we offered to bring her over here the other day to spend the day with us, she made up some silly excuse as to why she couldn't come." Aunt Sara paused as she contemplated. "Do you think I should try to talk to her again?" she wondered.

Papa threw up his hands as he shook his head.

"Aww, I don't know, Sara!" he answered, exasperated. "Like I said, I'm at my wit's end as to what to do for her! I'm just hopin' that maybe Isaac's comin' home tomorrow will draw her out."

"Oh, that's right!" Aunt Sara exclaimed, encouraged. "I forgot he was coming. Seeing him might be just what she needs."

"Well, I sure hope so!" Papa reiterated. "I don't think I can take too much more of this!"

"Well, besides the obvious," Aunt Sara queried, "how is she doing otherwise? Is she, at least, eating all right...keeping her strength up?"

"*No!*" Papa stated emphatically. "And that's got me worried, too! She's *losin'* strength if ya ask me, gettin' weaker by the day, although she'd never admit it as stubborn as she is! *I* can tell, though... it shows!" He sighed, clearly aggravated. "I just wish she could see she needs to be buildin' her strength to get well so she can get outta that chair of hers! Seems to me she's all but given up!"

"Well, hopefully this specialist can, at least, help her headaches," Aunt Sara tried to encourage. "Perhaps if she gets to feeling better physically, maybe then she'll feel like doing more."

"Well, again, I sure hope you're right!" Papa groused with a sigh. "*Somethin'* sure needs to change!"

*****

The next morning was absolutely horrible! I had to get up extra early to get ready to go to my appointment, and as seemed to be my lot anymore, I wasn't feeling very well at all! I had had another terrible night with little sleep, which, of course, caused another pounding headache, and I was fighting pain and fatigue something awful! We were meeting the specialist at the hospital where they'd performed my surgery, so I knew the drive was going to be a long and bumpy one (something that was likely to make things worse), and I was already in a cross mood, so having to deal with other people wasn't exactly high atop my list of things I wanted to do!

While I was lamenting my circumstances, Papa came knocking at my door.

"Jochebed, sweetheart, are ya ready to go?" he asked.

"I'll be there in a minute," I replied, trying not to sound too irritable. I sighed with angst, dreading what lie ahead!

304

I finished getting myself ready the best I could and wheeled myself out to the kitchen where Papa and Isaac were waiting.

"It's so good to see you!" Isaac expressed with a smile as I came into the room.

I nodded politely, trying to be cordial.

"It's good to see you, too," I told him in a less than enthusiastic tone.

"Ready to go?" Papa queried, upbeat, trying to lighten the mood as he brought my winter shawl over to me and helped me put it on.

"No, not really," I answered honestly, somewhat annoyed. "But I guess I have no choice."

Papa sighed as he took hold of my wheelchair, pushing me towards the door.

Isaac looked at me, concerned, as I passed; sensing that something was wrong, but he chose not to say anything to me right then. He simply walked to the door and opened it up so that Papa could wheel me outside.

As the door opened, the cold was bone chilling! The wind was blowing harshly, and it nearly took my breath away. Of course, anxiety immediately set in on top of everything else I was dealing with, and I instantly wanted to run back inside. I gripped the sides of my wheelchair as hard as I could and took a deep breath. This was truly turning out to be a miserable day!

When Isaac and I were settled in the back of the wagon, Papa climbed aboard and took off for the hospital. I lay there on my cot, so consumed with panic and fear that I didn't say anything. I was too distracted to even think about having a conversation.

"You seem really quiet," Isaac commented once we were on our way. "Is everything all right?"

"I'm fine!" I shot back somewhat tersely, not really wanting to talk. "I'd just rather be home right now, that's all!"

"But aren't you excited to see the specialist?" Isaac asked, trying to cheer me up.

"No, not really," I replied very negatively. "Nothing's worked so far. I don't suspect this will either."

Isaac frowned, troubled by my response.

"Jochebed," he questioned, concerned, "what's going on with you? You seem…"

"Nothing!" I snapped, cutting him off. "I'm fine! I just have a headache, is all! I'd much rather be home resting in my warm bed than jarring around, freezing to death in some old rickety wagon!"

Isaac was taken aback by my tone and obvious foul mood. I'd never spoken to him like that before, but I was so obsessed with my problems and so caught up in my worry that I was blinded to the person that I had become. I'd convinced myself that I was handling things, but clearly I wasn't! I didn't realize that I was pushing everyone away, including him.

"I'm…I'm sorry, Jochebed," he told me, feeling rejected.

We both stopped talking for a while, feeling badly, but after several minutes of uncomfortable silence, having had enough of my obfuscation, Isaac spoke up again.

"Jochebed," he pressed, "I don't mean to cause you any more distress, but honestly…I really don't think you're fine!"

That was it! I'd had it!

"You're right!" I shouted angrily. "I just told you - I have a headache! Now…if it's all the same to you, I'd rather stop talking…all right?!?"

Isaac sighed, more than a little troubled and frustrated with me, and rightly growing more concerned. He knew that there was much more to my irritability than just a headache, and he wanted to draw it out of me, but he could tell that I truly was hurting, and he didn't want to upset me further. Respectfully, he chose to let it go.

He sighed again as he looked at me with worry, but I just closed my eyes and tried to rest. He remained in the dark as to what was really wrong with me, as did everyone else.

Isaac and I didn't say anything else to each other all the way to the hospital.

When I fell asleep part way there, Isaac climbed up front to talk with Papa.

"Mr. Lowry, sir," Isaac began. "Is… is Jochebed all right? I mean, I know she has her headaches and all, but she doesn't seem at all herself lately."

Papa shook his head, discouraged.

"Ya noticed it, too, huh?" he quipped with a sigh. "Truthfully, she's been this way for weeks and we're all at a loss as to what to do about it!"

"Well, do you know what's bothering her, sir?" Isaac questioned.

Papa sighed again.

"Not for certain, Son," he admitted, "but if I had to hazard a guess, I'd say it still has somethin' to do with what happened to her back at the house when that man held her at gun point."

Isaac hung his head.

"I wondered how she'd handle that," he confessed, concerned.

"Well, from what I've been told," Papa revealed, "she's still scared, although, like I told her Aunt Sara, I really don't know why. The man who attacked her's in jail and he can't hurt her anymore, for goodness' sake! Ya'd think she'd let it go!" He glanced at Isaac. "It's been frustratin', to say the least!" he conveyed. "I know somethin' more's eatin' at her, but she just won't talk about it. She barely eats, doesn't sleep well, and I can tell it's definitely beginnin' to take a toll on her body. I just wish somebody could get through to her! Her Aunt Sara's tried, I've tried, *several times*, in fact, but she just keeps sayin' everything's fine and for everyone to just leave her alone." Papa looked again at Isaac. "I'll be honest with ya, Son," he said, "I was really hopin' that maybe you bein' here today would help her open up a bit."

"Well, I don't know about that, sir," Isaac lamented. "I'll sure keep trying, but she doesn't seem much like she even wants me here."

Papa nodded, understanding.

"Well," he tried to encourage, "don't feel too badly about it. Unfortunately, she doesn't seem like she wants *anybody* around right now!"

*****

By the time we reached the hospital, my headache was feeling somewhat better, but I still wasn't talking all that much to anyone. I just wanted to be home, alone with my thoughts, as it was easier for me to cope when I could concentrate on my worries and fears and not have to be distracted by other things. When I was alone in my room, I felt somewhat safe, but out here, I was just too vulnerable and too exposed. As you can imagine, it put me on edge and I just couldn't *wait* to be back home!

Papa and Isaac waited in the lobby, while the specialist examined me thoroughly. He asked me all sorts of questions, and I answered them the best I could. When he finished his evaluation, he told me that he thought he could help me but that it would require another surgery. The thought was not at all appealing! He was gracious, though, not pushing me for an answer right way, and in fact, recommended I talk it over with my family first. I nodded politely, agreeing to his suggestion, but deep down I was more than a little discouraged and even more upset than I had been before.

Before the doctor left, he asked me if I had any questions, but I honestly couldn't think of anything worth asking. I simply sighed, heavyhearted, and shook my head no. I just wanted to go home!

He accepted my response, and went to go find Papa and Isaac.

As I waited for them to come, I cried, growing ever more frustrated and angry for what lie ahead.

"I think I can help her, Mr. Lowry," the doctor told Papa and Isaac as they walked down the hallway towards the exam room.

"Why…that's great news!" Papa exclaimed, excited. "How? When?"

They came to a stop right outside my room, where the door was slightly ajar. I'm not sure I was supposed to, but I could hear every word they were saying.

The specialist looked at Papa and to Isaac.

"I'd have to perform another surgery on her," he revealed. "And, of course, there are always risks involved."

Papa looked disheartened and quite concerned.

"I know it's not ideal," the doctor sympathized, "but I really do think it would help her. I've had good success with other patients with similar problems."

"But another surgery," Papa lamented, shaking his head, pulling at his chin. "You're sure there's no other way? I mean…she's already been through so much! I hate for her to have to go through it all again."

The doctor kindly listened to Papa's concerns before expressing his opinion.

"Look," he said candidly. "She could continue to take her medicine like she's been doing and cope with her headaches the best she can, but I'll be honest, I don't think she'll ever improve much past where she's at, and from the sounds of it, her headaches are pretty debilitating. There's obviously damage there, and I think I can repair it. She may still have headaches, some may even be severe from time to time, but the frequency with which she gets them should lessen." He looked earnestly at Papa as he went on to explain. "I truly believe if I perform this surgery on your daughter, sir, that it will give her a much better quality of life!" He was quite confident in his pronouncement. "But listen," he acknowledged, "the decision's yours - yours and hers, of course. Nothing says you have to decide today. I would advise you to go home and think about it…talk it over. When you've reached a decision, just let Dr. Wellesley know and he can contact me with whatever you decide." He paused. "I don't say this lightly, Mr. Lowry," he expressed with all sincerity, "but if she were my daughter, I'd strongly encourage her to have the surgery. I really do think she could benefit from having it done."

Papa nodded, grateful as he shook the doctor's hand, thanked him for his expertise, and assured him that we would let him know of our decision as soon as possible.

The doctor nodded back, accepting, and went on his way.

As soon as I heard Papa and Isaac coming, I quickly wiped my tears, not wanting them to see that I'd been crying.

When they walked into the room, Papa looked across the way to where I was sitting, somberly staring out the window.

"Jochebed," he called out as he walked over to me. "I talked with the doctor, and…"

"I heard!" I interrupted sharply, not even looking in his direction.

Papa sighed deeply.

"I know this isn't what any of us expected to hear, sweetheart," he sympathized, "but it does sound promisin'. What do ya think about what the doctor said?"

"I think I just wanna go home!" I responded curtly, aggravated with the whole matter, nearly ready to cry again.

Papa looked at Isaac, who looked just about as discouraged as Papa did. Papa shook his head and looked back to me. It was obvious I wasn't ready to make any decisions about anything today, so he reluctantly took hold of my wheelchair and wheeled me out of the room. Isaac followed behind, neither knowing quite what to say or do.

On the way home, Isaac tried again to talk to me, but I barely said two words. It was all too overwhelming, and I just wanted to run away and hide. I just wanted to be alone with my thoughts and fears and have a really good cry. I tended to be very quiet and withdrawn when I was worrying, and even though I loved Isaac, I just didn't know how to talk to him - not now, not about all this!

I could tell I hurt him by my silence, and I honestly didn't mean to, but I was so weighed down and so preoccupied with all my troubles, I really didn't know how else to be.

LAYING IT DOWN
(Chapter 36)

It was late when we arrived home, and when we did, I briefly said goodnight to Isaac and went straight to my room. I was so depressed and so frustrated and so worried, I was only focused on being alone.

"I'm sorry, Isaac," Papa commiserated. "I really thought she'd open up to ya."

Isaac nodded, forlorn.

"Me too, sir," he replied, very disheartened and concerned.

"I know it seems too simple," Papa requested, troubled, "but I'd ask ya to pray for her. I know she needs help, and I think at this point God's the only One Who can give it to her. Heaven knows I don't know what to do for her anymore!"

"Absolutely, sir!" Isaac assured. "I have been, and I'll definitely continue to." It was evident Isaac was hurt and feeling dejected. "Well, I'd better be going," he said somberly. "I'll stop back by tomorrow if that's all right?"

"Of course," Papa agreed. "That'd be fine. Maybe things'll be better by then."

"I sure hope so, sir," Isaac expressed with melancholy. "I sure hope so!" With that, he said goodnight, and left.

*****

That night I lay in bed, weeping uncontrollably. It made me so sick to do so, but I couldn't help it. I was beside myself with worry over the possibility of another surgery, and still terrified over the man in the hat. It was all just too much!

As I lay there crying and fretting, it was as if I could actually feel the weight of the burden on my shoulders. I just couldn't see a way out of this awful tempest I was in.

Mercifully, eventually, I did cry myself to sleep, but not long after I drifted off, my nightmares returned.

"We're not finished, me and you," the man would say.

This time, a gun suddenly went off, jolting me awake. Frightened, I sat straight up, breathing hard, my heart racing as if I'd just been chased a mile. My head was throbbing, and I was trembling in fear. The wind was howling outside, causing the shutters to creak and bang against the house, and when I looked out the window, I could see the trees in the moonlight rustling in the wind. It was an eerie sight that only added to my fears.

"This has to stop!" I told myself. "Please, God!" I cried. "Please take this away!"

Unfortunately, I was restless throughout the rest of the night, tossing and turning, worrying the whole time, only catching a moment's rest here and there. I eventually gave up trying to go back to sleep, and decided to get myself up. I thought perhaps if I could occupy my mind with something else, I'd stop dwelling on all my troubles.

It was still dark outside when I got out of bed, and no one else was awake yet, but I knew the sun would be coming up soon, so I got myself dressed and headed for the kitchen. I managed to pour myself some milk, and I buttered a piece of bread to eat for breakfast.

As I sat there alone at the table eating, I was suddenly startled by an unexpected knock at the door. My heart nearly leapt from my chest as I choked down the piece of bread in my mouth.

Who would be knocking on our door at this hour of the morning? I thought to myself. *What am I going to do?* I sat there utterly panicked, convinced that it was the man in the hat returning for me!

As I sat there frozen in my chair, my eyes fixed on the door, I was unable to move, much less breathe. I thought that if I kept quiet, whoever it was would eventually go away, but unfortunately, I was wrong! Whoever it was knocked again and this time, they knocked much harder and much longer. I wished at that moment that Papa was still sleeping downstairs, but with the man in the hat supposedly caught, and with me now having my medicine at hand in my room, he didn't think it necessary for him to be downstairs anymore. I knew that Samuel would never hear the knocking (his bedroom was too far away), so that left me...alone...in the kitchen...just like before!

I thought for sure I was going to get sick right then I was shaking so badly! The person at the door seemed relentless, though, as they knocked again and again.

Feeling I had no choice, I slowly started to wheel myself towards the door to see who it was, but I was still trembling so badly, I had a hard time maneuvering my wheelchair. I was trying to move across the floor as quietly as I could, but it seemed with each turn of my wheel, I could hear every creak and noise in the floor. It was awful!

Finally, I managed to roll up to the window and peer out. There standing at the door in the moonlight, was a man...in a hat! Scared to death that my nightmares had come true, I screamed at the top of my lungs!

Suddenly, the pounding on the door got louder and louder and the man outside kept shouting.

"Open up! Open up!" he yelled, over and over again.

I screamed and screamed and screamed some more, until Papa and Samuel came bounding down the stairs in their nightclothes, guns drawn, ready to shoot!

"What is it?" they were shouting as they ran into the kitchen.

"The, the, the man!" I barely eked out. "The...the man in the hat, he...he's at the door!"

Papa furrowed his brow as he cautiously went to the window and slightly pulled back the curtain with the barrel of his gun. Peering out into the darkness, he tried to make out the image of the figure that stood on the front porch. When he was certain who it was, he lowered his weapon and went to the door.

"No, Papa!" I shouted as he turned the lock.

"Jochebed," Papa calmed as he began to turn the knob, "it's just the sheriff."

As soon as Papa cracked the door a bit, Sheriff Bradley came bursting in, gun drawn.

"Is everything all right?" he asked frantically, his eyes as big as saucers, searching the room.

"Everything's fine, Sheriff," Papa assured him. "Ya just frightened, Jochebed, is all."

"Oh, good gracious!" the sheriff quipped, letting out a big sigh, relieved. "I thought for sure someone was bein' attacked!" He holstered his weapon and looked over at me. "I'm sorry I scared ya, Jochebed," he said. "I certainly didn't mean to!"

I nodded, accepting his apology.

"What on earth brings ya out this early, Sheriff?" Papa asked. "Everything all right?"

"I'm sorry to wake ya folks," Sheriff Bradley explained, "but ya said to let ya know right away if we caught the other man involved in those string of robberies, and…well…we did! We just took him into custody a few minutes ago. Caught him tryin' to steel from the Hadley's place. Caught him red-handed, too! He was carryin' a saddle from the barn, ready to load it right into one of their wagons he'd hitched up to steal. Thought maybe y'all could rest a little easier knowin' he was behind bars along with his partner."

Papa looked over at me and then back to the sheriff.

"Well, thank ya, Sheriff," he said. "We do appreciate ya lettin' us know." Papa shook the sheriff's hand.

"You're right welcome," Sheriff Bradley replied. "And again…I'm sorry to disturb ya folks so early." He tipped his hat before looking over at me. "And Jochebed," he apologized again, "I am terribly sorry I frightened ya so."

I nodded again, again accepting his apology, although I was admittedly still shaking from the whole ordeal.

Papa opened the door for the sheriff to leave, but before the sheriff stepped out, Papa stopped him.

"If ya don't mind me askin, Sheriff," he queried, curious, "how long they gettin'?"

"Not sure," Sheriff Bradley admitted. "That'll be up to the judge. If I had to guess, though," he proffered, "given their string of crimes, I'd say they're both goin' away for a *very long* time."

Papa nodded, pleased at the thought.

"Well, thanks again, Sheriff," he said.

"No problem," Sheriff Bradley told him. "Ya folks have a good day now."

With that the sheriff left, and Papa closed the door behind him.

When Papa turned around, he looked over at me sitting there in my wheelchair, head down, eyes closed. I couldn't help it; I began to cry quietly as the stress of everything overtook me.

Papa walked over and put his hand on my shoulder.

"It's all right, Jochebed," he assured, trying to comfort me.

Nearly inconsolable at this point, I turned my chair abruptly and went to my room.

Papa sighed, discouraged, as he let me go. He just didn't know what else to do.

*****

A couple hours later, Isaac came over to see me. Papa and Samuel were both outside working, and I was sitting in the living room alone, trying to concentrate on some schoolwork.

When Isaac knocked on the door, my heart quickened at the sound, still not quite over what had happened earlier that morning. I knew Papa and Samuel were right outside, but still, it was rather disconcerting. Knowing I couldn't avoid answering the door forever, I took a deep breath, mustered my courage, and went to see who it was. When I saw that it was Isaac, I promptly let him in.

Isaac walked inside and closed the door behind him as I wheeled myself back into the living room. I didn't say anything, and neither did he. He followed in behind me and sat down on the couch, quiet and brooding. I was tired from lack of sleep and weary from all the stress, and I think he was still hurt from everything that had happened the day before. I'll admit, it felt strange, he and I not talking to each other, but I just didn't know what to say to him, and it seemed he didn't know what to say to me.

Finally, after a minute or two of uncomfortable silence between us, Isaac spoke up.

"How are you doing this morning?" he asked in a somber tone.

"All right," I answered timidly, barely looking up at him.

"Hmm!" he grunted in response.

Then nothing!

I fidgeted with my hands as I looked out the window, feeling nervous and ill at ease. The awkwardness between us was palpable, and the tension seemed to grow exponentially until it became almost unbearable as we sat there for quite awhile not saying anything else to each other.

After several more agonizing minutes, Isaac decided he'd had quite enough!

"Jochebed," he began, "do you remember Thanksgiving when I was home on break?"

I searched my mind, not sure where he was going with his question.

"I remember some things, I guess," I answered warily. "Why do you ask?"

"Do you remember the argument you're Uncle Mark and Aunt Sara were having at the time?" he queried.

I looked over at him, quite perplexed at his line of questioning. I thought for a minute.

"Yes," I replied hesitantly. "I think I do. They were arguing about Uncle Mark moving them here, selling all their things or something … right?"

"Right," Isaac confirmed. "And your Aunt Sara was angry because he hadn't told her. Do you remember?"

I nodded, indicating that I did.

"Well," he continued, "do you remember how worried you were for your Aunt and Uncle because they weren't talking to each other?"

I nodded again.

"Okay, then," he went on. "Do you remember the walk we took together the day after Thanksgiving - after everything had blown up?"

I shrugged.

"Sort of," I admitted, not fully recalling. "Why?"

"Well," Isaac wanted to know, "do you remember what you asked me that day, what you asked me to promise you?"

I sat there and tried my best to remember what he was talking about, but my mind was blank. No matter how hard I tried to force the memories, they just wouldn't come. I was beyond frustrated!

"No!" I confessed, more than a little agitated. "I guess I don't!"

"Then I'll help you remember!" Isaac said succinctly. "You made me promise that we'd always talk things out right away and be open and honest with each other."

I sheepishly lowered my head, fidgeting again with my hands, slowly beginning to understand where he was going with all of this.

Isaac went on to make his point.

"When I made that promise to you, Jochebed," he stated sternly, "I assumed that by you asking me that meant you were promising me, too."

I sat there, somewhat angry, because even though I couldn't remember *exactly* what he was talking about, deep down I knew he was right.

I was stubborn, though, and I didn't want to talk. I didn't want to share what I was going through or how I was feeling. I wanted to deal with things on my own, in my own way, and in my own time! I was so tired of everyone trying to pry things out of me, trying to get me to tell them what was wrong with me! I just wanted to be left alone to figure it all out on my own! I loved Isaac, I did, but I was just too afraid and too embarrassed to say anything to him right now.

"Jochebed," Isaac said earnestly, "I want you to hear me."

I could tell by the tone in his voice that he was very serious.

"If we're going to move forward in our relationship together," he conveyed with fervor, "then you *have* to talk to me! You can't just shut me out! You need to trust me with whatever you're going through - no matter *how* you're feeling about it!" He paused as he shook his head, clearly upset. "Jochebed," he said again, almost pleading, yet forceful, "I *need* for us to be open and honest with each other! …Can you understand that? If we're going to make it…we *have* to be!"

I was listening, *I was*, and I *did* understand, but I just didn't know how to respond. I kept quiet as I sat there staring out the window, feeling guilty and angry and frustrated!

Isaac waited patiently, hoping I would say something - *anything,* but I never did.

After a few strained moments, when I didn't reply, Isaac, hurt and disappointed, got up to leave.

"Then…I guess…I guess this is goodbye," he said, sounding as if he were fighting back tears.

In that moment, I knew how deeply I had hurt him, and truly there was a part of me that wanted to reach out and tell him how much I loved him and to beg him to stay, but with everything I was dealing with, I just couldn't bring myself to do it! My fear and stubbornness and my foolish pride won out over reason and love, and I just sat there in silence, letting him go.

Beyond devastated and heartbroken, Isaac slowly walked out into the kitchen readying to leave. As his footsteps neared the front door, my heart sank in utter despair as I began to cry uncontrollably over what I knew I had just lost.

As I sat there weeping, lost in my grief, I was suddenly startled by Isaac's voice. He had walked back into the living room unbeknownst to me.

"Jochebed," he implored with such anguish in his voice, "would you *please* just look at me!? *Please?* I don't want to lose you!"

While a part of me was relieved he'd come back, I still couldn't bring myself to turn around and look at him. I was just too ashamed!

"Jochebed, *please?*" he begged again with desperation in his voice.

I could tell, at this point, he was crying as he stood there waiting, and I felt so *unbelievably* horrible about it, and I knew in my heart that if I didn't turn around and say something I would likely lose him forever, but I just didn't know what to say! I honestly didn't know how to let him into my world anymore! I'd built up a wall so high, and locked the door so tightly, that even *I* didn't know how to escape the fortress that I'd built! I felt like such a failure for having allowed things to get so far out of hand.

I sat there shaking my head over and over again, *furious* with myself, beating myself up, tears streaming down my face. I wished like everything that I could bring myself to talk to him, but I just couldn't, or rather - I wouldn't!

Having waited long enough, Isaac suddenly cleared his throat.

"Well," he said with melancholy, distraught by my decision, "I...I suppose that's it then. I..."

"I'm sorry!!!" I finally blurted out, interrupting his thought. I buried my face in my hands and broke down weeping again. "I know you want me to talk to you, Isaac," I sobbed, "but I just don't know how! Not about this!"

Isaac rushed to my side, kneeling down, taking hold of my hands. Leaning in, he forced my gaze to his.

"Jochebed," he said with tears in his eyes, "I love you. Please...just talk to me! Whatever it is...you can tell me!"

"No!" I cried. *"I can't!* You don't understand!"

"Then help me understand!" he insisted.

I sat there crying, shaking my head, looking into his desperate eyes.

"Jochebed," he begged again, "Please! Please just let me in! Just tell me what's going on?"

I could feel rage building up inside of me, not at Isaac, but at myself. I was so tired of feeling the way that I did!

"I'm angry!" I shouted in tears. "I'm just *so very angry!*"

"All right!" Isaac accepted sympathetically. "Angry about what?"

"About *everything!*" I stated adamantly. "I'm terrified, Isaac! And I'm so tired of being afraid!"

I could tell by the look on Isaac's face that he didn't quite understand.

"Afraid?" he wanted to know. "What are you afraid of?"

I hesitated, not sure how to tell him.

"The...the man," I divulged, lowering my head in shame.

"Man?" Isaac queried.

I nodded.

He thought for a minute.

"Do...do you mean the man who attacked you?" he questioned curiously.

"Yes!" I awkwardly admitted. I felt so weak and embarrassed. *Why hadn't I been able to deal with this on my own?* I scolded myself.

Isaac was clearly concerned, but a little confused.

"But...why?" he questioned. "Why be afraid of him? He's in jail, Jochebed, and he won't be getting out for a *very long time!*"

I timidly looked up at Isaac through my tears.

"But you don't understand!" I insisted. I swallowed hard, trying to muster the courage to tell him. "He...he threatened me, Isaac!" I revealed.

Finally, it was out! The secret I'd been keeping for so long was finally out!

"He did *what?*" Isaac shouted angrily, taken aback by the disclosure.

I was reluctant and nervous to say it again, but I did.

"The man," I said, trembling in fear, "he...he threatened me. I...I've never told anyone, Isaac, but...he threatened me!" I began to cry again, overwhelmed by the thought.

Isaac moved closer and took me in his arms, hugging me tightly, letting me cry.

"I'm so sorry, Jochebed," he comforted. "I had no idea."After a minute or two, Isaac lifted my face. "Can you...will you...will you tell me what he said to you?" he asked, concerned.

"It's foolish, really," I admitted, knowing they were just words. Still, I had a hard time repeating them. "I...I know that terrible man's in jail," I acknowledged, "and I...I know he can't hurt me anymore, but he...he..." I just couldn't bring myself to say it.

"He what?" Isaac prodded gently. "What did he say to you?"

I took a deep breath and looked Isaac right in the eye, my heart pounding in fear at the thought of those awful words. As loathe as I was to speak them, however, I gathered my courage and did just that.

"He...he said he wasn't finished with me!" I sobbed. "Oh, Isaac," I cried, burying my face in his shoulder, "I'm so afraid! I'm so afraid of what he'll do to me when he gets out of jail! I just know he'll find me and kill me, and I don't know what to do! You didn't see his face. He was *so* adamant - so sure of himself! He really meant it, Isaac! I know he did!"

Isaac tried to calm me, but I was too upset.

"I thought I could let it go!" I explained, looking up at him. "Really, I did! I thought I could handle it! I thought I could deal with it on my own, but...it's only gotten worse! I've tried begging God to take it from me, but He hasn't, and I just don't know what to do anymore! It consumes me! My heart races every time I hear the rustling of the trees against the house or a knock at the front door. Oh, Isaac," I wept, frightened, "I just can't live like this anymore! I just can't! I feel like I'm locked in a prison, and I don't know how to get out!"

Isaac shook his head in sympathy and disappointment.

"Jochebed," he lightly admonished, "*why? Why* didn't you tell me about this sooner?"

I wiped a tear and then another, sniffing and stammering.

"I...I just couldn't," I shamefully admitted. "I didn't know how! I...I didn't know how to tell anyone, and then..." I looked away, not wanting to face him. "And then there's...you," I intimated.

"*Me?*" Isaac questioned, dumbfounded. "What...what are you talking about? Jochebed," he said, trying to get my attention, "look at me! What about me?"

I shook my head furiously as I bit my lip, afraid to say.

"Don't you see?" I stressed with angst, finally looking up at him. "I've failed you! *I've failed!*"

"*What?*" Isaac came back at me, furrowing his brow, clearly at a loss. "How on earth...how on earth have you failed *me?*"

I just stared at him, so sorry for what I had to say. Overcome with shame and guilt, I tried to explain.

"Isaac," I said, "can't you see? How could you *possibly* want me? I mean, what kind of a preacher's wife will I make if I can't even deal with my *own* problems, if I can't even face my *own* fears? How will I ever be able to help anyone else or...or be a help to you, for that matter, if...if *this* is how I react to difficult situations?"

Isaac was simply astounded!

"Wow!" he exclaimed, shaking his head. "Is that why you haven't told me about all this? You were afraid I wouldn't want you or...or that I'd think less of you somehow?"

I turned away and softly began to cry. Ashamed, I slowly nodded my head, indicating that that was the reason.

I could hear Isaac sigh in disappointment as he stood to his feet in disbelief. He paced back and forth for a minute, unsure of what to think or what to say. Finally, he came back over and knelt down in front of me. Tenderly taking hold of my hands, he looked up at me with pity and compassion.

"Jochebed," he conveyed so patiently as he brushed a tear from my cheek. "Don't you understand? I love you! *You! All of you*...and all that that entails! I don't *ever* want you to feel like you've failed me...because you haven't! I *know* you worry about things and that you struggle with fear, and...while I wish for *your* sake you didn't, it's...it's okay! I understand! We *all* have things we struggle with! No one's perfect!" He sighed, pressing on. "Jochebed," he stated, visibly upset, "what that man did to you..." He clenched his jaw, angry at the thought. "I wish I could've been there to help you," he lamented, "to stop all this from happening, but..." He looked down at the floor, shaking his head, and then back to me. "But the truth is," he pointed out, "*I wasn't there!* And I *couldn't stop it!* And what happened happened, and now...well...now we need to deal with it!"

I looked down, so self-conscious.

"I know, Isaac!" I admitted, feeling like such a failure. "But...

"Listen," Isaac interjected, "I know this is difficult for you to hear, but the only person who's putting you in prison *is you!* You're putting yourself there by worrying about something that you have *no control over!*" He looked up as if he were searching for the right words. "That man," he rightly pointed out, "he's just wicked! He's evil and vile and what he said to you, it was...it was hateful and awful, it was mean and cruel, and I know it's frightening, but, Jochebed, you *have* to trust God with this! You *have* to trust that He's in control of your life and that He'll *never* let anything happen to you that He doesn't intend to happen. Worrying about it won't change *anything!*"

"I know that, Isaac!" I snapped, so exasperated with it all. "Don't you think I've told myself that a thousand times? You don't understand! No matter what I do, I just can't seem to get past it! I hear him in my dreams! I can still smell him, I..."

"I know!" Isaac interrupted, trying to calm me down. He looked at me sympathetically as he squeezed my hands. "But, Jochebed," he told me earnestly, "you can't keep carrying this burden around with you. You *have* to lay it down! God's bigger than all of this, and He wants you to give it to Him. He never intended for you to carry it."

"Then why did He let it happen in the first place?" I angrily shot back. "Why, Isaac? Why?"

Isaac sighed.

"I imagine for the same reason He allowed your accident to happen," he submitted, "so that somehow, someway He could use it for good."

I turned away, upset, not wanting to hear it.

"Jochebed," Isaac went on, "I don't pretend to know everything, but I do know that God loves you, and that even though we can't see it right now, He *does* have a purpose for all of this!" He paused. "Look at me," he softly implored.

Reluctantly, I turned towards him, my eyes meeting his.

"Put it at His feet," he urged forcefully, begging me with his eyes, "and then leave it there! You have to! Otherwise, it'll keep you in bondage. Let go of it, Jochebed, and let God set you free! He's more than able to protect you, and He wants to…and He will! …Trust Him!" he strongly encouraged. "Just trust Him!"

I looked at Isaac, feeling so weak and vulnerable and helpless. I knew that what he was saying was true and right and for the best, but I just didn't know how I was going to let it all go. I knew that I wanted to and that I was ready to, but I knew, too, that I needed help to do it.

"Will you…will you please help me?" I asked, tearing up again. "I just can't do this on my own. I'm sorry, Isaac, I've tried, and I just can't!"

Isaac looked at me tenderly with pity in his eyes.

"You're not alone, Jochebed," he assured, squeezing my hands. "I'm here, and I'm not going anywhere. *I promise!* I'll help you anyway I can!"

"Will you pray for me?" I requested, desperate.

"You know I will!" Isaac stated passionately.

"Will you pray specifically that God will give me the faith and the courage to let it go?" I implored.

"Absolutely!" Isaac promised with a nod.

I looked at him, almost as if he were too good to be true. I just couldn't believe that I was so blessed to have such a patient, loving, caring, understanding man in my life. I shuttered at the thought that I had almost let him go because of my fear.

"I love you, Isaac!" I expressed with joy, overwhelmed in the moment. "I really don't know what I would do without you!" I wiped my tears. "I promise I'll try to get past this…*I promise!* But…please…please just be patient with me, okay?"

Isaac smiled as if he were confident everything would be fine.

"You have my word!" he replied sweetly. "I'm not going anywhere!"

THE DECISION
(Chapter 37)

Isaac spent the next few hours with me, praying with me and for me, and reading scripture with me. We talked about a lot of things, but mostly we discussed my worry and my fears. I was relieved that I'd finally told someone about what had happened between me and the man in the hat, and I was hopeful that talking things through would eventually help me to get past it.

As we continued to talk, however, the conversation gradually moved to the decision that I needed to make about my surgery. I was still apprehensive and unsure of what to do, and honestly, I hadn't come to any conclusions as of yet. While I was extremely tired of being incapacitated by my pain, and while I did want a more normal life, I was admittedly scared to death at the thought of having to have another surgery. It was high risk, and there was no guarantee that it would even help.

"I just don't know what to do," I told Isaac. "I worry that it'll make things worse somehow."

"Jochebed," he reprimanded, "there you go worrying again! I really don't think it'll make things worse. In fact, you heard the specialist, he really believes it will help."

"But another brain surgery!" I bemoaned. "Isaac, you know how hard it was on me the first time. What if…"

"What if what?" he interrupted. "What if you get better? What if you're able to live a more normal life? What if you stop having so many severe headaches? What if…"

"Okay, okay!" I conceded. I sighed, still apprehensive. "But what if things *don't change?*" I fretted. "What if things do get worse? What if my recovery's longer and harder than it was before? Isaac, I just don't think I can go through it all again!"

Isaac started to chuckle, and immediately I furrowed my brow, failing to see the humor!

"Well, I don't think it's very funny!" I protested, offended by his reaction.

"I'm sorry," he said, trying to contain his laughter. "I don't mean to laugh at you, but leave it to you to see the glass half-empty."

I continued frowning at him as I folded my arms in consternation.

"Listen, Jochebed," he pointed out, "the specialist is called a specialist for a reason. He knows what he's doing, and he knows what he's talking about. You heard what he said, he's had great success with many of his patients. Why would it be any different with you?"

I sat there silently, unimpressed with his arguments.

"I understand your concerns, I do," he sympathized. "And believe me, I don't exactly look forward to you having another surgery either, but if it could mean a more normal life, less pain, more mobility, well then…I think it's worth the risk!"

I shook my head, still unconvinced.

"I just don't know," I replied warily. "I think I need more time to think about it."

Isaac nodded, conceding.

"All right," he relented. "I know it's a big decision. I'll just pray that God will give you peace one way or the other."

"Thank you," I replied, grateful for the support.

"But I still think you should have the surgery," he quickly came back at me with a wink and a smile.

I just shook my head and smiled back.

Time slipped away, and before we knew it, it was time for Isaac to leave. He was heading back to college later in the evening, so he needed to get going. He gave me a hug and told me he loved me, and I thanked him for not giving up on me despite all my imperfections.

He smiled and told me, "Never!"

I told him I loved him, too, we said our goodbyes, and he left.

As Isaac walked away that day, I sat by the window in the kitchen just watching him go. I knew that I didn't deserve such an amazing man in my life, but I was so thankful to God that He had blessed me with him anyhow. I just couldn't get over the fact that God knew *exactly* what I needed! My heart was overflowing with gratitude and joy, and in fact, in that brief moment, I was completely free of fear. I was simply too overwhelmed by the wonderful blessings in my life to let my problems bother me!

*****

The next morning, I woke to a tremendous headache. It was as bad as or worse than the one I'd experienced at Christmas. I was in so much pain, it hurt to even move! I lay there so sick and faint not even sure I could get to my medicine, even though it was right there beside me on the nightstand. Needing it badly, however, I agonizingly stretched out my hand to try to reach for it. Unbelievably, it seemed a mile away! I tried to turn my head to see if I was even grabbing in the right location, but I was so dizzy I almost got sick right then and there. I immediately closed my eyes, trying to make it stop, and while it took several deep breaths and me swallowing hard to do so, thankfully, it finally did.

With my eyes still closed, feeling a little less dizzy and sick to my stomach, I took another deep breath, and reached out to see if I could feel for the bell. I knew there was just no way I could get my medicine on my own, so I'd have to call for help. Once I located the bell with my fingers, I grabbed hold, wearily picked it up, and began to ring.

"Aaa!" I moaned in sheer agony. The noise was deafening and it caused my head to pound even harder! I knew I had no choice, though, I needed someone to come. I took another deep breath, groaning in pain, and continued to ring and ring.

Thankfully, Papa heard from the other room and came right away to see what I needed.

"Jochebed!" he exclaimed as he came into the room.

He didn't say another word. He could tell as soon as he saw me that I needed help. He quickly came over and mixed my medicine, gently lifting my head to help me take it. I drank it down the best I could, but when the medicine hit my stomach, I instantly threw it back up again. I hadn't had this problem before, but for some reason, this time was different. I was so sick, I just couldn't handle it.

It startled Papa and he was frantic! He wasn't sure if he should give me another dose of medicine or not, and unfortunately, Samuel had already gone to church with Uncle Mark, so Papa couldn't send him to get the doctor. He knew he needed advice, and that I needed help, but he didn't want to leave me alone in my condition to go get the doctor on his own. He was at a loss as to what to do!

"Papa, *please!*" I begged, breathing heavily, fighting pain and dizziness. "Please...do *something!*"

Papa was reluctant, but he could hear the desperation in my voice. There was no doubt, something had to be done!

Growing ever more concerned, he decided he had no choice. He ran to the kitchen and got another glass of water. Swiftly coming back into the room, Papa mixed another dose of my medicine, and again, he carefully sat me up and had me drink it. Mercifully, this time, I managed to keep it down.

Papa gently laid me back down on my pillow and went to get a rag to clean me up.

While he was gone, I lay there, trying to stay as still as possible. I was in such dire straits; I thought for sure I was going to die! Terrified I may not make it, I silently prayed to God to spare my life.

Papa quickly came back with a cool cloth and tried to clean me up the best he could. He wiped my face and hand, and pulled the soiled blanket off of me, and laying it aside, he went and got a fresh one from the closet to cover me up again.

When he had me all tucked in and was finished cleaning everything up, he came over and sat down beside me.

"Jochebed," he expressed with grave concern, "sweetheart, it's obvious your headaches are gettin' worse. Ya can't go on like this!"

"Papa," I whispered, trying to reassure him, "it's only this one time."

"But it's not!" Papa countered, clearly upset. "What about Christmas? Ya went through this at Christmas, and it seems to me that this time's even worse!"

I let out a moan as a wave of nausea and pain swept over me.

"Sweetheart," Papa begged, "as much as I hate the thought of ya havin' to go through another surgery, please…I really think it's for the best!"

I couldn't answer him. I was simply in too much pain at the moment to discuss it. I lay there with my eyes closed, not saying a word.

Papa sighed, conceding I needed rest. He didn't push.

"Ya get some sleep now," he encouraged as he stroked my arm. "We'll talk later."

I could hear the worry and concern in his voice.

As I lay there trying to cope, waiting for my medicine to kick in, I thought about what I should do. I knew Papa meant well, but I also knew that I didn't want to have the surgery. I didn't want to have to go through everything again, and admittedly I was scared, and the possibility of the surgery *maybe* making things better wasn't enough to overcome all that.

Yes, this was an awful, *horrible* headache, no doubt, but as I began to feel a little better, I convinced myself that I was managing just fine with only my medication. I thought I'd be okay, and I wanted to wait and see.

*****

Over the next few weeks, my headaches came and went. Only a few were as severe as the one I'd experienced at Christmastime, but most were manageable. We'd discussed the surgery many times as a family (especially when I had a severe headache), but every time the headache would pass, I'd indicate that I wanted to wait. Grampa, Aunt Sara, and Uncle Mark all agreed with Papa that I should have the surgery; only Gramma voiced concerns that I shouldn't.

Papa was stubborn like I was, though, and he did his best to convince me to change my mind. He even went so far as to have Dr. Wellesley come and try to persuade me. I told the doctor that I appreciated his position, but that I still needed more time to think about it.

As hard as Papa pushed, and as badly as he wanted me to have the surgery, to his credit, he ultimately did leave the decision up to me. He determined that I was old enough to decide for myself.

Still, I was as obstinate as ever and absolutely terrified! I just wanted so badly for things to resolve themselves. I prayed and prayed all the while to that end, as did everyone else, but as the days wore on, things only seemed to get worse.

Regrettably, I could tell that my medicine was no longer working like it had before. Instead of taking my pain away completely, it only lessened it a little, and it got to the point where I was in constant pain almost all of the time. I didn't want to say anything to anyone, though, or let on as to what was happening, mostly because I was afraid of what everyone would make me do. I tried to hide things the best I could, but with each passing day, it was getting harder and harder to do so.

In those stressful weeks, I had miraculously managed to convince Papa to let me walk around in the house on my own. He made it intensely clear, however, that I was to do so *only* when he or Samuel was present. I abided by his wishes and did quite well.

I was glad that I was basically free of my wheelchair most of the time, but I was still housebound and missing a lot of school. Graciously, Papa arranged for a tutor to come and help me out, which was a huge blessing, but I still wished that I could be back in the classroom. I kept up with my schoolwork (most days) the best I could, and was able to stay up with my class, for the most part, but I still worried that it wouldn't be enough to pass the year. I did what I could and prayed a lot!

*****

My headaches continued to worsen on into February. The frequency and severity of my bad headaches were definitely increasing, and I was now nearly in constant pain. Still, despite all of my struggles, I refused to make a decision about the surgery (although, not deciding was in and of itself a decision).

Isaac had been home twice since my appointment with the specialist, and he, along with everyone else, could tell that I was getting much worse. He practically begged me, *several times*, to have the surgery.
I, of course, obstinately refused, still holding out hope for a miracle.

Most days, I tried not to think about it as I wasn't very good at making decisions anyhow, and one this big and important was, to say the least, rather daunting. I was so afraid of making the wrong choice, not to mention terrified of the surgery itself. I was more than content to push the decision off as long as I possibly could.

Little did I know that soon the decision would be made for me.

*****

It was a sunny day in mid-February, a Tuesday to be exact, and I was standing in the kitchen at the sink preparing some potatoes for supper. Papa was out working in the barn, and Samuel was upstairs quickly changing his clothes after arriving home from school.

As I stood at the sink, experiencing a dull headache, which was now part of my normal daily life, I suddenly felt a sharp pain shoot through my head. It was strong enough to make me stop what I was doing and take a deep breath. I paused, leaning forward, hoping the pain would subside, but unfortunately, it didn't. It just continued to get worse and worse the longer I stood there. I began to feel incredibly dizzy, and I was afraid I was going to fall down. I dropped the potato and knife into the sink as I grabbed hold of the edge, trying to steady myself. I tried to yell for Samuel, but I could barely get the words out. Needless to say, he didn't hear me, and the next thing I knew, I was waking up in the hospital with Isaac by my side.

When I came to, my head was wrapped in bandages, and I was completely disoriented. I had absolutely no idea where I was at or what had happened to me. I looked over and saw Isaac sitting there beside me, his head was down, and he looked to be in fervent prayer, but I was thoroughly confused as to why he was there. I moved my eyes around the room, and then it slowly began to dawn on me.

I've been here before, I recognized.

I let out a moan, trying to speak, and when I did, Isaac immediately leapt from his chair. He came close and got right in my face.

"Jochebed," he said frantically, "please tell me that was you! Say something - *please!*"

I looked up at him, bewildered.

"Can you hear me?" he asked, hopeful.

It was as if I was in a fog, but it slowly began to lift.

"Yes," I barely eked out. "What happened?"

Isaac started to cry as I watched relief sweep over his face.

I felt so lost and confused. I didn't know what to say or what to think.

"You're here!" he cried out so grateful. "Thank the Lord you're really here! We thought we'd lost you!" He smiled down at me through his tears as he took hold of my hand, unbelievably overjoyed.

"What happened?" I asked again. "Why am I here?"

Isaac was so overwhelmed he could barely speak.

"You had the surgery," he informed me.

"Surgery?" I queried. "But why?"

"You passed out in your kitchen," Isaac explained. "You hit your head, and started to seize. Your Papa had to rush you here to the hospital. Fortunately, the specialist was available, and he performed surgery on you, but you've been out for over a week. We didn't know if you were ever going to come back to us!" He leaned down and tenderly took me in his arms, holding me tightly, not wanting to let me go.

I could sense his desperation.

Knowing he couldn't hold me forever, though, he gently lay me back down and looked happily into my eyes. Sniffing, wiping his tears, he smiled.

"I should probably go get someone," he said. "I'm sure they'll want to examine you." He reluctantly left the room as I lay there waiting. When he came back, a nurse and the doctor were with him.

"You had us all worried there, young lady," the doctor said with a smile as he walked over to the bed and began to look me over. "I'm glad you decided to join us again!" He took his time, and examined me thoroughly, and while he was completely baffled as to why I hadn't come to sooner, he seemed pleased with what he saw. He indicated the surgery had gone well, and he was optimistic that it would help relieve my severe headaches. "Now," he pointed out, smiling down at me, "your recovery begins!"

A MORE NORMAL LIFE
(Chapter 38)

I was in the hospital again for another two weeks. Isaac was unable to stay with me this time, but between Papa, Uncle Mark, and even Mrs. Bell, and the hospital staff, of course, I had plenty of help during my recovery. I progressed reasonably well and seemed to be doing much better than I had after my first surgery. I didn't have nearly the trouble walking this time, although I still had bouts with light-headedness and had to be careful, and what headaches I did suffer seemed to be less frequent and much less debilitating. In fact, in the two weeks I was there, I only experienced one severe headache which kept me down for half the day. But only having one bad headache in that amount of time was very encouraging. I was hopeful that the surgery had actually worked!

While I was in the hospital alone, I had plenty of time to pray and think and read my Bible. I prayed a lot about my fears and worries and read verses that helped encourage me. In those two weeks, God allowed me to slowly but surely gain victory over my anxiety. I was so thankful and relieved, and I was looking forward to moving on with my life. I determined to put the man in the hat behind me!

I was so excited about the peace I'd found, that I couldn't *wait* to tell Isaac! He'd been such a help and encouragement to me during my struggles, and I knew he was praying for me; I wanted so badly to share my victories with him! He hadn't been able to visit me in the hospital (except for those first few days after I woke up), and I hadn't had a chance to write him during my recovery. I missed him terribly and wished I could see him! I knew, however, that he'd taken so much time off for me before that he needed to stay in school and catch up on his work. He'd told me before he left that he probably wouldn't be home again until sometime at the end of spring, and even though it was already March, his return seemed so far away. We'd promised to write, and that was one of the first things I intended to do just as soon as I was home and settled.

*****

On the way home from the hospital, Papa and Samuel filled me in on everything I'd missed while I was gone. I was amazed at how many things had changed in just a short amount of time. They told me that Aunt Sara was doing so well, that Dr. Wellesley had given her permission to get out of the house more often as long as she was careful and stayed in her wheelchair. They said she was ecstatic for the opportunity but that she never abused it. She only went out on certain occasions and always took care to protect herself and the baby. She was doing great, they said, and was really getting big with only a little over two months to go before the baby's arrival. I couldn't wait to see her!

They told me about Gramma, too. They said she was nearly all the way recovered, or, at least, as recovered as she was going to be. I was so proud of her! They said she was practically free of her cane and only had to use it if she got really tired or run-down. They explained how her personality was still different but endearing and how her speech, while it had improved a little, was still altered and would probably never get any better. She could communicate just fine, though, and that was all that really mattered. I couldn't wait to see her either!

When I arrived home from the hospital, I was able to walk to the house practically on my own, only needing a little assistance from Papa. I still had my wheelchair, of course, but I now only needed it just in case I got light-headed or if I got a severe headache. I was *so excited* to be back home again and *thrilled* to have most of my freedom back!

Papa told me he didn't want me attending school just yet until I was completely healed, and I told him I understood, graciously complying with his directive. I was just grateful that my headaches seemed better, and that I was allowed to walk around again on my own.

I have to admit I still tired easily, but I knew that I would regain my strength in time. Unfortunately, that meant I still had to sleep downstairs in the sewing room, Papa insisted on it! I understood, though, and accepted it, knowing it would be awhile before I could safely traverse the stairs on my own. Thankfully, however, Papa only put the restriction on me just until I had my follow up appointment with Dr. Wellesley. He said if the doctor okayed it, then he would be all right with me moving back upstairs to my old room. I was delighted and very determined to work as hard as I could so that I could do just that! My appointment was only a little over a week away, and I couldn't wait!

"Wow!" I exclaimed as I walked into the house. "It seems like forever since I've been here!"

"Well, you're about a week shy of a whole month," Papa reminded.

"I know," I commented, "but I almost feel a stranger in my own home."

"I'm just glad you're back," Samuel said as he brought my things in from the wagon. "It was too quiet around here without ya."

"Well thanks, Samuel," I said as I went to sit down at the kitchen table. "Believe me, I'm glad to be back, too!"

"By the way," Papa said as he pushed my wheelchair inside, "Pastor and Mrs. Scott wanted me to tell ya that they send their love and that they're lookin' forward to seein' ya in church on Sunday."

"I can't tell you how much I'm looking forward to seeing them!" I expressed with glee. "It's been..." I paused, trying to calculate how long it had actually been since I'd last sat in a service. "Gracious!" I finally concluded. "It's been...why...nearly three months now since I've been able to attend church! I miss it so much! I just can't wait to see everyone again and to thank them for their love and support and prayers. It's all meant so very much to me throughout this whole difficult ordeal."

Papa walked over and kissed me on the top of my head.

"It's so good to have ya back with us, sweetheart," he conveyed with love. "We've missed ya terribly!"

"Me, too, Papa!" I wholeheartedly agreed, looking up at him with a smile. "Me, too!"

"Hey," Papa suddenly remembered, "'bout forgot. Aunt Sara and Uncle Mark asked us to join 'em for an early supper over at Grampa and Gramma's tonight. Is there anything ya need to do before we go?"

"I would like to freshen up a bit and change my clothes, if that's all right?" I said, looking down at the gown I'd worn home from the hospital.

"I understand," Papa said with a nod. "Just tell me what ya need, and Sam and I can get it for ya."

"Thanks, Papa," I replied, "but that's all right. I'm pretty sure everything I need is still down here. I'll try to hurry."

"Okay," Papa accepted. "Just take it easy and let me know if ya need any help."

"I will," I assured as I carefully stood up and gingerly walked to the sewing room.

When I opened the door, it smelled a bit musty from the lack of use, but everything was still pretty much as I'd left it. I walked over to the closet and got out a clean dress and proceeded to get changed. I'll admit, I was a bit exhausted from the ride home from the hospital, but I pushed on anyway. I wanted desperately to see everyone again, and I wasn't about to let a little fatigue get in the way.

"Where's Samuel?" I asked as I walked back into the kitchen.

"Oh, he ran on ahead," Papa informed me. "Ya know him; patience isn't one of his strongest qualities." He smiled. "Ya ready to go?"

"Absolutely!" I replied enthusiastically. "I can't wait to see everybody! Just let me grab my shawl."

"I'll get it for ya, sweetheart," Papa offered.

He walked over and took it off the hook by the door, helped me put it around my shoulders, and walked me to the wagon. After he helped me climb aboard, he did the same, and we took off for Grampa and Gramma's.

When we arrived, it seemed odd to me that the house looked rather dark.

"Where is everybody?" I questioned as we pulled up.

"Don't know," Papa replied, playing ignorant. He helped me down off the wagon and on towards the house. "They're probably all just waitin' on us in the kitchen," he offered.

I shrugged, accepting his explanation as he and I walked up onto the porch together. He courteously opened the door for me, and I stepped inside. When I did, it was eerily quiet and quite dark. It seemed rather strange, but I could see a light flickering in the kitchen, so I assumed everyone was in there just like Papa had said. Even though I couldn't see or hear anyone, I headed on in that direction.

"Are you sure everyone's here?" I asked again, pausing, as Papa came up beside me.

"I'm sure, sweetheart," he chuckled. He took hold of my arm and I held tightly to his as he led me through the darkened family room towards the kitchen.

When we got there, everyone jumped out and yelled, "Surprise!"

I should have suspected, but I didn't, and it nearly scared me to death!

"Oh my! What on earth?" I exclaimed.

As I adjusted to what was happening, I could see Grampa and Gramma standing there together smiling and Samuel and Uncle Mark grinning from ear to ear.

Aunt Sara was over by the counter smiling happily, too, holding a cake with candles on it.

"Happy Birthday, sweetie!" she expressed with delight. "And welcome home! We've missed you!"

I was so overwhelmed; I couldn't believe it! In all my excitement of being able to come home today, I had actually forgotten what day it was.

"Happy Birthday, sweetheart!" Papa echoed as he gave me a kiss on the cheek. "I'm glad we were able to surprise ya."

"Well, you certainly did!" I assured. "Thank you all *so much!*" I walked around and gave everyone a great big hug and a kiss, and when I finished, I turned back around, and there standing beside Papa was none other than Isaac, thrilled to see me, and smiling broadly .I put my hand to my mouth in total shock and excitement. I beamed as I made my way over to him. "How did you?" I questioned, still amazed that he was standing there in front of me.

He took me in his arms and hugged me tightly lifting me up off the floor.

"Welcome home!" he whispered in my ear as he put me back down. "You didn't think I'd miss your birthday, now did you?"

"Oh, Isaac!" I exclaimed, beyond happy to see him. "I can't believe you're really here!" I hugged him again in my enthusiasm.

"Well, it'll be a whirlwind trip," he informed me, smiling down at me. "I can't stay long. I have to leave early in the morning to get back, but I didn't want to miss your special day."

"Well then, let's eat!" Grampa proposed eagerly as he motioned everyone to the table.

Everyone heartily agreed!

Papa and Uncle Mark lit some more lanterns and Gramma and Aunt Sara went to placing everything on the table. They'd graciously prepared all of my favorite foods, and everything smelled and looked delicious!

We all sat and ate and talked until Grampa couldn't wait any longer.

"Jochebed," he said, salivating, looking longingly at my birthday cake that was sitting over on the counter, "how 'bout cuttin' me a piece of that *luscious* lookin' cake over there that your Aunt Sara made for ya. Why…I've had to withstand temptation now for hours, and I'm growin' mighty weak! I just don't think I can hold out for much longer!"

Gramma looked at Grampa dubiously.

"Now, Ezra," she scolded, "you need be patient. I think you can wait till everyone finished. You certainly not going to die if you not get cake right now!"

Grampa let out a big billowy laugh.

"No, I suppose I won't," he conceded, "but I just might succumb to temptation, and that would be downright sinful now, wouldn't it!" He winked at Gramma with a huge grin on his face.

"Oh, you silly ol' man!" Gramma quipped, smiling back at him. "You not fool me!"

Uncle Mark jumped up to go get the cake and a knife.

"Wouldn't want ya sinnin' there, Pa," he said as he brought it over to the table. "Besides, if ya hadn't a said somethin', I was about to!"

Aunt Sara chuckled as she went to get the plates.

"You two," she teased. "You're worse than two little boys!"

Uncle Mark smiled wildly at her as he set the cake down in front of me and handed me the knife.

"You're the birthday girl," he announced with gusto. "Ya do the honors! And, hey," he added, raising his eyebrows up and down, "don't forget to make mine a big one!"

Everyone burst out laughing at his antics.

After we all enjoyed a piece of the delicious cake Aunt Sara had made for my eighteenth birthday and after I opened up my gifts, we all retired to the family room where we sat and talked and laughed well into the evening. It was such a wonderful birthday and an even more wonderful day! I was so thankful to be home and to have Isaac with me and to be surrounded by my loving family. It was more than I could ever ask for and more than I knew I deserved! As I looked around the room at all of my loved ones, I couldn't help but think how truly blessed I really was!

THE NEW ARRIVAL
(Chapter 39)

It had been almost a month now since I had come home from the hospital, and I was doing quite well. I battled with headaches from time to time, but most were very manageable. Only a few had been severe, and for that I was extremely grateful! I couldn't thank God enough for intervening on my behalf, making the decision about the surgery for me.

My follow-up checkup with Dr. Wellesley had gone very well, too, and he agreed with Papa to let me move back upstairs to my old bedroom. He also released me to go back to school, for which I was very thankful!

On my first day back to class, my teacher informed me that I had done a very fine job of keeping up with my studies, and that he saw no reason why I wouldn't pass the year. I was so relieved, as I had worried that my extended absence might harm my grades and prevent me from moving on.

Isaac and I had written back and forth over the weeks, I more than he, but I understood as he was just so busy with school, it was hard for him to correspond. Still, as you would expect, I dearly looked forward to every letter that he was able to send. I missed him so much! He had only been able to come home once since my birthday (and that was just for a weekend), and it was unlikely he would be able to come home again until the end of the school year. Needless to say, it was so hard to wait as I wanted him home so badly! It seemed like an eternity until his return!

The weeks continued to pass, albeit slowly, and now there was just four weeks to go before Isaac would be home from college, and I couldn't wait! I was so excited at the thought of being able to have him all to myself for the whole entire summer!

I was also very excited for Aunt Sara and Uncle Mark. Their baby was due to arrive within a week or so, and I was looking forward to it immensely! Aunt Sara and Uncle Mark had already settled on names for both a boy and a girl, but they were determined to keep them a secret until after the baby was born. That didn't stop Grampa from trying to figure them out, however, and try he did! Every day, *several times a day*, he would come up with some real doozies! Uncle Mark and Aunt Sara were gracious, but I could tell they were anxious for the baby to arrive, not only to finally have it here with them, but also to stop Grampa's relentless guessing!

*****

It was late in the evening on a Monday night, and Papa and Samuel and I were in the middle of supper, enjoying our food and conversation, when all of a sudden we were startled by Uncle Mark frantically bursting through the door.

"Michael!" he was shouting in a panic. "It's time! Sara's gone into labor, and I need Jochebed to come right away! Ma's with Sara, and Pa's gone to get the doc, but I don't know if he'll make it back in time! Ma needs Jochebed - *now!!*"

I promptly jumped up from the table and grabbed my shawl, scrambling outside with Uncle Mark to his wagon. We both quickly climbed aboard and took off as fast as we could!

Papa and Samuel closed up the house and followed behind us.

"Isn't she a little early?" I inquired as Uncle Mark tore off towards Grampa and Gramma's.

"Yes!" he responded anxiously. "Over a week! That's what's got Ma concerned!"

Practically before Uncle Mark could finish answering my question, we were at the house. Immediately, I hastily jumped down from the wagon and hurried on inside.

As soon as I entered the house, I could hear Aunt Sara yelling in pain as I ran to her bedroom. Gramma was there tending to her as I walked in.

"Good, Jochebed," Gramma expressed, relieved. "You here! Go get pan, warm water!"

I dashed off as swiftly as I could to do as Gramma asked, and Aunt Sara continued to scream out in pain. Her shrieks sent chills down my spine as I had never *ever* heard her yell out like that before. It was frightening, to say the least, and it sounded so excruciating!

I got the water started on the stove and went back to the bedroom as quickly as I could to see if there was anything else I could do.

"The water's warming," I informed. "What else do you need?"

"Get towel from washroom," Gramma instructed. "Bring lots!"

Aunt Sara was writhing in pain on her bed, and Gramma was trying to comfort her.

"There, there!" she kept saying. "It be okay. Just breathe."

I stood there transfixed, watching Aunt Sara struggling to breathe normally as waves of pain seemed to overtake her. It looked like such a strenuous, difficult task just for her to take a breath. I couldn't help but worry for her!

"Jochebed!" Gramma shouted ardently, jarring me from my thoughts. "Towels!"

"Oh, right!" I said, coming back into the moment. I promptly hurried off.

When I got back with the towels, I immediately set them down beside Gramma and went back to the kitchen to check on the water. It was warming, but not quite warm enough. I rushed back to the bedroom to see what else I could do to help.

While we were busy inside, tending to Aunt Sara, Uncle Mark and Papa and Samuel were all waiting outside. Uncle Mark was nervously walking back and forth, while Papa and Samuel sat on the porch step just watching him pace.

"Don't worry, Mark," Papa tried to bolster. "I'm sure she'll be just fine. Pa should be back with the doc any minute now."

Uncle Mark seemed to be in his own little world, hearing nothing Papa had just said. He was intently wearing a path in the grass as he walked back and forth anxiously waiting for any news. Aunt Sara's screams could be heard by all, and each time she yelled out in pain, Uncle Mark would stop with a worried look on his face, look in her direction, shake his head, and begin to pace again.

After about the third time, he looked over at Papa and asked fretfully, "Is that *normal?*"

Papa grinned and answered with a chuckle.

"Yes, little brother," he assured, "women have been birthin' babies for centuries. I don't think it's gotten any easier with time!"

Uncle Mark frowned at Papa as if it wasn't at all what he wanted to hear. He shook his head and went back to pacing.

"Sounds awful to me!" Samuel remarked, wide-eyed and troubled after hearing another of Aunt Sara's horrific outbursts. "Sure glad I'm not a woman!"

Papa tussled his hair and laughed.

Back inside, Gramma was trying to keep Aunt Sara calm.

"It be all right," she told her. "Just let it come."

"Oh, please!" Aunt Sara cried out, grimacing in pain, grasping the sides of the bed so hard her knuckles were turning white. "I don't think I can do this! Mama Lowry, it hurts so *badly!*"

"I know, Sara," Gramma sympathized, "but you strong girl. You can do this!" Gramma turned to me. "You go check water," she said. "Will need it soon! This baby not gonna wait much longer!"

I left immediately and headed for the kitchen, and when I got there, thankfully, the water was ready. I poured it into a pan and carefully carried it to the bedroom.

"Here it is!" I announced as I entered. "Where would you like me to put it?"

"Put over here," Gramma answered, pointing to the table she had set up at the end of the bed where she was now sitting.

"What can I do now?" I questioned anxiously.

"Go sit by Sara," Gramma instructed. "Take her hand. She need help pushing."

I went over and sat down beside Aunt Sara, taking the cool cloth that was there beside her, and wiping the sweat from her brow.

"Oh, Jochebed!" she said with angst as she took my hand and looked at me with such trepidation in her eyes. "I'm so scared!"

"You can do this!" I encouraged. "Aunt Sara, I *know you can do this!* Just think, in a few minutes you'll be holding your sweet little baby!"

Just then, another labor pain hit, and she let out a terrible scream! Again her shrieks sent chills down my spine, but then she squeezed my hand so hard I thought *I* was going to scream! My eyes got as big as saucers, but I managed to keep quiet.

"Aaaaaaaaa!!!" she yelled out in agonizing pain.

My heart skipped a beat, and then began to beat faster and faster. I knew childbirth was painful, but I'd never seen it up close before and never *imagined* it would be *this traumatic!* I have to admit it was definitely making me think twice about having children of my own!

"It coming!" Gramma announced abruptly. "I see top of head!"

Aunt Sara fell back to rest, but immediately sat right back up wincing in pain.

"I can't! I can't!" she exclaimed, shaking her head feverishly. "It hurts too much!"

I tried to calm her the best I could.

"Yes, you can!" I told her as I rubbed her back, holding her hand, encouraging her on.

"Push!" Gramma shouted. "Push!"

Aunt Sara bore down and pushed with all her might. She pushed and pushed until she just couldn't push anymore. She was exhausted! She lay back briefly to catch her breath.

"Next pain," Gramma insisted, "you really push hard! Baby almost here!"

Aunt Sara looked at me in desperation, her eyes pleading for help - help I couldn't give her. I felt so badly for her, but I just didn't know what to do! I wished like everything that I could take her pain from her, but I couldn't. All I could do was give her my support, and even though I wasn't sure it would help, I felt I had to do something!

"Aunt Sara," I said with all sincerity, "you're the *strongest* woman I know! I *know* you can do this! I know it hurts, and I know it's hard, but your baby's almost here. You can do this!"

Another pain hit and she instantly sat up.

"Aaaaaaaaa!!!" she screamed out as she bore down.

"Push! Push!" Gramma demanded over and over again. "Good girl! Good girl! Now...*again!*"

I could tell Aunt Sara was trying, but she was so tired and worn out she could barely hold herself up. She glanced over at me breathing heavily, drained and completely stressed. It was obvious she was spent! She shook her head wearily as she took a deep breath, trying to gather her strength. Giving it all she had, she bore down one more time.

"I can't do it anymore!" she cried out in tears. "I just *can't!* Please...make it stop!"

"You *can* do this!" I told her. "You're doing great! It's almost over!"

She looked at me, absolutely depleted, ready to give up.

I looked at her sympathetically but tried to cheer her on.

"You can do this, Aunt Sara!" I encouraged again. "Honest...it's almost over!"

She looked so pitiful, so tired...I couldn't help but feel sorry for her. She kept shaking her head over and over again as tears began to stream down her face. I had to fight to keep myself from crying, too, as my heart broke for her.

Finally realizing she had no choice, she took a deep breath trying to muster the strength to go on. When the next pain hit, she leaned forward and bore down with everything she had, squeezing my hand, pushing vigorously.

After the labor pain passed, she fell back in sheer exhaustion. It seemed she was at the end of her strength.

"That's it!" she said, trying to catch her breath. "I can't do it! I'm done!"

Gramma immediately stood up and looked her firmly in the eye.

"No you're not!" she insisted with earnest. "Baby ready to come!" She sat back down, and demanded again, seemingly with no compassion, "Now push!"

Aunt Sara sighed, distraught, and looked at me with the most helpless look on her face.

I forced a smile, trying to be helpful.

"Just a little more," I bolstered. "Come on. You can do it! Think about holding that little baby of yours! It's almost here!"

She closed her eyes as she took one more deep breath.

I helped her sit back up and she squeezed my hand again as hard as ever, bearing down, pushing , focused and determined.

"Aaaaaaaaa!!!" she screamed as she pushed and pushed.

"Little more! Little more!" Gramma kept saying.

Suddenly, Gramma's face lit up with sheer delight as Aunt Sara lay back in utter relief.

"Baby here!" Gramma exclaimed in excitement.

All of a sudden, the baby started to cry as Gramma began wiping it off. It was the most joyous sound I think I had ever heard!

Aunt Sara was crying, but now they were tears of joy!

Gramma brought the baby up and carefully laid it on Aunt Sara's chest.

"It a girl!" Gramma announced, beaming, as tears welled in her eyes. "And she perfect!"

I was so overwhelmed by what had just happened; I couldn't believe it! The baby was finally here and she was safe and healthy and *so beautiful!*

Gramma got a cloth to wrap the baby in, as Aunt Sara lay holding her precious little girl.

She couldn't stop smiling as she wept.

"Hello," she said, holding onto her daughters little fingers. Aunt Sara was so overcome with joy she could barely speak. "I never dreamed this day would ever come!" she confessed. "I love you so much!" She leaned down and kissed her baby's tiny, little, wrinkled forehead as the baby just lay there staring up at her, wide-eyed, contented to be in her mama's arms.

I couldn't remember a time when I'd ever seen Aunt Sara so happy! She was simply elated!

Gramma and I were both in tears as well!

"She's just gorgeous!" I complimented. "Amazing! Congratulations, Aunt Sara!" I sat there smiling, staring at this precious little life.

"What a miracle!" Gramma pointed out, wiping her tears. "I go tell boys."

Aunt Sara didn't take her eyes off of her little girl. She seemed mesmerized by every little feature: her deep blue eyes, her tiny little nose, her o-shaped mouth, and her dark thick hair.

"I just can't believe she's really mine!" she kept saying over and over again.

Just then, Uncle Mark walked into the room and I got up from the bed so that he could come over and join Aunt Sara. He stood there with tears in his eyes, a huge smile on his face.

Aunt Sara looked up at him.

"Come see your little girl, Papa," she urged, smiling.

Uncle Mark walked over and sat down on the bed beside Aunt Sara. He gave her a kiss and looked down at his little baby girl. He shook his head in disbelief.

"She's so tiny!" he remarked, overtaken with tears. "She's perfect!"

"So," Gramma prodded as she walked back into the room, "what her name?"

Papa and Samuel were standing at the door, and I walked over to join them.

Uncle Mark took his little girl in his arms and looked down at her precious little face. He sniffed and wiped a tear as he looked over at Papa.

"Her name," he revealed, "is Lydia...Lydia Grace."

Everyone looked at Papa to see his reaction. His lip began to quiver as his eyes filled with tears. He nodded, approving, overcome by emotion. He cleared his throat, trying to compose himself.

"That's real nice," he told them, overwhelmed. "I know...I know she'd be so proud." He pulled out his hanky and wiped his eyes. "Congratulations!" he said. "I'm so happy for the both of ya!"

Gramma commented.

"What lovely name!" she said. "She blessed little girl, and so beautiful, too!" She smiled sweetly at Aunt Sara. "I so proud of you, Sara," she told her. "You did wonderful!"

"Thank you, Mama Lowry," Aunt Sara accepted. "That's kind of you to say. And thank *you* for helping me through it. You, too, Jochebed," she added quickly, looking over at me. "I don't know what I would have done without the two of you!"

"It my joy!" Gramma declared.

"And mine, too!" I chimed in.

"And good thing I know what I doing, too!" Gramma stated a little upset, grabbing the conversation right back. "Gracious!" she quipped, looking over at Papa. "Did your father lose way on way to get doctor?"

Papa chuckled.

"I'm sure they'll be here soon, Ma," he replied.

As we all stood around admiring baby Lydia, Grampa and the doctor finally showed up.

"I see we missed the party," the doctor remarked, smiling, as he made his way into the room and over to Aunt Sara and the baby.

"They both doing fine," Gramma assured. "What take you so long get here?"

"I'm sorry, Mrs. Lowry," Dr. Wellesley explained. "I was out on another call, and your husband had to track me down." He smiled again at Aunt Sara and baby Lydia. "I see they were in more than capable hands, though," he complimented.

Uncle Mark stood up holding the baby.

"All right," Dr. Wellesley instructed, "everyone out for now. I need to look this young lady and her baby over. You can all come back in in a few minutes."

Uncle Mark leaned down and gently handed baby Lydia back to Aunt Sara. He gave Aunt Sara a kiss and told her he loved her, smiled affectionately at the both of them, and left the room with the rest of us.

"Wow!" I expressed with amazement as we all walked out into the family room. "That was the most incredible thing I've ever seen! Thank you so much Gramma and Uncle Mark for allowing me to be a part of it!"

"It is miracle!" Gramma reiterated as she squeezed me tightly. "God truly is good!"

"Amen!" Grampa concurred, beaming with pride. "Amen indeed!"

MOVING IN
(Chapter 40)

"Congratulations, Papa!" Papa said again to Uncle Mark as he gave him a big hug. "Now where do ya plan to put that little one?"

"Well," Uncle Mark said as he pulled at his chin, "funny you should ask. I've been thinkin' a lot about that lately, and I was wantin' to propose a plan to Ma and Pa, but just haven't had the time to discuss it."

"No time like the present, Son," Grampa said as he went to sit down in his chair. "What's on your mind?"

"Well, I know it'd be askin' a lot," Uncle Mark started, "after all, you and Ma have already done so much for Sara and me, so I'd understand if y'all were against it; but I was hopin' that maybe I could buy a small piece of land from ya. Ya know the section in the back corner of your property there? I was thinkin' that maybe I could build us a home on it. I know it'd be a lot of work and take a while to finish, but hopefully I could have us out of here within a month or so. Again, I know it's a lot to ask, but…well…what'd ya think? I'll pay a fair price!"

Grampa looked over at Gramma as he stood back up from his chair.

"Well, dear," he said, motioning for her to come with him, "shall we adjourn to the other room and discuss the matter?"

Gramma nodded as she got up from off the couch and walked with Grampa to their bedroom.

We all sat talking in the family room, waiting for them to return.

"How long ya been thinkin' in this direction?" Papa asked Uncle Mark.

"Actually, not all that long," Uncle Mark confessed. "As ya know I've been searchin' for a house for us to purchase for months now, but there's just nothin' available around here that I can afford. I was really hopin' to have a house ready to go by the time Sara gave birth, but…well… it just didn't work out. One night, Sara and I were talkin', and she happened to mention maybe buildin' somethin' somewhere, and that put my mind to thinkin'. One day, a few weeks back, Pa and I were walkin' the property, and it dawned on me that maybe this would be the perfect place. It'd put us close to family, and I know that's important to Sara."

Papa sat listening, nodding, agreeing.

"Well, if ya get Ma and Pa's approval," he assured, "ya know ya have my help."

"And mine!" Samuel volunteered.

"And I'll do what I can, too, Uncle Mark," I added, excited at the thought of having them all so close.

Just then, Grampa and Gramma came walking back into the room.

Uncle Mark stood up with a hopeful look on his face.

"So, what'd ya think?" he asked.

Grampa looked at Gramma as they smiled at each other.

"We'd love to have you and Sara here with us!" he answered. "The land is yours!"

Uncle Mark smiled, relieved and thrilled for the opportunity.

"Thank ya Pa, Ma!" he said as he walked over and gave them both a hug.

"Son," Gramma relayed sweetly as she hugged him back, "we want give you land. You our family. No need to pay. We not feel right take your money."

"Absolutely not!" Uncle Mark adamantly refused. "I insist! I'll pay a fair price! Ya've already done so much for us. I…"

Grampa put his hand up, stopping Uncle Mark mid-sentence.

"No, Son!" he insisted right back. "Your Ma's right. We wouldn't feel right takin' your money - now just accept it! Besides, the matter's settled! We've made up our minds. We're given y'all the land, and that's the end of it!"

Uncle Mark shook his head, more than a little uneasy with their decision.

"Are ya sure about this?" he questioned with reservation.

"Positive!" Gramma replied as she patted Uncle Mark on the cheek.

Uncle Mark sighed, reluctantly accepting their generous offer.

"All right, then," he agreed. "I don't know how we'll ever repay ya, though."

"Ya just take care beautiful daughter of yours," Gramma told him. "That payment enough for me!"

Uncle Mark hugged Gramma and Grampa again, overwhelmed.

"I can't thank ya enough!" he expressed with sincere gratitude. "This means more than ya know. Sara'll be so thrilled!"

Not long after the matter was settled, Dr. Wellesley came out from the bedroom.

"All looks good," he informed as he extended his hand to Uncle Mark. "Congratulations! You have a beautiful little girl there. She appears healthy as can be, and Sara's doing great, too. You should be proud!"

"Thanks, Doc," Uncle Mark replied. "Can I go see 'em now?"

"Sure," he allowed. "You enjoy that little girl of yours. She's a sweetheart!" He walked towards the door. "I'll check back in a couple of days," he said. "Congratulations, everyone!"

Papa nodded.

"Thanks, Doc," he told him. "We appreciate ya comin' out."

Everyone made their way back to the bedroom, wanting to see little Lydia.

When Uncle Mark opened the door, Aunt Sara looked up with a smile.

"Can you believe she's actually ours?" she commented, still so overwhelmed and pleased.

"I know!" Uncle Mark agreed enthusiastically as he went and sat down beside Aunt Sara. "Every time I look at her, it almost doesn't seem real!"

"Well now, let me hold that child," Grampa requested as he stepped forward and made his way to the bed.

"Here ya go, Papa Lowry," Aunt Sara offered as she gently placed Lydia in his arms.

"Oh, you be careful ol' man!" Gramma warned nervously.

"Now, Elizabeth!" Grampa chided. "This isn't my first time holdin' a wee one. I think I'll manage just fine!"

"It first time as old man!" Gramma quipped right back.

Grampa looked at Gramma, smiling wildly.

"Ya better watch it there, *old* woman," he teased. "Two can play at that game!"

"Well, I never!" Gramma huffed in consternation.

Just then, Lydia started to cry.

"See," Gramma jabbed, "ya make baby cry. She not like it when you call me old!"

Grampa just laughed.

"There, there," he quieted. "Shhh! You're makin' me look bad in front of your Gramma."

Lydia paid him no mind, and kept right on crying.

"All right, all right," Grampa relented, "back to Mama ya go." He carefully handed Lydia back to Aunt Sara. "She's beautiful there, Mama," he complimented, smiling proudly, "even when she's cryin'."

"Thank you, Papa Lowry," Aunt Sara replied. "I think she's just hungry."

"All right, everyone out!" Gramma shooed. "Let child eat. Scoot!"

Uncle Mark stayed behind as we all heeded Gramma's instruction.

*****

Throughout the next week, there was much talk and preparation for Uncle Mark and Aunt Sara's house. Papa and Uncle Mark started planning and designing the house (with Aunt Sara's input, of course), and Grampa decided to make an announcement at church that Sunday, inviting folks to help out if they'd like to. By the end of the service, all the men in the church, including Pastor Scott, had graciously volunteered to be a part of the project.

*****

By the start of the following week, Uncle Mark and Aunt Sara had settled on what they wanted, and Papa and Uncle Mark had gathered the materials necessary to start building.

With everything in place, that Wednesday night at church, Uncle Mark let everyone know that they planned to start on the house bright and early the next morning. Papa agreed to let Samuel and me take the next couple days off from school to lend a hand, but only if we got permission from our teacher and promised to keep up with our schoolwork. We both assured him that we would, and went that very evening to get permission. We couldn't *wait* to help out!

We all got to Grampa and Gramma's extra early that next morning and got started right away helping to get things ready.

"Oh, I'm so excited!" Aunt Sara exclaimed with restless anticipation as she walked into the kitchen carrying baby Lydia. "I just can't believe we're actually going to have our *own home!*"

"Oh, I know!" I expressed with delight, excited for them as well. "I'm just *so thrilled* that you all get to live so close to us! I'm absolutely *giddy* that I get to be around baby Lydia…and…you and Uncle Mark, of course."

Aunt Sara chuckled.

"Would you like to hold her?" she asked.

I smiled brightly!

"Very much so!" I accepted enthusiastically. "I'd love to!"

Aunt Sara walked over and gently placed Lydia in my arms.

"I just can't get over how tiny she is!" I remarked, looking down at her adorable little face. "She's just *so sweet!*"

"Oh, I know!" Aunt Sara concurred, beaming as she stood there admiring her precious little girl, so thankful and proud. "Sometimes I still can't believe she's actually mine."

Lydia was still asleep, and she looked so cute in her little lavender nightgown and light green blanket that Aunt Sara had made for her. Her dark hair was sticking up a bit, and her little hands were in fists up by her face. She was sucking on her tongue, and with

335

every breath she took, it seemed as if she were dreaming a happy dream. I felt I could sit there watching her all day long.

Everyone began arriving, though, the men from the church, along with their wives (they were there to help with meals and to see Aunt Sara and baby Lydia), so I knew that I could only enjoy her for a little while longer. Soon I'd have to give her back to Aunt Sara and get busy along with the rest. Until I did, however, I was going to savor every precious moment I had with her.

Outside, Uncle Mark, Papa, Samuel and Grampa had already started on the foundation to the house. As each man arrived, they jumped right in and began working alongside the others. With such a large group working diligently, by noon, the house was completely framed in, and some had already started working on the outside, while others began constructing the roof.

Inside, all of the ladies, Aunt Sara, Gramma and I were visiting, enjoying the conversation as we cooked and prepared and took turns passing Lydia around. It was such a busy but fun day! We made fried chicken, biscuits, corn and green beans, mashed potatoes and gravy, and plenty of apple and peach pies. We had apple cider and lemonade to drink and cold water and coffee as well. It was a regular feast, a lot of hard work, but no one seemed to mind. The fellowship was sweet, and Aunt Sara and Uncle Mark were all that much closer to having their own home.

By the end of the day, the men had the house under roof and had commenced to working on the inside. They worked as late as light would permit and then came inside for a late supper. We ate and fellowshipped, having such a grand time, until everyone had to leave to go home to get some sleep. The plan was for all to return early the next morning, and it would be upon us before we knew it.

*****

The next day, all of the men were back, working as hard as ever as were the ladies. I have to admit the time spent laboring was extremely hectic and exhausting, but it was also exhilarating at the same time. For all of the wonderful moments we got to spend with family and friends - helping one another, encouraging one another, laughing together, and fellowshipping, it made all the grueling work all the more worth it.

I had completely forgotten how rewarding days like this could be! It had been almost a year since anyone had needed anything built, and even though we had had plenty of church gatherings in that time, there was just something extra special about helping someone in need. It was that added blessing that seemed to make the fellowship all the sweeter.

*****

By Saturday, the house was finished to the point where Aunt Sara and Uncle Mark could start moving in. Aunt Sara was so thrilled that she finally had a house of her own and a room for her little baby girl. The house was relatively small - only two tiny bedrooms, a half kitchen, half dining room area, a small wash room, a little sewing room, and a quaint little porch on the front of the house, but Uncle Mark told Aunt Sara not to worry; there was always room for expansion on the back. Aunt Sara assured him that she didn't mind the house being small, though. It was hers, and for that, she was eternally grateful!

With everyone helping, it still took most of the day to get Aunt Sara and Uncle Mark's things moved into their new house. I didn't mind a bit, though; I got to watch baby Lydia while everyone else worked, and I thoroughly enjoyed every minute of my time with her. She was such a sweetheart and a delight to be around! I was simply enthralled with her tiny little features and her pleasant personality.

Particular as to how she wanted things arranged, Aunt Sara took charge of the move, telling everyone where to put things and helping to put things away herself. She took short breaks now and then to feed Lydia, but then she was right back at it. Uncle Mark worried that she might be overdoing it, just having had the baby and all, but Aunt Sara was strong-willed and determined. She was going to have them all moved into their new house and sleeping in their own beds that night if it was the last thing she did.

*****

Sure enough, by late evening, everything was all moved in. The house still needed some finishing touches, but Uncle Mark and Papa would take care of those over the next week or so. Aunt Sara couldn't wait to get started on the curtains for the windows, but first, she said, she just wanted to sit and enjoy her new home.

That night, as everyone sat down to the supper we'd prepared, Uncle Mark stood up to say a few words before we got started.

"I really don't know where to begin," he admitted. "All ya've done for us…" He paused, reaching down, taking Aunt Sara's hand. "I don't know how Sara and I can ever say thank ya enough," he went on, "or repay ya'll for your kindness and generosity. We're so blessed that ya've taken us into your congregation and that ya've made us feel a part. Thank ya all for your friendship and unbelievable support. It means more than words can say."

When Uncle Mark finished, Pastor Scott stood up to say grace.

As soon as he ended his prayer, Grampa bellowed, "Let's eat!"

Everyone laughed and we all dug in!

THE HARRIED DAY
(Chapter 41)

After church on Sunday, Aunt Sara and I spent the afternoon in her sewing room laying out patterns for the new curtains while Gramma came over to help us, and also to help watch baby Lydia.

"Oh, Aunt Sara!" I commented, approving."This material is just gorgeous! Wherever did you find it?"

"Mama mailed it to me in the last package she sent," Aunt Sara explained. "They knew from my letters that we were looking for a new home, and Mama always told me that new curtains helped to make a house your own. She wanted me to have something fresh and colorful." She held it up, admiring it in the sunlight that was streaming through the window. "I agree," she said happily, "it is beautiful! Then again, Mama always did have good taste. I can't wait to write her again and tell her about our new home! I just know she'll be so surprised!" Aunt Sara laid the material down and began to measure it out. "I'm hoping, though, that my parents will be able to see it for themselves this summer," she continued. "When Mark sent the wire letting them know about Lydia's arrival, they sent back saying they planned to come for a visit just as soon as time and money permit. I just can't wait to see them again!"

"Oh, I do hope they can come again soon!" I replied, so excited for Aunt Sara. "It'd be so nice to see them again, and I'm sure they just can't *wait* to see little Lydia!"

"Oh, I know!" Aunt Sara agreed as she started to cut the material for the curtain. "When they sent their congratulations, they said they wished like everything that they could be here with us now. I so hope they'll be able to come before Lydia gets too big."

"Well, I'll be praying to that end," I assured her.

Aunt Sara and I worked diligently all through the afternoon, right up until church time. We were able to get most of the curtains sown, and Uncle Mark and Gramma were able to hang some of them up around the house. It was neat to see as their house was really beginning to look and feel like a home.

*****

Over the next week and into the next, Papa and Uncle Mark finished up a lot of little things inside the house, and even began work on a barn to house Uncle Mark and Aunt Sara's horse and wagon. I was so grateful to have such a wonderful family and to have them all so close.

I couldn't wait for Isaac to come home from college so that he could see baby Lydia and see all of the changes that had taken place while he was away. His arrival was to be at the end of the week, but it still seemed like an eternity until he would be home!

School for Samuel and me had already come to a close, and, needless to say, we were looking forward to the time off. I made myself busy with chores around the house and sitting for Aunt Sara, watching baby Lydia, hoping that maybe my business would take my mind off of Isaac and make the time pass by a little faster, but unfortunately, it didn't seem to work at all! I missed him way too much, and he was pretty much all I could think about!

*****

"Penny for your thoughts?" Aunt Sara questioned as I sat there starring aimlessly, rocking baby Lydia while Aunt Sara prepared supper.

"Oh," I replied, being jarred from my thoughts, "I guess I was just missing Isaac. It's been so long since he's been home, and with only a few days to go now...well...it seems like time's slowed to a snail's pace."

Aunt Sara chuckled.

"Ah, young love!" she quipped. "How I remember it well!" She smiled sweetly. "You'll make it, Jochebed!" she encouraged. "I promise!"

I sighed, not so convinced.

"I'm sure you're right," I reluctantly agreed, "but still...I just can't wait to see him!"

Aunt Sara smiled again as she stirred the contents of the pot there in front of her.

"So," she queried curiously, "do you think he's the one?"

I perked up, smiling broadly.

"I do!" I answered confidently. "He's all I've ever prayed for and so much more! The more I get to know him, the more I'm convinced of it!"

Aunt Sara nodded.

"I can see that," she accepted. "He seems like a very decent, godly man, and he obviously loves you very much. Any talk of marriage?"

"No," I said, a little dispirited. "We've not broached the subject. Not having been courting all that long, I guess we've both been hesitant to bring it up. Not to mention with everything I've gone through this past winter, I think my health just took priority." I paused as I thought for a minute. "I know we've only been courting for awhile now," I submitted, reasoning it all out, "but we have *known* each other for a lot of years. It almost seems silly to wait at this point."

Aunt Sara abruptly stopped what she was doing and looked at me, surprised by my pronouncement.

"Now, hold on there!" she cautioned. "Somehow I don't see your father going for that! After all, you've not even officially been together a whole year yet, not to mention you still have another year of school to go before you finish."

"Oh, I know," I assured her. "It's just that when you've wanted something for so long, it's...it's *so* hard to wait!"

Aunt Sara nodded, fully understanding.

"I can empathize with that," she said as she walked over to Lydia and stroked her hair. "I look at her some days, and it still doesn't seem real. I wanted a child for *so long*..." She paused, taking hold of Lydia's tiny little hand. "And now look at her!" she smiled lovingly. "Be patient, Jochebed," she heartened, "it'll happen in time."

"I know," I sighed, understanding, but still desiring things to be different. "I just wish there was a way to speed things up!"

*****

After I enjoyed supper with Uncle Mark and Aunt Sara, I said goodbye and headed home. It was such a beautiful evening, and I was looking forward to the walk. There was a scent of flowers in the air, and the grass was gently blowing in the breeze. As I strolled along, I thought of Isaac, and I remembered back to the walks that he and I had taken together. It made me miss him all the more, and I just couldn't wait until the week was up!

By the time I reached home, lamentably, I could feel a headache coming on. I still had them from time to time, but they were a lot less frequent since my surgery, and the severe ones only bothered me on occasion. I tried not to take my medicine unless I absolutely had to, though, because it often made me drowsy, and I didn't like being tired. Most of the time, what headaches I did get were mild, and I could get by without taking anything at all. They simply lasted a short time and then passed on their own. I was hoping this one would do the same, but unfortunately as the evening wore on, the pain continued to worsen. I was reluctant to do so (I still had so many things I wanted to get done before bedtime), but I decided I should take some medicine. The headache just wasn't going away! As I drank my medicine down, I sincerely hoped that I hadn't waited too long. Sometimes if I did, it seemed the medicine was of little effect. When that happened, I'd be in bed for hours waiting for the pain to go away.

Papa was just coming in from outside as I was putting my medicine away, back in the cupboard.

"Is everything all right?" he asked.

I took a deep breath and sighed more than a little disheartened.

"Unfortunately, no," I answered, feeling rather sick at this point. My head was really starting to hurt, and I was feeling somewhat dizzy, too. "I'm having a headache again," I said as I brought my hand to my forehead, "and it seems to be getting worse. I took my medicine, but I'm afraid I may have waited too long."

"I'm sorry to hear that, sweetheart," Papa sympathized as he could tell I was in quite a bit of pain. He walked over beside me. "Maybe ya should go lie down," he suggested, worried.

"I think you're right," I whispered, agreeing, not feeling at all good. "If you don't mind, I think I'll just turn in for the night."

"I understand," Papa assured. "I'll help ya to your room."

"No, that's all right," I told him. "You don't have to. I think I can manage."

"Are ya sure?" Papa questioned hesitantly. "Ya don't look too good."

"I'm sure," I promised. I started to walk towards the stairs, but with each step I took, I kept getting dizzier and dizzier. I staggered over and leaned against the wall.

Papa quickly came up behind me and took hold of my arm.

"Whoa, there!" he expressed with concern. "You're definitely not fine! I'm walkin' with ya, and that's final!"

I was too weak and too sick to argue. I clasped Papa's hand and leaned against him as he carefully and steadily helped me up the stairs and into bed.

"Try to rest, sweetheart," he encouraged as he tucked me in. He kissed me on the forehead before going to get a bucket for me just in case I got sick. "I hope ya feel better, soon," he said as he set it down beside my bed.

"Me, too," I whispered back, my eyes closed, feeling terrible.

Papa looked at me sympathetically, leaned down and gave me another kiss on the forehead, told me he loved me, and left, quietly closing the door behind him.

After he was gone, I lay there just trying to breathe, swallowing hard, trying my best not to get sick as I was in so much pain. My head was aching something awful, and I was dizzier than I'd been in a very long time. It was horrible! I have to admit, feeling as dreadful as I did, I started to worry that maybe my severe headaches were coming back. I tried not to dwell on it, though, but as miserable as I felt, it was very hard not to. I lay there awhile longer and eventually fell asleep.

*****

The next day, I was awakened by the sun shining brightly through my window. It took me a minute to remember why I was still in my dress and not in my nightgown, but when I saw the bucket lying there on the floor next to my bed, it all came back to me.

Immediately, I sat up in a panic as it suddenly dawned on me that if the sun was shining this brightly, it had to be late in the day. I quickly threw the covers off and stepped to my mirror. I hastily fixed my hair up in a bun, changed into another work dress, and headed for the door.

When I threw it open, Samuel was just heading for the stairs from his bedroom.

"Well, it's about time!" he quipped when he saw me. "Thought we were gonna have to come in after ya."

"Oh, Samuel!" I fretted. "What time is it?"

"One o'clock," he said, laughing. "I think ya might be takin' this whole vacation from school thing just a little too seriously, don't you?"

"One o'clock!" I gasped in absolute horror. *"Are you joking? Please...*tell me you're joking!"

Samuel shook his head, grinning from ear to ear, seemingly enjoying my predicament.

I stood there aghast! I just couldn't believe that I had slept in this long. I mean...I hadn't slept in like this since...since before my surgery! I was completely beside myself!

"This is awful!" I exclaimed in consternation. "Just *awful!* Why didn't you wake me?"

Samuel put his hands up.

"Don't take it out on me!" he shot back defensively. "I was just followin' orders. Papa told me to let ya sleep. He said ya had a really bad night last night and that you weren't feelin' good." He abruptly turned and ran on downstairs.

I stood there a minute totally dumbfounded! I just couldn't *believe* that this had actually happened to me again!

Finally accepting that I couldn't do anything about it, I sighed in frustration, quickly gathered my dress, and rushed off downstairs behind Samuel.

"Have you eaten lunch yet?" I asked as I hurried into the kitchen.

"Are ya kiddin'?" he said. "Of course, I have! Wasn't 'bout to starve to death waitin' on ya to get up!" He grabbed an apple and headed outside.

I stood there shaking my head, staring at the door as I watched him walk out.

Once he was gone, I stopped and thought to myself.

One o'clock I contemplated. *What was I supposed to be doing today, and where would I be in my day if I'd gotten up on time?*

It took me a minute to think it through, but I finally decided that I was supposed to be at Grampa and Gramma's helping Gramma with some laundry and helping to peel apples for the pies she wanted to bake for tomorrow's supper.

I quickly grabbed my apron, an apple to eat on the way, hurried to the door, and left as fast as I could.

*****

"I'm *so sorry!*" I apologized as I scurried into the kitchen at Grampa and Gramma's, hastily tying my apron around my waist.

Aunt Sara was there with baby Lydia, and she and Gramma were both partway through a basket of apples.

"It all right, sweetheart," Gramma assured. "Your Papa tell us what happened. You okay now?"

"Yes, Gramma," I replied, still feeling awful that I was so late. "I feel much better, thank you. But I *really* am sorry! I should've been here hours ago!"

"Jochebed," Aunt Sara scolded, "stop fretting! It's all right! The important thing is that you're feeling better. Here," she said as she held out her knife, "you can take over for me. I have to go feed Lydia right now anyhow."

I nodded.

"Of course," I agreed, hurrying to take the knife from her. "But I *really* am sorry!"

"Stop!" Aunt Sara insisted. "It's fine, really!"

*****

I worked with Gramma and Aunt Sara for the rest of the afternoon, and when I finished, I rushed back home to start supper for Papa and Samuel. It was Wednesday, and we had church later that evening, so I needed to get things started right away so that we wouldn't be late. I hurried around preparing the meal, all the while lamenting all of the work I'd not been able to accomplish during the day due to my late start. I still couldn't believe that I'd slept in so late and lost so much time!

I kept looking at the house as I scurried about in the kitchen, noticing this mess and that. I remembered the mending I'd intended to finish and my room I'd wanted to clean, and the more I thought on it, the more aggravated with myself I became! Isaac would be home by the weekend, and I wanted to get ahead on my work so as to have extra time to spend with him. Losing most of a day was *not at all* in my plans!

As I finished up the meal, I went to the door to call Papa and Samuel in for supper. After I'd called them, I hurried into the living room to pick up a few things in there while I waited for them to come in.

When I got the things in that room taken care of, I scurried back to the kitchen and started cleaning up in there. I wasn't long started on it, however, when Papa and Samuel finally came in the house.

I left off what I was doing, joined them at the table, Papa prayed, and we all began to eat.

When we were finished, I began to clear the table, putting things away, and stacking the dishes in the sink. I worked diligently, but in my determination to get things done, I inadvertently lost track of time. Thankfully, I happened to glance at the clock but when I did, my heart sank! I hadn't much time left to get myself ready for church.

Needless to say, I abruptly stopped what I was doing, and headed straight for my room. Once there, I looked around at the mess I'd left and felt a bit dejected.

So much to do but so little time! I bemoaned.

I decided I'd not primp too long, but rather take some time to straighten up a bit. I quickly changed into my church dress, hastily fixed my hair, and immediately commenced to cleaning. I'd do what I could until Papa called me down to leave.

"Jochebed!" I heard him shout up the stairs. "Sweetheart, we need to be goin'."

I couldn't believe he was calling me already! It seemed as if only a minute had passed since I'd gotten to my room. I guess when you're busy and you really don't want it to, time simply flies by!

"Now why can't time pass like this when I want it to?" I lamented.

I quickly put away the books in my hand, grabbed my Bible, took one more hurried look at myself in the mirror and headed for the door.

"The rest will have to wait," I told myself as I frantically left the room. "I'm coming, Papa!" I yelled as I rushed towards the stairs.

The whole day had been maddeningly frenzied! It was as if I were in a race, a mile behind, and running like crazy to catch up!

While I was scurrying down the stairs, I noticed a bow on my dress that needed tying, so while precariously holding my Bible under my arm, I thought I'd attempt to tie it. Unfortunately, in my haste and distraction, I completely missed the last step at the bottom of the stairs and went screaming, careening helplessly into the wall across the way. When I hit, my Bible went flying, I bounced off, stumbled backwards, and my arms went flailing about, futilely grasping at air. Powerless to stop myself, I tripped on my dress and promptly landed with a thud on the floor.

Samuel, of course, saw the whole thing and was practically in tears, laughing at the sight.

I sat there a minute, stunned and embarrassed by my clumsiness.

Papa yelled at Samuel to stop laughing as he rushed over to help me up.

"Are ya all right?" he asked as he leaned over to grab my arm.

I could tell he was trying hard not to laugh, too.

"Yes, Papa," I answered with a shake of my head. "Just embarrassed is all."

As I stood to my feet, Papa picked up my Bible and asked again.

"You're sure ya didn't hurt anything?" he wanted to make certain.

I straightened my dress and looked myself over.

"No, I'm fine, Papa," I assured, feeling like such a klutz. "Really…I'm okay…thank you."

"If you're sure," he said, biting his lip, unable to contain his smile any longer.

I just sighed, starring at him, shaking my head as I took my Bible from him.

He started to snicker.

As we turned the corner into the kitchen, I looked up, and much to my surprise (and shock and horror) there stood Isaac looking half-concerned and half like he was about to break into laughter himself.

When the reality of the moment hit, I immediately felt all of the blood drain from my face and my heart begin to pound. I was mortified!

"It's…it's good to see you," he said, trying to keep a straight face, fighting hard to suppress his smile.

I looked at him, unsure of how to respond. I was so stunned that he was standing there, completely embarrassed by what had just happened, wishing I'd taken more time with my hair, and yet happy to see him all at the same time. It took me a minute to collect my thoughts, but I finally answered.

"It's…it's good to see you, too…I think!" I said, feeling unbelievably self-conscious.

Isaac came closer and gave me a hug, breaking out in a big grin as he did.

"I'm glad you're okay," he remarked. "And all in one piece, too!"

What could I do? I had to laugh.

"I'll have to say I'm glad to be in one piece, as well," I replied, hugging him tightly.

"Well, you two," Papa interrupted, still smiling, "I hate to break up this reunion, but we really need to get goin' or we're gonna be late."

Isaac looked down at me with a smile as he put his hand out.

"Shall we?" he offered.

I shook my head, smiling back, putting my hand in his.

What a day this had turned out to be!

SPRINGTIME SURPRISES
(Chapter 42)

"What *are* you doing here anyhow?" I questioned Isaac as we walked out and got into his buggy.

"Well, goodness," he teased. "I thought you'd be a little more excited to see me than that!"

"Oh, I...I am," I stammered. "I didn't mean...it's just that..."

"I know what you meant," Isaac chuckled. "And to answer your question, I was able to finish up early. I packed all my things up yesterday, took my last exam this morning, and decided to leave right away. I really wanted to surprise you!"

"Well, you certainly did that!" I quipped, still completely embarrassed. "I just wish I could have greeted you a bit more...well...a bit more - *properly!*"

Isaac grinned broadly.

"I wouldn't have had it any other way!" he chuckled again.

"Oh, thanks!" I said, feigning offense.

"Well, if you could've seen yourself!" he recalled, now laughing uncontrollably.

I gave him a look of consternation.

"All right, mister!" I came back at him, teasingly. "I think that's quite enough! I can walk the rest of the way if you'd like!"

He bit his cheek, trying to stop himself from laughing, but he just couldn't help it. He burst out again.

"Isaac Lewis!" I reprimanded, trying to contain a smile. "Now you stop that right now!"

"All right, all right!" he agreed, attempting to settle himself. He cleared his throat. "I'm sorry...you're right...I shouldn't laugh!" He looked straight ahead, trying his best to be serious.

"Well, now," I accepted, "that's more like it!"

I sat there, wary, keeping an eye on him, watching him bite his cheek again and then his lip. I could tell he was in agony, trying to keep himself from laughing.

We sat there in silence for a little while, but as the moments ticked by, he slowly began to let out a chuckle, and then another, until he just couldn't take it any longer! Suddenly, he exploded into raucous laughter as if the scene had just replayed itself over again in his mind.

I reached over and wacked him on the arm.

"I'm sorry! I'm sorry!" he apologized, trying to catch his breath he was laughing so hard.

I smiled at his jocularity as I shook my head, trying to maintain my composure. It was nearly impossible, though, as his laughter was just too contagious. I couldn't resist any longer! I started to laugh right along with him.

"Okay, enough!" I blurted out after several minutes of laughing so hard I was nearly doubled over.

Isaac was doing his best to stop, but he was in tears, nearly doubled over himself.

"I'm sorry," he said, rubbing his eyes, trying to keep the buggy on the road. He took a few deep breaths. "Okay...okay...I give!" he finally conceded.

Thankfully, he sobered enough that he was able to settle down. With him not laughing anymore, it was easier for me to stop as well.

"Goodness!" I remarked. "I've not laughed like that in such a long time!"

"Me either," Isaac related. "I needed it, though!"

"Me, too!" I agreed. "I've had a pretty rough time of it lately, so I have to admit, it's nice to be able to relax a little and let go for awhile."

Isaac furrowed his brow.

"A pretty rough time, huh?" he inquired, becoming a bit more serious. "How so?"

I sighed.

"Unfortunately, I had one of my dreadful headaches again, yesterday," I explained. "I got terribly sick and ended up sleeping half the day away today."

Isaac shook his head sympathetically.

"I'm really sorry to hear that, Jochebed," he told me, feeling badly for me. He sounded a bit worried and concerned. "Have you had a lot of them...I mean...severe ones?" he wanted to know.

"Fortunately, no," I answered. "That's the first one I've had in a long time." I hung my head as I began to fidget. "I'll...I'll admit it does have me worried, though," I confessed. "As terrible as it was, I'm afraid..."

"Now don't go borrowing trouble!" Isaac gently admonished.

"I know," I countered, trying to defend myself, "but it was *so* awful! I haven't felt that miserable in a *very long* time! I really thought my worst headaches were behind me, but..." I shook my head, distressed. "It scares me, Isaac!" I told him with angst. "I'm so afraid that maybe..."

"Maybe what?" Isaac pressed.

I could tell by his tone that he was disappointed that I was worrying again.

I reluctantly answered.

"Well," I hemmed and hawed, "I'm...I'm afraid that maybe..." I shook my head again, hesitant to say. "I'm afraid that maybe they're starting up again!" I finally blurted out.

Isaac's shoulders drooped.

"Jochebed," he started in.

"I know, I know!" I interrupted abruptly, somewhat angrily. "Don't go borrowing trouble!" I sighed. "It's just that..." I paused, so upset and aggravated with myself. "I guess sometimes I just wish I could have that day back again!" I divulged with a tinge of bitterness. "I wish I had *never* gone out in that terrible storm!"

Isaac let out a sympathetic sigh as he put his arm around me, squeezing me tightly.

"I know," he relayed sweetly. "I understand."

I laid my head on his shoulder as he held me close.

"Jochebed," he went on to say, "I know we've talked about this before, and I know it's still hard to understand, but I believe with all of my heart that God will continue to use this in your life...somehow, someway. Now, please don't misunderstand me," he was quick to add. "I'm not saying I want you to suffer one more headache, because I don't...that's not at all what I mean! It's just that...well...I know that God can take these trials, even your mistakes, and somehow use them for good."

I let out another sigh.

"I know," I lamented. "And I'm sorry. I guess sometimes I just get so tired of hurting. I just want so badly to be normal again!"

Isaac hugged me even tighter as if to say he understood.

I was so thankful he was there for me.

*****

When we arrived at church, everyone was thrilled to see Isaac again, and Pastor Scott even asked him to close the service in prayer. As you can imagine, I was so very proud of him and so happy that he was finally home. Despite my headaches and my worries, I was looking forward to the time I'd be able to spend with him over the summer.

"Will you meet me tomorrow?" Isaac asked as he helped me out of the buggy after driving me home from church.

"Of course, I will!" I replied enthusiastically. "When and where would you like to meet?"

"I'll pick you up in the morning," he said as we walked up onto the porch. "Ten o'clock sharp, if that's okay?"

I could tell by the tone of his voice that he was up to something, but I didn't know what.

"As far as I know, that should be fine," I answered, a little curious. "What do you have planned?"

"Nope!" he refused to tell me as he turned his head, smiling. "That's for me to know and for you to find out!"

I looked at him suspiciously.

"All right, then," I hesitantly agreed, trying to figure out what he was up to. "I guess...I guess I'll see you tomorrow then."

"Great!" he exclaimed excitedly. "I can't wait!" He was grinning from ear to ear as he tipped his hat to say goodnight. "I'll be counting the hours, my lady!" he announced courteously.

I smiled back, my heart so filled with love for this most wonderful man!

He stepped off the porch and headed for his buggy and as he climbed aboard, he waved and yelled out that he loved me.

I waved back as I returned the sentiment.

As he drove away, I stood there smiling, overwhelmed! He was just so amazing and so incredibly thoughtful. I absolutely *loved* when he had surprises planned for us! Morning couldn't come soon enough!

*****

When I woke up the next day, I woke to Samuel pounding on my bedroom door.

"Jochebed!" he was shouting. "Are ya ever gonna wake up?"

I rolled over and rubbed the sleep from my eyes, yawning as I groggily sat up. The sun was already streaming through my window, so I instantly knew that I was late yet again!

I quickly jumped out of bed and rushed to the door.

"Samuel!" I questioned anxiously as I opened it up, disgusted with myself that I'd overslept again. "What time is it now?"

Samuel chuckled.

"It's not all *that* late!" he teased. "Just eight o'clock is all."

"Eight o'clock?!?" I snapped back. "Samuel, that's late enough! You *know* I never sleep in this late!"

He shrugged his shoulders.

347

"Sorry," he retorted as he followed me back into the room, "I just figured you were havin' one of your headaches again. Papa left for town as soon as I got up, so...well...I didn't think to wake ya."

"Well, you woke me up *now!*" I groused angrily, hurriedly getting a dress from my closet. "What's so *magical* about eight o'clock?"

Samuel meandered over and plopped himself down on my unmade bed.

"I was *starvin'!*" he revealed, sounding desperate and almost as if he thought I should have known. "I need somethin' to eat!"

I abruptly stopped what I was doing, absolutely astounded by his admission. I turned with furrowed brow and looked at him in utter amazement.

"You mean to tell me that you couldn't have managed a breakfast for yourself, on your own, by *now?*" I said, aghast. "Good grief, Samuel! How old are you anyhow?"

Samuel looked at me deviously.

"Well...yah...I could have...but..." he smiled broadly. "Yours are just *better!*"

I shook my head in incredulity.

"Would you *please* just leave now so that I can get dressed?" I insisted forcefully, pointing to the door.

"All right, all right," Samuel chuckled, as he stood to his feet. "But could ya hurry? I'm *famished!*"

I was so annoyed by his impertinence that I threw my dress at him as he walked towards the door.

Naturally, he gave me a disgusted look and let the dress fall to the floor.

"Ha!" he laughed as he walked on out. As he stepped out into the hallway, he turned around, stuck his tongue out at me, and promptly closed the door.

I rolled my eyes and sighed as I walked over to retrieve my dress.

"Brothers!" I whispered under my breath as I leaned down to pick it up. "Good grief!"

I quickly got myself dressed, made my bed, and headed downstairs to make Samuel something to eat. When I got to the kitchen to ask him what he wanted, he, of course, was nowhere to be found.

Probably outside shooting his gun or in the barn messing around, I surmised. I ignored his absence and went to preparing.

I was in the middle of making his breakfast when all of a sudden there was a knock at the door. My heart instantly skipped a beat at the sound. Even though it had been months since the man in the hat had attacked me, I still got a sinking feeling every time I heard someone knocking on the door - especially when I was in the house all alone. I took a deep breath and glanced at the clock. There was still an hour to go before Isaac was to pick me up, so I knew it wouldn't be him. Feeling I had no choice, I hesitantly walked towards the door to see who was there.

As I got closer, I could hear voices talking back and forth, so I paused a minute to see if I could recognize them. Unfortunately, I didn't, but given past experience, I went to the window to check first before opening the door.

When I looked out, there was a man standing on the porch saying something to a woman sitting in a wagon. I had no idea who they were, but I decided they looked harmless enough, so I went to the door and opened it up.

"May I help you?" I asked, cracking the door just a little, still leery about the situation.

The man turned back around from talking to the woman and stepped forward a bit.

"Oh, good morning," he said very politely, tipping his hat. "My name's Evan Deerfield, and that's my wife, Alicia. I was hoping maybe you could help us."

I opened the door a little wider, not wanting to appear rude but still staying inside out of caution.

"Oh," I queried. "What do you need?"

"Well," the man explained, "it would appear that we're a bit lost. I'm looking for the Lowry house. Do you know where I might find it?"

"Umm," I answered, a bit puzzled, "you *have* found it! We *are* the Lowrys!"

"You are?" the man questioned, looking rather confused.

"Yes, sir," I assured him, unsure of what to make of his response.

We both just stood there a minute looking at each other quite perplexed.

Finally, he removed his hat and scratched his head.

"*This* is the Lowry place?" he asked again.

"Yes, sir!" I reiterated assuredly.

"Well, then," he commented, looking terribly bewildered, "I apologize. I thought for sure Mark said he and Sara lived alone in a one story house, just the two of them, with their daughter Lydia."

"*Oh!*" I exclaimed, realizing the misunderstanding. "You're looking for my Uncle Mark and Aunt Sara's place."

"Yes!" the man readily confirmed. "And...who might you be?"

"I'm Jochebed Lowry," I explained. "My Papa is Uncle Mark's older brother."

The man smiled with a nod.

"Well, that would explain it, then," he said, chuckling as everything began to fall into place. "What a small world!"

I stepped out onto the porch, feeling a bit more at ease, and pointed down the road.

"They live just on down there a ways," I told him. "If you keep driving about a half mile or so, you'll see a little house on the right. That's my Grampa and Gramma Lowry's place and my Uncle Mark and Aunt Sara live just behind them. Their house will be down the first long lane you come to."

"Well, thank you kindly, ma'am," the man replied. "It was nice to meet you."

"You, too!" I agreed with a smile. "But...if you don't mind me asking, how do you know my Uncle Mark?"

"Oh, I'm sorry," the man answered. "Where are my manners? My wife, Alicia there, she's Sara's sister. We're here to surprise Mark and Sara with a visit and to see that new baby of theirs."

"Oh my!" I exclaimed, looking out to the woman, suddenly recalling who she was. "That's right! I recognize her now! It's been so long since I've last seen her!" I smiled broadly, so excited for Aunt Sara. "Oh, I just know my Aunt Sara's going to be so happy to see you two!"

"And we her," the man replied as he stepped down off the porch. "Thanks again for your help," he called out as he hurried to his wagon and climbed aboard.

"You're welcome!" I shouted back as he went.

They both waved in appreciation as they drove off, and once they were gone, I went back inside the house to finish breakfast.

About that time, Samuel came walking out of the barn and ran up to the house.

"Who was that?" he inquired as he came inside.

"That was Mr. and Mrs. Deerfield, Aunt Sara's sister, and her husband," I answered excitedly. "They came to surprise her with a visit. Isn't that just *wonderful?*"

Samuel shrugged his shoulders.

"Yah, I guess so," he answered, completely indifferent. "Breakfast ready yet? I'm *starved!*"

"Oh, Samuel!" I complained, giving up hope for him. "You simply have no sense of what's important!"

"Sure I do!" he shot back, as he pulled out a chair at the table and sat down. "It's food, and I'd like some soon, please!"

I sighed heavily as I shook my head walking over to the table.

"Here!" I said as I placed a plate of bacon, eggs, and biscuits down in front of him. "Enjoy!"

"Now that's more like it!" he exclaimed, grinning from ear to ear, rubbing his hands together in anticipation.

He was just about to dig in when I yelled at him.

"Stop!" I shouted insistently. "Not before you wash those filthy hands of yours!"

Samuel looked up at me with a chagrinned look on his face.

"Go!" I adamantly persisted, pointing in the direction of the wash room.

"It's my dirt, and my mouth!" Samuel complained loudly. "What do *you* care?"

"You'll care when I take your food away!" I threatened. "Now go!"

Samuel rolled his eyes, clearly aggravated.

"Fine!" he groused as he got up from the table. He instantly started mumbling under his breath as he meandered towards the washroom. "It's *my meal!*" he grumbled. "Don't see what difference it makes to *you* if I want to eat with a little extra dirt on my hands...*bossy!*"

"I'm standing right here, Samuel!" I pointed out, shaking my head, hands raised in consternation. "I *can* hear you you know!"

He walked on not saying another word.

I sighed again, shaking my head as I went on to clean up in the kitchen.

Samuel soon returned and began to eat his breakfast.

When I was finished with what I was doing, I decided I'd better go and get ready before Isaac arrived. I quickly ran to my room, changed my clothes, fixed my hair, and sprayed some of Mama's perfume on me. I fidgeted a bit with this and that, and then it was time to go.

I carefully made my way downstairs and walked to the kitchen to wait as I expected Isaac to arrive at any minute.

Samuel had already finished his meal and was off outside again (doing what I don't know), so I took care of his dishes, straightened a few more things in the kitchen, and then went to the door to call for Samuel.

"Samuel!" I yelled out as I opened the door. I got no response. "Samuel!" I shouted again even louder as I stepped out onto the porch. "Where are you?"

Finally, the door to the barn opened, and Samuel came walking out.

"Yah!" he yelled back, wiping his hand with a rag. "What do ya want?"

"Isaac will be here to pick me up any minute now," I informed him. "When did Papa say he'd be home?"

"He didn't!" Samuel informed, half distracted. "Said he had a job to do in town for the Ansell sisters. Said it might take all day. Why?"

I walked to the edge of the porch.

"Because, I don't think you should be here all alone," I told him.

"Oh, good grief!" Samuel derided, rolling his eyes, as he walked towards me, arguing his side. "I've stayed home *plenty* of times before by myself!"

"Yes," I acknowledged, "but not for very long, and *certainly not* without Papa's permission! I think it'd be best if you go spend the day at Grampa and Gramma's. I don't know how long I'll be gone with Isaac, and I'd feel much better knowing you weren't here all by yourself."

Samuel came walking on up to the porch.

"Ya worry too much!" he indicted, perturbed. "I can handle things here by myself. Stop treatin' me like a little baby! I'm twelve years old - remember!? Besides, you'll probably be back before Papa gets home anyhow, so stop worryin'! I'll be fine!"

"I know you'll be fine," I insisted, pointing at the house, growing ever more agitated at his attitude, "because you'll be at Grampa and Gramma's! Now get in there and get a jacket so you'll be ready when Isaac arrives!"

"No way!" Samuel protested. "Ya can't make that decision!" He threw up his hands, infuriated. "Are ya hard of hearin' or somthin'?" he shouted. "I'm not a little baby anymore! I can stay by myself!"

By now I was fuming!

"This is *not* up for discussion, Samuel!" I stipulated angrily. "If you can get permission from Papa to stay here alone, then fine, but until then, I'm taking you to Grampa and Gramma's, and that's *final!*"

Samuel was having none of it! He stormed up onto the porch and got right up in my face.

"Papa's in town!" he raged. "Ya *know* I have no way of gettin' his permission! That's not fair!"

"Well, I'm sorry, Samuel!" I came back at him, bristling from his outburst. "Maybe you should've thought about that before he left! Now please, go get your jacket!"

He stood there seething, scowling at me, absolutely incensed!

I didn't flinch, though; instead, I stood my ground, staring back at him, hands on my hips, adamant!

Finally conceding, knowing he was whipped, he shook his head vehemently, let out a huff, and angrily tossed the rag he was holding down on the ground. Clenching his jaw, he stomped his foot, and turned abruptly to go inside. He furiously threw open the door, went on in, and slammed the door hard behind him, nearly shaking the entire house.

I sighed, disheartened, as I stood there on the porch by myself.

I have to admit, I did feel a little sorry for Samuel as Papa and I had failed to work out the details for the day, and now he was caught in the middle. Deep down I knew he was old enough to be at home alone, but I didn't have Papa's permission, and I didn't feel it was my place to make the decision myself. I hoped Samuel would understand.

I went and sat down on the porch swing and waited for both Samuel and Isaac. I'd only been sitting there for a minute or two, however, when Samuel came tearing out of the house. He had no jacket, but he did have his gun. He immediately jumped down off the porch, heading where, I had no idea! Frustrated with his obstinacy, I stood up and yelled after him.

"Samuel Michael!" I shouted. "Where do you think you're going?"

"None of your business!" he shouted back.

"Samuel, you get back here right now!" I demanded angrily, clenching my fists as I stepped to the edge of the porch.

Samuel intentionally ignored me and kept right on walking.

My face was red with fury as I watched him disappear into the barn, willingly defying my commands!

Just then, Isaac pulled up.

"Morning," he said as he slowed his horse to a stop. He jumped down off his buggy and headed towards the porch. "Whoa!" he commented as soon as he saw my face. "What's wrong?"

I furiously gathered my dress and walked down the steps.

"Samuel!" I blurted out tersely, completely at my whit's end at this point. "He's being simply *incorrigible!*"

Isaac walked up to me, meeting me halfway.

"Now I doubt it's all that bad," he offered, trying to calm me.

I shot him a look indicating the contrary.

"Okay!" he surrendered with a chuckle. "Maybe I'm wrong. Maybe it *is* that bad! What's going on?"

I shook my head.

"Oh, Isaac!" I lamented, absolutely at a loss as to what to do. "He's ruining our day with his stubbornness!"

"And how is he doing that?" Isaac questioned.

"He's refusing to go to Grampa and Gramma's," I explained. "Papa isn't home, and I'm afraid to leave him here all by himself. Papa didn't give his permission and…"

"Say no more," Isaac said, looking out to the barn. "Let me go talk to him."

"Huh! I wish you well with that!" I quipped cynically, not expecting much as he began to walk towards the barn.

He smiled back at me as if to say, *O ye of little faith.*

I shook my head and went back to the swing to wait.

Isaac opened the door to the barn and walked inside.

"So…what's going on, Sam?" he asked, as he walked over to him. "Your sister tells me you don't want to go to your grandparents today."

Samuel was standing at Papa's bench cleaning his gun. He was still so upset and angry, he didn't even bother to look up before responding.

"Humph!" he reacted annoyed. "I see she sent ya in here to get me, huh!? - *Ridiculous!*"

"No," Isaac corrected, "I volunteered to come and talk to you. I just want to know, why the reluctance to go to your grandparents?"

Samuel kept cleaning his gun, answering crossly.

"I'm tired of bein' treated like a little baby!" he barked. "I've stayed at home *plenty* of times before by myself! I don't know what she's so worried about. *It's absurd!* Besides," he continued to argue, "I have a gun now, and I know *perfectly well* how to use it! She worries for *nothin'!* I mean, seriously…what's gonna happen to me? *Not a thing!"* He paused as he looked over at Isaac. "No offense," he said in a very disrespectful tone, "but I don't need my *bossy* 'ol sister tellin' me what to do anymore! She needs to *mind her own business* and *leave me alone!"* He promptly went back to cleaning his gun.

Isaac took a deep breath, trying to keep his composure. Stepping a little closer to Samuel, he did his best to respond as calmly as he could.

"Well, Samuel," he replied, "I have to be honest with you, I do take offense! While I *can* understand your frustration with the situation, I don't think how you're handling it is right. Your sister's not trying to be bossy; she just loves you and wants to make sure you'll be safe."

"But I…" Samuel tried to interrupt.

Isaac didn't let him.

"Samuel," he kept right on going, "a mark of maturity is being able to submit to the authority in your life, whether you always agree with it or not. I'm sure if your sister knew that your father was okay with you being here alone today, all day, she'd have no problem with it, but she doesn't want the responsibility of making that decision, a decision she really has no authority to make, anyhow."

Samuel let out a huff as he shook his head, adamantly disagreeing.

Isaac ignored his impertinence and went on talking.

"And another thing," he added, "you need to be willing to take into consideration everything your sister's gone through this past year." Isaac leaned against the table. "Sam," he reminded, "she was attacked in her own home by a vicious, evil man, and the crazy thing is…she *wasn't even alone at the time!* Her fear comes from a reality that you and I can't fully appreciate." He sighed. "You have to understand…that traumatic experience, well…it changed her, and…" He paused, somewhat conceding. "Ok," he granted, "maybe you're right, maybe she's more cautious now than she was before, and maybe too much so, but it's only because she cares about you. You need to be willing to see the bigger picture in all of this. It's more than just a sister trying to keep her brother from staying home by himself."

Isaac paused again as he put his hand on Samuel's shoulder.

"I know it isn't easy, Sam," he acknowledged, "but…I guess what I'm asking you to do here is, be mature…be mature enough to recognize that you'll have plenty of days in the future to stay home alone. Today, be willing to put yourself aside and consider your sister. Can you do that for me?"

Samuel stood there listening, clearly still bothered, but starting to soften a bit. He sighed, reluctantly capitulating.

"Yah, all right," he relented. "I guess I can see your point." He shook his head begrudgingly. "Still doesn't mean I have to like it, though!"

Isaac nodded as he patted Samuel on the back.

"Thanks, Sam," he appreciated. "You're doing the right thing."

Samuel sighed again as he grabbed up his gun, visibly less than thrilled with the situation.

He and Isaac walked to the door.

I stood up as soon as I saw them exit the barn.

Isaac was walking a few steps behind Samuel who still looked rather upset but nonetheless compliant.

I looked at Isaac questioning, unsure of what to think.

He shot me a smile as if to say, *Everything's fine!*

Samuel walked straight to the buggy and belligerently climbed aboard. It was obvious he was not at all happy, but he did appear ready to go. I immediately ran inside to get his jacket for him, and as soon I had it in hand, I locked up, and hurried on to the buggy. I climbed in beside Isaac, and quickly glanced back at Samuel. Unfortunately, he was sitting there with his head down, brooding, clearly not wanting to be bothered. I looked over at Isaac and sighed, concerned.

Isaac just smiled back as he told the horse to get-up, and with that we were off to Grampa and Gramma's.

As we were going, I felt I needed to thank Samuel for his acquiescence. Turning partway to face him, I addressed him with reserve.

"Thank you, Samuel," I said, grateful. "I really do appreciate what you're doing."

He never looked up nor acknowledged me, and it made me feel quite awful, but I guess I could understand his reluctance. I just hoped he wouldn't stay angry with me for very long. Despite his negative reaction, though, I truly was glad the issue had been resolved, at least for now. He would be spending the day with Grampa and Gramma, and I could rest easy knowing he wouldn't be left alone.

When we pulled up to their house, Samuel immediately jumped out and ran to the back lot, not even going inside to say hello. I wanted to go after him, but Isaac advised against it. He said I should just leave him alone, and let him be. Reluctantly, I accepted it, and did as he asked.

Isaac got out himself and came around to assist me out of the buggy. He sweetly took hold of my hand and helped to lower me down. When I was clear, we made our way inside to inform Grampa and Gramma that Samuel would be spending the day with them.

As soon as we stepped inside, however, we were met with a pleasant surprise. Aunt Sara, Uncle Mark, and Mr. and Mrs. Deerfield were all sitting in the family room, visiting with Grampa and Gramma.

"Well, I'll be!" Grampa expressed with delight. "Look who we have here! Come on in, you two. It's good to see ya!"

Isaac and I walked on into the family room and said hello. I introduced Isaac to Aunt Sara's sister and her husband, told Grampa and Gramma about Samuel, and then explained that Isaac and I had plans for the day and that we couldn't stay long.

Everyone was gracious, and seemed to understand.

We visited briefly, readied to leave, and just before we did, Gramma invited us to join them later on that evening for supper. We accepted the invitation, said our goodbyes, and left.

While we were driving away, Isaac inquired about Aunt Sara's sister.

"Is that your Aunt Sara's older or younger sister?" he asked, wondering.

"She's younger," I informed him, "about two or three years…I think. Anyway, they've always been extremely close, and I truly think that was one of the hardest things on Aunt Sara when Uncle Mark moved them here from North Dakota, having to leave her sister behind."

Isaac nodded, seeming to appreciate the situation.

"Makes perfect sense to me!" he stated with empathy. "I can see were that would be very difficult. I know it would be hard on me if I had to be away from Andrew for any extended period of time." He shrugged. "It's hard enough, me just being away at college for as long as I am. He and I have always been close, especially after our parents died, so…yah…I can't *imagine* us having to be apart permanently!"

I put my arm through his as I scooted a little closer.

"I guess sometimes I envy that kind of closeness," I confessed. "I often wish that Samuel and I were closer than we are, but he doesn't seem much interested in a relationship with his 'much older' sister." I paused. "Anyway," I went on, "I'm just glad Aunt Sara gets to spend some time with her sister now."

"Me too!" Isaac agreed with a nod.

I hugged his arm tightly as I smiled up at him.

"So," I prodded curiously, "what are we up to today?"

Isaac just smiled.

"You'll see soon enough!" he replied evasively.

*****

Thankfully, the day was turning out to be an absolutely beautiful one. The sun was shining brightly, the birds were chirping playfully, and there was a slight but refreshing breeze in the air. Isaac and I drove on a little ways, and after awhile, we finally arrived at his grandparents' place.

Pulling right up to the house, barely able to contain his excitement, Isaac promptly jumped down off the buggy.

"Stay here!" he instructed as he smiled excitedly and ran on into the house.

"Okay," I replied, chuckling at his boyish enthusiasm.

After a few minutes, Isaac emerged from the house carrying a picnic basket. He quickly ran around to my side of the buggy, extended his hand, and helped me down.

"Come with me!" he invited eagerly, flashing the biggest grin.

Again, I chuckled at his zeal.

"All right!" I happily agreed, smiling in anticipation.

He squeezed my hand tightly, and whisked me away.

"I want to show you something!" he revealed as we hurried along.

I held my dress so as not to stumble, trying to keep up with his pace. I'd never seen him so excited or energized before. It was as if he were a restless schoolchild again, antsy for Christmas morning to arrive! I couldn't *wait* to see what he had to show me!

We walked quite a ways to the very back of his property, down a steep hill, and across a tiny stream. Just as we crossed through the water, Isaac abruptly stopped.

"Now close your eyes," he told me.

"What?" I laughed. "How am I going to see where I'm going?"

"Just close your eyes!" he urged. "Hold tightly to my hand, and I'll lead you. You trust me, don't you?"

"Well, of course I do, silly," I told him, "but…"

"Well then," he said, squeezing my hand, "let's go!"

I looked at him warily and reluctantly closed my eyes.

"No peeking, now!" he insisted.

"All right," I agreed, closing my eyes even tighter. "No peeking!" I held tightly to his hand as he slowly and carefully led me along.

We walked a good distance further, and then suddenly, we came to a stop.

"Okay," he said as he stood there beside me, "now…open your eyes!"

I did as he said, and when my eyes were opened, I couldn't believe what was there in front of me. It was the most beautiful rose garden I had ever seen!

"Oh, Isaac!" I exclaimed. "It's…it's *amazing!* Whenever did you find this?"

"My grandparents, Andrew, and I put it in a few years ago," Isaac explained. "We've been cultivating and expanding it ever since. I've been dying to show it to you forever, but I wanted to wait until the roses were in bloom so you could appreciate the full beauty of it."

I stood there in absolute awe!

"Well," I remarked, searching for just the right words to express how I was feeling, "it's...it's *gorgeous*...just...just *extraordinarily breathtaking!*"

Isaac smiled, pleased, as he went on.

"I think this is my absolute, most favorite place in the whole world to be!" he shared. "It reminds me of the beauty and wonder and magnificence of God!" He took my hand and began to guide me along.

As I looked around, I was astounded at the sheer beauty! There were so many different colors, and the wonderful aroma...my goodness...it was overwhelming! There were so many winding paths to walk down, and even a gazebo in the distance. It was truly a remarkable place!

"You know," Isaac commented as we continued to walk, "I used to think this garden was just about perfect, but...seeing you here, with all of *your* beauty...well...now I *know* it is!"

I looked away, blushing, completely embarrassed by his kind remarks.

"Oh, Isaac!" I professed, placing my hand to my chest, my heart aflutter. "You're simply too much!"

Isaac smiled lovingly as he stopped and plucked a pink rose from one of the bushes and carefully placed it in my hair.

"A beautiful rose for *my* beautiful rose!" he complimented so sweetly.

I couldn't help but blush again! I shook my head as I looked at him, overwhelmed by the love I felt for him in that moment.

"Thank you so much for sharing this with me, Isaac," I expressed with such gratitude. "It truly is *unbelievably* amazing!" I looked around before gazing back into his gorgeous blue eyes. "I could easily spend the rest of the day here with you!" I confessed, my heart completely full.

"Me too!" Isaac agreed as he took hold of my hand once again. He led me on to the gazebo where he and I shared a lunch and talked and laughed together for hours.

It was such a wonderful, beautiful surprise...something I would cherish...always!

THE FITTING
(Chapter 43)

After spending a lovely day together, as much as we hated to, Isaac and I decided that we needed to get going in order to be able to join everyone for supper later on. We picked up our things and headed for his house, needing to take care of a few things there, first.

When we got to the house and stepped inside, we were greeted with a wonderful surprise. Andrew and Isabelle were there finishing up some final details for their upcoming wedding that was to take place on the following Saturday, the last day in May. They were there at the dining room table with Mrs. Lewis - books, paper, and material scattered everywhere, trying to figure things out.

I could tell by the look on Isabelle's face that she was quite frazzled by it all.

"How's everything going, little brother?" Isaac asked as we walked into the room.

Andrew smiled hesitantly.

"Maybe you should ask Isabelle that question," he suggested.

Isaac flashed a grin.

"Gracious!" Isabelle exclaimed, exhausted, "I never knew getting married was so much *work!* I just hope everything comes together in time!"

"It will, my dear," Mrs. Lewis encouraged. "It will be a grand day, and you will make a *beautiful* bride!"

Isabelle smiled, touched by the compliment.

"That's sweet, Mrs. Lewis," she replied demurely. "Thank you!" Isabelle sighed, overwhelmed. "I'll just be glad when the day arrives!" she stated with earnest.

Andrew lovingly leaned down, put his arms around her, and gave her a reassuring hug.

She patted his arms and smiled up at him, appreciative of his support.

Isaac and I visited briefly with them, but then we were off to Grampa and Gramma's for supper. Time was quickly slipping away from us, and we didn't want to be late.

As we went, I expressed to Isaac how much I was looking forward to getting to know Aunt Sara's sister and her husband a little better while they were here with us. I relayed again how it was such a nice surprise that they had come all the way from North Dakota to visit, and how thrilled I was for Aunt Sara that she could have her sister around her once again.

Isaac nodded, heartily agreeing.

When we finally arrived at Grampa and Gramma's, it was already time for supper. Gramma and Aunt Sara were just putting the last of the meal on the table, and everyone was gathering around. Thankfully, Papa had finished up his job in town, and was able to join us, too.

We all had such a wonderful time of fellowship together, and as was always the case, the meal was simply superb!

Mr. and Mrs. Deerfield were such a sweet couple, and I was glad that they could be here with us for awhile. It was intriguing hearing about their lives back in North Dakota, and listening to Aunt Sara and Uncle Mark banter back and forth with them about the things they all used to do together when Aunt Sara and Uncle Mark lived there as well. It was obvious that they all missed each other terribly.

As I observed Aunt Sara and her sister, it was absolutely uncanny the similarities between the two of them. One thing I noticed right away was that they shared so many of the same mannerisms, and that they sounded an awful lot alike, too! Sometimes, if you weren't looking and one of them was talking, it was hard to tell exactly which one was doing the speaking. It was just fascinating to watch them, to see the two of them interacting with each other. You could tell by their words and their actions that they loved each other very much, and that they were very, very close. It was evident that Aunt Sara was overjoyed to have her little sister back with her again.

"So, how long do ya think you'll be stayin'?" Papa asked.

"Not sure," Evan replied. "We thought maybe a week or so…that is, if Sara and Mark can stand us for that long."

"Of course, we can!" Aunt Sara chimed in enthusiastically. "I wish you two could stay here forever!"

Aunt Sara and her sister smiled longingly at each other.

"It's more like if y'all can put up with *us!*" Uncle Mark teased. "Now that we have a cryin' baby at night, ya might find ya wanna leave a lot sooner!"

"Oh, Mark!" Aunt Sara rebuked, hitting him on the arm. "Lydia's a *good baby*, and you *know it!*"

"I know she is," Uncle Mark agreed, chuckling at her consternation. "But it doesn't mean she never cries. They're not used to havin' a cryin' baby wake 'em in the middle of the night. They might not take too kindly to it for very long."

Alicia looked at Aunt Sara, grinning from ear to ear.

"Weeelll," she said coyly.

"What!?" Aunt Sara exclaimed, ecstatic. "You mean…"

Alicia nodded, as her smile grew even bigger.

"Oh my goodness!" Aunt Sara squealed with delight. "I can't believe it!"

Alicia leaned over and hugged Aunt Sara.

"When? How long? When are you due?" Aunt Sara quizzed her.

"Well, I'm only a month along," she explained, "so I have a ways to go, but I just couldn't *wait* to tell you! That's one of the reasons why we came. I just *had* to tell you in person!"

Aunt Sara and Alicia hugged again, and everyone gave their congratulations.

Needless to say, Evan and Alicia were beaming, as was Aunt Sara.

It was wonderful news, and a perfect ending to an already perfect day!

*****

When the evening came to a close, Isaac happily drove me home, and Samuel came along with Papa. Thankfully, Samuel seemed like he'd come around a bit, and had actually enjoyed the evening.

When we got to the house, Isaac walked me to the door and reminded me that he'd pick me up in the morning around eleven so that we could go for our final fittings, as he and I were both to be a part of Andrew and Isabelle's wedding. I told him that I was looking forward to it, we both said I love you to each other, and Isaac left.

*****

The next morning, I actually woke up early, not because I had necessarily planned to, but because my head was hurting again something awful. I immediately got up and went to the kitchen to take my medicine, hoping it would help, as I didn't want my headache to get in the way of my fitting. Isabelle and Andrew had graciously asked me to be a part of their wedding, and I didn't want to do anything to jeopardize that.

Papa was at home today working in the barn, and Samuel was off with a friend, so while they were out, I went about trying to do some of my chores, wanting to get something done before I had to leave.

Regrettably, though, I didn't get much accomplished as the medicine I'd taken earlier wasn't helping, and my pain was gradually getting worse. Too, as the morning wore on, I began to feel sick to my stomach and rather tired. Knowing I still had a couple of hours left before Isaac was to pick me up, I decided to lie down on the couch in the living room for a little while, hoping a short nap would help me recover. I felt certain I could rest for a bit and still have time to get ready before he arrived.

Given my present state, it took me no time at all to fall asleep. Unfortunately, I'd greatly underestimated the severity of my condition, and ended up sleeping way longer than I had intended. Before I knew it, I was being startled awake by a knock at the door.

Sitting straight up on the couch, still groggy and tired, I tried to get my bearings. It took me a minute, but once I shook off the haze, I slowly started to get up from the couch. Lamentably, as soon as I stood up, I was instantly reminded as to why I had laid down in the first place. My headache was still there! As you can imagine, my heart immediately sank for what I knew it meant. There was no doubt this headache was a severe one, and it would likely not be going away any time soon!

Wearily and painfully, I made my way to the door to see who was there, and when I opened it up, much to my surprise, there stood Isaac. He was clearly confused, and a bit startled by my disheveled appearance.

He frowned, concerned.

"Are you all right?" he asked.

"Oh, Isaac!" I exclaimed, nearly beside myself, realizing what his presence likely meant. "Is it eleven o'clock *already?*"

"No," he replied, "not quite but almost. I take it you forgot?"

"No!" I assured him in a panic as I motioned for him to come inside. "I have a very bad headache, and I fell asleep on the couch. I'm *so* sorry! I'd only intended to sleep for a short while, but…I guess my headache was much worse than I thought. I'll go right now and get changed!"

"Jochebed," Isaac questioned as he reached out and took hold of my arm, "are you sure you'll be okay to go?"

I sighed as I struggled with the pain.

"All I can say is I'll try," I told him. "I don't want to be the cause of things not going right for Isabelle and Andrew."

"But, Jochebed," Isaac stressed, "I'm sure they can fit you another day. After all, the wedding isn't for another whole week."

"No!" I came back at him, perturbed (although not at him, but rather at my situation). "I want to go! Isabelle is *so* busy and still has *so* much to do! *This* is the day she scheduled to do the fittings, and I don't want my *lousy headaches* messing that up!" I shook my head, aggravated. "She was kind enough to ask me to be in her wedding," I pointed out, "and I'm determined not to make her regret that decision!"

By now, I was practically in tears out of frustration and pain. Unfortunately, it hadn't been quite long enough for me to take another dose of medicine, or believe me, I would have!

No, sadly, I would just have to wait this out, hoping my pain would subside on its own. I was unbelievably angry, though, so tired of my headaches getting in the way of *everything!* I just wanted so desperately to be normal again!

"I know I'm damaged and broken," I started to break down, "but still I…"

Isaac came close and gave me a hug.

"You're not damaged or broken," he tried to comfort.

I fought my tears as I looked up at him, distraught.

"But it feels that way!" I cried as a tear trickled down my face.

"I know," he commiserated. "But we'll get through this. We will!" He hugged me tightly as I hugged him back.

I sniffed and wiped a tear and then another.

"I should go get changed," I said, putting my hand to my head, closing my eyes, still struggling.

Isaac sighed, very uneasy with the whole thing as he looked at me with angst. I could tell he didn't want me to go, but I was stubborn and determined. I was going to the fitting, headache or not!

Much to Isaac's chagrin, I carefully made my way upstairs and changed into another dress. My head was pounding and I felt terrible, but I pressed on anyway. I quickly fixed my hair the best I could (trying not to tug too hard as it hurt my head even worse), took one last look at myself in the mirror, straightened a hair pin, and when I felt I could, I lethargically made my way downstairs to where Isaac was waiting.

"Oh, Jochebed!" Isaac lamented upon seeing me. "Look at you! You can barely walk you're in so much pain! This is just silly! You should be in bed, not going to a fitting!"

I appreciated his concern, but I was hearing none of it!

"I'm going, Isaac!" I insisted. "I'm sure I'll be fine! Please…let's just go!"

Isaac sighed, more than a little frustrated, as he gave me a look of disapproval.

"Has anyone ever told you that you can be *downright stubborn* sometimes?" he rightly charged.

I shot him a look that could kill, clearly indicating that that was *not* the thing to say to me in my condition!

"Ooookay!" he quipped, a bit taken aback. "I guess that'd be a yes!"

I glared at him, sighing, *so* not in the mood!

He hesitantly took my arm and helped me outside to his buggy.

After I climbed aboard, I sat there in pain, waiting, while Isaac went to let Papa know that we were leaving.

When he returned, I had my face in my hands with my eyes closed, taking deep breaths, trying to cope.

"Jochebed," Isaac started to say.

"Just go!" I abruptly cut him off.

He let out a huge sigh and reluctantly complied.

Not two minutes down the road, I was already beginning to regret my stubborn decision. The ride in the buggy was just about all I could take! The jostling and the jarring were killing my head, and I was desperately trying not to get sick as my stomach was tossing and turning! I knew Isaac was trying his best to be as careful as he could be as he drove, but the road was just too rough and I felt every rock and every dip, every bump and every jolt. I sat there in total silence, rubbing my forehead, clenching my jaws, eyes closed, praying the whole time that my pain would go away soon!

Recognizing that I was in utter misery, Isaac didn't say a word to me all the way into town.

As we were nearing Isabelle's home, where we were to try on the clothes that she and her mother and her two sisters had made for the wedding party, I was so ill I could barely move!

Mercilessly, I began to scold myself, suddenly realizing that in my haste to get going, I had foolishly forgotten to grab a dose of my medicine to bring with me.

When we finally arrived, Isaac pulled up to the house, and neither of us moved nor said a word for quite awhile. I was so disappointed that my headache hadn't gone away, and I think Isaac was a little upset with me that I hadn't listened to him. I knew that I owed him an apology, but I felt so horrible and sickly in the moment that I could scarcely talk.

After sitting there for a few more minutes, I took a deep breath and whispered as best I could.

"Isaac," I said.

"Yes," he quietly responded.

"I'm so sorry I did this," I told him, feeling awful. "I should have listened to you. I never should have come!" I paused, swallowing hard, trying not to get sick. "But, honestly," I defended, "I really did think I'd be better by now. I am *truly* sorry!"

Isaac nodded, accepting my apology.

"I understand," he replied. "What do you want to do?"

I sat there not saying anything, my eyes still closed, my head in my hands, unsure I even wanted to move.

"Do you want me to take you back home?" he offered.

"No," I whispered. "We're already here. I can try to get through it. Besides, you need to be fitted, too."

"I know that, Jochebed!" Isaac countered with concern. "But…are you *sure* you want to put yourself through this? You know how bad things can get sometimes."

"I know," I acknowledged, "but this is *so* important to Isabelle. I don't want to let her down. I'd really like to try. - *Please?*"

Isaac sat there weighing the situation, understanding how badly I wanted to be normal, but also realizing how sick I was. He hesitantly asked again.

"You're *sure?*" he wanted to make certain.

Again, I swallowed hard and took another deep breath.

"Yes," I affirmed. "With help, I think I can do it."

Isaac sighed reluctantly.

"All right," he agreed. "Then let's see if we can't get you inside."

Isaac carefully got down from the buggy, trying his best not to jar it too much, and came around to where I was sitting. He put out his hand for me to take it.

"Wait!" I rebuffed. I swallowed hard several more times, my stomach churning. "I think I may be sick!" I said. I sat there with my eyes closed, trying my best to keep everything down.

Isaac waited patiently, while I sat there for several more agonizing minutes, hoping the nausea would pass. Thankfully, it finally did.

"Okay," I whispered, "I think I'm ready."

Isaac slowly and gently helped me out of the buggy, and once I was on the ground, I had to lean on him for support. I was just too weak and feeling too poorly to walk on my own.

"Jochebed," Isaac said again out of concern, "this is just silly! You're way too sick to even walk, much less try on any dress!"

"Isaac, please!" I begged. "I want to try!"

Isaac stood there holding me up, clearly torn as to what to do.

Sensing his reluctance, I begged again.

"Please," I said, "we're already here. Let's just go inside."

Isaac shook his head again, sighing in aggravation.

"All right," he relented. "Do you think you can walk?"

"I think so," I whispered hesitantly.

Isaac held tightly to my waist as I held to his, leaning heavily on him for support. He carefully took a small step forward, and I did my best to shuffle along side of him.

Slowly and methodically we made our way around the buggy, and just as we were about to step onto the sidewalk, Andrew came running from the house to see what was wrong.

"Is she okay?" he questioned frantically as he ran up to us.

"She will be," Isaac assured. "She just has a really bad headache right now. Help me get her inside, all right?"

Andrew quickly came around and took hold of my other arm to assist me as I was so worn out at this point, I could barely walk. Nevertheless, I did my best to will one step in front of the other, determined to make it into the house.

After taking a few more steps, I happened to look up momentarily, and I was completely mortified at what I saw! *Everyone* in the wedding party had come out on the front lawn to see what was going on. I thought for sure I would die right there on the spot! I knew everyone was coming for their fittings, but I *assumed* they'd be off getting fitted! But no, there they were, every last one of them, much to my shock and horror, standing, staring, watching Andrew and Isaac practically drag me inside. I couldn't have been more humiliated if I tried!

What an awful sight I must be! I thought to myself. *Oh, why...why didn't I listen to Isaac?*

As these thoughts were running through my mind, Isabelle came rushing up to me as we were almost to the door.

"Jochebed!" she queried in a panic. "What can we do?"

"Nothing!" I whispered in pain. "I'll be fine. I just need to lie down is all."

Isaac finally determined that walking was taking far too long, so he abruptly stopped, reached around, and gently picked me up.

Andrew and Isabelle came along behind us as Isaac carried me into the house.

Once inside, Mrs. Chaucer (Isabelle's mother) directed Isaac to lay me down on the couch in their sitting room.

"Can I get you anything, child?" she asked after I was settled.

Part of me knew I might need a bucket just in case I got sick, but there was *no way* I was about to ask for one!

"No, ma'am," I answered politely. "I just need to rest. Thank you!"

The wedding party was now standing at the door to the sitting room, gawking at me as if I were a side show at the circus. They were whispering amongst themselves as they stood there watching me writhe in pain. Needless to say, I was beside myself with embarrassment and wished like everything that I could just disappear from sight!

I'd brought this on myself, though, and I knew it, and I would've given myself a good verbal thrashing for it, but I was so tired and in so much pain at the moment, reprimanding myself for my obstinacy would simply have to wait.

"Everyone out!" Mrs. Chaucer directed. "Let the poor child get some rest."

Everyone complied with her wishes, and she partially closed the door to the room as Isaac was still inside with me.

"You're sure you'll be all right in here by yourself?" he questioned, concerned.

"Yes," I answered. "You go and have your fitting. Hopefully, I'll feel up to mine in a little while."

"All right," he reluctantly agreed. "I'll go, but I'll be back to check on you as soon as I can. Don't hesitate to call me if you need anything, though, all right?"

I nodded the best I could, wearily looking up at him.

"I am sorry, Isaac," I reiterated, my eyes growing heavy. "I'm so sorry!"

"It's all right," he assured. "You rest. We'll talk later." He quietly turned and left the room, closing the door behind him, and thankfully, he wasn't gone but for a minute or two, and I was already asleep.

Apparently, Isaac had come back to check on me several times, but I never heard him, not even once. I was asleep for hours and didn't even realize it. When I finally woke up, it was evening time and everyone from the wedding party had already gone home.

Initially, lying there, practically in the dark, I felt a little out of sorts. I was completely disoriented, in a strange place I'd never been before, and it took me several minutes to reacquaint myself with my surroundings. Once I did, however, I sat up and tried to stand. At first, I was a little woozy, but thankfully it passed, and I managed to steady myself on my feet. My headache was much, much better, but I still felt groggy and a little hazy from having slept so long.

When I felt I was able, I carefully made my way to the door of the sitting room and peeked out. No one was there, but I could see light coming from a room in the back of the house. I wasn't sure where I was going, but I knew I needed to find someone who could tell me where Isaac was.

As I neared what I assumed was the family room, I could hear voices talking back and forth. At first, I didn't hear Isaac's, and I felt a little lost and alone, but then he said something, and I felt more at ease.

~

The Chaucers were a very wealthy family, and their home was very lavish. They were similar to Isaac's family in that they were very rich, but they were, well, for all intents and purposes, a little more pretentious, albeit not a lot. Given their proclivities, though, I have to confess, being in such a fancy setting made me feel rather small and extremely self-conscious. I'd never been in Isabelle's home before, and everything seemed so expensive and delicate. I feared I might break something if I weren't careful. I was completely out of my element and felt incredibly uncomfortable.

~

As soon as I rounded the corner to the family room, I spotted Isaac, and he spotted me.

"Jochebed!" he called out, standing to come greet me. "Thank goodness! I was getting a little concerned."

Everyone was sitting on the very expensive looking furniture, talking and sipping on tea. Mr. Chaucer was now home, and Mrs. Chaucer was sitting beside him on their settee, so prim and proper. Isabelle and Andrew were sitting together on one of the love seats, and Mimi (Isabelle's younger sister) was gracefully sitting on the floor, resting against a rather large, luxurious chair.

As you can imagine, I felt acutely self-aware walking in so disheveled and frumpy from my sleep. I nervously began fidgeting with my hair, hoping I didn't look too terribly awful, although that's *exactly* how I felt!

I think Isaac sensed my trepidation because he walked up to me, sweetly offered me his arm, and kindly whispered in my ear.

"Come on," he encouraged, "it'll be okay!"

I reluctantly smiled and nodded as I took hold of his arm.

He and I walked together over to another small couch that sat across from where Mr. and Mrs. Chaucer were sitting. I timidly sat down beside Isaac, again fidgeting with my hair and my dress, hoping to make myself a little more presentable.

"And how are you feeling, my dear?" Mrs. Chaucer asked.

"I'm much better now. Thank you, ma'am," I replied, completely embarrassed by everything that had happened. "I'm so sorry about all of this." I abruptly turned to Isabelle. "Please forgive me for messing things up for you today," I implored. "I had no idea things would get this bad."

"Oh, nonsense!" she dismissed enthusiastically. "You didn't mess anything up. I'm just glad to see you're feeling better!"

"Well, that's very kind of you," I relayed. "But, Isabelle, I..." I paused, nervous to say what I knew needed to be said. "I...I don't know if this is the time or the place," I anxiously continued, "but...I would completely understand if you wanted to ask someone else to stand in for me at your wedding. I don't want to take the chance of another headache ruining your special day."

Isabelle seemed a bit taken aback as she just stared at me for a minute. I could tell by the look on her face that she was bothered that I had even suggested such a thing.

"I wouldn't hear of it!" she finally stated. "You're who I asked and you're who I want." She shook her head. "I knew all about your condition when I asked you to stand up with me, Jochebed," she reminded, "and I'm not worried *one bit* about you ruining my day. Don't you fret yourself one more minute about it, all right?"

I nodded, timidly accepting what she was saying.

"No more talk like that!" she insisted. "I have no doubt you'll do just fine." She was polite yet stern.

Again I nodded, conceding.

I have to admit, after seeing and hearing her reaction, I felt a little guilty and ashamed for having said anything in the first place. Nonetheless, I was happy that she still wanted me in her wedding, and grateful that she seemed to understand.

"Thank you, Isabelle," I replied graciously. "Again, that's very kind of you."

I looked at Isaac and nervously smiled, as he smiled at me as if to say, *See, you're not damaged or too broken. You can still have a life!*

We all chatted a while longer (well, actually they did most of the talking while I just sat and listened), and before I knew it, Isabelle was standing to her feet, smiling over at me.

"If you're up to it," she suggested, "how about we take you and get you fitted for your dress?"

I smiled back as I nodded, standing to my feet.

As I stood up, so did Mrs. Chaucer, and she and Isabelle led the way as we all headed to a rather large sewing room where they kept the dresses and suits for the wedding.

I had my fitting, and when we were finished, we went back to the family room where Isaac was waiting to leave. I politely thanked everyone for their patience and for their understanding and also for their hospitality. Isaac graciously thanked everyone as well, gave Andrew a hug, shook Mr. and Mrs. Chaucer's hands, and after he'd assured them that he would tell his grandparents hello for them, he and I left for home.

I can't deny it, as we were walking out, I was kind of glad to be leaving. While the Chaucers were a very lovely family and admittedly very kind, I just felt so out of place and awkward being around them. I preferred the comforts of the country and the familiarity of my family and I was looking forward to being home.

"Well," Isaac commented happily as we made our way back to my house, "I think all in all that turned out rather well, don't you?"

"I suppose so," I answered with reserve.

Isaac could sense that something wasn't quite right.

"What is it, Jochebed?" he asked. "I can tell something's bothering you. What's wrong?"

I was hesitant to say anything, but I obliged.

"I…I guess I'm just…well…I'm still embarrassed by everything that happened today, is all," I told him.

"What?" Isaac questioned, surprised. "What do you have to be embarrassed about?"

I furrowed my brow, absolutely stunned at his cluelessness!

"Isaac!" I exclaimed, unsure of how it wasn't obvious to him. "You saw all of them! I mean, *gracious!* They were all just standing there staring at me - gawking at me for goodness' sakes! No one but family has *ever* seen me so bad off, I mean, excluding you, of course. I just felt so *foolish!* And then to sleep the day away like that, and in the Chaucer's home no less…I…I just felt so small and humiliated!" I looked down fidgeting with my hands as Isaac abruptly pulled the buggy to a halt.

"Jochebed," he demanded sternly, "look at me!"

I reluctantly lifted my gaze and looked at him, feeling so self-conscious.

"You *know* Isabelle and Andrew love you!" he started. "And they would never think…"

"Oh, Isaac!" I interjected, cutting him off. "It isn't about that! I mean…*oh…you just don't understand!"* I turned away, frustrated by the whole matter.

"No!" Isaac came back at me, exasperated. "I guess I don't! Please explain!"

I took a deep breath, trying to avoid having to say anything. I didn't know how to express how I was feeling, and I was afraid if I tried to explain myself, I might hurt Isaac in the process.

He was used to being around people with money, with all of their fancy things and refined behavior, but I wasn't! They were *his* friends, not mine (really), and he felt comfortable with them - I didn't!

Me...I was just a simple country girl with adequate manners and a limited vocabulary. I knew that money had never been an issue between Isaac and me before (I guess it had never really come up), and I didn't want it to become an issue between us now, but sitting there thinking on it, I realized it was a reality that we would probably have to face at some point. The problem was I just didn't know if I wanted to face it *today!* I mean...how could I deal with it without upsetting him?

Isaac and his family were rich, but they never acted like they were, and I never felt out of place around them. The Chaucers, on the other hand, were a different story. They were...well...quite a bit more...how shall I say...proper and sophisticated. They carried themselves differently, and even though they were very gracious and kind, they just seemed so...so...well...for lack of a better term - upper class.

And that was my dilemma! How could I say such things to Isaac without insulting him? He and his family and the Chaucers were very close, and I didn't want to say anything that would be taken the wrong way. I wished now that I had just kept my mouth shut!

"Jochebed!" Isaac prodded as I sat there contemplating. "I would like it very much if you would explain yourself."

I nervously sat there wringing my hands, still unsure of the whole thing.

"Jochebed!" he pushed again, this time a lot more forcefully. "I'm waiting! Please, explain what you meant!"

"All right!" I snapped back angrily, *really* not wanting to divulge my true feelings, quite perturbed at his insistence! "If I must!" I paused, dreading what I had to say.

"Well?" Isaac persisted, growing ever more impatient. "Let's have it!"

"I'm thinking!" I barked back. "I just don't know how to say it!"

"Then just say it!" Isaac demanded, irritated at my reluctance. "You *know* you can talk to me about *anything!*"

I took another deep breath, looking away, my heart racing, and my hands sweaty. I *so* did not want to have to tell him, but I knew he wasn't about to drop the matter. I shook my head, and mustered the courage.

"They're all just so rich," I blurted out, "so prim and proper! Isabelle and her family and Andrew's friends, they all come from money and...well...*I don't!* And then to be on display like that in front of all of them, so weak and so vulnerable, it...it made me feel so...so small, so self-conscious! I know it's no one's fault but my own, but I...I...oh, I just wish I'd never accepted the invitation from Isabelle to be in her wedding in the first place! *I just don't fit in!* I'm just so different from all of them, and there's no denying that!" I was almost in tears at the thought.

Isaac sat there completely stunned by my startling admission. Not knowing what to say, he looked away, dejected, deeply troubled and quite disconcerted.

As I looked over at him, I could tell I had hurt him badly.

He shook his head, collecting his thoughts as he finally faced me.

"I...I had no idea you felt that way about us," he confessed, visibly shaken and genuinely concerned.

"Oh, Isaac!" I begged, wanting to clarify. "Please don't get me wrong! I *know* it's just me! I know everyone's always been kind and courteous and gracious towards me, it's just that...well...I feel so...so out of place around them, almost as if I'm on pins and needles or something!"

Isaac furrowed his brow as he looked me square in the face.

"And me?" he questioned, very unsettled. "Is that how you feel around *me?"*

"No, of course not!" I frantically tried to reassure him.

I vigorously shook my head, absolutely furious with myself for what I had said!

"Oh, this isn't coming out right at all!" I lamented. "Isaac...*it's not you!"*

"But *I* come from money!" he countered angrily. *"My family* has money!" He shook his head, trying to wrap his mind around it. He sighed, exasperated. "We...we *never...*" He paused, visibly offended. "Is...is that how you feel around *my* family?" he wanted to know.

"Isaac, *no!"* I insisted adamantly, ready to flog myself for having said anything at all. "Oh, why...why didn't I just keep my mouth shut?" I scolded myself. I sat there feeling completely awful, wishing I could take back the last few minutes of my life.

Unfortunately, my words were out there, and there was no retrieving them! As much as I didn't want to, I pressed on in my explanation, my voice and mannerisms pleading as I spoke.

"Isaac, please believe me!" I implored. "Your family...they've...they've *always* been very kind to me, loving and accepting, but the Chaucers...well...I know they've been kind, too, but... it's just that they're...they're just *different* somehow, that's all! Maybe it's just because I don't know them very well. I...I...oh...I don't know!"

By now I was simply rambling, but for some reason, *oh, for the life of me*, I just couldn't stop myself!

"Sometimes," I posited, "I wonder if Isabelle didn't choose me to be in her wedding because she felt she *had* to because I'm courting *you!* I mean, she and I were never close in school, and all of Andrew's friends...well...they're older, and they're *your* friends, and...well...I...I...ohhh...*I just don't know how to explain this right!"*

Isaac sat there staring straight ahead, absolutely speechless. I could tell by the look on his face that he was truly troubled and profoundly hurt, and it seemed the more I spoke, the worse things got. I wasn't trying to offend him, honest I wasn't, I was just trying to explain how uncomfortable I felt around people with money. He looked so disappointed, though, and I knew I had upset him deeply. The trouble was...I didn't know how to make things right!

In that moment, I felt as if something had changed between us, and I didn't know how to change it back!

Much to my dismay, Isaac didn't utter a single word. He simply told the horse to get up, and we were on our way again.

As we rode towards home, I sat there quietly, feeling like such a horrible person, cringing at the sick feeling I now had in the pit of my stomach. I tried to think of something else to say, maybe another way of putting things, maybe a better way of explaining myself, but nothing - ***nothing*** would come to mind!

Thinking on it, I was completely beside myself with worry for what had just happened, wishing like everything that I could just take it all back, that I could simply erase the whole day and start all over again, but it was too late! What was done was done, and now I would have to face the consequences of my choices yet again. I was afraid and angry with myself all at the same time. *Oh, when would I ever learn?!?*

When we got to my house, Isaac pulled the buggy up to the house, and we both just sat there in silence. He kept his eyes straight ahead, indicating that he had no intentions of speaking to me. I'll confess it scared me but good as he seemed so different, not at all himself. It just wasn't like him to not want to work things out.

What have I done? I fretted. *Have I crossed a line that I can never cross back over?* My mind was racing with all sorts of doubts and fears, and my anxiety continued to grow. Even though I was sitting right there next to Isaac in the buggy, he felt a million miles away.

After waiting for what seemed like an eternity, I couldn't take the silence any longer. I *had* to say something!

"Isaac," I called to him softly.

He didn't answer.

My heart was beating furiously as I was so nervous and panicked.

"Isaac, please!" I begged in desperation. "I'm *so sorry*! Please…*please try to understand! I love you! I do!* I didn't mean to insult you or your family or the Chaucers, for that matter. It's just my insecurities talking… *I know that*, and *I'm sorry!*"

Isaac just sat there, staring straight ahead, saying nothing.

I was heartbroken, to say the least! Deep down, I knew that I had ruined things between us, and I was frantic to fix them!

I waited for him to respond, but he didn't.

Not knowing what else to say or do, I hung my head, biting my lip as tears welled up in my eyes. It was obvious my feeble attempts to make things right had failed miserably.

Not wanting things to end this way, I sat there for a few more agonizing minutes, hoping beyond hope that Isaac would say something, but he never did. Finally concluding that there was nothing else I could do, distraught and frightened, I decided to go inside. I let myself down from the buggy and turned to look up at Isaac.

He never looked at me once nor said a word.

"I'm so sorry, Isaac," I whispered again as a tear trickled down my cheek.

As soon as I stepped away from the buggy, Isaac immediately told the horse to get up, and he left.

As I watched him drive away, my heart was in pieces as tears streamed down my face. In that moment, I honestly didn't know whether or not I would ever see Isaac Lewis again.

FINDING ISAAC
(Chapter 44)

I waited and watched as he drove out of sight, and once he was gone, I hastened to the house, crying uncontrollably. Once inside, I ran straight to my room and slammed the door behind me. Completely overcome, I went directly to my bed, collapsed in a heap, and commenced to sobbing hysterically.

Papa, who had been in the living room, startled by my troubling behavior, immediately jumped up, and came to see what was going on. Knocking softly on my bedroom door, he inquired as to what was going on.

"Jochebed," he asked, concerned. "Sweetheart, is everything all right? What's happened?"

I didn't answer. I was too upset to say anything.

Hearing my sobs, and growing more concerned, Papa opened the door and let himself in. Seeing my distress, he walked over to the bed and sat down next to me.

"Do ya wanna talk about it?" he asked sympathetically.

I was so heartbroken and in such agonizing pain, I could barely speak.

"He's...he's gone!" I blubbered, sniffing and stammering, crying all the more.

"What?" Papa questioned, completely lost. "Who's gone? What are ya talkin' about?"

"Isaac!" I shouted distraught, trying to catch my breath. "He's...he's gone, and... and I've lost him... *forever!*"

Papa shook his head, more than a little bewildered.

"Now just a minute!" he came back at me, not fully buying it. "Turn over here and talk to me right. What do ya mean Isaac's gone?"

I sniffed and sighed and wiped a tear as I turned over to face him.

"Oh, Papa!" I cried, sitting myself up beside him. "I fear I've pushed him away!" I wiped another tear and reached over to grab a hanky from my nightstand. Wiping my nose, I sniffed and sniffed, trying to calm myself down.

Papa compassionately leaned over and took me into his arms.

"There, there, sweetheart," he comforted, hugging me close. "Tell me what happened."

Nodding, I sat back up and tried to compose myself the best I could.

"Oh, Papa," I began to explain, tearing up again, "I hurt him. I hurt him *so badly!* I said some *awful, terrible* things that I never should have said, and...I hurt him. I didn't mean to...but I did!"

Papa sighed, clearly troubled.

"Well...what'd ya say?" he queried as he shook his head, furrowing his brow. "What could ya have possibly said that could've hurt him that badly?"

I hung my head, feeling guilty.

"I...I brought up money," I replied in a whimper.

"Money?" Papa questioned, confused. "What about it?"

I bit my lip, feeling like such a horrible person for feeling the way I did.

"He...he's rich, Papa!" I exclaimed. "His family's rich, his friends are rich, his family's friends are rich, and I...I just feel so out of place when I'm around them sometimes. I mean, I know we're not dirt poor or anything, but when I'm with them, I guess...I guess sometimes I just feel like such a plain, little, peasant girl or something." I sniffed and sniffed, wiping my tears as I tried to press on. "They all have such fancy clothes and nice things, Papa," I blurted out. "They're all so refined and sophisticated, and…oh…I don't know, I just feel so awkward around them…so terribly uncomfortable!" I quickly looked at Papa. "They've never been unkind to me, mind you!" I promptly added, trying to assure him. "Please, don't get me wrong, it's just that…well…oh…"

I paused, so exasperated with it all!

"I tried to tell all of this to Isaac," I explained, "but it seemed the more I spoke, the more things came out all wrong, and the more I hurt him. I apologized profusely, I did, but…Isaac, he…he just sat there. He didn't say *a thing!* He wouldn't even *look at me*, Papa!" I shook my head, my heart in pieces. "There was nothing I could do!" I cried. "He just left!"

Overcome, I broke down again, sobbing.

"I just can't believe he drove away!" I wept. "I just can't believe he drove away and left me standing there like that…but he did!" I looked frantically at Papa. "Oh, Papa!" I fretted, absolutely worried. "I'm so scared! I'm so afraid that I've lost him for good!" I buried my face in my hands and began to cry yet again.

"Now, Jochebed," Papa calmed, "ya need to settle down. If Isaac really loves ya, he'll come around." He put his arm around me, trying to console me. "Is this the first time the issue of money's come up?" he wanted to know.

I nodded, sniffing and sniffing as I wiped my tears.

"Yes," I answered truthfully. "I don't think it was ever a thought before today. But being humiliated in front of all his friends like I was, I…I guess it just got to me."

"Humiliated?" Papa questioned, his tone quite troubled. "How were ya humiliated?"

"It was my fault, really," I confessed. "I foolishly went to the Chaucer's home for my fitting in the midst of a terrible headache. I should have known better, and Isaac tried to talk me out of it, but I just wouldn't listen. I didn't want to let Isabelle down and, too," I reluctantly admitted, "I guess there was part of me that didn't want to be the 'outsider' ruining the day."

Papa furrowed his brow again, taken aback.

"Outsider?" he questioned. "Why would ya feel like an outsider? Is that the way Isaac treats ya when he's around his friends?" Papa seemed genuinely upset at this point, and growing more and more concerned. "I wanna know, Jochebed!" he demanded, angrily. "Does Isaac treat ya differently because ya don't come from *money?*"

"No, Papa! Honest, he doesn't!" I assured him adamantly, vehemently shaking my head, trying to dissuade him of the notion.

"Does his family treat ya that way then?" he pressed.

"No, Papa!" I answered again just as adamantly. "No one has!"

Papa shook his head thoroughly confused.

"Then, Jochebed," he came back at me, scratching his head, "I really don't understand. Why feel that way?"

I sighed, disheartened.

"Because I'm foolish and insecure!" I stated bluntly, so angry with myself for what I'd done. I looked up at him in desperation. "Oh, Papa!" I cried. "What can I do?"

Papa let out a long, heavy sigh as he pulled at his chin, contemplating. I could tell by the look on his face that he felt sorry about the situation, but it seemed clear that he was struggling with how to help me.

"Maybe Isaac just needs time to think things through," he suggested, trying to sound hopeful. "Maybe upon reflection, he'll realize the misunderstandin' between the two of ya and see it for what it is." Papa took hold of my hand and smiled sympathetically. "I know he loves ya, sweetheart," he bolstered. "Hopefully, soon he'll be able to talk to ya about what he's thinkin'. I'm sure the two of ya will work things out eventually." He leaned over and gave me a kiss on the forehead.

I wanted to believe what he was saying, but Isaac had never *not* talked to me before; in fact, he was always the one trying to get *me* to talk to *him!* I felt so awful about the whole situation; I didn't want to wait another minute to try to resolve things. I knew it was late, but I asked Papa if I could please take the wagon to go talk to Isaac.

"Tonight?" Papa questioned, extremely hesitant given the hour.

"Please, Papa!" I begged. "I won't be able to sleep a wink tonight if I don't, at least, try to set things right! ...*Please?*"

Papa was reluctant, but he finally relented.

"All right, I suppose," he said, granting his permission. "But it's late. Ya gotta promise me you'll be careful, and that ya won't stay out too long."

I smiled, grateful!

"I promise!" I assured, hugging his neck, giving him a kiss on the cheek. "Thank you, Papa!"

He smiled kindly.

"I'll go hitch up the team for ya," he offered.

Right away, he got up and headed downstairs, and I quickly followed behind him.

When everything was ready, I gave Papa a hug and climbed aboard the wagon. Taking hold of the reigns, I took off as fast as I could, desperate to go find Isaac. I'll admit I wasn't sure what I was going to say to him when I found him, but there was an urgency inside of me that compelled me to try to do something!

When I got to Isaac's house, the sun was just setting, and everything seemed dim and quiet. I could see Isaac's buggy sitting in front of the barn, though, so I was fairly certain that he was there. I stopped the wagon in front of his house, promptly jumped down, and ran to the front door and started to knock. I just wanted to see Isaac so badly; it was all I could do to just stand there and wait. When no one immediately came to the door, I began to wonder if anyone could even hear me. Antsy and rather impatient, I knocked again a couple more times, only this time I knocked as loudly as I could.

Finally, after a few minutes, Mr. Lewis came to the door and opened it up.

"Why, Jochebed!" he said, surprised to see me. "What are you doing here so late? Is everything all right?"

"I just really need to speak to Isaac, sir, if that's all right," I told him, trying not to sound too terribly desperate.

"Well, that's fine with me," he answered, "but I haven't seen him yet this evening. I thought he was still out with you."

"No, sir," I replied, disappointed. "I'm afraid he isn't. I do see his buggy out here, though. Would you know where he might be?"

Mr. Lewis shook his head.

"No, I'm sorry, dear, I wouldn't," he answered. "But sometimes I know he likes to walk the property at night to think and clear his head. Perhaps he went on one of his walks. You're more than welcome to wait here for him if you'd like."

"Oh, thank you, sir," I politely refused, too anxious and nervous to wait. "But if it's all the same to you, with your permission, of course, I'd really like to go and try to find him."

"You're sure?" Mr. Lewis questioned, peering out, a little concerned. "It'll be dark soon!"

"I know, sir," I acknowledged earnestly. "But I just really need to speak with him!"

Mr. Lewis nodded, conceding.

"All right then, child," he agreed, recognizing my desperation. "You have my permission. But here," he offered as he held out his lantern, "better take this with you. You'll likely need it before too long."

"Thank you, sir," I replied, appreciative, taking the lantern from him.

"Well, I hope you find him," Mr. Lewis said optimistically. "You take care now."

I nodded, grateful, as he smiled and closed the door.

As soon as he was inside, I immediately turned around to begin my search for Isaac. Unfortunately, the Lewis' property was so vast, and Isaac and I had only walked it a couple of times, I really had no clue as to where to start. I looked this way and that as I made my way down off the porch, tentative and unsure of which way to go. Knowing I had to start somewhere, however, I finally picked a direction, and just started walking. I hoped beyond hope that I would eventfully run into Isaac.

Initially, not seeing him anywhere in the front of the house, I quickly made my way around to the back. I started to walk along the edge of the property, but even there I saw no sign of him. Nevertheless, I hastened on, purposely making my way towards the rose garden, knowing how much Isaac loved it and thinking surely he'd be there.

As I walked, the sun slowly sank below the horizon, and when it finally disappeared out of sight, I was very thankful for the lantern Mr. Lewis had given me to use. Losing the light of day, though, I began to feel quite uneasy being all alone in a somewhat unfamiliar place. Still, I hurried on, earnestly calling out for Isaac, making sure to look for him everywhere as I went. I desperately hoped I would find him soon!

Even though Isaac had only taken me to the rose garden once, I was fairly certain I could remember how to get there. It was a rather long walk, but I was determined, so I continued on. The further away I got from the Lewis' home, however, the more I began to worry that I may not even be looking in the right place.

Still, I reasoned, *I haven't found him anywhere else; the rose garden is as good a place to look as any!*

After much walking, I came to the steep hill that Isaac and I had walked down just before coming to the little stream. I made my way down the hill and across the water knowing that the rose garden lay just beyond. Sure enough, when I crossed the stream and walked on a little further, I lifted my lantern, and there in front of me was the gate that opened into the rose garden. I quickly made my way to it and opened it up.

When I entered the garden, I swiftly moved along one of the paths, calling out for Isaac as I went. I held my lantern up, swinging it this way and that, hoping to catch a glimpse of him somewhere, *anywhere,* but I never saw him.

After doing what I thought was a thorough search of the garden, I finally came to rest at the gazebo. I sat down on the little bench just inside, absolutely exhausted.

Of all the places he could be, I thought to myself, *I thought for **sure** he would be here!*

Needless to say, by this time, I was quite discouraged and beyond disappointed! I sat there, melancholy, not really sure where else to look.

Finally, recognizing the lateness of the hour and that I wasn't likely to find Isaac tonight, I decided to rest a minute longer and then head back to my wagon.

As I sat there upset and frustrated, I couldn't help but become more furious with myself for everything that had transpired earlier in the evening. I wanted so badly to see Isaac and to make things right, but I couldn't even find him!

With tears welling up in my eyes, I set the lantern down next to me on the bench. I knew I needed to get back, but right now all I wanted to do was have a good cry. I put my face in my hands and did just that!

Sobbing bitterly, my head down, tears flowing freely, I was nearly startled right out of my skin when suddenly I heard someone call my name.

"Jochebed!" the voice said.

My heart skipped a beat as it almost leapt from my chest.

Suddenly, Isaac came into view out of the darkness.

"What are you doing here?" he asked somberly.

I quickly wiped my tears as I sat up to look at him.

"I…I came looking for you," I replied with angst, hoping he wouldn't walk away.

He just stood there for a minute, staring at me, his brow furrowed, seemingly angry.

"You really shouldn't be out here all by yourself," he admonished, his tone serious and stern.

I looked at him nearly trembling as there was such a horrible awkwardness between us. It hung in the air like a thick, dark cloud, and it was excruciatingly awful, to say the least!! I didn't care, though. I knew we needed to talk, to try to work things out, so I sniffed and wiped a tear, trying to compose myself.

"I know," I finally admitted. "But I didn't want to go to sleep tonight until…until I saw you."

He shook his head, clearly aggravated. It was obvious he was still upset and hurt.

"Well, you've seen me!" he retorted impertinently. "Now what?"

I nervously stood up and stepped towards him, but when I did, he backed away. It was almost as if he didn't want anything to do with me anymore. My heart instantly sank, and I stopped!

"Isaac!" I started to cry again. "You're scaring me! Please…can't we just talk about this?"

He just stood there looking at me, giving no response.

"Please?" I implored again.

"Haven't you said enough?" he barked angrily.

I bit my lip as I looked at him intently.

"Isaac," I cried, my eyes pleading, "I'm *so* sorry! You *have* to believe me!" I shook my head, desperately praying for wisdom. "I don't know what else you want me to say!" I wept. I was nearly beside myself with worry and fear. "You told me I could talk to you about *anything!*" I reminded. "And well…I tried, but…it…it just didn't come out right!"

"Jochebed!" Isaac shouted gruffly, stepping on my words, his jaw clenched as he shook his head, clearly infuriated with me!

This was a side of him I'd never seen before, and I'll admit I was scared!

He sighed heavily, as if he were trying to restrain himself, trying to find a way to reply without letting his anger get the best of him. He shook his head again as he looked down and to the side, finally settling on me. He looked me right in the eye.

"You just don't get it, do you?" he charged crossly. "I've stood by you through *everything*, and I've never *once* treated you like you were somehow less just because you didn't come from money!"

I was taken aback by his tone, but I knew he was right.

"Isaac!" I tried to interject.

"Just let me finish!" he demanded sternly, cutting me off.

I immediately shut my mouth and listened.

"Never *once* did I treat you like that!" he reiterated. "And my family..." He shook his head again, his jaw clenched, his brow furrowed. "I don't believe they've *ever* treated you like that either...*not ever!*" He stepped a little closer, staring at me bewildered, almost as if he didn't even know me anymore. "I've *always* loved you, Jochebed!" he pointed out. "I've always loved you for *you!* Not for what you had or...or for what you didn't have, but for *you!* And I thought you felt the same way about me! I don't judge your friends, I don't judge your family, I just...I just..."

He sighed, exasperated, clenching his fists, trying to calm himself down.

"I don't think you understand!" he indicted. "My money, my friends, my family, I...I want them to be *yours* just as much as they are *mine!* I don't *ever* want you to feel like you don't fit into my world, but..." He paused, stepping yet a little closer. "If you can't accept who I am," he stated with resolve, still staring me right in the eye, "to *really* accept who I am, and who my family is, and who my friends are...if you can't feel comfortable around us, and if your perception of us is so...so *awful*, then...then I think that..." He stopped abruptly, looking away.

My heart was pounding furiously as I waited for him to finish his thought.

"Think what?" I finally prodded, too anxious to wait any longer.

He shook his head again as he slowly turned his gaze back to me. The look on his face said it all! I could tell he was reluctant to answer, but then he said it.

"Then I think," he suggested solemnly, "that you and I, we...we just shouldn't be together anymore."

Instantly, it felt as if someone had knocked the wind right out of me because I could no longer breathe! I was so shaken by his words, I could feel my heart breaking into a million pieces as it sank into the pit of my stomach. Immediately, I began to feel light headed and faint all at the same time. What I'd feared the most, Isaac had now given voice to, and I wasn't sure how to respond.

Reeling, I slowly turned around and walked back to the gazebo, holding my stomach, overwhelmed and sickened by the devastating situation I now found myself in. I sat down, dazed, staring at the ground in utter dismay.

How had it come to this? I thought in despair.

I tried to think of what to say, something - *anything* that would make everything all right again, but no words seemed adequate to fix what was broken.

Isaac stood there looking at me, waiting for me to say something.

I shook my head, completely at a loss.

"Isaac," I said, dispirited, "I...I don't know what else I can say that I haven't already said. I...I can't tell you how sorry I am that I hurt you, I...." Tears started to trickle down my face as I tried to explain myself once again. "I know it may not be much of an excuse," I defended, feeling badly that I had no eloquent words to sway him, "but I…I'm a very shy and insecure person…*and you know that!* I tend to be a homebody because that's where I feel safe and the most comfortable. I'm really only ever around my family, rarely around others, and….I mean, think about it," I pointed out, shrugging my shoulders, "my nickname is *Wallflower* for goodness' sake! I certainly didn't earn that because I'm vivacious and outgoing!"

I glanced at Isaac, hoping beyond hope that I was somehow getting through to him, wanting so badly for him to understand. Seeing the look on his face, though, I again felt like I was doing a very poor job of explaining myself.

"Oh, Isaac!" I expressed with earnest. "I truly didn't mean to offend you! I *do* love you for you! *Honest I do!* But…" I looked at him again, absolutely desperate, my eyes pleading. "We just run in very different circles," I argued. "That's all! I was never around your friends until now. It's just something I'm going to have to get used to." I fidgeted nervously, trying to get him to see. "I'm not saying I could *never* fit into your world, or even feel comfortable in it," I pressed on, "but I…I just think it's going to take me some time. I'm terribly self-conscious, I always have been, and well…to be humiliated in front of your friends like I was, it was…it was…it was just more than I could handle. I felt *so* unbelievably awkward and terribly out of place!" I sighed, so disgusted with myself. "I've always been that way around people who are older and more cultured than I am," I guiltily confessed. "It's a lousy excuse, I know, but it's the truth!"

I could tell Isaac was listening, but I wasn't sure if what I was saying was making much of a difference. The reason I questioned it was because, suddenly, he furrowed his brow, almost as if he thought I was including him in my last remark. It was obvious I'd struck a nerve.

"I'm not saying *you* ever made me feel that way," I quickly clarified, "because you *haven't…never… not once!*" I sighed so unbelievably frustrated with myself! *"Ohhh!"* I grumbled, looking up to the sky, annoyed and exasperated. *"Why* can't I explain this better?!?" I turned back to Isaac, depleted. "I just don't know how to make you see!" I said, giving up. "I just don't know how to make you understand!" I buried my face in my hands and began to cry again. "I don't want to lose you, Isaac!" I sobbed. "How can I make this right?!?"

Isaac didn't respond. He just stood there looking at me, seemingly lost in his thoughts, but the longer he stood there not saying anything, the harder and more intensely I cried.

After awhile, I assumed his silence meant that I had failed to persuade him, and that he was now just searching for some kind words to send me on my way.

Unexpectedly, though, after several, agonizing minutes, he walked over and sat down next to me on the bench there in the gazebo. He didn't say anything at first; he just sat there quietly, so I wasn't sure what to do, or what to make of it. Needless to say, it was rather awkward and disconcerting. I wished like everything that he would just say *something*.

I was still crying inconsolably, when I finally heard him clear his throat.

"Jochebed," he said, his tone dreadfully serious. "I want to ask you something, and I don't want you to answer me right away. Do you understand? I want you to really think about your answer before you say anything." He paused a minute before going on. "This is very important to me," he made clear, "and I need to know…I need to know the absolute truth!"

I looked up at him through my tears, wondering what on earth he could possibly be thinking. I waited nervously for his question.

"In all honesty," he began, "given *all* this - what you know about me…my family, my friends…*all of it*… and given what you know about yourself, can you…can you honestly, *honestly* say…and don't give me an answer based on some schoolgirl crush you've had on me for years, but…given what you know…can you *honestly* say that you want to be with me? Can you honestly say that you *really* want to be a part of *my* life?" He paused again, tearing up. "I guess what I'm really asking you is, do…do you really, truly love *me,* or…or do you just love the idea of me?"

I wanted so desperately to blurt out *yes*, with every fiber of my being I did, but I restrained myself, choosing rather to honor his wishes. I knew he was serious, and I knew I needed to think about what he was asking.

I wiped the tears from my eyes as I sat up and turned towards him. Strangely, all of a sudden, things became crystal clear to me. I finally realized that I truly did have a real decision to make. For the first time, I was face-to-face with the reality of our relationship. It was no longer just a budding friendship and romance with the man I had dreamed of being with for so many years, and it was no longer just a childhood crush come true, it was serious, very serious, and I needed to be honest about it - with myself, and with Isaac.

I looked out into the darkness as I began to contemplate the gravity of the choice in front of me. Isaac was absolutely right…I needed to face this!

Did I genuinely love him? I questioned. ***Did I?*** *Did I* **honestly** *want to spend the rest of my life with this man, accepting all that that entailed? Knowing the reality of his world, could I ever* **really** *feel comfortable in it?* It was such a contrast to what I had always known; *could I genuinely accept the differences?* Isaac was all I had ever dreamed of, but…*could I* **truly** *accept him for who he was? Or…was he right?* **Was** *my love for him based solely upon my ideal of who I thought he was?* I pondered all these questions, trying to be completely honest with myself. *Was Isaac Lewis really more to me than just a dream come true?* I took a deep breath as I looked over at him, all these questions still whirling around in my mind.

Suddenly, my heart began to fill with excitement as I realized that the answer to every question I was agonizing over was *yes! Yes,* I did genuinely love him! And *yes*, I did accept him for who he was! And *yes*, I did want to be a part of his life, no matter what! And *yes*, he truly was more to me than just a childhood crush, more than just a dream come true!

I believe in that moment, God was confirming in my heart and mind that Isaac was the man I was supposed to be with. He honestly *was* the man I loved, and he was the one, and *only one*, I wanted to spend the rest of my life with! A smile slowly made its way across my face as I solidified these feelings deep inside. Wiping a tear from my cheek, I began to share my heart.

"Isaac Lewis," I said, overwhelmed, fighting through my emotions, "you are the most honorable, loving, selfless, *wonderful* man I know! My perceptions were based on my own inadequacies, not on reality. I felt the way I did not because of who *you are* but because of who *I am*. I can only apologize and ask you to forgive me. While I'll admit I'm still more comfortable around familiar things, I know that I'm comfortable around *you,* and I know beyond any shadow of a doubt that I want you in my life - you and everything and everyone that comes along with you! I love you Isaac, with all of my heart I do, and no matter what happens between us here tonight, I want you to know that!"

I was crying so hard at this point, I could barely see through my tears.

"I promise you," I assured with zeal, "I'm being as honest with you as I possibly can be!" I sniffed and sniffed, as I shook my head, wiping my tears, hoping I hadn't lost him. I looked longingly into his eyes. "I love you so much, Isaac!" I told him with earnest. "I always have, and I always will!"

Isaac didn't readily respond as he looked back at me almost as if he were weighing the validity of what I had told him.

I'll admit I was worried sick! My heart was racing a mile a minute as I searched his face for any sign that he still wanted me. *Unbelievably* nervous, I could hardly sit still!

Had I convinced him? I wondered. *Did he believe me? Would he forgive me for my foolishness and be patient with me* **one more time?** *Could he overlook my immaturity and accept my insecurities, or had I revealed a part of myself that made me no longer desirable to him? Would he take me back? Did he even* **want to?** I couldn't help but think such thoughts as I sat there waiting. I was so absolutely terrified because I realized that what he was about to say next could change my life forever!

Finally, after what seemed like an eternity, Isaac began to speak.

"Jochebed," he said softly, his eyes welling with tears, "I'll be honest with you...this has really been difficult for me." He shook his head, trying to figure out how to tell me. "You have to understand," he explained. "I thought I knew you, but...when you said what you did, it...it caused me to question everything about you. I felt like you'd been dishonest with me somehow, like you'd kept your true self hidden from me, and well...when you expressed how you truly felt, I...I suddenly realized that there was such a stark contrast between us, something I'd not really ever seen before. I honestly began to question myself. How could I have been so blind to your perception of me?"

"But, Isaac!" I interrupted anxiously, wanting to make sure he understood my true feelings. "I didn't, and I don't..."

"Stop!" Isaac insisted. "I need to say this!"

I stopped as I took a deep breath, holding it in, incredibly worried for what he would say next!

"As I was saying," he continued, "I began to question your love for me, whether you truly loved me for me, or whether you just loved the idea of being with me, and I'll admit...it scared me! I was afraid I'd misread you."

A tear trickled down my face as I looked at him, fretful, looking for any signs of hope. I so desperately wanted him to still love me, to still want me, but he sounded so dire. I couldn't help but fear the worst!

"What you said," he went on, "it made me question *everything!* For the first time, it caused me to really think about our families, our differences, *all of them*, even the difference in our ages. I questioned my judgment and whether or not we could truly be together, being from similar yet very different worlds. Before this, I...I guess I never considered all those things because I never saw you as different, but...when I realized that *you did*, I...I guess I just didn't know what to do with that."

By now, I was sobbing as I thought for sure I had ruined everything! I was begging God in my heart that Isaac would forgive me and give me another chance to show him the sincerity of my love. I was so afraid; I didn't know what to do!

"Please, Isaac!" I wept. "Can you ever forgive me!? I'm sorry, I am, and I do love you, so much I do! Please...you just have to believe me!" I sniffed and sniffed, tears streaming down my face. "Please, Isaac!" I begged in desperation. *"Please!"*

Isaac shook his head, crying, too.

"No, Jochebed," he said. "I'm sorry!"

I was so startled by his words, I couldn't breathe, I couldn't cry, I couldn't move! My mind went blank as I sat there absolutely stunned! All of my fears, and all of my worries had just come to fruition, and I didn't know what to do with it! I didn't want things to be over between us, but suddenly they were! I just didn't know how to accept that this was really the end!

Overcome by unbelievable heartache and grief, I just couldn't be there with Isaac anymore! I had to get away! I just had to be alone! Overwhelmed by it all, I got up and started to run.

Confused and concerned, Isaac jumped up and came after me. He quickly caught up to me and grabbed me by the arm, stopping me in my tracks. Whirling me around, pulling me close, he hugged me tightly.

"Let me go!" I sobbed. "*Please*, just let me go!" I tried to break free, but he was holding me so tightly I couldn't.

"Jochebed!" Isaac insisted, squeezing me tighter, trying to get me to calm down. "Stop it!"

I was struggling as hard as I could, just wanting to get away from him.

"Jochebed!" he shouted sternly. "Stop fighting me and *listen!* I'm trying to tell you...*I don't care!* Do you understand me? *I don't care!* After considering everything, and hearing your explanation, I...I've come to the conclusion that *I don't care!* I love you! And I don't want to lose you! I know we can work through this together!"

I was crying so hard, I wasn't sure if I'd heard him correctly. I slowly stopped struggling and calmed myself down a bit.

"Wha...what?" I asked, sniffing and stammering, looking up at him through my tears.

He smiled at me so sweetly as he looked into my eyes.

"I love you!" he said unwaveringly. "And I don't ever want to let you go!"

Relief instantly swept over me as I collapsed into him, hugging him tightly.

"Oh, Isaac!" I cried. "I can't tell you how sorry I am for all of this! I love you *so much!*"

He looked down at me with tears in his eyes as he lifted my chin.

"I know you do," he assured. "I'm sorry I ever doubted you."

"Then you forgive me?" I wanted to be certain. "My immaturity, my insecurities, my foolishness...all of it?"

Isaac looked at me intently, as he wiped a tear.

"If you can forgive mine," he said graciously.

We both just smiled at each other, our eyes expressing an unspoken *yes*. We hugged again so tenderly, and as we did, I could feel that whatever had come between us before was now completely melted away.

I breathed a huge sigh of relief as we stood there holding each other, so thankful for forgiveness and restoration. I was with Isaac and he was with me and we truly were in love with each other. It was hard to explain, but I felt that in some strange way, this division between us had somehow brought us even closer together.

Once again, I was truly amazed at how God had managed to work something so awful into something so good. I was as happy now as I had ever been and excited for what the future now held for me and Isaac.

A GRAND DAY
(Chapter 45)

Over the next week, Isaac and I continued to discuss the issues between us, and we confirmed to each other again that we would always work to resolve our problems in a timely fashion.

Wanting to get to the place where I could feel as comfortable around his family and friends as I did around my own, I prayed to God, asking Him to give me the wisdom and grace to know how to be in Isaac's world. I knew it was important to him, and because I loved him, I wanted to try. I knew it wouldn't be easy, though, and that I would need God's help to get there, so I made it a matter of fervent prayer.

Having to deal with all the wedding preparations throughout the week and being around the Chaucers and Andrew's friends, it gave me the perfect opportunity to be gracious and to open myself up to their way of life.

All in all, I have to admit, it had been a very good week. I learned a lot about myself in that amount of time and a lot about all of them as well. I discovered that I was too quick to judge and that I needed to give others a chance. I needed to be willing to see them for who they really were and not just for who I *thought* they were based upon their status in life.

By the time the wedding rolled around, Isaac and I had spent so much time with the Chaucers and the wedding party, I felt as if I had gained a whole new set of friends. They were all so kind and accepting of me, and never once did they seem to look down on me because I didn't have as much as they did, or because I didn't dress as nicely. I was grateful that I'd been given the opportunity to get to know them better, and I could honestly say that by the end of the week, there was a comfortableness with them that I hadn't felt before. I thanked the Lord so much for opening my eyes to the way I'd been and for allowing my heart and feelings to change.

*****

It was early Saturday morning, the day of the wedding, and I was so excited! I just couldn't wait to stand up for Isabelle and Andrew. I got up extra early to get things done and to make certain I had plenty of time to get myself ready before the wedding started. Isaac was picking me up at nine, and I needed to be ready to go when he arrived.

I hurried around and got quite a bit accomplished before the sun ever came up, and by the time Papa and Samuel were finished with breakfast, I had just enough time to clean the kitchen and get myself ready.

Thankfully, Papa noticed my franticness and graciously helped me out. Needless to say, it was a huge blessing! With his help (and Samuel's, too - Papa had to make him), I could dress and fix my hair without having to be rushed.

~

The dresses that Isabelle, her mother, and her sisters had made for the ladies in the wedding party were just absolutely gorgeous! The material was a soft, silky, light lavender color with the prettiest white lace trim on the cuffs of the sleeves. A white ribbon ran around the middle of the dress and draped down the left side, twisting part way down the skirt. There was also a lavender hat that matched the dress, and it was beautifully decorated with white flowers. A lavender and white ribbon ran interlaced throughout the flowers, and it also hung in a twist off the left side of the brim. The final touch was the long, white silk gloves that went halfway up the arms. I couldn't help but feel like royalty wearing the gown.

~

After I finished dressing, I went downstairs to the kitchen to wait for Isaac to arrive.

When Papa heard me moving about, he came in from the living room to join me.

"Didn't anyone ever tell ya that it's impolite to outshine the bride on her weddin' day?" he flattered upon seeing me.

"Oh, Papa!" I blushed demurely.

He looked at me and smiled.

"Ya look just beautiful!" he complimented sweetly. "I sure wish your mama could be here to see ya now - so grown up!"

I walked over and gave him a big hug.

"Thank you, Papa," I accepted, grateful.

Just then, Samuel opened the door and came walking into the kitchen.

"Look who I found standin' outside all dressed up," he quipped.

Isaac stepped in behind him, all decked out in his top hat, black suit, and tie. His face instantly lit up as soon as he saw me.

"Wow!" he remarked, taken aback. "You look stunning!"

"Yah, ya kinda do," Samuel surprisingly interjected.

Everyone looked at him, shocked by his comment.

"What?" he countered, a little embarrassed.

"Nothing!" I replied with a smile. "I'm just not used to you being so polite."

"Well, even you can clean up nice *every once* in a while!" he teased.

I looked at him, chagrinned.

"Thanks, I think!" I commented warily.

Isaac jumped in.

"Are you ready to go?" he asked.

"I'm ready!" I replied with a smile as I gathered my things and walked over to him. I took his arm and we walked out onto the porch together.

"We'll meet ya there," Papa called out as he closed the door behind us.

Isaac and I made our way to his buggy, climbed aboard, and headed off for the church.

When we arrived, several people were milling about outside, and the photographer was unloading his gear from his wagon.

Isaac helped me down off the buggy, offered me his arm, I accepted, of course, and we walked into the church together.

When we got inside, Pastor and Mrs. Scott were in the narthex along with Mr. Chaucer and Mr. and Mrs. Lewis.

When Mrs. Scott saw Isaac and me, she came over to us and told me that I could go to the basement where Isabelle was waiting.

I thanked her and turned to Isaac.

"You look beautiful," he complimented. "I'll see you later."

I smiled courteously and headed downstairs.

Isaac left to go find Andrew.

~

The church was decorated so beautifully. Outside there were white and lavender ribbons that ran down the railings of the steps with tiny bouquets of flowers attached at the end, and inside the auditorium was adorned in magnificent décor. White and lavender bows were tied to the end of each pew, and flowers (white and lavender) were everywhere. With greenery showing through the bouquets, everything looked so elegant! There were candles lit strategically around the church, and even the piano had a beautiful array of flowers gracing its cover. It was so pleasing to the eye; it almost seemed like a picture straight out of a picture book. It was simply breathtaking!

"Oh, Jochebed!" Isabelle frantically called out when she spotted me coming down the stairs. "Thank goodness you're here! Mother insisted she be at the house when my cousins arrived from Maine, so she's not here at present, and Mimi and Alice are supposed to be on their way, but they haven't arrived yet!" She looked at me quite anxiously as she started to turn. "Would you please help me button up the last of my buttons here on my dress?" she requested.

I smiled, happy to help.

"Of course," I replied, walking over to her. I took hold of one of the buttons and started to slip it through its buttonhole. "Isabelle," I complimented as she stood there looking into the mirror, fiddling with her hair, "you look gorgeous! I've never seen you look lovelier!"

She smiled, timidly accepting the accolade.

"Thank you, Jochebed," she said, "that's kind of you to say." She looked back at herself in the mirror with a look of angst. "I still feel as if I have a thousand more things to do to get myself ready," she stressed, "but I'm so nervous, my hands just won't work right!" She turned a bit, holding out her hands to show me her jitters. Shaking her head, worried, she took a deep breath. "Is Andrew here yet?" she asked in a panic, turning back to the mirror, adjusting one of her hair pins.

"I haven't seen him," I admitted, "but I *think* he is. I'm pretty sure I saw his horse and buggy tied up outside. I do know Mr. and Mrs. Lewis are here, though."

"Oh, Jochebed!" Isabelle fretted. "What if he doesn't come? What if he's changed his mind?"

I chuckled, knowing that would never happen!

"Now that's just silly!" I chided. "That's simply your nerves talking. Andrew *adores* you, and he wouldn't miss this day for the world!"

Isabelle took another deep breath.

"I suppose you're right," she accepted. "I'm just so unbelievably nervous I can hardly stand it!"

"You'll do fine!" I encouraged as I buttoned up the last button on her beautiful gown.

Isabelle glanced back at me with a smile.

"Thank you!" she said. "You're a dear!"

Isabelle continued to get ready, and I did what I could to help her, but fortunately, it wasn't long before her sisters, Alice and Mimi arrived, and shortly after that her mother. They all took over the primping and fussing of Isabelle, and I again did what I could to help.

Before we knew it, it was time for the wedding to start, and Mrs. Scott came down to inform us that we needed to head upstairs.

When we got to the top of the steps, I could hear Mrs. Grant playing the piano in the auditorium, and I could hear the hushed murmurings of all the guests waiting inside for the wedding to begin. Mr. Chaucer was standing at the back of the narthex waiting to walk

Isabelle down the aisle, and the groomsman were milling about, waiting on us bridesmaids to come. The adorable little ring bearer and flower girl were standing by Mrs. Scott, who was patiently waiting to help get the wedding party situated.

While we were getting into our proper order, the ushers came to escort Mrs. Chaucer and Mr. and Mrs. Lewis to their seats.

One of Andrew's best friends, Dylan Stark, and I were walking down the aisle together first, so we stepped up, and waited for our cue to go inside. Settling in behind us was Mimi, Isabelle's' younger sister and maid of honor, and Andrew's other best friend, Adam Nolles. They were to head down the aisle next, after Dylan and me. Lastly, there was Alice, Isabelle's older sister and matron of honor (Alice was married to Mrs. Grant's son, Benjamin), and Isaac, Andrew's best man. They got in line together behind Mimi and Adam and waited their turn.

As we all stood there anxiously waiting, the song that we were to walk down to suddenly started to play, and I have to admit, I got a little nervous! As soon as Mrs. Scott opened the auditorium doors, everyone turned to look at us, and, of course, the church was jammed packed with guests, dressed to the nines, waiting in joyful expectation. I swallowed hard, and managed a smile as Dylan and I began the procession down the center aisle.

At the front of the church, Andrew stood on the stage with Pastor Scott, waiting, looking nervous but quite happy. I could tell he couldn't wait for his bride to appear!

Once the wedding party filed in, the Wedding March began, and everyone stood to their feet. Isabelle and her father appeared in the doorway and slowly began to make their way down the aisle. It was so sweet to watch Andrew and Isabelle gazing at each other the whole time as she approached. Neither would take their eyes off the other, Andrew beaming at her and her at him!

The ceremony was quite long but very lovely, and everyone cheered at the end when Pastor Scott pronounced them husband and wife, and Andrew and Isabelle kissed for the very first time. I couldn't help but be happy for them!

I smiled across at Isaac as he was smiling across at me. It was evident that he was overjoyed, and so very proud of his little brother.

It had been such a lovely, beautiful wedding, and such a wonderful testament to Andrew and Isabelle's love and commitment to each other. I was so thankful to have been able to be a part of it!

Deep inside, though, I have to confess, I couldn't wait for it to one day be Isaac's and my turn to stand at an altar and say I do.

PATIENCE
(Chapter 46)

The wedding reception was held on the Lewis' property and just like the wedding, it was grand! They had erected a large tent in the backyard and had plenty of food and drink for everyone. The party lasted well into the night, and Isaac and I had such a delightful, enjoyable time together! We mingled with friends and family and got to know some of Isabelle's relatives who had come in from all over the country - some from Maine, some from Vermont, some from Ohio, and even a great-aunt and great-uncle who had managed to make it all the way up from Florida. It was such a joyous, fun time; I hated that it had to come to an end!

Isaac and I stayed to help clean things up after Andrew and Isabelle left to go on their honeymoon. They had planned to drive all the way to New York to spend a week at a grand hotel, seeing the sites, and going to the ocean. I envied their trip, as I had never had the opportunity to visit any other state.

By the time Isaac drove me home, I was truly worn out, and a headache was slowly coming on. We said our goodnights; I took some medicine, and headed straight for bed.

As I lay there trying to deal with the pain, I praised the Lord that I had not gotten sick sooner, potentially ruining the day. While I wished I wasn't sick at all, I was, at least, grateful for that!

I painfully managed to struggle through my devotions and my prayers, and when I was finished, mercifully, I eventually fell asleep out of sheer exhaustion.

*****

The next day, when I woke up, I could hear voices conversing downstairs. I thought it sounded like Papa and Isaac, but I shrugged it off, thinking surely it couldn't be. It was so early, a Sunday no less, *and why*, I thought, *would Isaac be here anyhow?*

I quickly got myself dressed and went downstairs to see who it was, and sure enough, as I descended the stairs, I could better make out the voices. I was right, it really was Isaac, and he was definitely talking with Papa. At first, I was excited that Isaac was there, but the closer I got, the more I could tell that whatever they were discussing was serious, and it didn't seem to be going very well. I rounded the corner to the kitchen, but they were both off in the living room.

"No!" I heard Papa shout sternly. "I'll not hear of it! She needs the extra time!"

"But, sir!" Isaac argued, almost pleading. "If you'll just hear me out!"

I stayed in the kitchen so that they couldn't see me, knowing their conversation was really none of my business, but my flesh got the better of me, and unfortunately, I lingered to listen.

"Isaac," Papa continued, "ya've heard where I stand on the issue. Now, if that's all, I have chores to do before services!"

Isaac sighed in frustration.

"Yes, sir," he acquiesced.

I could tell by the tone in his voice that he was sorely disappointed about something, albeit what, I didn't know.

Suddenly, I could hear Papa coming, so I quickly darted off to the stairs so he wouldn't see me.

He walked into the kitchen and right out the front door, barely stopping to grab his hat before he left. He didn't seem very happy.

I continued to watch as Isaac came walking out of the living room and into the kitchen. He looked so discouraged and upset; I felt badly for him.

I slowly emerged from my hiding place and walked on into the kitchen just as Isaac was heading for the door.

"Good morning," I called out as I walked over towards him. "What brings you here so early?"

"Oh, Jochebed!" Isaac replied, startled to see me. "I didn't see you there!" He walked over to greet me. "I just had something I wanted to discuss with your father, is all," he explained.

"Oh?" I queried, curious.

He shook his head with a sigh.

"It's nothing," he dismissed, looking rather disheartened.

I furrowed my brow, suspicious.

"You're *sure* it's nothing?" I questioned.

I could tell he wanted to say something, but he seemed hesitant as to whether or not now was the right time.

He thought for a minute.

"I love you, Jochebed," he announced unwaveringly, "and…well…seeing Andrew and Isabelle yesterday it…it got me to thinking." He paused as a smile made its way across his face. "Do you have time to talk?" he asked excitedly.

I looked at the clock on the wall, disappointed. I knew my time was limited because I had breakfast yet to prepare and myself to get ready for church. I wanted so badly to hear what Isaac had to say, but now really wasn't the best time.

"Ohhh!" I expressed with aggravation. "I still have a lot to do before services. Do you mind if we talk while I prepare breakfast?"

Isaac contemplated as he shook his head.

"No," he declined. "I think it would be best if we could talk when we can be alone."

Just then, Samuel came meandering down the stairs and into the kitchen, rubbing his eyes, yawning.

"Mornin'," he said groggily. He suddenly noticed Isaac standing there in the kitchen. "Hey," he questioned, "what are *you* doin' here?"

Isaac just grinned, Samuel's presence putting a fine point on his previous statement.

"Had some business to tend to," he replied. He looked at me still smiling. "We'll talk later," he assured. "I really should be going anyhow." He gave me a hug. "I'll see you at church in a bit, all right?"

I reluctantly hugged him back.

"All right," I agreed. "Maybe we can talk this afternoon?"

Isaac smiled down at me.

"Sounds like a plan!" he accepted. "I'll see you later." He told me he loved me, and promptly left.

I went about preparing breakfast, my mind admittedly distracted, trying to figure out what Isaac could possibly want to talk about, and when I got to church, it was all I could do to concentrate on the message as I wanted so badly to find out!

Once the service ended, I was hoping Isaac and I could leave right away to go somewhere quiet and talk, but he said he needed to speak with Pastor Scott first before we could go. I understood, but secretly I hoped it wouldn't take too long!

While Isaac went to talk with Pastor Scott, I went to find Naomi to chat with her for a few minutes.

"Good morning, Jochebed," Naomi cheerfully said as I walked up. "Wasn't that just the loveliest wedding yesterday that you've ever seen?"

"Oh, I know!" I agreed enthusiastically. "Isabelle was *such* a beautiful bride, and Andrew, *my!* I don't think I've ever seen him look more debonair!"

"I would agree!" Naomi replied. "They do make such a handsome couple!" She grinned broadly. "Speaking of handsome couples," she prodded, "how are things with you and Isaac?"

I grinned, excitedly.

"Better!" I revealed. "We had some differences prior to the wedding, but I think we've worked them all out."

"Oh, nothing too serious, I hope?" Naomi questioned, a bit concerned.

"It was," I admitted honestly, "and it scared me but good, but we talked things through, and thankfully, we were able to reconcile our differences."

"Shoo!" Naomi responded, relieved. "That's good to hear! You two make such a wonderful couple, I'd hate to think of anything coming between the two of you!" She smiled audaciously. "So...," she wanted to know, "any talk of marriage yet?"

"Naomi!" I hushed, a little embarrassed, looking around, hoping no one else had heard. "Please, keep your voice down!" I shook my head, mortified that she would be so bold as to ask so openly. "No," I answered, "not so far."

"Well," she giggled, "if you ask me..."

I quickly motioned for her to lower her voice yet again.

Again she giggled as she looked around, leaning in.

"Well, if you ask me," she continued in a whisper so no one but she and I could hear, "I think you two should get married *soon!*"

"Naomi!" I exclaimed, surprised by her remark.

"What?" she countered. "You two were made for each other! Why wait?"

I looked at her with furrowed brow, my mouth agape.

"Umm, because I haven't finished school yet!" I not so subtly reminded her. "Not to mention the fact that Isaac still has another year of college to go, we haven't been courting a full year yet, and, *oh yah*, let's not forget the pièce de résistance...my Papa would **never** allow it! Shall I go on?"

Naomi shook her head, smiling.

"Well," she dismissed spectacularly, "I think school is overrated and *love...*should simply conqueror all!"

I chuckled at her dramatics.

"Naomi," I scolded, smiling coyly, "you're terrible!"

She chuckled back, smiling happily.

Just then, Isaac walked up.

"Ready to go?" he asked.

Naomi and I flashed a grin and giggled at each other.

Isaac looked at us both rather suspiciously.

"What are you two up to?" he questioned warily.

We chuckled, holding our secret between us.

"Oh, nothing!" Naomi answered evasively. "It's good to see you, Isaac!" She abruptly turned to me. "We'll talk later, Jochebed," she said smiling.

We hugged and she walked off.

I immediately turned back to Isaac so that we could get going, but when I did, he was looking at me with one eyebrow raised, still questioning what was going on.

"What?" I quipped innocently.

Isaac kept right on starring at me with reservation.

I grabbed his arm, smiling cagily.

"Shall we go?" I suggested.

"Uh huh!" he answered back hesitantly.

I chuckled and we walked out to his buggy together.

Isaac graciously helped me in, and when I was settled, he went around and got in on the other side.

"So," he asked, wasting no time, "is now a good time to talk?"

I smiled excitedly.

"Seems perfect to me!" I replied. "What did you want to talk about?"

Just as Isaac was about to answer, Papa came walking up to the buggy.

"Jochebed," he wanted to know, "are ya plannin' on bein' home this afternoon?"

"No, Papa," I explained. "Isaac and I have plans to spend the afternoon together. Why, did you need me for something?"

"Just didn't know if ya planned on bein' at Grampa and Gramma's today for lunch," he reminded. "With Evan and Alicia headin' back to North Dakota this afternoon, didn't know if ya wanted to say your goodbyes."

"Oh, gracious!" I exclaimed, shaking my head. "I completely forgot!" I looked at Isaac, unsure of what to do. I wanted so badly to talk with him, but I felt an obligation to family as well.

Isaac smiled, understanding.

"I guess family it is!" he announced, making the decision for me.

"All right then," Papa agreed. "I'll see ya there."

I sighed a bit melancholy as Isaac and I took off.

"I suppose we'll have to postpone our talk, won't we?" I lamented, disheartened.

"Well," Isaac offered, "we *could* start talking now, but...if it's all the same to you; I think I'd rather wait. It won't take all that long to get to your grandparents', and I really don't want to be in the middle of a conversation we can't finish."

I looked over at him so desperate and disappointed.

"Don't worry," he assured with a smile, noticing my angst, "we'll get to it sometime today, I promise!"

I sighed impatiently. The suspense was *killing me!* I just wished I could have one clue as to what was on his mind.

"Weeelll," I said flirtatiously, scooting over, snuggling close, hoping he would oblige. "Can you, at least, give me *a hint?*"

Isaac looked down at me, shaking his head.

"Oh, you're awful!" he indicted. "Just look at you trying to woo it out of me!"

I batted my eyes, shamelessly trying to cajole it out of him.

"Just *one...teeny...tiny... little...hint,*" I pressured, walking my fingers up his arm, tapping him on the nose.

"Jochebed Lowry!" he feigningly blustered. "You're *awful! Just awful!*"

We both let out a boisterous laugh!

"All right," Isaac finally relented. "I'll tell you this much."

I immediately perked up with anticipation as he nodded, seemingly ready to reveal some gravely important thing. I couldn't image what it could possibly be!

"Well!" I prodded impatiently. "What is it?"

He looked over at me with earnest.

"All I can tell you is this," he said so seriously. "It has to do with… you and me."

"Ohhh!" I protested, exasperated, whacking him on the arm, so not amused! "I may be thick, but I'm not that dense," I quipped. "I *assumed* that much! Can't you tell me *anything* more?"

Isaac chuckled at my consternation.

"Patience is a virtue, you know," he teased, trying to get a rise out of me.

"Oh, *now* look who's being awful!" I retorted.

Just then, Papa and Samuel passed us in their wagon.

"Come on you two," Papa shouted, "Gramma won't wait dinner forever!"

Isaac and I waved as they went on by.

*****

When we arrived at Grampa and Gramma's, everyone was there patiently waiting on us. I guess Isaac and I had let time slip away a bit, but fortunately we weren't too far behind Papa and Samuel. We enjoyed the meal and fellowship with family, but before we knew it, it was time to say goodbye to the Deerfields.

All of their things were already packed in their wagon and ready to go as they wanted to get a good start before nightfall. We all gave hugs and handshakes and wished them well, and when it was time for Aunt Sara and Alicia to say their goodbyes, they both broke down into tears. I knew how much Aunt Sara missed being with her sister every day, and I could tell she was just heartsick that she wasn't able to go back with them now.

As they stood there hugging and crying, frantically talking back and forth, Uncle Mark finally walked over and put his arm around Aunt Sara indicating that she needed to let her sister go. Desperately not wanting to, but understanding she must, she reluctantly stepped back, took Alicia by the hands, and gave them one last final squeeze. Alicia smiled at her longingly through her tears, before turning to climb into the wagon.

Her husband helped her up, climbed aboard himself, and they readied themselves to leave.

As Mr. and Mrs. Deerfield pulled away, Aunt Sara stood waving; tears streaming down her face. Her sister was turned, doing the same. I couldn't help but feel badly for the two of them, but I have to admit, selfishly, I was glad that Aunt Sara and Uncle Mark were staying behind with us.

Once the goodbyes were said, I stayed to help straighten things in the kitchen, and to help with the dishes, while Isaac visited with Grampa, Papa, and Uncle Mark in the family room. From time to time, Isaac would come in to check on my progress, clearly hoping that maybe he and I would have time to steal away and talk before the evening service, but even though I sensed what he wanted and did my best to hurry, there was simply no rushing Gramma. She was washing, and I was drying, and it was obvious she was *not at all* concerned about the time!

Thankfully, *finally*, Gramma came to the last dish, handing it off to me to dry. I dried it as quickly as I possibly could and walked over to the cupboard to put it away. Just

I was closing up the cupboard door, however, ready to be finished and to go find Isaac, Gramma suddenly asked if I'd do her a favor. Instantly, my heart sank in apprehension as one could never be sure what Gramma might ask.

I took a deep breath, letting it out slowly.

"What is it, Gramma?" I asked hesitantly.

"I need help icing and boxing cookies," she said. "I taking for Pastor Scott. Tomorrow his birthday and I want him to have them by tonight."

I got a fretful look on my face as I looked over at Aunt Sara. I was hoping that maybe she could help, but she was sitting at the table nursing baby Lydia and I didn't want to disturb her.

I thought of Samuel, *Perhaps he could do it,* I considered, but then suddenly, a vision of him covered in icing with cookies all over the floor went flashing through my mind and I quickly dismissed the notion. *Never mind!* I shuttered at the thought. *Terrible idea!*

Realizing I was the only one left to help, I hung my head, sighed again, and reluctantly agreed.

"Yes, Gramma," I unenthusiastically relented. "I'll help you with the cookies."

By the time Gramma and I finished icing and boxing up what seemed like a thousand cookies, it was time to go to church. Isaac and I would have to wait yet again to have our conversation.

Of course, Isaac teased me the whole way to church as he was insistent that we wait to talk until we could be alone, and have more time to do so. I was in *agony* wanting to find out what was on his mind! I could only imagine what it might be, and as one is prone to do, I had all sorts of scenarios running through my head. This was *truly* a test of my patience!

When we got to church, it took everything within me to concentrate on the message. When it was over, I was *determined* to whisk Isaac away - no more postponing, no excuses...no more delays!

Pastor Scott finally said amen and summarily dismissed the congregation.

Immediately, I grabbed Isaac's arm and started to urge him on towards the door. We were polite to those who spoke to us, but I wanted to make sure that we weren't swept up into any lengthy conversations. I vigorously kept us moving so that we could leave as quickly as possible. I'd already told Papa my plans to spend the evening with Isaac, so that was taken care of, and neither Isaac nor I had any pressing issues we needed to discuss with anyone.

As such, you would think our departure would be fairly simple, however...we were nearly out the door, almost home-free, when Pastor Scott yelled out to Isaac.

Of course, we both stopped, and right away I closed my eyes, shaking my head, anxiously thinking to myself, *What now?*

Pastor Scott came up behind us as we slowly turned around.

"Isaac," he said, "real quick! About what we discussed this morning, it's a go. Addie was able to work things out with her mother, so we'll be leaving after services on Wednesday. Thanks for being willing to fill in."

"You're welcome, Pastor Scott," Isaac replied. "Any time! I hope you enjoy your trip."

"Oh, I'm sure we will!" Pastor Scott stated enthusiastically. "And thanks again!" He smiled. "You all have a good evening, now."

Isaac nodded as he and I turned around and continued on.

"What was that all about?" I queried.

"Oh, Pastor Scott asked me if I'd be willing to preach for him next Sunday," Isaac explained. "He and Mrs. Scott are going out of town to celebrate his birthday. They weren't sure they'd be able to go, but it looks like everything worked out."

"Well, I'm happy for them!" I said. "And for you! I haven't heard you preach in such a long time. I'm really looking forward to it!"

Isaac smiled as we hurried on.

At last he and I reached his buggy where we climbed aboard and took off.

"Finally!" I exclaimed, relieved. "We're alone! Now please...*talk to me!*"

Isaac chuckled.

"I ought to make you wait until we get to the rose garden," he said with a grin.

Again, I was not amused! I gave him a look that could kill!

"Isaac Lewis!" I insisted loudly. "Don't you dare!"

He laughed hysterically at my insistence.

"All right, all right!" he relented. "I'll give you *one* hint."

"*Ohhh*, don't you *even* say it has something to do with me and you again!" I warned, in no uncertain terms.

"Well, it does!" he chuckled lightheartedly.

"Isaac!" I barked, overwrought. "You're jumping on my very last nerve! Now what is it?"

Isaac smiled.

"Okay," he surrendered, "all I'll say is this - it has to do with our future."

I'll admit I was a bit taken aback by the comment, as it was not at all what I expected him to say. I looked at him inquisitively, completely intrigued!

What could Isaac be thinking? I wondered. My heart raced with excitement and anticipation as I became quite antsy! I couldn't *wait* to get to the rose garden!

Sensing my excitement, Isaac set the horse to galloping.

We made it to his house in no time at all!

FINISHING EARLY
(Chapter 47)

When Isaac stopped the buggy in front of his house, we jumped down and raced off to the rose garden, laughing and being playful all the way. When we arrived at the gate, Isaac opened it up and ushered me inside.

"Now," he teased, acting aloof, "what would you like to do?"

"Isaac Lewis!" I protested - my patience at its end. "You know *very well* why we're here! Now talk!"

Isaac smiled broadly.

"All right," he agreed. "I guess you've waited long enough."

"I should say so!" I quipped.

The smile on Isaac's face slowly began to dissipate as a sobering look took its place.

"Isaac," I asked, perceiving the change in mood, "what is it? What was so important that we needed this time alone?"

Isaac lovingly took my hands in his as he looked me in the eyes.

"Jochebed," he started to say in such a dire and serious tone, "you know that I love you, right?"

"Yeess," I replied hesitantly, a little afraid and unsure of where he was going.

Isaac sighed troublingly.

"Well," he continued, "I know we haven't talked about it officially, and I hope I'm not overstepping my bounds, but after seeing Andrew and Isabelle tie the knot yesterday…well…it got me to thinking. Do you…" He paused a little nervous. "Do…do you ever think about *us* getting married?" he questioned.

I instantly breathed a huge sigh of relief, thankful it wasn't quite as dire as Isaac had made it seem.

"Of course I do!" I answered with a smile. "All the time!" I looked at him wondering as I sobered a bit. "Do you?" I wanted to know.

Isaac sighed again.

"I have…*some*," he admitted. "But…I guess yesterday, after seeing Andrew and Isabelle, it…it made me *really* think about it!" Suddenly an anxious look came across his face. "Don't get me wrong!" he was quick to point out. "I'm not asking for your hand right now, but I…I just thought that…well… maybe…maybe it was something that we should…you know… talk about. …What do you think?"

My smile quickly returned as we began to walk.

"Well," I told him honestly, "I do believe you're the one God has for me to marry, if…if that's what you're asking."

"Oh, I believe that, too!" Isaac promptly agreed. "But…I guess what I was wondering is…well…*when?*"

"When?" I queried, not sure I understood.

"Yes," he answered. "I mean…how long do you think we need to wait to…you know…set things in motion?"

I raised my eyebrows, quite surprised that he was asking, but admittedly thrilled that he was!

"Well," I began, not exactly sure how to answer, "I…I guess I…I guess I never really thought about specifics. I mean…well…I don't know! What do you think?"

Both of us seemed quite nervous, hemming and hawing about, hesitant to say what was really on our minds, dancing around the issue like it was taboo.

Suddenly, Isaac stopped walking, turned to me, and abruptly announced.

"I want to marry you sooner rather than later!" he stated nervously but confidently.

"Oh!" I expressed, taken aback by his declaration.

He furrowed his brow, concerned.

"You don't?" he questioned worriedly, thinking he'd said something wrong.

"Oh no!" I came back at him, trying to assure him. "It's not that! It's just that...well...I...I..." I got a very anxious look on my face. "Have you...have you spoken to my father about this?" I wondered.

Isaac took a deep breath and blew it out slowly

"Sort of," he revealed. "That's actually why I was at your house this morning. I hope you won't be angry, but I was trying to convince your father to let you finish school early by taking the state exam." Isaac shook his head, visibly upset. "He was having none of it, though," he conveyed, clearly disappointed. "Again, I'm sorry if I overstepped. Maybe you wouldn't even want to do that."

"No!" I replied vigorously. "In fact, I'll admit I've thought about it a time or two, but honestly, I quickly dismissed it on a count of I didn't know for sure where we stood with things at the time, and also on a count that I figured Papa would do exactly what he did...not allow it! I'd actually *love* to finish school early to be free to move on with my life! But..." I paused, contemplating. "Maybe if I tried talking to Papa about it," I suggested, "maybe I could get him to see!"

"No, Jochebed!" Isaac insisted. "I don't want to get you into any trouble with your father. He seemed pretty adamant about you finishing school. Besides, do you really think he'd let us marry?"

"Well, I'd hope he would!" I came back at him doggedly.

"No," Isaac clarified. "I don't mean would he let us marry *someday*, I mean, do you really think he'd let us marry...you know...sometime in the near future?"

I nodded, understanding, as a smile quickly made its way across my face.

"I guess there's only one way to find out!" I teased, tempting him.

Isaac grinned.

"I guess you're right!" he quipped back.

I giggled, overjoyed.

"I just can't believe we're actually having this conversation!" I expressed excitedly as we began to walk again. "I've dreamed of this for so long it...it hardly seems real!"

"I know!" Isaac agreed. "I guess it's something that's always seemed so far away...but now..." He smiled eagerly as he looked over at me. "Now...well...now I feel as if it's almost in reach!" he expressed with enthusiasm. "Seeing my brother marry...I can't deny it...it did make me envious!" He stopped again, turning towards me, taking me into his arms. "It made me realize just how much I love you, Jochebed," he said, gazing into my eyes. "It made me realize how much I love you, and how much I want to be with you!"

I gazed back into his beautiful blue eyes, smiling affectionately.

"I love you, too, Isaac," I affirmed, "with all of my heart!"

Isaac hugged me tightly, as I did him, and we continued walking.

"I'll speak to your father right away!" Isaac promised, determined. "I want to get this settled! I want you to be my wife!"

My heart was simply aflutter as I was grinning from ear to ear; completely overwhelmed with joy and excitement! I desperately hoped Papa would be willing to listen to reason, but admittedly, there was a part of me that feared he'd stand in our way. I tried not to dwell on the negative, however... I just wanted to enjoy this special time with Isaac!

Isaac and I spent the next hour together in the rose garden, enjoying each other's company immensely, talking some more about the future and reminiscing a little about the past. By the end of the evening, I couldn't have been more thankful to have him in my life. I knew beyond a shadow of a doubt that he was the one whom God would have me to marry, and I couldn't *wait* for that dream to come true!

After spending a lovely evening together, Isaac drove me home. We said our goodnights, and I went inside.

Surprisingly, Papa was waiting for me at the table in the kitchen.

"Did ya have a nice time?" he asked as I came walking through the door.

"Yes, Papa!" I answered happily, still excited from the day. "It was absolutely wonderful! Isaac and I had a really good talk."

"Did ya now?" Papa quipped. "Care to share?"

I walked over and gave Papa a kiss on the cheek before joining him at the table.

"We talked of all sorts of things," I relayed, a bit evasively.

Papa looked at me soberly.

"Did Isaac happen to share why he was here this mornin'?" he wanted to know.

I looked at Papa sheepishly.

"Yes, he...he told me," I replied hesitantly, afraid Papa would be upset that he had.

"And what do ya think about it?" he queried.

I was actually surprised Papa was even bringing it up, but it seemed he wanted to discuss it, so I obliged.

"Well," I explained, gaining confidence as I spoke, "I very much want to be with Isaac, and well...if that means I have to be done with school earlier than normal, then...I'm willing to study hard and take the exam!" I looked at him quite earnestly. "I love him so much, Papa!" I stated unwaveringly. "And I know he loves me, too! We're certain it's God's will for us to be together!" I shook my head, wanting so badly for Papa to understand. "So...given all that," I went on to say, pleading my case, "I...I see no reason for us to have to wait a whole other year before we can be together!"

Papa sat listening, nearly expressionless, indicating absolutely *nothing* one way or the other. I honestly had no idea what he was thinking. I was so afraid that maybe I'd said too much, but it was how I felt, and regardless of the outcome, I knew he needed to know.

I sat there nervously, anxiously waiting for him to reply.

After sitting there quietly for several minutes, doing nothing more than staring at me austerely, finally, *thankfully*, Papa spoke up.

"I'm assumin' Isaac told ya my position on the matter?" he questioned sternly, his tone ominous.

"Yeess, sir," I admitted reluctantly, fearful I'd made him angry.

Papa stared at me once gain quite seriously. Not knowing what it meant, I swallowed hard, fretful, worried sick for what he was about to say. As I waited, all sorts of terrible thoughts went running through my mind. I was trying not to think the worst, but I just couldn't help it! Papa seemed so unsympathetic and unyielding. I did my best to brace myself for what I thought was coming, but try as I might, I just couldn't!

When, he started to speak, I was *not at all* prepared for what he said to me!

"Jochebed," he began, "I've watched ya over these past months - everything ya've been through, everything ya've had to endure, and I...I've seen ya handle yourself with such dignity and grace. I know it hasn't been easy for ya, and I know ya've had your ups and downs, but I've definitely seen a real growth and maturity in ya."

Much to my surprise, Papa started to tear up a little, something I certainly wasn't expecting him to do. His emotion threw me, and I didn't know what to think.

"I've also watched Isaac through all of it," he went on, "and I'll confess, I'm impressed with how he's handled himself, how he's treated ya, how he's stood by ya and helped ya through your trials. It's obvious he cares for ya a great deal, and that he loves ya very much." He sighed, seemingly melancholy. "I admit that as your father, I wanna hold on to ya and protect ya forever," he told me, "but with everything that's happened over this past year, I...I've learned that that's not possible. As much as I wanna keep ya my little girl..." He paused, fighting back tears, clearing his throat, trying to compose himself. "As much as I wanna keep ya my little girl," he reiterated, "I can't! Ya've simply grown up into a fine young lady, and...I need to accept that." He wiped a tear and then another, before continuing. "I know I haven't always handled things the best," he humbly admitted, "but...well...I guess what I'm tryin' to say is...I've thought a lot about what Isaac proposed this mornin', and...if ya really wanna finish school early, then...then ya have my permission."

My mouth instantly fell open, completely stunned! I honestly thought Papa would *never* allow me to do such a thing! In fact, I was so shocked and taken aback by what he'd just told me, I almost didn't know how to respond!

"Papa," I managed to eke out, "I...I...I don't know what to say!" I shook my head, bewildered as I leaned over and gave him a big hug. I couldn't help it; I broke down into tears. "I love you so much, Papa!" I expressed, overcome, still hugging his neck. "Thank you so much! Thank you! You've made me the happiest girl in the world!"

"You're welcome, sweetheart," Papa replied, patting my back, smiling.

I could tell it wasn't easy for him, but he did seem genuinely happy for me.

I sat back, elated, as I wiped my tears, still amazed at what had just happened. I was so overwhelmed and thrilled for what it could mean; I couldn't *wait* to tell Isaac!

SUMMER STORM
(Chapter 48)

Monday morning, I awoke to rain pounding on the roof, thunder rolling, and lightning flashing across the sky. It was a dreadful storm, and I was a little worried. Tornado season was upon us, and we'd definitely seen our fair share in the past. The wind was blowing something fierce, and I could hear the shutters on the house banging and clanging terribly!

I quickly got up, got myself dressed, and went downstairs to see if Papa and Samuel were awake yet. When I reached the kitchen, Samuel was standing at the window, intently staring outside.

"What is it, Samuel?" I asked frantically as I walked over to him.

"I'm watchin' Papa," he replied.

"*What? Why?*" I questioned in a panic, surprised and concerned that Papa would be out in such a storm.

"A big ol' branch came crashin' down on part of the barn out there," he told me, "and Papa's tryin' to get it off!"

I quickly wormed my way in beside Samuel to see if I could see what was going on.

"He told me to stay inside," Samuel explained, as we both watched Papa struggling something awful in the wind and driving rain. "Said it was too dangerous for me to be out there."

"Then what in the world is *he* doing out there?" I exclaimed, infuriated by Papa's lack of judgment.

Samuel shrugged.

"He said he wanted to get the branch off the roof and patch the hole before the rain damaged stuff in the barn," Samuel answered. "I offered to help him, but he wouldn't let me."

I shook my head and sighed, exasperated!

What was Papa thinking! I blustered to myself. I stood there anxiously watching him as he fought the wind, trying his best to get the ladder up against the barn. Unbelievably, the rain was pounding so hard at times, I could barely see him. "This is *ridiculous!*" I charged. "That ladder's going to fall over with Papa still on it, or worse yet, another limb's going to fall right on top of him!"

Samuel shrugged again seemingly indifferent.

"I tried to warn him," he quipped.

We both stood there watching Papa exert himself, straining and struggling to climb the ladder, nearly falling twice before reaching the top.

"I can't take this any longer!" I blurted out, fearful! I went to grab my shawl, hastily putting it on.

"Where do ya think you're goin?" Samuel groused with a frown.

"To talk some sense into Papa!" I barked back, determined.

I quickly opened the door to step out onto the porch, but when I did, the wind was blowing so violently, it nearly blew me right back into the house! Pressing on, I stepped out into the storm, turned, and pulled with all my might to close the door behind me. When I turned back around, the rain immediately began pelting me in the face, stinging my cheeks something awful as it was coming down so hard and at such an angle. Barely able to see, I stepped forward, leaning into the wind, fighting to get to the post by the porch steps. Finally close enough, I grabbed hold and held on for dear life!

"Papa!" I shouted worriedly. "Come back inside!"

The wind was swirling and howling so loudly, Papa couldn't hear me over the noise.

"Papa!" I shouted again even louder. "Come in! You shouldn't be out there!"

Still, Papa gave no response.

As I looked to the sky, it looked frighteningly foreboding, and all around me I could hear limbs creaking and cracking as debris whirled about, and there was Papa drenched through with rain, relentlessly fighting the wind. I knew it was pointless to keep yelling, so I contemplated what to do.

Papa needed to get inside, I concluded, but knowing how stubborn he could be, I figured the only way I was going to accomplish that was to make my way out to the barn, and drag him in myself! I cautiously let go of the post I was holding on to, and struggled down the steps, fighting the wind and rain the whole time. As I managed to step off the last step, ready to head for the barn, suddenly there was a huge gust of wind, followed by a tremendous crash! Another huge limb had broken off and landed not three feet in front of me. Naturally, it startled both me and Papa at the same time.

Papa immediately looked up from what he was doing, saw me standing there, and motioned for me to go back inside. I stood my ground, however, motioning for him to do the same. He obstinately shook his head, pointed adamantly for me to go, and continued right on working.

Needless to say, I was furious! I was so afraid for him to be out there in this raging storm, but there was clearly nothing I could do about it.

Accepting that it wasn't safe for me either, I shook my head, aggravated, and reluctantly complied with Papa's wishes. It was all I could do to make it back inside.

"What, are ya nuts?" Samuel scolded as I came into the house, quickly shutting the door behind me. "Ya could've been killed out there!"

"Oh, Samuel!" I groused, completely drenched and miserable, "Papa shouldn't be out there either! What are we gonna do?"

"Don't think there's anything we *can* do!" he said dismissively, looking out the window again. "Ya know Papa, he's stubborn and *obviously* determined to get that roof fixed no matter what!"

I stood there shivering from the dampness, anxiously looking out the window with Samuel. The lightning and thunder were almost nonstop at this point, and the wind was blowing so hard I could hear the house creaking and actually feel it swaying from time to time.

As I watched the trees whirling and bending in the wind, and debris blowing about, I couldn't help but worry all the more for Papa! He needed to be inside out of this violent storm, but he just wouldn't listen! Frustrated, I found myself wishing Isaac was here so that he could give me some advice as to what to do. Sensing the growing danger, unsurprisingly, my fear began to grow exponentially!

Suddenly, without warning, there was a big flash of light and an unbelievable boom! The big oak tree that stood in front of our house had completely snapped in two and crashed to the ground with a jarring thud. When it hit, I instinctively let out a terrified scream!

Samuel, too, instantaneously jumped back from the window and shouted.

"Whoa, did ya see that!" he exclaimed with an excited chuckle.

Did I see it? Of course I did! I thought to myself. And now I couldn't see Papa anymore either! The tree was so large that it blocked my view of where Papa had been working, and the way it fell, I was afraid that maybe it had landed close to or on top of him. Scared that he may be hurt (or worse), I just had to go check!

I scurried towards the door to venture back out into the horrific storm, but before I could even get there, it started to hail, and I could hear the winds picking up speed. I'll confess part of me feared a tornado as the sky was black and threatening, and the tops of the trees were swirling about, but I didn't really care! I had to make sure that Papa was all right!

"Samuel!" I instructed frantically. "Stay away from the window just in case! I'm going to find Papa!"

"No, way!" Samuel protested. "That's just foolish! I'll go!"

I gave him a look of provocation.

"Have you lost your mind?" I came back at him. "There's no way you're going out there in this storm! As scrawny as you are, that wind will carry you clean away!"

"Hey!" Samuel scoffed, offended. "That's not nice! How dare ya call me scrawny?"

"Oh, would you just stop!" I yelled, perturbed. "I don't have time to stand here and argue with you! I'm going, you're staying, and that's final!"

Just then, the door swung open, wind blowing harshly, rain pouring in!

I startled and abruptly turned around!

"Papa, thank goodness!" I exclaimed, thrilled to see him standing there all in one piece.

"Get to the cellar, now!" he demanded sternly.

We all took off as fast as we could go!

To get to the cellar, we had to go out the back door that was in the living room. No one ever used it much, so it always stayed locked.

Papa quickly unlocked it, and we made our way outside. Fortunately, we didn't have far to go as the cellar was relatively close to the house, situated in the back yard.

When we got to the cellar, Papa lifted the heavy door and ushered Samuel and me inside. After we were in, Papa stepped in with us, closed the door on top of us, and latched it tightly. Once we were squared away inside the cellar, Papa told us what was happening. A tornado was nearby, and we needed to wait it out.

As we crouched inside, I could hear the wind howling something fierce overhead, and it was so loud, it sounded like a locomotive barreling down on us! It was violently throwing debris up against the house and onto the cellar door, and every once in awhile, glass would shatter from its force.

Visibly shaking, I was scared to death! I couldn't help but worry for Grampa and Gramma and Uncle Mark and Aunt Sara and little baby Lydia. I hoped and prayed that they were somewhere safe, and that they would be all right!

Thankfully, we weren't down in the cellar for very long when the wind started to die down, and the rain lessened to a drizzle. Within minutes, the sun was peeking through the clouds as the storm rumbled off into the distance. It felt a little strange just sitting there waiting, but Papa wanted to make sure that everything was passed before we tried to venture out.

After waiting a few more minutes, Papa tried to open the cellar door, and while it took several tries due to the debris that was resting atop it, after giving it one more good shove, he finally managed to get it open.

Once we were freed, Papa stepped out and looked around. He assessed the situation to determine whether or not it was safe for Samuel and me to leave the cellar, and when he decided it was, he allowed us to exit.

When we got to the top of the steps, we could see limbs and leaves lying *everywhere!* Apprehensive, we climbed out and made our way carefully back to the house.

Papa went first, making sure the path was safe, I followed and then Samuel. When we finally entered the house, amazingly, the living room appeared untouched. As we made our way towards the kitchen, however, we all just stopped and stood at the edge of the room, stunned in disbelief! The window had been blown out and glass was lying all over the floor, the door was wide open, banging against the wall, and it looked as if the outside had simply decided to come inside. Water was dripping from several places, chairs were over turned, everything was damp, and there were leaves and sticks and debris lying all about.

"Careful!" Papa cautioned. "I don't want ya gettin' hurt!"

Again, he went first, making a path for us to follow.

As we cautiously stepped over and around this and that, we all made our way to the front door to see how the barn had fared. Fortunately, it looked like it hadn't sustained any major damage, other than the initial branch that had fallen on its roof. Papa breathed a huge sigh of relief, thankful it had been spared!

Guardedly, Papa walked out onto the porch, but he told Samuel and me to stay back. A branch had fallen on part of the roof, causing a section of it to cave in a little, and he didn't want us out there not knowing if it was stable or not.

Samuel and I obeyed, standing just inside, surveying the widespread damage all around. Trees were down here and there, pieces of the fence that lined our yard had fallen to the ground, and with the limbs and leaves blown everywhere, it looked a bit like a war torn battlefield.

After the initial shock wore off, I anxiously looked at Papa.

"Can we go check on Grampa and Gramma and the others?" I asked, worried for their safety.

"I was just thinkin' on that," Papa said. "You and Sam stay here and get started cleanin'. I'll make my way to their house and check on everybody."

I nodded, agreeing, as Papa made his way down off the porch and on towards Grampa and Gramma's.

As Samuel and I turned to get started in the kitchen, the task at hand seemed overwhelming. There were so many things out of place, and the mess was impressive!

"Well," I sighed, "you start collecting all these sticks and limbs, and I'll find the broom to start cleaning up the broken glass. Just be careful, all right?"

"Yah, you, too," Samuel echoed.

Samuel and I got busy right away, but as we cleaned, I couldn't help but worry about my family and about Isaac and his. I couldn't wait to get word that everyone was all right and I prayed diligently that they were.

We cleaned and cleaned for quite some time and got a fair amount accomplished before Papa came back from checking on the family.

"How is everyone?" I asked earnestly as Papa stepped inside.

"They fared reasonably well." he explained. "Uncle Mark has a gash on his head from where he got hit by a limb, but they've managed to patch him up pretty well. Both houses and barns have minimal damage, but nothin' that can't be fixed. All in all, they were fortunate. Looks like we suffered the brunt of it here."

"Shoo! That's a relief," I expressed, grateful. "I was so worried for them!"

"I was, too," Papa admitted, "but God's good!"

I smiled, agreeing.

Papa smiled back before heading outside to get started on things out there.

Knowing my family was safe helped to lessen my worry a little, but I couldn't help but still be concerned for Isaac and his family. I hoped I would hear something soon, wanting desperately to know that they were all right!

Samuel and I continued to clean things in the house while Papa worked to get things squared away outside, and after about two hours or so of working, I looked out to see Sheriff Bradley riding up on his horse. He'd come by to check on us, making the rounds to outlying farms, surveying the damage, and making sure that everyone was all right. He only stayed a few minutes, however, speaking briefly with Papa before moving on.

When I saw that the sheriff had gone, I carefully stepped out onto the porch and called to Papa.

"Did Sheriff Bradley happen to say anything about the Lewises?" I queried.

"No, sweetheart," Papa called back, "I'm sorry he didn't. He's still checkin' on folks, though. If we don't hear somethin' real soon, maybe we can ride over ourselves and make sure they're all right."

He started to walk towards me so that he didn't have to yell.

I couldn't help but notice he looked troubled.

"What is it Papa?" I asked, concerned.

He shook his head quite dour.

"Sheriff said that the Motter's didn't fare so well," he informed. "Apparently, their house was completely destroyed, and Mrs. Motter and little Levi were injured badly enough that they had to take 'em to the hospital."

I immediately put my hand to my chest, completely distressed by the news.

"Oh, Papa!" I remarked, fretful. "I so hope they'll be all right!"

Papa nodded, agreeing, as he went on.

"Sheriff said the Clark's had significant damage as well," he told me. "They lost part of their house and their entire barn was destroyed. Two of their horses and a milkin' cow were killed, too." He sighed, distressed. "This storm sure did a number on quite a few folks," he commented as he shook his head again in disbelief. "The sad part is," he pointed out with concern, "Sheriff Bradley hasn't even finished checkin' on everybody yet."

"Oh, Papa!" I exclaimed again. "I surely hope no one else is hurt!" I looked around at all the devastation. "What a horrible, wicked storm this turned out to be!" I lamented. "I thought we had a lot to contend with here, but after hearing about what others have suffered, it simply pales in comparison. I'll definitely add the Motters and Clarks to my prayers."

"That'd be good," Papa approved. He went back to work, and so did I.

As I busied myself again, I kept thinking of the Motter's and the Clarks, and, of course, of Isaac and his family. I still hadn't heard anything as to how they were doing, and the more time passed, the more worried I became. I wanted so badly to run off and check on them, but I knew my help was needed here.

I worked as quickly and as diligently as I could to get the house back into some semblance of order, and while it took several hours to do so, it *was* coming along. Papa and Samuel worked outside on the big oak tree, trying to cut it up and get it moved, so that they could repair the damage to the fence. It was a long, arduous process, but they were making good progress.

As I was finishing up in the kitchen, I heard a wagon pull up outside. When I looked out the window to see who it was, my heart leapt for joy as it was Isaac driving up. As quickly as I was thrilled to see him, however, that's how quickly my emotions changed to one of concern when I saw that his arm was bandaged and hanging in a sling. I immediately rushed outside to see if he was all right!

In my haste, I completely forgot about the damage to the porch roof, and while Papa had already removed the branch from it, the roof itself was still unstable. Needless to say, when I instinctively closed the door behind me, the jarring was enough to cause that portion of the roof to give way right in front of me. I screamed in alarm at the sudden collapse.

Papa, Samuel and Isaac all came running to see if I was all right.

"Jochebed, are you okay?" Papa frantically called out.

As the last bit of debris finally drifted to the ground, coming to a rest there in front of me, I was stuck, standing between the house and a rather large pile of rubble. I looked out at all of them as they stood there eagerly waiting for me to answer. I quickly assessed myself, and shouted back.

"I'm fine, Papa," I assured, feeling completely embarrassed by my foolish mistake. "Just a bit shaken is all!"

Isaac and Papa immediately scrambled to the top of the heap.

"You're sure you're all right?" Papa questioned again, reaching out his hand to help me out of my predicament.

"Yes, Papa," I replied as I took hold. "I'm so sorry I forgot about the roof."

Papa and Isaac helped me up and over the debris and down off the porch. We all stood there staring at the extended damage.

"Well," Papa remarked, trying to put a positive light on the horrible situation in front of us, "that ol' porch's been needin' repairs now for quite a while anyhow. Guess I can't put it off any longer, can I?" He looked over at me as he gave me a wink and a smile.

"Sorry, Papa!" I cowered, feeling badly. Knowing there was nothing else I could say or do to change the present circumstances; I abruptly turned my attention to Isaac. "Your arm," I queried, "are you okay? What happened?"

"Oh, I'll be fine," he downplayed. "Just a minor fracture is all. It happened when I was trying to help my grandparents get to safety. In fact, I would've been here sooner to check on you, but the damage at our place was extensive, and I had to tend to my grandparents."

"Oh, Isaac!" I exclaimed with concern. "Your grandparents, are they all right?"

"I think they will be," he replied glumly. "They both got cut up pretty badly, and unfortunately, Grandfather broke some ribs, but once Dr. Wellesley came and bandaged him up and gave him some medicine for the pain, he seemed in better spirits. Of course, we had to wait quite a while for Dr. Wellesley to get there - as you can imagine, he's been pretty busy making the rounds, so Grandfather suffered in excruciating pain before he arrived. It was truly hard to watch!"

"Wow, I'm sorry to hear that, Son," Papa relayed with sympathy. "Is there anything we can do to help?"

"You look like you have your hands pretty full here, sir," Isaac replied. "I'm sure that once Andrew and Isabelle return from their honeymoon, we'll be able to get things patched up. For now, though, I'll do what I can, even though, unfortunately," he sighed, "I'm pretty limited." He lifted his broken arm, emphasizing his point. "I've moved us out into the shanty on our property," he informed, "and we should be all right in there until I can get the house repaired. Hopefully, it won't be too long until I can get that done."

Papa stood listening with a furrowed brow.

"That's just nonsense!" he blustered. "We need a town meetin' right away! We need to get together and assess who needs the most help and get busy puttin' things back together for folks!" He looked at Isaac. "Ya do what ya can in the meantime," he said. "I'm goin' right now to town to ring that bell and get the ball rollin'!"

Isaac nodded, smiling, encouraged by the plan.

"Sounds good!" he said excitedly. "I'll come with you!"

"No need!" Papa told him. "Ya tend to you and your family. We'll let ya know if we need your help."

"All right, sir," Isaac accepted. "Will do!"

With that, Papa took Samuel and left for town.

When they were gone, I turned and gave Isaac a big hug.

"I'm so glad to see you're all right!" I said with fervor. "I was so worried about you!"

"And I you," Isaac revealed as he hugged me back. "You were all I could think about when that tornado was barreling down on us. I'm so thankful for the Lord's protection!"

We both just stood there hugging each other for a minute, realizing how blessed we were to have come through the terrible storm as well as we had.

"Your arm," I questioned, concerned. "Does it hurt?"

"A little," Isaac admitted, "but it'll mend. I'm just glad it wasn't any worse."

"Me, too!" I said with relief as I hugged him again tightly. "I love you, so much!"

"I love you, too!" he echoed with a sigh, thankful.

We stood there a little longer.

"Well," Isaac finally said, "I so hate to leave you, but I really should get back to my grandparents."

"Oh no!" I insisted, "I fully understand! I'll come with you!"

Isaac looked at me with question.

"Are you sure?" he asked. "What about your place…and your father? You didn't tell him you'd be leaving."

"I'll leave him a note," I assured. "I'm sure he won't mind. Besides, there's not a lot more that needs to be done inside the house anyway, and I'm almost certain Papa wouldn't want me doing anything out here on my own."

Isaac considered it.

"All right," he agreed, "but…" He paused, looking over at the mess on the porch blocking the front door. "How on earth are you going to get back inside the house to leave a note?" he queried.

"I should be able to get in through the back door," I explained, starting to walk in that direction. "I don't think anyone locked it back after we came in from the cellar."

Isaac and I made our way to the back of the house, and sure enough, the door was still unlocked. I went inside, wrote Papa a note, gathered a few things, and then Isaac and I left in his wagon.

As we drove over to his house, the devastation from the storm was evident everywhere. There were trees down, fences broken, houses damaged, and animals that were supposed to be in pins, out roaming the country side, loosed by the storm. I couldn't believe how wide spread the damage was or how much it had changed the landscape.

I thought to myself as I took it all in how impossible it seemed that things could ever be back to normal!

COMING TOGETHER
(Chapter 49)

When we arrived at Isaac's house, I wanted to cry at the sight.

"Oh, Isaac!" I bemoaned as we made our way down the lane to his house. "Look at your beautiful home!"

"I know," Isaac agreed, shaking his head, disheartened. "I still can't believe it's as bad as it is. Fortunately, though, the damage is only in the front of the house. When you see the back, you'd never know anything happened."

Isaac pulled up and drove on past the house, continuing down the lane to the little shanty that sat towards the back of the Lewis' property. He stopped the wagon, helped me down, and we went inside.

Isaac's grandparents were both there; his grandmother was standing at a small table, trying to peel some potatoes for their lunch, while his grandfather was resting on a small cot in the corner.

"Grandmother!" Isaac reprimanded when he saw her. "You shouldn't be trying to do that! I told you I'd find us something to eat in the house when I got back."

His grandmother's arms were covered in bandages, and her hand was wrapped as well.

"Well," she defended, as Isaac took the knife from her hand and guided her to a chair, "I was going crazy just sitting here. You won't let me do anything in the house, and I feel I need to get busy doing *something!*"

"Rest, Grandmother!" Isaac strongly encouraged. "You need to heal first."

"Son," Mrs. Lewis chided, "I appreciate your concern, but I'm fine - a little sore perhaps - but fine! I'll not break if I try to help out!" She turned and looked at me. "It's good to see you, Jochebed," she said sweetly. "How did your family fare?"

"Well, at first," I confessed, "I thought we fared quite terribly, but after seeing and hearing of the devastation of others, the damage we sustained was really quite minimal. We have some damage to the house and barn, but no lives lost, thankfully, and only my Uncle Mark was injured."

"Oh, gracious!" Mrs. Lewis exclaimed. "I hope not too seriously!"

"No, no!" I assured her. "He has a minor cut on his head, but he should be fine." She sighed, relieved.

"Well, that's so good to hear!" she remarked. "Now," she continued, turning back to Isaac, "I think I can manage a few potatoes!" She stood up and put her hand out wanting Isaac to return the knife to her.

Isaac gave her a reluctant look as he sighed, shaking his head. Knowing she wasn't going to back down, he finally relented.

"All right," he reluctantly agreed, handing her the knife. "But promise me you won't over do!"

"I'll be fine!" she told him. "You go do what you need to do in the house, and I'll tend to your grandfather out here. But, Isaac," she implored, "you be careful in there! That house surely can't be safe!"

Isaac gave her a reassuring smile.

"I'll be careful, Grandmother," he promised as he kissed her cheek. "We'll be back in a little while."

Isaac and I left Mr. and Mrs. Lewis and headed back to the house.

As Isaac pulled the wagon up to the back door, I was immediately struck by the contrast. Isaac was right, to look at the back of the house, you'd never know anything had happened.

He and I got down and carefully entered through the back door.

"I want to gather a few things for lunch," Isaac said as we walked into the kitchen. "After that, I'll get started on the cleanup in here."

"What can I do?" I asked, eagerly wanting to help.

"Well," Isaac contemplated, "I guess *you* could get things together for lunch and take them out to Grandmother." He cocked his head. "That way, I could go ahead and get started in the front of the house. Is that all right with you?"

"Sure, that's fine!" I agreed. "But Isaac," I urged, "please do be careful, all right?"

He smiled.

"I will," he assured. "Don't worry! I have no desire to get hurt any worse than I already am."

I nodded, satisfied, as Isaac and I went right to work.

I gathered what I could for lunch and took it out to Mrs. Lewis. She thanked me, and busied herself preparing the meal using the small fireplace there in the shanty. I offered to stay and help her, but she said she could manage and that Isaac probably needed my help more. I agreed and went back to see what I could do.

As I reentered the house and made my way to find Isaac, it almost seemed eerie. The house was quiet except for the drip, drip, drip of water falling on the floor from the rather large crack in the roof. There were puddles of water everywhere, and the furniture was wet and moved about, some even overturned. A lot of the Lewis' things were broken and scattered throughout the house, and one of the walls had split in two and was leaning a bit.

I carefully made my way through the dining room and into the living room.

"Careful!" Isaac yelled out when he saw me coming. "That ceiling above you isn't stable! Here, walk over this way." He motioned for me to go around on the other side.

I immediately complied, slowly making my way to him, following his directions.

"Gracious!" I commented when I got over to him, overwhelmed by the scene. "I'm so sorry for all you've lost!"

Isaac put his arm around me as he stood there looking around at all the mess.

"It's just things," he pointed out. "Nothing that can't be replaced."

"I know," I understood. "But still, how devastating!"

He gave me a reassuring squeeze, and he and I went to work.

We did what we could to clean things up and to salvage as much as possible. We made sure to steer clear of any areas that were unstable and tried to be as careful as we could amidst the poor working conditions. We worked for about an hour or so and accomplished quite a bit despite Isaac being limited by his injured arm.

Before we knew it, Mrs. Lewis was coming to the back door, calling us to lunch. It was a welcomed break from all the grueling work I'd been doing pretty much nonstop since I'd gotten up that morning. I was looking forward to being able to just sit and rest for a little while.

After lunch, Isaac and I decided we needed to get back to work. Before we left, however, Mr. Lewis expressed how sorry he was that he couldn't help us out. Isaac tried to assure him that it was all right, and that we could handle things, but Mr. Lewis still felt awful that he was of no use. I couldn't help but feel badly for him.

Isaac and I thanked Mrs. Lewis for the meal and headed back to the house.

I suppose it'd been an hour or so that he and I had been working, when suddenly we heard wagons coming up the lane. We both peered out the cracked window in the front of the house to see who it was.

"I don't recognize that group of people," I remarked to Isaac. "Do you?"

Isaac looked again.

"No," he agreed. "They don't look familiar to me either." He set aside the item he was holding in his hand as he started for the front door. "You wait here," he instructed. "I'll make my way outside to talk to them and find out what they want."

I watched as the wagons continued to come; there were four in all, and each was full of men.

When they came to a stop, Isaac walked up to greet them, and I could just make out what they were saying through the broken window I was still peering out of.

"Good day!" Isaac called out as he walked up to the first wagon. "May I help you?"

A big burly man jumped down and walked over to greet Isaac. He looked a bit rough, but friendly as he extended his hand to shake Isaac's.

Isaac obliged as the man responded.

"No, sir," the man said. "Ya can't help us, but we can help *you!*"

Isaac looked at him a bit puzzled.

"I'm sorry, sir," he replied. "I don't think I understand. Do I know you?"

"Nope!" the man quipped. "At least, I don't think ya do. Me and my men here, why, we're from the surroundin' area and we heard about the devastation ya folks suffered over here this mornin'. We've come to help ya rebuild, and from the looks of it," he said, surveying the damage, "looks like ya could use the help."

A smile made its way across Isaac's face as he was pleasantly surprised and grateful.

"Why…I don't know what to say!" he exclaimed in disbelief. "That's…that's amazing! And mighty generous of you, too! Thank you! But…" He paused, realizing that others had a much greater need. "I know there are other folks hurting worse than we are," he told the man. "Perhaps if you're wanting to help, those families should come first."

"No need!" the man assured. "We have other men already on those jobs. Plus, I know your townsfolk have gathered a bunch of men to help out, too." He smiled kindly. "I think we've got it covered!"

Isaac was simply overwhelmed.

"Well, all right, then," he accepted, "if you're certain…we sure could use the help!"

"I'm *absolutely* certain!" the man confirmed. "Now, if you're willin', we'd like to get started as soon as possible."

Isaac extended his hand and shook the man's hand again, thanking him profusely.

The man gestured to the other men on the wagons, and they all got down and descended on the house.

Isaac came back in and got me, and we stepped out of the way just as a large group of men were making their way into the house. As you can imagine, it was an amazing sight to see! They got busy right away, and I just couldn't believe how quickly they worked and with such care and precision. They accomplished in just a short amount of time what Isaac and I had tried to do in an hour. I guess the saying really is true, "Many hands make light work."

Before supper was ready, the men had already repaired the roof, reset and repaired the damaged wall, cleaned up most of the water, and were starting to refurbish some of the damaged furniture.

I was just astounded that this group of strangers was so willing to give of their time and talents to help out people they didn't even know, and to do such a fine job on top of it!

By the time daylight was fleeting, the strangers had the Lewis' home livable again. There were still minor repairs that needed to be made and things that definitely needed to be replaced, but the major things were taken care of, and the Lewises didn't have to spend one night in the shanty.

Isaac was so appreciative, but yet at a loss as to how to repay the men. He tried to give them money, but they flat out refused. They said it was their pleasure and that they'd do it again in a heartbeat. Nevertheless, Isaac wanted to do something, so he insisted they stay for supper. They were hesitant, not wanting to impose, but they did finally accept his offer.

When they finished eating, they loaded up, and in no time at all they were on their way. I realized after they'd gone that I hadn't even learned most of their names. They'd all been so busy, working so hard that there simply wasn't time for a lot of chit chat. They came, did their job, and left. It was truly something to see and such a wonderful blessing!

"God never ceases to amaze me," Isaac commented as he and I stood there watching the last wagon pull away. "He's so good, far beyond what I can express!"

"I know exactly what you mean!" I wholeheartedly agreed. I paused, contemplating. "I wonder how the other families fared," I pondered aloud.

"Well," Isaac remarked, "if they got a crew half as good as ours, they ought to be under roof by now - or close to it. That was an incredible group of men!"

"It sure was!" I concurred. "Hopefully, one day we'll have an opportunity to repay them somehow."

"Oh, I hope you're right!" Isaac approved. "Although, I sure don't know how we ever could!"

Isaac and I turned around to admire the work the men had done on the house. It was simply amazing and unbelievably flawless! If you didn't know any better, you'd never even guess that a destructive storm had come through earlier that morning, wreaking havoc on the Lewis' home.

Isaac put his arm around me and pulled me close.

"God is just good!" he reiterated, squeezing me tightly. "He just is!"

STUDYING HARD
(Chapter 50)

The aftermath of the storm was lessened by the kindness of strangers, and while it took a few more days of hard work to get everyone back to normal, within the week, there was little evidence that a tornado had even come through.

The only tragedy of the storm that strangers couldn't fix was the loss of the Motter's five-year-old son, Levi. He'd been badly injured along with his mother when the tornado hit, and even though they'd been taken to the hospital for treatment, Levi's injuries were just too extensive, and the doctors were unable to save him.

When Mrs. Motter returned home from the hospital after recovering from her injuries, the town gathered on that Thursday to bury little Levi.

It was a beautiful service, and Pastor Scott did a lovely job. He and Mrs. Scott had postponed their trip due to the storm and, of course, due to the tragedy of losing Levi.

I couldn't help but feel sad and heartbroken for the Motters. They were such a wonderful, sweet Christian family, and they're loss was almost unbearable. Levi was the youngest of their eight children, and he was such a charming, adorable, little man - so small, yet so grown-up. He had the type of personality that would light up a room, and there was no doubt he was going to be missed terribly!

Unhappily, I could relate to what the Motters were going through as it was the one year anniversary of Mama's passing. Having lost her so unexpectedly, just as the Motters had lost little Levi, it made me very empathetic to their pain.

I have to admit, though, it was extremely difficult attending another funeral at this time of year. To see another family having to suffer the way my family and I had, it brought back floods of emotions that had overwhelmed me on the day that Mama was killed.

At the funeral, I cried a wealth of tears, not only for the Motters, but for missing Mama as well. As I watched the Motters go through their horrible anguish, however, I could see the extra measure of grace that God was extending to them. It made me realize just how faithful God truly is, for I recognized that it was the same measure of grace that He had given to me and my family in our desperate hour of need.

After the funeral was over, Isaac could sense that I needed some time away, so he whisked me off to the rose garden, partially to check on how much damage it had sustained in the storm, but mostly to give me a place of solitude where I could be alone and deal with what I was going through.

I was very quiet all the way from the cemetery to Isaac's place as I wept on and off, grieving over all that had happened. Isaac was a perfect gentleman, though, leaving me be, not prodding or pushing for any explanation.

When we got to his house, he helped me down from the buggy, and he and I began the long walk back to the rose garden.

As we went, I finally decided to talk.

"I'm not sure I want to see it," I confessed, very wary and downcast.

"The rose garden?" Isaac questioned.

I nodded, indicating that that was what I meant.

"But why?" he wondered.

"Because it may be gone, too," I explained, so worried, "and I just can't bear the thought of it not being there anymore!"

Isaac squeezed my hand as we walked on.

"Why don't we just wait and see before we get too discouraged," he said, trying to cheer me. "Nothing says that the storm destroyed all of it, and even if it did, we can always rebuild."

As we got closer to the garden, my heart began to pound faster and faster, nervous for what I might see. As we crossed the little stream that was now flowing quite rapidly from the extra rainfall, I could see the gate to the garden opened, looking a little askew. Instantly, my heart sank at the sight, thinking surely it was a sign of bad things to come.

Isaac noticed it, too as he squeezed my hand a little tighter.

"Come on," he encouraged. "We'll face it together!"

As we reached the gate to the garden, I just couldn't believe my eyes! The garden was unbelievable - breathtaking! It looked every bit as lovely and beautiful as the first day Isaac had shown it to me. Amazingly, it was as if the storm had never come, like somehow it had completely missed this wonderful place altogether!

As we stepped inside the rose garden and began to walk its paths, the gloom in my heart began to fade away, and happiness and joy slowly began to take its place. I was so thankful that God had seen fit to spare this magnificent garden.

"I wish I would learn," I confessed with a sigh, lamenting my stubborn weaknesses. "Sometimes I get *so angry* with myself!"

"Learn what?" Isaac queried.

"To not borrow trouble!" I answered, rebuking myself. "All the way here, all I could think about was what devastation we were going to encounter when we got here, fretting, and even dreading seeing the place. And now look! Had I just waited, I could have spared myself all that worry!"

"But the important thing is that you're learning," Isaac kindly pointed out. "You recognize the problem, and now the key is to try to change what needs to be changed."

"I know," I acknowledged. "But sometimes it's easier said than done."

"I can understand that," Isaac commiserated. "But never forget, with God all things are possible."

I nodded, agreeing, as we walked on to the gazebo.

Once there, we sat down, looking out for a few minutes, just taking in the beauty of the garden.

"Do you remember our last conversation here?" Isaac finally asked.

"Of course, I do!" I replied with a smile. "Do you?"

"Yes!" Isaac assured me, with a smile of his own. He took my hand, sobering a bit. "I know this may not be the best time," he admitted, "what with everything going on and all, but…I want you to know, I haven't forgotten about speaking with your father."

"Oh!" I revealed excitedly. "You don't have to!"

Isaac furrowed his brow, perplexed.

"I don't?" he questioned, surprised.

"No, you don't!" I confirmed. "I guess with everything that's happened, I completely forgot to tell you. Papa already changed his mind. He said I could take the exam and finish early!"

"Are you serious?" Isaac exclaimed, hardly able to believe it.

I nodded, grinning broadly.

"Jochebed," he conveyed, so thrilled by the news, "that's...that's *great!*" He sat there absolutely stunned that Papa had actually agreed to it. "Wow!" he expressed with amazement. "I just can't believe it! I mean, your father, he...he was so adamant against it when I talked to him Sunday morning. What changed his mind?"

I shook my head as I shrugged my shoulders, not really sure.

"I don't know!" I admitted. "I was just as surprised as you are! For whatever reason, he brought it up that night after I got home, and all he really said was that he'd been thinking about it, and that he'd decided I was mature enough to go through with it."

Isaac, too, shook his head, grinning wildly, still overwhelmed!

"Well," he stated cheerfully, "I couldn't be happier! And hey," he quickly offered, "I'll do what I can to help you study, all right?"

"That would be wonderful!" I accepted. "I'm sure I'll need all the help I can get!"

*****

Over the next few weeks, Isaac and I studied for hours on end. He was so patient and helpful and supportive as I plowed through a plethora of information. I studied so much during that time, though, I felt like I was back in school again. I literally studied from early morning 'til late at night, carrying books with me *everywhere*, even while doing my chores. I had them while I cooked, while I mended, while I cleaned, and even at night with me while lying in bed, many a time falling asleep with a book still in my arms.

It was truly exhausting, and a monumental task, but by the end of the month, I decided that I was ready to try to take the exam. While I knew that not everyone who took the test passed, I honestly believed that I was prepared, and so did Isaac.

*****

The morning of the exam, I woke up extra early, admittedly nervous, but definitely not wanting to be late! I hurriedly got myself ready, Isaac came to pick me up, Papa and Samuel wished me well, and Isaac and I took off as quickly as we could as we had to drive to a school in an adjacent town, due to the fact that it was the only school in the area administering the exam at this time of year. I, of course, took my books with me, trying to cram a little more on the way.

The closer we got to the town, however, the more anxious and worried I became. Isaac tried to calm me, but I was scared to death by the time we arrived at the schoolhouse.

"You'll do great!" Isaac encouraged as he walked me to the door. "I'll wait out here for you, and I'll be praying the whole time. Just take your time and do your best. You're ready for this! I know you are!" He smiled, put his arm around me, and gave me a big hug as I hugged him back.

Looking up at him, I took a deep, nervous, heart-pounding breath, letting it out slowly.

"I'll do what I can," I promised.

Isaac smiled sweetly and gave me another reassuring hug.

I gave a reluctant grin before anxiously walking into the school.

When I entered the room, it was deathly quiet. There were only two other pupils there to take the exam, both were young men and both looked as nervous as I. The monitor was sitting behind a desk at the front of the room, and much to my chagrin, he looked rather stern and mean. His glasses sat on the tip of his nose as he glanced over the top of them, looking at me briefly when I opened the door. Once he saw who I was, he went right back to whatever he was doing, never saying a word to me at all.

I swallowed hard, quietly closed the door behind me, and walked over to take a seat. My heart was pounding so furiously, I thought for sure it was going to pop right out of my chest! I couldn't *wait* for the test to be over!

After sitting there in silence for several agonizing minutes, the monitor glanced at his pocket watch that was hanging from his vest pocket and got up from his desk.

"All right!" he announced in a gruff voice. "You have exactly two hours to complete the exam there before you. On my say, you may turn it over and begin. No talking, no cheating!" He stood there austerely looking at his watch. "All right…begin!" he instructed.

I promptly and nervously turned over my test, not wanting to waste any time. I glanced down at the questions, took a deep breath, grabbed the pencil provided, and dove right in!

Amazingly, I seemed to fly through the questions on the first page, fairly confident of most of my answers, only questioning a few. I quickly turned the page over and proceeded on. There was so much more to do, but as I completed each page, I began to feel pretty good about my chances of passing. Not that I was certain, by any means, but definitely more hopeful!

Thankfully, I was able to finish early within the time allotted, so I used the extra time to go back and check my work. I was just finishing my final check on the last page when suddenly the monitor blew a whistle that nearly sent me flying out of my seat.

"Time's up!" he declared. "Put your pencils down and bring your exams forward. You can expect your results to be sent to you in the mail within the week."

After collecting my heart off the floor, I gathered my test and took it forward. I thanked the gentleman when I laid the papers on his desk, he nodded, acknowledging me; I nodded back and left.

When I emerged from the schoolhouse, Isaac was waiting for me by his buggy.

"How'd you do?" he queried anxiously, walking over to meet me.

"I think I did all right," I answered with measured confidence.

Isaac smiled, pleased.

"Good!" he expressed with relief. "I'm so proud of you!"

"Well, I haven't passed yet," I reminded him.

"Yes," he accepted, "but I have every confidence that you will! I know how hard you studied, and I know God will honor your efforts."

TRUST
(Chapter 51)

On the ride home, Isaac and I talked about the wonderful possibilities of what could happen if I passed the exam. He was determined to talk to Papa about us marrying sometime soon and I was excited, but admittedly, somewhat afraid all at the same time. I knew Isaac was the man God wanted me to marry, but the thought of such a huge change in my life was a little daunting. I felt mature enough to become his wife, yet doubted my abilities all at the same time. There was still so much unknown, and I wanted to make sure we weren't rushing into things.

"Isaac," I questioned, "but, where would we live? I mean, you still have another year of school left, and…well…what would we do?"

"I've thought about that," he assured. "I figure you can move with me to school. I would attend classes during the day and work at night to support us."

I looked over at him, concerned and a bit reluctant.

"I suppose," I replied warily. "But…what would I do while you were away for so long?"

Isaac shrugged his shoulders.

"I don't know," he said, "I guess wifely things."

"Wifely things?" I queried with a bit of a chuckle.

"Yah, you know," Isaac explained, "clean the house, cook the meals, mend the clothes…wifely things."

"I understand all that," I came back at him, still concerned. "But those things don't take all day! What am I to do with the rest of my time? Who would I talk to? Where would I go if I so desired?"

Isaac sat contemplating, seemingly having no answers to my questions.

I, however, *dearly* wanted to know!

"Isaac!" I pressed. "I'm serious! What would I do?"

I could tell he was seriously thinking about it, but I could also tell that he was at a loss as to how to answer me.

"I suppose I could introduce you to some of the people who attend the small church I go to while I'm away at school," he finally suggested. "And there's also some of the other seminary fella's that have wives. Maybe you could get together with them from time to time."

I sighed, less than thrilled with the prospects.

"Yes, I suppose so," I answered, quite hesitant at the thought.

I knew myself all too well, and meeting new people was not *at all* easy for me! Being with Isaac had helped with that *somewhat*, yes, but still, I tended to be shy, and I wasn't sure I wanted to try to start all over again in a strange, unfamiliar place, *especially* with people I didn't know!

I guess Isaac and I had never talked about this aspect of things before, and the more I sat there and thought about it, the more I realized how little I really knew about what Isaac's plans were for the future. Even though I knew he intended to be a pastor, I had no idea where he felt God was calling him to go. My heart sank at the realization that I may have to move away from my family and friends and from everything that was familiar to me. And then, my heart sank even deeper when I realized I had to answer the question: *was I willing to go?*

I wanted to be with Isaac (so desperately I did), but I guess I always thought I would marry and stay close to home. The thought of possibly having to leave was more than I could bear!

I stayed fairly quiet the rest of the way home, intently thinking about the quandary I was in. Isaac would say something here and there and I would acknowledge him, but for the most part, my thoughts were preoccupied with worries of the unknown.

I knew that Isaac and I needed to address these issues, but unfortunately as was my habit, I internalized the problems, worried about them, and tried to figure them out on my own. I guess my thinking was that I needed to come to a conclusion in my own heart and mind before confronting Isaac with them. I'll readily admit that it was foolish, but in the moment, I thought it was the best thing to do.

When we got to my house, Isaac told me that he couldn't stay because he needed to get home to deal with some things there. He said that he'd be back later on in the evening, though, and that we could spend some more time together then. I nodded as I got down off the buggy, fully understanding that he had to leave.

Surprisingly, he never asked me what was bothering me, but I suppose he was simply too focused on the jobs he had waiting for him at home to ever really notice my worry.

~

With Andrew no longer at home, and Isaac's grandfather still laid up from his broken ribs, most of the work fell to Isaac. While Isaac's arm was healing nicely, he was tired of being limited on what he could do and tired of his chores taking him twice as long because he could only use one arm. Needless to say, he was looking forward to being free of his sling! Fortunately, the doctor had told him that he would probably be able to get out of it in a week or so, if not before, but with all the work Isaac had to do on a daily basis, it just couldn't come fast enough for him!

Isaac's grandfather was progressing with his recovery from his broken ribs, but he still had a ways to go. He felt badly for Isaac that he had so much work to do on his own, but there really wasn't anything he could do about it. Moving about caused him so much pain, he simply had no choice but to spend most of his time relegated to a chair or lying in his bed.

When I found out about Mr. Lewis' limitations, I gladly offered him my wheelchair, and he graciously accepted it with much appreciation. Having it definitely afforded him more mobility (for which he was also thankful), but even with it, he was still very limited on what he could do to help Isaac out around the house.

~

Before Isaac left that morning, I was still preoccupied with all my worries, but I tried not to let it show, putting on a brave smile, and telling Isaac how much I loved him. I agreed I'd see him later on that evening, but as I was saying as much, deep inside my stomach was churning something awful with angst at all the things I needed to decide. I couldn't wait to be by myself and sort things out!

After Isaac pulled away, I ran inside, hoping to go straight to my room to think things through, but when I opened the door, there was Papa standing in the kitchen wanting to know how my test went. Not wanting to be rude, I paused in my haste and shared with him how I thought I did. He said he was proud of me and told me not to worry about it, sure that I had done just fine. I thanked him, told him I'd try not to worry, and headed up to my room.

Once there, I immediately closed the door behind me, walked over and put my things on my dresser, and went to my bed to sit down. I was so worked up about everything; I just needed time to think!

Sitting there, all the worries and concerns that I'd been fretting about on the way home came rushing back into my mind, not to mention the words that Papa had just said to me about my exam.

Don't worry about it, he'd told me.

I sighed, frustrated, because the problem was…I *was* worried about it! Not so much worried that I *wouldn't* pass, but now worried rather that I *might!*

If I failed, I reasoned to myself, *then that would solve my problem. Well, maybe not solve it, but, at least, delay it for another year.* I shook my head as I closed my eyes in aggravation, so infuriated with myself! *How could you have not considered these things before, Jochebed?* I admonished. *How could you have been so blinded by your love for Isaac that you failed to see these crucial issues?* "Ohhh!" I groused in frustration as I flopped myself back on my bed, the back of my hand coming to rest on my forehead. "How could these things have escaped me?" I lay there wrestling with the problem, vacillating back and forth. "I don't want to move away!" I fretted. "But I do so want to be with Isaac! I don't want to leave the comforts of my familiar surroundings, but, *ohhh*," I moaned again, forlorn, "it's a very *real* possibility!"

There was no doubt; I was in a very tough dilemma!

What am I going to do? I agonized.

Lying there, thoroughly exasperated, I couldn't help but beat myself up! I just kept scolding myself over and over again, thinking how it could even be possible that these things had never crossed my mind before! Ridiculously, I worked myself up so much about it, I actually found myself questioning whether or not I should even be with Isaac! Of course, part of me knew how silly it was to think that way (after all, I hadn't even talked to him about the matter), but part of me realized that I truly did need to answer this all important question: Was I truly willing to give up *everything* to be with him?

For the next thirty minutes, I tossed and turned, sat and paced, stewed and fretted over that very thought. I went back and forth numerous times.

Yes, I would tell myself confidently, *I **will** sacrifice everything for Isaac! I love him with all of my heart, and…* Then someone from my family would come to mind, and it would cause me to waver in my resolve.

The longer I thought about it, the angrier and more worked up I became. It got to the point where I just couldn't take it any longer! I needed to get out of the house, to take a walk, to clear my head. I thought that maybe if I could be distracted by other things, then maybe - just maybe - my worries would fade, and I'd feel better somehow. Admittedly, it didn't seem likely, but I had to try.

I immediately got up and headed downstairs, determined to do just that!

As I descended the stairs, I could hear someone rustling around in the kitchen. Sure enough, when I walked in, Samuel was there, messily making himself a sandwich. Of course, he had to stop me and ask me how my test went, but by this time, I was certainly in no mood to respond to the question.

Knowing Samuel was none the wiser of my current predicament, however, I courteously obliged him an answer.

"It went fine," I told him politely yet succinctly, just wanting to leave.

Samuel couldn't help himself, he quipped back.

"Must be nice bein' able to be done with school so early," he jabbed. "Guess this means you and Isaac'll be tyin' the knot soon and movin' away, huh?"

I instantly burst into tears, upset by his comment.

"How could you be so insensitive?" I blubbered.

Samuel got a terribly confused look on his face as he stood there staring at me like I'd gone stark raving mad!

I turned away, crying, and ran out of the house.

"Jochebed!" I heard him call out just before the door slammed behind me. "What'd I do?"

I wasn't going back to explain. I just wanted to run! I just wanted to run away from it all! It was all just too much, and I didn't know what to do with it. I ran and I ran until I came to Mama's grave, collapsing there beside it on the ground. I wept and wept and wept some more.

"Oh, Mama!" I cried. "I so wish you were here! You'd know exactly what to tell me! You'd know exactly what to say! How could I have let things come to this? How could I..." I was crying so hard, I couldn't speak anymore.

I knew in my heart that I loved Isaac, so *much* I loved him, *I did*, but I loved my family, too! I sobbed and sobbed, desperate for answers.

Finally, after finding no relief, I did what I should have done in the first place, I cried out to God.

"Please, dear Lord," I begged, "please...please help me to know what to do!" I cried and cried, and prayed to the Lord, desperately pouring my heart out to Him.

After awhile, I settled a bit, enough that I felt I could go back home. When I stood up and turned around to leave, however, much to my surprise, there was Aunt Sara walking towards me. I frantically and quickly wiped my tears, hoping she wouldn't notice my present state, but unfortunately, my face was already puffy and red from crying, and it readily gave me away.

"Jochebed," Aunt Sara questioned as she came near, "sweetheart, are you okay? Gramma said she thought she saw you run by earlier, heading in this direction. I just wanted to come and make sure everything was all right."

I stood there, caught, and admittedly conflicted. There was no hiding the fact that there was something bothering me, and I knew I needed to talk to someone about it, but part of me felt that that someone should be Isaac. I fidgeted a little, nervous and embarrassed, before finally coming to the conclusion that Aunt Sara would understand. I timidly proceeded to share with her what had me so upset.

"Well," I started hesitantly, "to be honest, I...I've been having some...well...some doubts about...about me and...about me and Isaac."

Aunt Sara furrowed her brow, concerned and surprised, but she let me continue.

"I'm just...I'm just dealing with some things that I hadn't thought about before," I confessed, still fidgeting, embarrassed to be in the dilemma I was in. "And now...now I...now I'm just not sure what to do!"

Aunt Sara came a little closer to me.

"Jochebed," she said earnestly, "you know I'm here if...if you ever need to talk...right?"

"Oh, I know!" I assured her. "It's just that...well...I haven't even...well...I haven't even spoken to Isaac about it yet, and I..."

Aunt Sara smiled sympathetically.

"I understand," she calmed. "But Jochebed," she encouraged strongly, "whatever it is, he deserves to know! You need to deal with this before things get too far out of hand." She put her hand gently on my arm, all the while sternly looking me in the eye. "Learn from your Uncle Mark and me," she warned. "Talk!"

She smiled sweetly and gave me a hug as I hugged her back, and after our embrace, we walked back towards her house. When we arrived, I hugged her once more and thanked her for her concern. She reiterated that she was there for me, and also assured me that she would be praying for the situation. I thanked her again, so appreciative of her support, and headed for home.

When I returned, Papa was working in the barn and Samuel was off busy with his chores. I didn't speak to either one of them, opting instead to go straight to the house to get started on supper. I washed my hands and began to prepare the meal, busying myself, trying not to worry, but of course, that was just about *all I could do!*

As time ticked away and it got closer to evening, I began to dread the thought of having to see Isaac. It was a strange feeling as I normally couldn't wait to see him, but with the weight of the issues that awaited us weighing heavy on my mind, I was full of trepidation.

This is just awful! I fretted to myself, nauseated at the thought of having to confront him. I sighed, very apprehensive. *There really is no way around this, is there!?* I lamented. I shook my head, knowing deep down that there wasn't. *Aunt Sara's, right, though,* I finally, reluctantly conceded. *Isaac deserves to know!*

I sighed again anxiously, determined I'd broach the subject with him tonight. No matter what, it needed to come out, and I'd simply have to let the chips fall where they may.

I finished with supper and called for Papa and Samuel to come inside, and after they washed up, we all sat down to the table to enjoy the meal I'd prepared.

Samuel was quiet and rather cold towards me, in fact, he wouldn't even look in my direction. I knew why, of course, I'd yelled at him and probably owed him an apology, but I didn't feel much like talking, so I just ignored it. We both just sat there and ate our dinner in silence. Papa tried to engage us both in conversation over the course of the meal, but he eventually gave up, realizing neither of us was in the mood.

When we finished eating, Papa and Samuel went back outside, and I started to clean up the kitchen.

As I was standing at the sink washing the dishes, Isaac came to the door, knocked, and peeked inside.

"May I come in?" he asked.

I startled at his voice, glancing over my shoulder at him.

"Of course," I permitted, calming a bit once I realized who it was.

He walked on inside and came over towards me.

"I sure have missed you," he said cheerfully. "How are you? How's your day been?"

I took a deep breath, starting to panic. I wasn't exactly expecting him just yet and hadn't rehearsed what I was going to say to him. I suddenly became so nervous; I didn't even turn to acknowledge him. I just stood there feverishly washing the dish I was holding in my hand.

"Jochebed," Isaac queried again as he came up beside me, "did you hear me? How are you?"

"I'm fine!" I replied succinctly, being less than honest. I continued vigorously scrubbing, never looking up at him.

Isaac leaned against the counter right beside me and gave me a curious look.

"Are you *sure* you're fine?" he asked, questioning the sincerity of my answer.

"Um...um..." I hemmed and hawed. "I will be...at least...I think I will."

Isaac looked at me warily.

"You're not fretting about your test now, are you?" he inquired.

I nervously grinned, glancing over at him, and then right back to my dishes.

"Well...sort of...I guess," I answered evasively.

Isaac shook his head, a little frustrated with me.

"Now, Jochebed," he tried to encourage, "I know you did fine! I'm sure you'll pass with flying colors." He playfully pushed against me. "Stop worrying!" he insisted, smiling sweetly.

"But that's what I'm afraid of!" I blurted out angrily, slamming my rag back down into the sink along with the dish I was holding.

Instantly, soapy water splashed up, landing everywhere - some on me, some on the counter, and some on Isaac.

"Whoa!" Isaac exclaimed, taken aback. "What's going on?"

"Nothing!" I snapped crossly. "I don't want to talk about it right now!" I irritably took hold of the bottom of my apron and started wiping the soap from my face.

Isaac shook his head passionately, scowling in incredulity.

"Now wait a minute!" he protested. "Didn't we just go through this not too long ago?" He was still shaking his head as he grabbed a towel to wipe the water from his arm. "No way, Jochebed!" he vehemently contended. "We're not doing this again! Now talk!"

I clenched my jaw, frustrated, as I took a deep breath, letting it out slowly! Deep down I knew Isaac was right, but I was so angry with myself, and so afraid of what the conversation might bring, I didn't want to say anything, so instead of revealing my misgivings to him, I just stood there, staring at the dishes in the sink, contemplating what I should do.

"Jochebed!" Isaac pushed, clearly perturbed. "I'm not going to ask you again! Tell me what's got you so upset!"

Finally at my wits end, my anger and worry overtaking me, I let it all come spilling out!

"I don't think I can be with you anymore!" I exploded. "I just don't think this is going to work!"

Isaac shuddered, completely caught off guard, stunned and shaken by my pronouncement.

"What on *earth* are you talking about?" he rightly questioned. "This morning, we were planning our future together, and now...now you're *breaking things off?!?*" He slammed the towel down on the counter, visibly furious! "What's going on, Jochebed?" he demanded to know. "What's gotten into you? What's this all about!?!"

I couldn't even look at him I was so ashamed. I didn't *want* to break things off with him, but I didn't know what else to do.

How could we plan a future together, I reasoned, *when I wasn't even sure I could be in it?* I shook my head, hesitant to speak.

"Isaac," I reluctantly told him, "there are things...things about us... things that I never...well...things that I never considered before, until...well...until today."

"Things?" Isaac questioned angrily, eagerly wanting an explanation. "Things like *what?!?"*

"Well…" I revealed, "things like…where you're going to preach."

Isaac gave me the most confounded, perplexing look.

"What?!?" he blustered, completely at a loss. "What are you *talking* about?"

I looked up at him, my eyes filled with desperation.

"I'm talking about you preaching somewhere far away from here!" I stated so sure of myself. "You'll be preaching far away…far away from my family, far away from my friends, far away from everything I know, and…" I paused, nearly beside myself. "Isaac!" I confessed, almost in tears. "I just don't know if I can leave everyone behind!"

Isaac rolled his eyes, shaking his head in utter disbelief!

"Who's asking you to?" he came back at me, raising his voice in consternation.

"Weeelll," I answered timidly. "You are…*aren't you?"*

Isaac threw his hand up in the air, completely exasperated!

"Are you telling me you've been worrying about this *all day?"* he asked, clearly upset with me.

Given how angry he was, I was very reluctant to answer.

"I…well…yes," I nervously admitted. "But Isaac," I quickly defended, "you don't understand! If I can't give up everything for you, then…then maybe I shouldn't be with you!" I shook my head, trying to clarify my thinking. "I've been worrying about it only because I couldn't answer that question for myself." I explained. "Don't you see?" I insisted adamantly. "You deserve someone who can support you *no matter where you go,* and I…well…I just don't know if I can do that! I mean, I think I would be able to, but…oh…I don't know! The thought of having to leave my family and friends behind…I just…"

Isaac was more than a little infuriated!

"Stop it!" he interrupted loudly. "Just stop it! We haven't even discussed these things, and here you've already come to some *crazy conclusions!"* By now he was pacing back and forth, fuming, absolutely livid and disconcerted! Suddenly, he stopped and walked right up to me. "I'll have you know that *I have* thought about these things, Jochebed!" he made clear, sternly looking me in the eye. "And while I'm willing to go *anywhere* God wants me to go, I believe, at least for now, that He's called me to serve alongside Pastor Scott *right here* in *this town!* Pastor Scott and I have been discussing it on and off now for years, ever since I felt God calling me into the ministry."

Isaac again threw up his hand in aggravation.

"I have no *intensions* of taking you away from your family and friends!" he announced with fervor, correcting my misguided assumptions. "And if you would've simply been willing to talk to me about these things, instead of keeping them all to yourself, you could have saved yourself a whole day's worth of worry and bother!"

I looked away, completely ashamed and embarrassed by my childish behavior. I felt so badly, I honestly didn't know what to say.

Isaac was seething as he stood there shaking his head at me, obviously disappointed and still upset. He took a few deep breaths, though, and began to calm himself down.

"I believe," he continued, in a much more measured tone, "that if you love God enough, and if you love me enough, then He'll give you the strength and the grace and *whatever else* you need to be able to handle moving *anywhere* He may lead us in the future."

I started to tear up, feeling absolutely horrible!

"But, Jochebed," Isaac went on to say as he reached out, gently putting his hand on my arm, his concern palpable, "if you truly feel that you can't support me in the ministry no matter *where* God may send us, then…then you're right…this won't work, and…as much as it pains me to have to say it, then…well…we really do need to end things now."

I sniffed and wiped a tear from my cheek as I turned to face him.

"Then you see why I've been worrying!" I argued in despair. "I'm *so* conflicted! I know that I know that I love you, Isaac, *I do*, and I honestly believe *with all of my heart* that you're the one God has for me to marry, but…"

"Then trust Him, Jochebed!" Isaac passionately interrupted. "If you *genuinely* mean what you just said to me, then…then your issue isn't about love, about whom you love more, me or your family, it's…it's not even an issue about whether or not you'll have to choose between them or me, your issue it's…it's one of *trust!*" Isaac put his arm around me and brought me close as he looked into my eyes with compassion. "Jochebed," he pointed out sweetly, "you need to trust God…number one, that He'll always meet your needs, and number two, that He'll *never* ask you to do *anything* that He won't first equip you to do." Isaac softly brushed aside a wisp of hair that had fallen in my face. "Trust, Jochebed!" he implored. "You need to trust God with all of this!"

What Isaac said hit me right between the eyes. Immediately, I realized what I had been doing. All of this time, I was worried that I had to choose between him and everyone else in my life - worried that if I chose the one, I'd automatically lose the other, when in reality, I didn't have to choose at all, I simply needed to trust God! Unfortunately, trusting Him with the whole matter had never even *once* entered into my thinking.

I shook my head, amazed at my foolishness.

Isaac was right…with God, I *could* go anywhere and it *would* be all right! I could see that now, and amazingly, as I began to shift my burden of fear from my shoulders to God's, an incredible peace swept over me that I just couldn't explain. It was as if in that moment, God was filling me with the assurance that everything would be all right and confirming once again in my heart that Isaac was the one He wanted me to be with.

Another tear came to my eye and slowly trickled down my cheek as I looked up at Isaac.

"I love you, Isaac!" I said as sincerely as I could. "I want you to know that. And…" I sniffed again and bit my lip, willing to confess my faults. "You're right," I admitted, "I wasn't trusting God, and…and I never should have kept all of this from you…and…I'm…I'm really sorry!"

Isaac nodded, seeming to accept my apology.

"I…I want you to know, too," I went on to say with earnest, "that…I believe I've given God this burden and…I know now that with His help I…I *really* can go anywhere with you, and…and…" I looked down as I started to cry, fearful that Isaac might not believe me. Wanting to convince him, though, I quickly wiped my tears, and tried to compose myself. I looked back up at him, my eyes pleading. "Please, Isaac!" I begged. "I'm telling you the truth! Honestly…I truly am willing!"

Isaac sighed as he looked at me with reserve, yet hopeful.

"You're sure?" he questioned, wanting affirmation.

With tears in my eyes, I nodded, assuring him.

Elated, Isaac's eyes filled with joy as he affectionately smiled down at me.

"Then I know that with God's help," he said with confidence, "we'll face whatever the future holds *together*…me and you, hand in hand, side by side, guided by His providence." His smile grew as he gazed into my eyes. "I love you, Jochebed!" he said unwaveringly. "I love you *so much!* Please…please don't ever feel like you have to figure things out on your own. I'm here for you, and…I want to be!" He paused as he looked at me very seriously. "Jochebed," he expressed intently, "*I need to be!*"

I again nodded with tears in my eyes, conceding his point.

Isaac slowly began to shake his head as a tender smile made its way across his face.

"I'm not going anywhere," he assured. "I promise! I'm yours - always!"

I hugged Isaac so tightly, overjoyed for his forgiveness, his patience, and his amazing love for me! He hugged me back just as tightly, and we stood there for quite awhile just holding each other, so thankful that things had been resolved between us, and *thrilled* that we were once again moving forward together!

In that wonderful moment, I was again reminded just how blessed I truly was to have Isaac in my life. I was determined *never* to let him go!

WAITING FOR RESULTS
(Chapter 52)

Now that Isaac and I had worked things out, I turned my concern to my test results. Whereas before I thought perhaps it would be best if I failed, now I began to worry that I might do just that, and now…well…I really didn't want to! I'd felt somewhat confident when I left the schoolhouse that day that I'd done reasonably well, but with each passing day, waiting on my results, that confidence began to fade.

Perhaps I did worse than I originally thought, I'd nervously worry on and off.

Honestly, though, I did try my best not to think about it *too terribly often!* The closer it got to the end of the week, however, the more my anxiety grew!

*****

"I thought for sure I'd have my test results by now!" I fretted to Papa.

It was late Thursday morning already (going on afternoon), and mine still hadn't arrived.

"They said we'd have our results within the week," I reminded him, "but I've not received mine yet!"

"I'm sure they're on their way," Papa stated confidently, "if not here already. I'm headin' into town later on today. I'll be sure to check at the post office for ya, all right?"

"Thank you, Papa," I replied anxiously. "I sure do hope I find out something soon. The suspense is killing me!"

Papa just smiled and kissed me on the forehead before heading outside to do some work.

I finished cleaning up the lunch dishes, and when I was through, I made my way to the sewing room to start work on some mending and to finish the special surprise I'd been working on for Isaac's upcoming birthday. He was turning twenty-one on Saturday, and I was looking forward to making the day a special one for him.

As I sat there working diligently, Samuel suddenly burst into the room.

"Here!" he said, throwing an old pair of work pants at me. "Can ya get those mended for me by tomorrow? Billy and me are goin' fishin' and I wanna wear 'em."

I grabbed the pants up off of me and glared at him, absolutely appalled by his behavior.

"Excuse me!" I barked angrily. "How rude, Samuel! I'm not your maid! The least you could do is say, please!"

He rolled his eyes cavalierly.

"Sorry!" he snapped. (Clearly not!) *"Pleeaasse,* mend them for me?"

I scowled at his deplorable attitude.

"Samuel!" I scolded. "You need to learn some manners!"

He shook his head dismissively, obviously none too concerned.

"Can ya do it or not?" he asked impatiently.

I sighed, exasperated, as I looked them over.

"Yes!" I finally affirmed. "I believe I can fix them."

Once Samuel had his answer, he immediately turned and left the room without so much as a thank you.

Incensed, I promptly got up from my chair with his pants in my hands, went to the door, and yelled after him.

"You're welcome!" I shouted tersely, shaking my head in disgust.

He kept right on walking without saying a word, summarily disappearing around the corner.

I slammed the door, infuriated, as I went back to my seat to sit down.

"Ohhh!" I groused. "That *never* would have happened had *Mama* been the one sitting here!"

I shook my head, flustered by the whole matter as I went to work on his pants. I have to confess, though, as I began to thread the needle, reflecting on his rudeness and bad behavior, I strongly considered sewing the legs of his pants together just to teach him a lesson! Straight away, however, the Holy Spirit convicted me with a verse of Scripture.

"Therefore all things whatsoever ye would that men should do to you, do ye even so to them."

I took a deep breath.

"All right, Lord," I conceded, "You'll have to be the One to take care of it!" I quickly put the thoughts of revenge from my mind and commenced to repairing Samuel's pants.

After I finished up all my mending, I got started right away on Isaac's surprise. I worked and worked and got so involved that I completely lost track of time. Before I knew it, I was startled by a knock on the sewing room door.

"Jochebed, are you in there?"

My heart skipped a beat when I realized that it was Isaac! I immediately stopped what I was doing and started to gather my things.

"Um…yes, Isaac," I called out, trying not to sound too frenzied. "I'll be out in a minute!" I was frantically trying to get everything tucked away in a basket, hoping that Isaac wouldn't open the door, potentially catching me with his surprise in hand.

"What are you doing in there?" he queried as I was banging around, dropping things, making a terrible racket.

"Oh, nothing!" I replied, trying to sound as innocent as possible. "I'm almost finished. I…I just have to straighten up a bit is all. …*Be there in a minute!*" Finally, I got things squared away, composed myself, and walked to the door.

When I opened it up, there was Isaac leaning against the door jamb, smiling, looking at me inquisitively.

"Sounded like it got pretty rough in there," he teased. "Everything all right?"

"Of course, it is, silly," I dismissed, walking on past him towards the kitchen. "I…I just had a lot of laundry and things lying about. I simply needed to get them put away - that's all!"

Isaac looked at me warily as he followed me to the kitchen.

"All right," he halfheartedly accepted, his tone clearly suspicious. He turned the corner. "You're *sure* you're not up to something?"

"Positive!" I lied. "Now, what brings you here so early? I thought you weren't coming by until later."

"Jochebed," Isaac pointed out with a chuckle, "it *is* later!"

"Oh…right!" I acknowledged as I looked at the clock on the wall. "Sorry, I guess I just lost track of time."

Isaac looked at me again very leerily.

"You're sure you're all right?" he questioned.

"Yes, of course, I am," I assured him. "I'm perfectly fine! Now, what was it again you had planned for us today?"

Isaac grinned at my forgetfulness.

"You really were preoccupied weren't you?" he quipped.

I furrowed my brow, feeling as if I'd forgotten something very important.

"We're going to Andrew and Isabelle's for an early supper tonight," he told me. "Remember? They invited us a couple days ago."

I gasped in utter dismay!

"Oh, Isaac!" I exclaimed. "I'm so sorry! I completely forgot! I'll be ready in a jiff!"

I immediately dashed from the kitchen and headed upstairs to my room. I scurried about as quickly as I could, changed my dress, made myself as presentable as possible, sprayed a little perfume on myself, took one last harried look in the mirror, and raced off back downstairs. I left a brief note for Papa reminding him where I'd be (he'd already left for town with Samuel), grabbed the pie from the window that I'd baked early that morning, gathered my shawl, and hurried out the door with Isaac.

"So have you heard back about your test results?" Isaac asked as we headed down the road towards Andrew and Isabelle's.

"Sadly no!" I lamented. "I was just telling Papa this morning that I fully expected to have them by now. He said he'd check on them for me, though."

"Well," Isaac stated confidently, "I'm not worried in the least! I know you did fine!"

"Well, that's good!" I quipped back, more than a little sarcastic. "I'm certainly glad *someone's* not worried about them!"

Isaac chuckled.

"I don't have to worry about them," he teased. "You do enough of that for the both of us!"

I gave him a disgusted look as I shook my head.

"All right," I granted. "Fair enough! But regardless…I sure do hope I pass!"

"Me, too!" he said as he leaned over, smiling. "Me, too!"

It didn't take long to get to Andrew and Isabelle's as they had purchased a farm just a few miles up the road from where my family and I lived. It was a very lovely house, not grand by any means, but very nice compared to ours. Isabelle had done an extraordinary job of decorating it when she and Andrew returned home from their honeymoon. I had a chance to see it when we threw Andrew and Isabelle a housewarming party to welcome them back.

"Come in, come in!" Andrew encouraged when Isaac and I arrived. He looked directly at me. "Isabelle's in the kitchen if you'd like to join her," he offered.

"Thank you, I think I will," I said as I handed him my shawl. "I'll go see if she needs any help."

I smiled at Isaac, took my pie, and headed for the kitchen.

He and Andrew went to the family room to talk.

"Oh, Jochebed!" Isabelle expressed with delight as I walked into the kitchen. "I thought I heard voices. I'm so glad you could make it! How are you doing?"

"I'm fine, thank you," I replied. "And yourself?"

"Wonderful!" she conveyed cheerily. "I'm absolutely *loving* married life!"

I grinned happily as I put the pie down on the counter.

"I can tell!" I chuckled. "Marriage suits you well, that's for certain!" I looked around at everything Isabelle had going. "Is there anything I can help you with?" I asked.

"No," she answered assuredly. "I think I have everything pretty much in hand. We just need to wait for the roast to finish cooking, and then I'll slice the bread and put everything on the table." She turned, noticing my pie. "My, but that pie looks delicious!" she complimented.

"Thank you!" I told her. "It was one of Mama's recipes. She was such a tremendous cook; I only hope it tastes half as good as one of hers."

"Well, if it tastes as good as it looks," Isabelle flattered, "I'm sure it will be delectable!" She smiled. "Shall we go join the men while we wait?"

I smiled back.

"Yes," I heartily agreed.

She and I started for the family room.

"Thank you and Andrew again for inviting us over," I said graciously as we walked.

"Oh, it's our pleasure!" Isabelle replied. "We've actually wanted to have you and Isaac over for a while now, but Isaac told us how busy you were studying for your exam. …Speaking of which, have you heard anything back on how you did?"

I sighed, disheartened.

"No," I answered, "I haven't yet, but I'm hoping to hear something soon!"

"There they are!" Andrew announced with a smile as he and Isaac stood up to usher Isabelle and me into the room. "Supper almost ready?" he asked, beaming at Isabelle, giving her a kiss when she came near.

"Yes, dear," Isabelle explained as they sat down together on the couch, holding hands. "Just waiting on the roast."

It was quite obvious Andrew and Isabelle were very much in love and more than excited to be newlyweds. As they sat there together, cuddling, they could barely stop smiling and looking at each other. It was thrilling and wonderful to see!

Isaac and I sat down beside each other on another couch that was situated across the room from where Andrew and Isabelle were sitting.

"So," Andrew finally inquired, "have you heard anything about your test results yet?"

I smiled courteously as I was getting a little tired of having to answer the same question over and over again!

I couldn't help but think to myself, *Perhaps I should have just worn a sign around my neck with the word NO written in big, bold letters on it!* I shook my head, collecting my thoughts. Not wanting to be rude, I politely obliged him an answer.

"Unfortunately, no," I replied. "I haven't heard anything yet. I'm still waiting, but I hope to hear something soon."

"Well," Andrew complimented, "if I remember correctly, you always seemed to do really well in school. I'm sure you passed with flying colors."

"Well, that's very kind of you to say, Andrew," I told him. "Thank you." I let out a long, deep sigh. "I certainly hope you're right about me passing," I conveyed with angst. "I just can't imagine what I'll do if I don't!"

Isaac put his arm around me and gave me a squeeze.

"Stop worrying!" he admonished. "It'll be fine!"

I gave a reluctant smile as I nodded, admittedly still worrying!

Andrew, Isabelle, and Isaac and I all sat talking a while longer before Isabelle and I finally excused ourselves to the kitchen to finish up supper.

While there (she and I being alone), we took the occasion to discuss the final plans for the surprise birthday party we were planning for Isaac.

"I have everything ready," Isabelle said in hushed tones. "Andrew has agreed to distract Isaac for the morning, so you and I will have the house to ourselves to decorate."

"And his grandparents," I wanted to confirm, "they're still on board with all of this, right?"

"Absolutely!" Isabelle assured. "I think they're as excited about it as we are!"

"Good!" I replied, relieved. "I just hope we can pull it off without Isaac finding out. I'm not sure if he suspects anything or not."

"Have you finished your gift for him yet?" Isabelle queried.

"Almost," I explained. "He just about walked in on me today when I was working on it, though. I hope I didn't give anything away by my frenzied behavior."

"Well," Isabelle pointed out, "even if he does suspect that you have a gift for him, I doubt he suspects a surprise party."

I nodded, hesitantly agreeing.

"I'm sure you're right," I accepted, my concerns momentarily dissuaded. Just then, my face lit up with excitement. "Oh, I simply can't wait!" I exclaimed enthusiastically. "Isaac's been able to surprise me *so many times*; I just hope this all works out for him!"

Isabelle smiled in agreement as we continued getting things ready for supper.

When everything was set, we called the men to the dining room, and once they were there, we all sat down to enjoy the wonderful meal that Isabelle had prepared.

As soon as we all finished eating, Isabelle immediately commenced to cutting the pie that I'd made, handing each of us a generous piece. Graciously, as we all ate it, everyone gave glowing compliments on how delicious it was. I was humbled by their generous remarks.

"I must get this recipe!" Isabelle announced. "This is simply divine!"

I smiled demurely.

"Thank you," I politely replied. "I'd be more than happy to write it out for you before we leave tonight."

"Oh, that would be wonderful!" she declared, pleased. "And, Isaac," she said, smiling across the table at him, "you're a very blessed man to have such a fantastic cook as this!"

Isaac smiled lovingly at me as he put his hand on mine.

"Oh, I know I am!" he concurred, glowing with pride. "She's not only a fantastic cook, though, she's also an *unbelievably* amazing person as well!"

"Oh, stop it!" I blushed, growing ever more embarrassed.

"Well, you are!" Isaac affirmed. "And I'm not ashamed to say it!"

I could feel my face getting redder and redder with each passing moment. Feeling rather uncomfortable with all the flattery, I searched my mind for something to say, *anything* that I could use to change the subject, but regrettably, absolutely *nothing* would come to mind! Mercifully, there was a knock at the door, and everyone's attention was drawn away to that.

"I'll get it," Andrew offered as he got up from the table.

As he went to answer the door, we all went back to enjoying our dessert.

"Who was it?" Isabelle asked as Andrew came back into the room.

"It's Samuel," he replied, "and he wants to talk to Jochebed."

"Samuel?" I queried, rather surprised. "Why…I wonder what he could want!" I excused myself from the table and hurried off to the front door.

When I got there, Samuel was milling about on the porch, waiting for me to come out.

I opened the screen door and stepped out to greet him.

"Samuel," I questioned, "what are you doing here? Is everything all right?"

"Yah," he said, holding out a rather thick envelope addressed to me. "Papa said he thought ya might want this right away, so he sent me down here to give it to ya."

I reached out and took the envelope from him, earnestly looking it over.

"Is…is this what I think it is?" I asked excitedly.

Samuel shrugged.

"That'd be my guess," he quipped. "Why don't ya stop starin' at it and open it up and find out!"

I was so nervous, I could barely move! My heart was pounding, my hands were sweaty, and I was more than a little anxious as I read the return address one more time just to confirm what I already knew. There was no doubt, it was most certainly my test results. I took a deep breath and let it out slowly, definitely wanting to know how I did, but somewhat afraid to look inside.

"Well!" Samuel prodded impatiently. "Aren't ya gonna open it?"

I glanced up at him with chagrin, before looking back down at the letter. I took another deep breath and began to carefully tear along the top of the envelope. Once it was open, my hands shaking, I reached inside and took out the papers it contained. In that instant, I think I actually stopped breathing for a minute! Swallowing hard, I nervously unfolded to the first page.

Immediately, my eye caught the word, *Congratulations!*

A wave of relief swept over me and a smile slowly made its way across my face as I continued to read.

Upon completion of your exam, and having obtained a passing grade, a certificate will be mailed to you in two weeks affirming your achievement.

I couldn't believe it! I'd actually done it! *I'd passed!*

I browsed the rest of the paragraph and then flipped the page to see my exam. I quickly glanced through each page, noticing a mark here and there, but I didn't care; I'd passed, and that was all that mattered to me!

"Well!" Samuel prodded again with a frown. "How'd ya do?"

I looked up at him with the biggest smile on my face.

"I passed!" I exclaimed. "I really passed!" In my excitement, I completely forgot myself and gave Samuel a big hug and a kiss on the cheek.

I think he thought he was going to die on the spot!

"All right! All right!" he shouted, extremely agitated, trying to push me away. "Ya don't have to get all mushy about it!" He quickly wiped my kiss from his cheek and gave me a disgusted look.

I chuckled a bit at his consternation as I smiled broadly. I didn't care! I was *so happy* and wanted to share it with everyone!

Samuel frowned, still reeling from my spontaneous display of affection, shook his head, and reluctantly asked.

"So," he wanted to know, "is it okay to tell Papa?"

"Yes!" I shouted enthusiastically. "You can tell him! And be sure to thank him for me for letting you bring this over here." I anxiously looked at the door and then back to Samuel. "Well, I'd better get back inside before they start to suspect something's wrong!"

Samuel nodded and promptly turned to leave.

As he stepped down off the porch, I quickly took the papers and tucked them back into the envelope, grinning from ear to ear as I did! I couldn't *wait* to share the good news with Isaac!

When I stepped through the door, I immediately tried to hide my enthusiasm, wanting to tell everyone at just the right moment, making it a huge surprise. As I got closer to the dining room, however, I found it extremely difficult to wipe the smile off my face. I was simply too excited!   I had to make myself stop just shy of entering the room so that I could try to compose myself. I stuffed the letter into the pocket of my dress (so as not to give anything away), put on the most somber look I could muster, steadied myself, took a deep breath, and calmly proceeded into the dining room, doing my best to act as normal as possible.

"Is everything all right?" Isaac questioned when he saw me walk in. "I was just about to come and find you."

"I passed! I passed! I passed!" I blurted out in exhilaration. "My exam, *I passed!*" I just couldn't help myself! My exuberance was like a bomb inside of me waiting to explode!

Isaac jumped up and ran over to give me a hug. He picked me up with his good arm and spun me around in excitement.

"Isaac!" I cautioned, concerned. "You'll hurt yourself!"

"I don't care!" he ignored, continuing to swing me around one more time before finally putting me down. "I'm so proud of you! I knew you could do it!" He was simply beaming!

"Congratulations!" Andrew and Isabelle joined in.

Isaac and I hugged again, elated!

"Now you're mine!" Isaac said in his excitement, smiling down at me. "You're finally free to be mine!"

SECRETS
(Chapter 53)

Isaac and I helped to clear the table, and when everything was taken care of, we all headed back to the family room to sit and visit some more.

It was such a wonderful evening, and everyone seemed to be enjoying it immensely, especially me, now that I no longer had the cloud of anticipation hanging over my head concerning the results of my exam.

Andrew and Isabelle, and Isaac and I talked on for quite awhile about all sorts of things, even discussing briefly Isaac's and my future together.

"So, have you asked her father for her hand yet?" Andrew prodded with a grin.

Isaac looked at me, and I at him.

"Well," he confessed, "I'm trying to think of the best way to approach him."

"Scared?" Andrew jabbed teasingly.

"I'll admit it, little brother," Isaac answered candidly. "I am a little nervous. I mean...let's be honest, given my record in talking with Mr. Lowry up to this point, you'd have to agree, things haven't *exactly* turned out in my favor very often."

"That is true!" I jumped in, backing up Isaac's claim. "Papa isn't the easiest person to get through to sometimes, but," I continued in Papa's defense, turning to Isaac, "I think he'll be open to hearing you out. After all, he did give in and let me take the exam."

Isaac nodded, conceding the point.

"You're right," he granted, "but this..." he shook his head. "This is a little more than just taking a test. I want to make his little girl my wife, and I'm just not so sure he's ready for that yet!" He sighed with a nod. "But," he went on, "hopefully you're right. Hopefully, your father will listen and give his consent." He paused, looking longingly into my eyes. "I very much want to move forward with things," he said with earnest, "and I want you by my side when I do!"

"Aww, how sweet!" Isabelle chimed in, smiling brightly. "You two make such a sweet couple! I'll certainly be praying that Mr. Lowry gives his permission. I would so love for the two of you to be able to experience what Andrew and I have experienced, thus far. It's been such a wonderful blessing being married, and an *absolutely* incredible journey!"

Andrew leaned over and gave Isabelle a kiss on the lips. She smiled at him as he smiled at her, so happy and contented with each other.

"I'll help you plan the wedding," Isabelle offered in excitement as she turned her attention to me. "That is, if you want my help."

"Now, now!" Isaac interjected, cautioning. "Let's not get the cart before the horse. Her father does still have to say yes, you know!"

Everyone just laughed at his retort.

I again looked at Isaac as he looked at me, both of us smiling affectionately at each other. We were so in love, and I felt so happy and overwhelmed in the moment.

As the evening wore on, we all continued to talk and laugh and joke together, that is, right up until Isaac realized the lateness of the hour.

"Oh, wow!" he said, almost in a panic. "I need to get you home!"

Andrew chuckled.

"That's right, big brother!" he teased. "You definitely want to stay in good graces with her father!"

Isaac looked at Andrew, playfully annoyed by the quip, while everyone else just laughed.

We all stood to our feet, Isaac and I thanked Andrew and Isabelle for their hospitality, Isabelle fetched my shawl, and we all walked to the front door together to say goodnight.

Just as we were about to leave, Andrew leaned in and gave Isaac a hug, wishing him well in his quest to talk with Papa. Isaac thanked him, he and I extended our gratitude to Andrew and Isabelle one last time, they said they thoroughly enjoyed the evening, and that we'd have to do it again sometime, real soon, Isaac and I heartily agreed, and he and I left.

"So," I inquired as we made our way home, "when *do* you think you might talk to Papa?"

"Oh, don't you worry any about that," Isaac said coyly. "I've been thinking about it a lot lately, and I'm pretty sure I have it all worked out." He smiled over at me. "And believe me," he assured, "you'll be among the first to know when I have an answer!"

I smiled broadly as I scooted over closer to him, leaning my head against his shoulder.

"I love you so much!" I expressed with fervor, absolutely giddy and excited for what the future now held!

"I love you, too!" he echoed with just as much enthusiasm.

When we arrived home, Isaac pulled the buggy up to the house.

"I'll see you tomorrow," he told me as I got down. "But hey, it may be a little later on in the day, though, all right? Doc said he'd take a look at my arm tomorrow and..." Isaac lifted his arm a bit. "Hopefully, this sling will be gone by the next time I see you!"

"Really?" I exclaimed, so excited for him. "Oh, Isaac, that's *wonderful!* I'll definitely be praying it comes off!"

"Thanks!" he replied with a nod. "Well," he said, adjusting the reins, "I'll see you tomorrow, then."

"Tomorrow it is!" I agreed with a smile.

Isaac smiled back, snapped the reins, and took off.

I stood there a minute watching him drive away, before finally heading into the house. As soon as I stepped inside, I heard Papa call from the living room.

"Is that you, Jochebed?" he asked.

"Yes, Papa," I replied as I hung up my shawl. "It's me!" I walked on into the living room to speak with him.

When I entered, Papa was sitting in his chair looking at the newspaper.

"Congratulations, sweetheart!" he said as he put the paper down. "I'm very proud of ya for passin' your exam!"

I smiled, grateful, as I walked over to give Papa a kiss on the cheek.

"Thank you, Papa," I told him. "And thank you again for letting me take it."

"Well, you're welcome," Papa replied modestly. He looked up at me smiling, filled with admiration. "So grown up!" he stated proudly.

I smiled demurely, a little self-conscious.

"So did ya enjoy your evenin'?" Papa queried.

"Yes, sir, very much so!" I answered with eagerness. "We had a delightful evening, a wonderful meal, and even better fellowship!" I smiled cheerfully. "Andrew and Isabelle are such a great couple," I conveyed. "I couldn't be happier for them! Married life really seems to suit them well!"

"Well, that's good to hear," Papa nodded, pleased. "And Isaac...how's he doin' with that arm of his?"

I chuckled.

"Funny you should ask," I replied. "Isaac just told me before he left that Dr. Wellesley's agreed to look at it tomorrow, and that he might be able to get his sling off."

"Hmm," Papa grunted, surprised. "Thought he wasn't due to get it off for another week or so?"

"That's what I thought, too," I revealed. "But I guess Isaac must have talked Dr. Wellesley into doing it sooner. I know Isaac's really wanted to be out of that sling for quite some time now."

"I can understand that," Papa sympathized. "Hope it works out for him." He put his hand to his chin. "Hey," he said, "speakin' of Isaac, how are your plans goin' for Saturday?"

I cocked my head back and forth, indicating that it was going so so.

"There coming along," I explained a bit worried. "Isabelle and I confirmed some things tonight, but I still have a lot more to do tomorrow." I sighed, more than a little anxious. "I sure hope I can get it all done in time, though," I said. "I'm so desperate for it all to work out! I just really want Isaac to be surprised!"

"Oh, I'm sure he will be, sweetheart," Papa tried to encourage.

"Well, thank you, Papa," I replied, not so sure. "I do hope you're right!"

"Stop worryin'!" Papa admonished. "It'll work. You'll see!"

I nodded, trying to accept it.

"Well," I relayed, "if it's all right with you, I think I'll go and work on his gift a little more yet tonight before I go to bed. I'm so wound up right now; I don't think I could sleep a wink!"

Papa smiled, understanding.

"That'd be fine," he allowed as he stood to his feet, putting his newspaper aside, grabbing his empty coffee cup. "But this old man's turnin' in. I need my rest!"

"Oh, Papa!" I protested. "You're hardly old!"

Papa chuckled at my disagreeance as he gave me a wink and a smile. Walking up to me, he sweetly gave me a kiss on the forehead, and told me not to work too late.

I assured him that I wouldn't, and we walked into the kitchen together.

"See you in the morning, Papa," I called out as I started for the sewing room.

Papa went to put his coffee cup on the counter.

"Love ya, sweetheart," he called back. "I hope ya get finished what you're needin' to."

I smiled over at him.

"Me, too, Papa," I agreed. "Love you!"

I went off to the sewing room, and Papa headed for bed.

When I opened the door to the sewing room, I quickly went and found Isaac's gift that I had earlier stuffed in a basket underneath some other clothes, pulled it out, straightened it the best I could, gathered my thread and needle, and sat down to begin sewing on it.

As I sat there working, I began to reflect back over the events of the day. It had been a very good day, and I couldn't be more grateful! Thinking about it, though, I was suddenly overcome by emotion. Tears of joy and happiness began to well up inside of me as I sat there so thankful for Isaac, so thankful for my family, and so thankful for dear, dear friends! Not only that, I couldn't help but be thankful for having passed my exam!

"Thank You, God!" I cried out, overwhelmed. "Thank You *so much* for *everything* You've done for me, and…thank You…thank You for what You're going to do!" I smiled and wiped my tears as I pressed on, trying to finish up my surprise for Isaac. Somewhere along the way in my quest to finish, however, I must have fallen asleep. Before I knew it, I was being jolted awake by the sound of Samuel rushing down the stairs.

"Oh, my goodness!" I moaned as I leaned forward in my chair, rubbing my neck and my shoulders. The stiffness I felt was unbearable! I instantly regretted my inadvertent sleepover in the sewing room.

Suddenly, the sewing room door burst open, nearly scaring me to death!

"Good grief, Samuel!" I blustered as I sat back, clutching my chest. "What are you doing?"

Samuel frowned, looking at me peculiarly.

"What am I doin'?" he retorted. "What are *you* doin'? Ya look awful!"

I glared at him, giving him a not so nice look.

He shrugged it off.

"Seriously, what are ya doin' in here?" he asked snidely. "I'm starvin'! Aren't ya supposed to be in the kitchen makin' breakfast?"

I rolled my eyes.

"Yes, Samuel!" I barked, still trying to work out the kinks. "I'm fully aware of my duties!" I shook my head, took a deep breath, and started to gather my things. Once I had them in hand, I leaned over to put them away, but when I sat back up, it hit me - a headache, and it was bad! I instantly grabbed my forehead in pain, closed my eyes, and began to rub.

Note to self, I thought, *don't EVER fall asleep in a chair overnight again - EVER!*

"Well, are ya comin?" Samuel nagged impatiently. "I told ya, I'm starvin' here!"

I sighed, nearly ready to explode!

"Yes, Samuel!" I snapped angrily. "I'll be there in a minute! Why don't you learn some manners?" I shook my head, appalled by his dreadful attitude. "And you know what?" I rebuked further. "While you're at it, why don't you learn some patience, too?"

Samuel huffed, rolled his eyes, and walked away.

When he was gone, I slowly stood to my feet and carefully made my way to the kitchen. I immediately went to the cupboard to get my medicine, mixed it up, and drank it down. I wanted to get it in me before my headache got too severe. I simply had *far too much* to do today to be laid up with another bad headache!

Fortunately, while I was in the processes of making breakfast, the medicine began to take effect, and I started to feel a whole lot better.

I finished the meal, went to the door to call Papa and Samuel, and sat at the table waiting for them to come inside.

They hastily finished up their chores, and eventually came to join me.

Papa ate, but he couldn't stay long. He was working in town today and wanted to get an early start. He quickly finished up, gave Samuel some further instructions as to what he wanted him to do for the day, gathered his things, and promptly left.

I told him I loved him and to be careful as he headed out the door.

Samuel, of course, never looked up from his plate. He sat there scarfing down his breakfast (as usual) completely unengaged. When he swallowed his last bite, he grabbed his milk, slurped it down, let out a very *rude* belch, (for which I instantly scowled at and scolded him for), never excused himself, jumped up from the table, and quickly ran off outside.

I was *absolutely* aghast!

*Would he **ever** grow up!* I wondered to myself. I sat there shaking my head, sighing, as I went back to eating. When I finished my breakfast, I got up right away and started cleaning up the kitchen.

As I was standing at the sink, washing up the breakfast dishes, I was surprised to hear a knock at the door. Wondering who it could possibly be, I set aside the dish I was scrubbing on, grabbed a towel to dry off my hands, and headed over to see who was there. Just as I was about to reach for the doorknob, however, Aunt Sara suddenly opened the door and walked in carrying baby Lydia.

I jumped, not expecting her to do that!

"Oh, I'm sorry, Jochebed!" she apologized. "I didn't mean to startle you. Samuel told me to come on inside."

I sighed, relieved that it was her.

"No, that's fine," I replied, calming myself down. "What brings you by?"

"I came to get that recipe of your mother's," she informed me.

I looked at her a bit perplexed.

"You know," she reminded, "the cake recipe you were going to give me, the one you asked me to bake for Saturday, the one for…"

"The one for Isaac's birthday party, of course!" I interjected, finally remembering. "Come on in!"

Aunt Sara walked on into the kitchen as I closed the door and followed in behind her.

"I'm so sorry, Aunt Sara," I apologized, feeling badly. "I completely forgot! I'll find the recipe for you right now!"

"Oh, no hurry," she told me as she pulled out a chair and sat down with baby Lydia. "Lydia and I are enjoying our day out, aren't we?" She smiled broadly at baby Lydia as she patted her adorable, chubby little cheek.

Lydia cooed back happily, smiling up at Aunt Sara with her bright, cheerful eyes. She was such a doll baby and a pure delight to be around!

"Well, thank you for doing this for me, nonetheless," I said, looking diligently for the recipe. "I know Isaac really enjoys this cake, and with everything else I have yet to do, I just don't know when I'd find the time to bake it for him…much less decorate it!"

"I fully understand," Aunt Sara replied. "I'm just glad to be able to help out. How are things going with the preparations anyhow?"

"All right, I guess," I answered, a bit frazzled. "I never realized how much planning goes into one of these things! I certainly hope it all comes together and that Isaac's surprised."

"Oh, I'm sure everything will work out just fine," Aunt Sara encouraged with a smile.

"Ah! Here it is!" I exclaimed, holding up the recipe. "Found it!" I walked over and handed the piece of paper to Aunt Sara as I smiled down at baby Lydia. "May I hold her real quick?" I asked.

"Why, sure!" she instantly obliged, carefully lifting Lydia to me, gently placing her in my arms.

"She is just *so* sweet!" I complimented, leaning down to kiss her soft little cheek. "I think I could just sit and stare at her all day long!"

"Oh, me too!" Aunt Sara heartily agreed, glowing with pride. "Some days I think that's all I ever get done!"

We both chuckled.

After a few minutes of doting on Lydia, I decided I needed to get busy.

"Well," I lamented, "as much as I'd love to keep her, I think I'd better get going. I still have *a lot* to do before tomorrow!"

"I understand," Aunt Sara said with a smile, lifting her hands to take Lydia from me.

I gave Lydia another kiss on the cheek and handed her back to Aunt Sara.

Aunt Sara adjusted Lydia's blanket, tucked the recipe I'd given her into her dress pocket, and stood up to leave.

"Thank you again for helping me with the cake," I told her, very grateful. "It truly is a big help!"

"Oh, not a problem!" Aunt Sara assured as she carried baby Lydia to the door. "It's my pleasure! I love to bake, so it's really no imposition at all. Now," she said, turning back to me, "you'll be sure to let me know if there's anything more you need me to do before tomorrow - right?"

"I will!" I promised. "And thank you!"

"All right then," Aunt Sara said as she opened the door. "I'll see you tomorrow if not before." With that, she left, and I quickly went back to work.

After getting as much done around the house as I could, I promptly headed for the sewing room to work on Isaac's gift. I desperately wanted to get it finished and wrapped before he came by the house. I wasn't sure just how much time I had, so I hurried as swiftly as my fingers would let me.

It took me about an hour or so, but finally, Isaac's surprise was complete! I held up the finished project and meticulously looked it over, thoroughly checking my work. I didn't gaze at it too long, however, because I still had to get it wrapped and hid before Isaac arrived. I quickly folded the gift and went to the closet for a box and some wrapping paper.

While I was in the midst of wrapping the present, Samuel came knocking at the door.

"Jochebed!" he yelled. "Ya in there?"

I was afraid that maybe Isaac had arrived, and Samuel was coming to get me.

"Yes, I'm in here," I answered. "What do you need?"

Without even asking or being invited in, Samuel came rushing through the door.

"Samuel!" I shouted, exasperated. "Shouldn't you, at least, *ask* before barging in?"

Of course, he was curious and nosy as to what I was doing, stretching his neck, bobbing about me, trying to see.

"What's in the box?" he pried.

I sighed, annoyed with his persistence!

"It's Isaac's gift, if you must know!" I stated hurried and none too happy. "Now, what do you need?"

Samuel gave me a snotty look before answering.

"I need those pants I gave ya to mend," he barked. "Billy's waitin', and I gotta get changed. Are they done?"

"Yes, they're finished," I said, just wanting him to leave. "They're over there." I pointed to a basket on the floor where I'd folded his pants and set them with the rest of the mending.

"Can ya reach 'em for me?" he had the gall to ask.

I turned and frowned, *furious* with his utter laziness and lack of honor!

"You're joking, right?" I replied angrily. "You do see that I'm trying to get this present wrapped? I mean…you can see that - right?"

Samuel rolled his eyes.

"Well, your closer!" he asserted. "Why can't ya just pick 'em up and hand 'em to me? I mean, seriously, it'll take ya what…all of two seconds?"

As you can imagine, at this point, I was absolutely fuming! I clenched my jaw, leaned over, grabbed his pants, and threw them at him.

Samuel caught them mid-air.

"Thanks!" he quipped with a grin. "I'm goin' fishin'!" He threw the pants over his shoulder, turned abruptly, and walked right out of the room without even closing the door back.

I huffed, growling at his insolence as I walked over to close the door. Turning swiftly, I went back to wrapping Isaac's present - quickly running out of time.

When I was finished, I placed the gift in the closet, straightened the sewing room a bit, and headed for the kitchen.

I decided to sit down for a minute at the kitchen table and go over the list of things that yet needed to be done for Isaac's surprise party. As I looked the list over, thankfully quite a bit had already been accomplished, but there was still much left to do. Needless to say, I was very grateful for the help of family and friends as I knew I could never get everything finished in time on my own.

While I was sitting there in the kitchen, all of a sudden, I heard the door start to creek as if someone were trying to open it carefully and quietly. I sat there frozen, unsure of what was going on. I waited, my heart pounding, trying to figure out what I should do. Finally, the door opened slightly, and in popped this arm waving up and down.

At first, I thought I was seeing things, and then I thought perhaps I was going crazy!

Why was there an arm waving up and down in my kitchen? I queried. Transfixed, I sat there staring at it, thoroughly confused and mystified. Just as I was about to stand up and go investigate, however, Isaac threw open the door the rest of the way and shouted, scaring me half to death!

"Surprise!" he yelled, grinning from ear to ear, still waving his arm. "See, I got it back!"

I instantly clutched my chest, sighing in sheer relief!

"Isaac!" I exclaimed, trying to breathe. "You do realize you were almost available again - right?!"

"What?" he questioned, chuckling, as he stood there smiling at my distress. "What do you mean?"

I shook my head, still clutching my chest as I gave him a look of disapproval.

"My heart nearly stopped when I heard the door creek!" I told him. "And then…then to have this *arm* just come reaching into the house, and with no body attached, I mean - *really!*" I scowled at him with a slight grin. "From now on," I chided, "I would appreciate it if you could please try to refrain from doing things that may cause my early demise!"

Isaac chuckled again, and then calmed a bit when he realized I wasn't laughing with him.

"Sorry!" he said in a boyish tone, looking innocently at the floor. He glanced up sheepishly. "Forgive me!" he implored with a smile.

I couldn't help but smile back at his playfulness.

"Yeess!" I reluctantly agreed.

"Good!" he quipped, grinning cheerily. He walked over a little closer. "So," he asked, staring at his arm, rubbing it up and down, "did you miss it? … 'Cause I sure did!"

I rolled my eyes as I shook my head, laughing at his silliness.

"You may have gained your arm back," I teased, "but I think you've *lost your mind!*"

"Hey!" Isaac protested, acting all offended. "Watch it there!" He looked down at his arm, rubbing it affectionately, holding it tightly to his body.

"Oh brother!" I howled, rolling my eyes again in disbelief.

We both burst into laughter as Isaac stepped a little closer.

"So," he queried inquisitively, calming down, trying to see what I had on the table there in front of me. "What do we have here?"

I furrowed my brow, quickly closing my notebook.

"None of your concern!" I insisted, snatching it up into my arms. "I simply have things I need to get done is all, and writing them down helps me to remember!"

Isaac smiled coyly as if he suspected something.

"Hmm!" he said. "Nothing wrong with being organized, I guess."

"Well, thank you for your approval!" I retorted, putting my notebook in my lap. "So glad to hear you appreciate good organization!"

Isaac grinned deviously as I got up from the table to go put my notebook away. Immediately, he started following me, acting as if he were trying to find out what I was up to.

Growing ever disconcerted, I stopped and turned around to look at him.

"Isaac Lewis!" I admonished. "Do you mind?"

"Who? Me?" he teased, pointing to himself, acting all innocent. "Why…am I bothering you?"

I looked at him chagrinned.

"As a matter of fact you are!" I stated emphatically. "I would very much appreciate it if you would please wait in the other room for me to return."

"But why?" he asked in his boyish tone. "Do ya have a surprise in there or somethin'?"

"A surprise?" I questioned, trying to sound like I had no idea what he was talking about. "Why would I have a surprise in here? A surprise for *whom?*"

"Ohhh, you know!" he intimated with a grin. "Somebody's havin' a birthday tomorrow!"

I frowned at him, feigning naiveté.

"They are?" I quipped, sounding even more lost than before. "*Who is?* Who's having a birthday?"

Isaac squinted his eyes as he cocked his head, looking at me a little worried.

"You're...you're just joking with me, right?" he asked anxiously.

I continued to act completely ignorant.

"Joking with you?" I replied. "Why would I be joking with you?"

Isaac sobered.

"You...you do know it's my birthday tomorrow, don't you?" he questioned, concerned.

I tried to look as shocked and surprised as I possibly could.

"*What!*" I exclaimed. "Now *you're* joking with *me*, right?" I gave him the most worried look I could muster. "Isaac," I cried hysterically, "please, tell me you really are joking!" I searched his face frantically, really playing it up. "Tomorrow's *really* your birthday?!?" I agonized.

Isaac nodded, indicating that it was.

I turned away, acting as if I was utterly distressed by the news.

"Oh, Isaac!" I said, sounding tearful. "I...I feel just *awful!* How could I have forgotten your birthday?"

Isaac came up behind me as I stood there acting as if I was about to cry.

"I...I didn't...it's okay!" he assured, trying to comfort me.

I sniffed a bit, still playing the part.

"I...I...I guess with all my studying and taking my exam and then...waiting on results, I..." I paused dramatically, trying to sound distraught. "Can you ever forgive me?" I begged, pretending to wipe a tear.

"Jochebed," Isaac replied, a little flustered, "it's okay, really! III didn't mean to upset you! It's not a big deal, honest!"

I kept my face turned away, trying so hard not to laugh.

"No big deal?" I blurted out, sounding beyond devastated. "But, Isaac...it's your birthday!" I shook my head. "I am *so* sorry!" I looked down at the floor, clutched my notebook to my chest, and headed straight for the sewing room as quickly as I could. I never turned back to look at Isaac, as I was trying my best not to burst into laughter. I bit my lip as hard as I could and hurried on down the hallway.

Once inside the sewing room, I promptly closed the door behind me, leaned up against it, put my hand over my mouth to muffle the sound, and quietly chuckled to myself.

After I'd settled a bit, I went and put my notebook away, rubbed my eyes a little to make them look like I'd been crying, (after all, I was supposed to have been overcome by tremendous guilt and emotion), and then I opened the door and walked out to go find Isaac. (He'd gone back to the kitchen to wait for me.) Before I turned the corner to face him, however, I made sure to put on a somber, melancholy face.

"Isaac," I said softly, drawing his attention to me. "I...I truly am sorry that I forgot about your birthday." I looked at him earnestly. "You'll forgive me?"

Isaac walked over towards me with a sympathetic smile.

"Don't think another thing of it," he encouraged, reaching down, sweetly taking hold of my hand. "I'm the one who should be sorry. I never should have said anything."

"No!" I asserted passionately. "You had every right to expect something!"

"But Jochebed," Isaac contended, "honestly...and I'm being serious...just forget about it!"

"Absolutely not!" I rejected, determined. "I insist! I have to do *something!*" I let go of Isaac's hand and started to walk further into the kitchen. "Perhaps I could..." I paused, acting as if I were actually thinking deeply about what I could do for him. "Perhaps, I'll... *nooo!*" I said, stopping abruptly, turning around to face him. "No!" I declared enthusiastically. "I think I'll keep it to myself and make it a surprise!" I nodded excitedly. *"That's it!"* I exclaimed, pretending I'd suddenly had some great revelation. "I'll make it a surprise! You've surprised me so many times before; it's my turn to surprise you! ...Why not!? It'll be fun!"

Isaac shook his head as he walked over towards me.

"Jochebed," he said, trying to dissuade me, "really...it's not necessary! We could just spend the day together taking a walk or something. That'd be birthday enough for me!"

"Nope!" I replied unwaveringly. "It's settled! I'll have a surprise ready for you by tomorrow. And no," I persisted, "you may *not* spend the rest of the day trying to pester it out of me!" (Although, as you can imagine, that's exactly what he did!)

Isaac smiled, furrowing his brow.

"You're sure?" he asked, very reluctant. "I mean, I feel so badly now, for having brought it up in the first place. You really don't have to do *anything!*"

I looked at him, smiling.

"I want to!" I assured. "I just wish I had extra time to do more."

Isaac came up to me and put his arm around me.

"I'm sure whatever you do, it will be absolutely wonderful!" he complimented.

"Well, thank you," I accepted. "And thank you, too, for understanding."

Isaac smiled, giving me a squeeze as I smiled back.

While my eyes may have been smiling on the outside, I was most definitely breathing a huge sigh of relief on the inside! I felt fairly certain that I had successfully convinced Isaac that I'd completely forgotten about his birthday (forgot that is, until he'd reminded me of it, of course).

I knew I'd dodged the proverbial bullet, for which I was thankful, and now I couldn't *wait* to carry on with my plans!

WIDE AWAKE
(Chapter 54)

Isaac and I spent the rest of the afternoon together (he, on and off, doing his best to try to pry my plans out of me, and me doggedly fending him off when he did), but after awhile, I finally told him that I really did need some time to prepare my surprise for him. He tried to insist again that I not worry about it, but I was hearing none of it! I insisted right back that I was going to do something, even if it couldn't be much. He graciously relented, and agreed to leave after supper. He helped me with the meal, we ate, and he readied to leave.

"I'll see you tomorrow at noon at your place," I told him. "So don't be late!"

He smiled inquisitively.

"Noon, huh?" he queried suspiciously.

I looked at him determined.

"You're not finding out!" I stated adamantly. "So you might as well stop trying!"

Isaac chuckled at my insistence.

"All right," he reluctantly granted. "Then I look forward to seeing you tomorrow."

He started for the door, and I walked with him, fully expecting him to leave without incident, but just as we got to the door, he looked at me with long, wistful, puppy eyes, trying to influence me one last time.

"Just one, teeny, tiny, little hint?" he begged. "Surely, you could tell me *something!*"

"Goodnight, Isaac!" I replied unyieldingly, completely unfazed by his antics, opening the door to show him out.

He stiffened as he folded his arms, feigning offence at my rebuff.

"Well, I never!" he quipped, walking on past me. "A bit *testy* there, aren't we?"

I smirked and rolled my eyes as I pushed him on out the door.

"Goodnight!" I reiterated cold-heartedly.

He laughed at my impertinence as he stepped down off the porch.

Just as I was about to close the door, I heard him call out.

"Goodnight, my love!" he expressed with theatrics. "See you on the morrow!"

I smiled breathlessly (so in love) as I closed the door. I leaned up against it and waited for Isaac to leave.

When I was certain he was finally on his way and out of sight, I scurried down to Andrew and Isabelle's to talk with them as they were in on my grand plan, and we had a few more things we needed to iron out.

When I got to their house, I explained the near disaster that I'd had earlier in the day with Isaac, but I assured them that I believed I had successfully handled it, and that all Isaac knew was that I had a surprise waiting for him at noon. They were a little concerned, but I told them I didn't think he suspected anything more. They were relieved, and we continued on with our planning.

I stayed for about an hour or so, and when we felt we had everything settled, I headed for home.

It was late when I got there and I was exhausted, so I decided to go straight to bed. I had to get up early, and wanted to get a goodnight's rest. Unfortunately, I was so excited for the next day to come; I had an *extremely* difficult time falling asleep! I lay there tossing and turning for what seemed like hours before finally closing my eyes. Before I knew it, the sun was up, and so was I. It had definitely been too short a night, and I was a bit tired, but I'd have to make due with what I got as I had a very full and busy day ahead of me.

*****

"Do ya really think he'll be surprised?" Samuel asked as we sat down to breakfast.

"Oh, I certainly hope so!" I replied anxiously, worried he might figure things out.

"Ya've done a good job of keepin' this from him," Papa complimented. "When I saw him and his grandmother in town yesterday mornin', he didn't seem any the wiser."

"I know," I lamented, "but that was in the morning. In the afternoon, when he came over, something happened, and I had to pretend like I'd forgotten all about his birthday altogether to keep him from asking too many questions and figuring things out." I sighed, doubtful. "I just hope I did a good enough job of coning him!"

"I'm sure ya did," Papa answered rather quickly. "Ya can be pretty convincin' when ya wanna be."

I looked at him quizzically.

"Thanks - I think," I said hesitantly. "I'm not so sure if that was a compliment or not."

Papa just chuckled.

"Anyway," I went on, wanting to confirm with Samuel. "Are you still going to be able to help us decorate this morning?"

"Yah, sure, if it's still all right with Papa," he answered.

"It's fine, Son," Papa agreed, giving his permission. "Just as long as your chores get done."

Samuel nodded.

"I'll go finish 'em up right now," he agreed. He grabbed the last piece of bacon off his plate and quickly headed outside.

After he left, I abruptly stood up and started to clear the table while Papa sat finishing his coffee.

I cleaned as quickly and thoroughly as I could, and when I finished, I gathered all the things I needed to take to Isaac's house for the surprise party (including his gift, of course), and started packing them into boxes so that I could more easily carry them. It was quite a lot, but Papa helped.

~

The plan was simple. Andrew was to take Isaac into town for most of the day where he and Pastor Scott would keep Isaac occupied until lunchtime. Isabelle was to pick Samuel and me up after breakfast, and we were to go to the Lewis' to decorate and prepare Isaac's favorite meal. Aunt Sara and Uncle Mark were to come help decorate as well, and everyone else was to arrive a little before noon to get into place to yell surprise.

~

Just as Papa and I finished packing the last of the things into boxes, Isabelle pulled up in her wagon. Samuel, Papa, and I loaded everything in, and we headed out. …So far, everything was going according to plan!

When we arrived at the Lewis', Isabelle parked the wagon out by the road, and we sent Samuel to stealthily go check to make sure Andrew had already left with Isaac. While Samuel was gone, we all sat anxiously, waiting for him to report back.

As we sat there, keeping our eyes peeled for him, Aunt Sara and Uncle Mark pulled up behind us.

"What we waitin' on?" Uncle Mark called out.

"Samuel's making sure Isaac's gone," I informed him. "We're just waiting for him to come back and tell us it's all clear."

I fidgeted nervously as we sat there waiting several more minutes for Samuel to return. Thankfully, he finally appeared down the lane, waving for us to come on. We pulled forward and proceeded on to the house.

"Oh, this is *so* exciting!" Aunt Sara squealed in delight as we started unloading things from the wagon. "I just absolutely *love* surprises!"

"Me, too!" Isabelle agreed, smiling broadly. "This is so much fun!"

In no time at all, we got everything inside the house, and Uncle Mark moved the wagons into the barn out of sight. When he finished, he came inside and began to help Mr. Lewis, Aunt Sara, and Samuel with the decorations. While they decorated, Mrs. Lewis, Isabelle, and I immediately went to work on Isaac's favorite meal. We all worked frantically and diligently over the next few hours, hoping to have everything done and in its place before it was time to hide and yell surprise!

As the time passed, people began to arrive, and Uncle Mark made certain that they parked their wagons and buggies in the barn out of sight. Once he was sure that that was taken care of, he showed the guests inside, and helped them find a place to hide.

The house was really starting to fill up, as we had invited quite a few people: some from church, a few of Isaac's friends from college, and, of course, family. It was quite a crowd, but fortunately the Lewis' home was plenty big enough to accommodate the extra people.

After working for hours, everything was finally in place. The only thing left was for Andrew to bring Isaac home, and for us to surprise him.

As the time neared for them to arrive, my heart began to pound faster and faster. I was *so* nervous! I just wanted everything to be perfect and to go off without a hitch! So far, thankfully, it seemed everything was humming along as planned.

At five till twelve, we all hid, quietly waiting for the door to open, and for Isaac to step inside. Just as the last person was getting into place, we heard movement out on the porch. It was obvious someone was out there, and it sounded like they were walking towards the door. We all instantly froze, readying ourselves, anticipating Isaac's entry.

As the handle on the door slowly began to turn, I closed my eyes nervously and took a deep breath! Isaac was finally here!

Suddenly, the door opened and the person who'd been out there stepped inside.

Immediately, we all jumped out and shouted, "Surprise!"

Unfortunately, it was Pastor Scott and not Isaac.

"Sorry! Sorry!" he apologized as he scooted on into the house. He quickly walked over and joined Mrs. Scott who had already arrived earlier in the day. "I believe Andrew's on his way with Isaac now," he informed us. "I left them a while ago, and I imagine they'll be here any minute."

We all hid again and excitedly waited.

It was all I could do to keep myself still as I was more nervous now than ever! Isaac would be here soon, and I just couldn't wait to see him, nor the look on his face when he realized what was going on.

Everyone waited...and waited...and waited some more!

Finally, we could hear a wagon coming down the lane, and as it got closer, Uncle Mark came rushing in the back door to announce that he was pretty sure it was Andrew's.

We all quieted again and readied ourselves for the big surprise.

As soon as the door opened, we once again yelled as loudly as we could, but regrettably, the surprise was on us. Again, the person wasn't Isaac, but rather Andrew, and curiously he was alone.

I stepped from my hiding place, puzzled, and a bit perplexed.

"Andrew," I questioned, growing ever concerned, "where's Isaac? He was supposed to be with you. Is he coming?"

I could tell by the look on Andrew's face that something was terribly wrong. He wasn't at all smiling, and he looked quite serious and stern. He walked over to me and quietly asked if he could talk to me in private.

My heart instantly sank in fear as I nodded, agreeing, but I just couldn't fathom what could possibly be so important that he couldn't tell me in front of everyone else.

Had something happened to Isaac? I wondered. *Had he fallen ill? Had he been hurt?* All of these dreadful thoughts went racing through my mind as Andrew and I excused ourselves to the kitchen. As the door to the kitchen closed behind us, I was near trembling in worry!

"Andrew, what is it?" I asked frantically. "What's happened? Where's Isaac? Why isn't he here with you?" I was so panicked by Andrews's ominous behavior; I didn't know what to do!

Andrew quietly walked over to the counter, leaned down, rested his elbows on it, and put his face in his hands with a sigh.

I walked up beside him, frightened!

"Andrew!" I demanded. "Talk to me! Tell me what's going on! You're scaring me something awful! Is Isaac all right?"

Andrew looked away, almost as if he were trying to avoid my gaze.

"I tried to get him to come inside, Jochebed," he said with distress in his voice. "Honest, I did! But...he just wouldn't come!" Andrew took a deep breath, clearly troubled. Finally, he looked up at me and conveyed with worry in his voice. "I've never seen him like this before," he confessed. "Something's going on, and it's eating away at him for sure." He paused, shaking his head, noticeably concerned.

My mind was in a daze, beset by what he was saying. I could barely comprehend it, much less organize my thoughts.

"Andrew," I queried, furrowing my brow, bringing my hands to my lips, trying to make sense of it all, "but I...I don't understand! Yesterday...yesterday he was fine...everything was fine! He was happy and...he was looking forward to seeing me....and..." I shook my head, thoroughly confused.

Without warning, I began to feel a little lightheaded, overcome by the stress of it all. I took a deep breath, hoping it would help.

"Andrew," I kept right on imploring, pushing through, desperate for answers. "What happened? Please...you have to tell me! ...*Surely*, Isaac told you *something!*"

Andrew shook his head as he lowered it, sighing heavily, seemingly in turmoil. I could tell by his actions that he was torn. It appeared to me that he might know something, but that he was just too much of a gentleman to say. (Or, at least, that's what I supposed!)

"Andrew!" I tried again, hoping to coax it out of him. "You have to have *some idea* as to what's going on! ...Please...just tell me!"

Andrew sighed again before reluctantly standing up to face me.

"Jochebed," he said earnestly, looking me right in the eye, appearing more despondent than I think I'd ever seen him before, "truly…I can't tell you. It's not my place." He took a step towards me, so somber and melancholy. "I really think it would just be best if you go find Isaac and talk to him yourself," he suggested.

I thought for sure I was going to die right there on the spot! It was more than obvious by the tone in his voice and by the look on his face that whatever Isaac had to tell me was not good! I nearly broke down crying right then and there.

"Well," I asked, shaking uncontrollably, starting to tear up a bit, "do…do you, at least, know where he might be?"

Andrew looked past me solemnly, almost as if he were fighting back tears himself.

"All I can say," he divulged as he cleared his throat, "is that…well…when we got here…Isaac, he…he jumped down and headed off on one of his walks." Andrew bit his lip with angst as he fixed his eyes on me yet again. "If I had to guess," he told me, "I'd say he probably went back to that garden he likes so much."

I was so distraught at this point, I could barely move! Nothing made sense anymore! I was simply *reeling* from this **unbelievable** turn of events! My palms were sweaty, my mouth was dry, and my heart was beating so furiously I literally thought it might leap from my chest! I put my hand to my cheek, feeling flush, as there was a sick, sinking feeling in the pit of my stomach that just wouldn't go away. It was so bad, I actually thought I might be ill right there in the kitchen in front of Andrew. I covered my mouth with my hand as I took one deep breath after another, trying to calm myself down. It was awful!! I just couldn't remember a time in all my life when I'd felt so nervous and so scared and so worried all at the same time!

Andrew stood there quietly, looking at me as if he genuinely felt sorry for me.

"Jochebed," he tried to comfort, "I'm so sorry for all of this. I know this isn't how you saw the day going and…" He shook his head, almost as if he didn't know what else to say or do.

I bit my cheek, my lip quivering, as a tear escaped my eye and trickled down my face.

Andrew kindly reached out and put his hand on my arm, trying to console me.

"I'll let the others know where you've gone," he offered. "You go! …Go find Isaac!"

I nodded as I wiped my tears, turning to leave.

Before I could step away, however, Andrew caught my arm, momentarily stopping me. I think he was trying to encourage me, but what he proceeded to say only caused me more worry and concern!

"Jochebed," he expressed with sincerity as I turned my head back to look at him. "I do hope things work out for the two of you. I…I really do like having you around."

I briefly froze, completely alarmed! I couldn't believe my ears!

What did he mean by that? I worried. *Why would he say such a thing?* I swallowed hard and nodded, biting my lower lip, trying very hard not to break down.

Andrew gave me a sympathetic smile and let me go.

I nervously turned to leave, dreading terribly what I now had to do. While there was a part of me that wanted to find Isaac, there was an even bigger part of me that didn't! I was so terrified for what was awaiting me, I just didn't know if I could handle it!

As I stood there agonizing over it, though, deep down I knew that I couldn't avoid whatever was going on forever, and as much as I just wanted to run away and hide from it all, I knew that I couldn't. I anxiously stepped to the door, gathered what courage I could find, took a deep breath, opened the door, and stepped outside with *much* apprehension and fear!

Once out there, I paused for a minute to look around, thinking perhaps Isaac might be near. When I didn't see him, however, knowing he was likely in the rose garden, I took hold of my dress and began to run as quickly as my legs would carry me.

All the way there, the most horrible thoughts kept racing through my mind. The tears that I'd fought so hard to keep back were now freely flowing down my face, and it was all I could do to brush them aside to see where I was going.

It was obvious that something had happened, obvious that something had changed, but for the life of me I couldn't figure out what. Of course, as was my bent, I fretted about it all the way to the rose garden. Several times, so upset and so distraught about it, I just wanted to fall to the ground and have a good cry. My perfect surprise for Isaac had turned into a horrendous nightmare for me, and I honestly didn't know how I was going to face it!

It all just makes no sense! I kept telling myself, over and over again. *But then again,* I reasoned, *life and love seldom do!*

When I finally arrived at the rose garden, I quickly made my way down the paths, searching desperately for Isaac. Row after row I searched, but to no avail.

Where could he be? I panicked. *I thought for sure he would be here!*

Nearing the last few rows of the garden, I worried that maybe he'd already gone, but then suddenly, there in the distance, I saw him.

Instantly, I froze, too afraid to go near.

Momentarily paralyzed by my fear, I stood there anxiously watching him. It was so disconcerting! I just couldn't understand what was going on!

Why was he doing this? I wondered. *What had changed?* I shook my head, wiping my tears, trembling at the thought of having to confront him. He looked so serious, so somber, so deep in thought. I loved him so much, and I *thought* he loved me, but now...

I let out a long, agonizing sigh as I slowly started towards him, my heart breaking from the thought of potentially losing him.

Why? I worried. *Why was this happening? Why?* No matter how hard I tried to figure it out, there was just no coming to any rational conclusion. As I gradually approached, I nervously called out his name.

"Isaac," I said, my voice quivering. I took a deep breath, trying hard not to cry.

Isaac glanced up, startled from his thoughts by the sound of my voice.

I looked at him with desperation.

"Why...why are you here?" I wanted to know as I inched ever closer to him. "Why didn't you come to meet me?"

Isaac stared at me soberly as he walked up to me, extending his hand.

"Will you walk with me?" he asked.

There are no words to express how scared I was in that moment as I put my trembling hand in his. There was something dreadfully wrong, I could sense it, and I had to fight every fiber in my being not to just run away!

Isaac clasped my hand, and we began to walk.

As we made our way down one of the paths of the garden, I couldn't help but notice the irony. The sun was shining, the birds were singing, there was a cool, gentle breeze rustling through the tops of the trees, and the roses were *absolutely* gorgeous, seemingly glistening in the sunlight. It was an unbelievably perfect, summer day, yet in my heart there was such an overwhelming shadow of gloom. It seemed a sinister cloud had formed, and the mood was melancholy and grave.

Isaac was *unusually* quiet and very distracted, even distant - not at all himself. It was horrible! His silence was *excruciating*, and my heart was pounding in anticipation of what he was going to say to me. I felt unbelievably weak and extremely sick to my stomach.

We were nearly to the gazebo, the place that had been our favorite spot, when I just couldn't take it any longer!

"Isaac," I implored, "please...tell me what's bothering you. Tell me what's going on?"

Unfortunately, he didn't answer me; instead, he just kept right on walking, seemingly lost in his thoughts yet again.

Needless to say, his silence scared me all the more! It seemed as if he was afraid to tell me what was on his mind.

"Isaac," I begged again, almost in tears at this point, "please...you have to talk to me! Whatever it is...I'm sure we can work it out!"

Finally at the gazebo, Isaac stopped and turned to me, taking my hands in his, looking me in the eyes.

"Jochebed," he asked somberly, "do you know that I love you?"

I have to admit, his question threw me. I furrowed my brow, not understanding.

"What?" I queried, confused.

He patiently asked again.

"Do you know that I love you?" he questioned.

Still, perplexed, I answered. "Of course, I do!" I told him, shaking my head, still not understanding. "And I love you, too! With all of my heart, I do! But...why ask me such a thing?"

Isaac hesitated, not readily answering me, his eyes searching mine as if he were contemplating what to say.

His odd behavior was simply more than I could bear! Naturally, I instantly began to think the worst!

Something's just not right! I fretted. *Why is he acting this way? Is he having second thoughts about us? Is he leaving and never coming back? Is he sick? ...Oh my, no! Is he dying and he just doesn't know how to tell me?*

"Isaac!" I cried out, growing ever more impatient and worried. "You're scaring me! Please, just tell me what this is all about?"

Again, Isaac didn't move. For whatever reason, he seemed utterly bent on torturing me to death! He just stood there staring at me not saying a word!

More than a little upset, I was just about to let him have it, when all of a sudden, completely without warning, everything began to move in slow motion, almost as if I were in a dream.

I curiously watched as a smile made its way across Isaac's face, as he was now staring at me with his gorgeous blue eyes, gazing into mine so tenderly, so adoringly. It was such a contrast from the previous moment; I didn't quite know what to make of it.

As I stood there, trying to make sense of it all, I felt Isaac let go of my hand. He slowly reached into his pocket and pulled something out, although, I couldn't see what.

Suddenly, he took my hand again and fell to one knee. By now, my mind was spinning, dazed and confused! I was simply dumbfounded! I honestly didn't know whether to laugh or cry! I could see his lips moving, and I knew he was saying something, but the sound was so muffled, I couldn't make it out. Strangely, it felt like I'd somehow been whisked away to another place, far, far away. I was most definitely in shock!

Could this be real? I questioned. *Could this really be happening?*

Floods of emotion came rushing over me as I stood there staring at the ring he held up to me on bended knee.

"Will you marry me?" he asked again as I stood there frozen for what seemed like forever. "Jochebed!" he prodded, his smile slowly fading. "Are you with me? Did you hear what I asked you? ...Well...*will you or won't you?*"

Will I? I thought. *Of course, I will!* But for some strange reason, the words formed in my head wouldn't come out of my mouth.

Finally, my eyes fixed on Isaac's.

What beautiful blue eyes he has, I thought, *what a perfectly handsome face, what a terribly furrowed brow! - Furrowed brow? Oh, Jochebed!* I scolded. *Get a hold of yourself before he changes his mind!*

"Yes!" I finally blurted out. "*A thousand times, yes!* I'll marry you! I will *absolutely marry you!*"

Isaac's furrowed brow turned into a soft approving one as he gently slipped the ring on my finger.

"Shoo!" he expressed with relief. "You had me worried there for a minute!" He abruptly stood up and pulled me close, holding me tightly in a warm embrace. "You've made me the happiest man in the whole world!" he whispered. He leaned back and looked at me, grinning from ear to ear. "Jochebed Lewis," he said with fervor, "that has a nice ring to it, don't you think?"

I looked up at him, smiling broadly, my heart overwhelmed with excitement, and now tears of joy streaming down my face.

"Absolutely!" I agreed. "It sounds *perfect!*"

In that moment, my mind raced back, remembering my dream. It was all so familiar, so unbelievable! This time, however, it wasn't a dream! There was no Samuel to wake me out of this perfect, fairytale moment. No, this time...this time, it was very real!

www.ingramcontent.com/pod-product-compliance
Lightning Source LLC
Chambersburg PA
CBHW030616250626
47154CB00006B/1813